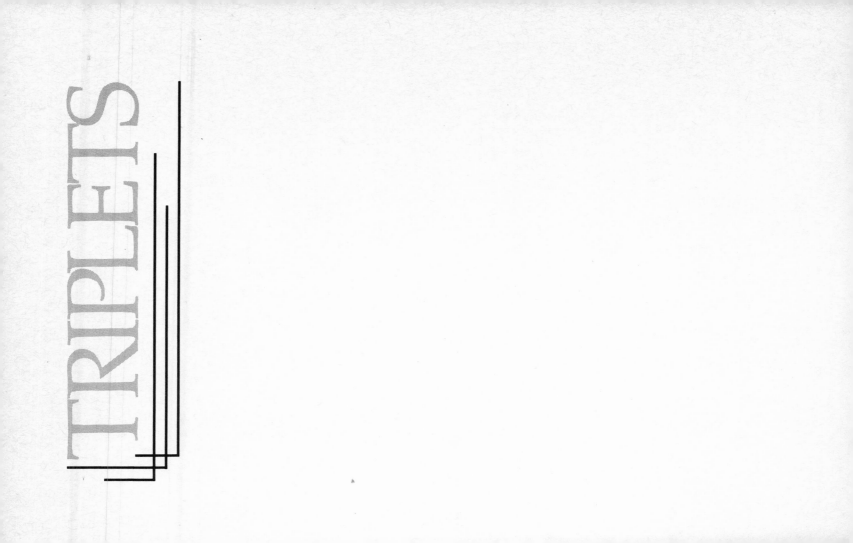

TRIPLETS

TRIPLETS

MOLLIE GREGORY

FRANKLIN WATTS
NEW YORK TORONTO 1988

Library of Congress Cataloging-in-Publication Data

Gregory, Mary Lawrence.
Triplets / Mollie Gregory.
    p.   cm.
    ISBN 0-531-15067-4
    I. Title.
PS3557.R43446T7 1988
813'.54—dc19   87-30705
                                       CIP

*To the sisters
and the brothers*

We will now discuss in a little more detail the struggle for existence.

Charles Darwin
Origin of Species

If this life be not a real fight, in which something is eternally gained for the universe by success, it is no better than a game of private theatricals from which one may withdraw at will. But it feels like a real fight.

William James
The Will to Believe

Though this novel, its characters and events, are completely imaginary, I have tried to make the backgrounds authentic. To this end I am grateful for the assistance of many people: to my cousin, Catherine Bartolozzi, and her husband, Ernesto, who assisted me with details of filmmaking in Italy and with translations; to Salvina and Cesare Taurelli, who introduced me to Rome; to Mark Fiorini, who gave me information on Cinecittà and the working life of actors there; to Dr. James Goldrich, the Triplet Connection, Gucciano Tataria, and Marie Stratton; and to Frederick Combs, Sam Adams, and others in Los Angeles who supplied experiences and stories on acting, directing, and the prices of fame.

This work of fiction is better because of the generous efforts of Pam Carter, Ellen Geiger, and Sybil Niden Goldrich, who read and commented on the manuscript, as did my literary agent, Elaine Markson, who believed in the book from the beginning.

My special gratitude goes to Krista Michaels, who always made skillful suggestions with humor and insight, and read the entire manuscript twice.

Finally, I am indebted to my editor, Ed Breslin, who was always keen, supportive, and sensitive to the work.

Mollie Gregory
Los Angeles
September 1987

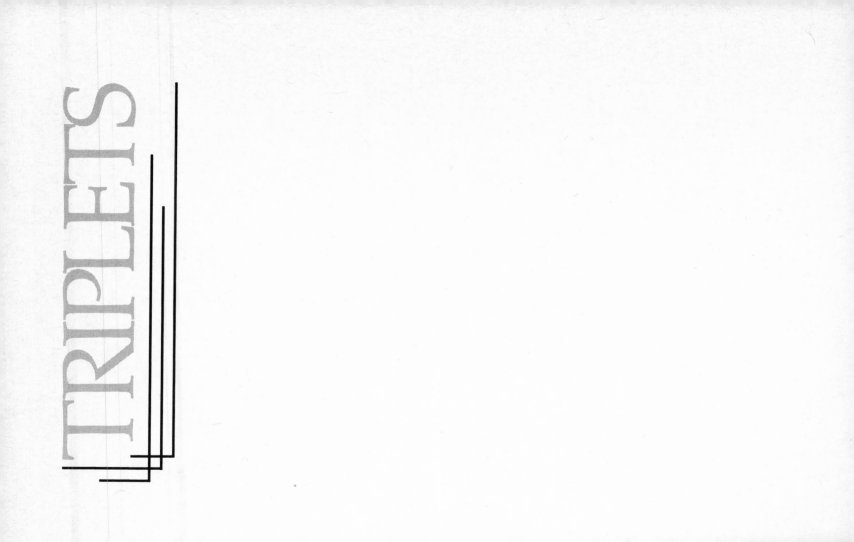

TRIPLETS

LOS ANGELES
1975

Growing up in the 1930's, two beautiful sisters and their talented brother reach for stardom in a world of betrayal, jealousy and murder.

Los Angeles is a young, hard, brash city with a soft underbelly. Its major art—an industry—turns dreams into universal folktales and can transform uncommon hardship into luxurious acclaim practically overnight, proving to the rest of the world that any fantasy can come true. But dreams made real are not without cost. The opposing face of dream is nightmare—sudden reversal that cripples hope and squeezes shut the bewildered human heart.

On June 15, 1975, a Santa Ana came in the night, whistling down Wilshire Boulevard, snapping through succulent palm trees. By morning, the wind had blown away the smog, and the San Gabriel Mountains emerged. They hunched in the bleachers of the vast city—impassive, proud—an audience waiting to be entertained.

Far up Beachwood Drive in the Hollywood Hills, Sara Bay Wyman drew down a shade in her sister's house. She could feel the crowd of fans outside taking possession of her sister, digesting their memories of her public face and acts. "I wish they'd go away," Sara muttered.

Her mother, Diana Wyman, barely heard her. She was thinking of Sky's black hair, her remarkable, penetrating eyes, and her chiseled porcelain face that had been world famous. Diana looked without blinking into the face of death. Nothing mattered—ambition, talent, beauty, compromise, or delay was useless. Fate sat in the shadows waiting like a cat to strike. The labor of a life could end in butchery.

"Why am I living on?" she whispered. "What could possibly justify me living on now?"

Five days before, Sky Wyman, age forty-five, had been killed. Her funeral had been held, flowers distributed, interment completed. Since her early twenties, Sky had been one of the most famous film stars in the world. She and her career had been one: Together they had skyrocketed, plunged, then escalated again, only to collide with the destiny of her own fame.

Sara was watching her seventy-year-old mother stare up at the beamed ceiling. Diana was the only woman she'd ever known who could be sympathetic and powerful at the same time. Sara, Sky, and their brother, Vail, were triplets. Sara was striking, too: Her mane of long, wavy, bronze-colored hair flew out from her head dramatically; her long hazel eyes, high cheek bones, and her full, rounded mouth—all were laced together by a bold, beckoning, almost wanton expression.

Sara pulled down another shade. The rampant press were interviewing everyone who'd ever worked with Sky, speculating wildly about her career swings and the violent nature of her death. By this process they were canonizing Sky into that rare assemblage that included Valentino, Harlow, and Monroe—other celebrities who'd died too young, thus assuring that they would live forever.

Sara looked around the living room. There was something wild and complicated just under the surface of its dreadful neatness. Behind the carefully selected French antiques angled between modern armchairs or 1900s wicker love seats, the room looked as if Sky had sought a different sense of order that was arranged disorder.

"It's so incredible," Sara kept saying. "We were back together, like the old days." She didn't expect a response. She kept seeing Sky's coffin being lowered into the grave. She and Sky were linked; death couldn't change that.

"Don't let that woman back in here," Diana said, speaking of Kitty, the only person Sky had ever loved.

Diana hadn't wept a single tear, at least none that Sara had seen. Did she weep at night? Sara wondered. What did she know that none of them knew? There had been times when Sara had hated her mother—for keeping her away from her father when he was dying, for her incredible management of Sara's only marriage, for the way she had pushed Sara aside when Sky went to Hollywood. But her alienation had been tempered with sorrow. Sara had her own litany of regrets, but she realized that though she and Sky had shared much, Sky had died without revealing what she felt about Diana, the mother who'd engineered Sky's career at Sara's expense.

Diana swept from the pale room, passing the dark and light shapes of furniture, and launched herself on the sea of what needed to be done. Her heels clicked on the brick red flagstones of the stairs that widened out to the tiled river of the second-story hallway and into Sky's bedroom.

Sara was in her wake. "Sky seemed so enthusiastic, Mother. Our picture together—we thought it was either going to make a whole new career for her, or—" Sara stopped. Or kill it, she thought. "What did she say when she called, Mother? Did she mention me? Did she mention that ugly, sad scene with Vail?"

"For God's sake, Sara, be still." Diana glanced at her crossly; Sara had always been emotional.

Sky's bedroom, an airy chamber with a skylight, looked as though Sky had just gone out to the garden below or had just left for the studio in a hurry. Diana blinked at the sunshine washing into the room, cleansing the disorder. Her eyes scanned a pair of crumpled linen slacks, several shoes, brimming ashtrays, and a marble dressing table cluttered with health store cleansers, lotions, oils, an ornate powder box, and a vase of white silk flowers. Typical of Sky, Diana thought, her public rooms relentlessly neat, the private ones a mess. Diana shied from the massive mirror, but when she turned from it, she found herself reflected in a wall of mirrors on the opposite side of the room. Sky had always been on display for herself as well as others. Outside, the indifferent birds chattered noisily from the huge palm tree.

Sara watched her mother slowly pick up the slacks from the floor. Age had not diminished her mother's power or her handsome good looks. She was a dynamo disguised as a lady. Her energies came in bursts quickly shut down into a false, self-possessed poise. Under wavy white hair, her dark eyes looked hooded and unnaturally bright. She had a soft, pretty voice, but Sara knew better than anyone the steel it sheathed. She wished she didn't love her mother so much.

Diana wasn't going to be drawn into any speculation about her dead daughter, yet Sara was driven to explore her mother's buried relationship with Sky. There had to be more there than simple infatuation for a famous daughter. There was a secret connection of need between them, just as Sara and Sky had been lashed together like the dark and light sides of the moon.

Sara had replayed the night of Sky's death a dozen times—viewing the film with her, Vail's surgical criticisms followed by his apologies, she herself going off when Sky had wanted her to stay. The more she examined the separate moments of that night, the less she understood of their lives together as triplets. Being triplets had been their special mooring and their greatest contest. "She seemed content," Sara said, lying a little. "She was worried about people's reaction to the film. But it was a new start. Didn't she say anything about it?" Sara had, after all, done something extraordinary by getting her that last picture. Sky had done something extraordinary by appearing in it. It had taken courage. But how had Sky really felt? Now Sara had a million questions that Sky would never answer.

"I saw the Levines the other night," Diana said, as if Sara had said nothing. "Such fine people, so comforting."

"Mother, I want you to talk to me about Sky!"

Diana turned as though Sara had whispered something important she couldn't quite hear.

"What on earth do you want me to say now?" Diana turned away. Sara was barely there to her; in fact, she was nearly transparent. But Sky was everywhere, curled in her unspoken thoughts, drifting behind her every gesture.

"I want to know what you really feel about Sky," Sara said softly, as if Sky were still alive. "You owe it to me."

Diana faced Sara with all the hidden power of a mother pressed to the breaking point. "There are a few facts *you've* never faced, Sara Bay. You've wasted so much of your life in envy and hate. Oh, I had such hopes for you. . . ."

The soft attack shocked Sara because it was so true and so false. After many failures, Sara was a film director in Europe. Had her mother ignored this major shift in Sara's fortunes? Or wasn't Sara's life important to her? Had it ever been?

Diana stared her daughter down. There had been a time when Sara had worn her inner sense of failure boldly like an emblem. She'd called herself a "former human being," quick to point out her own shortcomings and then laugh about them. Sometimes, late at night, Diana felt guilty about Sara. "I don't want to discuss Sky, dear."

Except for her coloring, Sara looked so much like Sky that it was painful for Diana to look at her. Clearly a sister, close to identical—the shape of her eyes, that captivating glance full of shrewdness and hesitation—so like Sky, but only for seconds, then gone.

Sara felt the sting of tears behind her eyes. There was so much she wanted to know, and she felt she wouldn't have another chance. "We don't have much time," she said. Vail would be there soon, and, for the first time, Vail would be in charge.

"I think you should take all these things before Vail gets here," Diana said. She held up an elegant silk scarf.

"I don't want her clothes!" Sara shouted, revolted. "Let Vail have them! Let him sell them, for all I care!"

Diana saw her daughter's baffling rage and pain and wondered what Sara would be like now that Sky was gone. Would she finally have what she'd always needed? Or would she drift? What exactly had gone on in the house the night of Sky's death?

Diana pulled out two suitcases, then walked into the dressing room—all mirrored—and found herself staring at one of the antique frosted light fixtures. She broke away and handed an emerald green silk evening dress to Sara. "Take it."

"You never wanted me to be like her before!" Sara cried. "Or to compete with her. Why are you pushing her clothes on me now?" Sara lurched away from her mother's outstretched hand that clutched the green dress. "Do you want a replacement?"

"I thought you'd want a remembrance," Diana said. "It's a very expensive dress. I certainly don't want Kitty to have it." Diana carefully folded the dress in a suitcase.

Sara stared down into the lush garden. Her mother put more clothes in the suitcase. They choked off grief in a conspiracy of silence. Diana clamped the first suitcase closed.

"Didn't you ever think what it was like for me to have a sister like Sky?" Sara said to the garden.

"Everyone loved you, sweetheart. You were always special and lively."

"You're not answering!"

"But you do such an outstanding job!" Diana said.

"Please don't flatter me," Sara said. "It's so patronizing." She dropped into a chair. "Did you know Sky?"

"I gave birth to her! To all three of you!" Diana, deeply insulted, sped across the room, away from her daughter. She stopped at the bay windows and looked out at the "lake," which was really a reservoir. "I know it was hard. She was always the actress!" Diana murmured, controlling herself. "Never a thought for us." She turned. "It was that Kitty who ruined her career—and her character."

"Kitty had nothing to do with it," Sara muttered, exhausted by her mother's jealousy.

"Sky wouldn't listen to me. She never listened to anyone . . . after . . ." Diana didn't finish. She stepped over a delicate slip embroidered with French lace. "Always so neat." She tittered strangely, sweeping up the lingerie and tossing it on the bed. "But she was generous, I suppose. Someone I met once said that neatness and generosity never went together. Remember that about Vail."

"Mother, you're harping on Vail as if he had anything to say about anything."

"He's the executor."

"Why don't you like him?" Sara countered.

"How can you say such a thing? He's your own brother, my son. Of course I like him!" she snapped. She was back in the dressing room, combing her hand gently down the sleeve of Sky's favorite jacket. "I did a lot wrong, I guess."

Sara felt that the chunky, guilty side of her mother was about to emerge. "Au fond," Sara said in the affected French they had used since childhood, "Sky loved only Kitty and her work. It had nothing to do with what you did or I did. That's the only thing Archie ever said that made sense."

"Psychiatrists! Detestable people!" her mother spat, then instantly drew the shreds of her dignity together. Archie was such a painful subject they hardly ever mentioned his name. While alive, he had filled Sky with shots and pills and God knew what else. Sky had not made a move without consulting him.

"I think, finally, that your sister could not tell the difference between the truth and a lie. She acted all the time. She admitted it once, tearfully. She wanted pity," Diana snapped. "Of course I had pity—loads of it. Who wouldn't? Sometimes," she added darkly, marching around the dressing room, "it was almost too much to bear. You, at least, tell the truth." Sara heard the scrape of a drawer. "Heavens," Diana said in a voice filled with innocent wonder, "look at all this beautiful jewelry." She came out of the dressing room carrying an ornate box.

Diana sat down on a satin chaise and put the box on the table between them. "You want me to give you what no one can give," Diana said, gently. "You want me to talk about Sky—the private things between Sky and me. About all my dreams—" She choked, a tiny explosive sound. "Then you would feel—what? Released? What is it you need? She's dead. Isn't that enough for you?"

Sara ignited from some inner pilot light. What metamorphosis was she approaching? Suicide? Or another kind of death, the personal inner kind that no one sees? Confidence at last? Splendor in middle age? Sara and Vail had always believed that Sky was their mother's favorite child—the child who'd fulfilled all Diana's ambitions, the most famous actress of her generation. Sara glared at the box laden with strands of pearls. Then she flashed again on her sister's coffin being lowered into the grave. The repetitive image skipped in front of her eyes, coming and going. Part of herself was going into that grave with Sky because, no matter what anyone ever said, she and Sky were joined. But Sky wasn't there anymore to define Sara, and Sara knew it. What was she going to do with the rest of her life? She felt she had less than a full right to be living. Death did not end the sisterhood. It just ended hope.

Diana lifted a framed studio portrait of her famous daughter from a little glass table beside the chaise. She was staring at it, crying without a sound, and whispering: "Look at that beauty. . . . So many times I looked at photos of her and marveled that I had given birth to her, formed those eyes and that hair and that mouth inside me. . . . She could be so cruel," she said from a deeply felt, long-sustained pool of pride and injury. "I never knew her at all." The tears, unleashed, flowed evenly, but no trace of her real grief broke in her voice. "What a Janus, a sweet fraud."

Sara whirled, her beautiful face twisted and perplexed. Yes, cruel sometimes. But a fraud? Sara clutched the box of jewelry. Had she, too, misjudged her sister? Had Vail, of all people, been right? No, she would not believe it.

The doorbell chimed out the tune from Sky's most famous picture. It had always sent Sara into gales of laughter. Now it sounded pathetic. Diana shook her head, holding one hand to her brow like a visor. "You and Vail and Sky— you didn't know what sadness was as children," Diana muttered. "My childhood was one long death. But I made your childhood a happy time for you. I made sure you had everything I never had. And you were all equal," she said firmly. "You were treated equally." She's so wrong, Sara thought, feeling the blood rush into her face. Diana looked at her daughter standing stiffly in the doorway. "What you did with your gifts was your business. I did my job. Didn't I?" she asked, her voice trembling. Again, Sara felt the claws of her mother's peculiar pathos. She had no idea how to comfort her.

She went downstairs and looked out the window. She could see the heads of the crowd below in the street and the roof of the permanently stationed television truck. On the porch stood a thin, balding man with a narrow, shrewd face. She opened the door. He thrust an open wallet at her.

"Miss Wyman? Sorry to intrude. I'm Detective Rollins. Homicide."

TRIPLETS

PART ONE

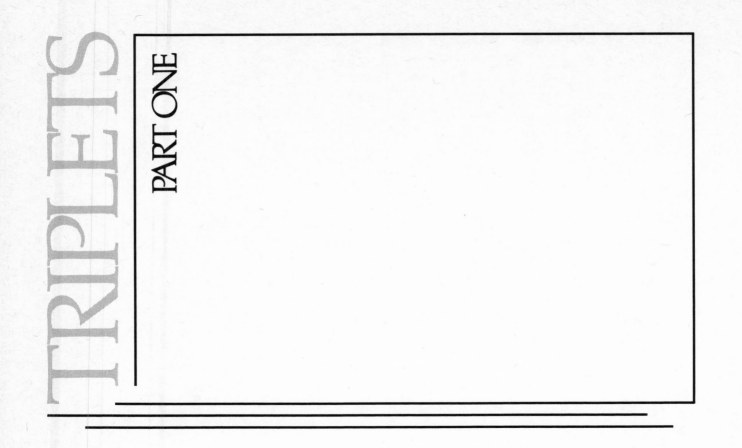

1

1915

Diana's earliest memory was the touch and smell of wet hair.

"Dee!" Virginia screeched, then plopped down on a high stool in the kitchen and began taking the pins out of her luxurious, chestnut-colored hair. Virginia was Diana's foster mother. She looked plump and pleasing—rosy, round cheeks, large blue eyes set close together, and a turned-up nose. She pulled a towel around her shoulders. "Dee!" With a practiced twist of her head, she tossed her hair forward. It tumbled down in front of her lowered face over the sink.

Diana was ten years old—bony, awkward, and timid. She came rushing in from the screened porch, wiping her hands on her torn skirt. "Get over here!" snapped Virginia from under the curtain of hair.

"I'm sorry," Diana whispered. She hopped up on a three-legged wooden stool next to the sink. Wetting Virginia's hair, she poured out a capful of sweet-smelling castile shampoo. Diana's small, pretty mouth tightened as she put her hands on Virginia's head and started scrubbing, working up a lather.

"Harder!" Virginia ordered. She was never satisfied. Diana redoubled her efforts, scrubbing until her fingers were pink and puckered. "Ouch! Not that hard!" Virginia commanded.

The last step in the washing of Virginia's hair was to pour the clean water from the blue china bowl over her head. Diana had to lift and pour with one hand while her other held the long hank of wet hair below it; Virginia's hair was never supposed to touch the sink.

"Careful!" Virginia warned Diana sharply. Soap in her eye or spilled water brought Diana a slap. Diana lifted the bowl, trying to be ever so careful. But her hand was still soapy, and as she started to pour the water, the bowl slipped from her fingers and fell into the deep sink, smashing into a dozen pieces.

Virginia's wet head jerked up, spraying soapsuds and water in every direction. "You careless, stupid child!"

"Please, I can do it right!" Diana cried out.

Virginia slapped Diana in the face with the flat of her hand. The blow knocked her off the stool, and she started to cry, holding her burning cheek with one hand, the other pressed to her wet apron. She was mortified and afraid. Virginia had that dangerous look in her eye, and her round, cherubic face was red with fury and pleasure.

She grabbed the child's long blond hair. "Stand up!" Diana scrambled to her feet as Virginia dragged her to the sink and pressed her face down. "Look what you've done! It can't be repaired! It's dead!" The sharp, broken pieces of the blue bowl lay in a bath of suds and stray hairs at the bottom of the sink.

Still holding Diana by her hair, Virginia jerked open a drawer and snatched up a pair of shears. "Hold still!" she ordered, giving the child's hair a yank.

"Please don't!" Diana pleaded.

Virginia cut off a hank of Diana's hair. Truly terrified, Diana screamed, but Virginia was frenzied. She cut and chopped. "This'll teach you that nothing in this house is yours!" she panted. "When you break something, you pay for it." When a pile of blond hair lay on the floor and in the sink, she flung the shears back in the drawer. She was sweating and strangely out of breath. "Clean it all up and go to your room," she ordered, throwing a towel over her wet hair.

When Virginia was gone, Diana felt her shorn head and burst into tears again. What would they do to her at school? It was bad enough that she didn't have a real mother, but now they'd make her a laughing stock. Sobbing uncontrollably, Diana picked the ceramic pieces out of the sink and

—12—

threw them away. She rinsed the sink, trying not to look at the bottom of it where the grate caught the hair in a nest. She rinsed the sink again and again to wash the hair away. But her hair and Virginia's were tangled together.

Diana shuddered and felt the familiar nausea rising in her. The worst part of washing Virginia's hair every week was cleaning the sink afterward. She steeled herself, picked up the grate, and pulled the clotted mat of hair out with her fingers. Her rising nausea was an engine, speeding her through the loathsome task. But not fast enough. As she scraped the last of the hair out of the grate, she vomited into the sink, clinging to the hard rim, riding out the spasm. She rinsed the sink, wiped the drainboards, looked all around—she mustn't leave a speck.

Outside at last, she took a deep breath of fresh air and ran across the yard to the orchard. She forgot she was supposed to go to her room.

The "orphanage" was a sprawling, three-story clapboard house in Multnomah County, a few miles outside Portland, Oregon. After two foster homes she didn't remember, Diana had lived with Virginia and Joe Whittaker since the age of three. Joe, a quiet, indifferent man, had an office job with a lumber company that took him into Portland most days. In the evenings he'd sit in his study off the hall and read books under the glow of a hurricane lamp. The son of a minister, Joe sometimes reached into the high shelves and gave Diana a book she could read.

This was the only home Diana had ever known. She was fed and clothed, but she lived in terror of displeasing Virginia. Diana had many opportunities for that because she washed dishes, scrubbed the floors with a cloth, dusted the downstairs rooms and staircase, helped prepare all the meals, made the beds, and helped with the ironing and laundry. After her chores were done, she could "play," which meant watching whatever younger children were roosting at the orphanage. After *that*, she could do her studies.

On the day Diana broke the bowl, the sun came out as she climbed an old peach tree and sat on a low branch. She tried to stop crying by looking up into its branches. The leaves fluttered against a sky lumpy with white clouds. Diana's loneliness had seeped into the marrow of her bones like a dye. She darted about her tasks, shoulders hunched forward, eyes wary, not knowing where the next blow might come from or why. She was neglected or ignored until she did something wrong. She'd never had a new dress or a toy all her own. She'd learned never to expect affection or understanding; she'd learned to work, to appease, to dissemble.

Diana forced herself to forget about the nauseating sink, her shorn hair, and the certain ridicule at school. She concentrated on the rare feeling of the sun on her scalp. She longed for warmth and light, but in Oregon the summers were short; in fall, winter, and spring the rain poured out of the sky and fell in sheets from the eaves.

Usually there were five or six children—all temporary boarders—living under the sagging roof of the old house. But this summer there were only two—May, a little girl of three, and Dave, about four. They were brother and sister, and they went everywhere together. The comings and goings in the house had ceased to interest Diana; she knew she was stuck there. But Diana dreamed of other, warmer worlds—worlds that swam before her eyes when she read about Sir Lancelot and the Lady of the Lake, Ivanhoe and Rowena, Jane Eyre and Mr. Rochester. They quickened her dreams: Maybe someone would come along the road someday and take her away to the city where she'd earn her fortune. Maybe if Diana worked harder, she could earn Virginia's love. The most precious dream of all was that maybe her real parents would come along the road, kiss her, and take her to a fine house and ask her forgiveness for abandoning her. Diana had asked Virginia before about where she'd come from, but Virginia never said the same thing twice: Diana had been left on the doorstep, Diana had been found in a bush, the state agency had assigned Diana to the Whittakers. Diana had stopped asking. She had no real hope that her mother and father would claim her. She was ugly; her dark brown eyes were long and narrow ("sneaky," Virginia called them); she had a long nose and a long neck. She was scrawny. No one would ever come for a child who looked like that.

When Diana remembered she was supposed to have

gone to her room, she froze. She'd get a licking for sure. She slid out of the tree and dashed toward the house. She crept through the kitchen, down the hallway, and was heading for the stairs when she heard Virginia's complaining voice coming from Joe's study.

"But her mother's got millions!" Virginia whined loudly.

"Why doesn't she send the money?!"

Diana stopped on the first stair and stole back to the study door.

Joe's lower voice was gruff and uninterested. "I haven't the faintest, Ginny. The letter came back unopened." Joe lived folded in upon himself.

"What are you going to do? Diana can't board here for free! They ought to pay! That was the arrangement!"

"What can I do? Put her on a bus and send her back? It seems to me she pays her way. She helps out."

Diana sailed up to her room on wings of hope. Her real mother was a fine lady like Queen Guinevere! Maybe her father was someone important like a businessman or a prince! She was dazed with joy. If her mother had money, oh, surely, she'd rescue her someday.

But Diana's mother never came.

Diana and Virginia were stirring the boiling tub of laundry in the back yard. Sometimes the slave labor of the laundry bound them together and made Virginia nicer to Diana. Diana asked again about her mother.

"She didn't want you!" Virginia sighed, dropping all pretense. She swept a strand of damp hair back from her eyes.

"Why didn't she want me?" Diana asked.

"She took one look at you an' knew you'd turn out to be ugly an' stupid!" Virginia laughed, shoving the stick deep into the writhing clothes. Diana felt a sob coming on. She kept her face immobile.

"Is she a fine lady?"

"Where'd you get that idea?" Virginia asked, suspicious.

"I heard you talking to Joe once."

"Oh, you did, did you? Aren't you the little snoop!" She came around the huge pot, then put her hands on her hips.

"Do I have to do everything? Give me that soap!" Diana handed it to her quickly. "We adopted you out of the goodness of our hearts."

"Maybe," Diana said, doing everything she could to keep her voice from shaking, "I should write her a note."

"What on earth for?" Virginia demanded, scanning the thin child.

"Just to thank her for putting me with such a nice family," Virginia let go of the stick. "Your parents don't want you. You don't belong with those hoity-toity stuck-ups."

Diana felt a sudden envelope of peace fall over her. She looked straight into her foster mother's eyes. "Yes, I do," Diana said.

Virginia's eyes widened at such audacity. She drew back her hand to box Diana's ears but Diana seized Virginia's wrist in midair and twisted it with all her strength.

"You devil!" Virginia squeaked. She would win the match and then she would set the strap on Dee so she couldn't sit down for a month!

Diana didn't care if her foster mother strapped her. She suddenly let go, sending Virginia backwards, off balance. Diana bolted. She ran far into the orchard and then into the pine trees beyond. She ran with grim triumph. Somewhere, her mother and father not only existed but were really fine people. If Diana worked very hard, maybe she could be worthy of them.

Diana set herself to read every book in Joe's study. When she had finished them—even a leather-bound Shakespeare—Joe overruled Virginia and let Diana stay an extra hour at the library close to her grade school. She read voraciously and indiscriminately—French history, children's magazines, etiquette books, books about art. By the eighth grade, Diana's teachers raved about her dedication to her studies, her aptitude in art—far beyond the norm for her age and upbringing—and about her quiet dignity. Most of the teachers saw but did not mention her sadness. Among themselves, they clucked about Virginia Whittaker, the neighborhood termagant who kept some of the state's wards.

In high school, Diana formed a crush on her homeroom teacher, Miss Ada Bentley, whose beautiful speech and delicate, studied gestures attracted her. Diana shyly asked her if she would teach her how to speak "like a lady." At first Ada Bentley didn't take the thin girl in the hand-me-down dress seriously. But Diana persisted. Miss Bentley informed Diana that, like many people in the Northwest, she had a "hard *R* sound." She demonstrated, sure that the girl would tire of the lesson. But Diana never tired. Slowly, the chance to mold Diana and to help her change her life seized Ada Bentley's imagination.

Ada Bentley was a forty-year-old, well-educated, but plain woman with wispy brown hair, a sharp face, and a slight cast in one eye. She taught Diana how to walk with her head high, looking neither right nor left, how to sit, how to make polite dinner conversation, how to hold a teacup, and which silverware to use. She took her downtown and showed her what good clothes looked like. Gossiping women gave Ada a pain; she told Diana that women should have a grasp of current affairs, and she infused the girl with her strong beliefs in woman suffrage. Ada had been on hunger strikes, and she still organized marches in the downtown Portland streets for the women's vote. Women were slaves, she told Diana. "We must dig ourselves out of the grave of economic dependence and servitude to which the men have consigned us."

As their lessons progressed, Diana confided to Miss Bentley that she knew her real mother existed and her fervent hope that she could someday find her. She speculated that her father was a fine gentleman in a big city. Ada Bentley was skeptical. She warned Diana that Virginia may have lied to her, but Diana wouldn't listen.

When the difference in Diana began to show, Virginia ridiculed it, heaping scorn on her and increasing her work load.

In the winter of 1922, Miss Bentley helped Diana apply to the state university for admission and for a scholarship. When she was accepted with a nominal scholarship, Miss Bentley helped make up the rest. Diana now had two foster mothers.

"I guess you're glad to be leaving," Virginia said, scowling, as Diana put her valise down next to the front door.

"I am pleased to be going to college," Diana said, calmly

putting on her one pair of gloves. She tried to keep the almost hysterical joy out of her voice. In less than five minutes, Miss Bentley would pick her up and take her to the train station.

"I guess we're not good enough for you," Virginia whined. Her hair was all gray now; Diana looked at it with passionate distaste. "You give yourself some pretty high airs, Diana. You'd be wise to just be yourself."

"This is myself," Diana responded, surprised at her foster mother's advice. Over the last couple of years, they'd had an unspoken truce, each doing her work and staying out of the other's way. Diana looked out the window for Miss Bentley's car.

Joe came out of his study. "So you're off then, is it?" He looked at her vaguely. "Does your mother know how to reach you?"

A horn honked outside. "No," said Diana primly, picking up her valise, "but Virginia does." She smiled in what she thought was a gracious fashion. "Good-bye," she said and breezed out the door, head high, shoulders straight. She had no intention of ever setting eyes on them again.

Diana had changed radically. From the scrawny, cowering, abused child of ten who'd broken the blue bowl, she had become stately. She was tall for a woman; her gestures were studied yet graceful, her voice modulated. Her almond-shaped eyes looked at the world intelligently, but despite her youth, they held no naïveté. Her mouth was pretty but a trifle ungenerous. She smiled quickly but the air of sadness, later to be tinged with condescension, never left her. She embraced Miss Bentley's political creed, believing that if women ran Congress, now that women had the vote, there would be no more wars.

Diana's first year at the university was an elixir of freedom. She had control over her life. She joined the sorority Miss Bentley suggested, she studied hard, and she constantly asked Miss Bentley's advice on which course she should take, which friends she should cultivate, and which teachers. During the summer in the sleepy university town, she worked in the most expensive dress shop in the county.

Since Diana was a good student, majoring in the fine arts, Ada Bentley advised her to leave the university after two years and try for Mills College, a women's college near San Francisco. This was a sacrifice on Ada's part, for it meant a true separation from the pupil who had become a surrogate daughter. She was not surprised when Mills accepted Diana.

"You will meet a better class of people," Ada said to Diana at the train station, "and I shall come and see you at Christmas." She kissed her on the cheek and wished her well. But that night she wept for hours. It would never be the same again.

Mills was the first women's college in the Far West. Small and elite, it was known for its fine arts department. Diana fit right it.

In the spring of 1925, her senior year, Diana met Edward Wyman at a dance.

"Oh, call me Ned," he said. "Everyone does." Ned, a senior at Stanford, was a handsome man of medium height with reddish blond hair, hazel eyes, and casual, easy good manners. He laughed a great deal and told charming stories. He didn't seem to have a care in the world.

Ned Wyman was immediately smitten with the willowy young woman who wrapped her honey blond hair around her head so enchantingly. She was clearly upper crust from her carriage and her speech, but she didn't seem spoiled or shallow. Her brown eyes were bold, and they said, I know what I want.

"You don't laugh enough, Diana," he said during a frisky two-step.

"I'm saving up," she replied.

"I hear you're all for women's rights."

"I'm proud of that," she said, waiting for him to make fun of it, like most of the young men.

"I'm for the women's vote," he declared, never having given it a thought. "I like a girl to have a good mind." He felt her back relax minutely under his hand. He'd never thought about girls' minds, either.

"Don't you know who he is?" Patty buzzed later. Patty was Diana's best friend at Mills. "His family has silver money! They have a house in San Francisco, and a ranch, and probably a house at Tahoe, too. Or maybe Hawaii—I don't know. He's very eligible."

The Wymans were storybook Californians. In the 1880s, Ned's parents had come to San Francisco after striking it rich in the Comstock Lode. They'd built a substantial house on Clay Street and owned a ranch in the Sierra Nevada foothills, east of Napa, and ran it with the mixture of people that California afforded: Chinese, Mexicans, Indians, and transient white cowpokes who'd lost what little they'd gained in the Gold Rush or the silver boom.

Diana was greatly relieved that the young man she liked so much came from a good family. It would have made her sad to have to give him up. Ned besieged her, sending flowers, taking her for rides in his Kissel Gold Bug, a two-seat speedster, and inviting her to theater parties at the Jenny Lind, to jazz parties featuring Jelly Roll Morton, and to picnics in Golden Gate Park. Both young and blond, they made a striking couple. Ned was completely infatuated with her.

All through college, Diana's terrible fear was that some-one would discover her lack of family credentials.

"Be truthful," Ada advised. She was still skeptical about Diana's belief that her parents were wealthy and powerful.

Diana wrung her hands. Family—the right family—was so important. But when Ned asked about her family it was in the most offhand, uninterested fashion.

She was invited to meet Ned's parents. Dressed in her very best, Diana nervously anticipated social disaster when they learned about her "family," the Whittakers. She decided on the phrase "in lumber." "In lumber" sounded good.

The Wyman house was of Queen Anne vintage, nestled between Nob Hill and Russian Hill. Built in 1891, it featured rounded corner towers, decorative columns, and bay win-dows in a powerful yet delicate combination. It was painted slate gray, pale blue, and white. Inside, Diana got her first look at real wealth—the elegant, curving staircase of satin-wood, the glistening parquet floors, and the rich, somber furniture in plum and pale blues and dark greens. She felt soothed and excited. Here the silverware would be heavy and the table linens like those she'd only read about.

Ned and his father were not close, but Ned was used to his mother's attentions. Mr. Wyman was a short man in poor health—bad circulation, Ned said. His mother was a proud, dignified woman with iron gray hair, a stern, nononsense air, and a hearty dislike for hypocrisy. She felt that Diana was too cool for her Neddie.

"My dear," Mrs. Wyman said, "will your people be coming down for the season?"

Diana's Rubicon lay before her. "No, Mrs. Wyman, my parents care nothing for the season. My father is in lumber, my mother has a weak heart. They are decent people but have not the resources to travel regularly."

Mrs. Wyman fixed her with a look, then softened. At least the girl was honest. "They gave you a good education," she said.

"Thank you," Diana said softly.

Mrs. Wyman gave in when Neddie told her he loved Diana for her strength and beauty and when, after a battery of rigorous tests, Diana's courtesy toward Mrs. Wyman never flagged.

Ned and Diana were married in December of 1925. Diana sent Virginia and Joe Whittaker a printed announcement. To Ada Bentley she sent the first-class train fare to be at her wedding, which was held in the Episcopal church, with a reception afterwards at the Palace Hotel. They set off on the first leg of their honeymoon in Europe.

"I love you, I love you so much," Ned whispered to Diana in their first-class compartment on the Union Pacific barreling across America. Ada, with her usual foresight and directness, had prepared Diana completely for her wedding night.

"Oh, I'm going to heaven," Ned breathed, his arms wrapped around his adored one, his lips tasting her soft cheek, her neck, her beautiful breast. "Do you have any idea how much I love you?" He raised his head and she could see the look of pure adoration in his eyes. She smiled and kissed him, surprised by the delicious sensations Ned stirred in her. She hoped it was modern, not sinful. Most of all, she loved Ned for giving her what no other human being had yet given her: safety and station.

When—after hours of somewhat painful but nonetheless promising lovemaking—they drifted into a rocking slumber, Diana had a dream that was to return to her again and again.

She was all alone in a vast sea of fog as thick and suffocating as cotton. Very faintly, she heard a woman seductively calling her name. She began to be aware that people, as still as statues, were hidden in the fog among giant trees. "Diana . . ." the tempting voice called again. She started forward, suddenly afraid and desperate. She reached out blindly into the fog and collided with a tree trunk. The earth began to move, shifting up, then dropping away. She clung to the tree trunk, panicked, terrified. The rough bark scratched her arms, her cheek, and her chest. The earth heaved, growling. Then the fog lifted. She was hanging in midair, embracing the trunk of the tree. The ground was far below her, writhing and rippling. Her arms ached. She felt them letting go, and she was falling and falling toward the buckling skin of the earth.

Ned's arms were around her. "You had a bad dream, sweetie," he said, cheerfully. "But I'm here." Diana started to cry.

When Ned and Diana returned from Europe, she assumed that Ned would go into the "family business." But there was none, really. His father kept an office on Montgomery Street, investing the money he'd inherited and made. Neddie was at loose ends. Moreover, he was a spendthrift, blowing money on horses, clothes, jewelry, perfume, gadgets, art. He disliked responsibility, office hours, business appointments. He was like a child.

Diana wanted him to get interested in something people would respect. He finally accommodated her by falling into brokering munitions. Though words weren't his strong suit with the people close to him, he discovered he could do the work with an offhand, indifferent charm. It gave him many opportunities to lunch at his club with convivial former classmates.

But that didn't last long. Soon Ned was lying to Diana; brokering munitions bored him, and after a while he found it distasteful. He much preferred spending time at his parents' ranch, riding horses, chatting with trainers and stable hands. That was really living. Diana wanted him in town.

She enjoyed giving dinner parties and teas, going to the opera, hosting a huge Christmas buffet for the members of the museum board every year. But her political activities were anathema to Ned's family. Her outspoken and scathing comments about Coolidge often brought dinner with the Wymans to an untidy close. She ignored their complaints: It was crucial to build on the passage of the Nineteenth Amendment that had given women the right to vote.

Ada Bentley was a frequent guest in the Clay Street home, but Diana's communication with the Whittakers remained distant and bitter. She sent them a Christmas card every year; when they said they wanted to visit, Diana wrote back that she and her husband would be abroad. She felt light-years away from them: She had worked hard to stretch the distance.

When Diana had first confessed to Ned that she didn't know who her real mother was, it struck him as "romantic." But he was uneasy when she said she wanted to locate her real parents. Ned didn't want her to be disappointed.

The matter drifted, unresolved, and, in truth, Diana was ambivalent about it. She wanted her real parents to see that the child they had cast out was now a person of worth and station. At the same time, she was afraid. She was well acquainted with rejection. Maybe Virginia *had* lied to her. Worse, maybe her mother was someone who would jeopardize her current life or turn Mrs. Wyman against her. Diana waited. And as she waited, she began to forget about the Whittakers. She began to invent her own past.

Ned was glad that Diana let it rest. There were much more important things to do than chasing after a rainbow called "finding her parents." He had an acute sense of dynasty and an emotional need that he found difficult to express. He wanted to be a father.

"We can't rush nature, darling," Diana said, sweetly. With Ned, she had tapped her own deep, underground current of sensuality in herself, to which, when they were alone, she gave herself completely. She was not displeased that she hadn't conceived; she led a very busy life. Besides, the doctor had told her there was nothing wrong with her.

In October of 1929, the stock market crashed, devastating Ned's father. Having nothing better to do, he had sunk most of the family's succulent cash flow into the market. Drawing a bead on his financial collapse, Mr. Wyman quickly realized that he was no longer tremendously wealthy. No one in the family would starve, but the fortune had vanished. Mr. Wyman never recovered from the blow and, as a consequence, he never met his grandchildren: He died of a heart attack that winter.

Diana conceived the month the market crashed. Ned was ecstatic. Since their marriage, they'd been living in the Clay Street house. Ned turned the whole top floor into a nursery, redecorating it lavishly, purchasing a hobbyhorse, an electric train, and stuffed animals. During her pregnancy, Diana and Ned grew even closer, spending long evenings reading to each other, selecting names for the child, and speculating on his or her nature and what he or she would look like.

"You are large for being only four months along," Mrs. Wyman observed only days after her husband's funeral. "Are you quite sure you have the date right?" Diana was quite sure. "Then I suggest you see the doctor again and put the question to him squarely. We cannot have any problems. I shall go with you."

Diana had been looking for a woman doctor, according to her principles, and had found a rare husband-and-wife team practicing obstetrics: Doctors Thomas and Victoria Giv-ler. Dr. Tom was a precise man with a young charm that had survived his forties, while Dr. Vicki brought to the partnership a peppy sense of order. They were certain nothing was wrong with Diana's pregnancy, but when she was five months along, they announced that they suspected a multiple birth. Ned and his mother were thrilled; Diana was shocked. In her sixth month, Diana took to her bed. It had become impossible for her to move around.

On June 1, 1930, the pains began. She was four weeks early. Ned, in a lather, crumpled the fender of the family's McFarlan sports sedan getting it out of the garage. At the hospital, Diana was rushed into the operating room, where the Givlers waited. She was fully dilated. One baby was

—24—

practically born. Diana was spinning in a cone of agony. They gave her a little ether. She shrieked for more.

She awoke in a pale green room not knowing if it was night or day. Ned, standing beside her bed with a white mask over his face, was crying with joy and surprise. Dr. Victoria Givler announced: "Mrs. Wyman, you're the proud mother of triplets."

Sara Bay Wyman was born first, Edward Vail an hour later, and five hours later, at dawn, Stephanie Skyler. The family quickly slipped into calling the boy Vail—Diana disliked Ed or Eddie. Stephanie Skyler became Sky, and Sara stayed Sara, except when she was bad—then she was Sara Bay.

Ned looked at his three tiny, fragile infants in their incubators. Each baby weighed between four and five pounds. Only Sky had hair—thick, black curls.

"Actually, we don't know much about triplets," Dr. Tom said to Ned as they stood in the corridor looking through the nursery window. "There are no studies I'm aware of." Ned kept shaking his head. He felt numb. "A childhood friend of mine had identical triplet boys," Dr. Tom persisted gently. "They're ten now." Ned did not look up. "Twins have a tendency to divide their world up in two equal parts, but the triplet relationship is inherently more unstable, since there are three of them." He ran a finger across his mustache.

"Are they breathing all right?" Ned asked. Dr. Tom assured him that they were and that Mrs. Wyman had done well to carry them for eight months.

"In most sibling relationships," he went on, determined, "one child is a couple of years older or younger. But the unusual thing about triplets is that they are exact contemporaries. They share most of the same understandings and experiences at the same age. This can lead to a profound bond between them, a kind of special harmony." Both men gazed at the three babies. "Course yours aren't identical," Dr. Tom murmured. "The girls could have been, but they're not."

"Oh, God," Ned murmured, "three of them."

Dr. Tom patted Ned's shoulder. "If they get on well with each other, they'll probably be very close for the rest of their lives. If they don't—well, anything can happen." He beamed at Ned. "Congratulations. Just having them makes you special."

In her hospital room, Diana leaned back against the pillows and stared out the window into the sky. Her triplets were an extraordinary gift. If she'd believed in God, which she didn't, she would have joined a church in thanks. Diana felt smug. *She* had created the triplets, not Ned. Twins ran in families, she'd heard. Could she have been a twin? Was that why she'd been left out on the Whittakers' rocky cliff while her twin had remained in the bosom of her unknown family? She pushed the painful idea away. She had to rest between feedings, for she'd insisted upon nursing her three babes. No bottles! Babies needed mother's milk. Diana began fantasizing about the triplets as adults: a concert pianist, a famous painter, a great beauty. Maybe Vail would be the Abraham Lincoln of his time. Sara might discover the cure for the common cold. Her triplets would have all the advantages that she and Ned could provide. Diana was sure they were unusual and gifted children. She was going to make them the very best they could be.

—26—

2

"You can do better than that, Sara Bay," Diana called to her on the beginners' slopes. "Let's all do it again." Diana pressed them to swim, ski, skate, learn languages, be "civilized," succeed, do better. She rarely lost her temper.

"I hate to ski!" Sara cried one day. "I hate being cold and wet."

"All well-brought-up children know how to ski, and I'm sure you will improve," Diana said.

"But you don't care what we want," Vail said. "We want to skate."

"That will do, children."

Diana never let up. The triplets were six, and she'd taken them to Garmisch in the Bavarian mountains. They were on a minitour of Europe "before it blew up," as Ned characterized it. Business had forced him to return to the States three months before, and they were alone with Diana. It was December 1936.

The triplets made a scene on the slopes of Garmisch and embarrassed Gretel, the young skier Diana had hired to teach them. They were sent to bed without their supper. In their beds with the lights out, a favorite and intimate time for them, Sky said maybe they ought to learn how to ski, but Sara and Vail maintained that skating was better, and it wasn't fair that they always had to do what the adults wanted.

This was their second trip to Europe with Diana. On the first, they had stayed in Paris and other places they barely

—27—

remembered. Wherever they went, people were always asking Diana how she did it or if they weren't a handful. They were, but Diana wouldn't admit it.

The triplets relished being the center of attention and actively collaborated with Diana to make their public appearances in identical clothing as noticeable as possible. They especially enjoyed the sailor outfits they wore on the *Normandie*, a luxury liner. After a few months in Europe, they had returned home to California where they had been put back into school. Then Diana had taken them to New York, and now they found themselves in Europe again.

Diana did not allow her educational plans to be confined by school schedules or even by impending wars. She cared nothing for rattling swords or marching armies piling up at borders. The triplets thought she was stronger than anyone. They loved Ned and his uncritical, diffident affection, but he was in an office and wasn't as available. When they returned from their travels, they brought him what they'd learned: a little French, a little German, some music, some poems, and knowledge of art museums and of geography.

In Garmisch, Diana realized she had a revolt on her hands and that, as usual, Sara was the ringleader.

"What's gotten into you?" she demanded of Sara. "You are always such good children, obedient, eager to learn."

Sara looked up at her mother, shielding her dark hazel eyes against the reflection of the snow, her brassy, wiry hair sticking out from under her ski cap. "We think we should learn what *we* want to learn once in a while," she said. Vail and Sky stood beside her in their "special lineup," as Diana called it, Vail in the middle. The lineup characterized them in many ways.

"You are children," Diana said sternly, "and you will do as I think best. Is that clear?" Each child reluctantly nodded. People on the slopes or heading for the chairs pointed out the identically dressed triplets.

In Europe's strange surroundings, the triplets had developed a strong sense of loyalty to each other. When their young French tutor scolded Sky for her messy workbook, Sara and Vail flew to her defense. When Diana punished Vail for being rude to the room clerk, Sky and Sara hotly

—28—

maintained he was just being "lively," their word for his quirky energy. Among themselves, they grew to expect understanding. As much as Vail liked to stir things up, he was the peacemaker of the three, often running interference between his sisters and Diana. But he could be very arch about his sisters, especially Sky's determined affections for her favorite doll, Sally. "Always talking dollie talk," he'd say about Sky, sighing deeply.

Diana suspected that Sara and Sky each practically knew what the other was thinking or feeling. But in nature, they were different. Sara was rebellious; she loved to cram her days with new experiences. Sky, the youngest, the sweetest, without the stature of being the firstborn like Sara or being male like Vail, followed their lead—until Garmisch.

Diana and her triplets were out of sorts when they all went into the village of Garmisch for lunch. Vail hadn't wanted to go. "Garmisch is bad," he said.

"Nonsense, Vail," Diana reprimanded him.

"It's scary! I don't want to go!"

Diana laughed. "Garmisch is a tiny, peaceful town in Bavaria. Now you all tell me something you've learned about it."

They were walking down the little street when a sedan carrying three Nazi officers pulled to an abrupt stop just ahead of them. Two of the men piled out and rushed inside a bakery. As the triplets and Diana stood looking in the window, the officers seized the elderly baker. One punched him and drew blood.

Vail shrieked. "Mama! Don't let them do this!" He tried to pull away but Diana held him fast.

"Don't move," she whispered fiercely to him, terrified he would draw the attention of the maddened officers.

The Nazis were literally clubbing the man to the floor. Blood poured from his face, and his agonized appeals for help went unanswered by the small crowd now gathered outside the bakery. One of the men grabbed his shoulders while the other grabbed his feet. With the old man swinging between them like a dead deer, they hauled him outside and threw him in the back of the car.

Vail was crying piteously. Sara and Sky held onto Diana

tightly, their faces pale. The car drove off. The street returned to normal as though nothing had happened. The triplets looked up at their mother and saw, incredibly, that their indomitable Diana was afraid. They moved closer to her. "We're leaving," she said. "Don't talk about what you just saw. It's too dangerous." Quickly, they made their way back to the hotel.

"You see?" cried Vail. "I told you Garmisch was bad." His feelings came and went. Sometimes they were like dreams; but sometimes after he had dreamed them, they came true. Vail's "dreams," as Sky and Sara called them, had become the family joke. Even after Garmisch, Diana laughed at them.

"No more skiing?" Sky asked hopefully. Her black hair and pale blue eyes with their dark rims gave her the look of an exotic young bird.

"Not here we won't," Diana replied, grimly.

But the next morning, as they settled into their compartment just before their train to St. Moritz in Switzerland was to leave, Sky discovered that she had left her favorite doll at the hotel. Diana, still shaken by what they had witnessed yesterday and anxious to leave Germany, said they would send for it.

"I won't leave without Sally," Sky said.

"Silly Sky," Diana said, stuffing luggage into the overhead rack, "we don't have time to go back to the hotel."

When Diana next looked around, Sky was gone. "Where is she?" she asked Vail and Sara, alarmed.

"She went back for her dolly," Vail said.

When a quick search of the train revealed no sign of Sky, all their luggage was taken off, and Diana, frantic and enraged, watched their train chug out of the station without them.

They found Sky a few blocks from the station, walking back to the hotel.

"I will not have this kind of behavior," Diana said, taking Sky's arm sternly.

"And I won't leave Sally behind," she said, revealing an intransigent side of her nature for the first time. When Diana thought about it later, she felt she had been too hard on Sky. But she excused her harshness. She had been afraid. No one had ever cared enough about Diana to feel that heart-stopping fear of the parent for the missing child. For the first time in years, Diana thought of Virginia and the long, frightening desert of her childhood.

They caught the next train. Sky was punished; she had to do extra French, she had to write on her pad, "I will not go off by myself," twenty times, and she couldn't have sweets for a month. It felt like a year. In Switzerland the unpopular skiing lessons resumed.

The preparations for war finally chased them back home. After Pearl Harbor, Diana started selling war bonds. For a while her social interests—the symphony and the museum—were forgotten. World War II gripped the nation—ration books, shortages, sorrow, and death. For the next few years, the triplets enjoyed the luxury of staying in one place—the Clay Street house in San Francisco.

The triplets still got attention by being a unique group. But, inside the family, the way to curry favor was to develop a special, individual talent. Sara took up the flute; Vail excelled in sports; Sky, her pretty charm hiding the steel beneath, offered as her talent the lack of a talent. The triplets conceded to each other a special interest that was inviolate. In smaller matters Sara loved trains, and in Europe she had been permitted to help choose the trains they rode. She kept the schedules and knew many by heart. Besides her dolls, Sky loved dressing up—for games or for every day. She knew styles and designers and always had an eye for quality. Vail danced elegantly, did an athletic lindy, and kept a diary.

There were events in their childhood that, in later years, the triplets tried to remember in detail. But they experienced their childhood like a dream, and the European periods were especially jumbled—like a jigsaw puzzle.

Garmisch had disclosed Sky's tougher side. In Lugano a little later, Vail had his first taste of inadequacy when he was unable to spare Sara Diana's anger.

They were staying that summer at the Hotel Splendide-Royal in the Swiss-Italian lake country, where the mountains rose straight up from the shoreline. Sky always remembered the cobblestone plaza, with its blue-and-white umbrellas shading the restaurant tables, but Vail remembered the nights. Just before bedtime, the triplets would stand at the window of their bedroom, watching the white boats on the lake. They were edged with lights, and as they sailed across the water, music trailed from them. Where are they going? he wondered. I want to go with them, he thought.

Diana rented a little cart and pony for a picnic outing in a meadow near the lake. Sara was restless, running around in the flower-strewn meadow, shouting. Diana suggested that they recite some French verbs. Sara balked. "I hate verbs!" she cried. "I won't do it!"

"Don't you speak to me or anyone in that tone," Diana said. "Or we will leave."

"I don't want to leave," Sara cried. It was heaven to be out of the hotel and out of their lessons.

"Apologize for your rudeness."

"I didn't say anything—"

"Then our outing is over," Diana said, picking up the uneaten food and packing it away. She motioned Sky and Vail into the cart, but when Sara tried to join them, Diana stopped her. "You chose to be separate by your rudeness, and so you shall be," Diana said, sitting down in the cart. She flicked the little buggy whip at the pony, which started into a trot. Sara ran after them, crying, but Diana would not relent. Vail and Sky looked back at their sister's humiliation.

"Mama," Vail said, "I think Sara's sorry now and wants to be with us."

"She can't," Diana said, urging the pony to go faster. "Sara was rude and disobedient. I will not tolerate it."

Sky and Vail eyed their mother. Her mouth was set in a grim line. They turned back to Sara. She was keeping pace with them, tears streaming down her face. Vail stretched out his hand to Sara but Diana saw him; she flicked the riding crop against his wrist. Finally, Sara stopped running.

"She's just standing there!" Sky screamed.

Sky started to cry. "Stop that," Diana said. Sky's sobs increased. "I said, stop that crying." Sometimes the triplets were like wild animals, quick to cry and shout and scream without any rein on their emotions.

Vail said to Sky, "Mama doesn't like to see us cry." Sky forced herself to stop, but the effort made her throat ache. Vail was looking back at Sara, who was growing smaller and smaller. "Mama! Stop!" he commanded. But Diana drove on, rounding a bend in the little cart path. He was frantic, but nothing he did had any effect. He sat down in the back of the cart and wept.

Finally, when she was ready, Diana stopped. "We'll wait here until she joins us," Diana said calmly.

Sara came pumping around the bend and crawled into the cart. Diana said, "You are children of quality. We have standards in this family, and I look to you to set examples. Rudeness is unacceptable."

An air of defeat hung over the triplets; they rode in silence back to the hotel. When they were alone, Sara said, "When one of us is punished, all of us should share the punishment."

Later that summer, in Paris, after a concert, Sara professed such avid interest in the flutist that Diana bought her a flute in a little leather case. A tutor was hired; Sara studied hard. She felt she was making up for her naughtiness in Lugano. She basked in her mother's special attention. She didn't even mind that she had to practice while Sky and Vail took riding lessons in the Bois de Boulogne.

The night before they left for the States, Sara and Sky were fast asleep when Vail awoke. He couldn't find his teddy. He'd been instructed to knock before entering the door that connected with their mother's rooms, but he forgot. Diana wasn't there. He looked around for his teddy, but the room was jumbled with trunks and stacks of clothing. The door to the bathroom was ajar. He heard water being poured and he peeked inside.

Diana was sitting in her bath, one arm outstretched ready to receive the sponge held in the other hand, the water dripping from it. She had her hair piled loosely on top of her head. Her back was to him. He watched the sponge skate down her glistening arm. She was humming, and the tune echoed in the huge, tiled room. Fascinated and afraid, the forbidden image held him. Suddenly, she was standing up, the water cascading from her white body. She was huge and pure, like a painting in the Louvre, but she was turning and her breasts swung into view. At that instant, Diana saw him.

"You are a nasty little boy," she said coyly, surprised and embarrassed.

"I'm looking for teddy!" he screamed angrily, running from the room.

Vail told his sisters, because they shared everything. But they didn't believe him.

"You're always making up stories!" they said.

"I am not!" he cried, stung. He'd show them; he drew a picture of their mother, naked. Vail was good at drawing.

"Okay," Sara said. "So what?"

"It just looks like the statue in the museum," Sky said shrewdly.

They forgot about the picture until Diana found it as she made her last sweep of their rooms. When the porter had left with their luggage, she took the drawing out of her purse. Years later they could still remember that moment.

"Who drew this?" Diana asked coldly. The triplets, standing in their line, did not respond. "Confess! What if it had been left behind? What would people think?"

"I drew it," Sara said.

"It's mine," Vail said.

"No, it's mine," Sky said, smiling.

Ned had inherited the Clay Street house and the Wyman ranch in the late thirties, but by that time, most of the ranchland had been sold off. All that remained of the once-fabulous estate was a collection of horses and some acreage. But Ned was optimistic; he loved the ranch more than any place on earth. "Animals," Diana was fond of saying with a brief smile, "always tempt your father away from real life."

The summer the triplets turned twelve, Ned gave them a chestnut filly with a white blaze down her nose and white stockings. Her neck arched demurely, and her coat shone in the sunlight. The triplets were good riders, and he said that if they took care of the horse, he would give each of them a horse when they were fifteen.

They were standing in front of the old ranch house,

—34—

gazing proudly at their new horse. Then the children let out a whoop of sheer delight; the filly started. "Less noise, darlings," said Diana. "You'll scare her." She put an arm around a beaming Ned. "It must be understood that you are never to ride without one of the adults present. Isn't that what you decided, Ned?" Diana asked.

"Your mother's right, kids. No riding without supervision."

"Don't worry, Mother," Sky said.

Vail smiled dangerously. "We don't want a sock in the kisser," he said. The triplets liked using the slang they picked up at the movies because it irritated Diana. But sometimes, like today, Vail could get a merry laugh out of her by using it.

The triplets named their horse Pegasus. They took turns riding her all afternoon, while Diana sat on the wide porch of the old-fashioned brick-and-shingled house. It stood on a rise that looked over the fields and the big, sprawling stables. It was a dreamy afternoon; the insects buzzed in the grass, and a sweet, warm breeze came across the meadow, crackling the leaves of the huge poplar trees.

"Maggie! Look!" the triplets cried. Maggie Caulfield was coming out of the stable. For fifteen years, she had worked for the Wymans on the ranch, which lay northeast of San Francisco in the foothills of the Sierras. Maggie ran the ranch from a small neat office off the study, and she had her own house down by the river that bisected the land.

Maggie wanted to get the stables painted a spanking white, but money was short, said Ned Wyman. The Wymans didn't know what short money was. Certainly Diana didn't. And what a tight rein she kept on the triplets—they never got a chance to blow off steam. If Maggie had heard Diana tell them to "be civilized" once, she'd heard it a hundred times. If one of them came in with a B from their private school in San Francisco, Diana smiled and said it was just fine, and then she'd say they could do better. Diana was hard to please, and Ned Wyman, he never disagreed with her—never.

Maggie was forty, wiry, and slim, and she wore her thick, stiff black hair in a bun on top of her head. Testy, that's what Diana called her. Maggie was black; she had plenty to be testy about and plenty to be grateful for. She'd been raised in Alabama; her son was dead, her daughter had two babies and no husband, and her own Iz, a man so black he looked like night coming for you—he'd been killed in jail. Yes, she was testy.

"You look good up on that sweet filly," Maggie said to Vail. At twelve Vail had a soft superior expression, but he was still his sisters' protector, the one who tried to patch up misunderstandings.

"Sara Bay," Maggie said, "why don't you ever run a brush through that brassy mop of hair? Look at Sky. Neat as a pin." She started up to the veranda. The triplets were good riders, but the girls seemed to feel best when Vail won in sports. It had upset their tacit balance with each other when Sky had finished first in the school relay race.

Diana watched her triplets and dreamed. She saw Sara in a concert hall, graceful and feminine, her eyes slightly closed, the tunes streaming from her flute. Gifted, her teachers had said. But Sara was also passionate and rash. Her approach to life was to open it like a piece of fruit and devour it. Old Mrs. Wyman had wanted Diana to curb Sara's quick intelligence "because a girl that smart would never get along with boys." But Diana had paid no attention to her mother-in-law on that one. Diana only tried to curb Sara's temper. It reminded her of Virginia's spells. So unseemly.

Sky's gift was sweetness. Diana had tried to find other gifts in her but ballet and art school had been dismal failures. She had a sensational doll collection. She sang nicely. Perhaps when Sky was older, her voice would ripen and she could sing professionally. Of the three of them, Sky remained the most tractable until she felt crossed. Then she was a tiger, sure of her ground and her rights.

Diana saw Vail as a cultivated man, perhaps an attorney or an art collector. Vail wrote nicely for his age but he needed discipline. He had an inquisitive mind. Diana thought he might do well in science, too.

"Vail, get off!" Sara cried. "It's my turn!"

"Children!" Diana called out. "Don't scream. Sara, another half hour and then practice."

Sara groaned. "Not today, Mother." Sara hated practic-

—36—

ing now. The flute was an albatross she couldn't shake. Sky was pulling on Vail's leg. Sky didn't have to practice anything; Sky still played with her dolls. Sometimes Sara hated Sky.

"We practice every day, Sara Bay," Diana said.

Vail got off Pegasus. Sara mounted, and Sky immediately climbed up behind her. They turned Peg away from the house and trotted off.

Diana dreamed on. Should her girls have marriages or careers—that was Diana's private quandary. They were too unusual, too beautiful; they deserved more than marriage and motherhood, though Sky seemed headed in that direction. But marriage was limiting; no one knew that better than Diana. She and Ned had been so close in those early years, but after the triplets were born, their relationship had changed. She had never regretted it; that was part of nature's cycle. Diana brushed some invisible dust off her sleeve, brushing away the poignancy of happier times.

The summer of 1942 changed Sara's life.

It was just before dawn a few days after Ned had given the triplets the horse they called Pegasus. Sara and Sky wanted to take her for a ride, but it would be hours before anyone was up to supervise.

"This is the best part of the day," Sky said.

Vail was sleepy and ambivalent about the whole thing. But the minute he saw Pegasus in her stall with the fresh dawn light on her rump, he knew that disaster hunched between her wide ribs and crawled along her broad back. "No!" he cried.

"Shut up, Vail!" Sara hissed. "They'll hear!"

He implored them not to go; they were set on it. Sara put a bridle on Peg and climbed up on Peg's back. "C'mon, Vail, you lead," she said. Reluctantly, Vail clambered up in front of Sara; Sky got on behind her.

"This is not a good idea," he muttered, guiding Pegasus out of the stables and along the dirt road that bordered the paddock, then urging her across one of the open fields toward the glowering, snowy mountains.

The air was crisp and bright. They were riding bareback, squeezed against each other, bumping along at a good trot.

—37—

Vail yelled and rolled her into a gallop. He gripped the bridle and clung to her neck, her mane flying into his face. Sara had locked her arms around his waist. "Faster! Faster!" Sara had screamed, and Pegasus had jogged into a bone-jolting ride, closing on the mountains. Sky, on the end, bounced on Peg's flanks, her knees gripping Peg's sleek brown body one minute, rising away from it the next. She wanted to scream at them to stop, but she couldn't get the words out. She looked up at the glistening mountains and thought she was going to ride right into them.

Peg had better sense and gradually eased off to a trot. Her riders gripped each other and looked around. Far behind them the white and brick buildings of the ranch were beginning to catch the sun. The summer morning resonated with bird song, the clop of Peg's hooves, and the smell of sweet grass.

"Let's get back before anyone catches us," Vail said.

"Not yet," Sky said.

"This is our secret," Sara said, quick to summarize their joint circumstances. "We'll always remember it!"

The sun was fully up when they turned Peg back toward the ranch. Pegasus was galloping, bouncing the children around on her back, when Sara, her hair streaming behind her, raised her hands above her head in sheer joy. Pegasus stumbled, breaking the rhythm of the ride. Sara grabbed for Vail, missed, and flew headfirst off the horse. She hit the ground solidly, chin out, and felt her teeth slam into each other. Vail pulled Pegasus to a halt. Sara lay crumpled on the ground, her mouth bloody, her eyes glazed and staring. They jumped off.

"Sara! Sara!" he screamed. She groaned and spit out a bloody tooth.

Sky cried out, "Jeepers, she's got no front teeth!"

The accident was a catastrophe.

When Sara got home from the hospital and oral surgery, she lay in her bed and listened to the house; it seemed unnaturally quiet. She got out of bed shakily and wandered downstairs and into the study.

Diana sat at a small Louis XIV desk in front of an oval stained-glass window. Vail, sitting very quietly with Sky at a card table, looked up at Sara solemnly. Since the accident he no longer denied to himself that something was wrong with him. He had known riding Peg would be a disaster, but he had kept it to himself.

"Go back to bed, darling," Diana said dreamily. Sara could hear the scratch of her pen on the thick paper.

"I'm sorry about the accident," Sara said thickly, her mouth aching. Vail rolled his eyes. He looked very sad.

"Yes, it's a shame," her mother replied. She tossed her head languidly. The pale sun shining through the colored glass cast a rainbow of light on her cheek. "No more music." Sara backed away. She felt she was being dismissed, that she was, simply, no longer a candidate with a future.

She looked at Sky, whose pale eyes stared back at her. Sara felt that Sky had somehow been taken from her, had switched from being an ally to a competitor.

Sky said, "You're in your bare feet, Sara." She had been jealous of Sara's high spirits, her courage, and the attention Sara had received for her music. Sometimes Sky had felt cowardly compared to Sara. But today the fruits of courage were bitter.

"Mama," Sara said tentatively. "We'll always ride with you. From now on."

"No more riding," Diana said. "I sold the horse."

Sara screamed. She ran up to Diana and beat her fists on her mother's arm, shrieking.

"What's all this?" Ned bellowed, appearing in the doorway.

"She sold Peg!" Sara screamed as the guilt ballooned inside her.

"I will not have this kind of behavior, Sara Bay!" Diana was saying. Vail and Sky, pale and shaken by the events that Sara was just discovering, did not know what to do.

"You will calm down immediately," Ned said.

"It was for your own good, and for Sky's and Vail's, too," Diana said.

Sara looked imploringly at her father. "Daddy, no!" she sobbed.

"I'm afraid so, chicken. You could have been killed." He felt immeasurably sad; Peg had been his special gift to them. "When you're older you'll have horses."

Sara began sobbing. They sounded so reasonable.

"Sweetheart, don't sob," Diana pleaded, gently, from the barricade of the little Louis table. "We did the right thing," she added hesitantly. She looked up at Ned.

From her perch at the card table, Sky silently cried out for Sara. Sky couldn't have put it into words, but she knew Sara was in agony because she felt responsible for the loss of their horse and because she had lost her unique place in the family. Sky knew that Vail understood it too.

In 1945, when the triplets were fifteen, America had won the war and was the greatest power in the world. It was a heady national feeling: Americans couldn't fail at anything. In San Francisco the streets rang with jubilation as handsome young men in uniform arrived by the thousands. Frank Sinatra sang "Swinging on a Star," and the bobby-soxers, among whom Sky and Sara numbered themselves, sighed. They read *Forever Amber* and went to see Joan Crawford in *Mildred Pierce*.

It was after they'd seen Ingrid Bergman in *Spellbound* that Sara announced she was going to be an actress.

"Oh, darling, that's absurd." Diana laughed. "It's so déclassé." But Ned liked the idea.

The triplets had acted out the movies they saw for years. Vail played William Powell or Cary Grant; Sky was Gene Tierney or Joan Fontaine; Sara played Claudette Colbert, Myrna Loy, or Jean Arthur. They reenacted most of the *Thin Man* series, *State Fair*, and *A Song To Remember*. Playacting had been a regular feature of their lives, only it was better than reality. It was a splendid and accepted dishonesty. They could shout and weep and get angry. Sky and Sara were confidantes, mirrors, and rivals in the great game of acting out movies. But around 1945, Vail dropped out. "I don't want to pretend I'm someone else!" he said.

"But you're the one who always said honesty didn't count!" Sky said.

"It does now!" he replied. "A sketchbook is honest, writing poems is honest, but not aping the movies!" He sat down heavily on the window seat and opened his sketchbook in which, Sky and Sara knew, he also wrote poems he never showed anyone.

"But we're doing it in assembly!" Sara said. "It" was

The Gang's All Here. Sara had decided they would play Alice Faye, Carmen Miranda, and Edward Everett Horton.

"When did *that* happen?" Sky asked, repulsed by the idea.

"I offered," Sara confessed.

"How could you do that without asking?" Sky demanded.

"I thought you'd be pleased," Sara said. Sky had always been a staunch supporter of the game.

"I'm not going to do it," Sky said. Sky was far more emotional than she let on. She wanted to be special, but she didn't think that she was. And though she dreamed of being admired and wearing beautiful clothes, being in front of a crowd with all eyes on her frightened her.

"I won't do it either," Vail said. He saw the crushed look on Sara's face. "It was okay when we were younger, but not now, Sara." Sky backed him up.

An impasse. It was Saturday afternoon. They'd been skating that morning and had come home for lunch. The house was empty.

Vail's sisters had a symbiotic bond. In school exams, Sara was never nervous. "Sky does that for me," she said. In turn, Sara protected Sky by studying for her and feeding her the information that might be asked of them in class. They went everywhere together, often dressed alike or in reverse (Sky in black, Sara in white). But now, Sky had taken Vail's side.

The telephone rang.

"Hello?" Sara said, picking up the receiver.

"Is this Sky?" asked a hesitant, querulous voice.

"Yes," Sara said. "Who's this?" She glanced at Sky sitting at the kitchen table with Vail.

"Ben Griffin." After a pause, he went on, "I want to invite you to the Christmas dance, if you'd like to go."

"Really?" Sara said, trying to hold back her giggles. Sky looked at her curiously. "Well, I'm not interested in that. I think it's stupid."

Ben was taken aback. "But you said—"

"Well," she said, "I've thought it over. I've no intention of going with you." She hung up and smiled at Sky. "He wanted you to go to the dance." Sara's laugh was a bray

—41—

that was full of joy. She fell all over herself, the furniture, the floor, throwing her head back and flinging her wild hair around.

"You didn't!" Sky screamed, rushing for the telephone.

"Oh, not again," Vail groaned.

"Yes," Sara choked, still laughing. "I did!"

"It's not funny!" Sky was dialing Ben's number.

"It *is* funny! And he's so very, very serious," Sara said, mimicking Ben.

"It's busy!" Sky banged down the phone.

"I will not escort you two to another dance!" Vail shouted.

The phone rang. Sky picked up the receiver. It was Diana. She was downtown working on a housing project for Negro veterans.

"Sara," Diana began, making the mistake everyone did on the telephone between Sky and Sara, "read me that letter from the governor. I left it on my desk, dear."

Sky arched her brow at Sara's questioning expression.

"I'm sorry, I have rehearsal now. I really can't stop for a minute." And she hung up. "That," she said, letting her words sink in, "was someone who thought they were talking to you!"

"Who?" Sara asked, guardedly.

"Mother." Then Sky's laughter broke from her, and she started hopping around. Sky always hopped when she laughed.

It was an old prank. Until Vail's voice changed, no one—not even Diana—could tell the triplets apart on the telephone, which gave them a sense of mischievous power.

Laughter had salvaged the afternoon. "Oh, never mind about the old movie game," Sara said. "It's silly."

But in a few years a single event was to change all their lives. The undertow would catch Sky first, suck Sara after her, and eventually engulf Vail.

3

By the summer of 1952, the Korean War was stalemated in truce talks, each side clinging to rocky real estate after desperate battles in Seoul and on Heartbreak Ridge. Americans thought of it as a minor skirmish in a country they could hardly find on the map. They wondered what U.S. troops were doing over there and why they hadn't won that war. They wondered who had started it, and why. Senator Joseph McCarthy, in a fever of denunciations, said that Americans were dying in Korea because of Communist sabotage in the United States government.

It was a time of distrust and anxiety. But the summer glowed with hope: The great American general, Dwight Eisenhower, had declared himself a candidate for president and was moving into the Republican Convention with strong support. Victorious Ike knew all about wars. Moreover, you could take one look at Ike and know he was loyal to the U. S. of A. Diana had nothing against Eisenhower, but she didn't think generals should be presidents. She was full of her plans to work for the Democratic nominee when the triplets graduated from college that June.

Diana had kept a tight rein on her children during their college years, and partly because of this, partly because it was the early fifties, they were naive for their age. Sara and Sky had gone to Mills College, and Vail had attended Stanford. Though they had not lived at home, Diana had insisted they spend frequent weekends and every vacation period in the city. They were never very far out of her reach.

As soon as graduation was over, Diana turned Vail into a clerk-messenger for Democratic headquarters, but Sara slipped through her fingers when she got a job for the summer at the Marin Theater Company. She talked them into auditioning Sky, too.

"But, jeez, Sky, give me something!" Jim Fry whispered to her in the wings of the little theater. They were in rehearsals; the first play opened in six days.

Jim was twenty, a jovial bearlike young man with a wide, mobile mouth and quiet eyes.

"I'm sorry," Sky said to him. "I'm doing the best I can." She laughed uncomfortably. "Sara talked me into this." She liked the idea of being in plays, not the reality.

Sara came off stage carrying her script rolled up in one hand. She looked like a sunburst in her yellow dress with her burnished curly hair radiating from her head. She frowned at Jim.

"Your scene is fine," Sara said to Sky. "All you need is a little confidence. C'mon, we're late for notes." She had worked in little theater before and had acted in plays at Mills; she was not about to let Jim push Sky around.

Jim flapped his arms at his sides and glared after Sky. "How can Sky look so great," he said to Vic Oumansky, the stage manager, "and be such a hopeless actress?" Jim was irritated at her, but it was hard for him to be angry because she was so beautiful. He sensed that she was just beginning to realize how beautiful she was.

"They are most the gorgeous creatures God ever made," Vic said, watching Sara depart. Sara and Sky were both wearing full skirts with big petticoats underneath. Their clinch-belted waists looked tiny.

Vic had an angular, assertive profile, straight brown hair cut in a duck tail, and blue eyes. He went to night school, majoring, at his mother's insistence, in engineering. Jim Fry, Vic's best friend, had helped him get the stage-managing job. Vic would have preferred set building. He lived on hopes and fanatasized himself as a Broadway set designer. His distance from that objective made him cranky and aloof.

Jim had studied acting in New York; he was playing the male lead in the company's first play of the season. He

—44—

knocked Vic on the shoulder and rolled his bulky, muscular frame into the green room for notes with the rest of the cast. Vic took a seat on a high stool near the door, and unrolled a pack of cigarettes from the sleeve of his T-shirt.

Lila Lewis, twenty-two, sat on the bench; she was the female lead in the play. Acting in summer stock all over the country since she was sixteen had made her a strong performer. Her carrot red hair was done in a poodle cut. Lila had a quirky sense of humor. She was the daughter of a celebrated thirties movie idol. She had made it clear that this was her last summer in little theater because she was on her way back to Hollywood.

The director, Sherman, was a short, intense man with a beard. He looked critically at the motley group before him. They were his punishment. At forty, Sherman had failed to win favor with the New York theatrical establishment. His original talent had turned into competence, and his dreams had died somewhere between 43rd and 44th Streets. Knowing he'd never be better than he was now, he'd accepted the job of artistic director at the Marin Theater. Sherman was afraid that their first play, *Caught in the Act*, would bomb. Part of the problem was Sky; she had a small but crucial role.

"Now, people, we've got a real problem in the second act, and it's not the play," he began.

During college, Sky had embraced acting with a silent and desperate ambivalence. But she hadn't confided any of this to Sara because she didn't want Sara to think she was just copying her. Sara was the family actress.

Acting soothed and terrified Sky. It was soothing because one minute she was herself and the next, on stage, she was someone else. She didn't know why acting terrified her. She ached to be good in the part Sara had wangled for her, but she felt mediocre. Sara declared that she had never been nervous. Sara liked rehearsals; Sky felt phony in them. She endured them nervously, speaking her lines flatly, trying to hide under an air of indifference her fear of acting.

"When are you going to show me something, Sky?" Sherman suddenly demanded. She jerked forward, aware that all eyes were upon her. "I want you to do Scene Two,

Act Two, with Jim after notes," Sherman steamed on, leaving Sky devastated. Why had she ever agreed to this play so she and Sara could spend the summer together?

After notes, Sky tugged at Sherman's jacket as she and Sara walked out of the green room. "I don't know why rehearsals are so hard for me," she whispered to him.

"She'll be great when we open," Sara said, staunchly.

"Everyone's got to play rehearsals like performances," Sherman said. "I have to see what you're going to do on opening night!" He clapped his hands. "Show time, everyone!" he yelled. "Let's give Sky and Jim an audience." Grumbling, they rearranged themselves in the small theater.

"Let's see what you can do," he tossed at Sky. Sherman had reluctantly decided to let Sky go and was figuring out who could replace her, and how he'd tell Sara, who played the second lead so well.

Sara groaned. "That's a bit much," she said, sitting down next to Vic.

"You want to have a cup of coffee after rehearsal?" he asked her, trying to get his mind off his problems by staring at her long, thick eyelashes.

She tilted her foxy head at him, and smiled. "You don't want to go out with me," she said. "Our mother interviews all our dates. So humiliating. Maybe some other time." Sara had a wide, full mouth, and she laughed a lot as though she were on display in a contest.

A few rows ahead of them, Sherman leafed through his thick notebook. "In this scene, as I am going to trust you know, Jim—Martin—is breaking off his engagement to you. He's bent on marrying your sister. It's foolish and cruel of him. You begin to feel 'the slip of madness,'" he said, quoting from Shakespeare, "and it's this rejection that starts sending you over the edge. Then you go into your monologue. Got it?"

"Poor girl," Betty, the woman who ran the lights, whispered to Lila.

"Poor girl, my ass!" said Lila. "She does a great audition, and that's the last work anyone ever sees out of her. It's like playing to a wood post." She pulled her white pop-it necklace apart and rearranged it into two tight chokers. Sara, sitting directly behind them, saw mean little lines of pleasure

—46—

crease either side of Lila's thin mouth. Sara clasped her hands together tensely.

Onstage, Sky was shivering. She felt completely hollow inside. She knew all her lines but she couldn't remember a single one. She sat down next to Jim on the sofa center stage.

"Whenever you're ready," Sherman intoned from the dark house.

Jim took her hand and felt it quiver in his. She was petrified. "Sue," he said, using her character's name, "don't be afraid." She smiled tightly.

He said his first line. "Dammit, Sue, that's what I've wanted to tell you for a long time." He looked at her icy blue eyes. She was fastened on him, connected to him suddenly in a way that made him shiver. Her riveting concentration sucked him into the world of the play instantly, completely.

Out in the house, Sherman slowly sat up. Sky was saying the lines as if they had just popped into her head, reacting completely to Martin's unconscionable confession. Behind him, Lila's smile vanished as she, too, was drawn into that other reality on the stage. Sara leaned back and relaxed; she knew Sky could do the scene. As the scene progressed, the cast and crew were held by the force of Sue's panic and misery, which had suddenly flown up like something wild in front of them.

Sky moved around the set, changing the blocking marked out for her in rehearsals, picking at a plant, trying to pour a glass of sherry and, failing that, using the business integrally with the subtext of what the character was going through. Well into her monologue by now, Sky sat down, stood up, took hold of Martin's hat at precisely the right moment—though that business, too, had never been discussed—and ended by wearing it. She was pathetic and courageous, naive and complex, emotionally out of control and struggling to save her sanity.

She ended up huddled on the floor by a chair Jim had just left. She said her last line, tipped the hat back on her head as she pressed her cheek against the arm of the chair in a gesture so moving that, when the scene was over, no one in the audience stirred.

Sara leaned over and hissed, "Whaddaya think of that, Lila dear?"

"Well, I'll be damned," Lila said. The cast broke into applause.

Sherman cleared his throat. "Guess she'll do," he quipped lamely, to cover how moved her performance had left him. Would it be like that every night? He went up on stage. "Very good," he said, pumping Sky's hand. He turned to the house. "Okay, everyone, that's it for today. Ten A.M. tomorrow, and remember—more energy!"

He turned back to Sky. "Let's talk." Sky waved at Sara and beckoned her up on the stage.

"How can he do that? Nixon of all people!" Diana was saying to Vail as she picked up Sara and Sky in the car after rehearsal. Sara was watching Vic walk away from the theater, his hands in his pockets. It would have been nice to have had coffee with him. "I've had experience with Nixon! Get in, Sara." The Republicans had chosen Richard Nixon as Ike's running mate. Diana had first seen Nixon up close when she'd worked on the 1950 senatorial campaign that pitted Helen Gahagan Douglas against Nixon, then an obscure California congressman.

Diana's blond hair fell in soft waves and was secured by a dressy clasp at the back of her neck. She had a closet full of dramatic hats, today's selection being a navy blue straw with a clutch of white ribbon bows on one side. Over the years, Diana had been, by turns, an obsessive or casual parent, for she could seize on an interest or issue and hardly notice the triplets for weeks. Then, with the issue resolved, she returned to them with renewed force.

"Ç'est Si Bon" floated out of the radio. Diana turned it off. "Nothing's ç'est si bon with Nixon a heartbeat from the presidency!" she snapped.

"Mother, Ike's not president yet," Vail said.

"Nixon's got the personality of a Fuller brush man and the ethics of Genghis Khan!" Diana said as she drove through Sausalito.

Vail lounged in the back seat, pretending to admire his new baggy pegged pants and suede shoes. But he was miserable and embarrassed. The memory of last night was too fresh.

—48—

Vail was a handsome male version of his sisters. He had a finely drawn face—"that foxy look," Ned called it—sharp and clever. His narrow eyes turned up at the outer corners, giving him a quizzical, playful look. He was resigned to being short—five feet, six inches short. To make up for it, Vail chased girls.

Being around his mother was stifling. He wasn't a teenager any more but she treated him like one. She was expecting him to be an attorney, a career of no interest to Vail. It didn't even interest his father because Ned simply expected him to be "someone worthwhile." Stanford law school sat at the end of his summer like a malevolent spider.

Vail had owned a used Chevy coupe since his sophomore year in college. He had souped it up into a real bomb of a hot rod. Last night, he and Dolores had been driving it back from Half Moon Bay. Remembering, he cringed now and looked out the window of his mother's car. He had known Dolores in high school when she had been stuck on him. She was a funny, brash girl who still wore braids looped over her head in a crown. Last night the moon had come up to light the narrow rural road. Rows and rows of artichokes radiated across the fields like an ancient design, gilded by moonlight. The air smelled of damp earth and hard leaves.

Dolores had made it difficult to drive. He had pulled over. "I'm crazy about you, Vail," she'd said. She had no guile in her. This was exactly what he had hoped for. But Dolores was greedy and possessive. She was climbing all over him, and he was aching to climb all over her, if she would only give him the chance. "Make me fly, Vail. Take me," she sighed. A performance was demanded. He yearned to make her fly, to reach her expectations, just as he strove to satisfy his parents'. It had been easy to make complacent coeds "fly," but Dolores was a handful. She was experienced.

He tried now to blot out the memory as he stretched casually in the back seat of his mother's car. But it kept returning. When it had become apparent that Vail was not performing up to standard, Dolores had cast a look at him—condescension, arrogance, frustration, disappointment, and superiority clustered in that one look and roasted him.

"Sky did a really good scene today," Sara said gleefully.

Sky floated, hearing over and over what Sherman had said to her. She had done something really good. Better than that, she'd known the scene was special while she was doing it. She said, "Sherman thinks both of us should go to New York to study!"

"The arts are significant but I want all of you to get more involved in current events. These are crucial times we're living in."

Sara and Sky looked out the window. They were crossing the Golden Gate Bridge. "If we were in New York," Sky said, "we could go see *Pal Joey.*"

"What would people say if I let you go off by yourselves to New York?" Diana said.

"Mother!" Sara shouted hotly. "Plenty of people our age go off by themselves! Two of my best friends are married!"

Diana made no response.

"Let's settle for seeing *High Noon* tonight," Vail said. "I hear it's terrific."

"That's nice," Sky said, pleased. When Vail wasn't thinking about his car, he was thinking about breasts, thighs, sex—girls. He didn't seem close to them any more but Sky knew that deep down he still felt protective of his sisters just as he looked to them for protection, too. "You would have liked my scene, Mother," she added brightly. "Sherman thinks we should study with someone like Mr. Strasberg."

"I'll have a talk with Sherman," Diana said. "We can't get our hopes up." She removed her hat.

Sara and Sky wondered silently why they couldn't get their hopes up. "I live on hopes," Sara said, giggling.

"So did the butterflies," Vail said lugubriously, "while the chipmunks were storing up nuts for the long winter."

"Squirrels," said Diana, smiling at him in the rearview mirror. "The grasshopper played all summer while the industrious squirrels stored up for the winter." She smoothed her hair back with the side of her hand in the odd, flat gesture she often used.

"Places! Places!" Vic hissed.

Sara was alone on the darkened stage. She could hear the audience on the other side of the curtain, murmuring and shifting. It was a thrilling sound full of expectation. The curtain parted and splashed her in a blaze of light. She felt the eyes of the audience on her like a caress.

In the wings, Sky clutched her icy hands together. Why had she ever agreed to this again? She was petrified. It was all Sara's fault. In a minute Sky would have to pick up a glass onstage and pour water into it from a pitcher. She wasn't going to be able to do it. It was a nightmare.

A small hanging mirror by Vic's stage manager's desk winked at her: Mirrors were her severest critics and her greatest friends. She looked at her reflection, hoping it would calm her. She pushed at her hair, brushed at one of her thick, black brows. She glanced fearfully out at her bubbling, confident sister onstage.

In the audience, Diana Wyman tilted forward in her seat as her husband, Ned, leaned back and folded his arms across his chest. Just look at Sara bailing out that actor's mistake! How beautiful she was as she swept across the stage, her head perfectly angled to catch the light, carefully timing her laughs except for that last one—she should have waited a moment longer. It was so easy now to see Sara as an actress. Diana leaned back and caught a whiff of Ned's last martini as he shifted beside her. She closed her eyes and let her daughters' voices lull her—gentle, colorful, full of power and music.

Sky heard her cue. She felt sick. As she walked onstage, the lights warmed her and she turned instinctively toward them, tilting her head. Suddenly she was assured and light-hearted. Sara and the others faded out; they were Martha and Pete and Sam, and she was their visiting cousin from Philadelphia. She reached for the glass with trembling fingers and pressed it against the lip of the pitcher.

Sara eyed Sky nervously from the distance of stage right. "Pete," she said to Jim, "how can we have forgotten our Sue?"

For some reason, Jim responded with a completely different line. Sky turned. Sara turned. Sky said, "You were always too clever, Peter," and laughed gaily. Sky had carried that one off perfectly. They were back on track.

In the audience, Ned shifted uncomfortably in the hard seat. He'd never thought Sky would wreck the play, and now he couldn't keep his eyes off her.

Ned Wyman was forty-seven years old, his huge frame

softening somewhat, his good tenor voice gone, and most of his ideals long forgotten. Being in the munitions business and being away from the ranch all these years had done that. It was necessary, of course. Triplets were expensive. Diana had done a good job, though. His hat was off to her on that one. He looked at her sharp profile, her head lifted a little, the old "nose-in-air" look, as he called it, loving it, resenting it. Her blond hair crested back from her brow in waves. She improved with age. She looked forty-six, yes, but she was still slender and somehow agile, compact. He ran a hand across his jaw, felt the loose skin, the sag under his chin. He glanced at Vail sitting next to him and tried to find his younger self.

Ned smiled. In August, they'd shut up the San Francisco house and go out to the ranch. They'd all ride, and he and Vail would go fishing, and Maggie would do up all those cold summer dishes out on the veranda. Nothing would ever separate him from the ranch again—no matter what Diana said.

A sharp, funny squeak from Sky brought Diana and Ned out of their separate reveries and back to the stage. Gradually, Diana began to notice that when Sky was onstage it was hard to see anyone else. Diana began listening very carefully.

The play was almost over. "Oh, God, don't let it end," Sara said to herself, gazing into the blinding lights. She felt whole, wanted, and visible when she was onstage. Sky felt exactly the opposite—invisible and safe: She didn't have to be Sky any more.

Backstage in their cramped dressing room, Sara was squealing to Sky, "You see? Wasn't that fun?"

Sky was dreamy, breathless, her eyes dancing. "I wish we could do this every night for as long as we live."

"Sweethearts," said Diana, coming through the door with a crowd of people in her wake, "let me be the first. You were splendid!" Ned was beside her, smiling broadly. He drew his daughters into a bear hug.

"Look what I have here!" he said, holding up a bottle of champagne.

"Oh, Neddie," Diana said.

—52—

Vail pushed through. "You were both terrible," he said. "Such a disgrace." He kissed them, cackling merrily.

"Sara, dear," Diana said, making a space for herself on a chair, "why didn't you do that business with the earrings? We worked so hard on it."

Sara laughed. "Can you imagine? I forgot! Isn't that ridiculous?"

"Next time. Now, here's the plan," Diana said happily. "We're all going over to the Mark Hopkins with the Bramsons."

"But Mother, some of the players—" Sara began.

"Just for a while, darling. Just a few friends."

Sara switched gears and hooked an arm around Sky's neck. "Wasn't Sky wonderful? A really powerful moment up there. Didn't you think, Vail?" He was leaning against the wall, his eyes snapping around the room.

"Magnificent." He was happy for his sisters' fun. He went over to Ned, who was struggling with the cork in the champagne bottle. Vail felt vaguely responsible for Ned and hoped he could live up to all his expectations.

The cork popped explosively. Ned started to dole out the champagne into tiny paper cups.

"Oh, Ned, for the children?" Diana said.

"Mother," Sky groaned, "we're almost twenty-two!"

"What do you think we did at college, Mom—study?" Vail hooted.

"Just a little toast," Ned said. He looked a trifle sheepish. The triplets all started talking at once. Ned laughed and handed out the champagne. "I should have brought another bottle," Ned said to Vail. Ned was looking forward to spending August with his son. "Why don't you and I go down to John's next week and have lunch, Son?"

"Sure, Dad." Vail instantly imagined what the lunch would be like. Ned was going to ask what Vail wanted to do with his life, a question Vail had ducked for a couple of years. Well, not this time. Vail wanted to write and he wanted to draw; he did not want to go into law. He could already see the expression on Ned's face when he told him that. Ned had never once sided with the triplets against Diana. What could Vail say, he wondered, to get his father to side with him?

A photographer materialized, taking shots for the *San Francisco Chronicle*. Flashbulbs went off. People squealed.

Reed Corbett stood in the doorway scanning the room. He saw a crowd of jabbering people around two beautiful young women in stage makeup. There was something flamboyant and glamorous about the one with the wild reddish blond hair. The other one, more aloof, was simply breathtaking. He went over to them.

"Congratulations to you both," Reed said in his deep voice. He introduced himself to Sara and Sky. "What a dreadful play, but you were very good in it!"

Sara's first impression of Reed Corbett was one of darkness—burning dark eyes, glossy dark hair. He was lean and well built, as though he was used to hard work. His expression was kind and attentive.

"Sara! We're going to some place called the Pit!" It was Vic and Jim calling from the hall.

"Come meet the family!" Sara yelled back.

They shouldered through. Sara made the introductions.

"Triplets," Ned said proudly.

"Really?" Reed asked.

"Sara's the oldest by an hour or so," Sky said to him, "and she's the hothead, too—"

"*Honestly*, Sky!" Diana snapped.

"And next is Vail—he's never very serious about anything—and then there's me!"

"Well, you and your sister are very talented," Reed said. He was about to say something else but changed his mind.

"Look, I'm on vacation this week for some sailing. I'm a film director in Los Angeles."

"Are you a famous director?" Sara laughed her famous bray and slapped Sky on the shoulder.

"No, but I've got a nice picture lined up," Reed said. Sara liked him; there was something solid and courteous about him.

"What's the picture about?" Sky asked. For all her delicacy, Reed sensed there was something straining for release in Sky compared to Sara, on whom the exaggerated gesture looked natural.

Reed had come backstage to ask Sky to do a screen test,

—54—

but he couldn't ask her in front of her sister. "It's too noisy!" he said, laughing. Conversation eddied about them.

Sara bent down to whisper something to Vail, who was sitting on the arm of a chair, swinging one leg. She held her wild hair to one side to keep it out of her face. Reed saw the nape of her neck: a V-shaped ribbon of hair trailed down her white skin. It stirred him. He glanced at Sky and smiled. Deep dimples appeared in his cheeks. Triplets! he thought. Lenny Kaplan, the studio's publicity chief, would have a field day with triplets! Lenny had more nutty, grandiose, and downright vulgar ideas per second than any other human being in America.

The crowd was thinning out. At the door Reed turned back and said, looking at Sky, "Don't lose your naiveté. It's all we ever have." His quiet voice was drowned out by Vic.

"Everyone down to the Pit!" Vic yelled. Sara took his arm and gazed admiringly at his broad shoulders. His eyes flashed with energy. "Vail, c'mon," said Vic. "Tell them to get a move on."

"They move on their own steam," Vail said of his sisters.

"We can't go," Sara was insisting to Vic. "Mother—"

Lila stood right behind him. "Whaddaya mean you can't go? Everyone's going!"

"Sky," Jim said, taking her hand. "Please come down with the company and bring your triplets!!" He laughed so musically it was impossible not to laugh with him.

Reed had followed Ned and Diana out the stage door. He reintroduced himself. "Do you think Sky would be interested in a screen test?" he asked.

"Sky?" Diana said, drawing back. "You mean Sara."

"No, Mrs. Wyman, I mean Sky."

Reed Corbett had been raised in the mountain community around Shasta in Northern California. His mother and father owned a gas-station-bar-grocery-store there and had, by working sixteen hours a day, raised five children. Reed, the eldest, had had a hard, decent childhood that he looked back on with respect and affection. When he was twenty-one, with three years of college under his belt, the Japanese had bombed Pearl Harbor. Reed joined the Army and spent four years slogging through action in Europe as a foot soldier, having the youth pressed out of him. Yet he never lost his innate capacity for compassion or his optimism. He could have been an officer, but he preferred his corporal's stripes and, later, his sergeant's stripes. For four years he slept in the mud, protected his men, and he buried some. Though he was not wounded once, he was changed.

When he got out he went to Hollywood, and through an Army buddy who'd been an assistant director before the war, he began working as an assistant director, too. People liked him, he made friends easily, yet he was nobody's hack. He wanted to be a good director and maybe someday make a film that would do some good. He wasn't ambitious in the feral way many people in Hollywood were; just by directing one film he had gone beyond any ordinary dreams in his family.

Under the noble, high-beamed ceiling of the Clift Hotel's Redwood Room, Reed's dark eyes regarded Sky unflinchingly. He knew in his gut that he'd found the lead for his film—the film that had defied casting for six months. "If you were just beautiful, I'd be out on the Bay in a boat instead of in this turn-of-the-century salon. It's your concentration on stage, your emotion. Very real."

Sky was so excited that she couldn't eat. Diana, sitting beside her, was nodding at a friend across the room. "You didn't have a lot of lines, Sky," he went on, "but you weren't just standing around waiting for your cue—you were listening to what people said in the scene."

"Isn't that the way to do it?"

"Of course!" he cried joyfully. "But it usually doesn't happen! Most people don't participate in a scene." He smiled, and his dimples popped into his cheeks. "Which means they're distracted by nerves or by their costume or by the fight they just had with their agent or by where the camera is."

"I think Sara is a beautiful actress, too, don't you?" Sky said loyally.

"Yes, she is. And she'll get better. So will you if you keep on acting. You know, I had to be dragged to that play you're in. This is fate."

The waiters swooped around them as women wearing

wide hats and long skirts on their summer dresses left clouds of powdery perfume behind them as they passed. Reed picked up part of his club sandwich.

"Sky and Sara have been talking about acting classes," Diana said, examining one of the women who passed their table.

"Oh, God, I wish you'd think that one through," he said, his mouth full of sandwich. He chewed and swallowed furiously. "You don't really want to take classes, do you?" Sky shook her head. The whole conversation made her intensely emotional. She could feel her heart pounding in her chest. "You have such fire in you. Classes might take the artist right out of you. Of course, some people learn a lot at the Studio in New York. You could study there. Do you understand anything that I'm saying?" Sky nodded. "But you don't trust me. No matter. You will." He bit into his sandwich hungrily. "Eat." He sipped his coffee. "My film is about a mother and a daughter. The mother is very genteel," he said mimicking the stereotype of gentility. "The daughter is very reserved, shy, held back. But she's a powerhouse of emotion, all repressed." He spoke intensely, telling them the complete story, outlining every character.

Sky knew Reed Corbett could change her life. She wanted to be able to tell him how she felt about acting, about being on her own, about being a different person onstage, but she couldn't say any of those things with her mother there.

He looked at Diana. "The studio system is breaking down. They aren't cultivating actors the way they used to, making sure they get good scripts, the right vehicles for them. And that's where I come in. It's true I only have a couple of films behind me; I'm comparatively new. Now, you could go into Hollywood and make the rounds and you'd get work—but it's the quality of what you're in that's important." He was pitching too hard and sensed Sky withdrawing. What if he went way out on a limb and she failed miserably? He'd lose what little credibility he had.

"Are you saying that Sky is more talented than Sara?" Diana asked.

"No, I'm saying that I have a role that is perfect for Sky."

"Sky's not really interested in acting, Mister Corbett,"

Diana said, arching her narrow brows and smiling coolly. "We've never discussed films." Diana was beginning to realize how the news of Sky testing for a movie would affect Sara. It would be a terrible blow, but she could see that Sky was eager to do it, no matter the cost.

"Sky is not a stage actress," Reed said. "I'll bet my bottom dollar on it. Sara might be, but Sky's a film actress."

For all her excitement, Sky was a little afraid of Reed; she didn't know whether she could trust him. "Come to Hollywood and do a test for me," Reed said to her.

"Oh, I don't think so, Mister Corbett," Diana intoned, checking her watch. "Movies sound . . . cheap. I don't think they're very serious, and I don't know what her father would say if—"

"You don't mean that," he said shrewdly.

Diana examined him and smiled. "I am not about to let my daughter disappear into Hollywood all alone." Reed dumped sugar into his coffee. "Let's stop playing games. Do you want Sara to come too?"

4

When Diana told her about the lunch with Reed, Sara felt as if she were chasing the cart in Lugano again. She wanted to scream at her mother and sister, *Didn't you think of what I wanted?* Her head was full of crazy things, like Sky betraying their special trust, like Sky taking over Sara's special place in the family. But there was nothing Sara could say.

She couldn't look at her sister.

"It's just something that happened, Sara," Sky said.

"It's not a question of you or Sky," Diana said. "Mister Corbett has a role that he thinks would be suitable for Sky, and he wants her to test for it." Diana's eyes caressed Sky briefly, and Sky was aware of it. She'd felt closer to Diana in the last two hours than she had in the last two years.

"Do you want Sky to say no?" Sara shook her head miserably. "He's going to think of you, too," Diana said to Sara, patting her shoulder.

"Sara," Sky said breathlessly, "it's just a test. I don't know anything about acting, and it won't amount to a thing. But I want to do it. I've never been good at music or studies like you, or a good dancer or writer like Vail. Oh, Sara, I want to do this so much. But when we were with Reed I hardly knew what to say to the man."

Sara looked at Sky, who suddenly seemed much more beautiful than she had a minute ago.

Diana was taking off her hat. "Let's all have some tea," she said. The discussion was closed.

"I don't want any tea," Sara said. "I want to be alone for a while." Sara was on her feet and heading for the front door.

"Sara!" Sky yelled.

"Let her go, darling," Diana called out. "Sara exaggerates everything. You know that."

"She feels deeply!" Sky said.

As Sara walked down Clay Street, she began to cry. She was furious at not being able to be happy for Sky and furious about feeling like an outcast.

The trees on Clay Street were in full summer bloom, and their scent mingled with the smell of the Bay. Sara walked angrily, beating at the pavement with her loafers. She'd walk it off; she'd be all right. She walked for an hour, then climbed on a bus and rode all the way out to the Cliff House, where the ruins of the old Sutro Baths clung to the rocky cliff above the pounding surf. Later, she got back on another bus that dropped her near Union Square. It was late in the afternoon. Her legs ached, but she didn't want to go home. She felt like an idiot but she couldn't face them. There would be a lot of hangdog looks and pity. She wished she didn't need any of them.

Tourists jostled her as she plodded down to Powell and Geary. A line of cars screeched to a halt at the light. One of them was Vic's blue Ford convertible coupe with white-wall tires. She stepped off the curb and grabbed the door handle.

"Hey!" he yelled. Then he recognized her. She looked grim and sort of nutty. "What's wrong?" The light changed. Horns honked. "Get in or stay out." She got in.

"What are you doing down here?" she asked.

"I'm just bombing around running errands. I was going to return some books to Jim's mother on the way to the theater."

"I'll go with you," she said dully.

Surprised, Vic went through a red light. She looked wild, with her dark gold hair sticking out and those long, hazel-green eyes rolling around looking at the crowds.

"How'd you meet Jim?" she asked. She glanced at his handsome profile as he drove out toward Sausalito where Jim lived with his parents. Vic's chin had just the right thrust to it; his nose was straight and strong, his lips curved and full. She'd never been alone with him before.

"Jim's mom and my mom went to college together—Cal. Jim sorta puts up with me, and I sorta put up with him. His mom married well and mine didn't. I'm older than he is, and he's a lot richer than I am." Vic laughed.

"Did you ever feel like you just wanted to disappear from everything?" she asked, staring up into the orange girders of the Golden Gate Bridge.

"Sure. In the Army!"

Jim's large old house was surrounded by trees and overlooked the bay. No one was home. Sara was disappointed. She wanted to see new people and places, and she'd settle for Jim's folks. "I have a key," Vic said. When they were inside the still house, Sara felt a curtain of desire for Vic brush against her and she instantly knew he felt it, too.

"Wanna cup of coffee?" he asked jauntily.

He didn't wait for an answer. He dropped the books on a table and swung gracefully into the kitchen, lifting the pot from the stove as he moved in the same unbroken liquid way to the sink for water. He had large, bony hands and talked a streak about how great the GI Bill was for poor guys like him, about how great Jim was, about working since he was ten, about wanting to be a set designer or maybe an architect. "You're very quiet," he said as he put the coffee on the stove to perk.

Sara leaned against the doorjamb. He was someone her mother would never approve of. "I was just watching you."

"Let's go into the living room," Vic said. "Jim ought to be back soon. Then we'll all go to the theater."

"Yes, the theater," she said dreamily. She had always heard that a really professional actress could go on no matter how she felt.

The living room was pale blue with high ceilings and white woodwork. Glossy antiques that had seen better days surrounded a large grand piano. Vic sprawled in an armchair, one leg cocked at a ninety-degree angle over the other, his trousers hiked above his ankles. The quiet house sighed. He was very aware of her. She was quite pretty but immature, like a glamorous schoolgirl. "You just graduated from Mills this year, didn't you?"

"Yeah. Very dull, Mills."

"You don't look like a Mills girl."

"I wasn't. But I got through it."

"What are you going to do after the play's over?" he asked.

Sara shrugged. "Something dramatic." Vic smiled. Except for Sherman, their director, he was older than almost everyone at the theater. It made him seem dangerously tempting. She arched an eyebrow at him. "Did you graduate this year?" Did she sound as stiff as she felt?

"Nope. Night school takes longer." He rose, retrieved the coffee with a clatter of cups, and put the tray down on a small brass-trimmed butler's table in front of the sofa.

"Where do you work during the day?" she asked.

"At a furniture factory. That's temporary. I've been thinking of applying to the Globe Theatre for next summer."

"Shakespeare," she muttered, thinking of Sky, Diana, and the screen test. "Pretty hot stuff."

"That's me. Nowhere to go but up!" He poured her a cup of coffee, took his own in one hand, and leaned rakishly against the mantel.

"What kind of a name is Oumansky?" she asked.

"Russian. The old man was a Red. No, actually, he was just a poor slob whose parents came over on the boat."

His light brown hair glinted in a streak of late afternoon sunshine that slipped through the venetian blinds. A thin leather belt threaded through the loops of his gray slacks; his waist was lean and tight. She wanted nothing about him or the room or the soft house to change, but she was afraid that Jim would walk in any moment and wreck the sudden exhilarating thrill she felt. He took a sip of coffee, put his cup down on the mantel, and shook out a cigarette from the pack in his shirt pocket.

"You're upset," Vic said casually. "What about?"

"I'm not upset."

"Not yet."

"Sherman fire you?" he asked.

"Well, what then?"

"Sky's going to test for a movie in Hollywood," she said.

"Oh, bad break. Yeah, I'd be jealous, too."

"I'm not jealous," she said. "I mean, it's more than

that—and less. It's like—Sky and Vail and I have always had a special understanding—'' He was looking at her attentively. "I can't describe it. We're real close in a lot of ways, and now—''

"Sure, that's tough, her getting the test over you—''

"No, it's not that—well, it is, but we weren't competing—'' She looked down at her hands. "Oh, shit.''

"Did you think you were all going to live together when you grew up?''

"I didn't know we were grown up yet.'' She smiled crookedly. "See, I didn't know she wanted to act that much.'' That wouldn't make any sense to him either.

"Listen, from what I hear, Hollywood's nuts. She probably won't get the part—they test hundreds of girls down there! She's just one in a crowd.''

"She's never one in a crowd!''

"Well, *you* sure aren't! Listen, so she's treading on your special preserve or something. You just be yourself. You're a real unusual person,'' he said.

She got up and walked across the old Persian rug to him. "Thanks,'' she said. "Can I hug you?''

Vic's dark eyebrows shot up and one hand moved involuntarily as she shyly slipped her arms around his slim waist. She'd been in clinches with boys before, but she'd never made the first move. She stared at the knot in his tie while she collected the courage to look up at him. He did not move. The silence between them grew wider and deeper and heavier. If she did not move, or he did not, she thought she'd burst. She raised her head.

Vic's heart was pumping wildly as she turned her face up to him. Isn't this a surprise? he was thinking. His arms lifted but he didn't dare embrace her yet. She was a rich, spoiled girl from Nob Hill who felt pushed out of her family for the moment. For all his good breaks at school, he felt inferior to her socially. He also felt she was trouble.

Sara looked into his eyes. They were a dark blue, his lashes very long. She moved closer. At last she felt his open hand against her back. She trembled violently. He was suddenly the most bewitching person she'd ever met, and she knew he didn't care anything about her.

She lifted herself on her toes and brushed her lips against

his. His skin was soft and he smelled of the fresh sea air.

"I know you don't care about me, but I won't apologize for kissing you," she whispered, afraid of his passivity.

"I don't want you to," he breathed. He felt the heat of her kiss spill through him and a delicious uncurling deep in his groin. His one hand tightened gently against her back, his other wound around her waist as he softly drew her close. His kiss was like a bird's wing fluttering against her lips, then coming to rest, sweetly drawing at the moist skin. She leaned against his slender frame, shuddering. She heard him moan softly as he drew her lips toward his again, pressing deeper, rubbing against her gently, running his mouth to the corner of hers, sliding up her cheek to her temple. He sighed and clasped her head to his shoulder. She was spinning, held upright only by his arms that gripped her tight. Every contour of his body became clusters of separate sensations to her: the hollow of his cheek right under the bone, the space between his rib and thigh for his waist, the hub of his groin pressed gently against her inner thigh. His hands moved across her back and shoulders, slipped over her ribs with a gentle unhurried pressure. To be embraced by one so known and unknown, so alien and so strangely familiar, was like coming home to rest. They kissed again, young, hungry kisses, he pushing his tongue into her mouth. She rocked against him.

Vic was on fire, a sweet agony. He wanted to lift her even closer so he could spread the burning that consumed him. But if he did that, he thought, she would run, and he didn't want that. He pushed his hesitations away and kissed her again. He felt her shaking against him, could hear the breath being pulled in and out of her. He was almost certain she'd never been this close to a man before.

The key in the front door sounded like a battering ram. They jumped apart.

In the days that followed, when Sara wasn't with Vic, she was thinking about him: the way he walked; the way he sat in a chair; the liquid, languid way he moved, head tilted up, hat back. She was obsessed with him; she'd never felt anything like this before. She wanted to be with him forever; He took the pain away. She sat beside his chair in the wings of the theater, secretly curling her hand in his; she watched his muscular arms reach up for the ropes when he opened and closed the curtains. She waited for him behind the flats to steal long kisses in the dark, to feel his lean flanks pressed against her thighs, to feel his lips drawing lines on her neck.

But the sudden advent of the sexy Vic in her life did not erase Sara's increasing sense of isolation from the family. She stayed later and later after the show, pressing her advantage with Diana, who was distracted by her work for the upcoming Democratic convention and campaign and by the trip to Hollywood. Sara pretended that Sky's departure didn't concern her. She passionately confided her feelings about Vic to Sky, hoping to reinspire their former loyalty, but both of them could feel their relationship tilting precariously.

On the third night that Sara got home late, Diana was waiting for her.

"Who drove you home?" Diana asked.

"Mother, I am not a teenager!" Diana stared at her. "Vic and Jim."

"If you are dating this Vic person," Diana said, "I think you'd better bring him over here for supper on Monday night."

"I hear it's inspection time," Vail muttered to her as they passed in the hallway the next morning. "Inspection time" had haunted their high school and college years.

Monday night was the night before Sky and Diana were leaving for Hollywood. When Sara heard the doorbell, she scurried back into the living room, picked up a magazine, and tried to look casual.

From the way Diana extended her hand, barely allowing it to touch Vic's, Sara knew that the evening was going to be rocky. Ned was mixing martinis and being jocular and democratic. "It's been a while since Sara's brought a gentleman caller to the house," he said. Sara cringed. The only boys she'd brought to the house were kids from school who'd arrived to escort her to dances, probably under protest, bearing their cross and their corsages. In college it was slightly better, but not by much. Diana seated herself in an armchair. She was wearing a curvaceously cut, tasteful silk dress and a large gold pin.

Conversation was brutal. Sara sat next to Sky, poking her to join in, to make it easier, and Sky rose to it a couple of times, but she was by nature so retiring socially that she couldn't be counted on. Sara stared at Vail, her eyes pleading for his help. Vail began talking horses.

"Do you ride much?" Vail asked.

"Rode a rental horse in the park once," Vic replied.

That ended that. They settled on the Korean War, truce talks, the Democratic convention, and the national fever to build bomb shelters. Sky brought up the UFO sighting in the Arizona desert.

Sara was relieved when Mrs. Shogutsi announced dinner. Diana had hired Mrs. Sho as their cook right after the war, when Mrs. Sho was just out of the internment camp near the Mojave Desert. Mr. Shogutsi had died of appendicitis in that camp. Before the war, the Shogutsi family had owned a big garden nursery out on Van Ness, where Diana had long purchased shrubs and flowers. But the nursery had been taken away from the Shogutsis during their internment, and their son had been killed in the Army's Japanese-American infantry unit during the Italian campaign. Mrs. Sho always reminded Sara of the difference her mother could make in people's lives.

During dinner Diana deftly questioned Vic about his family. Everything came out. His widowed mother; his runaway father; his home on the Avenues, that repository of unacceptable "Frisco" people, the people who wore "paper collars"; his stint in the Army after the war; his GI Bill education. Later, all Sara could remember of the evening was Vic's stony gaze, Ned's stifled yawns, Diana's slight nod and faint smile at each new piece of information, her cool good manners like a scrim to cover what Sara felt was her disapproval.

Dinner seemed to last a year. Sara made excuses that she and Vic were to go to Jim's house for dessert, and they were able to escape about eight.

Vic pulled the sputtering Ford out into the traffic on Clay Street and drove in silence to the marina near Buena Vista cafe, where he parked. Sara felt humiliated by the ordeal and began apologizing.

"I don't know what you told them we were to each other," he said coolly, "but I am not in a position to become involved with anyone. I hope you understand that."

"I didn't tell them anything."

"They obviously have higher hopes for you."

"Well, I have my own plans! I'm my own person!"

"Fine. Let's just be friends. Kisses aren't proposals. Tell your parents not to worry—I'm no suitor." He sighed deeply. He felt used and was surprised how keen his disappointment was. He didn't want to go to Jim's house; he wanted a stiff drink. How'd he ever gotten involved with this young girl?

"I'll take you home," he said.

"No! Please, we've got to let a little time go by—" Sara was acutely embarrassed. "Never mind. Just let me out here. I'll walk around and then get a cable car."

"I can't just let you wander around the city!" he said angrily. They sat in silence. "I've got to check on a friend's house," he finally said. "They moved out last week and I'm keeping an eye on it until it's rented. We'll go out there. That'll kill some time. Then I'll take you back home."

They drove over to the Sunset district. The fog was coming in, and the repetitive, low warning notes of the foghorns sounded over the shore. The house, close to the ocean, facing the Golden Gate Park, was somewhat larger than most in the area. Vic inserted his key in the lock and snapped on the hall light. The vacant house creaked as Vic walked through it, testing the doors and windows. It was completely empty, and his footsteps sounded loud, precise. Sara drifted upstairs into a large room with bay windows. She looked out at the dark ocean. Vic came up the stairs. "Oh, Vic, this is beautiful!" She could see herself living there with him.

"Yeah," he said gruffly. He was standing behind her in the doorway. She stuck her head out the window and breathed in the fog and the smell of the sea. He approached. "Close the window. I'll take you back."

She put her hand on his arm. "I don't want to go back." She sat on the edge of the windowsill. "I wish we could stay here forever." Vic lit a cigarette; the interrogation at dinner had unnerved him. "I don't think my parents want what's best for me," Sara said after a moment. "I always did think that—even when I didn't agree. But it's all different now."

"Why?" He blew out a plume of smoke.

"When I was a kid, I fell off a horse and snapped out two front teeth. I couldn't play the flute again."

"So what?"

"Playing the flute was everything to my mother. I hated it, all the practicing. . . Anyway, I could stay inside the family when I played the flute well. Vail did it with sports, and Sky—she did it with charm, I guess. But when I fell off the horse and couldn't play anymore, it was like I was—this sounds really corny, doesn't it? It was like I was being shoved out of the family. I feel just like that now." She looked up at him. "You should have seen them after opening night," she said. "It was—everything was different. I didn't exist. I mean, I do exist, but it's like I'm suddenly on my own." She stared out at the roofs of the smaller houses that reached toward the sea. "I think I'm in love with you. Oh, don't worry. I know you don't love me. It's okay." She wondered what her next line would be if she were in a play. "I just wanted to say the words to you." She combed her fingers through her thick bronze hair.

Despite his sensible bargain with himself earlier and his anger at her family, he could not ignore her. He recognized pain when he heard it, and he sympathized. "You'll forget all this. Sky will go to Hollywood, have a ball, be tested, and no one will hire her. I told you that."

"Do you think so? You know, being a triplet is different. We're very close. It's hard to understand if you're not a triplet, but we can practically read each other's thoughts."

"C'mon."

"No, really. And we always understand each other. That's why this is so upsetting. Sky knows how much I'm hurt by that guy asking her to be tested and not me. She knows how much I want to be an actress. But maybe I won't be one after all. Maybe I'll do something else." Her voice held a pathetic truculence that irritated him and made him want her at the same time.

He stomped on his cigarette and drew her into his arms. "This is crazy," he said. She leaned closer to him, fitting her body into his, and kissed him furiously.

How long had they stood knitted together against the window? She remembered later that he'd taken off his jacket and spread it beneath her. She could see the moonlight through the windows and the way the light hollowed out his cheek. She could remember exactly the way his lips tasted, tangy and full, and the tremendously exciting weight of him as he rested on her. When he gently entered her, she'd bitten back a cry and had dug her fingers into his back. It hurt.

"No hurry," he said. His voice was very soft. She looked up into his eyes and at the shadows of his face. He was looking at her so tenderly she felt a sob catch in her throat. "I love you, I love you," she murmured. He moved a little inside her, stopped, looked at her, stroked her once, twice, then stopped, never moving his eyes from her face. He dipped his lips into her, drew away, stroked her, stared deeply into her eyes. She felt suspended in the dark shadows of his eyes; it took the pain away. The shell of the house around them sighed. Suddenly, he lifted his body from hers, withdrawing roughly, and fell onto his back on the floor.

"What's—wrong?" she gasped. He did not respond. "Why did you stop?" He sat up, hunching over, his shoulders shaking, his back to her, the moonlight touching his hands, which hid his face. A sob—he was crying! She moved to him and took his hands away from his face. "Are you sad? Are you afraid?" He shook his head, struggled stiffly to his feet, pantless, and sat down again under the windows, putting his back against the wall.

"I'm in love with someone else," he said. "Her name is Pam, and she's getting married this weekend. I'm sorry."

Sara looked away. She didn't know what to say. Her stomach was knotting up. She hunted for her blouse; she wanted to be covered. "I thought you were beginning to like me."

"Well, I do," he snarled, then put out a hand to erase the roughness of his tone. "You're very beautiful and—alive.

I noticed that when Jim introduced us, but I guess Pam's just one of those things."

Recklessly, Sara tossed her head in the shadowed room and said, "I don't care. You're going to marry me."

"You did it? You made love?" Sky whispered.

Sara nodded smugly. "It's about time, isn't it?"

Sky quietly closed Sara's bedroom door behind her and sat down on the bed. "We were going to wait—till we got married," Sky reminded her. "Oh, what was it like?" Sara was so daring.

"I just can't explain it," she replied. "You just—it's like you're in the grip of something bigger and sweeter than anything else. Like you're being swallowed up with him. It's like my soul was going away toward him and his was coming toward me. . . ." She wanted something of her own, as romantic and exotic as Hollywood. "And it hurt, too."

"A lot?"

"Enough. And then it gets better. Sort of."

"Are you going to marry him?" Sky asked.

"Oh, no," Sara said, "but I'm in love with him. I just had to experience something deeper."

That night they talked a long time, whispering and giggling, both relieved that they each had something. Finally Sky got up. "Wait," said Sara. "You're leaving tomorrow."

"Yes. I'm scared," Sky said, sitting down again.

"Knock 'em dead. And don't let mother make all the decisions."

Sky looked around at Sara's room—at the "Billy Budd" poster from the Broadway show, at the other of Edith Evans, and at the stacks of *Theatre Arts* magazines. Sara had made a model of the Lyceum Theatre when she was fourteen; they'd worked on the curtains and the paper dolls for it together. It was sitting on top of her bookcase.

"Sky," Sara said, "I'm awful upset about you going down there for the test. You know that. I feel so hurt—" Sara started to cry and angrily brushed the tears away from her cheeks. "I don't know what to do."

"I wish it were different, but I can't not go!"

"I know that!" Sara said. "I want you to go! But if I

hadn't told you, I'd never be able to talk to you again about anything."

"You can't change any of this with Vic," Sky said.

"That's separate. He doesn't have anything to do with you and me."

"I don't want to lose my best friend," Sky said.

"Me neither."

Hollywood studios were virtually autonomous fiefdoms. In each one, thousands of people toiled toward a single goal: making pictures. Laboratories, business offices, mills, blacksmith shops, police and fire departments, a school, a theater, a commissary, and a hospital could exist within the walls of a studio. Their huge warehouses were stocked with collections of costumes, furniture, vehicles, and scenery from every era, and miles of narrow paved streets wound through their stucco canyons—the exterior walls of the cavernous soundstages. Replicas of French villages, Italian piazzas, New York's Park Avenue or 42nd Street—all were scattered over the back lots of the studios. And at MGM the blackened ruins of Atlanta, torched for *Gone With the Wind*, once cast ghostly shadows—a set that eclipsed all others in size and cinematic history.

An entire system of work and life, of union rules, political courtesies, and a stratified social register—A list, B list, depending on money, fame, or power—whirled around the central nurseries of the studios.

But in the summer of 1952, this system that had sprung up from the orange groves in a single generation was in the grip of monumental change: The blacklist sowed betrayal and fear, the arrival of television competed, and the Paramount Decree amputated the studio's theater chain from the body of its productions: Automatic distribution was gone. Though the pain was real and widely felt, few people re-

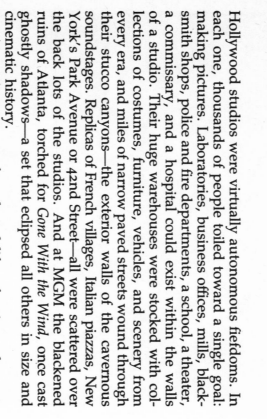

alized that the apparatus of the studio system was being dismantled.

Sky let her fantasies roll. A press corps would greet them with cameras and questions at the Pasadena train station. She would answer demurely, then step into a limousine, and drive off to a fine hotel in Hollywood.

This picture faded out when they arrived not at the famous old Pasadena station but in Los Angeles, where a surly driver met them in an ordinary Chevrolet sedan. He deposited them at the Hollywood Roosevelt. No fruit baskets or flower arrangements welcomed them, only a brief note saying a press photographer would arrive to take Sky's picture. He never showed up.

The hotel was definitely passé. Since the Bel Air was booked, Diana quickly moved them to the Beverly Hills Hotel. Sky didn't care—she was in a state of euphoria.

The day began with a fight: Diana wanted to accompany Sky to the studio for makeup and wardrobe; Sky, intractable, resisted, and won.

The guard at the gate directed a jubilant Sky to the makeup building. Inside, a man with slicked-down hair analyzed her face and found it wanting. She didn't want her face changed and refused to participate.

She strode outside and down a warren of little streets. She asked a half-dozen people, some in costume, where she could find Reed Corbett, but no one had ever heard of him.

"What's up with you?"

Sky whirled. A tall man about her age with azure eyes and a thatch of blond hair was looking down at her. "Lost?"

She laughed. "I just don't know what I'm doing here!"

"Oh, I think you belong here," he said, staring at her.

"Have you ever heard of a man called Reed Corbett?"

"Sure! I'm on my way over there! You want a little tour?"

"Okay. My name's Sky Wyman," she said, sticking out her hand.

"And mine's Patrick O'Mara." When he smiled, he looked like a model.

They wandered down twisting alleys, past soundstages and offices. Out of the open windows floated music, dialogue, singing, hammering, and jagged pieces of passionate arguments.

"Now over here," Patrick said, flinging out a long, graceful arm. "Marlon Brando's going to be shooting *The Wild One*. Down the road a piece is a movie called *The Big Heat* with Glenn Ford and Gloria Grahame. It's just wrapping. Then there's *From Here to Eternity*. That's a big movie. Those'll probably be released next year. Did you see *A Place in the Sun?*" He looked at her solemnly. "George Stevens directed that."

"Sure. Everyone saw that. *A Place in the Sun* was based on the Theodore Dreiser novel," she said.

"Oh, a reader, huh? Yup, that's right. Paramount made it. Paramount's Alfred Hitchcock's home. Martin and Lewis are over there, too."

"Who are they?" she asked. They were walking for blocks and blocks.

"A new comedy team. Slapstick stuff." Taking his self-appointed job as guide seriously, Patrick escorted her from one soundstage to another and past a line of doors labeled Projection Room. She had not realized how big a lot could be. "Over at Paramount," he said, "they've also got Alan Ladd in *Shane*. Brandon de Wilde's in it, too. Now, Warner Brothers, they're out in Burbank. And here's Reed's office!"

They'd stopped before a low building whose window boxes sported bright red geraniums. She could see Reed inside hunched over a large drawing.

"Reed!" she shouted. Patrick started to leave; she touched his arm. "This nice guy found me outside makeup. They want to make me look like Bette Davis! I left!"

"This nice guy?" he repeated, coming over to the open window. Patrick affected a country-boy attitude, hanging his head and shuffling his feet.

Reed threw back his dark head and laughed, hanging onto the dormer window for support. "Meet your costar in the test!" he yelled. "Come in here. We have to start rehearsing!"

Two hours later Sky was back in makeup. She sat down again in a plastic-covered chair.

"I want her to look natural," Reed explained patiently. "And don't touch her hair."

One of the men sniffed. Reed Corbett was not an important director. The hairdresser took a handful of Sky's hair, put it on top of her head, and looked questioningly at Reed. Reed shook his head. "She's supposed to be sixteen and it's the eighteen-eighties."

"Ace!" the hairdresser called out. A tall man on the other side of the room with a perky, very short man looked up. "Help them!"

Ace advanced languidly. He had a long, open face, high cheekbones, and blond hair. He wore an insouciant, wry smile as if it were part of his clothes. "This a test?" he asked, putting his hands behind his back and walking all the way around Sky. "We'll put it in curlers to give it body and pull some of it back like this, let the rest hang, maybe a ribbon, a few bangs?" He had a soft, direct voice.

Ace motioned the short man over. "This is Cage," Ace said. He had a handsome, almost pretty face, with warm brown eyes.

"My first name is Roland. You can see why I use Cage." Sky didn't see. Cage put a little soft rouge on her cheeks, a pale blue liner on her eyelids. "Maybe a little lavender for highlight if we want to be revolutionary. She doesn't need false eyelashes. Won't everyone be jealous!"

"That's it," Reed said. He drew Ace to one side and said, "I need this film as much as you do. I'm in your hands." Then he sent Sky off to Ladies Wardrobe, which was not far from Makeup.

A bent gray-haired woman led her into a huge room where racks of clothing from every era hung from floor to ceiling. The old woman, Valerie, chewed on the inside of her lip and moved slowly. She had come from Vienna, a dancehall girl who'd fallen into the movies in 1910, doing Willam Selig serials. She had worked with Universal, and by 1912 she was a star, making pictures with D. W. Griffith, and with Lois Weber, another director. But by the late twenties she was a has-been, and by the late thirties, she'd spent every nickel she'd ever earned. The studio had made a home for her in wardrobe, where she'd worked ever since.

Valerie's sharp brown eyes skipped over Sky. A long

checked skirt and frilly blouse lay on the table, but, clucking and shaking her head, Valerie pulled out a pale blue cotton dress of the same period and held it up. "Yes. Mit eyes, yes. You wear that tomorrow. Shoe size?"

Another room held racks of shoes sorted by size and period. Varerie selected a pair. "Hair like that?" asked Valerie. Sky nodded. "Maybe a ribbon?" Sky nodded again. "You come here tomorrow after Makeup." Valerie had a beautiful voice that didn't sound nearly as old as she looked.

The next morning the whole process was repeated. Diana was joining Sky on the soundstage at ten.

At that hour, Makeup was a beehive of activity: Thelma Ritter sat in one chair and Gloria Grahame in another. Sky sat in a corner. Other famous people wandered in and out. They were all getting ready for work, just like she was! She waited until the celebrity crush thinned out; then Cage put her in one of the chairs and brushed on her makeup while Ace put her hair in curlers and stuck her under the drier. When the two of them had finished with her, she gasped. Her hair was very girlish and her makeup much thicker than she ever wore it. "You can't imagine what the lights do to a face," Cage said. "They wash it out."

Nervously, Sky went on to Wardrobe, where Valerie was ready for her. She put on the blue dress, adjusted the ribbon in her hair, then stood back critically. "Hat, I think." She went away and came back with a small summer straw. Once again she surveyed her work. "Good," she said.

"Thank you for all your help," Sky said.

Valerie watched her rush out. They came young and left old. She hoped the change wouldn't overtake the girl who called herself Sky too soon.

Stage 8 was a great, echoing, dark barn. Far off, at one end, lights shone and people scurried around. Men arrived, men left, men climbed things, pulling at cables and shouting. All this for her? She drew back. A chubby man came up to her. "Are you Sky Wyman?" She nodded. "I'm Jake, Mister Corbett's assistant director. Your mother is at the gate. They just called. Come this way." They walked toward the lights. Reed rose from a camp chair.

"Good morning! Everything okay?"

"I'm awfully nervous."

"That'll pass. I want you to meet Ernie Ping, the cameraman."

Ping, a Chinese American, was about thirty-five. He had a plain round face, high short eyebrows, and sharp black eyes.

"Welcome aboard, as John Huston always says. Let's see what Makeup did." He turned her head this way and that.

"Go over there in front of the picket fence—watch the cables," Reed directed. He pointed at a spot in front of the lights, and she stepped into their chamber of warmth. "Stop there." She turned. She felt exposed. "Stay there." He went back to his chair beneath the huge camera and spoke to some of the men. Then he came back to her. "Bob!" A man lurched out of a corner carrying an open satchel. "Bring the mouth out a little. And take the hat off." Reed smiled and stepped back. Bob took her hat off. "Who put that hat on you?"

"Valerie."

"Yeah, it's good. Use it in the scene if you like." Bob fluffed her hair.

"I want her face pale and oval and surrounded by a black forest," said Reed. He went back to confer with Ernie Ping, who was peering at her through the lens.

Until this moment it had been hard for Ernie to concentrate. He and Marjorie, his wife, had quarreled that morning, a rare occurrence in their marriage. He focused the camera, bringing it up on Sky. The lens did something to her. He waved Reed over. "Look at this," he said.

Reed put his eye to the camera. "Ha!" He grinned at Ernie.

"Let's hope she can act," muttered Ernie, who'd grown up in Los Angeles's Chinatown during the Depression and knew how cutting disappointments could be.

"Oh, she can act," Reed whispered.

"I'd like to use a lot of footcandles and a sharp, sharp focus," Ernie said.

"Try that Garbo shot—"

"I was just thinkin' of that myself," Ernie said. It wasn't that half of Garbo's face had been kept in light and the other in darkness. It was more that the camera tried to peer into her eyes to see what was there. Sky had very long lashes.

Could he bounce some light from above her so that her lashes cast shadows on her cheek? He set to work.

A park bench suddenly appeared, and she was placed on it. The scene was going to happen on the bench. Someone rushed in with a few pots of flowers. The fence was moved back. They were in a backyard. Ernie moved quickly and precisely, his stubby fingers pointing to what he needed as he called out lights. He'd look at the effect, the back of his thumb against his upper lip; he never seemed quite satisfied.

"What's he doing?" Sky asked Reed.

"He's lighting to find your best features," he said, strolling away. He wanted to accent them strongly, especially her pale eyes with the dark borders around the iris. He wanted to get right inside those eyes.

"Which side, Ernie?" Reed asked.

"Right side's best," he said, meaning Sky's face.

Lights went out. Lights went on. Sky looked out at the crew. Except for a petite woman—the script coordinator—sitting near Reed's chair, everyone on the stage was a man. Big men, small men, men with protruding stomachs, lean men, old men, young men, bald men. Sky remembered as a child cutting her arms badly in a collision with a French door. Rushed to the hospital, she'd lain on the operating table under the hot, bright lights, frightened out of her wits but trying not to show her fright by chatting up the scrub nurse. She'd told Diana that she'd loved every moment of it, and Diana, in later years, had repeated how brave Sky had been and how much she loved new experiences. When this terror today was over, Sky would be telling Diana how much she loved it all. And she would never mention her fear.

Reed came back to her. She was trembling. "That's good. Tremble. Don't put on airs, don't fake your feelings. Don't squint into the lights. Ignore them."

The assistant director came up to them. "Pat's here."

"OK, bring him over."

Patrick looked like a paint box in his bright red evening coat, black trousers, blue vest, and yellow hair. "Hiya," he said, seeing her terror. "I'm a friend." He grinned. Reed gave them their positions and went back to his chair. Diana arrived and was given a chair near the perimeter of the equipment circle that surrounded the patch of light on which all efforts were concentrated. Sky smiled distantly at her, then turned her back to move into place. The clatter and noise and shouts continued unabated while Reed sat in his chair like a prince, calling out courteous and friendly orders. Finally, Jake nodded at Reed.

"Okay, let's go," Reed said happily.

Jake bellowed, "Quiet!! Quiet on the set!"

Someone off in the distant acreage of the soundstage yelled "Quiet!" and a stillness fell. "Rolling," said the sound man. "Action," said Reed quietly.

There are moments in life when you know you cannot lose, that all will come to you. For Sky, this was one of those moments. Under the strained artificiality and the confusion of the set peopled with strangers, working with Patrick made it possible for her to find her feelings again. All the havoc fell away as she said her first line and listened for his reply. She was home.

The screening room was a small, marginal space with a tired, shabby air. Long-expired cigarette smoke clung to the worn carpet.

The studio had assigned Raymond Sordo to oversee the production of Reed's film, *The White Queen*. Sordo was in his thirties. He was a plump, nervous man with a pencil-thin mustache and an ingratiating smile. He kept his hands in his pockets. The day after Sky's test, Sordo was walking up and down between two rows of seats in the screening room.

"I don't want that Chink shooting 'Queen'!" Ray was shouting at Reed. "There's all kinds of great guys we can get—Sheldon *likes* this picture!"

"I won't stand for it, Ray," Reed said airily. "Ernie's test of her is gorgeous. I'll take this all the way up—"

At that moment, Ernie and Jake, Reed's assistant, came into the screening room, followed by Sky, Ray, a man who slouched, mumbled at them. Everyone sat down to watch the test. The lights dimmed.

A clapper stick snapped on the screen, showing her name and Reed's, and someone yelled "Take three!" on the sound track. Then a closeup of her face came on. Her face started talking. The camera pulled back; Patrick was lounging against a post at the end of the fence.

Sky covered her eyes. It was grotesque. She looked like a giraffe, the way she walked. Then came another closeup. Her face was distorted somehow—like a mask. And her words—wooden, dull. She slipped down in her seat and prayed the lights would never come up. What would she say to Reed, who'd been so kind? Clearly he wanted her to see the test so that she'd understand why he couldn't possibly give her the part. Well, she'd go back to San Francisco and work for her mother in Adlai Stevenson's campaign. His victory over Ike and Nixon was more important anyway.

The lights came up. Reed turned to her. "What do you think, Sky?"

"Not good enough," was all she could manage. The two other men were looking at her strangely. They'd probably been on a hundred tests. They knew a hopeless case when they saw one.

"Of course you can do better, but it's pretty good as it is," Reed said. "We're showing it to the production chief and the head of the studio today."

"You *are*? But it's terrible!"

"Terrible? God, no!" He'd hoped that when she saw the unusual quality she had on the screen it would give her confidence. "Get some rest," he chuckled. "You look all done in."

As she left the little screening room, she heard Ernie say to Reed, in a hushed whisper, "Jesus, Reed, she captivates that camera!" Sky pressed herself against the dark wall of the alcove by the projection booth that led to the outside door. Ernie's voice was building. "The current between her and the lens—like a zap of lightning! Zap! When she gets some experience—!"

She heard them getting up. She carefully opened the door and slipped out. The sunlight slapped her. She was afraid to believe that it was happening to her. She'd won.

"Such cheap girls," Diana observed to Sky as hopeful teenagers, dressed in bathing suits, strolled past the bronzed men on the other side of the pool. Diana and Sky were sitting poolside, under a rush overhang that shielded them from the wicked, damaging sun.

"Mother, if Jane Russell walked by, you'd call her déclassé," Sky murmured.

"And so she is, dear, the poor thing."

Sky felt feverish and ill; there were dark circles under her eyes. A month ago she hadn't cared much about the movies; now she felt that her life hung in the balance. She couldn't sleep, and she hated sharing a room with her mother. It was a dreadful time.

A teenager in a bellcap's uniform marched through the lounging, golden bodies. "Sky Wyman," he called. Sky waved to him. He carried a telephone, which he plugged in at the end of a line of empty lounge chairs. It was Reed.

"You've done it! You've got the part! They're writing up the contracts as we speak."

Sky felt her heart leap. "Mother, I've got it!" Two sunning teenagers narrowed their eyes at her through their dark glasses.

"Of course you've got it. They're not fools," Diana said, obviously pleased.

"Come out to the studio, meet the chief," Reed was saying, "and sign the contract—it's their standard seven years of servitude, then on to Publicity—"

Sky broke in, "A contract for seven years? I thought it would be for just this picture."

"No," he said. "Listen, can you drop by Wardrobe today? Ask for Valerie."

"But, Reed, seven years—"

Diana took the phone from Sky. "We'll call you back." She replaced the receiver brusquely. "You have what every girl dreams of. What are you doing?"

"I just want to think about it. It doesn't feel right. Seven years is a long time."

"All right, don't take my advice." She picked up the telephone and called a friend in San Francisco who suggested she see Mel Winters. "He's a brother to the head of the studio. Don't worry, he's used to the other side of the table. Besides," her friend finished, "things are different in Southern California." Winters couldn't meet them until late, so Sky went over to Wardrobe first.

"I now take all your measurements," Valerie said.

"But I'm not sure I'm going to take this seven-year contract thing," Sky said as Valerie slipped a tape measure around her waist. She wrote the number in a black leather notebook.

Valerie stepped back. "You are an odd girl," she said. Her eyes looked like half-moons, crescents, which gave her a perpetually happy expression.

"I don't know anything about anything. I don't want to make a mistake—"

"Everyone makes mistakes," Valerie said. She liked Sky, who had been courteous on that first day. Valerie remembered how she'd felt when she first arrived in Hollywood—a flat little town in the middle of orange groves; she hadn't known anyone or anything either. Of course no one had been throwing seven-year contracts in her lap, just five dollars a role and a sandwich for lunch. But Sky was a lovely naive girl in a town full of sophisticated sharks.

"Come," she said. "We take tea back here." She led Sky to a tiny windowless room the size of a closet. A hotplate, some cups and tea bags, and a pot of jam. "I tell you advice."

"Fine. I'm seeing a lawyer later. What would you say to him?"

"In the end, you will take the contract, if that is what you want, because you have no choice except to go back to your town." She dipped a tea bag in a cup of hot water, then put jam in the cup. "I have been here a long, long time," she said, and told Sky a little about herself so she would listen. "Maybe you show them you can't be pushed around? Fine. That is good for them to know as long as you do it with a smile." She pointed to her lips, then suddenly turned them up at the corners. "Now I tell you about Mel Winters. He can be very helpful."

Mel Winters was a square, compact man. He wore a checked jacket that made Diana's teeth ache. He had short, choppy gestures and a robust voice. His office was full of cigar smoke. Valerie had said that Mel came from a legendary Hollywood family. His father had been one of the industry's first major agents; his mother, a silent movie queen; and, of course, his brother, Sheldon, headed the studio that had offered Sky the contract. They had a younger brother, David, who had been cited by the House Un-American Activities Committee as a Communist. Mel was deeply embedded in the effort to save actors and writers from the hands of the committee by counseling them to cooperate, not defy it as David had done. Valerie had contempt for this side of his work, but respect for his power and his knowledge of the business.

Diana described their situation in two sentences. "Sky's been offered a seven-year contract. And she doesn't want to take it."

Winters studied the luscious young woman who was so closely attended by her mother. "Why not?" he asked.

"Because they will control what pictures I'm in for seven years."

"Then don't take it. But you oughta know that it's probably one of the last such contracts coming out of the studios. The system's changing. There are benefits in being under a studio contract—they'll supply your lessons—voice, speech, dance, movement. They'll build you."

"I don't want to be built. I am already."

"What do you want?" he asked, frowning. *Where'd this girl come from?* he wondered.

"I want a contract just for Reed's movie now, or a contract with Reed for his next two pictures."

"He's not powerful enough. If you want to do that, you want to go with real strength, Willie Wyler, Fred Zinneman."

"Then get me that."

Winters appraised the young woman who looked so retiring and wasn't. "I can't. There's only one person who cares a damn about you right now, and that's Reed Corbett. Take the offer. I'll do the paperwork for you."

Mel was shrewd and pragmatic; he saw the makings of a star in Sky. There was no telling, of course, he thought, but nevertheless he put his cigar out, opened a window, and turned on the considerable if rough charm at his disposal. He wanted her to trust him. Sheldon needed some fresh talent; his studio was fully rigged but it was one of the smaller studios. Sky looked like someone he might cash in on down the line, if all went well—you never knew.

In the end Sky agreed to the contract. She sent a bouquet of pink tea roses to Valerie that evening.

The next day Diana and Sky went to see Sheldon Winters. To reach his office they walked through a covey of secretaries and assistants, through door after door.

Believing that he would live forever, that square footage symbolized power, and that there was no such thing in the universe as illness or misery, Sheldon had naturally created an office the size of a basketball court. He sat behind a luxurious desk at one end of the room in front of a large American flag, a new prop; the House Un-American Activities Committee was still on the rampage, stirring things up. Most of Sheldon's furniture was a ripe, reddish brown leather with brass studs. The walls were paneled in leather. There was a fireplace and a grand piano. He had three phones on his desk, color-coded with the furniture.

The studio had started a new life when Sheldon Winters took it over in 1941. Until then it had languished in the ranks of Monogram or Republic, churning out Grade B features, with an uncut diamond now and then by accident. Sheldon had a nose for hits and coming actors. He said he could smell a hit from the mimeo ink on the pages of a script, and a star from the nervous pores of young waitresses. Armed with these instincts and a superb business sense, Sheldon had lifted the minor league studio into the Academy Awards: Directors wanted to direct his pictures, actors wanted to be in them, and writers fought to submit their scripts. The studio had taken chances, and the studio was booming. But to do this Sheldon worked like a miner, eighteen hours a day.

The key to Sheldon Winters was his pride in his power. Though he was a handsome man of distinctive, electric charm, inside he was a cone of cold loneliness.

He rose and greeted Diana and Sky warmly. Mel had already spoken to him. Sheldon was curious about Sky, about why she hadn't wanted a contract that other girls would have been on their knees under his desk to sign.

Sky regarded him. He was tall; had thick, straight, sandy hair; and a long, handsome face with closely set, enigmatic eyes. He didn't look anything like his brother. He wore beautifully tailored clothes. They weren't one minute into the conversation before he brought up horse racing. Sky mentioned that her father was also devoted to it.

"He is? What's he got?"

"A colt named Fireball."

"Who's the sire?"

"I don't know." She turned to her mother. "Do you?"

"No, but perhaps Ned can come down when you start shooting and tell Mister Winters himself."

"Fine, fine." He started to talk about Reed's film. He said he was glad it didn't have any "phony artistic pretensions." He said that Reed was going to be an important director.

Diana and Sky were whisked over to Lenny Kaplan's domain. He was head of Publicity, Promotion, and Exploitation.

Lenny was nimble and short. He had lots of curly brown hair and a swift smile. He talked very fast. "Welcome aboard, Miss Sky. Welcome aboard." He repeated everything he said. "Now just sit down there and we'll do up some info on you." He pressed a buzzer on his desk. A woman in a print dress and very high heels came into the office. "Rhonda, this is Sky and Mrs. Wyman. Take some notes." He turned to Sky. "By the way, the chief wants you to have a new name."

"What's wrong with her old name?" Diana asked coldly.

"Nothing! But he thinks Sky Lark would be best for publicity."

"Ridiculous. Come along, Sky." She rose.

"It's in the *thinking* stages, Mrs. Wyman! Please sit down." Diana sat. "Sky Belvedere is another choice." He started firing questions at her: Where and when she was born, what her hobbies were, brothers or sisters—?

"Triplets," Diana supplied. "She's one of three."

Lenny stopped. "Triplets?" His eyes widened. There *was* gold at the end of the rainbow. "Do they look just like her?" he asked, breathlessly.

"Her sister does—almost. The boy, of course, looks like a boy," Diana said coolly.

Lenny rose, rubbing his hands together. "Wow, wow," he murmured, walking around his office. "I see Sky in her part in this picture, and the other two in bit parts! I see—

rewrites. I see interviews—triplets on the set, inseparable. I see—Rhonda, get Corbett on the phone. Get Sheldon. Jesus."

Diana cut in. "Rhonda, wait a minute. Mr. Kaplan—"

"Lenny," he urged her.

"Lenny," she repeated distastefully. "Sky's brother and sister have their own lives. They don't want to be involved in all this—hoopla."

"Mrs. Wyman, this 'hoopla' is the movies! Triplets! Do you realize what this means? *Time! Life!* Growing up together, sharing identities, loves, experiences! *International Publicity!*" He was speaking so fast his words were running together. He couldn't wait to capitalize on the triplets. A matched set! "Surely you can see the benefits," he pleaded to Sky.

Sky knew she could override her mother, that Sara and Vail would be on the next train. But she said nothing.

"Her brother and sister will not be in her pictures," Diana said.

"Let's leave that up to the director and the head of the studio." He nodded at Rhonda, who snatched the phone. The idea of triplets in a movie thrilled her, too.

Winters punched his desktop with enthusiasm when he heard that Sky was one of three. Reed Corbett, who already knew, was less sympathetic. He telephoned Sky that evening at the hotel.

"I got a couple of fights on my hands," Reed said. "I need your help." First he explained the situation about Ernie. "Frankly, there are other DP's—that's director of photography—who could do the picture, but I don't think anyone will do it as elegantly. The problem with Ernie is that he doesn't have as many credits as the others, and"—he paused significantly—"he's Chinese."

"I like him," Sky said immediately, "but what can I do about this?"

"I want to go right to the wall with it. I want you and me to say we won't do the picture unless Ernie's on it."

"Would they really give it to someone else?" she asked.

"I don't know. I don't think so. Well, they could, but I think they'll back down. But they might not. It's a risk—particularly for you. I'm asking a lot, Sky."

She hesitated, putting a bony fist to her mouth. There was a life decision every single hour down here. "Well, okay, let's go to the wall!"

"Atta girl!" he said.

"I don't see why they'd pay any attention to me about it," she mumbled.

"It's a matter of solidarity," he said. "The studio's rotten about Ernie. Now, listen, second, Lenny's making a lot of noise about rewriting 'Queen' to include small parts for Sara and Vail. I don't really want to do that. It's a stunt."

"What?" She was amazed at how fast Lenny had moved.

"There's never been an actress who came from a set of triplets! They want to use it as a draw to the picture. They want to publicize it by adding parts to the script! Your brother and sister might get a kick out of it. Sara would probably love it—well, it's hard to say. But I have to think of the picture, and I have to think of you. And that's why I'm less than enthusiastic. The fact that there are three of you, especially another sister who's beautiful and a good actress, makes you less than unique. Know what I mean?"

There was a long pause. Sky was glad her mother was soaking in the tub at the other end of the suite. "Don't do it," she finally said softly. "Fight to keep the picture the way you want it."

"We'll settle for an interview with the three of you for the publicity and that's all," he said. "Talk to you tomorrow. Bye."

Sky sank down in a chair. She had just done something selfish, maybe immoral. Sara, I'm sorry, she said to the couch.

6

"Do you feel each other's pain or unhappiness?" a reporter asked.

Lenny Kaplan was publicizing the hell out of the triplets to promote *The White Queen*. His first press conference for them was exactly the kind of extravaganza he'd wanted. Reporters from *Variety*, *Hollywood Reporter*, and assorted fan magazines, and both Louella and Hedda were busily firing questions at the triplets who sat on a platform in one of the meeting rooms of the Beverly Hills Hotel. Lenny stood to one side, beaming. Attractive triplets were a great gimmick.

"What do you mean? Do we have some special hookup?" Sara asked, enjoying every moment of it. She and Vail had arrived yesterday with Ned and Diana; they hadn't stopped for a moment since. The phone in the hotel room rang constantly. Now, on the platform like an exhibit, they absorbed the frank looks of jaundiced interest from the reporters. "Yes, we do understand each other maybe better than most brothers and sisters."

"Is this for real?" a woman from *Variety* asked Lenny as he bit into a doughnut. "Are they really triplets?" Her voice dripped with disbelief.

"I swear!" Lenny cried. "Ask them!"

"Sky! Sky! Over here!" a photographer yelled.

"Did you fool your boyfriends?"

"Sometimes," Sky answered. "Sara and I do have the same voices, as you can hear."

—88—

"Could you fool your teachers?"

"With hair like this?" Sara laughed, lifting a wing of her curly hair like a sheet of ribbed bronze. The reporters smiled and wrote. Flashbulbs went off again. The triplets were disarmingly ingenuous.

"Who was the best student?"

"Sara," Vail said.

"Vail," Sara said.

"Does that mean that Sky didn't study?" asked Louella Parsons, who sat in the front.

"Next question!" Sky exclaimed, laughing.

"Did you help each other? I mean, in special ways."

"Sure," Sky said.

"Was there an odd man out?" someone at the back shouted. Everyone laughed.

"That's me!" Vail said.

"In a way, it was Sky," Sara said, more seriously. "She was the youngest. And the smallest."

"The runt," Vail supplied. The reporters hooted.

"When did you all know you were different?"

"When did I know I was different?" Sky asked, too quickly.

"We were always triplets!" Sara answered. "We were always different."

"How do you feel about your sister having a part in the movies?"

Vail said, "We think it's a great break for her."

"Do you want to be an actress, too, Sara?"

"Yes, I always did."

"Always? Before Sky?"

"Are you studying to be an actress?" a woman at the back asked. "Are you coming to Hollywood? Are you an actress, too?" the reporter insisted. Sara looked at Sky.

"I do want to—" Sara began, feeling pushed and confused.

Sky broke in. "Right now, I'm what you have in the actress department." She smiled dazzlingly. Flashbulbs.

"How about you, Vail? What are your plans?"

"I'm—I want to write," he said.

An hour later they were upstairs in the suite the studio had provided for Sara and Vail. "How could you have said that?" Sara yelled at Sky as soon as they closed the door.

"It just came out!" Sky said. "I'm sorry! It's *my* first press conference, too."

"But you just pushed me aside!"

"I didn't!" Sky knew she'd done exactly that. "I didn't mean to."

"Knock it off," said Vail, from an easy chair. "It's over. Forget it."

Sara was persistent. "You've only been down here two months, but you're like a different person! It's like we just don't matter to you!"

Sky rounded on her. "That's not fair, Sara! I do care, but I also have to look out for myself down here. It's a strange place."

"Illusion, illusion," Vail said, hiking himself off his chair. "All life is an illusion of one sort or another. Get used to it."

They stared at him. "Are you as casual about life as you sound?" asked Sara.

"You don't think what's happening to me down here is *real?*" Sky cried.

"For the moment, my dear Sky, for the moment." Vail was not as disillusioned as he sounded, but law school and a bunch of unappetizing courses were staring him in the face. He was only twenty-two, yet he felt locked in on a course of life that he strongly disliked. Ned had not supported his hopes about writing. His sisters seemed to have sorted out their lives: Sky had her Hollywood movie, and Sara had her passionate affair with Vic. What did he have?

Sky went back to the bungalow the studio had located for her in the Hollywood Hills. Vail and Sara just didn't understand. Being an actress in Hollywood was very demanding. In the last two months, while Reed got the production together, she'd gone from one lesson to another, and no one had liked anything she did. Her speech wasn't crisp enough, she didn't enunciate, and her *L* sound was wrong, and her voice—"Pitch it lower, lower!" the woman kept shouting at her. And then there was her walk, tilted slightly forward—"A disgrace!" her movement teacher said. It was ego bruising, but no one cared about her feelings. Learn or get out.

That night, Raymond Sordo, the studio's producer of

The White Queen, took them all out to dinner at the Brown Derby on Vine Street.

Heavy, brilliant chandeliers hung over the Derby's huge dining room. Below, the red booths were full of people cataloging arrivals and departures while they carried on conversations without looking at their dinner companions. Vail grinned; it was like being in a great king's court where the careers of anxious courtiers depended on the way they looked, the information they knew, and how they transmitted it. Information was currency.

They were eating their salad, and Sordo was telling them how great the picture was going to be—that Sheldon himself had said so—when Lenny came bouncing over to their table.

"You kids were great today!" He larded on the compliments, especially for Sara, squeezing her hand confidentially before he darted away across the room.

Sara felt warmed by the glare of his attention. But five minutes later, she thought she was going mad. Lenny's voice, soft and persuasive, was coming from the corner of their booth right next to her ear. But Lenny was on the other side of the room at another booth, talking to a couple of people in evening dress. "Isn't Sky great?" Lenny's voice was saying. "The sister, Sara's, okay, too, but no contest with Sky. Reed says Sky's a gifted actress—another Garbo."

Sara looked at Sordo, whose face was reddening. "Waiter!" he boomed out. "Let's have some champagne over here!" Sky looked very pale. She started to babble at Sordo about other movies he'd produced.

"What's going on?" Sara asked Sordo directly. She could still hear Lenny's voice, going on about Sky, contradicting everything he'd just said to them.

"Quirky acoustics," Sordo said loudly at her. "Eighth wonder of the world! I guess the architect wanted to hear the agents' deals!" He laughed insincerely. "Don't mind Lenny—he's just trying to promote the picture, you understand."

It was 5 A.M. on the first day of shooting for *The White Queen*. From the bedroom of their little house in Burbank, Ernie Ping could hear his wife, Marjorie, preparing breakfast. She was also Chinese American and should have been as delighted as he that Reed had won the battle: Ernie was going in as the cinematographer on *The White Queen*. But Marjorie had been only momentarily pleased. Now she was urging Ernie to think about directing. He realized what he had never faced before: Marjorie would never be satisfied. The knowledge made him unhappy and lonely.

On this same morning, Ace leaped out of bed at 6 A.M. and selected a pair of cream-colored slacks and a brilliant, peacock blue shirt. He was new at the studio, far below, in station, the hairdressers the stars took around the world with them. But because of his work on Sky Wyman, Reed had put him on the payroll as assistant to the hairdresser on the set. His easygoing, unrippled life-style was improving. He was pleased with himself. Life was good.

As she got out of bed that morning, every bone in Valerie's body ached. She groaned audibly as she moved unsteadily to her tiny kitchen. Reed had also improved her position in life by requesting that she assist the wardrobe on "Queen" and go with them on location. She put water on to boil to make the strong coffee she'd learned to love in Vienna. She wondered if she was too old and too disappointed to feel happy. She was glad her stultifying routine had changed, thanks to Sky, and she was glad she'd been able to help Sky. In the hall, on her way to the bathroom, she passed a poster of herself in *The Duchess of Danby, 1917*, without even looking at it.

Sky hadn't slept all night. Her "shakes" had taken over, and she'd imagined all kinds of embarrassing horrors—losing her voice, knocking over one of the big lights, stepping on Anne's dress, losing her lines, behaving like an idiot, and being ridiculed. She stared into her mirror: It told her she looked like hell.

Sara's room at the hotel connected with Vail's. She lay in bed that morning and wished she were lying in Vic's arms. She wondered if he'd read all the trashy mush the fan magazines had concocted out of their interview. A clear thought popped into her head: "The only set I want to be on is my own." She rolled over and wondered if she could pretend to be ill.

Reed was up at four that morning, and in his office at

—92—

six with Ping and Jake. The picture was not a big one, it did not have great studio support, and as for stars, Anne Abbott was the only one. The supporting roles were played by unknowns, among them a fresh kid called Robert Wagner, who'd had some stage experience and had one film under his belt. And then there was Sky. But with Ping's help, and if Reed could keep Anne sober, they had a chance of making a good picture that might surprise everyone.

By nine o'clock the set was crowded with visitors, fan magazine writers, a few curious actors from other sets who wanted a look at the triplets, a billionaire who invested in movies and was thinking of forming his own company, the pitcher for the New York Giants, Miss America of 1949, the director of a Utah opera company, and an admiral. Jake looked around and murmured to his assistant, "Gee, for a small pic we have a great turnout." But then, the triplets had gotten a lot of publicity.

As Reed set up his first shot, Vail and Sara moved to one side of the set near a chair that had "Sky" written on its back. Anne Abbott was standing near the 1880s dining room set, watching Frederic March and Doris Day approach her. She felt old, tired, and disillusioned, and it made her cranky. This Corbett production was beneath her—she who had been plastered all over billboards in the thirties and forties. She'd worked with William Powell and Clark Gable then. But that was a long time ago. Now her debts had forced her to take the role in "Queen."

Sometimes she was at peace that she'd had her ride and it was over. At other times she fought her fate: the knowledge that she'd lost—that she'd never be the actress she'd dreamed of being. Money had seduced her; her precise beauty had melted down; sometimes it was all she could do to keep from bursting into tears in the middle of a scene.

Vail found chairs for his mother and father on the other side of the set, then wandered over to Sara. He watched Frederic March and Doris Day chatting with Anne Abbott and noted the formality of great stars meeting for the first time on a set. He thought they seemed stiff and courteous, like great blue herons in a new marsh. Were they as much in awe of each other as he was of them? He wondered shrewdly if they had any sense of their own fame. He supposed they did, but what did it feel like to be that famous?

Sara watched people deferring to Anne Abbott, who held a Pekingese on a silver leash. March and Day broke off and went over to Reed. Abbott drifted in Vail's direction, cooing at her dog, nodding regally to other visitors and crew members she appeared to know well. She sat down next to a crisp young man. Sara was fascinated by Abbott's sexual power, which, though middle-aged, she was flaunting with every exaggerated movement. She even winked at Vail, the drooping eyelid heavy with innuendo. Reed had said that Abbott was obsessed with proving that she could get any man she wanted. As Abbott stroked the man's cheek, Sara leaned forward to catch what Abbott was saying to him, something breathy about all the men on the set wanting her. She segued neatly into a lascivious story about one of her recent or historical sexual encounters.

Tedium quickly replaced formality on the set. Sky was standing far outside the circle of light until Reed forced her into it. Her hands were shaking, her head, her legs. She worried about what Reed was thinking of her, that he would have to replace her after the certain shambles of this day; she worried about what the crew was thinking, particularly Ping, who was so important to her career. Patrick put an arm about her, but she barely noticed him. The visitors drifted away; she saw her parents sit down near Sara and Vail. Diana smiled and mouthed, "Chin up." Sky knew her blocking, she understood the scene, but now she couldn't remember any of her lines. She was sweating, spoiling her makeup.

"All right, Sky, you wanna move to your mark?" Reed said. "Patrick, over here. Good. Makeup!" Cage rushed out of the darkness beyond the lit set and started powdering her face.

"I'm so sorry. I know I'm wrecking it," Sky whispered to him frantically.

"Don't breathe," he said, "and don't sweat anymore! Just pretend you're dead." He smiled, gave Sky's arm a quick squeeze, and darted away.

All the lights went on, blinding her. Sky squinted and wanted to crawl into the darkness of the vast stage, where it was cool and anonymous.

Sara watched her terrified sister. If she were out there in Sky's place would she be as scared? she wondered. To be that scared was her desire. Coast, she told herself. She fought to anesthetize the envy curling out of a deep recess inside her. She glanced through a forest of light stands at her mother who sat straight as a board in her chair. Sara rose.

"Where are you going?" Vail whispered. "Sit down. Everyone will see you." He pulled at her sleeve. She sat down.

"I can't stand it."

"Quiet on the set!" Jake called out, looking at her. Someone echoed the order: "Quiet!"

"Rolling," the sound man said.

Sky took a step forward in the lavish dining room set, looked down at the silverware, and straightened a knife.

Patrick came up behind her, carrying a bunch of flowers. "Estelle," he said.

She reacted and turned. She smiled dazzlingly at him as he extended the flowers. "For me?" she asked hesitantly, afraid to believe it. "Oh, William." She took the flowers, pulling them to her, and pressed them to her chest, a gesture at once fearful and provocative.

Anne Abbott watched Sky as if she were a mirror of her own past youth. She remembered her jittery, thrilling first morning on a set. She ground her teeth. What she wouldn't do to be that young again.

"Cut," Reed said. He went over to Sky. "I like that with the flowers, squeezing them to you like that. Keep it."

"I had to," Sky said shyly, "to keep them from shaking."

The next scene was between Abbott and Sky. Reed gallantly escorted Anne to the set from her chair, reintroducing her to Sky, who felt like curtseying. After Reed had left them, Abbott said to Sky under her breath, "Just stay out of my light, and don't ever try to take my scenes with your pathetic nerves."

Well into the take, Sky flubbed her line.

"Cut." The line was read to her as Abbott, smiling at Ping, fanned herself and called for her personal makeup man.

On Sky's third fluff, Abbott turned away so quickly that her heavy skirt flared out and almost knocked over a chair. "I declare!" she said in a piercing falsetto. "What's become of this majestic profession when we have to put up with amateurs?" She whipped her fan open, bellowed for her hairdresser, leaned across the table, and whispered so loudly to Sky that the whole crew could hear, "Don't cry, baby. Just do your job!"

Diana froze. Reed, wearing an air of happy fatigue, rose to go out to them when Sky said, quite loudly, "It's my first day, Miss Abbott. Please don't mock me. I'm sure you were once nervous, too, a long time ago."

Reed broke in as Abbott was working herself up for a fight. "Miss Abbott, you have more experience than anyone on this set, with the possible exception of Frank." He nodded at a slender handsome actor of sixty who stood to one side. He took her arm and said quietly, "I need your help to make the picture the kind of vehicle you will be proud of."

They went into the next take, which was perfect, and broke for another setup. Abbott and her young man went out to her trailer. Ace started combing Sky's hair. She was fighting back tears when Reed came over to her.

"Let's take a walk," he said softly. They went deep into the stage. Reed was gallant, generous, and soothing. "Everyone knows you're nervous," he said. "We all were, too." He chatted on, putting her arm through his, as though they were making a tour down Fifth Avenue. He talked about directors and actors—how good directors, in his humble opinion, gave actors confidence. "I try to whisper instructions or ideas to the actors," he said, "so the crew and whoever else is out there during the take won't stand around waiting to see if the actor does what I suggested." He turned and led her back to the set. "But often a director's a traffic cop. Making pictures is a physically grinding process. It wears you down, and we all wait while the light's going, makeup isn't right, horses aren't on time, the rail's off."

"You've made me feel much better."

He bowed. "Miss Abbott is a mite jealous. It's hard when you grow older—especially for someone like her. Be kind."

The next take used a different area of the table and different props: The meal was over. Abbott and Sky and Patrick sat at one end as a maid with a tray cleared the table. It was the first scene in which the girl begins to defy her mother.

"Quiet! Quiet on the set!"

Jake was standing beside Sara's chair as, on the set, Sky rose from the table in character, shaking with repressed fury at Anne Abbott. The take was over in a minute, but it had power and went perfectly. I can do that, Sara thought, watching her sister. I can do that. Jake bent down to Sara and said, "Isn't she great? She's got all the internal stuff, all natural. You must be real proud."

Sara rose and smiled as Jake hurried off. She couldn't stand it. Vail eyed her. "I'll come with you," he said.

"I'll only be a minute."

She walked out of the circle of light, into the cool darkness of the stage, pulled open the heavy door, and strode into the hot sunlight. Outside the studio, she walked to a café and called a cab. She was perfectly calm. She took a cab to the hotel, got into the elevator, rode to the fifth floor, and let herself into the room. She slammed the door, hurled her purse across the room, and fell on the bed, sobbing, biting into the pillow. She gripped the headboard, screaming and howling.

Sky came home that weekend to pick up more clothes. Vail dropped Diana and Sky off at Magnin's and his father at the garage where Ned's Buick was being fixed. "You go on and see how Sara's doing," Ned said. Sara had come home a day earlier. "I'll pick up Sky and Diana. They'll need a big car for the packages."

And so it was that Vail found the note propped against the mantelpiece when he got in late that afternoon. It was unsealed; he read it, his heart pounding. He wanted to destroy the note, but what good would that do? He couldn't reach any of them and if he could have, what would he say? It wasn't something he could talk about over the tele-phone.

In anger and dismay, he waited with the news that would punch everyone in the face. An hour passed, two, then three. He sat in the study, the smoothed-out note on the table next to him. About five o'clock they arrived.

Vail hesitated. "Here. It's from Sara," he said, giving his mother the note. Sky's hand flew to her mouth; she could tell that something was terribly wrong.

"How could she do this to me?" Diana wailed. "What will people think?"

Ned grabbed the note and read it. He sank into a chair.

"But why? Why would she do that?" He looked up at Vail.

"What's she done?" Sky asked timorously.

"She's eloped," Diana said.

"Oh, no." Sky sat on the couch.

"Did you know about this?" Vail demanded.

"No! I didn't—"

"What will become of her?" Diana was murmuring, over and over.

"Mama," Sky said. "Sara will be all right. She's strong." Diana shot her daughter a look that silenced her.

"Sky," Vail said, "you just don't understand."

"But she loves him a lot, doesn't she?" Sky asked.

Ned put his face in his hands. "She wasn't happy here, I guess."

"Stop that, Ned," Diana said. "Of course she was happy here. She's behaving like a fool, all caught up in passionate adventures! Oh, why couldn't she have waited? What will people think?"

As their parents wrangled, something invisible was hap-pening to Sky and to Vail.

Sara had torn their triplethood apart. They'd always formed a solid front, cohesive despite quarrels or petty jeal-ousies. No major decisions had been undertaken without consulting the other two. Agreement did not always follow, but sharing, not agreement, was the crucial element. Sara had betrayed that covenant by acting alone, secretly. Sky felt abandoned by her.

Vail was standing outside himself and looking at Diana—

the woman who cared only about herself and what others would think. He felt he was separating from them all, freed by Sara's rupturing, reckless act.

A week later he enlisted in the Army. A month after that he was shipped to Korea.

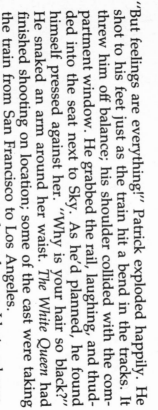

"But feelings are everything!" Patrick exploded happily. He shot to his feet just as the train hit a bend in the tracks. It threw him off balance; his shoulder collided with the compartment window. He grabbed the rail, laughing, and thudded into the seat next to Sky. As he'd planned, he found himself pressed against her. "Why is your hair so black?" He snaked an arm around her waist. *The White Queen* had finished shooting on location; some of the cast were taking the train from San Francisco to Los Angeles.

"You're the one who wanted to rehearse. I hate rehearsing!" she said, slapping her script down on his lap.

"Oh, do it again," he begged her.

Giggling, she hit him playfully on the shoulder. A columnist had hailed Patrick as a young Clark Gable—a hunk with a mind. His attractive animal charm was tempered by intelligence, whimsy, and a brittle, childlike sensitivity that poked out of him at surprising moments. Sky had learned that he was the son of a four-star general and that Patrick's mother came from a famous manufacturing family. She pictured his father dressing in black for dinner and shaking his son's hand instead of a goodnight kiss. Patrick could be amusing about his father, the general, but Sky knew he longed for attention from the man who barely noticed him. He spent a lot of time talking about the high standards his father set for everyone; inside, he was afraid he'd never reach them.

"I intend to use every moment that Lila isn't in this roomette," he said, staring solemnly into her eyes.

"Lila's probably doing things we don't want to know about," she said, coyly.

"What, our Lila?" he cried in mock horror about the aggressive redheaded actress who had joined them in Tomales Bay when the woman who played Sky's best friend in "Queen" broke her hip. "Oh, I forgot," he said, chastised. "You knew her in San Francisco, didn't you?"

Sky nodded primly. "Lila's father was Reggie Lewis," she said, naming the once-celebrated matinee idol. "And Lila wants to be just as famous."

"Aw, forget Lila. You're a much better actress," Patrick said.

Sky was trying to be Lila's friend. She felt sorry for Lila; just being Lewis's daughter made life hard for her: She didn't know who she really was. To most people, she was simply her father's daughter. "I won't hear a bad word about Lila," Sky said.

"Bad? From me?" he said. "I won't say a word. But she's jealous of you."

Sky fascinated Patrick and he was more than a little in love with her. During the months of delays, rehearsals, studio shooting, and location work on "Queen," Sky had lost her baby fat—that slight, affectionate rounding of her features. As it vanished, her face emerged with the crisp, brilliant beauty she'd have the rest of her life. He catalogued her. The color of her pale blue eyes changed with the light or her mood; she widened them when she wanted to be heard or wanted to pretend she was interested. He had the feeling sometimes that she was creating herself, shaping a style of unapproachable, challenging sexuality that, combined with her vulnerability, made her irresistible to Patrick and to many others.

The train was snaking through Monterey in Northern California. "C'mon, last scene," Patrick said, flipping the pages of the script.

"I know every line."

"Estelle," he said in character, "I'm not going away. I can't leave you."

Sky sighed. "but you said—"

"I know what I said, I just can't now. Let them come after me, let them jail me, it's over anyway for me." Patrick reached out and stroked her cheek with the back of his fingers. "You'll never know how much this means, just to have this moment . . . like this . . . beside you. . . ."

Patrick leaned in for the kiss. She bent toward him, too, eyeing her script, and felt his lips brush hers. She started to move away, then turned back, feeling the soft pressure of his palm on her cheek. Suddenly, they were kissing for real.

Patrick wanted to wake her. When he kissed her on the set, it was like kissing a sleepwalker. In this desire he was competing with half the company including their producer, Sordo, who had so fallen under her spell that he'd successfully urged the writer to add even more lines to her role. But now Patrick could feel her bending toward him, giving herself fully to the kiss. It was erotic to kiss her without people watching. Walls fell away. He clasped her to him, aching for her. She put her palm on his chest and gently pushed.

"Oh, Sky," he sighed.

"Yes," she said. She was surprised. Usually, she didn't like being touched and had had no sexual experience except embraces from college dates. Adoration was not new to her, but something in Patrick stirred her deeply. "We should go on," she said, fumbling for her script.

"Of course." They spoke another page of dialogue that brought them to the chasm of another kiss. She looked up sharply at him. He was no longer in character. He curled her into his arms and kissed her, running one hand up from the base of her neck into her thick hair. She tingled all over, pressing her lips against his. When their bodies parted at last, Patrick said, "Whew! Don't do that again!" He made a show of putting his script facedown in his lap.

"You're out of character," she said, smiling.

"Oh, no," he said, grinning at her, "I'm entirely in character!"

Sky lifted her script and peered at it, said her next line. She was a fast study; she'd stopped apologizing for her indifferent rehearsals. Acting released her from strains that didn't yet show on her face. But acting was also self-discovery and she feared the cowardice and the rage she'd found inside herself. She'd dive into her part to escape them. She was rewarded for total self-involvement. That was the job.

She often thought of Vail in Korea, and of Sara living with Vic, the man no one knew. Once so close, they were no longer a part of her reality. Would the three of them ever have their special alliance again?

Patrick took her hand and raised it to her lips. "It's all different now, isn't it?" he said, giving voice to her thoughts. In the beginning, at rehearsals, his talent to read her had been eerie. It was almost like being with Vail or Sara, and for that reason Sky was drawn to Patrick as to no one else she had met. "Yes. Quit reading my mind."

Patrick slipped an arm around her waist and pressed his face against her black hair. "I'm falling in love with you. Are you just a little bit in love with me?" He was trying to pick the right moment—and it had to be just the right one—to make love to her.

"I've never been in love," Sky said with complete candor. "I don't know what that feels like, but I guess when it happens I will." She took out a packet of gum and offered him a stick of it. He shook his head. "I'm sorry, Patrick. Maybe we can just be friends right now, okay?"

He nodded sadly. He'd settle for anything with Sky.

"The Reds are right over the next hill!" Colonel Danton yelled, slamming down the receiver. "Get the fuck out!"

Vail and Bondy Goldstein, a lieutenant from the Bronx, grabbed papers and gear from the Twenty-fifth Regiment's command post on a hill that had been behind the lines until now. Vail's fatigues were filthy, his fingers stiff with cold. The single light bulb strung from the ceiling went on and off in time with the burp guns and artillery fire from the valley.

It was late October of 1952. There had been little ground fighting for months since the large scale U.S. bombing raids had been pounding North Korea. Then, after the truce talks had broken down, General Van Fleet, commander of the Eighth Army, had launched Operation Showdown. He had ordered IX Corps to seize the hills of the "Iron Triangle" north of Kumwha, a fair-sized town, where the Communist forces were entrenched. He had predicted that he could capture the objective in a few days, but the Red resistance in the mountainous terrain had been unexpectedly fierce. All along the rocky ridges on the line the UN soldiers—Turkish, French, Australian, and American—had been over-run by waves of North Koreans and their Chinese Communist allies.

Twenty-four hours later, Vail and Bondy joined what remained of the rest of the outfit on one flank of a pincer movement headed toward Kumwha. It was freezing; snow and ice covered the frozen mud. Everywhere, ragged stumps of trees poked up as though a huge animal had come through and chewed down a meal of timber. From ahead and from the north came the sound of mortars and artillery.

Vail walked in the colonel's retreating column. When he'd been processed into Camp Pendleton, he'd been considered too small and light for regular infantry, but he'd tested bright (a moron, he'd said, would test bright in the Army) and was assigned to the colonel's intelligence staff. In addition, he had a good ear for languages. Four weeks later he'd been activated and sent over to Pusan, a port on the southeast tip of Korea. When Vail got transportation to the Twenty-fifth, up north in the hills, not far from Heartbreak Ridge, he knew he had landed in hell. The Korean War had inaugurated a new kind of slaughter—human wave assaults without respect to human life. Vail had just been learning how chaotic and confusing intelligence work was in America's "police action," when everything blew up in the bunker. The regiment's various battalions and companies scattered.

It was late afternoon, and the thin gray light was going. Refugees had joined the column—they were everywhere—an entire nation on the road carrying bundles. A woman passed him, bent over from her load, a baby strapped to her chest. The line snaked into a valley and came to a halt near a town, but Vail didn't know which one. Suddenly the shelling began. People were running in all directions. Vail leaped away from a jeep and into a ditch. He landed next to Danton, Bondy, and a sergeant with part of his platoon. A two-year-old girl sat beside Danton, squawling. Her body was covered with mud.

Just under the roaring whine of the mortar rounds, Vail could hear the clacking sound of the T34s, the Russian tanks. One of the biggest problems they'd had was not being able to stop those tanks. Their bazookas were too small, and firing one of them at a tank was the same as throwing a rock at it: The shells bounced off the armor.

"Goddamned leftovers," the sergeant muttered. He was fumbling in the cold to set up the bazooka. "The fuckers didn't work in World War Two and they're not working here." He gripped a dead cigar in his teeth.

Vail saw the low silhouette of a line of Russian tanks limned against the darkening night sky. The sergeant and Danton got the bazooka ready and fired. Nothing. The tank was spewing out machine-gun fire off to their right. The men buried themselves in the icy mud of the ditch. The baby howled.

Vail knew he would never live through the night. "They really want this town," hissed Bondy, a jolly, irreverent man of Vail's age. "We gotta get outta here."

"Keep your head down!" Danton shouted.

All Vail's youthful enthusiasm to join some effort larger than himself and his family, and to run from the collapse of triplethood, had long since drained out of him. Now he just hung on. In the middle of that long, dark night, a rain of mortar fire fell on their ditch. The baby and a corporal were killed, and Danton took one through the chest. "Medic!" Vail heard himself screeching into the deafening night. He fumbled with his CO's body, put his head down, tried to listen. The gurgling and choking told him Danton'd been hit in the lung and it was collapsing. He felt along his back and found the hole where the bullet had gone clean through. Willing his stiff fingers to work through his own panic, Vail clamped one hand over the bloodiest part of Danton's chest and the other over the hole in his back. He began to breathe more normally. The Russian tanks moved on, diagonally to the east. "Medic!" he screamed again, as Bondy shook some sulfa powder on Danton's wound. It felt like hours later, long after he and Bondy got Danton bound up, that the first stretcher-bearers arrived.

In the morning they started searching for their unit, and by afternoon had found sections of the First Battalion of the regiment crawling and running out of the rocks and farms and shacks to the top of a hill. Below them was a large town sitting in a mountain-rimmed basin. "Is that Kumhwa?" Vail asked Bondy.

"I dunno," he answered. Corsairs dove down from the sky, then swooped back up, leaving behind puffs of black smoke and soft explosions. A pall of smoke hung over the town, and many buildings were on fire. Everyone was waiting for the truce talks to work, especially men like Bondy who had almost all his points to get out of the madness. But Vail had just arrived, and the talks had dragged on since 1951. Vail spat out a laugh, looking at the burning ruins. "Sure am glad I brought my dress uniform," he said bitterly, remembering his sergeant who declared he could use it in a few weeks to celebrate the truce. War was miserable and cruel and filthy; there was nothing to celebrate.

Word came up the line that they were to take back the town and advance from here. Exhausted, the men picked up their M1s and carbines, shouldered their bazookas, and entered the outskirts of the town. All he and Bondy could see on either side were ruins and enemy roadblocks made from hunks of wood, sandbags, steel beams, and rocks. As the snipers from the buildings picked off squads on the street, his freezing and dangerous command post in the hills looked pretty good. They went from street to street and house to house, tossing grenades inside. "We gotta get hooked up," Bondy kept saying. "We're intelligence, not infantry.".

Vail flung himself into a doorway as bullets ricocheted around them. They were part of the advance to seize this town, and he saw no way out of it. If they went back to where headquarters used to be, they risked open fire and running into the Red army.

A staff sergeant came out of withering fire and dove into their doorway. "Jesus fucking Christ," he breathed. "Ain't seen this kinda fighting since Okinawa." He was a marine. He glanced at them. "What the fuck you guys doing here?"

"That's what we'd like to know."

"Well, it's all going to hell now."

A platoon advanced cautiously into the street ahead of them, threw down as much fire as they could to find out where the opposition was, and then four men, two on each side of the street, leapfrogged the street, one group firing into a building while the others worked their way next to it. They tossed grenades through the windows and rushed it. In the afternoon, they came to a warehouse and set up near it. Vail was behind an alley next to a long, deep sewage ditch full of stinking filth. Then a line battalion pulled in and got everything organized. Heavy mortar and tank fire began again as the North Koreans knocked hell out of the roof of the warehouse, shooting out the windows with machine-gun fire. Wood and glass and steel fell all around Vail and Bondy and the squad they'd joined. The din was deafening.

As they cleared one area, the South Korean civilians rushed out from God-alone-knew-where and helped the platoons and squads carrying their wounded. When they ran out of stretchers, the Koreans gently carried them on doors. Vail and Bondy advanced cautiously into another street and peeked around a corner, trying to get their bearings because they had no maps—and most of the officers had none either. What Vail saw riveted him.

A snow leopard was sailing over a ruined barricade and the chunks of concrete. He watched it like a vision, completely enthralled as it loped high and easy, coming on, ears flat against its big, gray, spotted head, yellow eyes gleaming, gaining ground toward the zone where he and Bondy stood. Was the big cat grinning, free at last? It looked soft and flabby; had it escaped from a zoo? The North Koreans on the other side of the barricade up the street from which it had emerged held their fire. Now less than a few yards away, Vail could see its luxuriously thick coat dotted with black rosette markings. The whole hard-contested street fell silent as the big cat, its huge tail high, bounded left, then right, searching for a way out of the rubble. Bondy said, "That's the only sonofabitch dressed for winter!"

A single shot rang out, whether from the North Koreans or the Americans, it was impossible to say. It missed! No one moved in the hushed street. Vail could hear someone whispering in Korean a few doors down. The shot had turned the cat; now it was headed for him and Bondy, its huge front paws reaching out, stirring up rubble. It raced past Vail, its eyes wide, its tongue hanging from its mouth. And then it was gone.

Still no one moved or fired. Vail pressed back against the side of the building in this fight that seemed to have no front and no rear. Had the big cat been grinning? Vail laughed out loud, feeling lightheaded, as if the cat had awakened him from a terrible dream about war. The sound of his laughter echoed. A bullet snapped out of an upper-story window and hit the concrete beside his head. He ducked down as the machine guns from the barricade opened up again. But Vail was smiling. Smiling and sweating.

A few tanks from the Twenty-third Tank Company were coming up the street, and the first one that began to pound the barricade made a lucky hit and ripped the turret off the T34 stationed behind it. Bondy cheered. The Russian tank burst into flames, and the shells inside it exploded.

By three o'clock in the afternoon of the longest day of his life so far, Vail walked behind Bondy in a single-file column of men down a residential neighborhood untouched by the devastation. The streets were elaborately terraced, the tree boughs graceful and unbroken. They came to a boulevard. The shops were burned out, plumes of smoke rising into the cold air shedding sparks and ashes. They trudged toward some distant trees. Things were winding down. Bondy pointed to a park beside the trees; it was gemlike and undisturbed. They sat down on some steps by a small, half-frozen pond and closed their eyes, remembering as vividly as a dream the vision of the snow leopard leaping down the broken street.

A week later, as Vail's units moved back into the hills of the Iron Triangle, Diana was going through her mail in the breakfast room of the Clay Street house. The house looked

—108—

manicured but the last months had been painful, and inside, Diana felt disorganized.

Eisenhower had defeated Adlai Stevenson, which put Richard Nixon, as Diana had feared, a heartbeat away from the presidency. Around the same time her tutor, mentor, and substitute foster mother, Ada Bentley, had died. She mourned her deeply. Diana hadn't heard from Sara, but she knew Sara and Vic were living in a rooming house in Berkeley; Vic was still going to school, and Sara was working as a file clerk. Diana's deepest concern, the one that had drawn the thin, hard lines around her mouth, was Vail. They heard from him often, when he had a chance to write, but sometimes she'd catch Ned looking at her with tears in his eyes. She knew he was thinking about Vail, wondering if he was dead or alive at that moment.

She put down the letters and drew the lapels of her dressing gown tightly around her neck. She'd been thinking about Miss Bentley, the woman who had saved her. Suddenly, she saw the hair clotted in the bottom of Virginia's sink. She had fought so hard, with Ada's help, to get out of the prison of her youth, and now here was Sara throwing her youth away! Dammit, she wasn't going to let Sara do it! She pushed her teacup away.

Three hours later, she had located an astonished Vic Oumansky in his morning class. "Let's get some coffee, Vic," she said when he joined her in the corridor. "It'll be worth your while."

The Twenty-fifth Regiment had been pulled out of the line around the Iron Triangle and put into reserve near division headquarters. The fighting had petered out; the Allies had won only a few feet of ground and at enormous, bloody cost. Vail and Bondy had three-day passes.

Seoul crackled under a particularly cold wind. Ice had formed on the Han River. The capital was wrecked. It had changed hands a couple of times, and the streets were full of rubble and rock. Portions of the main library, the capitol building, most of its tanneries, textile mills, and railroad repair shops had been blasted away by the mortars. Refugees poured into the city from the north, sharing the wreckage with inhabitants who'd been there for generations. Thousands of orphans lived in the streets, silent, shocked, wailing, starving, wounded. "It's the kids," Vail kept saying. "Oh, those poor kids." He doled out money and chocolate, took them to hospitals and to the orphanages.

Much as the children made his heart ache—up in the hills, on the roads, down in Seoul—the snow leopard haunted him. He'd even gone out to the wrecked zoological gardens in Seoul on a fruitless search for it, but of course it was not there. He couldn't stomach the trapped animals clinging to life under such appalling circumstances. Like the people of the city, they didn't have enough to eat, but the animals were trapped in cages, and many of the keepers had fled or been killed. Vail had wrenched open some of the cages and let the arctic foxes, some of the birds, and all the monkeys out. That night he'd gotten very drunk.

Vail and Bondy stood in front of a huge bronze bell cast in the fifteenth century that hung from a horizontal timber inside a wall-less structure. In the wreckage of the ancient city, the bell seemed lonely and out of place.

"We can make better use of our time than staring at this friggin' bell," Bondy drawled. Vail smiled. He'd been drawn to him for his perpetual but not foolish good humor. Nothing could depress Bondy. He sang in the mornings while everyone else grumbled and cursed; he had cheerfully come through the siege of the Iron Triangle when everyone else came back hollow-eyed. Bondy loved life.

Evening was approaching. Vail suggested a slice of the nightlife. Bondy agreed, and they headed into the red-light district of Seoul, where the bars were filled with young, beautiful shack girls, where the drinks were watered and the music loud.

It was still early in the evening but that made no difference at the bar just off Ma-Po Boulevard where they finally landed. Like a hospital or a train station, it was a ceaseless concourse of comings and goings. Australians, Indians, Dutch, black and white Americans—men of all colors and nations—leaned against the bar, or danced on the tiny dance floor to deafening, tinny music. A woman calling herself Lee slipped up to them and put her hand in Vail's. She was tiny. Her heavily made-up oval face smiled wearily at him. She tittered and spoke a peculiar and broken English that constituted communication. She could get them anything. "Screw?" "Drink?" "Dance girl?" "Blow?" They shook her off and went to the bar, where they drank for two hours. Lee returned with a friend. Bondy went off with May, the friend, disappearing into the now jammed and smoky dance floor. Lee hooked her arm through Vail's.

"Twenty dollah screw," she said, zeroing in on the deal.

Vail wanted to screw someone but he was afraid of screwing her. He'd seen grotesque Army movies about the clap, and he had a horror of disease. He began to feel sorry for himself, lost in the asshole of the world. He remembered Dolores, the girl in the artichoke fields who had mocked him. Even from this vast distance, he felt embarrassed all over again. He looked down at Lee.

She was rubbing against him in the close, crowded bar. Her hand gripped his arm. "Ten dollah blow," she chimed. Her voice was like a little cracked bell. He couldn't catch anything from a blow job, and the idea of it warmed him in an excited rush. It would wipe out the memory of Dolores. He nodded.

She led him through the packed room, ducked under some red curtains at the back, and opened an iron door to the hallway at the rear of the building. The air smelled of garbage and urine and dead animals. It was much worse than the artichoke fields. Her hand came out for the money as the iron door slammed behind them. He gave it to her. He was fumbling with his fly, and she was helping when the first blow fell. It split his skull open. The second blow rammed into his kidneys as he was dropping to his knees. He remembered thinking that he was not unconscious as he saw two bantamweight Koreans dart from behind him. One took hold of his collar as the other kicked him in the stomach. Vail flew backwards into a pile of wet garbage. Someone was stripping his jacket from him as someone else rolled him over and grabbed his wallet. He couldn't see. His blood was blinding him. He had a sense of floating in air. He saw his mother, huge and white and pure, turning in the bath, the water cascading from her. She towered over him, turning and smiling. Then the universe expanded, and it was very quiet except for the whisper of people's feet dancing around him. A hailstorm of blows bombarded him. He heard his leg snap twice and felt someone jumping on it. He tried to crawl away, but someone caught his head and snapped it around, holding it in the cradle of his arm while unnumbered fists popped into his face. His nose cracked; he was choking on blood. My God, he thought clearly, I'm going to die. Mama, I'm going to die.

Ned was spending most of his time at the ranch, or at the training barn at Tanferan near San Mateo looking at the colts, talking to trainers, and racing Fireball, his new quarter horse with a white blaze and frisky, intelligent eyes.

He was at the ranch when Bondy telephoned. At first Ned couldn't take it in, and spent one full minute trying to figure out which of Vail's commanding officers this Bondy was.

"Vail's been hurt," Bondy shouted again.

Ned swallowed, picked the phone up, and pulled it across his study to the cabinet where he kept the vodka. "Is he dead?" he croaked, seizing the bottle with one hand.

"No, sir."

"Oh, thank God," he babbled, hooking the phone under his ear and pouring a huge drink. The static on the line was fierce.

"He's in the hospital in Pusan, sir, very badly hurt."

"Where's he hit?" Ned gulped half his drink and shivered.

The horrible story with its seedy, vicious circumstances came out in pieces through the hissing static. Ned leaned against the wall and felt the perspiration popping on his brow. "Is he going to be all right?"

"They think so, sir. I hope so. He's a great guy. But he's taken a bad beating. It leaves its marks. Can you come out, sir?"

"Can I talk to him?"

"No, sir. His jaw's wired, broken in three places."

"Oh, Jesus."

"And he didn't want to write. He can't write anyway. He didn't want to upset his mother. He felt you were—"

"Yes, yes."

Ned carefully constructed a story for Diana. Vail had

—112—

been wounded in action and was recuperating in the Army hospital. When he left the next day for Pusan, Diana picked up the telephone to call Sky. She could feel the tears beginning at the back of her throat. She replaced the phone until she could control her voice. Then she began again.

8

In Los Angeles, Sky stared at Sheldon Winters, the head of the studio. His hand was clamped around her wrist.

"Please let go," she said.

He lifted his hand and slid back in his chair on the other side of his desk. "It's a beautiful part," he said. "Made for you. Wyler's a great director. Why don't you unfreeze a little?" His light blue eyes narrowed.

"I'm—I can't, Mister Winters," she said, squeezing the words out. She turned away to hide from him.

A soft knock sounded at the door. Sheldon's chief secretary, Dan Thayer, tiptoed into the room. "Robert Taylor is here, sir," he whispered. Sheldon gave no sign that he heard. Thayer tiptoed out.

"You've got a contract with this studio, Miss Sky," he reminded her. "You'll do the pictures we assign you. I can get other actresses for Wyler's picture. Maybe you'd end up with something like *Dead of Night*," he said, naming a B picture RKO had just released. "Or maybe I'll put you in *Beach Ball*." He looked up at her sharply. "I am not overstating my control. I can make you the most famous actress in the world. Or I can wreck you. You're only as good as the pictures you're in."

After seeing the final cut of Reed's film, Sheldon had been elated by Sky's beauty and performance. He had decided to turn Sky into a sexy, modern "second Garbo." But while promotion was gearing up and Lenny was poised to bombard America, Sheldon exacted his tribute. One of the

—114—

expressions of his power was his flamboyant sexual use of his starlets.

Sky opened her eyes wide and adopted a look of injury. "I won't sleep with you. It would destroy me." She had heard all kinds of rumors about casting couches, but this was her first brush with that infamous love seat.

Sheldon laughed. "Who said anything about sleeping?" He enjoyed her naïveté. "Nothing so quiet as sleeping." He beckoned her to his side of the desk. Stiffly, she approached, then watched, horrified, as he unzipped his pants and fumbled within. A slightly erect penis popped out.

How could this be happening to her? She was frantic. There were people outside typing and eating Danish. Reality had tilted with a terrible jolt.

"Kneel here," he said quietly, pointing to the front of his chair by his thigh. Sky couldn't move. "What's the matter with you? Get down on your knees!"

She felt herself bending down. His free hand shot out and grabbed her shoulder and pressed. He was very strong. Her knees buckled and sank into the soft carpet. His hand seized her hair and pulled her toward him. Her cheek brushed his leg. She didn't know what he wanted. Was she supposed to gaze at him or put her hand on him? What did he want?

"Open your mouth," he commanded quietly.

As she realized what he wanted she began pulling back against him. He yanked her hair and seized the back of her neck with his other hand.

"I can't!" she said through her teeth, frightened out of her wits. What could she do to make the room real again? This was a nightmare.

"C'mon, kid, lick."

"I—I'll get lipstick all over you."

"Joey loves lipstick," he said. He found her resistance enjoyable. Years of couplings had jaded him; only power and control were fruitful aphrodisiacs. The image of her tied to a bed sent a spurt of excitement through him.

With a quick, panicked movement he wasn't expecting, she ducked and jumped to her feet. She looked wonderfully scared.

"I didn't know I could get so lucky," he said, realizing that she was a virgin. She was hurrying across the room.

"Come back here," he ordered. He strode to the door and blocked her way. "I won't release *The White Queen* until you come around." "That wasn't quite true; he couldn't delay it forever. "Or you can start production on "Beach" in two weeks!"

Sky broke from Winters's office into the outer chamber where the courtiers, as she'd called them, waited to see the Sun King. Bewildered, hurt, degraded, feeling everyone's eyes on her, she rushed down the hall until she reached the rest room. Inside, she washed her hands and face twice. Did she really have to do that with him to get the picture released? Her teeth were chattering as if she'd been out in a storm. She started to cry as she reached for the paper towels. Then she realized anyone might walk in. She fled.

Reed and Sky were dining that night at Ciro's on the Strip. As they walked down the club's inside staircase, Sky felt like a character on display in a Busby Berkeley movie. She saw Gary Cooper, Van Heflin, Myrna Loy, and other celebrities jovially engaged, glancing up at them. Sky felt dazed: Was this spectacular scene real, with these tantalizing people whose faces were as familiar to her as her mother's? Or was the image of Sheldon unzipping his fly real? Were the releases the studio publicity machine cranked out about her real? She knew they were not—not really—but she wanted to believe what they wrote about her. She lifted her chin to give the chilly, glamorous look one article had described. But she felt like a phony, and for Sky that was the worst thing to be in the world.

"You're awfully quiet tonight," Reed said, taking her hand after they'd settled in at their table. Sky looked magnificent in a dark red evening gown that fell off her shoulders and long gold earrings. Valerie had been busy.

Sky smiled automatically at him. She'd grown quite fond of Reed since they'd finished the picture. She trusted his advice and his honesty. But she couldn't tell him—or even Valerie—what had happened in Sheldon's office that afternoon.

"What's the matter?" he pressed gently. "You look so sad. Problems with Sara? Your mother?"

"Oh, I was just thinking about Sheldon. I don't think he's interested in good acting." She smiled at her lonely joke.

"No, not really. He's interested in what makes money for the studio. Basically he has contempt for the audience."

That's not all he's got contempt for, she thought. She said, "When do you think 'Queen' will be released?" She was skirting dangerous territory, but she couldn't stop.

"Don't know," he said, leaning away from her as their drinks arrived.

"What if it isn't released?"

"Ha! Disaster for me! For us all. Well, not exactly that, but it's a film that can certainly make careers, if I do say so. Mine, yours—even Ernie's. Don't be gloomy—they'll release it. No reason they shouldn't." He leaned in closer to her. "You should start thinking about your next picture."

The night was like a fantasy as she found herself dancing on the same floor with Cary Grant, Elizabeth Taylor, and Montgomery Clift. Before this night their familiar voices had come floating out of huge screens; now they were as close to her as Reed. Just people, she kept saying to herself.

She gazed at the lovely women, some quite celebrated. Did any of these beautiful people have to do what was being demanded of her? She couldn't believe it. Would they, in her place, just laugh it off? What would they say to Sheldon? Oh, put your thingy back in your pants and give me the role? Or had every single one of them done something demeaning and shameful to get the roles that had made them into the people whose sculptured shadows floated over America?

When Reed pulled to a stop in front of her little bungalow, he drew her into his arms. "I'm getting quite mushy about you, Sky, my dear." He gently tilted her chin up and kissed her. It felt like a heavy feather. It felt good. "You seem fragile, Sky."

"I'm not," she whispered, enjoying his closeness and the sense of harmony and security she felt with him. She breathed in, smelling the faint odor of salt and cedar coming from him.

"Reed, Sheldon's talking about putting me in a beach film."

"What? No, that's crazy. Where'd you hear that?" he asked, smoothing her hair back from her brow.

"Oh, I was talking to Mel," she fibbed.

"You talk to him again. I think Sheldon wants you in Wyler's picture." He kissed her lightly. "Maybe you're coming down with something," he said. "Are you going to be well enough for the races tomorrow?"

She nodded. Reed's brother and sister were visiting him.

"Is this the brother who's a minister?" she asked again, a running joke because he had so many siblings she kept getting them mixed up.

"No, this is the brother studying engineering. And the sister who wants to be a reporter."

"Oh, yes, I've got it now."

"Make sure you do."

She hoped Sheldon wouldn't be at the races.

Sheldon called her the next morning. "Have you decided?" he asked as if he were asking about a menu selection.

She started to cry. "I—can't. I don't understand why—"

"Then kiss your career goodbye," he said quickly and lightly. "And Reed's, and Ernie's." He hung up.

Her bungalow looked out on a little courtyard. A woman was sunning herself and painting her toenails. She wore very short shorts with tiny, rolled up cuffs. Sky envied her. She looked so contented. The phone rang.

"What are you doing?" Mel Winters demanded. "Come and see me."

In his office, he came right to the point. "Look, I'm sorry. These things happen. Quid pro quo and all that. My brother can be your best friend or your worst enemy. He's fond of you—"

Sky sneered. "Don't treat me like a fool."

"All right, he hates you. That's why he wants to make you the second Garbo." He glanced at her and started moving his pen set around on his desk. "You can go far, Sky, but you have to learn the rules. You have to show you *want* it. And you have to show your appreciation." Mel squirmed. He'd never heard Shel so coldly furious or so dangerously engaged in the stupid struggle. Damn him. Mel detested this. He shifted his angry frustration to Sky. "Why are you being so stiff-necked?"

"It's degrading!" she yelled. She started to cry. "It's degrading even to talk about this with you! I can't stand it."

"I thought you were tough," he said.

"If this is what it takes to be an actress—I don't want it. I'll quit. I mean it."

"You can't quit!" he yelled. "You got a contract. If you quit, Sheldon can ruin you. You'll stay and make beach pictures for seven years and take Reed right down the tubes with you. He'll never work in this town again."

"Why does this involve Reed? He hasn't done anything!"

"Leverage," Mel said. "Revenge. All that good stuff." He stood up and walked to the window, his hands in his pockets. "You're already an actress. You know how to do that. But this is something else. This is what it takes to get to the top. And today this is what it takes to get the *picture* released. I'm sorry you got so much on your shoulders, but I'm telling you, you don't know what trouble is if you don't do it."

"But . . . but . . ." she spluttered, "I've never slept with anyone! I didn't even know what he wanted, when he—" She started sobbing.

His heart was aching for her. Mel put his hand on her shoulder. "Oh, kid, just bend a little. It's nothing, it won't take anything away from you. When this is over, I'll have Sheldon right where we want him, I promise you. You'll have the best roles in the world."

Sky appeared at Sheldon's office without an appointment. Thayer pouted at her. He asked her to wait. She sat down in one of the huge flowered chairs and gripped her hands together. Sheldon kept her waiting half an hour.

Inside his office, she shut the door behind her. It's a role, she kept saying to herself. I'm onstage, and it's just a role.

He leaned back in his chair, his arms folded behind his head, admiring her slim waist as she approached. She stopped at the side of his desk. He took her hand and stroked it delicately. He had had no doubt that he would win the contest. She stared at the American flag behind his head. Her heart pounded.

"We don't have to rush," he said. "But I do like a display of eagerness."

He reached for his trousers. "How about a little smile?" he said. He tugged on her hand. He wanted her to kneel. His pressure on her hand snapped her out of her role.

"I won't!" she cried. "How dare you?" She felt herself fly out of control, and in that outer space she let her career, and Reed, go. "I'm not someone to be prodded! You sit there and gloat and take away my dignity! I won't let you have it! If you never release the picture that's fine! It'll be your loss!"

Astonished and enraged, Sheldon had dropped her wrist. "Get out of here, you little ninny! *Get out!*"

On a wet night in February of 1953, Sara arrived at the Clay Street House by taxi. She looked pale, her bronze hair standing out from her head in disarray. She paid the driver, then stopped on the first step and pretended to get a better grip on her overnight bag. But she was really getting a better grip on herself for her entrance.

She stared up at the two second-story windows she'd always thought of as eyes. It was her first visit back since she eloped. She breathed in deeply. Vail, who hadn't answered any of her letters, was inside. She knew from Sky that he'd been badly wounded and that until a couple of weeks ago he'd been in a hospital. How would she find him? Did he hate her? She climbed the steps and stood on the front porch, making faces at the door to relax her face. She didn't want to give anything away until the time was right. Just as she was sticking out her tongue and crossing her eyes, the door opened.

"Oh, darling, how good to see you," Diana said as if Sara had been away at camp. "Dad's in the study with Vail, but I wanted to be the first. Now, don't think anything is wrong—it's done now, and we all hope you're happy. How is Vic?"

"Fine, mother," Sara lied.

At the end of the hall, Vail sprang out of a doorway, a cane raised in front of him like a fencing sword. "En garde!"

he yelled, lunging toward her. His knee buckled and he collapsed.

In the study Ned was remembering Diana crying and crying the night Sara had eloped and her frantic telephoning the next day to put the right notices in the paper, to "square" everything with her friends. He heard Vail and Sara yelling at each other out in the hall and added more vodka to his drink before they returned. As he raised his glass to his lips, he smelled Willa's perfume on his fingertips mixed with the musky organic odor of her body. He told himself that he had to do it tonight. The change would be hardest on Willa, but she knew how to roll with the punches. He conjured her image, easy to do after their year together: a plump, motherly, outspoken woman (Diana would say vulgar, if she met her, which she wouldn't), who enjoyed a good drink as much as he did. Nothing pretentious about Willa.

As Vail limped into the room with Sara on his arm, Ned knew instantly that Sara was in trouble. That son of a bitch called Vic had done something to her, and she was home for good. Ned smiled his best "I'll-pretend-as-long-as-you-want-me-to" smile and drew his passionate, heedless daughter into his uncritical arms.

"It's nice to be back," she said softly. She watched Vail ease himself into a chair.

"Oh, I'm fine," Vail said deprecatingly, picking up on her thoughts. A thin, jagged scar slanted down from his hairline across his forehead to his eyebrow. His lean face held a fashionably cynical expression, but Sara saw the deep pain in his eyes. He pointed to his leg. "It might get better with exercise. I can—"

"—still ride," she completed for him. He nodded with a sly smile, pleased that their instant reading of each other had not diminished. But clearly, she thought, Vail's easy sporting grace had vanished with his innocence.

Mrs. Shogutsi came into the room with a tray of canapés.

"Mrs. Sho!" Sara cried, happily, then kissed her warmly on the cheek. "I'm so glad to see you!" Sara put an arm around her.

"You are happy with your husband?" Mrs. Sho asked her.

Sara smiled and was about to launch into a complicated

lie that would please Mrs. Sho when Vail said cheerfully, "It's lonely here without you and Sky."

"How is Sky?" Sara asked.

"Just fine, honey," Diana asked.

"Oh, let's not talk about movies," Vail said quickly.

"Let's talk about Sara."

"Let's talk about why you never answered my letters," said Sara briskly.

"Everything I had to say to you—couldn't be said."

"You're a wounded war hero now," Sara said.

Ned was the only person who knew the truth about that one, he thought. Whenever he looked at his father, Vail felt guilty. Vail had come home changed, but Ned's expectations for him had remained unchanged. Ned had spoken about the ranch, about raising racing horses together, to which Vail had responded vaguely. He couldn't get going in any direction; he was frozen.

"You've heard about the Rosenbergs, I suppose," Diana said to Sara. Ethel and Julius Rosenberg had been sentenced to death for passing atomic secrets to the Russians. "I'm working on a committee to get the sentence commuted to life imprisonment. The anti-Semitism this whole thing has released is simply not to be believed."

"Diana," Ned said, "they are guilty of treason."

"It's the atmosphere," Diana said. "That's what sentenced that woman and her husband to death." Diana rose to a well-worn argument. "If you'd have come with me, you'd have seen."

"Seen what?" Sara asked.

"In New York—the pickets around the Federal Building. Let's fry the Jews,'" she quoted, adjusting her necklace angrily.

"Did the signs say that?" Sara asked.

"No, that's what the people carrying the signs said. I tell you, these are terrible times."

Ned sighed deeply. "Oh, let's not get into current events. Sara, would you like a drink?"

Diana felt the letter in her pocket. What would they think of it? she wondered. She remembered sitting in the branches of the peach tree in the Whittakers' back yard, and trying to imagine her real mother and father, how all through college and long after she had married Ned, she'd avoided speaking openly about "her family." The triplets had been absorbed by "the mystery of her real parents" when she had told them about her foster parents, cautioning them over and over not to mention it, ever, to anyone.

Diana said: "I got a letter today." She removed it from her pocket. "Mrs. Whittaker has died," she announced, and couldn't help adding, "finally."

Sara and Vail smiled uncomfortably. She'd always brushed off her childhood with, "It was very unhappy and I want you to have better." She'd rarely talked about it.

As Diana read the letter from the executor of Mrs. Whittaker's estate, she couldn't suppress the smile curling along her lips like a little wave of pleasure. How she'd hated and feared that woman. "It seems that Mrs. Whittaker has left me a bequest of one thousand dollars—and an apology."

"What kind of—apology?" asked Ned, pouring himself another drink.

"Mrs. Whittaker, in her wisdom," Diana said sarcastically, "explains that there was some mystery attached to my birth, and that they were paid a stipend to care for me."

Vail shot a look at Sara. This was better than the thousand dollars!

"They had taken me in as a foster child. After a few years, the money stopped coming, which Mrs. Whittaker, in her letter, fears she took out on me." Diana looked up at them. "She certainly did."

"You were abandoned?" Ned gasped.

"So it seems. And, children, not a word about this to anyone."

"Who did that? Who left you?" Ned stammered.

"They don't say." Crisply, she folded the letter and re-placed it in her pocket. "That's what I'm going to find out."

It was a conversational sensation that they continued into dinner.

"But why won't you tell us more about your childhood?" Vail demanded at one point.

"Because it was very unhappy, and it brings back bad memories," Diana snapped. "I worked every minute. I grew up working." She bit her lip, and Sara felt a rush of compassion; there was so much that was hidden in her mother.

"Let's talk about the present," Diana said, wearing a false smile. "Tell us all about your life in Berkeley, Sara."

That was the last thing Sara wanted to talk about, but none of them would let her out of it. To their endless questions, she piled lie upon lie, hating herself.

"And Vic—maybe I should call him Victor—does he like his work?" asked Diana. "What's he doing? Just studying all the time?" Mrs. Shogutsi came into the dining room.

Ned bailed Sara out. "Let's not all gang up on Sara." He felt the buzz he enjoyed so much from his martinis and the wine. He wanted to speak before the buzz evaporated and left him exposed. "I've made a decision that I want to talk to you all about. You better stay, too, Mrs. Shogu—" —because it's going to require some changes."

Diana put her fork down. Vail heard the note of bravado and apology in his father's voice.

"I'm selling my partnership in the business. I'm sick of guns and tanks and planes—and business."

Diana gasped. Sara stared at her father. Was it because of Vail's brush with death that Ned was doing this? she wondered. Had Vail told him things he hadn't told the rest of them?

Ned's words were slurring a little. "I'm going to become a gentleman farmer. Well, not exactly that—isn't enough land out there on the ranch to farm!" He shot a quick self-conscious smile around the table. "What I mean is, I've decided to get the racing stock back. Vail and I are going to race the horses."

Sara looked at Vail, who appeared to be astonished. Diana was too shocked to notice. "You mean, give up this house? Live out there?" Diana asked. "We can't do that, and besides, Neddie, racing horses is cruelly expensive!"

"No, no, we'll live here, but it will mean we'll have to cut back a bit. But you kids are grown up. Sara's married. Things are changing. I just have to change, too." Nakedly, he looked at Diana for her acquiescence.

"My, that's a lot to take in all at once," Diana breathed.

"Too good," he grumbled.

The conversation got back on track, and Mrs. Shogutsi

excused herself. She went to her room behind the kitchen and reached deep into a drawer where she kept her savings in a soft cloth pouch. She sat down in a straight wooden chair and started carefully to count the money.

Diana knocked at the door. When she was inside, she said, "Don't worry. Nothing's going to change."

They had coffee in the living room without the festivity Diana had planned. Vail let Sara carry the burden of the conversation. He was in the same room, but he was adrift. He put his cane between his legs. Sara's envy of Sky in Hollywood exhausted him—especially, he thought, since he was the only one who saw it. He could see it plainly. He closed his eyes, listened to the rise and fall of the voices, and watched the snow leopard lope along the devastated street. He wanted to tell Sky and Sara about the big cat, but now the thought of the leopard didn't uplift him as it once had; it reminded him of the Seoul alley. He opened his eyes. He was staring directly at Diana, and for a moment she resembled the leopard—cool and pale and sleek. He tapped his cane absently. He saw his mother rising out of her bath, the water dripping from her. He closed his eyes. What was he going to do with his life?

Diana was pasting articles about Sky from the fan magazines into a large scrapbook. She started at the top of a clipping, moist with glue on the reverse side, then slowly moved the flat of her hand down until she reached the end where she gave it a little tap-tap. She turned the page and started on another. There were a dozen in all. "Oh, I do wish Victor had come up with you," Diana said to Sara, to fill another yawning hole in the conversation.

"Mother, please!" Sara said. "You don't have to go on pretending," Vail opened his eyes.

Diana drew back, shocked. "Sara Bay, how can you say that? I only want what's best for you."

"I know I've made a mess of everything—married below me and all that—embarrassed everyone—"

"I certainly never led you to believe any such thing," Diana said.

"Mother! Stop that!" Sara yelled.

"Yes," Vail said. "No one here liked or trusted him. Let's be honest."

"You could have come to me," said Diana, ignoring Vail,

—125—

"and we could have worked it out. You would have had a decent wedding instead of some hole-in-corner—"

"I couldn't come to you!" Sara wailed.

"Now, now," Ned said, "Vic can come up this weekend. I'll take you both out to the ranch. Call him up. Tell him he can't say no."

"He's not coming this weekend or any weekend. He's left me," Sara said heavily. "Are you pleased, Mother? You see, everything you said was right!"

"I knew it!" Ned snapped, outraged and appalled. "The bastard."

Sara's beautiful face crumpled. "I can't stand it any more, pretending that everything's fine. It's not."

Diana rose, moved behind the couch where Sara was sitting, and slipped her hand under Sara's quivering chin. Her hand felt extremely soft and warm. "There, there," Diana said. "You've had a tragic first love." She withdrew her hand and sat down on the arm of the couch near Sara.

Great tears rolled down Sara's cheeks. "I came home four nights ago from my job, and I could feel that he wasn't there any more. It was so *quiet.* I went into the bedroom and opened a closet, and there wasn't one thing of his left. Nothing. He left me a note." Sara looked up. "It said that he couldn't stay any longer, that he just didn't have the courage to stay. That I was above him somewhere, and he'd never be able to reach me." She looked beseechingly at her father. "I've wrecked my life!"

"How can you say that? Sara! You haven't!" Diana said. Ned rose unsteadily and went over to her. "Now, chicken, nothing's changed around here. We all love you, and anything you ever do will be great."

Sara pulled back. "But it *has* changed. *I've* changed. Oh, God, I'm too old to—"

"You're never too old to come home," Ned said sternly. "Listen, Sara, you and I will get an apartment," Vail said. The instant the words came out of his mouth, he thought of all the reasons why that would not be fun.

"No, that won't work," Sara said, rising nervously and walking away from them toward the bank of windows at the end of the room.

"Sure it would, chicken," Ned said. "You and Vail'd have a great time. And we'd all be together, Vail and me—"

"It won't work!" Sara yelled. "I'm pregnant!"

Diana clapped a hand over her mouth and stared at her daughter. "My God," Diana gasped, "I never thought!"

When Sara was noticeably pregnant, Diana explained to friends that "Victor" was stationed in Korea. Sara said nothing. It was hard to behave normally when she didn't feel normal. She couldn't see her friends—what would she say? The lies her mother had so quickly made up depressed her. She spent her time at the movies or walking or reading or sleeping. She thought of Vic constantly, wondering where he was, missing him, wanting him. By abandoning her he had taken on sharper significance and she genuinely mourned him as she grieved for the woman she had once been. She feared she'd never be young again; she was ashamed of her failure. She took no joy in being pregnant; she and "it" were in the same prison for an indeterminate sentence. How was she going to support it? What was she going to do? She wanted to put it up for adoption, but under the circumstances, given her mother's own abandonment as a baby, Sara could not and would not consider it. She was trapped.

Belinda Victoria Wyman was born early that summer after the "night of long knives," as Sara referred to the ordeal of giving birth. Briefly, she basked in the look of unqualified love that swept Belinda's little face when the baby nursed or woke up from one of her long sleeps. The terror and pain of the delivery faded. "I am going to call you Lindy," she said, "because you look so spritely."

But Sara had no sense of being Belinda's mother; she felt like an aunt or a guest. The only person she felt she could talk to was Mrs. Sho. All Ned's soft threats about belt-tightening had been hollow. Mrs. Sho moved into a new position as head nanny; Diana increased her salary.

Then Sky came back.

"Oooh, I'm an aunt!" were her first words to Sara.

Sara winced but recovered quickly. "Sure! Easy! She's already as pretty as you are!"

"Prettier, I'll bet." Amazingly, Sky started to cry when she saw Belinda. "I don't know why I'm doing this," she blubbered. But the sweetness of the child stirred her; she felt profoundly connected to her.

"Here, put this cloth on your shoulder," Sara said, noticing Sky's beautiful silk dress.

"Ohhh, you've done something so wonderful."

"You want her?" Sara laughed. It was like playing dolls again.

"Oh, yes!"

At two o'clock the next morning, Sky and Sara were sitting cross-legged on Sky's bed in their pajamas, surrounded by Coke bottles, by part of a chocolate cake, and by an ashtray full of cigarettes. Throughout her pregnancy, Sara had been trying to decide what to do with her life. After Belinda was born, she had started to think about going to an acting school in New York.

Sara broke off a sizable piece of chocolate cake and crammed it into her mouth. "Mother's cutting out all the clippings about you. I've read a few. Who's that Patrick you're dating?"

"That drivel—the studio puts those things out. We aren't really dating."

"He's almost as good looking as that Reed Corbett," Sara said.

"Oh, Reed's wonderful." Sky sighed.

They'd been sitting there for hours, but Sara couldn't find the words for what was on her mind. She'd wrecked her life and she had to repair it. She touched Sky's hand. "You haven't mentioned one word about the movie."

"I was afraid to," Sky said. "I know how upset you were, but believe me, Hollywood's a nutsy place. It isn't a garden of roses."

"What's going on with the picture?"

She looked up at Sara's pretty face. What would Sara have done in her place with Sheldon? Refused outright, as Sky had finally done? Sheldon had been enraged, but Sky had felt good; she had not betrayed herself. And then, for a long time, there had been silence. Reed had gone crazy, trying to find out why his picture wasn't being released. Finally, Sheldon had ordered some reshooting and another cut. Mel had told her to keep her head down, that Sheldon might end by respecting her.

"I don't know when the picture will be released," Sky said. "Maybe this fall, maybe later." As the price of her disobedience, Sheldon was forcing Sky into the beach movie. Just yesterday she had stormed into Mel's office. He was "working on it." "Isn't it funny the way it worked out? None of us is where we thought we would be?" Sara said.

"I don't want you to feel bad," Sara said.

"Bad?" Sky asked sharply.

"Bad about you getting the break and making the movie, and not me. I was so angry at you—and at everything. But I'm getting over it."

"Are you?" Sky asked. "In your place, I don't know if I'd ever have gotten over it." She reached over Sara's leg and plucked off a piece of cake. "I know it was rough on you." She ate the cake. "On me, too," she finally said. "I want to do good work, not just this dumb beach movie. I've read scripts you wouldn't believe! Every part calls for me in a bathing suit! Or a nightgown! And now Mother wants to come down and stay with me."

"Do you want her to?" Sky shrugged. Sara picked at the cake, not looking at Sky. "You've changed," she said.

"How?" Sky asked.

"I don't know." She laughed lightly. "We're all growing up, I guess. Look at Vail."

Sky groaned. "Yes, he's just lost, isn't he?"

"Because of his injuries. He'll get back. But Dad's putting a lot of pressure on him."

"Wait till he finds a girl," Sky said.

"Sky, I was going to tell you earlier—at one point I just gave up, when I thought you were going to have to do the acting for both of us. But now—"

"Acting isn't everything," Sky said, lighting a cigarette. "It is to me."

"You still want to? I thought, with Vic and everything—"

"Vic's gone! He's not coming back—I can feel it," Sara replied bitterly. "I've been thinking. There's an acting school in New York. I'm thinking of applying."

"But Lindy—"

"Yeah, I know, I've got a lot to figure out now. But—how would you feel if I did that?"

"I'd feel fine," Sky said.

Sara raced on to other subjects. She knew that her acting

in New York didn't seem very real to Sky. It didn't seem very real to Sara, either.

Sky went back to Los Angeles, and Sara went out to the ranch. "What're you doing out here?" Maggie demanded. She'd just seen her daughter and three children off and had been hoping for a little privacy.

"Came to see you," Sara said, flopping into a chair in Maggie's office. She thought of the way Sky looked—sleek, confident, and cool.

"There ain't nothing out here to ride," Maggie replied tartly. "Your dad's real particular now." Maggie sniffed. For all the money that man was spending on horses he could feed half of South Sacramento. She peered at Sara with a look of long experience. "What's wrong?"

"I need advice." Maggie had already had one child when she'd put herself through agricultural school.

Maggie clucked. "You're eaten up with envy and sadness, and you got no pretense in you to deny it." Maggie started pulling files out of a desk drawer. "What are you doing about it? Nothing! You're just standing around watching the fuss everyone's making over Sky and gettin' mad. But you got nothing to do except tend to that baby." She slapped a pad of paper down on the desk and picked up a pen. "I swear, you and Vail. What's he doing for himself, huh? Just moping around as if he's the only man'd ever been in a war. Plain sickening! When are you going to quit feeling sorry for yourself and do something?"

Sara smiled. "That's what I came to talk about. I'm going to need your help—with Belinda."

Later that afternoon, Sara found Ned smoking a pipe and nursing a glass of whiskey as the boy-groom he'd hired curried Fireball, his colt. She and Ned walked around the paddock twice as Sara described what she wanted to do: live and study in New York.

"Forget the dramatics," he finally said, turning back toward the stables. "I know you have to get out. Tell me how much it's going to cost, and I'll tell you if I can do it." He raised his glass to his lips, drank hungrily, and disappeared back inside the stable.

"I guess that's a yes," she mumbled. "Thanks."

—130—

Back in San Francisco, Sara spoke with Mrs. Sho. When Vail got home that night, she took him out to dinner and asked him to help her. Vail got slightly tight, told her not to worry, to go do what she wanted, that acting in New York was a damn sight better than acting in Hollywood. "It's all a crock in tinsel town. She won't be allowed to do anything good down there." He seemed disconnected, criticizing everything, from the political state of the Union to the creative state of the arts. "You don't even know if you have any talent," he said.

"I gotta find out, Vail. Or I'll go crazy."

"Yeah, well, I can understand that. Count me in," he said, indifferently. "You remind me a lot of a snow leopard," he said suddenly, smiling. Sara was bounding over rubble under fire, but she probably wouldn't make it.

"A what?" Sara asked, disconcerted.

"Nothing."

"Vail, what happened to you in Korea?" Vail was hiding something, and she'd sensed it that first evening at home with him.

"Got wounded," he said. "Bad. Right here." He pointed at his heart. He didn't have to say anything more. Sara started to cry. He touched her hand. "There's been enough tears. Korea can wash the world in tears."

When Sara told Diana what she wanted to do, her mother's reaction came, as usual, on two levels: accusatory and practical.

"If you do this crazy thing," Diana said finally, "I want you to sign Belinda over to me." Sara was too astonished to speak. "I know what it sounds like, but babies get sick, mostly not serious, but if anything happens, you'll be three thousand miles away and I'll have to act. I have to know I can act in her best interests always."

They had gone to Diana's little workroom at the top of the house for privacy. "You know I'll do everything I can for Lindy and so will Daddy. She's very special, and she's a lot like you as a baby. You were never any trouble and you were always so happy." Diana's lip trembled, and she put a hand over her face, thinking of the morning she'd met with Vic. She shook her head violently; recriminations were for the weak.

Sara misunderstood Diana's silence. "I know I've disappointed everyone," Sara said shakily.

"No, no," Diana protested, waving her hand weakly. "Only yourself. Only yourself."

"I meant about Lindy, leaving her, not taking the responsibility."

Diana wiped her eyes. "She'll be well cared for," Diana said. "I think you ought to have a chance to do what you want to do, make a life for yourself. I do think one actress in a family is enough." She looked at Sara fiercely. "Don't try to compete! It can't be done. You'll only bring more grief on yourself."

On the day Sara's acceptance from the New York School of Dramatic Arts came in the mail, San Francisco was glistening under a late summer rain, and the streets sparkled. A rolling bank of fog bunched in the west, gathering itself for an assault on the city.

Sara stood over Belinda's cradle and took her baby's little pink hand. "Bye-bye, sweetheart," she whispered. The baby gurgled happily, half asleep. "I don't know if I'm doing the right thing. I hope I am. If I'm wrong, I hope you'll forgive me." Lindy's blue eyes gazed at her. "You can't get worse from my mother than what I got. You might do better. A lot of it depends on you." Sara looked up at the ceiling, her mouth a tight line. Oh, God, she thought, this is so hard, leaving her. Please don't make this the biggest mistake of my life.

Mrs. Sho stood in the doorway. She was the only one who saw the tears in Sara's eyes.

9

Reed loved his 1949 Ford convertible. The outside was bright red, the inside white. It was small enough to park easily, big enough to hold friends.

"You don't care that your car is two years old and that it's not a Mercedes, do you?" Sky said as they drove along the Pacific Coast Highway. "I like that." It was a lovely morning; they were on their way to Zuma Beach for a swim and lunch.

Sky's hair billowed out behind her head in the soft, fast air. "That stupid girl in the beach movie doesn't do anything except moon around after the guy," she said. "I just read the rewrite."

He laughed. "And she gets into trouble, right? Quit thinking about it," he said. "Mel will get you out of it. That's what he does best. You're not the first actress to be cast in a beach movie," he said. "Though I can't imagine what Sheldon's thinking of. It's all wrong." He hoped she wasn't typecast as a pretty sexpot, because she'd never be allowed to act.

She looked out at the turquoise Pacific. "He owes me a good role," she said. It was more insulting than Reed would ever know; it was her punishment for not obeying. She hoped Mel could fix it.

Reed heard her tone. From a shy, introverted girl, Sky was remaking herself into a woman to be dealt with. She had an aura about her, a wholly unconscious power like an energy field. And he was caught in it. "Looks like 'Queen' is back on schedule. Going to be released early next year," walked on the beach, as they swam and ran or simply a woman. She kept walls around the secret, vulnerable core within her, from which all her emotions and talent came. The real Stephanie Skyler hid behind those walls. Outside, she looked delicate, ladylike, eager to please. Inside those walls, she was tempestuous, dramatic, emotional. He'd seen inside those walls when they were working on "Queen," and he'd watched her tunnel under them into her secret self when she acted—into anger, joy, sorrow, pain. The essence of the woman he loved was her drive toward creative truth and her impulse to hide.

All through that day, as they swam and ran or simply is back on schedule. Going to be released early next year," Reed observed the girl growing into

It was dusk as they walked on the beach. "I'm pooped," Sky said. They went back into the house, whose western wall was all glass, so that from any point within they could see the ocean without. She flopped down on the couch and leaned against the big soft pillows. Reed was making coffee. She was getting nervous again. It was like this when they were alone.

The first time Reed had gathered her into his arms and kissed her, she'd tolerated his embrace while feeling close to Reed the man. But she'd kept her actor's mask firmly in place. She'd slipped away from him. But when she wasn't with him, she longed for him and even pursued him: They had sailed to Catalina, done a turn on the merry-go-round in Griffith Park, and, like today, spent hours together like children. It had ended each time he drew her close to him— and she whisked away like a minnow in the shallows.

Tonight was going to be different.

They were lying on the deck. He was holding her, aching for her. Her eyes half-closed, she felt him bending in to kiss her throat. He stopped. "Please, don't accommodate me," he said, realizing that she was playing a part. He sat up and turned away.

"No," she whispered. There were tears in her eyes. "I'm sorry. It's not that." Her memory of Sheldon in his office stood between them when she was in Reed's arms. But tonight other, more powerful emotions were moving within her.

She put her arms around Reed's neck and kissed the back of his ear. "Please be patient with me. I'm worth waiting for," she whispered.

He turned, put his arms around her, and rocked her. "I never thought you weren't," he said. "I love you."

"And I love you, Reed." She pressed her open palm to his cheek and gazed into his eyes without flinching. She felt lightheaded and excited. "Now."

They made love on a big soft couch, the door open to the deck, serenaded by the rolling sound of the sea.

In New York, Sara was on a small stage pretending to be a tree.

"*Stones!*" Miss Ilani had yelled resonantly at the twelve freshmen sitting in the house. "If you want to make *Stones* act, teach them the Method!" She had hung her head in a trite rendition of sorrow. "Talent is a word of the past."

Irene Ilani was built like a steamer trunk from the neck down. Her colossal head, heavily covered with dark tan makeup, was capped with dyed black hair fixed in masses of tiny curls. Many antique chains of beads and silver baubles dangled from her neck. Her bracelets clanked dramatically when she gestured. She had been the toast of Broadway in 1920.

Sara's tree was supposed to come to life, trot around (in the "character of the tree"), see its image in a pool of water, laugh delightedly. Then her tree was to find itself rooted once again to the earth, whereupon her tree was to cry. That was Irene's first exercise for them, and Sara was up first. Acutely conscious of the strangers who were her classmates, Sara stood on the bare stage in front of them. She decided to be a Douglas fir. Becoming free of her bonds, Sara stiffly shuffled around like a walking Douglas fir, bending her head. Her long curly hair flapped like a truncated mop over her face. She tried to pretend she wasn't making a fool of herself by pretending to be a tree.

Someone out front giggled. Sara's tree stopped and looked down at the "pool of water." She saw floorboards. She opened her lips, and choked out a high, painful, unhappy sound—the antithesis of laughter. Wretched and embarrassed, she implored herself to laugh, but her state was so

—135—

far removed from anything remotely amusing that she gave up, turned stiffly in a circle, then began rooting herself into the ground again so that her Douglas fir could sob, which it did "with great expression—very believable," Irene said when the catastrophe had ended.

"That was absolutely the worst tree I have ever seen. You looked like some kind of robot. Walking." Teddy Monroe, nineteen, was the ringleader of the school's intelligentsia. He was tall and thin. His mouth sneered charmingly, and he wore heavy, black-framed glasses that gave his boyishness a varnished air of adult speculation. "Wait till you see mine," he went on. "I was thinking of a pomegranate tree." His black eyes snapped with malicious enjoyment. "My name's Teddy Monroe. Teddy for short." He cackled.

After Irene Ilani's spectacular opening class, Teddy and Sara walked through the marble hall under the vaulted ceiling of the School of Dramatic Arts. The main building was set majestically on a corner in Manhattan's East Seventies. There were about three hundred students from all levels in the school, and they all seemed to be in this hall, which echoed with their complaints, jokes, and ambitions.

"Where are you from?" she asked him. Though he was younger than Sara, he seemed sophisticated, older.

"Traumatown, New Jersey," he snapped. "That's what I call it."

They moved slowly through the waves of students. Teddy told her about the half-duplex he'd rented in the Village with three other men: Bertie Heather, Dirk Simons, and John Lands. "We are the elite of the elite," he said.

"Oh, are you *those* guys?" She laughed. They were suddenly playing a scene.

"Yes, Marjorie, the same," Teddy said in a fair British accent. "I hope you will come to luncheon soon." The accent fell away. "You can check out the stifling Republican aura of our flat with Bertie and the rest. Distasteful as hell." He peered at her. "But I always have gin, beer, or scotch. They make it all bearable."

"I'm a Democrat, so you're in good company."

"Oh, my dear, don't I know? What else could you be with that gorgeous face? Anyway, Traumatown, N.J. Filled

—136—

with artists, musicians, Communists, little factions of people. Brilliant. I've been living in the midst of all that for the important, formative years of my life. But all the kids of these artists, yours truly among them," he added, heavily accenting the words, "grew up too fast, I might say, and that is where my limited education about things artistique derives. What about you?"

Sara gave him an abbreviated sketch, omitting Belinda, and mentioning only that she also had a brother and a sister.

Gilbert Weisl, who commanded the school, came steaming down the hallway, his pumping arms propelling him. He was a tall, thin, agile man of fifty who spoke in a high nasal whinny, a voice easy to imitate. He waved at them.

GW, as he was universally called, had come to the United States in 1910 as a child. His family had amassed a department store fortune. Dipping into his inheritance, he had dotted New York with his theatrical failures. But these forays on Broadway had not distracted him from his charges at the school. He saw every entering student personally. Just before she became a tree, Sara had had her "welcome appointment" in his office, where the bookshelves were crowded not with books on drama but on psychology. In later months she came to feel these selections were appropriate, considering the school's many neurotic students.

As GW disappeared down the hall, Teddy—a first-rate raconteur and purveyor of all "campus" gossip—hissed, "He's a fiery Jungian, you know. He calls kids into his office and explains their compulsive tardiness, insubordination, or licentiousness in Jungian symbols. I was in his office my first week," he said proudly. "Did you notice that huge polar bear rug in his office?" Sara nodded. "GW had me sit down on it, and before we were through, he was tearing whole tufts outta that poor ol' bear in his fervor to help! He's a card." He winked at Sara.

Diva Baron taught speech. She was sleek, had a long face, and reminded Sara of a temperamental racehorse. Diva rapped the class sharply to order.

"You think you're all going to be actors, but you're going to end up as speech teachers like me, so you'd better pay attention in this class." Sara thought she was nuts.

"You must learn to use your organ properly," Diva went on. Titters rippled over the room. "Your organ," she continued, ruinously, "is your most important instrument."

"She'll get no argument from me," Teddy whispered.

The girl sitting next to Sara scowled at her, then smiled timidly. A big girl with big bones that would have seen her over the Rockies on foot, her uncombed hair was so thick and brown that it looked like clumps of underbrush. "Do you have a nail file?" she whispered. Her eyes were as round and sad as a seal's. Sara shook her head. The girl looked down at her long, thick nails painted a deep red. Her name was Anne Mehan.

An acting major like Sara and Teddy, Anne tagged along for the next class, Actors' Orientation. It was conducted by Georgie Cavanaugh, one of the school's acting teachers and its primary director of student productions.

"Wanna know the skinny on Georgie?" Teddy whispered. They were now sitting in the main auditorium, a baroque hall from another era. "He takes *girls* home with him!" Sara frowned. "It's a mark of distinction," Teddy added irritably. "You're very naive, aren't you?"

"Most people from the West are, Teddy," Anne said in her husky voice.

Sara gazed at them. She felt older and more experienced.

"Our other acting teacher, Fred, is a gem," Teddy announced. "But we won't have him until we're sophomores."

Georgie was friendly yet businesslike. He had dark brown hair, a reddish beard, and an open, let's-all-pull-together manner. But even in this first meeting, he showed a snappish side, labeling questions stupid or dishonest or tiresome. He described the freshmen's duties, called Crew, providing the labor for the productions in which the older, senior students acted; the freshmen made costumes and sets, attending their seniors by cleaning or mending those costumes and generally waiting on them hand and foot.

"Such a tired old system," Teddy moaned as they left.

"I've heard he's a good director," Sara said.

"He's a peach. Let's have a drink."

"No. Dance class now." Sara and Anne dragged him along.

—138—

It wasn't a real gym, just a big exercise hall on the top floor, where the dancing and fencing classes were held.

Rags Kipper was a Canadian who had perfected her voice and speech a half-century ago and had feet like eagle's claws. She was thin, wiry, blustery, warm, and tireless. So conditioned was her body over many years of teaching dance and gymnastics that she could fold up like a camp chair. She wore bright blue leotards and carried a portable Indian tom-tom that she began beating as Sara and Teddy stripped off their jeans and cords and fell breathlessly into line.

"Down on the floor," Rags cried. "Uh one, two, three—" Rags put them through their paces. Groans and cries arose from the fifteen bodies that twisted on the floor. Rags shouted, *"Move! Move!"* Teddy got up after ten minutes and limped out of the room, winking at Sara as he passed.

When class was over, and the hardiest of the group were feeling pretty peppy, Bertie Heather sauntered over to Sara. He was very blond, almost to the point of whiteness. His tights showed off his muscular legs and his tangerine jersey stuck to his well-developed chest. He introduced himself.

"How'd you like to go to a dance, Sara?"

"What dance?" Sara snapped. She smiled to counteract it.

"The Art Students League. Costume ball."

"Jesus, do we have to wear costumes?"

Bertie's face fell. "No, but I thought it would be fun."

"Oh, all right," she said. She smiled again. "Thanks."

She picked up a load of voice and speech books and her dance gear and headed home. She didn't have time for dances.

Sara's apartment was on Twenty-fifth just off Third Avenue, a studio with kitchen and bath and a little terrace overlooking the backyards of the ground-floor dwellings. It cost her forty dollars a month and represented her first free space. She put up photos of Sky, Lindy, and Vail and some posters; bought a reed rug, a couch, bed, and desk and some secondhand Depression dishes that had originally come from the movie houses, which had given them away in the thirties. She got her cigarettes from the cigar store on the corner and ordered her coffee light at Max's on Third. She wrote skimpy letters back home for everyone's consumption and thought about calling Sky but kept putting it off. She was busy separating herself.

Bertie gnawed delicately on Sara's ear and pressed her tightly to him. The hall was jammed with people dressed as animals or exotically costumed in sequins and cardboard. One woman had come as a house—an elaborate structure that fitted over her. Her head stuck out of the chimney, and a red-brick stovepipe hat completed her ensemble. It was an eccentric group, but when they began tearing down the decorations, Sara wanted to leave.

Sara tried to feel free to be young again. In the cab going home, Bertie put an arm around her shoulders and kissed her. Slowly he moved his hand under her skirt and stroked her thigh. She was a little drunk and let him go on. He lifted her skirt and slowly bent down to kiss her thigh. As his lips moved, she put her back against the seat and gazed out at the dark buildings fleeing past. She combed his hair with her hand and touched his ear and felt the blood beating in his temple. Bertie's head came up and he kissed her lips, slowly, drawingly, moistly. "You like?" he asked, smoothing her dress down. She nodded. "How about some more back at your place?"

"I don't think so."

At her apartment, he dropped her reluctantly and somewhat coldly. Why had she let him do that in the cab, of all places? she wondered. What was wrong with her? She'd wondered the same thing after she'd slept with Vic that first time. Diana would call her cheap. Fleetingly, she compared herself to Sky. "Oh, screw it," she said, unlocking her door. She gave it a kick for good measure.

In a San Francisco attorney's office, Diana fingered her gloves as she listened to the private detective her attorney had hired describe the difficulties. At last she could listen no longer.

"Mr. Vaughn, I don't care what your problems are with this assignment. Either do it, or tell me you cannot so that I may hire someone else."

Vaughn shot a look at his old friend, Maurice Hyman,

the attorney. The woman wanted the impossible. She wanted breaking and entering. Since neither the orphanage people nor the state would give her any confidential information about her parents, she wanted him to get into an office and a private file cabinet.

"We've been to the orphans' court records in Multnomah County," Hyman supplied. "I'm afraid it's the end of the road unless you can pull something out of the hat, which is what I've told Mrs. Wyman here," he said to Vaughn.

"All right, let me see what I can do," Vaughn replied, irritated. He had uneven teeth and a wide unselfconscious smile. "I've got a few connections in Portland."

Diana fingered her squash-blossom necklace and returned his ugly smile warmly.

At home that night, Ned broached a subject that had always embraced both mystery and indifference for him: money. "I'm asking you to stay your hand before you go off like a nut hiring private eyes and more attorneys, Diana. I simply cannot afford it!"

"*You* can afford to start a racing stable and hire a lot of grimy men for God knows how much; I guess you can afford to help me!" She was exasperated with him. She'd helped people all her life, and Ned was complaining about the one thing she wanted to do for herself.

"I'm telling you, the money's running out! You don't have to find your parents this year—find them next year after I've got some wins under my belt!"

They both continued to do exactly what they had done before, except that Ned—perhaps seeing Armageddon ahead more clearly—began spending wildly and secretly.

Kismet had opened on Broadway during a newspaper strike which had cast a long shadow over the season. Sara was walking in the Village, the hub of Off-Broadway where *End As A Man* and *Threepenny Opera* were playing. Being so close to the center of the new American theater invigorated her until a car came rolling by blasting "Doggie in the Window" into the street.

"What a thrill to see you," Teddy said sleepily as he opened the door for Sara. He was dressed in an open blue plaid robe. His legs, nude up to his Jockey shorts, were sprinkled with brown hair. He wore dirty white wool socks. His light brown curly hair stuck up in a cowlick on top of his head.

"I was in the neighborhood," said Sara. "It was an open invitation, wasn't it?"

"As open as I get. Enter." The house Teddy shared with Bertie, Dirk, and John was on Macdougal Street in the Village. Some of the houses sported window flower boxes; all were in an advanced state of deterioration, yet the neighborhood as a whole had a rickety charm.

Sara and Teddy walked in silence up the stairs. "I've got a hangover," he announced as they reached the living room. Teddy surveyed it critically. "We had to paint the whole thing over, of course," he said. "This room was pink." It was now dark gray with black woodwork. There were two long windows on one wall that faced another building. Moldy secondhand furniture sagged against the walls; the carpet breathed dust. "My mother hates this room," he noted.

"How are your parents?" she asked.

"Cold, very cold." He pointed to a Lautrec print on the wall. "Dirk's," he sneered. "Don't mind Dirk."

It was not quite noon. In the kitchen, Dirk and Bertie were hunched over their coffee, stirring slowly, staring at the sticky, yellow-flowered oilcloth covering the table. Dirk was dark and lanky, a sharply pointed nose protruding from his Italian Renaissance face. Bertie glanced at Sara but didn't smile.

"Coffee's over there," Teddy said to Sara, "and get some for me, too." He turned to Dirk. "I just can't stand it." He pointed to Sara. "Look at her. Fresh as a daisy, and I'll bet she made every little class this morning, didn't you?"

"Yes, I did." Sara didn't look at Bertie. Teddy poured cream into his coffee and added three spoons of sugar.

Dirk contributed a grunt. He had very long eyelashes. He was reading the *Times* theater section. Silence hung over the kitchen. Sara felt uncomfortable. Had Bertie told what they'd done in the cab? The kitchen was chilly; someone had turned on the oven and opened the door. It made the room smell oily and close. Fragments of curtains clung to the windows, their last outpost before the ragbag.

"And how was Rags this morning?" Teddy asked.

"Wonnnderful class," Sara breathed, leaning back in her chair and stretching. "We have a new exercise now. We lie on our backs, raise our feet—"

"Stop!" Teddy commanded, holding up a bony hand. "I can't bear it. I have to pull myself together and meet John. We're having lunch, it seems."

"Where?" Sara asked.

"At the Oak Room of the Plaza," Teddy said, getting up and pulling his plaid bathrobe about his tall, slender frame like a toga. He'd lost the sash. "Then to a new play, some expressionistic social drama about loneliness or rebellion against authority."

"There'll never be another *Come Back Little Sheba*," Dirk intoned from his newspaper.

"And just who is John?" Sara asked, hoping he'd ask her to go along.

"John . . ." he said to a pot of jam. "John is a contemporary Keats, only smarter. Wholly enjoyable. Surely you've met John." Sara pretended she was trying to place him. She and Teddy were acting out another scene, and only they knew it. "Well, someday we'll take you to lunch, too." His lips formed a slightly mocking smile and he wheezed an explosive laugh. "But not for a while." Instantly, Sara knew that Bertie had told him about their evening—the dance, the cab. Maybe Bertie had embroidered the experience. Teddy was jealous. "I must go," he said. "Farewell." He drew his bathrobe around him again, lifted his chin, and padded down the hall.

Sara rose. "You're a pig," she said to Bertie.

"I don't like teasers."

She straightened, slapped by the word. Dirk got up and left. "I am very fond of Teddy."

"You won't get anywhere with Teddy. He likes small, dark-haired girls, not—"

She ran down the hall and started pounding on closed doors. "Teddy! Teddy!"

A door opened. He stood there in his underwear. "Oh, lordy, Wanda Mae, why didn't you tell me you were coming!"

"Shut up, Teddy. Get inside."

"What will people think?"

Sara shut the door behind her and leaned against it.

"I like you a lot, and I don't want whatever Bertie's told you—"

He put a hand over her mouth. "Don't worry. Bertie's a bourgeois fool. I know everything he said was true!" He laughed.

She shut her eyes. "Oh, shit."

"I like you. Just the way you are. Now get out of my room."

10

That winter Reed gave a party to celebrate the studio's release of *The White Queen*. For a little film it was developing major pretensions.

Reed's house was above Sunset Strip on Londonderry Place. The art director on "Queen" had naturally saved the first sketches of the set; he'd strategically decorated Reed's bar, the living room, and the terrace that overlooked Los Angeles. The hi-fi was playing, "In the Cool, Cool, Cool of the Evening."

Sky, wearing a black lace dress, entered the bubbling room nervously. She was almost reclusive. Parties were difficult for her. The men stood around in a bunch talking about the movies they were making, while the women took refuge in another part of the room. They had about them, these wives, an air of vague sadness or surrender. The only emissaries between these two segregated groups were the famous women—always welcomed by the powerful men— or men like Reed who enjoyed talking to women.

"Hello," Reed said to her in his deep voice. He kissed her cheek. "I hope you can stay after the festivities." She nodded, and he put an arm around her waist. "I love you," he whispered.

She smiled. "New sweater," she said. It was a brilliant emerald green.

"Mother made it," Reed said, proudly. He was always getting something from his family, and it was always handmade. "Listen, the power brokers from the studio are getting here around eight, then we all eat dinner, then I show the picture. Sheldon won't stay for it, of course. Then we hope everyone leaves."

She had resolved to be politely attentive and faintly aloof to Sheldon, though it was still very hard to be with him at all. Mel had somehow extricated her from the beach movie, and, moreover, he'd extracted a promise from Shel that if "Queen" were a hit Sky would receive a bonus. Mel had assured her there would be no more beach movie threats. Sky arched her eyebrow and straightened her shoulders: Contracts and money were the only means a beginner had to measure how well or badly she was doing. But Sky hadn't escaped punishment completely: Sheldon had given the part in the Wyler picture to Lila Lewis.

Rosemary Clooney was belting out "Come On-a My House" on the hi-fi. "I'll get you a drink," Reed said, over the music, "and then we'll circulate."

"I'm so bad at this, Reed," she confessed. "I just can't make conversation."

"You don't have to. They will," he said, smiling. "Have you met Donna Reed?"

But he was the host and, instantly called away by arriving guests, he bounced from one group to another with glee. Reed had so much energy, he was always doing something—softball with the Directors Guild team, writing letters to his family, playing the harmonica, working on charity benefits.

She watched him. Reed was the kind of man, she knew, who made lasting commitments; when he said he loved her, it was forever. She was completely caught up in the strong, silvery passion of their love affair. Everyone thought they'd be married, and Sky dreamed about it, too. Except for Sheldon, her life had a precious, unbreakable charm. But she knew that almost more important than her first picture, the choice of the second could make or break her career. She and Reed had talked about it a lot, and now that the danger of the beach movie was behind her, she knew that just refusing pictures wasn't the answer. She needed a plan.

Sky circulated as someone put on the records of Kismet. She wasn't used to the duality of life in Hollywood. On the surface, society seemed informal and democratic, full of per-

—146—

formers, health nuts, and sunshine. But that was only the surface. Underneath, life was rigidly stratified, depending upon the job one had, the amount of money one made, and the quality of one's connections. To the Hollywood professional or afficionado, motion pictures—the obsessional culture of the city—were the only aspect of world endeavor worth talking about. The guests chattered about sets and percentages, gross and net, who was making which picture, and negative costs.

In the corners of the room and outside on the terrace, people murmured about the blacklist. Hollywood was in the grip of panic. The House Un-American Activities Committee rode high in Washington. People were still being denounced as Communists, losing their jobs, friends, and sometimes their families. Books believed to be "Communist inspired" or "pinko" were being torn from library shelves. A mass madness was in the air. Only the youngest people in the room, like Sky, had little to fear. As Reed said, "You couldn't have joined the Communist Party at ten!" But Reed could have joined at twenty, and even if he hadn't, she knew that anyone might denounce him out of jealousy or out of fear. Fear sat at everyone's table these days, and betrayals were as common as the aggressive birds of paradise that bloomed in every Hollywood garden.

Sky saw Ernie Ping's wife, Marjorie, and Lila Lewis chattering nervously and confidentially in the "wives'" part of the room. A former script girl, Marjorie had given up her job in pictures when she had married. The barrier against Chinese Americans was almost insurmountable. She was a small, extremely pretty woman who wore her straight black hair high on her head.

"I just wanted to say hello," Sky began, softly.

"Hi," Marjorie said. "Lila and I were just talking about Brando's work, ah, in 'Streetcar.' " Sky realized she had interrupted some confidence, and they had quickly made up a subject.

"I liked him in *Julius Caesar*," Sky said.

"There's one we forgot," Lila said. Both women eyed Sky archly; they had been classmates at Hollywood High, Sky suddenly remembered.

"I heard that you're doing great in Wyler's picture, and

that you stand a good chance of getting that part in *Artists and Models*," Sky said to Lila. Since joining "Queen" in San Francisco, Lila had stayed with Hollywood, feverishly raking up the dust for roles.

"Did you?" asked Lila, preening slightly. "Do you think the role is a good one? I mean, she's really a headstrong career girl."

"I think it's a wonderful part," said Sky. "There's loyalty and determination in her."

Lila amused Sky because her conversational range was so limited. She couldn't talk about books or plays or current events—she barely knew that Eisenhower was president. But she knew everything about Hollywood: who was starring in what, what they wore, what it cost, where they got it. She constantly asked advice about what she should do —should she take this part or that one? Should she wear this dress or that to this or that premiere? Sky called her "the little star," but she meant it affectionately, and she had hoped that Lila and she would be friends. Now she was beginning to doubt it.

Conversation was difficult. Marjorie was a trifle jealous of Sky because Ernie was so infatuated with her as an actress, and Lila had practically thrown herself at Reed, but he'd demurred. It had been embarrassing.

Lila and Marjorie started talking about the Dior show at Magnin's, pointedly ignoring Sky, who finally drifted away.

"When you said that about Brando—!" Lila hissed as soon as Sky was gone. "Well, at least she didn't tell us about how all the *real* actors are studying the Method and getting in touch with their emotions. That just bores the hell outta me." Even though she was working with Wyler now, Lila envied Sky: People were crazy about Sky. Lila had another scotch, then thought bitterly and briefly about her father, the former matinee idol, who was too drunk to help her now.

"Strangers in Paradise" poured over the room in syrupy sounds. "I love this song," said Marjorie. Lila nudged her and tilted her head toward a nuclear physicist in his sixties, a playful man who was married to someone else. "Don't you think he's cute?" she asked.

—148—

"This is for you, Sky," Ernie said, handing her a glass of champagne.

"Ernie, do I do the right thing in rehearsals?" Sky asked. "I mean, for the camera?"

"Don't change anything," he said. She was barely adequate in rehearsals, and she'd probably never improve. It was part of what made her sizzle in front of the camera. She couldn't turn on until it was "for real." "I read a script today that I could just see you in," he said. "It's a Western, a special Western."

"Like *High Noon*?" she asked.

"Well, a little, but the woman's role is more pivotal."

There was a commotion at the door. It turned out to be Vail. He was drunk. He was carrying a six-pack of beer he'd dropped on the stone steps. He was laughing and apologizing. A maid scurried out with a towel and a broom.

"Jesus, Reed, those steps are so high!" Vail shouted, laughing.

"Come on in. Sky will be glad to see you. She feels out of touch with you all."

Vail stumbled inside and managed to remain upright. He knew he was drunk, but the room wasn't spinning yet so he couldn't be that drunk. Maybe no one would notice. He peered into the room as Reed chattered beside him. God, so many famous people. So dull. He giggled to mask his fears.

In the last months, Vail had taken a small apartment on Russian Hill in San Francisco and had started a literary magazine to publish poets from the Bay Area. The magazine didn't turn any profit, indeed its subscribers only totaled forty-five, but Vail had borrowed the money from Ned to keep it going. Every few months he assured his father that next month it would make a profit. Both of them knew it never would. Ned still wanted him to come up to the ranch and work with the horses. But Vail had refused. His father had looked forlorn. It had made Vail cringe.

"Vail!" Sky called. She dived into his outstretched arms as everyone watched this touching display. "You *did* come! Where's Sara?"

Vail drew back. "Where's *Sara?*" He laughed. "Where's

the *punch bowl*?" Sky realized with a shock that her brother was drunk. "Punch bowl, punch bowl," Vail was chanting, drawing her through the smiling and tittering crowd. "I'm Sky's famous derelict brother." He nodded at them wolfishly. "I run a magazine up north in the old homestead."

"Coffee," Reed said to the maid.

"Nah, let's have champagne! Can't you guys afford champagne?"

Sky was acutely embarrassed. No one had seen any member of her family since the first day of the shoot. She realized that their parents had reason to be concerned about Vail. "Let's go out on the terrace, Vail," she whispered.

"Nah, let's have a drink. *Then* we'll see the view!"

"How's Sara?" she asked again to distract him. She cast a frantic look at Reed, who grabbed a glass of champagne from an approaching waiter and gave it to Vail.

"Why, thank ye, sir, mighty decent of you." He drank it down in a gulp. "And one more for the road." Vail turned to Sky. "Sara's in New York." The room returned to its conversational buzz.

"Oh," she said, relieved. "I'm glad she's getting some time off. It must be hard living with mother and Lindy."

Vail hooted with laughter and snagged another glass of champagne. "What stories you tell, sweetie! Did you just come up for air or what?" He peered playfully at her, then at Reed. "You ought to let her out more often."

Reed said, "It has been a rather heavy schedule here—"

"Vail, I don't understand," Sky said, annoyed.

"Didn't mother tell you?" He drained his glass. "God, that's good." He seemed to be calming down a little.

"Tell me what?" Sky demanded.

"Sara's living in New York. Jesus, Sky. She was accepted. She's studying acting."

That night Sara didn't get home until after midnight. Crewing a play made her days so long and her nights so short that when the phone began ringing at 1:00 A.M., she put a pillow over her head. But it kept ringing. She yanked the pillow off, flung her arm out, found the receiver, and lifted it.

"Sara!" came the distant voice.

"Sky!" God, Sara thought, I should have called her long before now.

Sky was babbling. There were dim party sounds in the background. "Why didn't you tell me?!"

"What?" Sara was trapped. "I just assumed that mother had—" She propped up on her elbows and tried to pay attention. "Sky, I'm sorry—"

"Mother never said a word."

"Don't blame me! I've been just as busy as you have. We work very hard here—"

"But you could have—"

"Called, yeah, I know. Let's not fight," Sara said. "Mother thinks I'm competing with you. That's probably why she's—"

"Makes me feel rotten to learn this—"

"Yes, but I was afraid you'd think that, too. It's an uncomfortable—

"Just because I fell into this caper down here," Sky said hotly, "doesn't mean I don't want you to do what you want."

"I'm glad to hear that I have your permission," Sara said. She rolled over on her back and hunted for her cigarettes in the dark. "Sorry. I'm not studying here out of vindictiveness or anything," she added. She found a cigarette and lit it. "Mother's done this, Sky," Sara went on. "I really thought you knew I was here, and when I didn't hear from you, I thought maybe you'd changed your mind about me acting too. It put me off calling."

"I want you to do what you want to do!" Sky yelled. It still sounded like permission. "Can we cut Mother out of our conversations?"

"Glad to."

"Well, how do you like it?" She didn't wait for an answer, but rushed breathlessly on. "How many boyfriends do you have?"

"My great weakness," Sara mumbled.

"How do you do it?" Sky asked. "You're so open."

"I'm sure some would call it loose," muttered Sara. She thought of Teddy, how she missed him when he hadn't been at school last week because of the flu. She thought of

—151—

acting her midterm scene with Teddy, whose high good humor had got her through the ordeal. Georgie had been up to his old tricks, urging people along in a hearty, democratic way and then switching suddenly into his nasty criticisms.

"Do you remember Patrick?" Sky asked, running forward with the bit in her teeth. "He's got a nice little Broadway role in *The Caine Mutiny*. Why don't you look him up? And give him my best. We left things a little raw, I have to admit."

"What do you mean? I thought he was really crazy about you," Sara said.

"Oh, he got too serious. I had to cut it off. I don't want to be involved with anyone except Reed."

"You're serious about Reed?" Sara asked.

"Yes."

"Very serious?"

"I think so." On the other side of the continent, Sky put her feet up on Reed's desk in his study and let herself float, thinking of Reed's warm embraces. "I told Patrick that—well, I can't remember what I told him. But he's a really nice guy."

"C'mon, Sky!" She was suddenly livid. "I don't want your old boyfriend and I'm sure he doesn't want me!"

Maurice Hyman called Diana. "He's done it!" Hyman sounded jubilant and guarded, a combination only a lawyer could master. "The name of your natural mother is Faith Venner."

That afternoon Diana heard about her real mother.

Harry Venner, her grandfather, said Maurice, had been a Western railroad king. He'd started as a storekeeper in Sacramento and had got into railroading during the Civil War when a desperate nation had handed over four hundred feet of rights-of-way, alternate square-mile sections of public lands for every ten miles of track, and the bonds to finance the tracklaying.

Harry's success had rivaled that of the Huntington-Pacific group and provided Harry with real power. "I mean," Hyman yelled, thumping his desk with the flat of his hand, "you and I can't imagine that kind of power. He could strangle the growth of California by his line's high freight rates. Example," he said, whipping out his papers. "It was cheaper to send a cargo of nails by ship from New York to Antwerp, then discharge the cargo and reship it on a British vessel around Cape Horn to Redondo Beach, California, than to use Harry's direct rail!"

During Harry's reign as railroad baron, he'd stomped out Indian wars, spawned holding companies to smother competition, bribed state and federal legislators. "No California governor was nominated without Harry's nod. He controlled police commissioners in San Francisco, judges, United States senators, the Railroad Commission, the price of land, the California press! He ruled like a king."

"Is he still alive?" Diana said, overwhelmed.

"No. Died in nineteen-twenty. Don't let me get ahead of myself here. It's complicated. In the early nineteen hundreds Harry had a spoiled, angry son and a very lively daughter. That's Faith. Faith fell in love with, or had some kind of affair with, someone—this is speculation. She got pregnant. She no doubt confessed it to her mother, who told Harry. When you were born, they farmed you out to the Whittakers. They might have offered to pay them."

"They did pay. But they reneged," Diana said. "Who was my father?"

"The birth certificate says, 'Unknown.' " He passed her the copy the detective had made in Oregon. Diana looked at the florid scrawl. Her hands were shaking. The dates were correct, that was her birthday and the year of her birth, but she hardly dared believe she had found her mother. And what about her father? Would she never know him?

"There's no trace of him?" she asked.

"No. Your mother married a man named Moberly after her father died. She must have been in her thirties. She and Moberly had one son, called Arch."

"I have a half-brother?" Diana sat back against her chair and drew out a handkerchief. She felt feverish.

"Yes. But Moberly left Faith after a brief marriage and before Arch was born."

"Oh, the poor woman. Why did he leave?" Diana asked.

"Probably because Harry left all his money to endow a university in his son's name. The son was killed in an auto accident." Hyman checked his papers. "Obviously, she's

—153—

got some money and has the old mansion up on California Street, but no millions."

"I don't want to get rich off them!" Diana exclaimed, as though he'd accused her. "I simply want to see my mother, talk to her. Can you help me do that?"

11

Vail had disconnected himself from the family.

He felt guilty about it. To avoid dealing with it, he hid out with his "gang" in the pool halls around Mission Street. Bondy Goldstein had never returned to New York. Scruffy young girls clung to them. Most of the men were vets from the "Big One," men who looked down on runty Korean vets like Vail. Korea was the war no one understood or wanted to hear about. That was fine with Vail—he didn't understand it either, and he certainly didn't want to talk about it.

Vail met Schurl at the Cafe Puccini; he met Jerry at Ferlinghetti's City Lights Bookstore in North Beach. Both of them hung out with other well-educated, miserable, rebellious men of Vail's age who gave themselves to showy, jaded laughter. Schurl was an anthropologist from Ohio, a sturdy, blond man with compact muscles. Jerry, a dropout from Harvard, was into Zen and had made himself a scholar on the subject. Lean and dark, with hooded eyes, he'd hit the road for the West, a "dharma bum." Bondy's infectious smile promised heaven right there on Mission Street; he wrote poetry, and he had taken up backpacking in the backwoods. As he waved his cue around the dingy halls, Bondy proclaimed urban life was "one long, demented suicide." Bondy lived in the city only long enough to earn money to live in the woods.

Their exuberant, fragile circle included the daughter of a cashier in the Jolly Roger, a painter with Brillo hair and a

—155—

mean smile, a waiter from Sausalito, a clerk from Woolworth's, a guitarist shacking up with a violinist from Tanglewood, and a novelist who worked at Macy's. They were all staving off bill collectors and hallucinations; when things got too bad, they retreated to their parents for brief respites.

Vail began living in Bondy's shack in Marin. Occasionally they worked as parking attendants, security guards, hotel clerks. After one victoriously drunken brawl, the three of them found themselves in a tent near Fresno and spent the next month picking beans and panhandling. They were outside what most people called real life, yet they felt they knew the inside track to the truth that someday, through their writing or criticism, they would display to the public. But first, the costs of life's experience beckoned with a tantalizing sneer.

Suffering turned Vail on—whether it was his own or another's. After all, all existence was suffering and pain. To experience that cracking edge of pain molded the artist. But as Vail rushed at life to make him an artist, he fled from his painful humiliation in Korea and the nagging envy he had for Sara and Sky.

The beat generation was just beginning. Actually, it had already begun but it had had no name until Kerouac, Rexroth, and Ginsberg came along. The words reverberated when Vail spotted an article called "This is the Beat Generation" in the *New York Times Magazine* after a gargantuan Saturday drunk with Bondy and Jerry and Schurl. They were sitting in the hot tent with Carol, the slovenly and ridiculously cheerful woman they'd all been sharing for three weeks. Vail's hands were calloused from picking beans.

"How old is this article, anyway?" he asked, turning the tattered pages. "Jesus, six months!"

"Don't you think it's weird that we're sitting up here in a field near Fresno reading the *Times*?" muttered Bondy.

That article told Vail that being "beat is a nakedness of mind, ultimately of soul." It was an appealing thought. He looked up. "I think we should get back to the scene," he said.

After the bean-picking episode, their quartet broke apart. Vail left them and hitched out to Ned's ranch. He wanted

—156—

to see the horses, to smell them, to lean his cheek against their firm necks. His father was nowhere about, and Maggie scolded him for his dirtiness. He cleaned up for her, rode one of the blanket nags, the lead ponies for the classy stuff Ned now owned, and felt the wind in his hair again. Ned arrived from somewhere.

"Son, when are you going to settle down?" he asked gently.

"Dad, I know I'm disappointing you, but I just have to get out and see life. Later I'll settle down." His father was watching his colt, Fireball, work out. "It's all too certain," Vail added. He liked risk; it had come to signify reality. His restlessness swept him back to the musicians, poets, addicts, and petty criminals in San Francisco. His quartet re-formed.

By the time he got back to his friends, Schurl had met Sammy—a fair-haired girl with a ski-jump nose whose father was in the merchant marines. They were living together in dull harmony in the shack in Marin, across the bay from San Francisco. Jerry was singing buddhist chants, writing poetry, and darting in and out of quick, fervent love affairs with dark, muscular boys. When Vail thought of love, he thought of the artichoke fields and the desperate, shaking, shaming lovemaking with the girl whose name he couldn't remember anymore. Had that experience driven him into Seoul alley? Vail didn't want to be in love. He wanted to concentrate on the synthesis of human experience in a few punchy words on paper. His San Francisco was one big mimeo machine grinding out poetry in midnight blue ink.

Vail got a job as a hotel clerk at the Simmons, a low-life flophouse near Eighteenth and Mission; he hung out at the Buena Vista; and he started to read Wilhelm Reich, which lit him like a fuse. He called Sara and demanded that she read Reich's *Function of the Orgasm*; he said that she would dig it, that it would make her whole. Thanks to his Reichian readings, coupled with Kinsey's new study on female sexual behavior, his poetry took a wild, sensual leap. He started hanging out at the poetry clubs in North Beach.

He was sitting at a beery, damp table at a place called the Cellar, scribbling in his notebook, when Bondy came weaving toward him with two girls on his arms. One was the most beautiful woman he'd ever seen, and that included his sisters. Before he knew what he was doing, he was rising from his chair and pulling out another for her.

Her name was Riva, and she was French-Chinese from Indochina. Her straight black hair fell below her shoulders like a wall of ebony water, her olive skin glowed over her high cheekbones, and her black eyes glittered like onyx. She wore an Indian feather in her hair, long beaded earrings, and dramatically fringed clothes. The electricity between them snaked over the filthy table and scattered their friends like old leaves. They decamped for her place on Oak Street in the Haight, an apartment she shared with four other people, give or take one or two. They listened to Charlie Parker, drank red wine, and plunged into a soul-to-soul talk that revealed her intense understanding of the levels of life. She dazzled him. Her grainy voice and superior vocabulary, derived from Wellesley and Cal, inspired the first tenderness he'd felt in years. Even as he made tentative motions toward making love to her, he found himself talking to her about Reich, poetry, life on the bum, feelings, dead civilizations.

"Just do it, man. Don't talk it," she said. A sliver of fear went through him. He would never be able to pretend with her. He pulled out his ace, that he was a triplet and started reminiscing.

"Stash that," Riva said, unimpressed. "Let's fuck."

They saw each other every day. Bondy, Jerry, and Schurl respectfully drew back. He squired Riva to clubs for drinks, to poetry readings for soul nourishment, to parties in Marin to show her off. His connection to her took on ecstasy: She was so hip, so cool. He felt special, worthy, when he was with her. He cultivated a goatee that made his sharp, hand-some face even sharper. He forgot he was short. But Riva was tightly wired and prone to dangerous fits of depression. In their swirl, she'd lash out at him with eviscerating, verbal knives that found deadly marks. She taunted him to stop drinking because when he was drunk he'd rail against her intellectualism, her downbeat, dead-end intensity, her ten-dency to think in categories—a ridiculous assertion, he knew, because Riva thought in galaxies. She was far too close to the core of him.

"You scare the shit out of me," he said loudly to her

—158—

one night at a very quiet poetry reading at the City Lights bookstore. Kerouac was going around collecting coins in his cap to buy jugs of wine. Rexroth—the headman of literary San Francisco—was introducing each poet. Riva narrowed her beautiful dark eyes at Vail, took Kerouac's arm, and went over to the other side of the room where she sat down next to Bondy.

Rexroth introduced Vail, and he read some of the poems he'd been working on for months. "Sweatdrenched fecund wings, sorrow stretched in windless corridors at world's end . . ." he began. Someone was shouting "Go! Go!" as he read, as though he were a baseball player on third with the bases loaded in the bottom of the ninth. The crowd was enthusiastic but also drunk. Vail never thought his poetry captured the roasted flesh of life on the spit the way Kerouac's did.

It turned out to be Ginsberg's night. He recited parts of a long poem he was working on called "Howl." It was like an explosion that left imprints on the insides of their eyes. Across the room, in the afterglow of "Howl," Vail watched the woman he loved and feared; she made him feel trapped in death because he was alive. Their lovemaking had deteriorated. He left with Ginsberg, who was living over in Berkeley, where he hid out for five days. He kept on drinking. The snow leopard leaped around in his dreams, and he thought about Riva a lot. She seemed to affirm life in the midst of death, exotic freedom in the midst of bondage. Something—the leopard—had broken loose! Would he?

But he couldn't bring himself to reach out for the lethal closeness he'd felt with Riva that first night, and he couldn't cleanse himself of his brutal need for her.

He was sitting in a North Beach bar, well into a prolonged bender, when Bondy and Riva came staggering in, their arms wrapped around each other like vines. He hailed them and pretended to be nonchalant. They all drank for an hour in harmony. Then Vail stood up and said, "Time to be gettin' on, Riva. Let's go." Bondy nodded, understanding.

But Riva wasn't going anywhere, and she let Vail have it, his drunkeness, his tardiness, his tyranny, and his bad poetry. "Laughable!" she flung at him in her gravelly, sexy voice. Heads turned. Bondy tried to joke her out of her attack, but when Riva was in one of her moods, and high to boot, she was a windmill with machete sails.

Vail knew what she was going to say before she said it. When she said it out loud, it sounded like an echo. "He's impotent!!" she shrieked. As her rage bit into him, making Bondy wince and pull at her arm, Vail was drunkenly aware of the levels of it all—his gargantuan love for her, his terror of her, the chaos of his life, and the certain knowledge that he would never feel as close to anyone as he felt to Riva. "This great believer in Reichian love! Phony! Phony!" she spat at him out of the profound depths of her disappointment.

He threw his beer in her face. Overcome with remorse, he lurched to the bar, got a napkin, and tenderly wiped off her face. "A lot of what she says is true," he said to Bondy. "I'm afraid of her." Riva had calmed down. She took the damp napkin from him and dabbed her neck. "Let's all go somewhere else," Vail said. "It feels dangerous in here."

They hit the street, but the feeling of danger dogged Vail. Riva took his arm. "Is forgiveness in your lexicon?" she asked. He nodded. She did a little dance step. Bondy, who loved to dance, took her arm and they started to waltz in the street. Vail leaned against a telephone pole and watched them humming and twirling.

The car had no lights, and Vail heard it before he saw it. He leaped toward them, pushing them with stiff, outstretched arms, knocking them down. The wheel of the screeching car ran over his ankle. He heard the bones snapping and felt the familiar pain rush through him. Then he passed out.

Vail woke up in the hospital. He had the vague impression he'd been swimming somewhere in icy water. Then he felt the throbbing pain.

Bondy was sitting on the floor, talking melodiously about getting back to nature. Maybe they should all go to the Grand Canyon or to Yellowstone. They were, Bondy muttered, living in a police state: A-bombs were going off in

—160—

Nevada, the perfume of radioactive dust was drifting down on their houses, and Orwell's 1984 was just around the corner.

Vail groaned. Riva swam into view. "You saved us," she whispered, taking his hand and staring at him with love. She had a nasty bruise on her cheek. Bondy got up off the floor and came to the other side of the bed. "Get well, pal, we're going to go back to nature. Armageddon's comin'," he said with a smile.

Riva said she hated nature and she'd see them when they got back. Vail gazed at her. "Twenty trains on the Union Pacific," he murmured to her, "couldn't carry the love I have for you."

When he got out of the hospital, Vail looked everywhere for Riva. He hobbled along to all the old joints. Bondy looked, too. "Man, she's just disappeared," Bondy said. "But she'll be back."

Vail and Bondy bought and stole bedrolls, a pup tent, and some canned goods for their excursion into nature. They were on their way to heist a car, or to borrow one, when they stopped in a bar at Third and Howard for a drink. The sawdust floors and the grimy, slick walls smelled like an abattoir, and the eyes of the men were cold and hard and deadly. Bondy started dancing with a woman who had a hunting knife in the back of her belt.

Riva was at a table near the back. Now out of his cast, Vail hustled over to her.

"I thought you were going to nature," she said. A man with a beard and long brown hair was sitting next to her, nursing a beer.

"We still are. You come, too," Vail said.

"Not me," Riva said, briskly. "I like Armageddon." She stroked the man's thick wrist. She didn't introduce him.

"Wanna dance?" Vail asked.

"No, I'm off dancing," she said. "Too dangerous."

"How about hearing some Yeats tonight, over at City Lights?"

"No, thanks."

"Jeez, Riva, I looked everywhere for you. Where have you been?"

"Around."

The man next to her stirred. "Get lost."

"When am I going to see you again, Riva?" Vail asked, desperately.

"Never."

"Man, I'm telling you, leave it alone," Bondy said when they'd left the bar.

"But something's wrong with her," Vail insisted. "I'm sorry, but I can't leave town right now."

Bondy was irritated, but he had a lot of roll in him. He shrugged. "It's pretty late in the fall anyway," he said.

"I gotta get her away from that guy. He's bad news," Vail said.

A week later, Riva was dead. "She was knifed!" Vail cried, his shoulders shaking. Bondy put his arm around Vail's shoulders and led him away from the bar to a back table at the Buena Vista.

"Eat something," Bondy said. A cheerful waitress came over and Bondy ordered eggs and bacon and plenty of home fries.

Riva's body had been found stuffed in a garbage can on Howard Street. Every time Vail thought about it, he shuddered. The image haunted him. When he couldn't think of it any more, he flashed back on Bondy and Riva waltzing in the street. "Oh, Bondy, what am I going to do?"

"She was one of those chicks," Bondy said philosophically, "who wasn't meant to be part of this life. She'll be around another time."

Vail woke up in the Troy Hotel down by the waterfront. Someone next door was either dying or screwing his brains out. He cranked himself out of bed. Every muscle ached, and his hands shook uncontrollably. His mouth was raw and sticky, tasting of blood and dust. He made for a small sink fitted into a corner like a leech. A tiny mirror hung crookedly above it. He didn't recognize the mask that looked back at him, it was so ugly and alone. Like a snapshot he'd once seen, his face resembled one he faintly remembered, one that had been handsome. He didn't know what month it was. How long had he been here? Where was Bondy? Like a thud, he remembered where Riva was.

He leaned on the sink because he couldn't stand up. He wanted to go home. He was only a mile or so from Clay Street—the distance between Mars and Jupiter. He began crying as he thought of Sky and Sara like tiny pinpoints of light in a night of blackness and decay. He knew he'd be okay if he could just find Sara and Sky. But when he did, they'd ask him what he was doing these days, and he had no answer for them. He thought of his father. Jeez, Dad, forgive me. I don't know what I'm doing anymore. I'm sorry. In his imagination, he had an hour's conversation with Ned. He felt better trying to explain why he couldn't "get with" suburban or even urban life, the way they wanted him to live it. He told his father how poetry rocked him to sleep at night but that when he was absolutely sober, he couldn't hear its soft songs any more. He told Ned about Riva and how frightened he'd been of being close to her, how the panic had made it impossible for him to make love to her, how deeply he'd loved her, how much he missed her.

He went out on the street looking for a drink and found himself, after a day of panhandling, outside the Co-Existence Bagel Shop. Jerry materialized, took his arm, and steered him to Marin where Bondy was hiding out from the woman with the knife he'd met in the rough bar.

"We gotta change our lives," Vail said.

Jackson Pollock and Willem de Kooning had come screaming onto the New York art scene in the late forties, and, by the fifties, abstract expressionistic art had linked up with the beat scene, riding a current of jazz, poetry, and the Cold War.

On a January day, Teddy and Sara came out of the Trans-Lux Theater: Fellini's *La Strada* had left them limp with admiration. They drew their coats and scarves tight around them and headed into the stiff, cold wind blowing from the east. The touching love of Richard Basehart for Giulietta Massina made Sara feel that there was tenderness in the world.

"I was married before I came here," she said to him.

"You were? Who to?" He was startled.

Sara ducked into the doorway of a building. He followed.

"I just had to tell you, Teddy. I'm so fond of you, I don't like pretending or anything."

"Well, what happened?" he asked. His nose was red.

"He left suddenly. I've never heard from him since."

"Jesus, that's rough."

"It was rougher with a child," she said.

"You have a child?" He was actually pointing at her. She nodded. "Well, Christ, this is hard to get used to!"

"She's wonderful," Sara said. "She's with my mother and Mrs. Sho." She explained how it was possible for her to go to school, how she was always looking for little things to send home for Lindy—a stuffed horse, a rattle, a dress. How guilty she felt about leaving her, that it was corrosively present inside her unless she was working really hard. "Or unless I'm with you," she added.

"Why didn't you tell me sooner?" he asked, stamping his feet to keep warm.

"I didn't think you'd like me as much," she admitted. "Eloping, having kids, sort of excessive—not what you'd expect from a serious actress."

"Aw, Sara, you're always excessive. It's one of the great things about you. C'mon, let's walk."

After a block, Sara said, "I can't stand this anymore. I'm a sybarite. Take me to the nearest bar."

They ducked into a dark, polished cell just off the avenue. It was three o'clock in the afternoon; the lunch trade had left; a bartender was smoking a cigarette behind the bar and reading a newspaper. A mournful rendition of "I Believe" drifted over the room from a speaker near him.

"Give us a couple of martinis," said Teddy. They sat down in a plush red booth. "So, what's her name?"

"Belinda Victoria." She smiled. "I call her Lindy."

"I like kids a lot," Teddy said. "They always smell so fresh, like the skin is all new." He was stripping off layers of clothes—coat, overshirt, scarf, gloves. "I'm glad you told me." He put all the clothes, hers and his, in the corner of the booth. "I read that scene from *The Rainmaker*," Teddy said, speaking of the scene she would be presenting after the Christmas break. "You'll be brilliant again." Sara shrugged lightly. It was hard to switch gears so fast. The bartender brought their drinks and slipped away. "I don't know how 'brilliant' I'll be moaning on a cot with Marvin's teeth rammed against mine. God, he's like a giant rabbit with giant teeth, and he presses them right into my mouth during the kiss." She counted on Teddy. With the images of *La Strada* swimming in her mind, she touched his knuckle with one finger. "I love you."

"Don't tell me that," he laughed. "I might take you seriously. Then I'll have to tell you how I feel." He made a show of leaning back in the booth and looking around the almost empty room.

"I wish you would."

He hunched forward. "Listen, I'm worried about my scene. When I play it without characterization it's pretty honest. As soon as I play my character, it's phony. I can't integrate the two when I play a thirty-year-old man with problems."

Sara settled for a conversation on acting. "Maybe you don't like your character."

"I hate my character. You are much more interesting intellectually and emotionally than my character."

"Good, now we're getting somewhere," she said.

But Teddy slipped away again. "I am bored, apathetic, devastated, uninterested, tired, sick, and deadened." He smiled. "Tell me what Georgie told you." Each member of their class had been evaluated by each faculty member, a midsemester chat about the state of his or her work.

Sara sighed. "Georgie told me I was a well-rounded person doing well—don't you hate that?—that it took a lot to interest me, and that I sought deeper things."

"Bullshit."

"He was really making a pass," Sara said. Teddy was twisting a napkin around his finger. "Irene mumbled dramatically about my great talent and my feet. She said that I was very expressive. How about you?"

Teddy rolled his eyes to the ceiling. "Georgie told me I have a voice problem—he's very right—and that I have a tendency to underplay, which is true, and so consequently when I play a scene with someone who gives me a lot, I steal that scene even though I'm not giving my partner a damn thing. He's right. Irene went into a glorious mono-logue about my nimble ankles and my beautiful movement and projection. She's a goddamned jewel. What an idiot." He drained his martini and looked around for another. "I like you because you're one of the few people who can hold up a strapless bra and an intelligent conversation at the same time." Sara didn't know why but his words made her feel bad. He saw it and added, "You're—" he searched for the words "—vital as hell."

She snapped her nail against his hand. "You're very phony today."

"Yes, I guess I am."

"I want you to start taking me seriously. I'm taking what I feel for you very seriously. Teddy, I love you."

He pulled his hand away and looked at the table. "What can I say?" He forced himself to look up at her. His heart was beating wildly. "I don't think anyone has seriously said that to me before. It's upsetting."

"Oh, great." She ate her olive.

"I'm being honest! I'm just not sure of anything."

"Take a chance," she said coldly. She wanted to share all the complicated feelings she had for him, now that she'd surrendered to the powerful drive to tell him all about her-self—especially about Lindy, but the look on his face dis-tanced her. Teddy was frightened.

"Cigarette?" He shook two out of the pack, handed her one, and lit it. "It would be nicer if I were drunk and it just happened." He smiled crookedly. He lit his cigarette and took a long drag. "How's this? I love you today!" He put out his cigarette. "I never said that to anyone before." He bent stiffly toward her over the table and slowly kissed her. His nose was in the way; his lips landed on the side of her mouth. His hands came up and clasped her wrists.

On that same January day, Diana was sitting in her car across the street from the Venner mansion. It was sand-wiched between huge apartment buildings erected after the earthquake. Compared to them, the once-imposing and op-ulent home of the Venners looked solid but sad. Diana had lived all these years just a half-mile from her mother. The revelation had shaken her. Was her real mother inside now? How did she spend her mornings or her afternoons? Diana wondered, staring at the gray stone building. What if she simply went up to the door and announced herself? Why had she been shut out of this once-fine home, handed off to strangers in another state? Diana pressed her gloved hands to her face and wept.

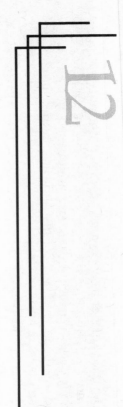

12

In February, Sara was assigned to the costume crew for one of the school's more elaborate productions. By silent, mutual consent, Sara and Teddy had spent less time together. By doing nothing, Teddy had rejected her; she felt lonely and dulled.

Late one afternoon she sat alone, stitching and clawing her way through a quilted vest and, to amuse herself, pretending to go insane while trying to cope with a sewing machine twice her age. Snow floated past the tall windows.

"Hi."

She looked up. It was Patrick O'Mara. He looked magnificent. She suddenly felt old and undernourished. "If the mountain doesn't come to whatever, then whatever comes to the mountain," he said with a winning smile. "Sky told me where you were." He sat down on a stool.

Sara!" Bertie appeared on the doorstep. He looked cross. His blond hair was nearly as white as the snow outside, and his face was red from the chill. He marched in and planted himself in front of her sewing machine. She introduced them. Bertie was pleased to meet Patrick, once he knew he was in *The Caine Mutiny Court Martial*, and Sara was not above feeling smug that Bertie, of all people, had found them together. Bertie would soon spread it around that she entertained Broadway actors in Wardrobe.

Sara solved Bertie's costume problem while Patrick waited patiently. Finally, with a phony, cheek-breaking smile at both of them, Bertie left.

—168—

The only time Sara had seen Patrick had been on Sky's set that first day of shooting. He was tall and very handsome, with large, sleepy blue eyes beneath a slab of blond hair. "How's Sky?" she asked, abandoning the sewing machine and lighting a cigarette. "Did she send you out here to check on me?"

"She's fine. Going Hollywood. That's the place where grown men earn wages by telling each other stories," he said, trying to get past her skepticism. "I prefer the theater, don't you?"

"Well, sure," Sara said.

"Sky didn't send me, but she told me you were here. I just thought I'd offer you a house seat to the show." He gazed at her. It was eerie how much she looked and sounded like Sky. If it weren't for the color of her eyes and all those brassy, electric curls, she and Sky would look identical. Sky was his drug, and he missed her horribly.

"C'mon, Patrick. What does Sky want?"

"Nothing," he said, truthfully.

Patrick looked disarmingly clean, as if he'd just stepped out of a shower. Drifting in the air around them was the odor of bay rum. He was gazing at her with a kind of soft wariness. There was something irresistibly sleek about Patrick. She imagined him lounging against expensive sofas.

"Why don't you come to the show tonight? Then we can have supper after," he said.

Sara was complimented. He took her to Sardi's and they ate crab and drank white wine. He told her about his father, the general, and his mother, heir to a manufacturing fortune. "My father used to shake my hand to say goodnight," Patrick said.

"How sad," she said.

They talked about the play, drank more wine, then zeroed in on directors, love, for God's sake, Patrick as a sorrowful, unloved child, Patrick as an adult, Patrick meeting Sky, Patrick's first play, the change in Patrick, great love scenes from Sophocles to O'Neill. For two hours Sara forgot about school, Teddy, the play, Belinda, her past life, and Sky.

"Sky's premiere is coming up soon," he said. "Are you

—169—

going?" The studio's publicity guy, Lenny, had called Sara; he had a "great" publicity stunt in mind: the triplets at the premiere, lined up in matching clothes. She'd refused. He'd kept calling. "Let's go together," Patrick said, whipping a card and pen out of his pocket.

"You're crazy!" she cried. "You can't take that kind of time off from the play, and I know I can't." He was nutty and wonderful. Sky was right, bless her.

"Okay! We fly! Takes about what, nine hours? It's on a Monday night, we're dark; we leave Sunday night right after my performance—" He pressed a hand to his chest and let out a tenor scale that made the people around them giggle. "And we're back by Tuesday night, just in time to get me to the theater." He clapped his hand on hers. "See? Nothing's impossible."

The streets were white and soft and silent. She took his arm and they walked nearly ten blocks before they found a cab. She leaned against him in the back seat, trying to get warm. He bundled her up in the curve of his arm. She thought of Teddy, wondering where he was that night. Did she still love him? She missed him terribly. Had he loved her? Would they be friends when they were old? Nestled against Patrick's arm as the cab slowly maneuvered the snowy streets, she tilted her head up and stared boldly into his handsome, glamorous face. Was he just a substitute to fill the void Teddy had left? No, Patrick offered something quite different, but she didn't know what. Was it possible to get him into her bed? She didn't think so when he gently patted her cheek, brushing his lips against hers. As he withdrew, she said in the voice she knew sounded like Sky, "Kiss me." Groaning, he put both his arms around her and kissed her fully. They were nearing Twenty-fifth Street. She said, "Don't go home. Stay with me."

Inside, she put a Handel record on as Patrick drifted over to the front windows and watched the snow falling against the glow of the streetlight. Shedding her coat along the way, she went over to him and put her arms around his waist. He moved away. Then, immediately, he turned back and seized her arms. "You are very tempting."

"I mean to be."

"But let's call it a night. I'll phone you." He grabbed his coat, waved, and rushed out. She leaned against the window, feeling the cold glass ease smoothly into her flesh. Her breath formed little wisps of fog on the window.

The searing cold of the night tore into her lungs as she ran after him. "Patrick!" This was crazy, she thought, leaping down Twenty-fifth Street at two in the morning. She hadn't even grabbed a coat. But it was more romantic without one. The insistent cold nuzzling into her body made her feel electrified and light. The snow choked all sound; a car's wheels whispered by. She pushed herself and slid on the icy pavement beneath the new snow. He was just ahead, walking slowly. She skidded to his side. "Pat!"

He stopped. Sara moved close to him and put her head on his shoulder. He slowly wrapped both arms around her. "You should have let me go, Sara." He patted her back absently, thinking of Sky.

"I don't think I want to."

The glare from the giant lights stationed outside the theater bounced around the dark skies. The premiere of *The White Queen* was in full swing, its proceeds to be donated to the Children's Hospital. Crowds surged forward as limos snaked up to the marquee and discharged their resplendent occupants: Sheldon Winters and his wife, Susan, the chairman of the board, B. B. Cohen, who happened to be in town, and lesser studio brass. Held back by a velvet cord, the press snapped countless pictures. While older, better-known columnists like Hedda Hopper chatted with the stars and executives inside, outside energetic youngsters in the radio business rushed the celebrities, thrusting mikes at their famous faces, rattling off questions.

A blond, crew-cut radio announcer who used to be a lifeguard on the Santa Monica beach was covering the premiere for a national radio audience. Between limos, he held the mike close to his face, disclosing tidbits of gossip about the arriving personalities—whatever he'd read in the latest fan magazines. When the limos arrived, he held the mike away from his face and shouted out the names of the celebrities.

"And here's Anne Abbott, accompanied by Mel Winters, her attorney and agent, I believe. Oh, Anne, please say a few words to our audience! How magnificent you look!"

Anne smiled. "Hello, all you fans out there in radio-land," she said, gliding past him.

"A great star, ladies and gentlemen, what a great star! We haven't seen her on the screen for a while—and, we'll be right back after these words." He broke off as another limo disgorged its passengers, people he didn't recognize. His harried assistant consulted a sheet. "T. K. Kyle, a member of the board of directors, and his wife," she shouted at him.

"Bat shit," the announcer said. "Nobody knows them."

Inside a huge limo waiting in line to draw up in front of the theater, Vail, Sky, and Sara were drinking champagne. Sara and Sky were tipsy, Vail smashed. He'd been drinking for hours. Patrick was keeping up with him, while reciting flowery, basso passages from *Romeo and Juliet.*

Sky was on one side of Reed, her parents on the other. Reed was trying to keep up with Ned's observations about the Preakness Stakes, past and present, and the general state of the Santa Anita track.

From Marin, Vail had brought a slip of a girl who looked about twelve but who insisted she was eighteen. Her first name was Nancy, but nobody could figure out what her last name was. When Vail said it, it sounded like Nematolla. She had her hair in long braids with bright gold Christmas wrapping ribbon at the ends in bows. He said she was his art director on the magazine.

Diana and Ned were crowded together pleasantly, but their view of their children at this moment was not sanguine. "I think it's difficult to see your children drinking," Diana said to Ned later.

Diana's hair was stacked on her head. She winked and clacked gently when she moved because her dramatic outfit was composed of huge sequins. Giant triangular onyx-and-gold pendants hung from her ears. Ned thought she looked striking. He ran a finger around the collar of his tuxedo and helped himself to the champagne.

"I'm writing a review of your movie for my magazine," Vail revealed to the crowd. "Did you hear that, Mom?"

Diana nodded absently. She and Ned were worried about Vail. Ned had done everything he could think of to get Vail home. Nothing had worked. He was throwing his life away. It was terrible to contemplate, so Diana turned her thoughts to her natural mother, Faith Venner Moberly. A week ago, Maurice Hyman had brought bad news. The Moberly family was adamant and insulted: Miss Venner, her name of choice, had never had an illegitimate child, and if the attorney or his client pressed any such charge they would sue. Diana pressed her fingers to her temple and slipped her arm through Ned's. "I think I'll have a drink, dear," Diana said, "if we're going to spend the night in this car."

"Righto," he exclaimed, supplying it. "You look mighty sexy in that dress, darling," he whispered, squeezing her thigh. When Diana got dolled up, nobody could top her, he thought.

Sky felt short-circuited; Reed's body next to hers kept her centered. She'd been surprised to see Sara and Patrick show up for this circus. As Sara leaned against Patrick's large and accommodating frame, Sky knew that Sara was hungry for his body. Sky envied her easy and passionate surrender to emotions. Sara lived so well within her body. Patrick whispered loudly in Sara's ear, "What are you doing later tonight? Think we can bust out of the party?" He glanced up at Sky.

"I said," Vail snapped, "that I'm going to write a review of your movie, Sky."

"I heard you," Sky said. The dynamics between the triplets were changing. She was in charge now, and she realized, seeing Vail's annoyance, that he'd just realized it, too. A wintry smile flitted across his face. She glanced at Sara; Sara was all bound up with Patrick and wasn't paying attention. Sky rolled down a window.

As their car crept closer, they could hear the low roar of the crowd punctuated by shrieks from the fans. "It's like an execution chamber, isn't it? Waiting for them to kill us," Sky said.

Sara was thinking about the running comments Teddy would have offered had he been with them, how his zany laugh would acknowledge and mock the ceremony that kept them locked in a car for an hour. She thought of the way

Teddy's lips turned up at the corners even when he was sad.

Suddenly the limo was in front of the marquee. The door opened, exposing them. "Triplets first," said Sara, and she stepped out. Sky followed and a wailing scream went up from the spectators. Lenny had really done his job; everyone knew about *The White Queen*. The press surged forward. Vail joined his sisters. They stood in a row as flashbulbs popped like the Corsairs over the Iron Triangle. Sky turned and took Reed's arm. A blond, crew-cut announcer thrust a mike in her face.

"Sky! *Sky!*" he was yelling. "Please say a word to your fans! How does it feel to be a new star?"

"Am I?" She laughed and whirled past the media artillery.

"And here's her sister and brother," the announcer went on without missing a beat. "They're triplets, as all the world knows by now."

Sara froze, suddenly aware she was in the central chamber of a national media splash. What would Teddy say? Maybe he'd like her more. Would that be better?

"*Please*," the announcer was imploring her as Vail stumbled up behind her. "How's it feel to be Sky's sister?"

"It's been great so far!" she snapped off as Patrick joined her.

"Patrick O'Mara!" the announcer cried. "The picture's costar! What was it like to work with Reed Corbett and Sky?"

"Simply divine. I hope everyone loves the picture," Patrick said smoothly, trying to move Sara and Vail ahead.

"And Vail—have you seen the picture yet?" the announcer asked.

Vail's eyes focused slowly and with disdain. "Nope. But I'll be writing a review of it for my magazine, *The Poetry—Ooops!*" He tripped on a cable. Sara took his arm and steered him away.

"And behind them are—" the announcer said, his voice rising, then falling as he identified them, "Sky's parents, I guess."

"Are you really writing a review, Vail?" asked Sara. "Do you think that's wise? I mean, you're not objective the way reviewers are supposed to be."

"Who said reviewers are objective?" he countered. "Besides, I'm an essayist as well as a reviewer."

Inside the theater, the lights went down, and people scurried to their seats. The studio emblem came up on the screen.

Sara sat between Vail and Patrick. The first huge closeup of her sister felt like a blow. That was the girl who'd lost her dollie in Germany, who'd sat beside her in the fields when Sara had fallen off Pegasus and knocked her teeth out. She listened to Sky's lines, hearing the tone of her own voice coming out of her sister's mouth, and watched her sister walking the way she herself did, tilting slightly forward. Her sister was being created in front of her. Sara hung somewhere between fury and admiration.

Vail hissed, surprised, "My God, she's good!" Sky seemed more intimately connected to the emotions of the scenes than the other actors up there on the oversize screen. At the same time, she was turned inward provocatively. He sneaked a look at Diana down the row. Her large, fine-boned head was tipped up proudly. She was rapt.

The reviews of the film were extraordinary. Sky was an overnight sensation. Within a month, Reed zoomed from a young director of promising B films to one of the most sought after directors in town. Ernie Ping, the cinematographer, suddenly commanded a bigger price and his pick of scripts with other good directors. *The White Queen* changed everyone's lives. But most of all it changed the triplets.

On the night of the premiere, Ned and Diana got a sense of what life was going to be like with a famous child. Reporters at the party besieged Diana with questions about raising triplets and about Sky as a child. "But Sky's only a young girl," Diana kept wanting to say as one stranger after another flew at her with questions, adding their own summaries of Sky, "stunning," "compelling," "sensitive but strong." One newspaper reviewer summed it all up by saying she was "the symbol of the introspective woman today, the 'new' woman who knew her own mind but had not lost her femininity to find it."

When Sheldon Winters wasn't talking horses with Ned, he danced with Diana—"Such a gracious man," she told

Sky later. She had just finished dancing with Sheldon and was sitting in a chair, watching Sky dance with Reed. "They make as handsome a couple as we did at their age," she said to Ned, who flopped down beside her. "And they'll have such beautiful children," she said, dreaming on.

"They're not even married yet," Ned panted, just off the dance floor.

"But they will be, dear. Just look at them." It was then that the idea about Belinda took shape.

In another part of the room, Sara was still dazed. She couldn't come out from under the spell the gargantuan close-ups of Sky had cast over her. Even as she was caught up in the general celebrations, she felt she was in mourning for the youth she'd shared with Sky; she felt smothered by the monumental shadows on the screen.

Diana came up to her. "Darling, let's have a little chat soon. I was just thinking about Lindy. It's not right that she be brought up by old women."

"You're not old, neither's Mrs. Sho," Sara said. "Besides, I'll be there for her."

"But I'm trying to think of what's best for her," Diana insisted. "She needs a steady mother, someone to play with her. Sky would be ideal, and Sky loves her, Sara."

"You mean, give Lindy to Sky?"

"You want your own life now, don't you, darling? But it's not settled yet, the life of a New York actress never is. Don't deny Lindy what Sky could give her, Sara."

"I can't make this kind of decision now."

"Of course not," Diana said, patting her knee. "But think about it, won't you? It might be just the ticket for little Lindy."

Vail knew nothing of this. He laughed, danced like mad, fell down, got up, and drank. He danced with Lila Lewis, who was so jealous of Sky that she could talk of nothing except how Reed had been able to "pull Sky's performance out of her." One minute Vail lounged in a chair next to Sara, the next he was jumping to his feet and swimming upstream against the tide of well-wishers and last-minute arrivals. He finally beached in the men's room. Going into a stall, he quickly opened a small flask, took a pill from his pocket, and downed it with whiskey. Hearing voices, he

—176—

flushed the toilet for verisimilitude, leaned against the wall, and felt the familiar wave of happy numbness encase him. He was rejuvenated, he could handle the evening, he could even enjoy it. Lightheaded, he came bursting out of the stall, grinning like the snow leopard, free.

13

"Jesus Christ! That's Sara!" Teddy exclaimed, staring at a picture of her in the *New York Times*. A beautiful dark-haired woman and an equally handsome man stood beside her.

"New Star Is Triplet," the caption proclaimed. An enthusiastic review of *The White Queen* commended the work of "newcomers" Sky Wyman and Reed Corbett.

"What Sara?" Dirk mumbled.

"Our Sara! Sara Wyman!" Teddy cried.

Teddy, Bertie, and Dirk were getting ready to go down the street to the Kettle of Fish Bar. Bertie craned his neck and tried to look at the paper Teddy was excitedly waving.

"I'll be damned," Bertie said. He took the paper away from Teddy. "Geez, look at the brother. He looks just like them! I didn't know she was a triplet, did you?" he asked Teddy.

"I knew, but she swore me to secrecy."

"Why?"

"How do I know? Maybe she didn't want to be a triplet any more!" Teddy said.

Bertie stared at the three oval faces with the same wide smile and upturned eyes. Three Saras. He had the tantalizing feeling that he knew exactly what Sky looked and felt like under her dress.

"Let's see if Sara's in town," said Dirk. "We'll take her over to Loew's, see the picture, and then go on to the Vanguard."

Teddy had a sinking feeling in his chest. Dirk had never had the time of day for Sara or for anyone he considered beneath him—which was most people.

"Christ, did you read this review?" Bertie said. "May be the greatest single actress of her generation, and is without a doubt, in looks alone, the second Garbo.'"

Sara wasn't home. Dirk even called backstage to see if she was on crew. They went to Loew's anyway and came out breathless. It was like Sara up there with black hair: same voice, same face almost, same odd little movements. It was weird and heady.

When Sara got back from the coast the next day, the reviews from the *New York Post* and the *Times* were up on the main bulletin board. She didn't see them as she floated down the hall to her early morning Voice and Speech class more asleep than awake.

Diva Baron was just beginning diphthongs when Sara crept in. "Good morning, Sara," Diva said, a wide, subservient smile spreading across her face. Heads turned. Teddy waved and she stumbled toward him. "Congratulations," Diva said. Sara stared at her, bewildered, then collapsed in a seat beside Teddy.

The air of a huge "wow" hung over the classroom. Students who had never noticed her nodded and smiled. "Class, class," Diva said reverently, "we must return to work." But the class as a body had dreamed of the storybook fame Sara's sister had been awarded; no one could stop them from whispering, grinning, and staring. Those nearest Sara asked hushed questions. Teddy put his hand over hers and smiled like a lunatic.

After class, GW corralled Sara in the hall. He remonstrated gently with her: She'd never mentioned her sister's acting experience on her application forms (which he'd reviewed that very morning) or that she was a triplet. He wanted Sara to ask Sky to speak to the school on her next trip East.

Georgie slapped her on the back playfully and told her fame had a price and that he expected her work to be extraordinary. Dirk asked her to lunch. Rags nagged about her body movement. "You are just like your sister. You tilt forward when you walk."

Irene invited her to a soiree at her thunderingly huge apartment in the Dakota. Sara asked Teddy to go with her; Teddy insisted Dirk and Bertie come with him. Irene didn't care as long as Sara was there.

That Sunday afternoon an article appeared about Sky's "new acting style—natural, movingly emotional," the writer exclaimed, relating Sky's technique to Brando's. The energy of the Method as a style of acting was sweeping the country. It was acting that demanded the practitioner plumb the character's emotional depths to achieve truth, not the phony superficialities with which Hollywood had long been linked. Marlon Brando in *A Streetcar Named Desire*, first on Broadway and then in the movies, was more than an actor—he was a force. Sky Wyman, this reviewer said, was his consort.

Irene served martinis in heavy, fat glasses, making a great display of waving the vermouth bottle over the silver shaker of straight gin. Irene called weaker martinis spring water. She'd seen *The White Queen* and spent the afternoon declaiming about Sky's acting style.

"That reviewer's mad!" she bellowed. "Sky doesn't depend on the Method! She simply is! What a great talent," Irene said to Sara. "How proud you must be." She sighed dramatically. Teddy tittered. As the worshiping soiree advanced, Irene consumed five martinis. She bumped into the furniture, moving upholstered chairs aside as she swept out to the kitchen for more gin.

Seeing Bertie grovel gave Sara a smug pleasure. "I just hadn't the slightest idea!" he exclaimed, hitting his palm against his jeaned thigh. "Why didn't you tell anyone?" She shrugged, a mountain of indifference. "I hope our little misunderstanding is all forgotten. Lord knows, *I've* forgotten it! I always thought the best of you!" he panted. He asked her out to lunch at the Plaza, but she said she was too busy.

As she looked back on it later, this early period of Sky's fame made Sara's life at school glow. She had no need to earn approval from anyone, everyone wanted to be next to her, to learn her story, to hear about being a triplet, a twin to Sky Wyman. They'd listen to her childhood memories of Sky for hours. No one was indifferent to her. She had the right to be boring.

—180—

Teddy remained unchanged toward her, cynical, humorous, whimsical.

"I just can't do anything wrong any more!" she laughed as she and Teddy waited on the main stage to do their scene for the spring midterm exam. Every student in class had wanted to do a scene with her but she'd selected Teddy.

"Everyone wants to be Sky's sister's best friend," Teddy murmured, going over his lines. He hadn't memorized them, as usual.

"Sara!" Georgie bellowed. "Let's do it!"

The theater was stuffed with students from every level who had come to see Sky's sister's scene. Sara took her position with no doubts or fears. She had worked hard and knew the scene would be accepted as enthusiastically as everything else she did. She launched into it with appetite.

When it was over, the students applauded. Georgie, sitting down front with his legs extended and his arms folded behind his head, did not move. He looked grim. He pitched forward and landed on his feet. "Why don't you listen to your partner?" he demanded of Sara.

"I was listening!"

"You were not! Your concentration was way off. The beautiful thing about Sky's work is that she's focused. It's all internal stuff. She doesn't try to be funny, she just lets her character react to the situation."

Teddy said, "Hey, Georgie, this here's Sara, not Sky!"

"When I'm ready to talk to you, I'll talk to you," Georgie snapped. "If I want to draw analogies with Sarah Bernhardt or Helen Hayes or Sky Wyman, I'll draw them, pal." To Sara, he said, "The scene's poor. Come back next week. Both of you."

Someone in the house hissed at Georgie.

"So she isn't as good as Sky, so what?" someone else whispered.

"Whaddaya mean? Sara's great!" It was Anne, sitting in the front row.

"Don't feel bad," Teddy said when they got out into the hall. "Georgie's cracked. We'll work this weekend."

All the rules had changed again—and drastically: There was another yardstick out there for her, and she was just beginning to see it. "I can't work this weekend." She struggled into her coat. She wanted to be alone. "Patrick and I are going out to Long Island." She went outside into the chilly spring afternoon. Teddy ran after her.

"What is this with Patrick?" he demanded.

"We're good friends," she said hastily over her shoulder.

"What about me?"

"What about *you?* I didn't get a lot of encouragement, remember? I suppose now you feel differently, like everyone else!"

"Hey!" He grabbed at her arm. "Stop right there. I'm not like everyone else, and you know it. I don't jump into bed with people just like that!" He snapped his fingers. "It takes time to develop feelings, deep feelings."

"Am I supposed to divine what your feelings are, Teddy? You expect a lot of people!"

"Damn right I do!" he shot back.

"You're not willing to be close to anyone," she said, sadly. "I wish you were. Maybe you think intimacy is square."

Later that night, he lay on his bed, drinking beer, listening to Ella Fitzgerald, and nursing his ambivalence—toward Sara, toward life. Sara was right: He wanted to be admired and desired, but he was afraid to be vulnerable. Why was that? His parents had been kindly if remote, given their economic struggles. He wished his father had been more available, but that was the way of fathers—they weren't around much. His older brother was getting married in the summer. What if he had suddenly become famous? he wondered. Would his brother's fame change everything for Teddy? Would he, like Sara, be trapped at the edges of that fame, not of it but still held firmly in its circle of light? An unnatural life. Sometimes, when her head was up and she was tilting into the wind, moving out fast to some destination, Sara reminded him of a beautiful racehorse—sleek, cool, determined to win. A horse was not made by nature to pull a wagon but many did. A huge sadness for Sara engulfed him. Was she, because of Sky, in danger? He hoped not. He loved her.

Sky stood in the middle of her bedroom, trying on a new hat, clumsily holding the phone in her other hand. Diana was on the extension by the table. "This hoopla will die down," Sky was saying to Sara, who was in New York. "In the meantime, mother's enjoying it. She cues me on my lines." Sky smiled in Diana's direction.

"How are you, Mother?" Sara asked. She was sitting on the couch in her apartment, pouring herself another cup of coffee. From the window she could look out on the dismal little garden below.

Diana was reeling with delight. Before she'd left for Los Angeles, all her friends had been over; she and Ned were constantly invited out. "Daddy loves this," Diana said to Sara on the phone, "but he's all tied up with that damned colt. He lost another race and he keeps telling me we're going to the poorhouse. What a nuisance. He wanted to buy some other horse, a yearling, one of those things that can't run or can't be broken or has to be saddle trained or *something—*"

"How about the Venners?" Sara asked.

"You know that we've had a little setback," Diana said. "They refuse to recognize my claim. But I've hired a genealogist! I've traced Harry Venner back to the Smiths in Nebraska, the Doyles in New England, and the Matheny family in Tennessee."

"Who were they?" Sara asked, lighting another cigarette.

"Nobodies, really, dear. Farmers, small businessmen. But Faith's mother's family are distinguished—the Seymours, Paynes, Greens, and Pikes—all from the East until her father, Faith's grandfather on her mother's side, started investing in land in the West." Sara stopped listening but her mother rattled on, elated that she could finally recount her family history where, before, a white space had existed.

When Sara came back to the conversation, Diana had switched to Sky's triumphs. The *San Francisco Chronicle* had been out to the house for an interview and was running pictures in the Sunday paper of the three of them as children. Diana was in heaven.

"Where's Belinda? Is she with Mrs. Sho?" Sara asked, cutting into Diana's aria.

"She's down here, dear," Diana said. "Sky's got a sweet room fixed up for her—"

"She's so well behaved, Sara," Sky said. "She's got a new trick. When she wants attention, she stands up in her bed and rattles the mobile you gave her."

"You've fixed up a room?" Sara asked, dismayed. It sounded as if Diana had moved Lindy into Sky's home.

"She's so cute, Sara," Sky cried. "If I can help raise her, I'd be so proud." Sky put the hat she was trying on aside. "Oh, do say yes, Sara."

"Mother spoke to me—" Sara said.

"I'm only thinking of Belinda, darling," said Diana.

"But I don't feel right—" The transfer of Lindy made Sara feel rotten, guilty, and second best.

"I do love her, Sara," Sky said.

"I know. I just want to think about it."

"Of course!" Sky cried. "Listen, let me tell you what's happening out here! I can't go out of the house except in an armored car! The studio's moved me to a house in the Hollywood Hills—more secluded, you know."

For Sky, everything had jelled, frighteningly, while she'd been shopping at Magnin's last week. Very slowly, she'd realized that the women in the cosmetic department were looking at her. They were strangers, but they recognized her. One of the clerks had asked, "Aren't you Sky Wyman?" The woman's face held a mixture of awe and anger. Valerie had once said that fans were the life and the death of a star.

"Well, aren't you?"

Sky had replied, "No, I'm not. You're mistaken." And she'd fled. Now, in front of the mirror, she tried on another hat and told Sara about the episode at Magnin's. "Why did I deny it?" Sky asked.

"Because you belong to them," Sara said slowly. "Or they want you to belong to them, but you didn't agree to it. You're theirs now."

"I'm not theirs!" Sky said. "I'm me! I'll always be me!" She waved at Cage who had just come in the door. "Did you see Vail's article about 'Queen' with the picture?" she went on to Sara. "It was reprinted in *Atlantic Monthly*."

Sara, in New York, twisted the telephone cord around her wrist. "Yes," she sighed, still thinking about Lindy. Vail's article was a rambling memoir about growing up with Sky and Sara, but it was primarily about Sky. The picture was of a ten-year-old Sky trying to balance on a fence, her face twisted with fear.

"He's raiding all the old albums. I want him to stop that!" Sky said sharply. "Those are *my* pictures."

"I gave them to him," Diana said on the extension. "At least he liked your movie."

"Can you imagine what it would be like if he hadn't?" Sara asked.

"Listen, the car's here," Sky cried. "I've got to do an interview with *Photoplay* magazine. I'm doing *Life* in a few weeks—I'm going to be on the cover! I'll call you tomorrow. Kiss-kiss." Sky hung up.

Sara looked at the receiver in her hand. "Kiss-kiss? Mother? Are you still there?" she asked.

"Yes, dear, right here."

"Mother, I'd like to come home for spring vacation. I miss Lindy so much."

"Oh, darling," Diana said impatiently, "you just got there. You'll only have a few days—she's settling in nicely down here. I've asked Mrs. Sho to help. Don't worry about anything."

"Well, I just have to see her," Sara said.

When Sara hung up she realized her mother hadn't asked her anything about school or about what she was doing.

Patrick's family lived on a part of Long Island where the estates had names, not addresses. The O'Maras called their manse Whiteclyff. From the boat that had taken them across the Sound, Patrick waved indifferently at a four-story structure sitting inland like a resort hotel. "Fifty acres," he said. The boat docked, and he helped Sara out. A waiting car drove them to the entrance where a uniformed butler took her bag.

They caught up with General and Mrs. O'Mara in the sitting room, a chamber as intimate as a hotel lobby.

"Father, I'd like you to meet my friend, Sara Bay," Pat said.

"How do you do," said the general. He was a short man with a deep chest. His bald head glistened. "May I present Mrs. O'Mara?"

"I'm delighted you could join us for the ball, dear," she

said softly. Mrs. O'Mara was reed thin and had white-blond hair and a nervous subdued manner. "We love the theater," she said. "I met your sister once, just after *The White Queen* was filmed."

The general said: "Patrick, I'm assuming you're home for a while."

"Yes, sir."

"So that play's finished," the general said.

"No, sir, but I've got a movie role waiting back in Hollywood. It's a—"

"Hollywood," the general said with disdain. "It's okay for girls to act—they don't know any better—but a man—" His father eyed him coldly. "Why don't you grow up?"

"Frank, please," Mrs. O'Mara said.

"Oh, Miss Wyman will forgive me," he said with a frosty smile at Sara.

Patrick and Sara made their escape by touring the mansion's spacious rooms and halls, full of priceless antiques; the projection room and small theater on the ground floor, the ballroom and a banquet hall the size of a baseball diamond on the second floor; the family and guest suites on the third floor. The fourth floor was for the thirty-odd servants and had once housed Patrick's nursery. When they got outside to tour the garden, Sara said: "Does your father really hate the theater?"

"No, he just hates *me* in it. He calls me 'that fruit' because I'm an actor. He thinks all the men in the theater and movies are fruits." He looked away. "The stables are over there," he said.

A maid was waiting for Sara in an upstairs guest suite where the closet was bigger than Sara's apartment. The maid had unpacked and put out her clothes and was drawing a bath. Patrick had sent up a bottle of champagne. After Sara's bath, the maid helped her dress and did her hair. Violin music drifted up from downstairs, and the grounds of the palace sparkled with lights. Guests were arriving by boat from across the Sound. A string of launches was docked in front of the estate.

Downstairs, surrounded by Diors and Balenciagas, Sara plucked self-consciously at her dress. The guest list was a roll call of Eastern Seaboard families in business, government, or the armed services. Patrick never left her side, except to allow her to dance with eligible, young, tight-jawed millionaires to whom he introduced her as "Sara Bay."

The O'Maras retired the instant the last guest roared away in a launch. Pat winked at her. "See you upstairs," he whispered.

After the maid left, Sara flung herself into the cozy warmth of the bed and waited for Patrick. He arrived an hour later, quite drunk, and as he struggled out of his tuxedo, he knocked over a table on his way to her bed.

On the night of the big snow, she'd found him a tender and possessive lover. But tonight he was a demon—rough, selfish, and urgent. He slammed his mouth against hers and squeezed her breasts too hard. She cried out and beat her fist against his shoulder.

But as soon as he was inside her, he calmed down. "Sorry," he mumbled. He kissed her eyes and her throat. From the glow of a lamp across the room she saw his glittering blond hair and his sleepy eyes staring out of his slightly flushed face. He looked down at her bare breasts and kissed them as he combed one hand through her hair. She nuzzled against him as his wide shoulders cradled her. He wound his arms around her, lifting her from the pillow, as he strained through his alcoholic haze to reach his expectations, he murmured, "Oh, Sky, I love you so much...."

She stiffened. Had she heard that right? Riding in his own dream, he exploded inside her, shivering. His head fell into the pillow as if he'd been shot. She wriggled out from under him. "Get up, you bastard!" she said to him. "Get up!" He didn't move. She grabbed her robe and angrily walked around the pretty room. Finally she sat down at the window in a stuffed chair. He began snoring lightly.

The night had been grotesque. How could she have done this to herself? She had never been anything to Patrick except a substitute.

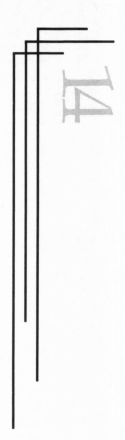

14

The sun was coming up over the Sound, turning the water pink and silver. Maybe, she thought, that's why he had tried to leave her that snowy night on Twenty-fifth Street. He hadn't wanted an understudy but she had flung herself at him. She felt she was sitting at a high stakes table without the money to ante up.

The house was utterly still as she walked into the sitting room adjoining her bedroom and shut the connecting door. She telephoned Vail.

He sounded alert. It was four o'clock in the morning there. "What are you doing up at this hour?" she asked him.

"Haven't gone to bed yet. Why are you calling?" He didn't sound very welcoming. She told him about the ball.

"You sound weird," Vail said.

"I guess I'm tired of being Sky's sister."

"I'm getting some of it out here, but do I mind?" Vail said. "Shit, no."

"Is that why you're drunk all the time?" Sara hung up. There was no point talking if they were going to lie to each other.

Across the country, Vail stepped over a poet from Oregon who was sleeping on the floor of the magazine's office. He opened another beer. Not one paper was out of place on his desk; the pencils were all sharpened, and the copies of his magazine were all stored neatly, by date and issue,

—188—

in racks on the wall. A stack of new paper lay beside the old typewriter. Vail hadn't worked there for quite a while.

He sat down heavily in his chair facing the one window that looked out over the San Francisco rooftops. Of course it was going to be rougher for Sara, being another woman and all. He *was* enjoying the media attention. It wasn't going to last forever, why didn't Sara see that? He took a bottle of scotch from a bottom shelf and poured a generous amount into his beer can, put his thumb over the hole, and shook it.

At that moment Vail experienced another premonition. They came and went, part of the currents of his life. Sometimes they turned out to be true, like his dread about Pegasus; sometimes they faded, unrealized, like discarded dreams. They had been thickest in childhood. Whatever they were, they had become part of him.

He saw the foyer of a large house. On the landing was a big, round window framing the tumescent fronds of a palm tree. Heavily, in his waking dream, he moved up the stairs and looked out the window. In the distance, a woman stood with her back to him beside a body of water that looked like a lake. There was a man behind her. He seized her. A geyser of fear rushed through Vail. The woman started to scream.

That is what he saw. It seemed more real than real, and he felt it powerfully, as he felt all of them. But he could never tell if he would actually see the round window one day, or not.

"Let's go fishing." The poet from Oregon stood in the door.

"No," Vail whispered, shaken by his vision. He looked at his watch. "I think the fish suffer. I'm not going anymore."

Sara left the O'Mara mansion and took a cab to the station. The slow Sunday train gave her plenty of time to think. She had been blind and she had blinded herself. From Grand Central she took a cab to the Village. She pounded on Teddy's door and rang the bell. Dirk answered it sleepily. She brushed past him.

Teddy was asleep. Sara leaned against the closed bed-room door, her open hands pressed against the cool wood, and stared at the back of Teddy's head. She wanted her own life, not Sky's; she could not steal her life from Sky by proxy, either. She took off her clothes and nudged her way into Teddy's bed.

"Huh, huh?" he groaned, turning over. "Sara!"

"Shhh!" She kissed his warm cheek. "Just hold me, Teddy. Hold me."

"Bad time on Long Island?" he whispered. He smelled stale and sleepy. He reached out clumsily and put his arms around her. "Jesus Christ! You don't have any clothes on!"

"Don't think about it," she said.

"It's a little irregular to find a naked woman in my bed." He laughed uncomfortably. She moved closer to his bony, long body. He was sleeping in his underwear. "That's your breast!" he gasped. "Sara, this is serious!" He moved away. She drew him back to her and slipped her hand into his Jockey shorts.

"Aren't we good friends?" she whispered.

His back and legs stiffened. "This good?" He started to pant. "The truth is, I don't have the faintest idea what to do next."

She didn't believe that for a moment. He was playing a scene. "Fortunately," she said, "you don't have to do any-thing. The woman does it all." His body felt hot. Her hand gently squeezed his penis, which was small but erect. "If you keep panting, you'll hyperventilate and I'll have to put a bag over your head."

"I'm trying to stop panting. I can't."

"That's because you're excited."

"I hate wild feelings," he said, his lips curving up at the ends. "I like privacy, being alone." He rose on his elbow and pecked her lips with his, then touched her breast with his hand. "Very pretty," he said. He gazed at her. He was nearsighted without his glasses. She was a sweet blur, and she smelled of the outdoors. "I'll try to be more sophisticated than this." It was embarrassing. He was admitting too much. "Being in bed is really rather silly, isn't it? Two adults lying next to each other without any clothes on and playing with each other's private parts. It's absurd!"

—190—

"You aren't playing with mine, so you're okay." She laughed out loud, and suddenly she couldn't stop. It was his tone of panic and whimsy, his search for analysis to give him distance, his dark, quizzical, squinting eyes. Rippling with laughter, she clapped her hand over her mouth, but that only made it worse, and she couldn't breathe, so she took her hand away and howled out loud, leaning back on the pillow, clutching his thin shoulders, struggling to get herself under control.

"What's so funny?" he hissed.

"The person you're trying to be!" She hiccupped and frowned and turned her mouth down grimly. "Two adults—!" She was off again, boiling with laughter, pounding on the bed with her hand, sitting up, lying down, trying everything to stop, failing to stop. She felt tears on her cheeks. "I'm okay," she said, crying for release and for escape. "Really I am. I mean—here I am—in bed, making this big offer—!" She couldn't go on. The muscles in her sides were cramping and again she broke with laughter, screaming and hallooing, her breasts jiggling and bobbing. She lay back on the bed. She pressed a corner of the sheet to her damp eyes and wiped her cheeks.

"I guess if I wanted to go to bed with a woman, I'd pick a maniac like you," he said, smiling widely, holding out his arms. She fled to them and started weeping from the pain on the other side of the laughter. He held her solemnly, feeling her nipples dotting his chest, waiting patiently.

"Okay, I'm okay. I'm ready," she said after a few moments of silence.

"You lie on your back," he said.

"Let's not make a science about this. Just relax. Don't organize it."

"I'm not organizing it! Jeez, Sara, if anyone's organizing it, you are." He ran a hand through his hair.

"You lie on *your* back," she said.

"Why?" he asked, guardedly.

"Just do it, Teddy. You'll like it."

With an air of accommodation, he shifted out of their embrace and lay on his back. "Now what?"

"Haven't you read or heard anything about making love?" she asked, inching the sheet down from his body.

"Is *that* what we're doing? Oh, I've heard a little," he said, pretending to examine his nails, "but what do a bunch of college boys know, and besides—" His size had been a subject of ridicule all his life and he feared her reaction deeply.

"Besides?" She pulled the sheet off him.

"Well, besides, I have many more important things to do! I read a lot, as you know. I have many friends and acquaintances, a heavy class load, and making love is, well, it's always struck me as being something you don't do casually like taking a piss!"

"How vulgar of you."

"You know what I mean!" he cried, sitting up and snatching back the sheet. She pressed a hand against his hairy chest. He lay down again. "Making love to someone is special. I'm only nineteen, Sara! Give me a break!" She began removing his Jockey shorts. "Now that's where I draw the line," he said, pulling them back up.

She yanked the sheet over them like a tent and dived beneath it. "How can I kiss you if you won't cooperate?" she said from beneath the sheet. "You'll like it. I told you, the woman does everything. All you have to do is lie back and enjoy it. And then, at the right time, I'll tell you what to do next." She was working at his shorts.

He stared at his Charlie Parker poster. "Like get on top of you, I suppose," he said, morosely, above the sheet.

"See! You do know!"

"Come up here!" He grabbed at her with surprising strength and pulled her above the sheet.

"One human being on top of another—except when they're riding a sled—is ludicrous," he said, staring into her eyes.

"You don't have to be on top of me. I'll be on top of you," she said, working at his shorts under the sheet. "You'll crush me."

She started to laugh again. She loved him, his sarcasm, his insouciant wisdom, his sour laughter at himself and others. She kissed him and he responded, shuddering. "More," he breathed. "More."

In no time, he was on top of her, nestling his head into her shoulder, slipping inside her, holding her tightly, his

—192—

face transformed. She felt closer to him than to any other human being, and closer to herself. She felt at peace. He leaned down into her lips and drew his first true kiss from her before sailing away.

Diana flew into New York. She pronounced Sara's apartment "charming" and then took her out to buy a new rug.

"I wish you'd brought Daddy," Sara said as they were walking back to the Westbury where Diana was staying.

"He was so involved in those horses that I just skipped out," she said gaily. "I needed a little rest. And I wanted to see you, dear."

They swung into the polished lobby, collected a telephone message from Ned, and went up to Diana's room. She tossed her packages on the bed, and carefully removed the small, veiled hat from her head. "Whoo! That feels better!" Diana looked critically at the view from her window for a moment and then turned to Sara. "Have you given any thought to what you want to do about Belinda, dear?"

"Yes. I don't feel right about giving her up."

"I understand, dear, but you have a very grave choice to make." She was peeling off bracelets.

"I'm aware of—"

"Are you going to stop your acting classes and take care of her? Does your apartment building allow young children? Could you afford a woman to take care of her while you're—"

"Mother, I've thought of all these things!"

"Darling, why are you making this so hard? Sky's there, she loves Lindy—she calls her Lindy for short, too, now. Such a cute nickname. And Sky's got all the financial resources—"

"Wouldn't you and Daddy help me if I could manage to make the right arrangements here?" Sara demanded.

"Of course we would! But we cannot go on supplying you with money! Daddy's paying your tuition, which isn't cheap, and I know he sends you a little extra, but his financial position isn't what it used to be! Now, Sky, she's going to make a lot of money, and she wants to spend it on Lindy." She took off the jacket to her pale blue suit. "I think the only way this makes sense is to let Sky raise Lindy as her daughter."

"But why that way? It's so—" Final, she thought. Diana whirled away. "It's not unnatural! A child should have a mother, Sara Bay."

"I think it's unnatural!"

"You wouldn't say that if you really understood what I'd been through without a mother!"

"How can any of us understand that when you never talk about it?" Sara said.

"I'm not up for discussion, Sara," Diana said, turning to face her daughter. "We're talking about Belinda." Diana's expression softened; she touched Sara's arm gently. "I know it's hard, but grown-up life is hard. If you want to be Lindy's mother, you will have to give up acting. And you know that."

Sara left the hotel and walked beside the park. The sky was elephant gray, low and heavy. Some of the little trees were bravely in bloom. Lindy was nearly a year old now. If she kept her, she would have to quit her classes and get a job. And even then she would have to hire help to take care of Lindy while she worked. But what was she prepared to do with her life to earn a living? The only thing she'd ever wanted to be was an actress. If she held to her design, she would have to give up Lindy.

The solution Sky offered seemed so easy, yet Sara resisted it. She felt cowardly that she was unable to do the strong, right thing by her own child: sacrifice. Yet Lindy would have an easier, maybe a happier life with Sky. Sara fought with herself: Would she be able to watch Lindy being raised as Sky's daughter? There lay the central agony of her decision. She walked all afternoon, pitting what seemed best for her daughter against what seemed best for herself.

Finally, at nightfall, Sara returned to the hotel and went up to Diana's room.

"You came here just to get my answer, didn't you?" she asked Diana.

"Why, darling, Belinda doesn't know who to call mother! It's time we all made some decisions."

"Then let Sky have her," she said. "I think it will be best for Lindy." Sara burst into tears.

"Oh, Sara, you'll never regret it. Though it's painful

—194—

now. Let's have a little supper together, and then we'll call Sky."

Sara, in the act of sitting down, straightened and stared at her mother. "Let's have a little supper?" she repeated softly. She was being dismissed. In that split second Sara realized that by giving up Lindy, she had severed one of the last cords to her family. The horrible irony of it stupefied her. She weaved on her feet, lightheaded. Then she turned and stumbled out of the room. Diana decided not to stop her.

In Hollywood Sky sat on a set made to look like a nightclub. Tab Hunter sat beside her. They were on a "date." The photographer snapped pictures, while the writer for the "big spread in *Life*," as Lenny had called it, sat at the edge firing soft questions at her. "Pose like a star," the fool photographer had said. Cage and Ace looked on, giggling and egging her on to greater heights of artificiality.

"Now the beach," Lenny said. Sky had a maid, Ace for her hair, Cage for her makeup, Valerie for her wardrobe, and Sam, her press agent. Sam, the cynic, could boil the layers of life down to the snap of a camera shutter. He was supposed to be the best in the business. Sky thought he was a dictator.

They all moved across the lot to Stage 5, the beach set.
In the dressing-room trailer, Valerie helped her out of her evening gown and into a bathing suit; Cage dusted her makeup, Ace puffed up her hair.

Sky's sense of herself was changing. She was on a journey and her constant companions were Ace, Valerie, Cage, and Reed. She knew she shouldn't believe everything written about her, but it was very hard not to. She felt important and completely phony at the same time. She wondered if she had arrived at her destination and would have to walk from now on. At night, when alone, she didn't feel glamorous, yet she was determined to live within the image.

"I want a hat," Sky said. "I always wear a hat now."
She smiled at Valerie, who reddened slightly, pleased. Valerie fished it off a shelf and gently put it on Sky's head.
"Oh, God," Sky said, "I'm so tired. Isn't all this a nuisance?"

She wished Sara or Vail were with her; they would have understood how silly and fun it was to her.

Valerie knew that Sky loved it, for she had once had this kind of attention. She also knew how cold and ordinary life could be on the other side, after the attention had faded. "Fame is fickle," she said to Sky, adjusting the brim of the hat.

"Now just remember, Sky, you're in charge of your face, how it looks, how it's photographed," Ace said, brushing away Valerie's philosophy. "Anything out there doesn't feel right, just stop."

Out on the set, Lenny was arguing with the designer of the photo session's beach set. Several other people stood around: Ping, who'd consulted with the photographer on the lighting, two electricians, a grip, the art director, and Sam. Lenny controlled the conversation. "She brings an idealization of womanhood to the screen," Lenny was saying to the writer and the photographer. "It's overpowering. That's what we want to show here."

The photographer sneered, "She's gorgeous, sure, but it's her job to be photographed!"

"I'm telling you, don't try for that cheesecake stuff. Rules don't apply to her. She even inspires the big guys in the front office to do their best for her. Don't try to make her like Betty Grable!"

"She ain't got the legs, Lenny!"

The press wasn't interested in her political opinions, or in her ability with languages, or in what she read at night. They wanted to know who she was dating, when she first started to date, how she felt about men, the kind of man she wanted to marry, and whether she'd give up her career for her husband.

Everyone stopped talking when Sky came out of the dressing room. Lenny looked at her with cold, appraising eyes. "Very nice," he said.

"Let's dump the little jacket," the photographer said to Lenny, referring to the beach coat that came down to her knees.

"No," said Sky. Lenny's eyes shifted from the photographer to Sky. Even though Lenny had told her the rules— "Cooperate with the press. Give interviews. Pose for pic-

—196—

tures. Then you'll be a star and win an Oscar"—there was a point beyond which she would not go. She was not a magazine model, and she would not "dump the little jacket."

She sat on the beach, posed demurely, and answered every question. She felt alone under the hot lights and the concentrated stares of the men.

The reporter, a middle-aged man, had interviewed Churchill and Eisenhower, Ethel Merman and Gandhi. He was shrewd and tough. As he rose, ending the interview, he looked into her ice-blue eyes with the dark circles around the iris. Sky Wyman was bold and candid, yes, but he saw a ghost within, afraid, thin-skinned, vulnerable, nervous. It was only a hint. She'd done the interview off the top of her head, and in a year she'd have it down pat. He knew he wouldn't see the bewildered little ghost in her eyes then. She'd know all the seductive tricks to keep her own secrets safe.

"Sky," he said, putting his notebook away, "what effect will your fame have on your family—your sister and brother?"

The question jolted her. She took off her hat and pulled the beach coat around her legs. "Why, I expect they will enjoy it, too," she said.

"No, I mean really. I'm not taking notes. Your sister's studying acting in New York."

"Sure."

"Does she have talent?"

"Why, I don't know. We'll find out, won't we?"

Ace looked sadly at the woman he was charged with making even more beautiful. She could have said Sara had a lot of talent, he thought. She could have said that.

TRIPLETS

PART TWO

15

NOVEMBER 1958

In the fifties, doubt and distrust had seeped into the central system of the national body. Though it seemed intact, the old beliefs were breaking down. World War II had ended in victory, the Korean War had been negotiated, family and safety seemed to be the goals in life, yet America still felt itself threatened—by the A-bomb, by the H-bomb, by the Communists—first in Russia, then in China, and now within America itself. Castro was taking over Cuba, and Latin America hated its big neighbor to the north. Beatniks were part of the culture; music had changed, rock and roll had come banging into the beat; the Russians had sent *Sputnik* into the skies; the blacks in the South weren't going to settle for less than justice any longer. The winds of change were blowing hard. In their wake came a vague sense of betrayal: America's hard won security had vanished. The fifties were the perfect loading dock for the sixties.

In this period, Sky Wyman had made the transition from girl to star. But she had left her innocence behind. *The White Queen* had been released in 1954. Since then she had made an updated *Camille*; a ballet movie called *Adagio*; *Fifty Minutes*, in which a handsome psychiatrist helped a woman recover from amnesia; *Lisbon*, a World War II spy glamour film with Joseph Cotten; and a remake of *Anna Karenina*. Her film image was that of a vulnerable, sweet, intelligent, and androgynously sexy modern Garbo. Like all successful film characters, it was allied with her own personality.

Though the big-budget films had capitalized on and increased her stardom, Sky had chafed under her contract with the studio. She'd been put on suspension when she'd refused to do *Susan Slept Here, Peggy Ann's Dream,* and *Woman's World*—pictures "with no merit," her favorite expression.

"Why can't I have a *Sunset Boulevard* role like Bill Holden had?" she'd demanded of Sheldon. "Or how about an issue movie like *Bad Day at Black Rock* for me?"

"You have *those* bad days all the time," he'd shot back at her. Sometimes he was patient, sometimes he was furious.

Sheldon Winters was a fixture of power in her life. They never referred to her aborted "initiation rite." But her resentment about it, and the quality of her roles, fueled her complaints.

"You guys don't seem to understand that a woman can be an actress without being a sex symbol," she'd said at one exasperating point.

"But you're the most beautiful woman in the world!" Sheldon had yelled. "You want to be dressed in a barrel?!"

"I don't want to wear this!" she'd cried, tossing a sequin-studded costume that looked like a bathing suit with feathers at him. "The woman in this picture is nothing more than a high-class prostitute who wants to go straight!"

"It's a beautiful role," he'd yelled back. "No one can do that role but you! I tailored it for you!"

"Thanks," she said snidely. "I'm not walking around the screen in a slip, either."

But she'd played the role, which at least had been adapted from a good thirties novel. She'd worn the slip, but with a knee-length silk dressing coat Valerie had designed. The reviewers had loved her; the public had gone to the theaters in droves to see her.

Her contract with the studio had a year to run and a renewal option after that. She had been loaned out to Warner Brothers to film the Anna Karenina remake. Now she was back at Sheldon's store for a film called *The Ginkgo Tree,* which she'd signed for more than two years ago. Taking place in the 1890s, it was about a new bride on a tea plantation in Java; Stewart Granger was her costar, and it was being shot entirely on the back lot.

Sky's bungalow suite on the lot contained a kitchen, bedroom, sitting room, hair-dressing and makeup room, wardrobe and fitting room. It was refurbished every year. In addition, she had her own impressive trailer on the set, a portable dressing room. On location, she was given a specially rigged trailer. Sky Wyman tried to feel as glamorous as her screen image.

Cage called mirrors Sky's "daily analyst," "her watering hole," her "confessor." Mirrors dominated her makeup room, a pale blue chamber in her bungalow. But recently, Cage noticed Sky's lack of interest in her own face. Mirrors had been reduced to checkpoints. Sky seemed bored and distracted.

In such a mood, Sky was sitting before her dressing table, whose huge mirror gave her a view of the whole room. She was going over her lines while Ace's slender, artful hands crafted her glinting, black hair. Cage was adjusting the depth of Sky's rouge for the lights.

"Oh, I always hate it when you do that," Diana said to Cage. Diana was resting on a striped love seat. She was wearing a modified peasant blouse of her own design, a belted, flaring skirt, and her wrists were encased in heavy Indian jewelry.

Cage knew Diana didn't mean what she said; it was just a way to keep herself a part of the scene. Sky's mother lived in San Francisco until Sky began preparing for a new picture; then she'd return to Los Angeles imperially concerned about Sky "wearing herself out." She stayed until the production wrapped. Cage liked Diana's forceful personality and her charm, but she wore Sky down in ways that were hard to analyze. Cage had stopped trying.

He deepened the rouge as Diana talked about "being a family again" for Thanksgiving in the house that Sky had just bought, about Sara's graduation from acting school and her search for work in New York, about her relationship with Teddy Monroe, about Lindy, about the new necklace Diana had found for Sky, about the family's money problems, and about generosity.

Sky wasn't listening to Diana. She'd sunk into herself, getting ready to go on the set, reacquainting her body and her emotions with the silly, shy character of Lydia, the nineteenth-century bride.

A face Sky had never seen before slid across her mirror: black hair and eyes, wide cheekbones, an impertinent mouth. The face disappeared. Reflected in the glass Sky next saw the AD, the assistant director of *The Ginkgo Tree*, coming through the doorway.

"Miss Wyman," said the respectful AD, "I'm sorry to disturb you, but you wanted to meet Kitty Hightower." When Sky did not respond, he added, "Your new stand-in?" Kitty, the face in the mirror, had retreated to the doorway, her hands in the pockets of her skirt. Diana scanned Kitty briefly, then went on talking about how Sky could help Vail.

Sky interrupted her mother and directed Kitty to sit down. "No, not there. Over there," she said turning back to her mirror. She nodded at Cage and Ace to continue. Ace twisted a hank of hair up onto the crown of Sky's head, and her mother chattered on. Sky watched Kitty.

Kitty Hightower was twenty-eight, the same age as Sky and of the same height and weight. She'd spent the last ten years as a stuntwoman; her specialty was horses—falling off them, swinging from them onto trains, leaping onto them, roping them. Of the few stuntwomen in the fifties, Kitty Hightower was considered one of the most daring. Some men in the stuntmen's union resented her, preferring to dress up their male members as women for the stunts, but others admired her audacity. Her last stunt, falling off a horse tripped by a wire and going over a waterfall, had cost her a broken collarbone, three cracked ribs, and a concussion. She'd nearly drowned.

"Why did you do stunt work?" Sky asked her.

"Danger, excitement," Kitty replied briskly. "I couldn't stand a tame, dull life. Danger kept me alive."

"I do most of my own stunts," said Sky. She was proud of the activity that unhinged the front office. An excellent rider and good driver, Sky was fearless and intolerant of physically weak people. "Don't think you're going to do my stunts."

—204—

"Don't worry. I'm too old and broken up." She smiled. Kitty had dimples and looked disarmingly young.

"Can you live without danger?" asked Sky.

"We'll see. I can't live without pictures, I know that. But my flesh just can't take the pounding anymore." Retired stuntmen often became stunt coordinators or second unit directors, handling the action sequences. But those avenues weren't open to a retired stuntwoman, who would have a hard time getting the stuntmen to follow her orders.

"Being a stand-in is pretty dull after all that excitement," Sky said, eyeing her.

Sheldon Winters still took a proprietary interest in every aspect of Sky's professional affairs. When the studio began looking for another stand-in for her, he had sent her a full report on Kitty.

Kitty had been raised on a ranch outside Butte in Montana. The ranch had gone bust when Kitty was twelve. Her father, half Assiniboin Indian, had moved them into town where he worked as a school janitor; Kitty had become a soda jerk at the drugstore. In high school she'd won most of the women's athletic events and all of the trick riding. At eighteen, she'd floated into Los Angeles and hired out as a wrangler for Warner's.

"You'll do," Sky said. She knew that the men would listen to Kitty as stunt coordinator if Kitty had Sky's blessing. But for the moment, she'd do what she was hired to do—stand in.

Kitty rose. "Then I'll see you tomorrow," she said.

"Nope! Tomorrow's Thanksgiving and even I get to visit with my family. Monday."

Kitty nodded at the breathtaking woman and withdrew.

Outside the bungalow the fresh air had a delightful snap to it. Kitty breathed in and opened her arms. She was working again! Not only that, she was working with one of the top stars in town. The job would help pay off her mortgage, the back stable fees for Chuck, her quarter horse, and feed all her cats and dogs.

Kitty walked a few steps, then sat on a big rock, that marked the entrance to the bungalow. She stared up at the bright sun. The word out on Sky Wyman was that she surrounded herself with people she'd worked with before;

that if you were in, you were in for life. She thought of the people close to Sky. Sherman Davies, a stage director from the old days in San Francisco, was now a film director of modest but competent talents; Jim Fry, an actor she'd known in San Francisco, worked every picture; Lila Lewis, the daughter of the matinee idol, had done very well playing Sky's sister or best friend, though it was well known that Lila felt the parts were beneath her. Of all Sky's old associates, Lila was the only one who openly criticized her. Ace and Cage were permanent courtiers in the retinue. Whenever Sky could, she used Ernie Ping, who'd built a substantial career by being her cinematographer. She had given new life to Valerie, who was now her personal wardrobe mistress. People were critical of Sky for surrounding herself with such a closed circle of friends and associates, but on balance Kitty found her loyalty admirable. Ah, she thought, watching two actors, one as a clown and the other as a pilgrim, walking down the lane eating doughnuts, life was good. Life was, at last, fair. She had deserved a break.

Kitty was a few yards away from the bungalow when Sky emerged from it. One hand was pressed to her bosom like a Southern belle in a bad melodrama; the other hand was holding a sun hat on her head. "Ace!" Sky yelled. "The damn hat's coming off!" Her mother, right behind her, winced. She hated to hear even a "damn" coming from Sky's perfect lips.

At that moment Lila's car came roaring around the corner of D Street. It was an open convertible driven by a man who looked like an aging surfer on leave from the beach.

"You're nothing but a rat!" Lila shrieked from the back seat. "You *know* that was my part! Things must be *desperate* if you have to stoop to tricks like that!" Her driver, his face blank, tooled the car slowly past the bungalow. "Don't think Sheldon's not going to hear my side of it—because he is!" The driver speeded up.

"Good Lord," Diana said, "was that Lila?"

"Yes, Mother," said Sky, still fighting her hat. "Ace!" Diana watched the car round the corner. "But what on earth was she yelling about?"

"It's about *Once in Nashville,* Mother," Sky snapped. She was nearly an hour late. "Ace!" she called out impatiently.

—206—

Ace came rushing out of the bungalow. "Sorry," he said.

"Can't you keep your hands off Cage for one minute?" Sky said, laughing.

"Sky!" Diana said, shocked.

"Fix this," Sky said, snapping her finger against the brim of the hat. "I'm sorry Valerie ever started me on these damned hats."

Sky's Mercedes slid to a stop in front of the bungalow. "How's it today, Miss Sky?" Wade, her driver, greeted her cheerily. "And you, Mrs. Wyman, how goes it?" Wade was perpetually optimistic. Like most of the drivers at the studio, he was a mine of information, opinions, and criticisms.

Ace helped her into the Mercedes. Sky sat down with relief, catching sight of Kitty leaning against the door in the shadow of Stage 4. She looked engagingly confident. She tilted her head and saluted. "See Kitty over there?" Sky asked Wade as he started for the back lot where *The Ginkgo Tree* was being shot.

"Yup. What about her?"

"What do you know about her?"

He gave her a complete rundown that matched the studio report and added: "Real nice person, all told. Fiber. She was fearless!" He slapped his hand against the steering wheel.

"But not anymore?"

"Don't know," he said, truthfully. "She took an awful beating on that Brazilian ranchero picture. Rumor was that the stunt coordinator had it in for her. He set the trip wire too late. But the guys liked her, mostly."

Ordinarily Sky encouraged Wade to natter on, for in many ways he was her daily *Variety*, but today she lit a cigarette and put herself into neutral. There was no glamour in working sixteen hours a day. She was exhausted.

"Mrs. Wyman staying over Thanksgiving?" asked Wade. "Going to have a big turkey?"

"Yes, and all the trimmings." Sky knew it was only a matter of time before Diana announced her permanent move to Los Angeles with Ned. The inevitability of it filled her with nervous fatigue.

Except for the immediate family, and Reed, Lenny, and Sheldon, Belinda was Sky's daughter. Lenny had helped create the scenario—an early husband killed in an auto accident—and he'd been glad to do it to give Lindy "a real mother," and to spare the family embarrassment. He assumed Sara had had the child illegitimately and did not pry further.

Lindy was the most important person in Sky's life. But Sara was arriving today, and it made Sky uneasy about Sara's reaction to their arrangement. Sky wanted her to approve of the way she was raising Lindy. She wanted Sara to have no regrets, an impossible wish, but Sky feared the price of regrets.

She pushed her apprehensions away and tried to concentrate on the work ahead of her. Today she was to be Rosa Morris, painfully shy, trapped in a loveless Victorian marriage by mail order. She'd played a girl like this several times—in *Adagio* and in *Stage Left*, as the stage-struck debutante who fell in love with Van Johnson.

Sky crushed out her cigarette. *The Ginkgo Tree* script had not been changed as she'd demanded, and the director was an ass; it was a vehicle that would not test her abilities or raise her stature. But Sky had learned that sometimes the pictures that seemed the silliest turned out to be the best in release. The only certainty was the script: A good director and actress could not save a bad script, but a good script could survive bad direction, even bad performances.

Sky was lonely. Ace and Cage were loyal and fond, but they were more like listening posts; they weren't real companions. She'd tried to make Lila a friend, but Lila's raw competitive energy wouldn't let her be anyone's friend. Everything had come to a head when they had both wanted the role of the tomboy faith healer in the South in the "Nashville" picture. Poor Lila.

Sky's affair with Reed had collapsed. They had quarreled on *Brandenburg Gate*, the World War II drama in which she'd played a demimondaine saved from suicide by her lover. The rupture had been building between them and came to a head when she refused to marry him. Diana was furious. Later Sky and Reed had calmed down and talked about what they wanted. She had realized that she wanted Reed to be more like Vail—a cheerful comrade who always understood her needs and moods. But Reed had wanted a wife. A few months after that, he'd taken a job in England and had stayed for two years. Now he was back and he seemed distantly affectionate.

She'd missed their closeness. It had been in his absence that she'd realized how alone she was. She'd watched the affairs between players uncurl like blossoms on her sets, and she'd wondered at the ease with which people folded themselves in and out of passion. For her it had never been easy. Sara, whom she thought of now as her "little sister," had sped from elopement to affairs at acting school, though she'd finally settled down into an uneasy relationship with Teddy Monroe. Vail went from woman to woman with all the ease of buying a newspaper. But she, Sky, held back.

Wade pulled up at the set, and Sky got out and went immediately into her trailer.

Sky had concentrated everything on her career. She attended to her fan clubs, tolerated her publicists, and reserved herself for her work. She sweated, she learned lines, she endured the crushing boredom of the set. Her life was glittering drudgery. The reality of fame, compared to her youthful dreams, had stunned her. She'd never expected to be chased, beaten, grabbed, or adored. Her status shone out of people's eyes and made her admirers unnaturally shy or aggressive. For reality checks, she could only count on a few people who'd known her at the very beginning. Sometimes even they failed. Fame was a tiger's embrace; sharp claws of loneliness hid in its soft, warm paws.

Vail was on a train headed for Los Angeles and Thanksgiving. He dreaded it.

His magazine had gone down the tubes and with it his attempt to change his life. He hung out with Bondy and Schurl at the Cafe Puccini or at Ferlinghetti's Bookstore for midnight poetry readings. He had all but overcome the effects of his humiliating beating in Korea, but suffering still turned him on—more than joy. He knocked almost everything—national politics, hypocrisy, phoniness, pretentious arts. Real artists suffered and were truthful. For Hollywood especially he reserved his sharpest scalpel. He was jealous of Sky's fame and a little bewildered by it. He was the boy in the trio; it was unnatural that Sky was famous and he wasn't.

He could brush away his envy by revealing his proximity to Sky. The first time Sky's beautiful face bounced up at him from the cover of *Life* magazine, he did a double take because for an instant she looked like a stranger *and* like she did when she was twelve! It was quirky. Bondy knew that Sky was Vail's sister, but almost no one else knew. At the time, Vail had been seeing a girl called Abby whose parents were both dentists in San Rafael. Abby was puritanical; she'd refused to sleep with him, but when she'd seen that *Life* magazine and Vail had exclaimed, "That's my sister!" Abby had slept with him that night. It had taught him that when he felt outside a group, or unwelcome, he only had to reveal Sky. Sky was instant acceptance.

Vail had decided to write poetry seriously. To this end, that summer he'd taken a job as a fire lookout around Shasta. He took weather readings, kept an eye out for lightning strikes, and made daily radio reports. He had plenty of time to write. He cooked his own meals on a Sterno cooker and washed in buckets of stream water. He sang songs to the cruel, black peaks and yawning canyons that held his little station like a toy in their giant fist. He bellowed poems into the silence. Time and peace became the enemies that running in place and pushups did not dispatch. He dreamed about Riva and awoke sweating and weeping.

When his month was up, he was grateful to leave the huge void of nature hugging its terrible secrets to itself. He hitched back to San Francisco with a batch of poems he feared were no good.

At the bars and coffee houses everyone was just where he'd left them, but Bondy looked thinner and hyped. He said he was taking Dolophine, "a great new drug." Bondy had become a Texas entrepreneur in Vail's absence. "Help me harvest my marijuana crop! We'll bring it back up here and sell the hell out of it."

It was backbreaking, cutting down the primitive green branches, drying them, and loading them on the back of the little flatbed Bondy had somehow gotten hold of. It was quite a haul. They drank beer all the way through New

Mexico and Arizona and played metaphysical word games and sang old folk songs and devised intricate plans for the distribution of their profits. The cops stopped them outside of San Jose. Bondy was drunk and started a fight. Vail backed into the truck, the old terror sweats seizing him. They had Bondy down on the gravel and were stomping on his head. They were killing him when Vail flew at them.

He woke up shivering under a thin blanket in a slimy jail. It was some kind of holding pen. Bondy was not there. Jesus, Vail wailed, they'd killed Bondy! He put his head in the crook of his arm and cried.

When they let him, he called his father.

On a train riding south to Sky's house and turkey dinner, Vail cringed, remembering Ned's reaction when he'd called him from jail. His father hadn't yelled or made demands, he'd only sounded miserably disappointed in Vail. Ned had come to the jail, clapped him unhappily on the back, asked him again to come out to the ranch and recuperate, told him he'd get a good lawyer for both him and Bondy. Vail couldn't look at his father, and he didn't know what to say. He'd given his father a big hug.

Vail looked out at the glass ocean as the train steamed along. He couldn't remember when he'd last seen Sky or Sara. His hair was long, almost down to his shoulders. He was twenty-eight, and he had lines in his face, lots of lines; his hazel eyes were a little less hazel, he thought, cloudier. But he hoped his charm was intact. He also hoped the girls wouldn't expect too much of him. After all, he'd just spent a month in the can. As the train devoured the tracks beside the sea, he rehearsed the way he would thank his father for getting him off with five years' probation.

16

As Sky became the family's silently acknowledged leader, her house, SkyHigh, became the family's nerve center.

The house was tucked into the once-fashionable Hollywood Hills, far up Beachwood Drive, a location that irritated Diana. Sky made as much money as any star in America, yet she'd deliberately sought a home outside Beverly Hills or Bel Air.

It resembled a small castle whose days as a fortress had passed. Narrow granite stairs climbed from the gate below on the dirt road to the structure perched above, which sprouted a few modest turrets and towers. The forested hill was home to great horned owls, to deer and coyotes; the gardens, carved out of the trees, had been improved with a fountain, a fishpond, and a swimming pool in the twenties. About a thousand feet north lay the reservoir, dubbed Lake Hollywood by residents. Through the jacaranda and eucalyptus trees, it looked like a lake.

Inside, the rooms were airy and bright. A circular window surmounted the landing of the grand staircase. Sky had started to buy antiques to season the anonymous modern furnishings—Florentine chairs, a prized carved French screen. Off the living room, a terrace overlooked Lake Hollywood. When Sky was inside her palace, she felt isolated from the other houses on the hill—Lila and her father's being the nearest—which were hidden in the trees below.

Sara burst through the front door of SkyHigh to see her sister skipping down the stairs into the high-ceilinged foyer. Sky looked like a girl, holding out her arms to Sara. They

—212—

collided in a hug that released for both the instantaneous intimacy of childhood. Behind them, Teddy staggered into the hall, carrying two large and battered suitcases. "Is this the famous Teddy Monroe?" Sky cried.

"*Infamous*, my dear, *infamous*," he replied as coolly as he could. Not only was he out of breath, he was delightfully shocked to see Sky in the flesh. Her eyes looked like a winter version of Sara's summer warmth. She was simply breathtaking. He dropped the bags and shook Sky's hand, trying not to stare.

"Isn't she beautiful?" Sara cried, holding Sky away from her, displaying her.

"She's great," Teddy said, sitting down on one of the suitcases, panting.

"Mother doesn't like unmarried people sleeping in the same room," Sky said conspiratorially. "We had a 'discussion.'" She hooked an arm around Sara's neck.

"Where are they? Where's Belinda?" Sara asked.

"Everyone's napping. Quick, into the study before they wake up!" She threw a practiced glance at Teddy—his curly hair, his skeptical air so carefully devoid of adoration, his horn-rim glasses, his tall grace. He'd do.

A television set, an audio tape deck, and a hi-fi were fitted into the wall of the study like technological paintings. In the corner a full bar, from which the glasses winked like gems, was built into the glossy pale oak paneling. The furniture was upholstered in soft green, the wallpaper was dark green. The room felt like a forest grove—woodsy and secret.

"Do Mother and Daddy live here now?" asked Sara, puzzled.

Sky shook her head. "Mother's down here a lot, but Dad's mostly at the ranch."

Teddy glanced around. "Just put a drink in my hand and let me wander."

When he'd disappeared, Sky settled into a soft sofa and asked Sara, "When are you and Teddy getting married?"

"How about you?" Sara countered. "The magazines never tired of recounting your long affair with Reed. Now that he's back—"

"We're not in love in that way!" Sky said sharply. "We're good friends!"

"Preposterous!" Sara fell over herself, laughing. "Reed's

the handsomest man I ever saw! And one of the most respected directors in the country. I can't imagine you not marrying him! Weren't you lovers?"

"Certainly," Sky said. She changed the subject. "Do you like your life, Sara?"

"It's okay. I've got big competition."

They had plugged directly into the center of the unspoken rivalry between them.

"Me."

"Sure," Sara said.

Sky looked away.

"Hey! We could have done that a thousand times!" Sara said. "You were in New York last year on your way to Paris, but you didn't have time to stop in."

"I know." The house was perfectly still.

"And I can't fly around the country on whim."

"Do you need money?" Sky asked. "I don't have a lot—my expenses with Mother and Daddy—"

"No. No money. You're caring for all Lindy's—"

"But I love Lindy," Sky protested.

At that moment, Belinda appeared around the corner of the study door. She was wearing a rumpled pair of overalls and a T-shirt. Belinda, five years old, small and delicate, had brown hair, large light blue eyes, and the look of a waif. But she was stubborn, willful, and spoiled.

"Honey!" Sky cried. "Come and see Sara!"

Belinda came into the room, keeping her eyes on Sara. She came to a stop at Sky's knee. "Mommy, who's that man out there?"

Lindy's "Mommy," directed at Sky, wrenched Sara.

"That's Teddy, Sara's friend. Go kiss Sara," Sky said. Sara ached to hold her. Every time she saw Belinda, the decision to let her grow up as Sky's child, so that she could have what Sara couldn't give her, became harder. Sara hugged the willing little body of her own child. She looked into Lindy's pale eyes and saw Sky's landscape; but from Vic she got her straight light brown hair. Sara saw little of herself in her child.

"Mommy, may I eat with everybody tonight?"

"Of course, dear."

"I was here last summer when you were learning to ride," Sara said softly. "Do you remember, Lindy?" The child nodded, staring gravely at Sara. "I have a present for you."

"What is it?" Lindy asked.

"It's clothes, but I won't tell you what kind yet. That's the surprise."

"Off with you now, Lindy," Sky said, relieved. "Mrs. Sho has your juice." Obediently, for once, Belinda trotted away.

"Oh, God, it's hard seeing her," Sara said.

"She's in a great private school here," Sky said, "and she takes all kinds of lessons—"

"I know, I know," Sara murmured.

"Tell me about what you're doing," Sky said, looking at her with the cool intensity she brought to her roles, an expression that Sara remembered well from childhood.

Sara started an automatic report, but she was thinking how deeply Sky had influenced her life.

The fallout of Sky's fame had been fun at first. Strangers had come up to her in stores or on the street and had said, "Haven't I seen you before?" to which she'd developed the reply, "Only in your dreams." She'd thought the brouhaha would die down. But Sky's second role, in a romantic Western, *Ride On*, had swept the nation. Its phenomenal success had sealed both their fates. Everyone Sara had ever met had seen that film. By Sara's third year in acting school, she knew that Sky's national ghost was lashed to her back.

"Things would be easier for you if I weren't—well, acting must be hard—I just can't imagine—" Sky said.

"Teddy urged me to quit," Sara admitted. "He said it was going to damage me psychologically." She laughed shortly and stared at a woodland print on the study wall. "Excruciating consequences," was what he'd really said. Sara remembered that they'd been walking in Central Park; she'd been quite angry with him.

"Don't you think I have talent?" she'd yelled.

"Sure you do," he'd said, "but it's got nothing to do with talent. It will grind you up."

"I'm not letting Sky run me out of acting!"

—215—

"Then face your own responsibility for the pain, because it's not going to let up. No matter what you do, it won't be good enough. Sky's your standard."

She knew he was right, she was trapped. But she'd stayed in school, riding above the daily comparisons—some casual, some mean. The school had given her good roles because she was a draw to their plays. She was Sky Wyman's sister. For a while, she'd performed as she thought Sky would perform, toning everything down, becoming more frail and pristine. Later, she'd broken out of that shell and made everything larger, more passionate. But Georgie, elevated to the school's top director in her junior year, became her enemy, screaming at her with such frequency that in one rehearsal she'd finally rounded on him.

"Just what is it that you really want? Do you want me to hide in some house as someone's wife? Do you want me to get off the stage because my sister makes movies? Shall I kill myself? What do you want?!"

Georgie, facing her stage center, took her elbow and turned her away from the other actors. "You're a terrific actress," he whispered viciously. "I want you to quit. You can't compete. Sky's the greatest actress of her generation." He squeezed her arm painfully. "You make me want to weep. Why don't you give it up?" She'd run off the stage and locked herself in the dressing room. She hadn't felt like herself, she hadn't felt like Sky. She'd pulled hard on a hank of her bronze hair; she wasn't *enough*—because she wasn't Sky! "You're a loose cannon on the family deck," Vail had said when he'd come up for air briefly. "Why don't you go into farming or advertising?"

Sara sipped her drink in Sky's woodland study and wondered if she could ever explain to Sky what her life had become. "I don't know how to answer you," Sara said. "Life is better now that I'm out of school."

"Why didn't you quit?" Sky asked.

"No. I'll never quit." Sara looked away. GW had loved having her there. He'd praised her and watched his enrollment and his donors grow. Irene had flattered her, had said she was gifted, and had told her that no exercises would ever improve her. "You know," she said, "the worst thing

—216—

is the hypocrisy." She remembered Bertie looking at her with servile awe telling her everything she did was great. Only Teddy had remained unchanged. "In a way it's because of you that I'm with Teddy today. He loved me before."

"Well, what about Patrick, my dear?" Sky said, archly, putting on a movie-star voice. "Didn't you love him?"

Sara laughed. "In a way. I was flattered that he seemed to prefer me to you." As she rose, she felt the liquid heaviness from the drinks. "Until I found out that he'd never left you. You were a bitch to him, Sky."

"He knew how I felt about Reed," Sky said, watching Sara. "I couldn't change that." Sara opened a can of nuts and scooped out a handful. "So what's next for you?"

"I'm making rounds in New York. At night I work at the club." She'd been working there since her junior year when Ned stopped sending the checks. He'd almost gone bankrupt, but Sky's intervention had saved his colts from auction.

"This is a fitting place for you to live—right on top of the world!" Teddy declared as he came back into the room. Distantly a melodious doorbell pealed out the first bar of the theme song from Sky's most famous film so far. "Bless me," Teddy sighed, "do I hear the theme song of *Ride On?*"

"My laywer gave it to me for Christmas last year," Sky explained a little sheepishly.

"I guess there's not much you need," he murmured.

Sky went to the study door and peeked out into the foyer. A stranger in long hair and torn jeans was arguing with Lester, her houseman. Lester was becoming shrill. The man replied laconically, "Just tell her, man."

"*Vail!*" Sky yelled. Sara bounced off the sofa and both women dived through the door. Vail turned and saw the two pinpoints of light he'd once imagined in one of his dark days transformed into his gorgeous sisters. They looked unchanged. He felt like an old man.

Teddy watched them from the study door. They were all about the same height, and if they'd had a Maypole they would be dancing around it. If this was joy now, he didn't understand why over these last years they'd stayed apart.

Was this delirium an act? Could they only act with each other?

Once they were all seated in the study's forest grove, they joked relentlessly about Vail being in jail, about their father's horses, about the time Sara dyed her hair black to give the finger to Georgie during a main stage production—boy, did Teddy ever remember that night! The little study rocked with their derisive laughter and inside innuendos—it was like being in a pit of jolly snakes. They were obviously triplets: Their gestures, tone of voice, lifted eyebrows, and the famous laugh were identical. Vail's long hair accentuated his resemblance to them, except for his saving goatee. Vail was bartending, mixing martinis with Sky's high-class gin, describing his sojourn as a bartender in a brothel. "You didn't!" his sisters squealed. He nodded solemnly.

A large spotted cat about the size of a shepherd dog ambled into the room. Mrs. Sho was right behind it, full of apologies. "That's okay, Mrs. Sho," Sky said. Sara, Teddy, and Vail drew back. It was a half-grown cheetah. "This is Nigeria," Sky said, patting the cat's head.

For one instant, Vail thought the snow leopard had leaped out of his head into the beautiful room. The cheetah's body was long and narrow, its back slightly swayed; dark lines ran from the corners of its eyes to its mouth like exotic African makeup. Its claws were out.

"Aren't those dangerous?" Teddy asked, staring at its paws.

"Nope, cheetahs can't retract their claws. Niger's about eight months old now." "She seemed charming if a little cranky." He looked at Sara. "She seemed charming if a little cranky."

"What was she doing?" Sky asked.

"She was sitting at a table on the terrace, drawing."

"Oh, yes, she loves to draw. Like you, Vail," Sky said.

"She looks a little like Vic," Sara said, waving her empty glass at Vail. The conversation depressed her.

"Where is Vic?" Vail asked.

"I met a little girl outside," Teddy said. "Is that Belinda?" He looked at Sara.

"What was she doing?" Sky asked.

It threw itself down on the rug heavily. Sky stroked its head. "I'd rather have her this way than on my back in a coat," she said.

—218—

"I don't know," Sara said. "Does Lindy ask about her father?"

"Not around me," Sky said. "Ask Mother."

"I wonder what Mother says?" Sara muttered uneasily. "We should talk about that, Sky."

"I think she's happy here," Sky replied, feeling defensive. "She loves Daddy and the ranch and Maggie. She spent all last summer there."

A woman's screech soared into the later afternoon shadows.

"Good Lord!" Sara exclaimed, rising off the sofa. "Who's that?"

"Sit down. That's only Lila," Sky said. "The 'li'l star,' I call her."

"She doesn't sound little."

Sky explained to Teddy how she and Sara had met Lila at the theater in San Francisco, that at the time Lila had had her sights on a movie career, that Lila's once-famous father was a sad drunk who hung out at the Polo Lounge, all dressed up in an ascot. They heard the distant voices of a man and a woman arguing. "Lila's house is right below this one," Sky said, waving an arm toward the east. "The hill is full of houses built in the twenties and thirties, but you'd never know it because the trees hide them. C'mon outside."

They were crossing the foyer when Vail stopped. "Jesus," he said, looking up at the round window on the landing of the stairs. It framed the fat fronds of a palm tree growing outside.

"What?" Sara asked.

Vail did not answer. He moved up the stairs to the landing like a sleepwalker. He didn't want to look out the window. He knew what he would see.

"Vail, what's the matter?" Sky asked.

Vail saw the blue water of the reservoir that looked like a lake and the wide path around it. The spot where he'd seen the man attacking the woman in his waking dream was empty.

"It's nothing," Vail muttered. "Forget it."

They went through the living room to a large flagstone terrace and dropped into wicker chairs. Beyond the garden and through the trees the glassy plate of the "lake" shone under the perpetual sun. "Lila's house is right over there," Sky said, pointing down into some trees.

The voices had stopped. The afternoon was silent. Sky lit a cigarette. "Lila was so much more ambitious than I." Vail said, "What's that mean?"

"I got parts which, had I not been here, she might have had. She cared more, that's all. Now she's drinking a lot, taking dope, whatever." She looked at the end of her cigarette as the unmistakable sound of breaking glassware wafted over the trees. "Then, just yesterday, I got a role that she wanted very badly. Anyway, poor Lila. She'll be drunk for several days. I've tried to help, but she doesn't want it."

"How ghastly," Sara said, noting the distant way Sky spoke and remembering the rambunctious redhead from the summer stock play in Marin.

"Didn't you hear something about Vic last year?" Vail asked Sara.

Sara shot him a look. "From Jim Fry—they used to be friends. He'd heard that Vic was in Sierra Leone." She looked into her new drink. "Mrs. Sho is good for Lindy, too," she said, remembering her daughter's eyes looking at her politely as she would look at a stranger.

Ned was in heaven. His three glorious children were all together again with him. He was pleased and slightly intimidated by them. From his end of the table, he could look out on the dim lights illuminating the terrace and the dark hole of the water beyond. After his fifth glass of wine, bolstered by the martinis before dinner, he minded Vail's ridiculous long hair less. He'd always been happy to see Sky's icy eyes looking at him from the covers of magazines, and it was true that in a way, Sara looked like a pale copy of her more dramatically colored sister, but up close, like tonight, she seemed definitely her own person—high-spirited. All the long talks Diana had foisted on him over the years, about how Sky and Sara looked and sounded too much alike to make acting anything but a quicksand for Sara, faded away. It had all worked out, just as he'd thought it would. Little Belinda was behaving herself—she had a strong temper—and she was all dressed up in a ruffled outfit

Sara had brought her. Vail had promised Ned he'd find a job—wasn't he thinking of working for that insurance company, the one that insured movie productions or something? He was also planning to write some critical essays on the side. "If you're not a poet," Vail had said to him, "then be a critic, right, Dad?" And Ned had chuckled with approval.

Like a toothless old lion who'd stayed in the pride past his prime, Ned watched the conversation swirl around him, excluding him. He never let on that he knew it.

Diana wore a low-cut Dior cocktail dress. She moved her head gracefully, occasionally tilting it seductively at Ned, a gesture she remembered. Her hair was done up in a twist. She glanced at Teddy and smiled. His looks were disappointing. His face was angular and intelligent, but without style, she thought, and though he seemed well educated, he didn't have a nickel. She looked back at Sky.

"All I'm saying, darling," Diana's low voice wheedled, "is that you're in a position to help Sara now. She's proved she can do it—"

"Mother, for God's sake," Sara hissed. Across the table, Teddy tensed. Sky's eyes were so shielded by thick lashes that he couldn't make out what she was thinking.

"Anger, fear, and sexual arousal all come from the same spot in the brain," Vail announced suddenly, in a merry voice.

"Darling, don't hiss at me," Diana said to Sara, ignoring Vail's extraordinary comment.

"Vail's going to be a critic," said Ned. "Isn't that what you said, Vail?" Ned was smiling warmly. Everyone looked at him, but he didn't go on. Diana sliced a ribbon of butter for her roll. Sometimes Neddie made her so mad she could kill him, Diana thought. Why *was* that? He was so sweet and helpless.

"Yes, Dad," Vail was saying, bathing, for once, in parental approval. "That's right. I've given up poetry, you'll all be glad to hear." He flicked his hair back over his shoulder with an oddly masculine gesture.

Diana went on as though no one had said anything. "Sky's one of the most powerful people in the world now."

"Don't believe my publicity, Mother," Sky said thinly. She was about to launch into what happened to people who believed their own publicity, but her mother took the helm back.

"The studio will do anything you want. They *need you*, isn't that right, sweetheart?" she asked Sky.

"Sheldon Winters," Sky replied, thinking of his long, severe face, "does exactly as he pleases."

"I need a little more wine," Teddy said into his plate.

"Have I gone too far?" Diana asked, smiling broadly at Teddy. She obviously didn't care if she had. "It's a mother's duty to support her children."

A faint shriek, like a distant comet, tailed by an angry male voice, arched over the silence at the table. "Don't be alarmed," Sky said. "That's the li'l star letting off steam. She's having a rough time."

"Sounds like her husband is, too," said Teddy as the male voice bellowed an obscenity. It sounded as if they were standing outside on the terrace.

"She's having an affair with, er, Patrick O'Mara, I think. I lose track," Sky muttered, glancing at Sara.

"I thought Patrick was back in New York now," Sara said.

"No, he's here. Trying to piece his career together. His face is going. Not quite the handsome man of yore." She smiled gently at Sara. "Sorry."

"Yes, I am, too. One thing about Patrick, though. He'll never starve."

"He might," said Sky. "His father's tightening the purse strings. He threatened to cut him off without a penny."

"Because he's still an actor?" Sara asked, remembering the general and his meek wife.

"Drinking. I haven't seen Pat sober in a year."

A sound like a car backfiring rang out. "Oh God, she's at it again," Sky sighed.

"That's a pistol?" Ned asked, aroused from his martini buzz.

"Yes, she waves it about and sometimes it goes off. This is a bad night."

"Maybe we should call the police," Diana said.

"We will if it gets worse."

"You mean if someone gets wounded?" Vail said, laughing.

"I love excitement," Lindy said, scrunching back in her chair.

"Not this kind," Sara said. "This is a very bad kind."

"It would be exciting if my daddy came back," Lindy said, peeking at Sky. "Did you know my daddy?" she asked Sara.

Everyone stared. Sara said, "Yes, I did."

"I had a dream about him last night," Lindy said, primly.

"He was meeting me at a car somewhere."

"Now, Belinda," Sky said.

"He was a coward," Diana put in coldly. "He left without a word and never came back."

"I didn't think he was a bad man," Sara said pointedly. "Maybe he left because he thought he couldn't take care of you the way he wanted." She touched Belinda's little hand.

"But is he coming back?" Lindy asked. She was delighted. No one had ever talked about her father before.

"I don't know," Sara said.

"What do you think of that Rockefeller being governor of New York, Sara?" asked Diana.

"I like him," she said absently, staring at Lindy beside her.

They talked about Vice President Nixon's hostile reception in Latin America, a conversation Diana could lead with energy. "They hate us down there, after all we've done to them," said Diana. "I can't think of a nicer person to spit on than Richard Nixon." Diana's interests were shifting, she said, toward the remarkable work of Dr. Martin Luther King. No one but Sara had heard of him. "His people helped get the buses desegregated in Montgomery, Alabama," Diana said. "It's terrible what's happening in the South, closing all those schools down so the Negro children can't attend them. And what are we doing to help integration?" Her question lay on the table like a stone. "Nothing. We're not doing a thing."

Sara thought, Yes, she's right. "I don't know," she said truthfully.

"Well, think about it," said Diana. "There's no sin worse than not being involved in your times. Some judge like Learned Hand said that." Teddy looked at Diana with guarded respect. She was complicated.

—223—

"Whatever happened to the Venners?" Vail asked in his perkiest voice. Sara knew he would never have asked if he hadn't been drinking.

"Now, I can see through that, Vail," Diana admonished. She plucked at her pearl necklace tenderly. "I will not be deterred, but for the moment I will answer." She addressed the table. "The Venners have not responded to any inquiries. Daddy himself sent a letter but—nothing. I've half a mind to go over there myself and just knock on the door."

"Good idea, Mom," Vail said.

"Well, it's a terrible idea," she said, laughing.

"Oh, give it up," Sky suggested.

"I will not," her mother responded.

Ruinously, Teddy said, "Which Venners?"

"Well, really, Sara Bay," Diana said, "haven't you explained anything to Teddy? But perhaps he's not interested." Sara rolled her eyes toward the ceiling. "The Venners, Teddy," Diana said, "started the railroad in this country—"

"Brigands with the law on their side," Sky said, smiling.

"Granny's family," Lindy said, solemnly.

"I see Lindy's all tuned in," Sara commented wryly.

Diana ignored her. "Now Ned's family had a successful claim in a silver mine in Virginia City—"

"Oh, that's great!" Teddy exclaimed to Sara. "I had no idea you were an heiress."

"Forget it," Sara said. "The money's gone, and the Venners won't recognize Mother. It's a long legal thing."

"Won't recognize her how?" he asked.

"Honestly, Sara, if you'd let me finish." She turned back to Teddy. "Faith Venner was my mother," Diana said with sweet dignity, "but due to circumstances, I was raised by other people. I am her only daughter, though she has a son by marriage."

"God, that's amazing," Teddy said, truly enthralled.

"Of course, money has nothing to do with it. Miss Venner had a modest trust fund—"

"A modest trust fund from a railroad fortune must be pretty substantial," Teddy broke in.

Diana ignored the interruption. "But money's the last thing on my mind. It's a matter of family. I've done some

—224—

genealogy on the family and I know quite a bit about both sides, but I won't talk about it at dinner."

"She'll talk about it later, though," Vail said with a wide smile.

"Now," Diana said to Sky, changing gears, "you're your own person. You don't need me. But Sara's still struggling. So is Vail," she added, almost happily. Sky no longer asked Diana for advice on her roles or even discussed them with her. Moreover, Diana was jealous of anyone close to Sky.

"Help Sara," Diana said. "She needs a good part, darling."

"Oh, Mother, please," Sara groaned. Maybe, Sara thought, Diana is the reason Sky still hasn't married.

I think I am going to kill her, Sky was thinking, feeling acutely embarrassed for Sara. Wasn't it enough that she was practically supporting Diana and Ned? Ned didn't really try to race horses for money anymore, and she was sure that everyone at the tracks laughed behind their hands at him. Just today, after she'd come off the set dog tired and sweating like a pig, Diana had asked her, very circuitously, for more money—the vet bills had been particularly high that month. Sky had refused; Ned had to get rid of some of the horses. Later, she'd felt like a heel when Ned had quietly told her that he would sell three of the ponies.

Diana was gearing up again. Sara glanced at Ned, hoping that just once he'd step in, but he was applying himself to the pumpkin pie.

"Mother, leave it!" Sara yelled passionately.

"It's just a question," Diana muttered. Something had shifted, but she was not willing to admit it. "I never knew why you had to compete with your sister anyway, but now you have, and you got some parts, dear, didn't you? I want you to get some of the breaks, too, that's all." She laughed her little trilling laugh and nodded at Ned as though he'd said something agreeable. "I mean, you've given up everything to act," she said, looking at Belinda.

Teddy rose. Belinda was a red flag to Sara. "Sky, I've always wanted to have coffee with a cheetah. I'll carry the pot," he said, seizing the silver tray that held the coffee set. He tilted his head at Diana. "Can you take the cream off before I spill it?"

Sara sank back in her chair. Teddy was so great in public;

why was he so difficult in private? Since graduation he had realized he was virtually uncastable as an actor; he wasn't old enough to be a character actor or handsome enough to be a lead. His charm was brittle and intellectual. Yet he doggedly pursued his acting and brought all his animosities home with him at night. As the months rolled on Sara had seen his sarcastic, cruel side more often than his wit. They were desperately paired.

The living room had a vaulted, beamed ceiling, white walls, and the out-of-fashion antique wicker furniture Sky loved. At Teddy's urging, Ned guided him through a checkered summary of the Venners that proceeded in fits and starts, approaches and retreats, people contacted, contacts broken.

"I've almost given up on the Venners," Diana said, knotting one loose thread of the conversation. "But not quite." She winked at Teddy, shook her gold bracelets, and touched her long drop-pearl earrings.

Vail had to hand it to her. She looked glorious, a handsome woman in her prime, artfully and dramatically dressed, unmistakably individual. Her curvaceous dancer's legs showed beneath her skirt; they were like parts of a beautifully designed machine, strong enough to get her across the plains with the covered wagons, yet lovely to look at. Maybe Ned had been drawn to that combination in her.

Diana's bewitching smile made her eyes tilt up. "All of you are the only family I need."

"Until the next campaign," Ned muttered.

The doorbell chimed its theme song. Vail laughed at it. A moment later Kitty Hightower came into the room. Sky regarded her with surprise.

"I'm so sorry to intrude," Kitty said in her soft voice. "Here are the new script pages for Monday. I thought you'd like to see them over the weekend. I was told these are closer to your version of the sequence." She extended the script to Sky.

"Thank you, how nice of you," Sky said. "Please sit down and have some coffee." Sky introduced her to everyone. "Kitty was a stuntwoman," Sky said, "and I'm thinking about making her my coordinator."

Kitty was so startled by that announcement that she

—226—

almost dropped the china cup Teddy was handing her. "Well, thank you!" she said. "But the guys aren't going to like it."

"They'll get used to it," Sky said, naming the man who had coordinated her stunts for the last couple of years. "I like doing things my way." She smiled at Kitty.

Muffled exasperated voices could be heard coming up the stone steps outside the front of the house. Then someone began pounding on the front door with ferocious energy. Mrs. Sho's quick steps tapped through the foyer as the unmistakable voice of the li'l star bayed from the front porch, "Sky, you bitch, come out here!" This order was followed by a shot.

Belinda screamed, and Sara caught her up in her arms. But the child wriggled away and fled to the foyer and Mrs. Sho, who picked her up.

"Jesus!" Ned cried, rising. "Sky, call the police!"

"Mrs. Sho!" Sky was already calling out like a sergeant. "Police!"

"And take Lindy upstairs," Sara cried.

"You deliberately took that part!" Lila shouted.

Sara heard Patrick's sloppy, angry voice on the other side of the door, "Gimme that, damn you!" followed by sounds of a scuffle, then another horrifying shot. A body thudded against the door.

"I'm going out there!" Ned yelled, striding across the room.

Vail caught his arm. "Dad, wait!"

"Is the door locked?" Kitty whispered.

Another shot went off. "Is anyone counting?" asked Teddy, who looked afraid. Sara said there had been three. Diana had crouched down beside the couch, putting it between her and the foyer. Ned went over to her and put his hand on her shoulder, pressing her down. Sky stood near Vail and Ned by the sofa, while Kitty and Teddy pressed themselves against the wall.

Sara ran across to the window and peeked out. She could only see a corner of the well-lit porch. She dropped the curtain and headed toward the door. "I'm going to make sure it's locked," she whispered.

"Get away from me!" Lila yelled, out on the porch. "Or I'll shoot you!"

At that moment the front door burst open, and Lila was upon them, brandishing her pistol, her fiery red hair whipping around her head, her blouse torn, her face pink with exertion and exaltation. She raised the pistol and fired into the ceiling.

"Lila!" Sky cried.

"Don't you 'Lila' me! I know what you call me behind my back! The whole studio knows!" Lila pointed the pistol at Sky and cranked out a terrible laugh. "Now you're not so haughty, are ya?"

Patrick came pumping into the room and stopped short. "Oh, God," he wailed. There was blood on his hand. His handsome face was beet red and twisted with remorse and exertion.

No one moved. "Lila honey, give me the pistol," Patrick said, breathlessly. He was slightly behind her and to her left. Lila stepped away from him so that she could unquestionably command the room.

"Now," she said, swallowing, staring at Sky with venom, "I want you to apologize. I want you to get down on your knees," she said, warming to her control of the situation, "and beg forgiveness for ruining my career." An evil smile slid onto her face. Vail, shaking, reached out for the arm of a chair to keep his legs from doubling under him. Sweat was running down his back.

Sky, standing almost dead center in the room, alone, had gone white. She knew that Lila would shoot if she didn't do it. The question was, did Lila have any bullets left? Sky was almost sure she did. She saw a movement out of the corner of her eye.

Sara took a step forward. "Don't you think introductions are in order?" she asked, her mouth dry as dust. Teddy took that moment to slip unnoticed around the corner and into the foyer.

"Shut up! I know who you are!" Lila snapped. "*Get down on your knees!*" she shrieked at Sky.

"I will not," Sky said, with an ethereal, shaky note in her voice.

"I will," said Kitty. "I'm the stand-in." She moved into the room, facing Lila.

Vail saw his moment and moved in front of Sky. "Vail! Don't—" Sky cried.

"Now shoot," he said, frightened.

"Get out of the way!" Lila screamed, waving the pistol wildly.

"If you shoot, you'll hit him, and I'll get you," Kitty said in an amazingly calm voice.

Diana, from the floor by the couch, began crying, her arm reaching out to Ned imploringly. He put his arms around her protectively.

Vail was focused on the maddened woman not three yards from him. "I'm not moving," he said, flicking his eyes at Patrick, wondering if he was going to move or not. He decided Patrick didn't have the guts. He glanced at Kitty and decided she did. "Put it down and we can all go home," Vail said, trying to sound stern. Sky put her hand on Vail's shoulder. He was weaving slightly, his face splotched. Sky felt so frightened that she didn't know if she could stay upright.

"Just put the gun down," Vail said to Lila again.

Kitty, from her station to his right, backed him up. He could see that she was gauging her attack. "No sudden moves," Vail said quietly.

Slowly the room was growing calmer. Then Sara took a step. Ned could see that she wanted to get behind Lila, but Lila's gun followed her for a moment. Sara stopped. The gun slid back to Vail and Sky. "If I get you," Lila lisped in a baby's voice, suddenly young and cute, "I'll get Sky too. Why doesn't Sky just do what I said? *Then* we can all go home," she mimicked him. Lila was drawn to Vail's terrified courage. It had become their contest. "You don't think I have any bullets left, do you?" she sneered. "Shall we play Russian roulette?" Sara imagined she could see lights turn on in Lila's eyes. It was eerie. Lila smiled sexily at Vail, feeling powerfully in charge of her part, as she slowly raised the barrel of the pistol. She inserted it into her mouth and sucked on it obscenely. It was a horrible gesture. Kitty was ready to spring, when Lila removed it and pressed the end of the barrel into her chin. Then she tilted the pistol at Vail again. "You don't think I'll do it, do you, kiddo?"

"No, of course not. You don't want to hurt anyone." His shirt was wringing wet, and a drop of sweat rolled into his eye.

Horribly, from her vantage point, Sara could see Belinda coming down the stairs holding a doll.

Lila put the pistol in her mouth again and sucked on it. Her pretty mouth puckered around it, then curved up in a cement smile. "Num-num," she sighed. Lila pulled the trigger.

The sound was deafening.

17

Lila's brains flew out of her skull. In the bloodstorm, as Lila crashed backwards, Ned reached up toward his daughter, and Sara heard Teddy sigh, "Oh, shit."

"Daddy," Sky moaned as she collapsed.

The room was resoundingly quiet, but the echo of the shot filled their heads. Time altered. They were frozen in tableau: Patrick bending over Lila; Kitty kneeling beside her; Diana still crouched by the sofa with Ned; Vail crawling to Sky, one arm bent over his head to protect it from mortars whizzing into the room from another era; Sara looking up at Belinda, who was sitting on the stairs.

"There are too damned many guns in this country," Patrick said.

Suddenly, the room was full of police whose heavy feet shook the floors. Questions were shouted, Sky was carried upstairs. Lindy, agog at the violence, and trembling, took Sara's hand when it was offered. They huddled in the kitchen with Vail, Diana, and Teddy. Gooey red dots spattered Sara's dress. Later still, Reed, Lenny Kaplan, and Sky's attorney, Mel Winters, arrived. Mrs. Sho was serving stiff drinks. Diana was directing her, keeping her voice low with dramatic calm. Reed came over to Sara, where she was now sitting on the bottom step of the main staircase with Teddy. "Are you okay?" Reed asked gently. She nodded. Lenny and Mel were making furious phone calls, their voices climbing out of the study. Reed put a hand on Sara's shoulder.

—231—

She looked up into his dark eyes and discovered they were warmly compassionate.

"This changes a lot," Reed said mysteriously. He was calm, yet seemed undone in some seminal way. "How's Belinda handling it?"

"She seems okay, excited by all the drama, though I think she was very frightened." How nice of Reed to remember Belinda with her.

Around midnight, Reed sat on the edge of the bed beside Sky. Her hand, draped over the side, listlessly stroked the top of the cheetah's head as the animal sat on the floor, ancient and wild, beside her. Kitty and Diana sat in the matching black and white chairs by the bow window that looked over the dark lake.

"You are lucky to be alive," Reed said to Sky. "That's all we have, you know. The present moment. Makes you think." He took her hand and pressed his cheek against it. Kitty brought her a glass of water. "He's right, isn't he, Kitty?" Sky said.

Kitty nodded. "Life is fragile," she said.

Sky drank the water, then pressed her face into the pillow. "Oh, God, am I to blame for this?"

Diana had come to the other side of the bed. "Of course not, darling. Don't think it."

"But people will believe it," Sky moaned.

"Nonsense," Diana said. But Kitty and Reed knew Sky was right.

The night passed in broken, dark moments. From somewhere deep on the grounds of the house, the cheetah let loose a growling moan. The sound of the gun kept exploding in Sky's head, and she kept seeing the halo of red spurting from Lila's hair.

Early the next morning, Sara walked around the garden by the pool with Ned.

"I feel like a coward," Sara said. "I didn't do enough."

The horrendous self-murder encouraged confidences that ordinary days would have silenced.

"You did fine, chicken." He stopped and touched a gardenia.

—232—

"No, I didn't," she insisted. "For one moment I wanted to know what my life would be like without Sky."

"Don't say that, Sara!" He was shocked and very angry. "You don't mean it!" He ripped a blossom off and pressed it to his nose, childlike.

"No, I don't. I can't say that," she murmured, accepting the flower from him. She saw Vail coming toward them.

"You and Sky are twins, and you love her," Ned said.

"You were very brave," she called out to Vail. "You're the family hero."

"Takes more than standing in front of Sky to make me a hero," he snickered.

Ned reached out and put both hands on Vail's shoulders. "If you never do another thing in your life, it's okay because of what you did last night. I'm proud of you, Son." Ned's eyes were watering.

Vail looked away, embarrassed and pleased. "I'm going to walk around the lake. Wanna come?" Sara shook her head.

When he was gone, Sara and Ned took up their per-ambulation of the garden again. As Sky's star had soared in the family, it had been the loss of Ned's attention that had grieved Sara most. She had lost Diana before that. Sara touched her tongue to the back of her false front teeth, and remembered the flute Diana had wanted her to play "bril-liantly."

"I think I fell off Pegasus deliberately," she said.

"What?"

"At the ranch," she said. "When I snapped out my front teeth. So I wouldn't have to play that damned flute any more." Sara had felt the implications of Diana's dismissal like a blow. And Pegasus's fate—that, too, had been her fault.

Sara and Ned walked around the pond where the golden fish glided among the lilies. She was thinking about her jumbled childhood years. "Didn't we come back to the States in nineteen thirty-eight?" she asked.

"Nineteen thirty-seven, just under the gun," he said.

They had returned to Ned and to the States, but Ned's readmittance into their circle was clouded by the loss of a lot of money. The feeling in the house was that he had done something stupid that had made life tougher for them all. Sara had been drawn to him because of it. She had felt they shared an unspoken bond, deeper, maybe, than the male bond he shared with Vail. But as Sara had warily approached her father, he'd vanished, too, lured away by the family's attention to Sky. "What is she to you, Dad?"

"Sky? She is the most vulnerable," he said. He didn't say all that he meant—she was tough and delicate, too.

"Sometimes I can't stand it, I'm so jealous of her," Sara confessed.

"That's a crock," he said roughly, falling into a jargon that seemed unnatural yet was perhaps more natural to him than any of them knew.

Sara spun on him. "I want you to love me, too!" she said with intense feeling. "Mother hasn't really cared about me since I broke my teeth!"

Ned was truly startled. "This shooting has upset you, chicken. I love you, and so does your mother. We're both proud of all of you." He turned away, patting her shoulder. "Better go inside. I don't want to hear any more of this crazy talk." They started up some stone steps. "You tell me about your Teddy."

Sara felt bereft. She looked wildly around the garden, conscious of a feeling of derangement. The too-red bougainvillea was choking the gazebo.

Ned was at the top of the steps, looking down at her vacantly, expectantly. "Tell me about Teddy," he repeated.

She thought of telling him that Teddy made jokes to keep people from touching him, or that Teddy sometimes drank a lot, but her father might take that as a snide criticism of himself. She wondered if Teddy trusted her—or anyone.

She said, "He's from Traumatown, New Jersey." He looked at her, puzzled. They walked back into the house.

That evening, Diana knocked on Sara's bedroom door. "Darling," Diana said as she came through the door not waiting for a reply. "Daddy said the most disturbing thing and I just want to clarify it with you."

Sara tensed. Her mother's voice held "that tone." She was lying on the bed in her slip, reading a book of plays. "Is Teddy here?" Diana asked, looking around.

"No, Teddy's drinking with Daddy."

"I was so shocked," Diana said, sitting on the edge of the bed. "And I know these dreadful events influenced you to say it. But Daddy and I do love you, and we're very proud of you. I haven't given a thought to your little accident with the horse for years," she went on. "I only knew that you loved music, that it made you laugh." Under her arching, pencil-thin eyebrows, her long, cool eyes rested on Sara, waiting for an acknowledgment.

Sara didn't have the energy or the courage to tell her mother what she really felt about the flute. "Just once I wish that I could have a conversation with Daddy without him running back to you with it. Did you see us from the window or what?"

"I certainly wasn't spying on you, if that's what you mean," Diana huffed. "And Daddy wasn't telling tales, he was simply concerned. We all are."

"Are we all concerned?" Sara snapped.

"Well, of course. The path you've set for yourself in the face of Sky's success is going to be so hard."

"What's really hard, Mother, is seeing Lindy look at Sky as her mother and look at me as a stranger. *That's* hard."

"I know it is, dear, but we all agreed it would be best for Lindy, and Sky loves her so, and here you are embarking on the career you always wanted—"

"How about later, Mother, when her questions about Vic can't be put off so easily? Is Sky going to pretend she was married to him?"

"I could say he was killed in the Korean War," Diana said.

Sara stared at her mother. "That's ridiculous. What if Vic showed up?"

"Well, we would all be very surprised," Diana said. "But I don't think he will. Daddy and I looked everywhere for him. He's gone, dear."

"Lindy ought to be told that I am her mother and that Sky is taking care of her so she has, well, two mothers, as you did, sort of." Sara was aware of how clumsy she often sounded with her mother.

"If you do that," Diana said, twisting her bracelet gently, "it will break her heart and Sky's. Just leave it alone for now. Concentrate on yourself. We all want it to be easy for all of you. Easier."

"It doesn't have to be easy," Sara said, "just fair." She felt defeated.

Diana let out a little puff of impatience.

Lenny Kaplan and Mel Winters were old hands at keeping the lid on and calling in favors. But even they couldn't extinguish the raging brushfire of publicity that fired the Hollywood skies after Lila's public suicide. The press laid siege to Sky's house, and the long holiday weekend became an internment. Mrs. Sho and the cook were attacked with questions and snapping flashbulbs when they entered or left. Anyone who came to the gate below the house was interrogated. Inside, the house had the unwholesome atmosphere of a prison. The family took refuge in their bedrooms, appeared for dinner, spoke little, and waited for it to end.

Vail basked in his role as family hero. But underneath, Lila's suicide had profoundly shocked him. "Women killing themselves, other women springing for them, sisters fainting, mothers weeping. God, what a time!" The way he said it sounded funny. Sara laughed.

"I can't do anything with him," Diana sighed. She looked at Sara for female support. "What on earth do you mean, Vail?"

"Sara knows," he said. "Ask her." He left.

"What did he mean, Sara Bay?" Diana asked.

Sara drifted away. "He's talking about the power of the pistol when women get hold of it, Mother. He was joking—sort of." She disappeared into the dining room.

Teddy thought that their incarceration was like being on a mountaintop in a blizzard. Only a few hardy souls could get in with supplies. But Teddy was loyal, and he said they should stay as long as necessary. "The bar and the view are both good," he added.

Reed and Lenny wanted everyone to stay on deck. The family must show support for Sky. Sky had dwelt in the sunshine of universal admiration for so long that the tornado of press speculations threw her off balance. In Saturday's paper one columnist asked the question, Had Sky's ambi-

—236—

tions driven Lila to madness and suicide? The press was well acquainted with Sky's snappish, private nature. Now they speculated whether her shy disdain in public had been masking her inner coldness. Sky exacerbated the situation by refusing to give interviews about "the accident," as Lenny called it. This more than anything else encouraged a New York columnist to print a damaging report: "Could Sky Wyman's family be concealing the full truth?" he asked. "Was she responsible for Lila's death?" The halcyon years between Sky and the press were gone.

On Sunday night Reed braved the press and the fans below to join the family for a morose dinner. Sky announced that she intended to work on Monday as usual. Diana threw up her hands and begged her not to submit herself to the hordes outside the studio and the certain questions inside.

Sky flared. "I will go, Mother!"

"I only meant—" Diana said.

"It won't get any easier to face people if I wait a week or a month."

"Then I'll go with you, if that's your decision," Diana said.

Reed hadn't seen the dynamics between Sky and her mother for some time. He had forgotten how controlling Diana was. Ned remained above it all. Reed felt that Ned's cowardly infatuation with Diana was just as dangerous for the triplets as their mother's demanding ambition.

Reed stepped into the tilting ground between Sky and her mother. "Diana, Sky needs to work tomorrow." Diana shook out her bracelets, annoyed at his intrusion.

It was finally decided that Reed and Sara would accompany Sky to the studio. That morning, Wade, Sky's driver, was uncharacteristically retiring. A deep silence settled in as the big car glided south on Vine.

Outside the studio gates, the swarming press had swollen the motley ranks of women in sunglasses, wearing the hat that Sky had made famous, and teenagers in penny loafers. As her car came into view, her fans waved their autograph books and reporters shouted questions. One man bellowed, "Who owned the gun?" a question that struck Sara as so bizarre that she gave him the finger and immediately felt better. The dark limo swept past the yelling crowd, its speed and purpose contemptuous of their long vigil. It came to rest at Sky's bungalow. Inside, sprays of flowers filled the room—from Sheldon, from Anne Abbott and members of the cast, and from her director, Nathan ("Pitcher") Steinmetz. It smelled like a mortuary.

Pitcher was a wiry, excitable man who suffered from high blood pressure. For years he'd felt like a phony. To mask his fear that people would find out that he didn't know what he was doing as a director, he'd behaved like a tyrant. He had cultivated this camouflage so assiduously that he was now known as the most sadistic director in town. His apparent contempt for actors was legendary. But from the first day on the set of *The Ginkgo Tree*, he'd fawned on Sky. This uncharacteristic behavior had made it difficult to direct her and had created a vacuum in the management of the production. Sky had filled it by directing herself. Pitcher, intensely aware that the picture was out of control, had not been able to bring it back under his command. His dreams at night were full of mayhem; his days were awkward and thorny. It was an unhappy set. His blood pressure had shot up to 280.

On this Monday morning, Pitcher was costumed in his director's garb—jeans, Eisenhower jacket, and his Orioles baseball cap (to cover his increasing baldness). Seeing Reed escort Sky onto the set fanned Pitcher's insecurities. He loathed Reed's liberal Director's Guild politics and feared any powerful competitor.

"The set's closed, just as you wanted, Sky," Pitcher said.

"Do you really feel like working? I mean, if you—" He stopped himself. He hated the way he sounded with her, and he particularly didn't want Reed, standing beside her, to pick up on it. Cool as ice, Sky said she was ready.

William Holden, her costar, was joking around with Clifton Webb and Dorothy McGuire at one end of the large set. Kitty stood under the warm lights. It was her first day as Sky's stand-in. When Ernie and Pitcher finished the first setup, Kitty joined the quiet commiserating group around Sky.

"This woman is one in a million," Sky said, patting Kitty on the shoulder. "She was there. She can tell you what happened." Sky liked the merry twinkle in Kitty's dark eyes. Instead of adoration it held respect.

Ernie's weekend had been hell, shocking in the first place because of Lila's suicide, doubly difficult because of Marjorie's long attachment to her. His wife blamed Sky for Lila's death. His morning had started on his front porch when a reporter tried to bribe him to shoot candids of Sky on the set today—letting the camera run after the director called "Cut!" Some cinematographers made a lot of money that way, catching actresses in unguarded moments, usually half-dressed moments. The editor of any film of Sky's could make extra money by selling the outs. Everyone wanted sexy shots of her thighs, crotch, and breasts. Ernie and Reed had caught a greensman on the set once with a camera taking shots of her cleavage.

Ernie shoved a stick of gum in his mouth. He was trying to give up smoking.

Sara took a seat on the edge of the set. "Jesus," she thought, "I'm back on this goddamned set." As the cast took their places, asked about their marks, or about their Thanksgiving turkeys, Sara watched people defer to her sister. Was it because of "the accident"? Sara decided not—their deference had an air of long familiarity. When Sky laughed, everyone laughed. When Sky turned rudely away, everyone pretended not to have seen it and, most of all, to be unaffected by it. From the grip to the director, Sara could see that everyone felt the heat of Sky's spotlight. People worked because of her.

Reed stood a little distance from Sara. When he had gone abroad, he had been trying to put some distance between himself and Sky, but her fame had followed him. Getting away from Sky was like trying to get away from the Cold War or Ike—they were omnipresent. Even in Bombay, giant painted images of her had smiled down on him from billboards surrounded by tangles of signs advertising Indian romantic adventures.

From the yawning shadows at the edge of the set, where Pitcher had consigned him, Reed watched Sky work for the first time in two years. Sky had once told him that under the lights, she felt freed. A director's call of "Action!" liberated her emotions for the take. She was sensitive, honest, and generous to the inexperienced. But she was also tough, demanding, selfish, and mercurial. Reed could picture her gloating to Lila when she'd won the part that poor woman had craved so much. Yet, as Reed watched her work, he was struck by her innocence. Her acting revealed the human heart.

Reed loved Sky. There had been a time when he was *in love* with her, too. But it had all come to an end when they were doing their third picture together, *Lisbon*. He had pressed her again to marry him. They had been sitting on Stage 9, just back from location. It was 1955. The electricians were shutting down, the actors had gone home. "I'm sorry," she'd said, "I'm not in love with you that way."

"I don't understand, Sky."

"Ask Vail."

"You triplets! You always say that when you don't want to answer!" he'd yelled at her, furious and hurt. He'd seen it coming, of course, but he hadn't let himself believe it.

Reed came out of his thoughts and looked at the woman he had always envisioned as his wife. People changed, and he understood the inevitability of those changes, but he mourned them, too. Sky had changed deeply, and Lila's suicide was going to change and isolate her even more.

Sky came off the set and sat down next to Sara while Pitcher set up the next shot. Ace fussed with her hair, and Cage repaired her makeup. Her press agent—the rapaciously competent Sammy—came up with a sheaf of papers.

"I don't want to say anything to the press. You make something up, Sammy." Sky saw Kitty moving onto the set. "Kitty was there. She'll give them a fair interview. She's smart." Sky waved him away.

"You've got to!" he cried.

"I don't have to do it!" she said. "You fix it." Sammy hustled off toward Kitty. "God, it's so draining," Sky moaned to Sara. "You just cannot imagine. The fans, the crowds. And the mail!—proposals of marriage, threats, awe, advice, pathos. Kids sleep outside the studio in sleeping bags to see me drive by. Whoever would have thought there were so many people in the world?!" she exclaimed. "It's so—"

"Lonely?" Sara asked.

"Yes."

Sky rose, sweeping her gown around her.

Pitcher was standing in front of them. "We're ready."

Pitcher insisted that Sky remove her hat for the scene, but she wouldn't do it. An embarrassing argument about the meaning of the scene erupted.

"Rosa just sits there, not doing anything," Sky snapped.

"She's got courage, Pitcher!"

In the midst of her tirade against the script, Sheldon Winters arrived with a clutch of dignitaries in three-piece suits. He tried to mollify her, enumerating for his startled East Coast financiers the recent tragic events that had victimized her, but Sky overrode him. "We're talking about artistic issues here!" she yelled. "Not business!" Pitcher was enraged but he wouldn't show it. It would be all over the lot that his set was out of control. Sara, open-mouthed at Sky's scene, could find no trace of the tractable twin who'd played with dolls. Pitcher finally found a way to close the argument; egos were appeased, Cage danced onto the set to powder Sky down, and the next take commenced.

Reed looked at Sara's sharp, beautiful profile. Her chin was resting on one fist as she gazed at her sister. Something in the tilt of her head—a fragile, crazy determination—moved him. He went over to her. "Come on. Let's get out of this hothouse." He took her arm and walked her out of the sound stage. They were on a little back street lined by the flat rumps of the sound stages. "Forgetting that fracas, what do you feel when you watch Sky acting?" he asked.

"Groan, groan. I don't call screaming like that acting," she said. He pressed her. "All right, sometimes I'd love to be Sky. Not today," she said.

He smiled boyishly at her. "Let's get some coffee. This way." They sat in the commissary drinking watery coffee among people in tricolor hats, coonskin caps, and medieval ball gowns. "I've watched you from a distance for years, but I don't know much about you," he said. Sara shrugged. "You and Vail are the only people who have double vision when it comes to Sky, seeing the old and the new. Sky will never change back, Sara. I'm glad you stayed today, but it was selfish of me to ask you."

"Why?"

He thought for a moment. "Because I wanted to have this talk with you."

"What?"

He weighed his next words. "Something so outrageous happened this weekend," he said, looking at his hands. He went on very slowly. "It makes everything we do now seem pathetic unless we're absolutely honest. Do you know what I mean?" She nodded stiffly; she had had the same feeling with Ned the morning after the shooting. "We're not very close; yet I feel I know you even though I don't know about you."

"Just say it."

"I think you should stop acting, find another life so you won't always be compared to Sky." He looked a trifle apologetic but firm, too.

Sara felt her cheeks burn with anger. "Oh, you do, do you? I guess it's just never occurred to you, the big Hollywood director, that I need *work*. In the theater. Sky doesn't know anything about the theater. She thinks Molière is my agent! You could help me get work instead of trying to push me out of the business like everyone else. Jesus, Reed, you of all people—"

"I'm trying to help!"

"Well, don't bother! Better people than you have tried, and I guess I'll just live my life my own way!" She jerked her chair back and jumped to her feet. "You could do a lot for me, and I haven't pestered you at all, have I? Just bug out!" She strode down the center aisle of the commissary. Heads turned.

He caught up with her just outside the door. "Calm down, will you?" She shook his hand off. "I'm on your side!"

"The hell you are!" She dodged around him.

"Stop a minute!" he yelled. "I'll give you the name of an agent in New York!"

"I suppose that's someone who will take me on as a favor to you!"

"Of course they'll do it as a favor to me! How do you think people *get* agents? She'll audition you, she'll send you out on casting calls, and what you do with it is up to you."

"No thanks! I'll help myself. I've been doing it a long time."

He watched her go, cursing himself. For a graceful guy he had certainly screwed that up.

At the actors' end of the lot, Sandra Dee, Sal Mineo, and Fess Parker were taking time out. They sat on the porch of their dressing rooms, their feet up on the rail, and talked about what role Sky had played in Lila's suicide.

18

Teddy sat in the darkened theater, his hands on the back of the seat in front of him, his chin resting on his knuckles, watching Sara play the role he'd written for her. She was skilled, determined, passionate, but it was utterly impossible to look at her and hear her without thinking of Sky. He knew the reviewers would dredge it all up when the play opened. He shuddered. The sign on the marquee had gone up, but he'd held off his own aching anticipation until he and Sara could see it together. He looked around for Marissa. Where was the little bitch? Off stealing kisses from someone else? On-stage, the patter of the dialogue he had written played on. Very briefly, he let himself bathe in his own brilliance.

When rehearsal was over he took Sara's hand and led her outside. The sharp spring wind slapped them as they came out on the street and looked up at their names painted on the marquee of the Circle in the Square, an Off-Broadway theater.

"I don't deserve that," he said. "You do, but I don't. What an accident." He giggled. He gently drew her scarf around her throat to protect her voice.

Sara barely heard Teddy undervaluing himself, a self-scorn that was to grow between them like a malignant plant. She was proud of him, and she was proud of herself. They'd earned it.

For months after Sara had returned to New York, the image of Reed thrusting his card at her, the look in Lindy's eyes,

—244—

and the horror of Lila's suicide haunted her. Sara made her rounds with feverish determination; it helped her to forget.

"So, tell me a little about yourself," was usually the first thing the casting directors said to her.

"My name is Sara Wyman," she'd begin.

"Any relation to Sky Wyman?" they'd ask, chuckling.

She'd take a beat, then say, "I'm her sister."

"Oh, really?" they'd say, and they'd smile.

Or the faceless office clerks, as anonymous as dust, and as annoying, would say, "The speaking parts are already cast—there are some walk-ons. The play has a lot of atmosphere. Leave your name and address. You look familiar. What's your name again?" If she felt up to it, she'd tell them she was Sky's sister. If she didn't, she'd go on to the next office or theater—the Broadhurst, the Plymouth, the Barrymore, the Majestic, the Booth. It was a turnstile—the actors' tough rounds to get noticed, to get cast, to be made real.

"Rounds" meant looking for work, going from producers to casting directors to agents. It meant smiling when she felt like punching people out. Some days it was degrading. She talked to silk vests and to corduroy vests; to nasty men and to compassionate men; to bitter, aging secretaries; and to polished, manicured producers. Young or old, they all crept back to their big or tiny apartments at night only to spill out of them the next day in their costly shoes from Churches or in their high spike heels from Leeds. All of them oiled the machinery of the theater.

She'd kept her job at the club on Second Avenue, fending off malicious or drunken men who "thought they knew her from somewhere." She worked in a merchandising office collating reports, walking around and around a huge table, picking up sheets of paper, number by number. She'd filed accident reports in an insurance office.

Sometimes agents or producers would see Sara because they knew she was Sky's sister. She was, after all, this oddball actress who looked and sounded like Sky but who wasn't Sky. Just when she thought no one would hire her she landed a small part Off-Broadway at the Cherry Lane Theater. It was the spring of 1959. They were well into rehearsals when the director said to Sara, "No, honey, let's do a bit here. Move like Sky does, just a hint, like a raising of the hand and that twitchy expression she gets on her face. Sort of sullen and pure. You know what I mean." Sara had had a bad morning: Her cat had escaped from the apartment and had been run over; she and Teddy had had a mean argument the night before; and she hadn't been able to find her new snakeskin shoes.

She flung years of frustration at the director. "Just where do you think Sky got that twitch and the little lift of her hand? From *me!* you fucking mouse! From me!" She'd stomped off the stage. She was fired.

Since then, she'd gotten other bits and walk-ons, little character roles that, had she been anyone else, she might have been able to use to begin building a career. Then, at a party, she met Arlene Sayers, an agent who didn't seem to care whose sister she was, an agent who'd liked her looks and her abilities.

Arlene Sayers' gray hair was cut in a strict page boy, her trademark. Narrow blue eyes surveyed a corrupt world; her strong, unforgettable face was as motionless as a statue's. "The first thing we have to do," Arlene said to Sara, "is separate you professionally from your sister." Sara had gone home to Teddy that afternoon feeling like a new person.

Living with Teddy in the apartment on Bleecker Street was like teetering on an outer edge of daily life—honest, thrilling, amusing. At night, they'd tell each other the disappointments or the lunatic adventures of their separate days. Bad as her days could be, Teddy's were worse.

"I'm a good actor!" he'd yell, pacing their minimal apartment with the butterfly chairs and the black tables. But the only role he'd had since leaving school had been as a butler. In desperation, he had started working as a gofer for Mort Kahn, a theatrical producer. It was a demanding, demeaning job that took the heart out of him. Mort loved to watch his underlings cringe and cower. Teddy spent many hours telling Sara why Broadway was dead, his diatribes laced with his condemnations of the plays Mort slapped on his desk. "Dreck. Pure, unadulterated dreck," Teddy said.

"Then write your own play!" she'd screeched one night. To show her that Broadway, and especially Mort, wouldn't know a good play when they saw it, Teddy wrote a play that weekend. Mort took one look at the title page and laughed at Teddy, "the gofer who thought he could write, ha!"

But the play, called *Sudden*, was good. Even Mort could see that. He paid Teddy five hundred dollars as the playwright and told him to rewrite it. When Teddy finished, Mort got the backing and mounted it Off-Broadway. Teddy had written in a meaty, supporting role for Sara. It had been a battle to make sure Sara got the part, but Teddy had fought courageously for her and won.

Sudden was a play about emotional corruption and betrayal within a marriage. The cast was small—the husband and wife, the wife's mother, a neighbor, and the husband's brother.

It was March of 1960. *Sudden* was opening in April. Sara felt she had become the play, the character, the set, the theater. Everything else was secondary, and anyone not connected with the play was hopelessly outside reality. They rehearsed twelve hours a day. At night Sara studied lines; the play spun in her dreams. She was closer to her fellow actors than they were to their husbands or wives. Teddy was wildly cutting and revising, typing up the script changes at night and handing them out in the morning. Each rehearsal became a skein of new lines weaving a confusing vine around the old. Everyone stumbled over new and old lines, terrified of "going up"—saying the wrong lines during performance. It was bad enough in final dress rehearsal—actors were going up all over the stage, stammering around, making it up until they found their way back to the revised script. Sara loved the chaos and the risk.

Even on opening night, she wasn't nervous. She couldn't wait to get onstage, and she hated getting off. Toward the end of the second act, she'd come out of the green room early to wait in the wings for her cue. The audience was warm, and the performance, considering the lunatic rehearsals, was smooth and powerful. She looked across the actors onstage to the stairs on the other side, which wound up to the dressing rooms. Teddy was standing under the stairs, his cheeks flushed, his hands in his pockets. It was such a big night for him, yet he looked forlorn. She wondered why he wasn't out in the house.

The lines told her that she had about two minutes to go. She looked back at Teddy under the stairs. Marissa, an understudy, had joined him. They were kissing passionately.

Sara heard her cue in a sea of numbed pain and stumbled onto the stage. She acted badly; her concentration was gone; she flubbed her best line.

Marissa and Teddy were sitting next to the first act flats, drinking brandy out of paper cups, when Sara exited on their side of the backstage area. He saw the injury and the accusation in her eyes, and he knew she knew. He was glad she'd seen that other women were attracted to him. He wanted her to know that.

Sara watched him bob up energetically. He whispered how good she'd been. His flattery disgusted her as much as his dalliance with Marissa; he'd sounded just like her mother, who'd always said she was good just to placate her.

The party afterwards was at a small restaurant on Greenwich Avenue. Teddy spent most of the time with Mort, the man he loved to hate, and with Marissa. Sara spent the most exciting night of her life with old friends from school and with Arlene, her new agent. They were all plastered by the time the reviews came out, but Arlene could still read.

"A brilliant play full of anger at the small betrayals that can corrupt a marriage," one reviewer said. Another hailed it as "the new drama." It was a surprise Off-Broadway hit. Sara's reviews were good, but they did not sing as Teddy's did. "A steady hand with big emotions," one said. "Sky's sister throws down the gauntlet," wrote another. Others were less kind: "Sky Wyman's sister, Sara, while passionate and at times exhilarating in her part of Donna Jean, should leave the acting to her extraordinary sister." Teddy, and even Mort, were outraged. "That's a cruel review! You're much better than that!"

Around dawn Teddy and Sara walked home.

"So now you know," Teddy tittered. "But I'm sorry you had to find out tonight. You really were very good."

"Just what is it that I've found out?" she asked. "That you are moving out? That you don't love me? That you never loved me?"

"No!" he declared. "You know how weak I am. I just couldn't stand the temptation. Marissa idolizes me. I've never been idolized." He felt guilty. He was a bastard. He put his head in his hands and groaned dramatically as he walked. Sara put her arm around him. A man walked by them, checking them out with his eyes. "I love you," he said through his hands. "Only you. It will never happen again."

About a month after *Sudden* opened, Sara and Teddy were returning home after practically closing the Village Gate, a jazz club. He'd been sober when the evening started, but now he lurched across the living room of their apartment, no shred left of the sweet, classy man she loved. She was learning that when drunk, Teddy was a monster.

"How'd you think it went tonight?" she asked, removing her coat and scarf.

"You were terrible, my dear, just dreadful."

"Thank you. Your play stinks, too, but we're doing our best to salvage it onstage."

The fight escalated, helped along by Sara losing her temper completely. That was a real mistake with Teddy. They shouted and cried, thrusting at each other with the arsenal of weapons lovers own. Finally, exhausted but still discontented, Teddy tripped and landed on the edge of the blue sofa. His backbone collapsed, and he hunched over his hands, clasped in his lap. Sara thought a truce had been called.

"You are a phony and a liar," he said, softly, more devastating than any shriek.

Absorbing the pain of his words, she stared down at the carpet and started to count each tiny blue thread.

"I never loved you," he said. "Your pathetic struggles against your sister. Why don't you just give up and kill yourself?" He laughed, then headed for the bedroom.

"You stay here!" she ordered. When he disregarded her, she plunged into the bedroom after him. They tussled; he slapped her hard, then passed out on the chaise.

She slept on the sofa in the living room. The next morning, he bounced in, joking about her sleeping on the couch. But as her head came up from the blanket, and he saw the reddish blue welt from her temple to her chin, he knew he had hit her. But when? He couldn't remember. He sat on the floor by the sofa, weeping. He begged her forgiveness. How could any man hit the woman he loved? There was something horribly wrong with him.

"Why don't you stop acting?" he said gently, sitting beside her. "We could have a baby, our own baby!"

Sara went into the bathroom, the only place she could be alone. What would happen to that baby, should they have it? she wondered, thinking of Belinda. It was noon; she had hours before going to the theater. She wanted to stay in the bathroom all day. Teddy was outside, hesitant and contrite, suggesting breakfast at the Plaza.

At the theater Sara shared a dressing room with two women, Dee and Sally, both solid actresses. Dee played the sexy neighbor in the show, and Sally played Sara's mother.

When Sara appeared at the door that night, she'd put her street makeup on with a trowel to cover the bruise on her face. But it didn't work; Sally noticed immediately. "God, did a bus hit you?" she whispered in her low theatrical voice.

Sara had a strong reply all ready that she gave with professional gestures and intonations, all about the angle of the dining room door. But later, as she left the room, she heard Dee say, "I think she found out about Marissa, and the bastard hit her."

"I doubt that," said Sally.

"Well, she's bound to find out," said Dee, who was close to Marissa. "Marissa says that he's just carrying Sara anyway."

"Don't believe everything Marissa tells you, Dee," Sally admonished. "Sara's good in that part."

"Yes, but she'd never have gotten it without Teddy!"

Instead of running and hiding, which she felt like doing, Sara stepped back into the doorway and stared at them with all the righteous venom she could muster. Dee ducked; Sally met her eyes and drawled, "You got a lot of grit, Sara Wyman."

The horrendous cycle of her life with Teddy found its engine. Afraid that she would leave him, he stayed sober for a while, began writing another play, and started teaching. But gradually, he slipped into the boredom that had led to excess. He was becoming well known and sought after. The play was enjoying a long popular run.

Sky called with congratulations. She and Sara laughed and giggled—it felt like old times. "Have you heard from Vail?" Sky asked. Sara had not. "He's sent me a play!" Sky went on.

"I hope it's good," said Sara.

"It's terrible. This is the second one he's written. How can I tell him?"

Shortly after that, Sara received a play from Vail, hand-written from edge to edge of the paper. "I can't read this," cried Teddy, tossing away the variously colored pages that had been written in every state in the country. The play was all about how white people put down black people.

"Except for Maggie, Vail didn't see a black person until he went to Korea!" Sara said.

All through the summer and fall of that year, Teddy sank into another bad period. He boasted of drinking a quart of vodka a day and lacing it with Percodan or Demerol. He always had marijuana, coyly called Mary Jane by many, and as he got richer, he passed it around at parties. Sara nagged him about getting his life together so that they could *have* a life. New friends told him Sara was jealous, that there was nothing wrong with him, that he was the O'Neill of the sixties and would soon have a play on Broadway. Sara and Teddy stopped making love; often she slept in the study to avoid the sweet, pungent odor of vodka that blossomed from his pores.

The play kept running. It was easy for the youngest, angriest playwright in America to flirt with adoring women. Soon he was sublimating his macho drives in other ways. He ordered Sara about at dinner parties; he took foolish risks, walked in front of speeding cars, or started fights in restaurants. "It's your fault," he'd often say after she got him home. "You don't understand what sort of man I am. I'm sensitive, high-strung. But you just want a big cock." Once she found him squeezed behind the stove, all curled up. "What the hell are you doing there?" she asked him.

"Hiding," he said, and passed out.

Teddy kept writing, wedging the shorter work periods in between drinking bouts. Sara's friends urged her to pull out, but she loved Teddy. She was harnessed to a far deeper fear than his excesses while he was drunk; that she would never find another man who loved her for herself. Vail sent another play.

On the surface their life had the best that the early sixties in New York could offer. *Fiorello!*, *The Best Man*, *Toys in the Attic* were all playing on Broadway. The streets were full of the strains of "Never on Sunday"; every secretary on the subway was reading a battered copy of *Advise and Consent*. By the end of 1960 the Eisenhower years were over; John F. Kennedy was president. There was an unspoken expectation of renewal everywhere.

"Got room for two more?"

It was Vail! His reddish brown hair stuck out under his cap, and his hazel eyes glowed with the surprise of his arrival. Behind him stood a tall, dark-haired man who was introduced to Sara as Bondy Goldstein.

"For you, anything!" Sara cried, giving Vail a big hug. He smelled of tobacco and the December night air.

"Guilt's chasing me!" he declared, dropping his knapsack on the new couch. "I couldn't face going home to Sunday dinner with Diana. Hi, Ted, how's it goin'?" Teddy gave him a drink. Vail looked a little wan but maniacally cheerful. Sara hadn't seen him in two years—since Hollywood, since the suicide.

Vail had written an essay on Resnais's *Hiroshima Mon Amour* which had been picked up by the *Village Voice*. He'd come to New York to do a series of reviews and essays on foreign films. Bondy had accompanied him and was off to the Bronx to see his folks. Bondy had a luxurious head of thick, silky hair that matched his dark brown eyes. His liquid smile saved his pale face from being a hard mask of sorrow, and his relaxed style was a good foil for Vail's animated high spirits.

"You were the one who saved Vail in Korea!" Sara cried, suddenly putting the pieces together.

Vail leaped off the couch. "Jesus, let's not talk about the war!"

"Yup," said Bondy to Sara. He grinned. "Pulled old Vail right out of the ditch."

"What happened?" Teddy asked.

"Nothing happened!" Vail said. "I'm here, end of story." He glanced at Bondy nervously. "I saw Sky recently. Boy, is she in trouble," Vail went on to Sara. "She won't do any press interviews, hasn't since the suicide. Fans are mad at her. Studio's furious. She's so stubborn! Did you read any of my plays?"

"Oh, sure," Sara said when Teddy didn't respond.

"I know the world isn't ready for them yet," Vail exclaimed. "I'm on the outer edge. I'm trying to bring out the truth of life, the way we learned it in Korea as opposed to all the crap that's around today." Once he got going, he was unstoppable. "Sky's bound hand and foot in tinsel. I write with my guts."

"They would be easier to read if you typed them," Sara said.

"Fuck that. If someone's really interested, they'll read them. My plays're honest."

The three of them stayed up till three listening to records—Billie Holiday and Thelonius Monk. The next night, Vail and Bondy went to Teddy's play. "Not bad," Vail said afterwards. "Pretty hip." He thought Sara was great, better than Sky could have been in the part.

For the next week, after performances, they hit most of the spots Sara and Teddy knew or dropped in on parties chockablock with actors acting. "God," Vail said, "much as I need company, why is everyone hung up on noise in this town?" He found the music overpowering, the laughter false and irritating, the pot pedestrian. They went from the Kettle of Fish Bar on Macdougal Street, right around the corner from Teddy's old place, over to the Village Vanguard where they heard higher-class jazz and where they bumped into Kerouac trying to read poetry again. But he was too drunk to do anything but curse the audience. Vail lectured Sara and Teddy about how New York's intelligentsia ignorantly dismissed beats as petty criminals who sidebarred in poetry. "Unwashed eccentrics who need love," the *Saturday Review* had just labeled them. Teddy and Sara hauled him out of the Vanguard up the basement stairs to the street. They went uptown to a club on Second Avenue where they danced their guts out to ten-decibel rock and roll.

Sara came panting and sweating off the tiny mirrored dance floor and flung herself into a plastic chair at the table Teddy's influence had won them.

"I guess you're really making it in Teddy's play," a familiar voice yelled at her. It was Patrick. She hadn't seen him since Lila's suicide. He was with an older man he didn't bother to introduce. Sara started to introduce Vail, but Patrick had gone on with his conversation with the older man. It was peculiar. She shrugged at Vail and looked back at Patrick who was starting toward the door. He turned and came back to Sara and Vail. His blue eyes were bloodshot. He said, "You hurt me. Just by being alive. I can't stay, and I can't talk to you. You just remind me too much of Sky and all that pain. Sorry." He turned and stumbled off.

"Such a sweet guy," Sara said bitterly to Vail.

Vail was yelling in Sara's ear over the music: "You and Sky have bought in and sold out. You're not being honest with yourself. You're freeloading on Teddy. How come you never get anything on your own? You're still young and pretty."

"I don't need this," said Sara, breaking away from him and hurrying off the dance floor. Vail thought she was going to the ladies room. She never came back.

About one in the morning Vail was sitting in the club with a woman he'd never met. Teddy and Sara had disappeared. He dumped the woman and went back to the Vanguard; the uptown places didn't interest him anyway. Bondy showed up with some good dope—Vail's first real chemicals in the city's playground of heroin, Dolophine (Bondy's favorite), pot, and barbiturates. He called Sara, apologized for whatever he'd said, and told her he was going to stay with Bondy somewhere below Canal Street.

New York's Village and the large, crowded areas south of it became Vail's second home, because everyone there read all the books he read, like Sartre and Beckett; they were cynical and anti-Establishment, cared as little for patriotism as he, and were cool: Relationships were held at a distance, while coupling was as common as a cold and about as passionate. Vail swung between that scene and the drug scene. He stumbled into Paula, a curvaceous blond prostitute, who

—254—

got minor detonations by removing and swallowing the cotton strip inside Benzedrine inhalers.

One night in February he was sitting on a rag rug, high on goofballs, watching someone shoot up, when Paula's sister, a fragile, sullen girl, keeled down the stairs in a junkie nod and broke her neck. Vail was not too dopey to know enough to get out.

The next day his essay on Antonioni's *L'Avventura* and *La Notte* appeared in the *Voice*.

Sara was putting on makeup in her dressing room when Vail appeared. "Your Antonioni piece was great!" she said.

"I'm slipping back through the mirror to you," he announced. He looked awful. Dark circles ringed his eyes. "Bondy's been shipped to the city jail." He flopped down in a chair. He knew Sara would give him Bondy's bail money, but he didn't want to ask her. "You liked it, huh?"

"Sure. You should stick to essays and reviews."

"How's every little thing?" he said.

"Not good." Over the last few months, Teddy's binges had been frightening. Whenever Sara tried to help him, he'd strike out at her, feel guilty, sober up, say he'd never drink again. Overjoyed, they'd see friends, dine out, spend long weekends in the apartment making love. Then he'd start drinking again. She never knew what she would find when she got home from the theater. But she stayed with him; she couldn't believe that the cycle couldn't be altered. She didn't have the strength to reprise it for Vail.

"Teddy's finished his new play," she said. "He's with his agent right now." When Teddy got back—if he had good news—they were going to celebrate with dinner out and probably end up at the Metropole where Dizzy Gillespie was working out some odd sounds. "You can come, too," she said.

Five minutes before she was to go on, Teddy burst into her dressing room. "It's a great play! That's a direct quote, sweetie!" He threw his arms around Sara and danced her about the room. "Wait till you see it, Vail. It's going to be on Broadway! And it's got a smashing part for Sara, completely tailored for her." He kissed her. "She's been through hell." He went over to Vail and shook his hand. "I put her through hell, but no more. No more!" He whisked back to Sara. "Bob's taking bids on it! They want to put a movie star in the male lead. Movie stars are box office now."

"They've always been box office," Vail mumbled.

"Bob's his agent," Sara told Vail. "A top theatrical agent."

"We're really going to celebrate tonight!" Teddy declared.

Vail didn't want to be around happy people, especially Teddy, whose plays were being produced. All he could do was write about the creative work of other people. "I'll catch up with you later," he said, lifting himself out of the chair.

"But Vail—" Sara cried.

Vail waved and smiled from the door and disappeared.

Vail called Schurl, who was still hanging out in Marin. Schurl said he didn't have the bail money for Bondy but suggested Jerry who was in Eagle Rock, Los Angeles; but, Schurl added morosely, Jerry never went further south than Sunset Boulevard for his connections. This meant that Jerry was in virtual hiding and wouldn't have any money.

Vail still didn't want to ask Sara for the money, so he got a part-time job as a desk clerk at a hotel on the Upper West Side. He moved into a cold water flat on Ninety-seventh Street near Amsterdam Avenue. It was part of a line of old brownstones with spaces in the back where gardens used to be. He didn't have any electricity, having taken the place over from a friend who frequented the Macdougal scene and had disappeared into it, so Vail used candles. They cast an eerie, soft glow over the two little rooms. It was particularly lulling to bathe by candlelight. He wrote with a sensual demonic energy, killing loneliness with marijuana. In these moments, sitting in his candlelit bath, writing and smoking, he felt that Riva was truly dead. The grass dissolved memories of Clay Street and of Sky's mansion; he could hunt for his mother's face and, gratefully, not find it.

When Bondy got out of the pokey, he brought some hash over to the Ninety-seventh Street apartment. Prime stuff, he called it. High together, in a mad fit, they moved down to the Lower East Side to Tenth Street between Avenues C and D. This apartment had flowered wallpaper. But when Vail got high there, all the flowers on the wall opened out to him like grasping, tumescent, female genitalia. They were swallowing him up. Like a victim trussed for the sacrifice, he couldn't move and couldn't scream. He was stupefied in his private terror.

"At least you're feeling something, Vail boy," said Bondy, flying high and happy. He was leaning against a flowered wall that did not reach out to get him the way it did Vail. "The worst crime is *not* feeling at all. We're living in apathy. Technology has us by the nuts." Someone had left a TV in the apartment; Vail turned it on to make the flowers hold back for a while. Somebody was talking about the John Birch Society. Vail thought of his mother. He changed stations, but the commercials made him sad. They were a symptom of the plastic apathy engulfing the land. "Torpor," he muttered, "a goddamned national torpor." He started shrieking: His heart had atrophied and he had felt it stop.

Bondy telephoned Sara from the pay phone on the corner. She took a cab over and almost fell back from the smell of garbage and urine and wine. Vail was huddled by the bed, crying, his knees pulled up to his chest. "You are behaving like an idiot," she said. "Now get up and get dressed. Here, I brought you a change of clothes. Put them on right now."

"She saved me," Vail wrote to Sky. "I was about to be sucked into that hell beneath the sea. I would have drowned. I'm writing a play about it. When are you going to see Sara in *her* play?"

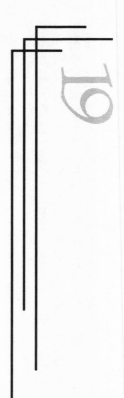

19

Sky was already planning to see Sara in New York on her way to the Bahamas, where her next film, *Paradise Key*, was to be shot.

"We'll all go," Sky told Kitty as they lounged in the warm afternoon on Sky's patio. Nigeria, the cheetah, was stretched out on the warm flagstones near the two women, her eyes closed, her giant paws at rest.

"Sara will like that a lot," Kitty said.

"Look at me!" Belinda shrieked from the pool. She was an avid swimmer. She climbed out of the pool and hopped on the diving board. Sky and Kitty turned. Lindy ran, bounced up, and hit the water in a rashly conceived swan dive. Sky waved as Lindy did a breaststroke to the end of the pool.

Kitty and Sky went back to the script which Kitty held, cuing Sky on her lines. But they couldn't really pay attention to it—they were laughing too much. Since "the accident," the family's euphemism for Lila's suicide, Kitty had become a pal, the confidante and real friend Sky had never had. Kitty did with grace and competence whatever was needed. And Sky preferred running lines with Kitty, who had a robust sense of humor, lively ideas about character, and who knew the personalities of the writers and directors.

Sky was also fascinated by Kitty's treasure trove of stories—about her father, about growing up near the reservation in Montana, about the history of the Assiniboin Indians, who came from the country owned by the Blackfeet and the Crow and the Sioux. She was just as entertaining about the stuntmen in Hollywood—"good old boys" with scars and muscles, grins and little kindnesses, courage and jokes. They were an exclusive brotherhood, bonded together as much as the Indians were.

Kitty told stories about directors being catered to, about those who had no idea what a stunt involved, who demanded more and more from the men, who whispered "Action" softly, whose egos needed to be cranked up hydraulically like their cranes, who expected applause after every shot. She talked about bike stunts, about falls off roofs, over waterfalls and rapids, out of planes, about faked fights, about driving cars over cliffs, about explosions that didn't go off, and about those that did.

"I have more fun with you than with anyone," said Sky, keeping an eye on Lindy.

For Kitty's part, Sky was the best friend she, too, had never had. Sky always kept her eye on the main track, something Kitty had trouble doing. Sky had supported her for stunt gaffer on *Once in Nashville*, which had given Kitty's career a giant boost. But Sky was not a ladder for Kitty. She was a challenging friend, someone who inspired protection and loyalty. She was the loneliest person Kitty knew, and the most sensitive. Sky could walk into a room and tell Kitty in five minutes what the temperature was, who was angry at whom, who was involved with whom, who was phony, and who wasn't. They gossiped ceaselessly with each other.

"But when he fell—" Kitty said.

"Into the air bag—"

"Sure, but—" They were screaming with laughter so much they could hardly speak.

"And," said Kitty, drawing herself up and looking glum, "the director said, 'Dumb, dumb, double-dumb. Can't we do something different?' The guy's just practically killed himself—"

"Was that the stuntman you had the affair with?" Sky asked.

"Yeah. That was Hank. The sweetest man who ever lived."

Diana's silver bracelets clinked as she came through the side door. "My! Such a good time!" she called out. "Hello, darling," she called to Lindy. Diana sat down beside them.

"I just came along to see how you were and to help you with your lines."

"Oh, don't bother, Mother," Sky said, seeing Diana's pale classically manicured hands curl around the script lying on the tile. "Kitty's already cued me on them."

Kitty was becoming a fixture. "Oh, I don't mind, dear," Diana said, picking up a pencil. "I haven't even read it yet." It had been Diana's habit to run lines with Sky since her first film. She leaned back on the chaise and slipped on her shaded, bifocal glasses with the white frames. Sky scratched the top of Nigeria's head. "And how are you, Kitty?" Diana asked.

"Very well, Mrs. Wyman."

"Come along, Sky," Diana said. "Let's have a few lines, at least."

"Mother, Kitty's cued me!"

Diana lapsed into silence. She was beginning to feel supplanted. "Vail wrote me the other day," Diana said. "It's tragic about him really, I don't know what's the matter with him, but I guess he's making ends meet by writing those articles. He says Sara's really good in her play."

"We were just talking about that," Kitty offered. "Sky thought of stopping in New York on her way to the Bahamas and the location shoot."

"Splendid, darling." Lindy pulled herself out of the pool and ran over to them. She did not look like Sara except around her mouth when she laughed. She was lean and promised to be tall like her errant father, Vic. She had Sky's eyes and her father's light brown hair. Moving with a coltish grace, she flicked her eyes coyly at Sky. Lindy's passion in life was riding. Sky, who kept her own horse at a riding club near the lake, had bought Lindy a horse for her birthday, and Lindy spent most of her time on it. She was also a fine student, getting good marks in everything, particularly history and arithmetic.

"Is it noon yet?" Lindy asked.

"Oh, sweetcakes, I'm sorry," Sky said, "but I can't ride today."

"But you promised!" Lindy shot back.

"Belinda!" Diana admonished her.

"But she promised. We almost never get to ride together!"

"Riding in public is very hard for Sky," Diana said.

Kitty watched the battle lines being drawn.

Belinda was proud of her famous mother, and she loved the envy of her riding club friends when she rode with Sky. But today was special. A new boy in her class who'd said he didn't believe she had any connection to Sky Wyman had grudgingly agreed to meet her at the stables at noon. Lindy had told him she would be riding with her mother, Sky.

"I'm really sorry, Lindy," Sky said. "But I'm going on location soon, and there's a million things to do." Sky waited for the blowup. She was not disappointed.

Lindy screamed and stamped her bare feet and flung down her towel and jumped on it. "You always disappoint me!" she shrieked. Nigeria sat up, looking uneasy. Sky hooked her hand through its collar.

"Belinda, go to your room this instant!" Diana ordered.

Sobbing, her face red, Lindy wailed, "Why can't I have a normal life like everyone else?" Instead of leaving, she sat down in a chair. Sky and Diana pointedly ignored her. Lindy's screams of rage and frustration increased. "You're afraid of the press!" Lindy yelled at Sky.

She hit her mark. Sky shot out of her chair. "If you do this for one more second, I shall never ride with you again!"

Lindy stopped screaming abruptly and swallowed hard. She looked up at Sky blankly. "Will you ride with me tomorrow?"

"All right. But we'll have to do it at six in the morning." The press had caught on to her habit of riding with Lindy.

Lindy smiled at Sky, the moment when she looked most like Sara. "Promise?" Her long lashes were wet with tears.

"I promise," Sky said.

Kitty said, "I'll ride with you right now!"

"Okay," Lindy said, appeased. She liked Kitty, and when she rode with her, Kitty did stunt tricks on her horse, Nutmeg. Kitty could pull a crowd of people in no time. She was a good substitute.

When Lindy and Kitty were gone, Diana put a hand to

her temple. "You and Sara used to have tempers like that," she said, "but you got over it."

"Oh, Mother," Sky groaned, "we never did."

"You most certainly did! Don't you remember that terrible scene Sara caused in Geneva?" Sky didn't remember. "She rolled on the floor of the hotel lobby, shrieking as though I'd stabbed her, which is what I wanted to do. So shameful."

"Why was she screaming?"

"Oh, I don't remember," Diana said.

Though she remembered nothing like Belinda's tantrums in her own childhood, Sky said, "How did you cure us of them?"

"I never gave in. Our family had standards," she said, implying, Sky imagined, that Vic's family had none because bad genes were incurable.

Though Kitty made life much more enjoyable, Sky wasn't satisfied with her own work. She wanted to do roles that challenged her. But her public was satisfied with anything, and the studio wanted her to coo at her leading men and wear fewer clothes. Sky had thought of producing, as many stars were beginning to do, but she didn't know how, and no one, except Kitty, encouraged her efforts in that direction.

She hadn't been on location in several years, and she eagerly looked forward to it. Yet no sooner had the studio bought the script for "Paradise," a big-budget, romantic mystery, than problems on the billing began. Her costar, Sonny Somaine, wanted top billing; his career was in high gear and he expected it. But Sky always got top billing. Mel was negotiating for her, and Sheldon was trying to keep everyone happy. That was impossible. What Sky demanded infuriated Sonny, and his ultimatum for top billing enraged her. Normally Sky's billing came above the title and was 100 percent bigger than the title; unless she gave her permission, no one else's name could be above the title. Sky resolved this explosive problem with Sonny by relenting marginally to allow the letters of his name to be the same size as hers, but his would come forward *after* the title. Sonny, who was also looking forward to the balmier climate in the Bahamas, finally agreed.

Sky won every other negotiable point. Her retinue consisted of Kitty, Valerie, Ace, Cage, and her press agent, Sammy. Their expenses would be covered by the film's budget, as well as Ping's, since she rarely made a film without him. These were the people who protected her from unwanted visitors and who supplied hours of entertainment on and off the set. In addition to a clause that stipulated her approval of the director and that she wouldn't work during her period, she had two penthouse suites in the Lyford Cay Hotel at her disposal, three thousand dollars a week for her own living expenses, plus fifteen hundred for Kitty, who would be "getting her to work on time."

With these tiresome arguments behind her, only one obstacle remained: how to go on location without her mother. Sky hated scenes, and she particularly hated them with Diana.

Diana had a sixth sense about almost anything that had to do with Sky. She removed the glasses from her nose, folded them, and rose from the chaise. She smoothed her wraparound skirt from her still-lean body. "Darling, we've both put off seeing Sara's play too long. Lindy and I will come to New York with you, but after the play and a few quiet days on the island, I think we'll just come back home. You won't mind, will you?"

Belinda's room in Sky's house was decorated with posters from Sky's pictures, with miniature saddles, statues of horses, and a saddle blanket that had belonged to Tom Mix. As she pulled on her riding boots, her fury barely controlled, she began thinking about her father again. She was sure that if he had been around, she wouldn't have been subjected to so much meanness. She remembered the day Diana had first told her about her father, out at the ranch when she was five. Sara was there that day, just back from the East. But Sky was off making a picture. To Lindy, Sara was magical, a golden-haired beauty who appeared with presents from New York and disappeared with a gentle smile, the woman who never punished and always seemed to approve. It had been Sara who had said that Lindy's father was handsome, that he'd had a wonderful laugh, that she'd been sure he'd loved her.

Lindy had had the impression that Vic might be coming back, and she had looked forward to that day. But when she had pressed Sky about her father, Sky had made it clear that she had only contempt for her father—the lustrous, happy Vic of whom Sara had drawn such a glowing picture. Diana had told Lindy that Vic was never coming back.

Lindy had learned not to discuss her father.

She gave her boot a last tug and stomped her heel smartly on the floor. She went over to the mirror and peered at herself. She wished she had golden hair like Sara, or black hair like Sky. That was probably why her father never came back—Lindy wasn't beautiful like Sky or even like Sara. She winked at herself; when she was older she'd find her father.

Lenny Kaplan, the studio publicist, had released Sky's intention to see Sara's play. As a consequence the street outside the theater was swollen with crowds barely contained by mounted police. Diana tried to talk Sky into driving around to the back, but Sky refused to bend. "I will not sneak in the stage door," she said. Belinda's accusation that she was afraid of the press had nettled her.

As Sky, Diana, Lindy, and Kitty emerged from the limo, the crowds broke through, screaming for autographs, rushing at them, pushing Kitty, Lindy, and Diana out of the way. Compared to Sky, they were no one.

"My God!" Diana hissed as the crowd fought and shrieked and wailed. "They'll kill us!" Someone ripped the hat from Sky's head. Lindy was terrified. She clung to Sky's coat, her face white.

Kitty picked Lindy up in one arm and regained her firm grip on Sky, but she, too, wondered if they would emerge without injury. All she could see in any direction were frantic, bulging eyes, fixed expressions, and hands reaching out. Kitty felt fingers close on the strap to her purse. The police seemed to be trapped beyond the outer perimeter of the mob surrounding Sky.

"Let's get back in the car!" Diana cried.

But Sky was not to be intimidated. Her head came up arrogantly as she yelled at the crowd, her well-trained voice resonating. It was only then that Kitty became afraid. Shouting orders at a crowd of maddened fans was not the way to get them to disperse. "You're not immortal," Kitty said in Sky's ear.

Sky gave her a short smile. "Oh, yes I am," she replied. They were being tossed about in the sea of people. Kitty sensed that the crowd knew in a collective, animal way that Sky was helplessly surrounded. Sky let out another sonorous demand that they let them through. Her pale eyes glistened. The mob hesitated. "Let me pass!" Sky yelled. The mob's momentary indecision gave the police a sudden edge. They plunged into the opening and formed a flying wedge that delivered them into the lobby.

Their clothes were torn, Diana's purse and Lindy's hat were gone; they looked like battered if-once-wealthy refugees. "I simply cannot imagine what possessed you to do that," Diana was saying. She had been frightened; her voice was shrill. "You know what it's like, and to put me through it, or Belinda, it's just so selfish." No one except Sky was in the mood to see the play. "How can we walk into the theater like this?" Diana demanded.

"Oh, everyone will understand," Sky said smoothly. She looked as if she was enjoying herself. Kitty put Lindy down. "You okay?" Sky asked the child. Lindy nodded, but she knew she'd never forget the experience.

People in the lobby were staring at them and murmuring apologetically. Some offered unsought congratulations for having gained the safe ground of the lobby.

"I don't even have a comb," Diana wailed. Sky's pressman, Sammy, came rushing up to them.

From a corner of the lobby, a theatrical producer, Rolf Martin, had been in conversation with Bobbie Schaeffer, Teddy's theatrical agent, when Sky and her entourage blew in the door. Bobbie was trying to interest Rolf in Teddy's new play.

"She looks glorious when she's all mussed up," Rolf observed. He had long admired Sky's film work. "Why don't you get a vehicle for her, Bobbie?"

Backstage, the actors and stagehands buzzed with Sky's arrival. But Sara had lost her anticipation. Their arrival in her theater was long overdue.

When the play was over, Diana led Kitty, Lindy, and Sky into Sara's dressing room as if she'd been backstage at the theater every night. She brushed away the stage manager and opened the door, saying to Sara, "Darling, it was so silly of me, I thought Off-Broadway had finally come to its senses and given you the lead!" She kissed her daughter lightly on the cheek.

"Oh, Mother, you always say the nicest things," Sara quipped. "Lindy, my love!" Sara kissed her daughter gingerly, aware that her sweaty face was caked with makeup.

"How'd you like the play?"

"Oh, very much, Aunt Sara. Especially the part where you laughed and laughed!"

"That's the easiest thing to do in real life," Sara said, "and the hardest thing to do on stage."

"You remember Kitty," Sky said. She tossed a towel aside and sat down in a chair. "The play's divine," she went on. "Acting in a play is so much more difficult than acting in films."

Diana began describing their rocky arrival and how it had affected her enjoyment of the play.

"There are easier ways of getting into a theater, Sky," Sara said.

"Oh, of course. I don't know what came over me," Sky replied. Shyly, Sally and Dee stuck their heads into the dressing room. Sara introduced them to everyone, but Lindy saw that they only had eyes for Sky. When they left, Sky said, "It's a nice long run you're having. Has Teddy finished his next play for you?"

"Yes, and his agent loves it! I'm very excited about it," Sara said.

"I'd love to do a play," Sky said.

Lindy was gravely looking at Sara's makeup box. "You and I are spending the day together tomorrow," Sara said to her. "You must start thinking about what you want to do."

Sara didn't look very happy. "Why don't you come to the Bahamas with us, Sara?" Sky asked her.

Sara laughed too hard. "And just turn my role over to the understudy?" Suddenly, she wanted them all to go away and leave her with Lindy. She couldn't tell them about the deteriorating situation with Teddy, or about Vail disappearing in and out of the Village, or about the extent of her own loneliness. She'd looked forward to having them see her in the play, but it didn't seem nearly as important to them as it had seemed to her. They acted as if they were backstage with her every day.

20

Sara took Lindy all over New York—to Central Park, on the Staten Island Ferry, to the ballet, to the Museum of Natural History, to Radio City Music Hall. Vail came out of the Village to see them all, arriving at Sara's dinner for them with corsages for everyone and a red rose for Teddy. He seemed gentle and attractive with the now-much-more-grown-up, nearly ten-year-old Lindy.

"Are you happy, Lindy, at home?" Sara asked her. Lindy smiled and nodded.

In the backstage dressing room, Sara was making up her own face while Lindy gleefully followed instructions and made up hers. "Cage does this for Mommy in the bungalow," Lindy said.

"Well, in the theater, we usually do it ourselves." She gave Lindy a quick hug. "How would you like to stay with me for a while, like you stay with Grandpa on the ranch?"

"I don't know," Lindy said with the candor of childhood.

"I have my horse—"

"Oh, I know how it is with horses," Sara said. "But there are stables here, too." Lindy's large round eyes were looking at Sara boldly. "We don't have to decide now. You just think about it."

On Monday night, the theaters dark, parties sprouted around town like nightshades. Sara had said good-bye to Lindy that afternoon at Sky's hotel; they were all leaving early the next morning for the Bahamas. Sara was going to a party at Arlene's East Side apartment, "an important party,"

—268—

where Sara could meet the producers and television folk who controlled so many careers. Arlene had pointedly not invited Teddy.

Mercifully, for her family's visit, Teddy had been involved in meetings with his agent on the new play. When he'd made appearances, Teddy had been on his best behavior. But it was an act. Life with Teddy was a tangle of recriminations, pitched battles, and remorse. On this of all nights, Sara had not mentioned the party to Teddy and had secretly asked Vail to escort her. Vail had entered into "the conspiracy," as he called it, with verve. He loved secrecy followed by surprises.

Sara smoothed the pink silk dress over her hips and turned slightly to examine herself in the mirror. She liked the combination of pinks and lilacs with her bronze hair. She was thinking about Lindy, about having her with her in New York, about the dainty way Lindy held her head and laughed. She was wondering, as she had a thousand times before, if she'd done the right thing, if it was too late to be Lindy's mother.

The front door slammed and she stiffened. She grabbed a raincoat from her closet and quickly put it on to cover the dress.

Teddy blew into the room. "Well, well, you're home! How long has it been since we've met in this room?" He was slightly drunk.

"I'm just on my way out," Sara said, keeping her back to him and stuffing some makeup into her purse.

He cocked his head, eyeing her and the room around her warily, like a fox catching a scent on the wind. "I see," he said. "Where are you going?"

"Meeting Vail."

Sara snatched up her purse and an old rain hat. Teddy stood in the doorway, still looking at her carefully, one arm folded across his chest, the elbow of the other touching it, his fist against his cheek. She brushed by him. It was then that he saw her pink satin shoes.

"You're going out!"

"Of course I'm going out. I'm heading for the door right now."

"I mean *out*! To a party! Without me!"

—269—

She denied it, making for the door, but he pursued her and flattened himself against it to prevent her from leaving. "How can you do this to me? Don't you love me?"

She glared at him; her evening was crumbling. The man who had been her biggest booster was now her greatest liability. "You're too drunk to go. When you get there, you'll drink more, and then you'll make a scene and embarrass everyone. I'm sick of waiting for you to make some stupid, cruel remark at my expense, sick of counting your drinks or trying to figure out ways to get us both *out* before you make a fool of yourself, and I'm sick of being your punching bag!"

She put her hand on the knob, expecting him to hit out at her or to start screaming. Instead, he slowly sank to his knees on the carpet and began sobbing. "You bitch, how can you hurt me like this?" America's new angry playwright wouldn't be invited until he stopped creating his legendary public scenes or until he had a Broadway hit—when people would put up with him.

Sara wrenched the door open and sailed out feeling like a traitor.

Arlene's apartment was in the East Forties overlooking the East River. Theater and television people fanned out from a marbled and mirrored bar in a corner of the gray green living room; a large glass table in an alcove held a stunning array of foods. The party had the quiet murmur of confident people who enjoyed the respect of their peers and who behaved themselves most of the time. Arlene, wearing a silver lamé and black velvet gown, escorted Sara and Vail around the room, introducing them gracefully. They were important people to Sara, now that her career was taking on a little color. Most of them had seen her in Teddy Monroe's play, and many spoke flatteringly about her performance. Sara felt safe and happy; Vail would not betray her.

"You look like a peach in that pink dress," he said. Vail's boyish charm had returned; the drug episode had chastened him considerably. Arlene bolstered Vail by mentioning his recent essay in the *New Republic* on *La Dolce Vita*.

"Well, thanks," Vail said. Arlene moved away, and he fell into conversation with her husband, Dick, a university professor. He didn't feel nearly as out of water as he'd imagined, though the crowd was considerably different from his Village acquaintances. He watched Sara, and realized he was totally bored with his life except when he was writing reviews. He didn't have any goal in life, as Sara and Sky did. As he was wondering why not and half listening to Dick, he remembered that he'd dreamed of the snow leopard last night. He saw it again, loping along the battle-torn street, and suddenly, he was telling Dick all about it.

Dick had a jaunty, determined air. "Magnificent," he said. "That leopard keeps coming back because you're not free yet."

"But of what?" Vail asked, thinking, It's the beating, the shame of the beating.

"Oh, I don't know—stress, childhood. That leopard is an affirmation of life in the midst of death. It means, you, too, can break loose and do what you want."

"It's my familiar," said Vail. He was completely attuned to Dick.

"Oh, yes! A supernatural spirit embodied in an animal. Maybe your leopard is a protector—against yourself."

Sara was speaking to a crisp, clean-shaven NBC executive named Woodruff when she heard Teddy in the foyer. He was not loud, but his voice had an angry underpinning that only a trained ear like Sara's could hear. Arlene crossed the room, her pleased, patient expression fashioned for a late guest. Sara didn't know what to do and briefly pictured herself swan-diving out the huge window. She blanched as she saw Teddy enter the living room with Arlene, whose expression had changed to one fixed in cement. Woodruff marched his conversation with Sara forward. He was telling her why he'd liked her in the play.

Teddy took command of the peaceful room by announcing his presence loudly. Heads turned, conversation stopped. An out-of-town guest who didn't know any better went up to him and started to ladle out the compliments about the play. Arlene urged both of them over to the hors d'oeuvres, but Teddy, pretending not to see Sara, appropriated the bar, downing a glass of champagne. "Have one," he said to his new companion, "they're cheap." Most of the people in the room knew who Teddy Monroe was and that he and Sara

—271—

were a couple. But few had seen Teddy's tricks up close. In the way of small groups, they made a civilized attempt to ignore his slightly drunken condition by absorbing him without fanfare into conversations so that the evening could continue unruffled.

But Teddy liked drama. Sara knew he was there to voice his outrage and to punish her. At first, he was just a bit noisier than everyone else, his sharp, bad-boy wit carrying a sense of fun. Teddy, that inveterate reader of trade magazines and gossip columns, knew enough about the people in the room to have something to say to everyone. Sara, like a rabbit under a bush, began to relax, lulled by a false security. When he at last came over to her and took her arm tenderly like a lover, she was able to smile. Together, they worked the room, Teddy describing his new play and the incredible part he'd written for Sara. The party got rolling.

Vail whispered to Sara, "He's switched to scotch." He nodded at Teddy. She was talking with a casting director she'd admired but had never seen outside her office when Teddy staggered up to them.

"Miss Sandler," Teddy said thickly, "there's something I've always wanted to tell you." Rhonda Sandler looked at him benevolently. "You can't cast a cartoon," he said sweetly. "You've got the taste of a boot and the experience of a whore." Arlene and Woodruff, standing nearby, turned. Sara was mortified. Arlene's face was now carved of adamantine granite. Sara motioned to Vail. She prayed they could get Teddy out of the room in time.

It was not to be. "Why are you so cruel to me?" Teddy cried, breaking away from her. "I adore you." He turned to the guests. They were just beginning to be aware that something awful was going to happen. "Don't you all agree?" Teddy roared, throwing the question open to the crowd. "Isn't she adorable? Why are women so cruel? I love her so much it hurts. I write all my plays for her." He staggered back to the bar, every eye on him. "But you know what's happened? Honey, let me be the first. We've got a producer for my new play." People murmured. "Yes, Rolf Martin's going to do it on Broadway!" There was light, hesitant applause. "But there's a snag. He'll only do it if Sky's in your role."

"The part's for Sara," Arlene said through her teeth. "You wrote it for her."

"Ah, but that's why they think it will be so great for Sky!" He tittered, and glanced around his audience. "I'm sorry, Sky—ooops, I mean Sara."

Without warning, without a change in expression, he lowered his head slightly and vomited copiously, over the rug, over part of the bar, over Arlene's silver lamé dress, and over Woodruff's brilliantly polished shoes.

The cab driver drove like a robot. Sara hunched against the door, thinking of the elegant anger and wit of Teddy's new play, *Elephant House*, of Sky in her part, of her life with Teddy—a fistful of diamonds he was casually strewing behind him in garbage heaps. She kept remembering the frozen faces of Arlene's guests as they drew back at the moment of eruption, and their murmurs of horror, pity, and superiority as they pulled into themselves.

When they reached the apartment, Sara turned Teddy over to their doorman, who was used to his problems, and told the cab driver to take them to the Pierre.

"A confrontation," Vail muttered. He felt lightheaded after his conversation with Dick. "Do you think Ted was telling the truth?"

"I think so," she said. "He doesn't have the credits yet to force producers to put me in his play."

Vail patted her on the shoulder. Women were always strong. "I'm sorry for Teddy. He's really a great guy underneath all that crap."

"Maybe," she said, "he's only a great guy on the surface and underneath is all that crap."

In Sky's large suite, Sara got right to the point. "Are you doing Teddy's new play?"

Sky had adjoining rooms with Diana and Belinda on one side, Kitty on the other. She was wearing a dark blue dressing gown that billowed out behind her when she moved across the room to shut the door. Then she turned and faced Sara. "I didn't seek it out, Sara. I had nothing to do with it. Martin came to me." She moved back across the room to the bar where she poured herself a Coke. "Help yourself, Vail."

"No, thanks," he said, watching his sisters. Sky looked back at Sara. "Oh, Sara, I don't know what to do! I know it's your part—"

"Are you taking it?" Sara demanded.

"I'm so bored with these movie roles. They're very limited—"

"But Teddy wrote it for Sara," Vail said quietly, pouring himself some seltzer water.

"Vail, the producers won't give it to her. If I don't take it, they'll get another star. It's an expensive production—all those sets—and they have to have a star." Sky was sitting on the arm of a chair. "I won't take it if you want to make a stand for it."

"Of course I want to make a stand for it!"

"If I thought there was any way they'd give you that part," Sky said, "I'd tell them to take a flying leap."

Suddenly Sara lost her composure. "Don't do this to me!" she screamed at Sky. "You took my identity, my daughter, and now—"

"Hush up!" Sky whispered, terrified Belinda would hear.

"Sara, I'm not doing anything!"

"My worst enemy," Sara said, almost hysterically, "and she isn't doing anything to cause it."

"She had nothing to do with it." Diana stood in the doorway of a connecting room. "It's just fate!" She shut the door behind her and approached Sara. "I told you and told you not to try to compete, darling, but you never listened. Sky didn't ask for the part! She might not even take the part!"

"If you only knew what it cost me to keep Teddy writing that play," Sara whispered. She turned on Sky. "Please don't take that part away from me," she begged, hating herself, hating Sky.

"I'm not taking it away from you. The part is not yours or mine or anyone's. There's too much money involved." She wanted to reach out to Sara, to comfort her, even to make it possible for her to have the part. But she couldn't do any of those things.

"Then refuse it," Vail said. "Don't make her read about you in that role."

"How can you ask her to do that?" Diana snapped at him.

"Easily," Vail replied.

"Mother, Sky doesn't need the role," Sara said. "I do."

"I see. If you can't have it, she can't have it either," Diana said. "Honestly, Sara, make sense. I know it's hard, but Sky didn't create this problem."

"Neither did Sara," Vail said from the bar.

"Why don't you cry?" Vail asked Sara in the cab back to her apartment.

"Too blown away, I guess."

He wanted to tell her that something very remarkable had happened to him that night by accident, but the timing wasn't right.

"Thanks for saying what you did," Sara said to him.

"I hate being between you two. Wasn't I between you two in utero? I guess that's my fate in life." He turned away. "I don't think that Sky went after the role," he said. "I think it just happened."

When Sara got home, Teddy was stretched out on their bed, fully dressed, sleeping. Sara lay down on the living room chaise, a blanket over her knees. She looked out the tall window into the quiet street and tried to cry. But her insides had turned to stone.

She awoke about dawn. Teddy was curled on the rug below the chaise, mumbling. He was filled with remorse. She didn't move, didn't open her eyes. He went on and on, a monotone of grief and fear.

"Sweetheart, it's the only way I can stop the pain. . . . My whole life is pain. . . . I hate myself, I'm no good. I've fooled all those people with my play. I can't write. I tried so hard to save your part for you . . . but I've never had anything on Broadway. They don't want to risk their fucking money on an unknown playwright without a star. . . . Don't you realize how miserable I am?" Sara watched the wall emerge from shadows as the pale dawn brushed it. "I'm so weak," Teddy went on mumbling, "I'm failing. I'm ruining my life. I've got terrible guilt, you'll never know." She drifted in and out of the monotone on her own sea of injury and disgust. She kept thinking that she had to save herself. "Honey, I need you so much. You're the strongest thing in my life. I want to marry you. Then I'll never drink again." He reached up and grabbed her wrist with surprising strength. "Just tell me you'll marry me! What a great life we'll have. I'll write you another part. . . . I promise. I promise."

"I can't marry you," she said flatly.

He dropped back onto the floor. "Why are you so cruel?"

"*Me* cruel?" she cried, sitting up. "You don't even care what you did to me last night! You think you can just say you're sorry and get some forgiveness, like a medicine or that fucking Percodan you keep taking, and then go off to do it again!"

He leaped to his feet. "No! No! you're all wrong! I'll quit! I won't take an aspirin, I won't drink a glass of water!" His hands waved desperately in front of him, pleading with her. For a second she was snared in the sweet net of pity, sacrifice, and remembrance.

"Just stop it!" she screamed. "I won't marry you!"

At the end of the hall, she saw a door opening. Vail had awakened. He signaled her that he was there if she needed him.

"You're doing this because of the part!" Teddy yelled. "I'll write you another one, better! If Sky does this play and it's a hit, I'll have bargaining power. I'll get you into the next one—"

"It's not just the part!" Sara cried, exhausted. "I hate this life! You're killing me!"

He peered at her, knowing it was over, knowing she was right to leave, admiring her intractable sense of survival. Suddenly, Teddy was on the attack. "You bitch. You cold bitch. You're afraid of loving. You can't love anyone, and you haven't the faintest idea what loving is all about. It's about pain and wounds and being open. It's about shame and emotions! I'm talking to a wall here. You don't have any emotions!"

"You're talking about yourself!" she shrieked. "*You* can't love! I *can*, if I can ever get out of here!"

She ran down the hall. "Help me pack, will you, Vail?" In her bedroom, as she dragged a suitcase out of the closet, she could hear Teddy howling.

Two weeks later, Sara discovered she was pregnant.

21

Underneath the flat, riverless Bahama islands, underground passages tie their mangrove swamps to the smooth, emerald ocean. When Sky and her entourage arrived for the filming of "Paradise," the Bahamas were entering a new phase: tourism. Men in Bermuda shorts and madras shirts and women in straw hats roamed the islands that had been controlled by the British for generations.

The Bahamas have stirred both dreams and passions. Their aborigines were quickly exterminated. The British imported black slaves from Africa to work the cotton plantations. Blackbeard and other pirates haunted the islands' bays. Loyalists to the crown fled to these islands from the American Revolution, bringing with them their conservative politics and their slaves. Their great-grandchildren ran the blockades into Southern ports during the Civil War, and during America's Prohibition Era, their descendants turned the Bahamas into a lucrative rum-running center. The islands' weather has been as unpredictable and violent as its history.

The filming was to take place mainly on Paradise Island across the bay from Nassau, and at the Victoria Hotel, a crumbling Bahamian "Raffles" in the center of town. The Hollywood production descended on the island community, stirring up eddies and strange currents. They took over the exclusive Lyford Cay Hotel, which was located a few miles outside Nassau. Like a tropical palace, it was surrounded on three sides by thick, pale pink walls that enclosed a sculptured garden of hibiscus, palm trees, and croton shrubs. On the fourth side, spreading away from the hotel like a luxurious apron, the lawn ran down to the emerald sea.

The chemistry in the early days of the shoot seemed particularly good. Ping was more relaxed than he'd been for years; Valerie's rheumatism soaked up the hot, healing, subtropical sun; Ace and Cage fairly romped through their work; and Sammy, in plaid Bermuda shorts, greeted the press on the beach. Kitty, as usual, made the bother of going on location easy, even fun, for Sky.

Diana, pleading fatigue and a dislike for humidity, took Lindy back to Los Angeles after only three days on the island. "Are you sure about the play, dear?" Diana asked Sky on the morning of her departure.

"Mother, please. The price is too high. It's not worth it." Sky had made up her mind to decline it. In doing so, she had been aware of what Kitty's reaction would have been, had she taken it.

Diana kissed her good-bye. "You are a good sister to Sara," she murmured. Sky was delighted to see them go.

In preproduction meetings with the director, Robbie Beaudine, a graceful man whose shiny black hair resembled patent leather, Sky had told Beaudine that she would tolerate no funny stuff from Sonny. "He's pompous, and he thinks all women are his personal consorts." Beaudine could have told Sky that Sonny's opinions about women were a great deal more degrading than that. Sonny's only yardstick for women was how good they were in bed. Sonny Somaine, a "hunk," who was reaching his thirty-fifth birthday, had the reputation of compulsively romancing and bedding his leading ladies, in which efforts he enjoyed enormous success. He said that without the "real thing" he couldn't make love to them in front of the camera.

After the wrangle over their credits, Sky was prepared to publicly insult him if he tried any such tricks with her. But the balmy island breeze soothed the handsome, square-jawed Sonny and brought out the sweet side of his nature. Beaudine, a man of infinite sensibilities and delicacy, was also a well-organized director who believed that a smooth location shoot should include plenty of rest. Everyone took this seriously.

Sky was stretched in a beach lounge chair one afternoon, a huge straw sun hat on her head, dark glasses perched on her nose. The placid beauty of the place felt cleansing. A bunch of palm trees swayed over a round grass hut where a collection of waiters, two bartenders, and a calypso band were assembled. The bartenders whipped up fanciful drinks and chatted cheerfully with guests sitting on the barstools. Sky watched the black Bahamian waiters in their pink coats trudge sullenly around the tables by the bar. One of them, called Johnson, fanned out from the bar, plodding through the soft sand with a tray of decorative drinks for recumbent guests.

"Put some oil on my back, would you?" Kitty asked, sitting beside her. When Sky had done that, she lay back on her chair, adjusted her hat, and felt the blanket of sun caress her. She wanted to put her arms around Kitty's waist and hold her close. It was a most unacceptable thought. She closed her eyes against it, but Kitty's shoulders and her seawet hair were printed on the lens inside. She opened her eyes and gazed at the sunbathers around her—members of the cast and crew, two British couples, and another from Germany.

"Something's wrong with this picture," Sky murmured to Kitty who glistened with sun tan lotion. "Look at Johnson."

Kitty looked at the fifty-year-old man. He handled the silver trays with dexterity as he made his rounds among the lethargic guests. Johnson walked out to the Germans, his expression hardened with distaste. But when he bent over to deliver their drinks, a smile pulled his lips apart. He looked servile and disgusted.

"I see what you mean," Kitty said. It was one of the great things about Sky—her attention to what was going on around her.

Both of them sat up a little, watching Johnson trudge through the hot sand in his street shoes. It wasn't Johnson's dislike of the Germans or of the British—it was his barely concealed loathing for all the guests. Sky surveyed the lounge and the grass hut bar. Very little moved except Johnson and his compatriots. The calypso combo played its repetitious tunes; the effect of the rhythmic music was at once irritating and lulling.

"Wasn't Calypso the siren who detained Ulysses on his way home from Troy?" Sky asked.

"I think so," Kitty said.

"This music is seductive in a wearing way. It deadens me." Kitty strained to understand the lyrics but they were unintelligible. She wondered if the words were dirty or insulting.

Sky sat up. She felt hated because she was rich and white. She had never felt that way before. She imagined the calypso band arriving on the sand and opening up their instrument cases to take out not guitars and bongo drums but machine guns, which they trained on the lolling white bodies, riddling them with bullets. A few rose and tried to escape, scattering over the beach—too late. A final spray; everyone fell bleeding and screaming into the sand. The combo struck up its cheeriest number; the bartenders, laughing, toasted each other.

Sky shot to her feet. The calypso band was still improvising its folk songs, the man with the drums was still smiling as he always smiled—permanently—and Johnson was plodding through the sand. But Sky felt endangered; the placidity of the place seemed combustible.

"What's the matter?" Kitty asked, propping herself up on her elbow.

A chill swept over Sky. A monumental cloud had blocked the sun. The emerald sea was streaked with dark gray ribbons. The air was hot and close and smelled rotten. The lean, graceful palm trees slowly began to move, their mammoth fronds dipping and rising. Little gusts of powdery white sand blew up. The light kept dropping as though some huge dimmer had begun a thirty-second fade. Far away, like a memory, she could hear the scrape of shuffleboard disks and the thwack of a tennis game.

Kitty saw a bank of clouds knotting into a deep menacing gray block on the horizon, waiting. Just above them, puffy white clouds skimmed the ocean's dark green surface. Glassy and still just moments ago, the surface now was puckered with flecks of whitecaps. The band broke off in the middle of a tune.

Johnson was standing beside them, holding an empty tray. "Storm," he said. "Coming soon." Sky turned. Was he speaking symbolically of the islands, or of the weather, or was he, with second sight, foreseeing a storm inside her? Johnson was grinning. It looked genuine.

"What are storms like here?" Kitty asked.

"Oh, everything fresh, clean."

"Violent?"

"Sometimes." He laughed out loud.

I don't feel safe here, Sky thought. "Changes," Sky muttered.

"That's okay, isn't it?" Kitty had a brisk, pert smile.

The next day they were shooting on the wide veranda of the old Victoria Hotel in town. Beaudine was setting up the last shot in which Sky would move across the veranda to Sonny by an ornate post. Ping was adjusting the lights and constantly checking the falling light level.

It had been gray all day; the air felt lugubrious and thick. Some of the crew were whispering about going "over the hill" to the black part of the island, where a famous limbo club operated. Standing on her first mark, looking out at the twisted branches of a giant banyan tree, Sky couldn't shake a feeling of disaster.

"I'll stand," Kitty said softly, coming up to her. "You sit." Sky shook her head. Very distantly, she heard thunder; it had an alien basso note as though it were rolling up from the bottom of the world. Suddenly everything got darker.

"Well, shit," Ping said brightly. The light variations were a real problem. "What happened to the contract stream of bright sunlight we were promised?"

"How long?" asked Beaudine.

"I'll set it up for what we have now, but that doesn't mean it won't change the minute we roll," Ping said.

Kitty and Sky had moved to the ornate pillar; they looked out at the sea. A gunmetal lump of clouds sat on the horizon. Instead of moving in en masse, it approached in sheets like a shimmering curtain limned against the thunderheads behind.

"There's some kind of real storm brewing out there," Sky said dreamily.

Suddenly, a sharp, jagged spear of lightning on the horizon cut into the sea. The curtain advanced, the bulk of the storm filling the vacancy behind it, as another spear of lightning stabbed into the dark sea. It was three o'clock in the afternoon, and it looked as if the sun had already set. Sheet lightning began, a sharp explosion of immense light that illuminated the entire horizon, and then went out.

"There goes our sound," said someone.

"Just hold it," said Beaudine. "Let's not surrender."

The entire horizon was a menacing gray. Far out to the right, anchored behind the breakers, they could see a sleek cruise ship, its stacks slanting gracefully back. Its brilliant white shape hovered motionless against the dark horizon.

"What's the matter?" Kitty asked.

"Nothing," said Sky. "I was just thinking about Sara." She felt as if she were speaking to Kitty from a great distance.

Beaudine surrendered. "Let's go back to the hotel," he said laconically. "Everyone started packing up. A half-hour later, the company stood on the city side of the veranda, smelling the wet dirt of the gardens as the rain poured out of the sky.

Suddenly it stopped. The crew threw the gear into their rented jitney and rolled away down the circular drive. Beaudine, Sky, Kitty, and Sonny were about to get into the other jitney when their driver, an old man named Bow Tie, got out.

"Not leaving now," said Bow Tie, looking up at the sky through the thick old palms dancing high above them.

"Sure now!" said Beaudine, a man whose high spirits never flagged.

Bow Tie shook his head. "Hurricane," he said.

"Hurricane?" Beaudine repeated. "Ridiculous." Behind him he heard a series of sharp cracks. A hotel clerk was slamming the shutters of the old building.

Bow Tie said, "Hurricane's about two hundred miles southwest. Heard it on the radio, but I don't need no radio."

He pointed at the sky.

The first arm of the storm reached out to embrace them.

The winds tore at the banana trees in the garden, followed by torrential rains. Inside the hotel, Sky and Kitty and Beaudine eyed each other; Sonny had settled down in a wicker chair with a gin and tonic.

"I want to get back to Lyford Cay," Sky said.

"Oh, we will," Beaudine said. "It'll quit in a while." He was repeating what the hotel staff had said. The rain was falling in solid sheets like sails, billowed out by the gusting winds. Gargantuan bursts of thunder sucked all other sound out of the air, and the force of the thunderclaps shook the building. Lightning lit the preternatural darkness like day.

"God knows what's happened to the crew," Beaudine said a half hour later as the storm raged outside.

Kitty was exuberant, and Sky caught a part of her mood. It was like playing hooky; the natural texture of the day had been guiltlessly interrupted. They joined Sonny for a drink.

As predicted, the rain suddenly lessened, and the thunder ceased.

"Take us back to the Lyford Cay," Beaudine said to Bow Tie, but the man was immovable.

"It's not raining! It's over!" Sonny said.

"Just beginning," Bow Tie said in his soft Bahamian English.

"Oh, let's drive ourselves," Sky said. "How about it?"

Everyone piled into the jitney. Sonny appropriated the wheel and tooled slowly down the wet driveway into Bay Street. It was much darker than they had expected. Sonny turned on his lights.

"Geez, look at all this water on the road!" Sonny shouted, sloshing the jitney through six inches of rain. "Don't they have any drainage system?"

As they drove in the lull of the storm, their headlights picked up shredded palm fronds and other debris lying across the dark, watery road. Sonny couldn't tell if it was six inches or six feet underwater.

"Whaddaya think?" Sonny asked, slowing down. It was a deserted spot. Their hotel lay at least two miles up the road.

"Back up and get a running start on it," Beaudine suggested.

Kitty laughed. "That's the worst thing you can do. Creep

through it." Sky was sitting next to her, looking out at the dark clouds and the rain dripping from the broad banana leaves. Sonny suddenly gunned the motor. "No!" Kitty cried. They hit the flooded road with a mighty splash, spraying out skirts of water. In the middle, the car stalled. Water began seeping in.

"Great, Sonny, just great," Kitty said.

"It's an adventure, isn't it?" Beaudine exclaimed.

They looked around. Casuarina pines and palm trees lined the road. In front of them, their headlights shone on a waveless pool of water.

"It's really wet back here," said Sky, picking her feet out of the water soaking into the car.

"Maybe we should get out and walk, what say you?" Sonny suggested, trying and failing to start the car.

Beaudine leaped out and sank up to his thighs in water. "Jesus!" he said, making for the front of the car and yanking up the hood. "The engine's still dry," he called back, "but not for long."

Kitty watched Sky's taut face looking at the pine trees near by. The winds were picking up. A spear of lightning blazed behind them, and thunder boomed directly overhead, rocking the car. Beaudine hopped back inside. Sonny tried to get it started. The storm broke, lightning crackling all around them.

"Christ, we have to get out of here," Beaudine said, as the rain broke out of the sky and fell solidly. He felt certain that the next bolt would strike the car and fry them all. "We're going to have to walk."

"We can't!" Sonny yelled as a coconut was torn from a tree and narrowly missed the windshield. Sky seized Kitty's hand.

"We can't sit in this water and get electrocuted," Sky said tightly.

"Try to get it going again, Sonny," Kitty urged. Miraculously, the engine caught. They cheered as Sonny crept out of the lake and drove slowly along a slightly higher strip of road. They crawled past the golf course, now flooded, and finally made it back to the hotel.

The first person they saw was Ping, sitting with Ace in the front lobby of the Lyford Cay. They were watching the activities director put up a hurricane map to chart by longitude and latitude on the hour the progress of Adelaide.

Ping said brightly, "Adelaide is about one hundred miles away, coming straight toward us." His plain, round face surveyed them. "Boy, you guys are really wet!"

"Gear okay?" Beaudine asked.

"Yup."

Ace was lounging in a rattan chair. "The staff says that we won't be able to get back to Nassau for a few days because all the roads will be out."

"Great," Beaudine said, thinking of the producer who was supposed to be flying in tomorow. "Great."

Much had changed since they'd left early that morning. Leaks had sprouted in the dining room, in the bar, and behind the front desk. There were rumors of an eighteen-foot tidal wave, which thrilled many of the cast and crew who peppered the lobby, drinking and chatting. Since the hotel sat right on the beach and both the bar and the dining room had huge plate glass windows facing it, some of the European hotel staff were arguing about whether to board them up or not. The majestic stretch of lawn commanding the ground between the hotel and the sea was slowly slipping underwater. The winds began to howl. People milled around in the lobby; a few predicted disaster, one saturnine grip proclaiming that the hotel would be blown away before morning.

"C'mon," Kitty said to Sky, "upstairs. You gotta get out of those wet clothes."

They had adjoining suites facing the ocean through wide plate glass windows. Sky was going to take a warm bath but the sound of the howling wind was too thrilling. She ducked under the shower, washed off the stagnant rainwater, toweled off, and slipped into a huge bathcoat. She was sitting at her window, feet up, when Kitty knocked. She had brought a tray of champagne, some sandwiches, and fruit.

"It's really wild downstairs," Kitty said, putting the loaded tray down on the table. "The general manager is rushing around, bellowing orders. Most of the staff saw it coming and headed home, so we serve ourselves tonight direct from the kitchen!"

Sky had turned the lights off to watch the lightning on the horizon fire up the image of palm trees bent forward. Debris was flying through the air. The next second, all was dark. The pitch of the wind rose higher. The day hovered in an unnatural space between night and day.

Kitty poured out two glasses of champagne. Sky watched her in the half-light that was regularly streaked with the brilliant and vital lightning. Of all the people she'd met after her public life began, Kitty had never seemed intimidated by her.

"I feel so strange," Sky said. "Like I'm suspended, that nothing's real. Normal life's just stopped." She gazed out the window. "I was afraid back in the car—"

"We all were," Kitty said.

"But it was wonderful! I haven't felt so petrified and keyed up since my first screen test." She glanced at Kitty. "I'm beginning to feel good about not doing the play. I didn't, at first."

Kitty tried to imagine what it would have done to both Sky and Sara had Sky accepted. She started to quarter an apple. A thunderclap smacked the sky overhead, its sonorous and echoing waves booming backward into the distance.

In the silence the thunder left behind, Sky said: "Sometimes I don't know who I am any more." Kitty looked up sharply; Sky turned away. "I'm in danger."

"Of what?" But Sky only shook her head. Kitty was uneasy; Sky rarely shared anything about herself. She steamed through life, protecting her soft center with her sleek exterior. Kitty admired Sky's self-navigation, her rigid adherence to her work, her principle that people close to her worked when she worked, her usually grave courtesy on the set, her generosity, her preparation for even the silliest role. But would she ever put aside the shield of her public face?

"I've been looking for a role like the one in Teddy's play for years," Sky said.

"Then why do you do so many pictures?" Kitty asked.

"You could live in New York, or travel. You could—" She was about to say that Sky could have married Reed, could still marry and have a family, that she didn't have to be on

—286—

a set year after year. What was Sky proving by making some of these pictures? Why didn't she expand her circle of friends?

"Why didn't you marry Reed?"

"It would have sapped me."

"Wouldn't you like to have children?"

"Not really. I don't feel like reproducing," Sky said. It sounded pompous. "Isn't that an awful thing to say?" Kitty didn't answer. "I'm close to Lindy," Sky went on, thinking about the mischievous and bewitching girl. She swallowed the last of her champagne and looked at the storm outside. She couldn't remember what it was like *not* to be famous, and it made her feel phony and afraid. "I feel unreal sometimes."

"You are perfectly real to me." Kitty tugged at Sky's hair, then squeezed her shoulder. "Mighty real. Let's not talk about all this."

Sky ignored that. "My life is controlling me."

"No!"

"It's worse than that, even. I am becoming a part to me. I can feel it." With that Kitty agreed. Lately Sky kept telling the same little things about herself in conversations—supposed confidences as if those were her lines. Maybe that's why nothing seemed quite real to her anymore. "I'd like to be anonymous again, but my work doesn't have any value if nobody knows me."

"I don't want to talk about this, Sky."

"Being famous was so important to me. I dreamed and I prayed that there was something special I could do, like Sara and Vail, that I was worth something, too."

Sheet lightning lit the sullen sky, casting the silhouettes of the palmettos into dark relief.

Sky threw back her head and laughed at herself. "Everyone wants a ride on the back of the tiger, Kitty! You climb up and keep your balance as best you can. One day you look down and see that it is a *real* tiger and that he wants you *off his back*. Pretty soon, it takes all your energy just to stay on." A horrendous peal of thunder drowned her out.

As the sound rolled away, Sky stretched out her hand across the immensely deep abyss she felt opening between them. "I don't know what's going on any more. Kitty, I feel so many things for you. I value your friendship more deeply than any I have, I count on you. I am afraid of you."

"No, Sky, not afraid, never that." Kitty held her hand. "I've been thinking all day about you, about fear, about things being upside down, about storms."

Kitty wanted to tell her about her longing on the other side of friendship, but she didn't trust words. She slowly opened her arms. As Sky went into them, the tension inside her loosened. Kitty put her cheek against Sky's, held her, not daring to move.

"I want you to know—"

"No," Kitty whispered. "Don't. Whatever you say, it's the same with me." She sighed, holding the all-too-human woman in her arms.

After a few minutes, Sky raised her head and ran her lips along Kitty's smooth, soft cheek. "I was looking at the back of your neck earlier, and I was thinking about putting my arms around your waist, and then I was thinking about how awful I was to be thinking about that."

"Shhh, Sky. Let's not think." She pressed her mouth to Sky's salty lips.

The next morning Ping and the hotel manager stood in the dining room that overlooked the wide back lawn, the beach, and the open sea. They were staring at the route Adelaide would take into the hotel. Water had been leaking into the dining room and had turned the carpeting to mush. "This is the worst," the manager kept saying. The crew had renamed the dining room Hurricane Alley. It and the bar provided spectacular views of the stormy show.

Gale-force winds shrieked around the corners of the hotel, ripping off the plumes of palm trees bent in half; blasts of rain beat against windows; and debris shot through the air—palm fronds, croton bushes, knots of seaweed, and masses of hibiscus blossoms like clusters of shooting stars. A beach chair swept by the window and collided with a palm tree, its plastic arms sticking out on either side of the trunk in a stiff embrace.

Ping went into the bar where the cast and crew were guzzling brandied coffee and flowery rum concoctions. Someone was trying unsuccessfully to count the number of coconuts the storm was hurling about like cannonballs. The outdoor pool was about to overflow (someone had forgotten to empty it), and it now threatened the accounting office.

In the lobby, the activities director received a new bulletin: Adelaide was at seventy-five degrees latitude and twenty-five degrees longitude. He drew a vertical line on the map to indicate the new coordinates. Adelaide was getting closer to Nassau.

Upstairs, Sky turned over, reaching out for Kitty. "Did you see that one?" she asked. She felt as if she'd been living in fragments until this moment when all the pieces had come together.

"The coconut? Yes." She stroked Sky's hair and held her close.

Sky felt another tremor—of how unacceptable and strange it was to be lying in bed with Kitty. Would the feelings evaporate when they got off the island or when the storm stopped? "What are you thinking about?" Sky asked.

"That I love you."

"Have you ever done this before?"

"Been in love?" Kitty murmured.

Sky laughed, pulling away from Kitty.

"It's a big feeling, isn't it?" Kitty whispered.

Far beneath the island, the underground passages were flooding, sending the brilliant fish to smoother waters at the bottom of the sea.

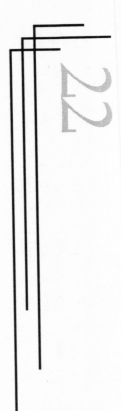

22

Sara was listening to whirling sprinklers. She felt groggy and disoriented. She opened her eyes and focused on a wall of dirty white clapboard siding. She was lying on a cot on a screened veranda. The smell of damp, freshly cut grass was reassuringly ordinary.

A shadow was materializing into the shape of a bulky man at the side of her cot. "How d'ya feel?" he asked. "Okay?" He was wearing a sweater vest and dark trousers. He looked about sixty. She wasn't sure how she felt, but it was her habit to claim anything that was needed. "I had to give you gas," he said. "You started to scream."

The image of the kitchen came bursting back to her like a shot, a yellow kitchen with a broad table and a spice shelf by the stove. He'd been standing by her feet; she was lying on the table. His voice had been rehearsed, smooth. And then the pain had started, wild and searing, strangling her.

"You'll have to stay here a few hours until the gas wears off. Is someone going to pick you up?" She shook her head; she had come alone and not told anyone. "Then you'll have to take a cab back to the city," he said. He leaned down. "Now how about a nice kiss for the guy who did such a great job?"

His face approached hers, dropping steadily like a boulder, till his plump, wet lips landed on hers, where they lingered, sucking at her. Weakly, she began to fight. He withdrew and disappeared.

The next thing she remembered it was morning, and she

was sitting in a cab, driving back to the city from Long Island. She was staring at the gravestones, thick as tiny skyscrapers flashing by on her right. She passed out.

Someone was shaking her. It was the cab driver. He was upset. Her doorman stood behind him.

"It's okay," she muttered, drawing the fare out of her coat pocket.

"Miss Wyman, you're white as a sheet," the doorman said.

"I'll be okay," Sara said. "Just help me inside."

She stayed in bed for that day and the next until she had to go to the theater. It was the last night of their long run. By the time she got down to the theatre, she was bleeding a little, and she felt lightheaded. Her dresser took one look at her and said, "You're too sick to go on. Where's Teddy?"

Sara gave a short laugh. "In Chicago with potential backers. He'll be back tonight." She fell into a chair. "I'll be fine. Just help me."

Out in the wings for her last performance, she had the stage manager bring her a chair. The dizziness returned in Act Two when she had to dash across the stage in wild pursuit of her neighbor. She knocked into a little table and sent it flying against the sofa. She steadied herself and managed to get through her speech while the stage tilted precariously. In many scenes she took unscheduled seats. Her ears rang. She clung to furniture. When the curtain finally rang down she had no sense of the final triumph or the applause that was drawing a part of her life to a close. She was wringing wet when she made it to her dressing room and collapsed. Her understudy rushed in.

"There's a big party at Sardi's! I'm so thrilled! And I just want you to know that I never wanted to go on. I think you are so great!" Impulsively, the young woman leaned down and kissed Sara. "Ooooh, you're so hot. Do you have a fever?"

Sara went to the party. The first person she saw was Teddy. "You look awful," he said, leaning in and kissing her cheek. "Up too late last night?" He was comparatively sober and contrite. He wanted rapprochement. It had been a month since their big fight. She'd moved to a hotel for a week, but she'd moved back to the apartment. Teddy had worked hard to prove to her that he could handle sobriety.

The next person she saw was Arlene. Arlene was with Bob, Teddy's agent, a tall, distinguished man with white hair, black eyes, and a wistful smile. "Let's talk a little shop," Sara said to Arlene grimly, excusing them from Bob.

Arlene followed Sara into a booth. "Do you feel all right?" Arlene asked.

"I'm fine. Tired." Her head spun. She gripped the table. She felt nauseated. Arlene ordered brandies. Sara was watching Teddy across the room. He was talking with Bob. "I feel like I'm losing myself," she said to Arlene. "I can't explain it." She took a gulp of the brandy and felt it hit the back of her throat like a tiny explosion.

Arlene looked at her sharply. "If you'd leave Teddy and get your own place, you'd feel a lot better."

"It's not as simple as that. Can you get my part back in Teddy's new play?" Arlene could not. Sara nodded. "I can't go on with Teddy like this. I want to go away; I want to work somewhere else. Obviously, I'm hard to cast," she said, referring to Sky. "But I want to leave *for* something. Is there anything I could do in Europe for a while?"

She sounded confused and overwrought to Arlene. "Rome is pretty active," she said, handing Sara a tissue. Sara wiped her brow. "There's an American producer I know who's starting a film there. Well, there are a lot of Americans in Rome." She sipped her brandy. "But giving up New York right now—that's crazy, Sara. You've worked hard. Think it over." Sara looked miserable and ill. Arlene felt sorry for her. She put her hand over Sara's. "Never damage your own character," she said suddenly.

The clatter in the restaurant started to ring in Sara's ears, and she knew she was fainting. She heard her own voice at the end of a huge tunnel. "I'm sick. Help me." Her head dropped to the table and she slid sideways out of the booth into blackness.

When Sara woke up in the white room, her mother and Vail were sitting in chairs near the window.

"You're all right, Sara Bay," her mother said, coming over to the bed. "But it was a close call. What possessed you—"

"Mother!" Vail said sharply.

"What's happened?" Sara asked faintly.

"You hemorrhaged," Diana said. "But you're all right."

"What day is it?" Sara asked.

"Well, you closed the play last night, and Arlene got you to the hospital about midnight, and it's almost five in the afternoon, next day," Vail summarized. "Mother got here an hour ago."

Sara looked at her mother and started to cry. "You came," she said.

"Of course I came. You were at death's door. You had a transfusion. It was very serious. Fortunately, Vail wasn't perambulating the country so there was someone to call me."

A shout and sounds of a scuffle came from outside. Teddy burst through the door, carrying a bouquet of flowers. His face was red. "You bitch! You killed my child!"

A doctor rushed in after him. "Mister Monroe! She's much too ill for this kind of behavior. You must leave now!" The doctor was young. He had a pencil mustache and rangy good looks.

"Oh, get away from me!" Teddy said.

"C'mon, Teddy, just can it," Vail said.

"How could you do that?" Teddy cried, flinging the flowers at Sara. He spun around, crammed his shoulder into the wall, slumped there, put both hands to his face, and began sobbing.

"It nearly cost her her life, whatever reason she did it," Diana said coldly, "and she'll never have another child."

The words struck Sara in the face like a slap. She looked at the doctor, who put a hand on her shoulder. "I'm sorry you had to learn it like this," he said, softly. "It's true. Whoever did the abortion bungled it badly. We just barely saved you. I'm so sorry."

"Please leave," Sara said. "All of you."

The next day, Teddy came by early in the morning. He had been up all night and had charmed a nurse into letting him see Sara. "I came to apologize," he said. "I don't know what got into me."

"I do."

"Sara, can't we fix things up? The new play's got backers now; it's going to be a hit. I'll be able to talk anyone into

—293—

anything on the next play. I want to get back together with you, like the old days, honey. You know I didn't fall in love with you because you could have children. It was just the shock of it all, the abortion, everything. Say you'll come back and everything will be okay."

"Where's Vail?" she asked.

"Oh," he said vaguely, "I think he and Bondy are getting ready for some trip."

"Diana?"

"She's at the Pierre. I'm sure she'll be here in a while."

Honey—"

"Teddy, if I stay with you, I'll die. I lay here a long time last night thinking. I'm going away. I can't stay in New York without you, and that's one of the things I just hadn't faced. New York and you and me—they're all one, they always have been."

"Come back!" he pleaded.

"No, never. You're killing me. It's that simple. I'm going to Europe."

"God damn you," he said, hating what she was saying, knowing it was final. He sat on the edge of the bed and pressed his head against her breast. "Oh, God," he moaned. "I've done this to you. I'm to blame. I'll never forgive myself."

Sara turned away. "Yes, you will. In about an hour," she said.

23

By the 1960s, Rome was known as "Hollywood on the Ti-ber." A diverse group fueled its international product: fading actors and actresses who couldn't get work in an America infatuated with "Our Miss Brooks" and "Leave It to Beaver"; aspiring cinematographers and impertinent young directors, recently disgorged by film schools from Stockholm to Paris; actors or directors running from their alimony pay-ments or their assault and battery charges; and the profiteers of the business—American producers, primarily, looking for big profits from cheap products. Americans and Europeans converged on the Eternal City; they ground out films like pasta.

When Sara arrived in December of 1961, *Cleopatra* had been shooting since September and was already legendary. The more modest film Sara was slated to do was called *The Mongol Hordes*, a historical picture loosely based on the twelfth-century Mongol invasion of Europe. John Barrymore, Jr., was signed for the lead. Sara had met Frank Pepper, the producer, in New York before she left. He'd outlined the story of the film for her to prove that Sara's role as the Mongol leader's consort was meaty. Pepper said he was hiring Sara for her stage experience and for her gorgeous bronze hair. He said he was trying to lift the film out of its class into "something important." He had big plans and needed an actress of her caliber to take a risk with him. Arlene asked her not to do it; it was beneath her. Arlene said that Pepper was hiring her for the value of Sky's name with his European backers. Arlene said Sara was running away.

"Maybe. But a few months in Rome won't hurt me," Sara replied. "It might even be good for me."

Carmen Giretto, one of Pepper's assistants on the Mongol movie, was assigned as Sara's translator. They met at the airport. Carmen was twenty, full of gentle, high spirits. Sara liked her immediately.

"You will not need me much," Carmen said in her very good but accented English. "Most people speak Inglese—English—some." Her dark hair, piled loosely on top of her head, and her pale hazel eyes reminded Sara a little of Sky. "You are sister to the famous Sky Wyman," Carmen said as they drove away from the airport. "We have big stars here, too," Carmen went on, "Elizabeth Taylor, Rex Harrison, Eddie Fisher. Maybe sometime your sister come."

"I doubt it," Sara said cheerily. A feeling of unreasoning anticipation seized her as they drove into Rome. She felt like a young girl. "It smells different here," Sara said, hanging out the window. She saw the tall spires of cypress trees grouped in threes, rising from the flat fields, and then suddenly the wide country road gave way to crowded, narrow streets. They had plunged into Rome where networks of tram wires crossed ancient stone facades on buildings centuries older than any in America. Sara breathed in deeply. Italy smelled of warm stones, sweet decay, and cypress.

Carmen took her to her hotel and helped the ancient porter lug her bags up three flights to a large, airy room with high ceilings and ornate trim. The room's little balcony looked out on the Spanish Steps.

"Domani—tomorrow—I pick you up in the car at the bottom of those steps and we go to Cinecittà. We costume fit you, make up you, and meet your director, Marco Isolantini. Molto gentiluomo—nobile. He's a very good man. You will like him." She had a small, pretty voice like a bell.

The next day Sara waited at the bottom of the steps in front of a fountain. At nine-thirty, Carmen's car jerked to a halt. "I am sorry for the lateness. I know all Americans are on time. Here it is a little different." The day was overcast;

Carmen was wearing a flowered kerchief around her head.

"I don't mind," Sara said, and she didn't. For the first time in her life she was nervous about meeting everyone, nervous about appearing in her first film. She felt like a wounded survivor, and Rome was her cure.

The car was very small, and Carmen drove like a demon, zipping through traffic with aggressive yet casual grace. They sped past the Roman Forum and the Arch of Constantine, and turned onto the Via San Gregorio. Another huge arch loomed in front of them, then disappeared behind their speeding car, the Porta Capena. "I am going now on the Via Appia Antica," Carmen announced. "It is the old road so I give you a little tour, and then we arrive at Cinecittà."

"You speak English very well," Sara said.

"Grazie. I learn it in American movies!"

Beyond the Baths of Caracalla, they met the old city wall and passed under the Porta San Sebastiano, a massive two-towered structure. The countryside began—quiet meadows dotted with conical cypress trees and the ruins of churches or monuments dating from the early Christian Era. The road was narrow and uneven—some of the original stones put down in the third century showed through the asphalt. On either side high walls of stone, showing the tops of poplars or towering pines, edged the big estates on the Appia Antica. Along the side of the road broken blocks of weathered white marble from antique buildings long since gone lay in pieces in the grass.

After they had driven a few minutes, they came to the Grande Raccordo Anulare, where the old Appian Way crossed the highway that ringed Rome. "Jesus," Sara murmured, looking at the four lanes of speeding cars rushing past them. Carmen, fearless, unaided by anything so handy as a traffic light, zipped boldly out, into the oncoming cars. Sara shut her eyes. Amid a blare of horns, they accelerated across and barreled down the Appia Nuova.

Cinecittà, a few miles outside Rome, was the great studio Mussolini had built in the thirties. As they neared it, Sara could see pine trees poking above a reddish Mediterranean clay wall. A cluster of people surrounded the main gate.

"Waiting for work?" Sara asked, remembering the cattle calls for actors and dancers in New York.

"Waiting for Elizabeth Taylor!" Carmen cried. "Or Burton! Not so much Eddie Fisher. My boyfriend works on the *Cleopatra*. It is very dramatic." She laughed happily.

A guard waved as they drove up, but Carmen didn't stop; she just said something in rapid Italian and pushed on. "Va bene," he called out.

"You are well known," Sara said, thinking of the Hollywood studios' tight security systems and of the protracted conversations with the gate guards while they checked their lists.

"Not really. We come and we go here," Carmen replied.

The main thoroughfare was cobblestone pavement lined with pine trees. The dry pine needles crunched under the wheels of the car. Carmen pulled into a parking spot. "Now, I take you around." She jumped out.

Cinecittà smelled of the pungent pines. Like Warner's or MGM, Cinecittà was a small town, but much less formal. Carmen and Sara were standing in a little grassy square. To the right was an espresso bar and behind that a restaurant with a terrace under the pine trees. On the other side were editing and screening rooms and producers' offices, all small, simple, reddish buildings.

"That's Fellini's over there, Numero Cinque—Number Five," Carmen said. "Then there's Wardrobe, and offices of the executives. All close to the center—the bar!"

There, a number of men had congregated to sip their espressos and read their newspapers. Two beautiful Italian girls passed, reaping a harvest of appreciative looks and murmurs. Carmen pointed to the door they had entered. "Casting," she said, "also close to the bar. Naturally!" She laughed merrily.

Hollywood's organized method of making films had collided with Italy's improvisational tactics in the 1950s when the first Hercules epic was born. *Hercules* made its obscure Italian producer a millionaire overnight, enticed American investors to Italy, and eventually spawned more than a hundred mythological brethren that were distributed all over the world. Historical blockbusters shot in Rome became the rage: Biblical, Greek, Egyptian, Christian, and Amazon epics rolled out of Cinecittà, produced by German, French, and English outfits joining in the Italian-American deals. The first multinational production companies had arrived. The films were made quickly, postdubbed, and released in a rush for fast profits from 1957 to about 1965, when the mythological and historical he-men bit the dust.

But the golden stream of inflated historical films was only one small part of Cinecittà's busy schedule. Antonioni's *L'Avventura* had been released in the States in 1959, followed by Fellini's *La Dolce Vita* and Pietro Germi's *Divorce, Italian Style*. These were the kind of pictures Sara expected to see at Cinecittà. She was not disappointed; Fellini was shooting on Stage 11.

The set looked like a huge bathhouse where a dozen extras milled about in togalike sheets. Fellini, spinning his cinema web of fantasy, sat on a crane with his cameraman about ten feet above the stage. Laughter, talk, and confusion filled the huge, brilliantly lit space.

Between Stages 6 and 7, they ran into Sergio Leone ambling along with a tall, lean, almost pretty actor. Carmen had just finished working for Leone as a production assistant on his *Colossus of Rhodes*. Leone greeted her effusively as Carmen introduced him to Sara. The lean man stepped back politely.

"I am very happy," Leone said to Carmen. "I am beginning soon a new film, an American Western!" He felt the big myths had run their course. "I borrow a little from *Yojimbo*," he said, twinkling with enthusiasm, "the Kurosawa film. You have seen it?" Sara had. "Kurosawa himself borrowed from an American novel to make *Yojimbo*. You know that?" Sara had not. "I put in a touch of James Bond, ecco——" he exclaimed, having finished his recipe "—a new Western!"

"What's it called?" Sara asked.

"*A Fistful of Dollars*. It stars——" Leone glanced around. The tall young man was leaning against the side of the sound stage. Leone beckoned him over. "Meet my star—Clint Eastwood."

The actor nodded at them shyly. Leone started off again, calling out to Carmen in Italian. Eastwood tipped his cowboy hat and followed Leone.

On Stage 6 the family-loving Italians were mass-producing erotic films. This one was called *The World by Night*, and the set consisted of three adjoining bedrooms, each done up to resemble a different décor—Chinese, French, and Indian. A delicious-looking woman was playing cards on one of the beds with a carpenter who had a hammer sticking out of his back pocket. The crew swarmed over the sets, fastening and moving lights, lugging cables, and shouting.

Stage 7 contained an interior set for Antonioni's new film, *L'Eclisse*. This set seemed slightly more formal than Fellini's, but not by much. Certainly, the actors were better dressed.

When they were back outside, Carmen said, "It looks like many people here, but the heart of our film work is still held in the hands of a few men. Most are working in films during the war. Their experiences then still influence stories and the look of their films." They turned down a narrow street. "You know de Sica?" Sara nodded. "We called him the 'Vittorio Nazionale'—Italy's national victory—our Number One actor. That was in the forties! And Roberto Rossellini—"

"The man who stole Ingrid Bergman's heart—!"

"Sì! He was producing films during the war with a young assistant called Antonioni! But the bombing made it hard to shoot—even Cinecittà was bombed. Rubble."

"How about Fellini?" asked Sara.

"In 1943 Fellini hid out from the Nazis in his mother-in-law's apartment. He was afraid he'd be seized and sent to a slave labor camp. Many were. Then Rome was liberated in 1944. Rossellini discovered him drawing cartoons of the GIs, and took him away to cowrite a film called *Open City*."

"I saw that film!"

"Good!" Carmen cast a coy look at Sara. "You like this tour?"

"Yes!"

"Ecco, right after the war, Antonioni made his first short; Bertolucci was a little child; Pasolini was writing poetry; Raf Vallone was a cinema journalist; Zeffirelli was a young actor and he painted sets, too; Dino de Laurentiis, who started as an actor, produced his first movie; and Mastroianni acted in amateur groups. *Open City* made everything different;

then de Sica made *Bicycle Thief*, and de Santis made *Bitter Rice*. And now Carlo Ponti is producing films; Visconti, de Sica, and Monicelli have just finished making *Bocaccio 70*; and Pasolini gave Bertolucci the chance to direct his first film. So you see, they all work together."

Part of the back lot was an open field with tall grass. "Bond comes out here next week," said Carmen, eyeing the men building what looked like a silo. "Bond is lots of fun."

Wherever Sara and Carmen walked, from a sound stage to the back lot to the bar, the air rang with a half-dozen languages.

"They don't know what they're missing," Sara said, as they walked back to Wardrobe.

"Who?"

"Hollywood. New York."

"But we have many Hollywood people here," Carmen said. "In fact, we have a saying, 'Go Hollywood in Rome.'" Carmen cocked her head. "It means 'go crazy.' Pazzo! Dance and sing, drink wine. Play! End up in the Queen of Heaven prison for the night!"

A man came rushing out of one of the small offices at the front of the lot waving papers at another man who was about to get into his car.

"Fox press people," said Carmen. (Twentieth Century-Fox was producing *Cleopatra*.) The two men huddled together. Suddenly the second man yelled and beat his fist against the hood of his car. The other man hooted with laughter. They both ran back inside.

Carmen took Sara to Stage 9 later that morning to meet the director of the Mongol film. The set was the portcullis and central courtyard of a castle. Beyond the drawbridge, the "meadow" was strewn with boulders. Hundreds of extras were standing around in peasant or military costumes from an indeterminate medieval period.

"But where are the camels and the little boys?" Frank Pepper yelled at the Italian production manager and the Italian director.

"They were held up."

Pepper seemed undone by this news. "The script calls for camels and little boys!"

"We will shoot something else," the director said equitably.

"Shoot fuck-all!" cried Pepper, washing his hands of it.

At that moment, the director of photography, an American, yelled at his Italian cameraman, "Jesus H. Christ!" The cameraman, Salvatore, had moved some of the extras to the left, and as a consequence he was moving a boulder to accommodate them.

Pepper erupted again, shouting, crazed.

"Mister Pepper," Sara said.

He turned around abruptly and recognized her. "Shit, I thought you were coming a week ago. I had to change everything around."

"Sorry. I didn't know."

"No one knows fuck-all around here." He took her by the arm and steered her aimlessly, here and there, around the stage. "I'm trying to get a little organization to make sure this fucking movie gets made. I'm spending half my dough just trying to do it like the pros. But it's goddamned impossible! You'll see! Outside of Barrymore you're the only American in this piece of shit."

"Gee," Sara said. "Is my movie a piece of shit?"

Pepper raged on, ignoring her. "No Italian producer has ever spent a penny to make sure the fucking production runs smoothly!" His lined, puffy face squeezed up like a raisin.

The director reappeared. "I am sorry for the delay. These things happen," he said with an effortless and graceful shrug. "It will all work out." He smiled at Sara. Pepper did not introduce her.

The Italian cameraman, Salvatore, rushed over, excitedly recapping in Italian something about the fracas with the American cinematographer, who was called Davie. The director remained calm. "Si, si," he nodded, then clapped Salvatore on the shoulder.

"Well?" demanded Pepper.

Davie was upon them. "I can't work if he keeps moving the set around. They've got to learn that the grips do that. And tell the grips to keep their hands off my lights!"

"Italians are used to taking care of everything," the director said to Sara. His attitude was one of patience for the stubborn American children who might someday learn better manners. "If there is no electrician, the cameraman will gladly take his place. But we understand what is needed

—302—

here. Only one person is allowed to move the chairs or the rocks on the set." The director smiled at Sara, took her hand, and raised it to his lips. "Welcome. I have seen your beautiful sister's pictures. We are happy you are here."

"Marco Isolantini," Pepper said gruffly. "Our director."

"Delighted," Sara said.

Marco had a fierce smile and a piercing gaze that somehow seemed gentle. He introduced her to Salvatore and Davie.

Davie's sour expression slid from his face. He smiled and said, "I worked with Ernie Ping a coupla times, once on one of Sky's pictures." He shook her hand.

"Ahhh," said the Italian cameraman, Salvatore. "The actress Sky Wyman?"

"Her *sister*, knucklehead," said Davie.

Salvatore's face was full of secrecy and shrewdness; his eyes were alert. He was attractive. Carmen translated for him. When he understood, his eyes lit up and a melodious stream of Italian flowed from him. Carmen said, "He admires your sister very much and is pleased to see you."

Sara forced a smile. "Thank him for us."

Marco took over. "Perhaps you can recite for me a little American poetry," he said in his beautiful voice.

Startled, Sara said she knew very little American poetry, though she did know a few poems in French.

"Yes, yes?" he said, waiting.

Somewhat self-consciously, eyeing the mass of extras and the irritated Davie, she recited a poem by Verlaine. When she had finished, he said, "And you know more?"

"A little."

"Good actors must know many, many poems by heart," he said, his expressive eyes fastened on her.

"Poetry, schmoetry," Pepper said. "Let's get on with the Mongols!" He turned to Sara. "Wardrobe all fixed up with you?" She nodded. "Good. Carmen, get her here at seven A.M. sharp tomorrow morning!" He looked at Sara sadly. "Time means nothing to the Italians."

Carmen took Sara to lunch in the restaurant behind the bar. As they sat on the pine-shaded terrace, Elizabeth Taylor and Roddy McDowall in full costume, accompanied by Eddie Fisher in ordinary attire, came whirling through the restaurant to claim a large terrace table. They were jabbering away with much laughter, momentarily safe from the ever-vigilant paparazzi, that horde of reporters who, like bumblebees, trailed after Taylor everywhere except within the studio walls.

Carmen clapped her hands and leaned in toward Sara. "You want to know about la produzione *Cleopatra*?" she whispered. "I mentioned my boyfriend in the cast, part of the Antony group, and I have another friend who assists the second unit people. So I have all the news." Her eyes glittered. "It is said that La Taylor and Signore Burton are having an affair! It is said that La Taylor and Signore Burton are having an affair! She does not want Fisher anymore."

"She hasn't had him very long," Sara remarked, looking at the jovial threesome who were welcoming Rex Harrison. He was decked out in Roman dress armor, a British trench coat thrown dashingly over his shoulders. The four of them were the center of attention, and they clearly loved it.

The *Cleopatra* production was chaotic for many reasons but the persistent rumors of the potentially explosive Taylor-Burton liaison was only one of the picture's trials. Though they had shot for months at Pinewood Studios in London before coming to Cinecittà, Twentieth Century-Fox still didn't have a picture. Key scenes remained unfilmed; Rouben Mamoulian, the director, had been fired. He had been replaced by Joseph Mankiewicz, who was directing during the day and rewriting at night. They were shooting around unwritten scenes. The cost of production had set a new record: twenty million dollars. *Cleopatra* had turned into the Augean Stables of the movie world.

The waiter arrived with a generous serving of pasta mixed with little clams. "It doesn't look like anything's wrong with their marriage," said Sara, glancing at the merry *Cleopatra* table where Taylor and Fisher were kissing.

"Oh, but, there is," said Carmen. "And everyone's afraid the affair might end before the picture." She waved her hand in front of her face and made a little 'yi-yi' sound.

Carmen had been born and raised in Siena, an ancient walled town near Florence. When she was fifteen, she'd come to Rome to be in the movies.

"Isn't that very young?" asked Sara. They were driving back to Rome from Cinecittà.

"No, not so, but we were very poor. I have younger sisters and brothers, and my mother a vedova—widow. I came to work. I work in the fumetti. They are photo-cartoon strips. Fumetti means smoke, which is what the circle that contains the dialogue looks like—a puff of smoke. Anyway, I was paid twenty thousand lire, about thirty dollars. I sent it back home."

"Do you want to be an actress?"

"No! I want to direct like Liliana Cavani or Vittorio de Sica. They are very different kinds of directors, Cavani is more like Bertolucci—very radical. De Sica, of course, is a god here. So special."

"Do you go to school to learn directing?" Sara was looking at her more carefully now. She would never have thought Carmen would be entertaining such high ambitions.

"I didn't go to the Centro Sperimentale di Cinematografia—the cinema school. Bertolucci went there. He and Cavani are part of a new movement in cinema here, against the Establishment, against mechanized ideals," Carmen said with passionate spirit. "Movies should be subjective, and the structure of a film should be an expression of the film's idea." Carmen glanced at Sara. "We go to see Cavani's new documentary if you like. It's about good and evil."

"A solid theme," Sara said.

"Si. Importante. She hopes to do a feature soon about Saint Francis of Assisi."

"Do women direct here?" Sara asked.

"Oh, yes, but it is hard. Some of the men don't like it," she said airily. "Bah." She grew thoughtful. "Women don't count much. They stay home, have children, keep their mouths shut. The men feel stronger when they think women are nobodies. But that's going to change," Carmen finished. She leaned into a curve on the road.

The next day, costumed in a comically hybrid outfit between a Turkish harem dress and a nineteenth-century Russian cloak, Sara appeared on the set. She met Barrymore, Jr., who had a bad hangover. Sara was apprehensive, and her voice felt constricted. But after a few hours, Marco's jovial informality had made her and everyone feel at ease.

"Prego," he said, after a scene. "Cut. Cut." He approached Sara. "You have face of an angel, a face that takes you anywhere, and you have the powerful emotions. Did you go to acting school?" She nodded. "It is good. You are trained. I applaud. Now unlearn what you were taught."

He stood behind the camera in her line of vision showing her what he wanted by his expressions and gestures. She couldn't converse with him all that well, not understanding some of his heavily accented English. Besides that, being in a movie was a new experience for Sara. She was used to building emotions through an entire scene and carrying them over to the next scene or the next act. But here the "scenes" came in bursts, sometimes for only a line or two, for which she had to weep or stomp around or coyly tease Barrymore, who alternated between stony boredom or frenetic papery emotion.

But as the production rolled on, foundering here, righting itself there, moving from the giant set to the back lot where the Mongols overran Germany, Marco's vitality occasionally made her take risks she'd never dared before. "Act with your whole body," he'd say. "Concentrate, listen. Don't wait for your cue—participate!" And always "Energia! Energia!" Sara also learned the physical labor and the stultifying boredom of being on the set. But whatever her mood, Salvatore beamed at her. He embraced the world; like Marco, he was in love with living, and he had a touch of the elegant aristocrat about him.

"Oh, I love this so much," Sara said one morning as she threw herself into Carmen's little car. Rome was the perfect antidote to the dark canyons of New York. "Will I be doing anything so fun a month from now?"

Carmen cackled. "In Rome tomorrow takes care of itself. Whatever you want to do, you should be doing it right now. Why make arrangements for the future? There is always a future."

24

Kitty was anxious and worried. It was bound to come out. She was fond of Lindy and had grown close to her. How would it affect her, and Sky's work—and everyone? What would Sara or Vail do? More immediately, what would Diana do? She was already jealous of Kitty.

Kitty's instinct was to advance slowly, not to be carried away on the wave of passion that held both Sky and herself in its curl. She decided to go up to Montana and spend a couple of weeks with her father.

Sky agonized about repercussions—about who she was and what loving Kitty meant. She looked back on the Bahamas as an enchanted interlude cut from time and space. Now gravity was back. In moments of courage, she wanted Kitty to move in because she couldn't live without her humor and her love. In moments of weakness she counted her connections and responsibilities looming before her, magnified and changed by what had happened. In the vanguard stood Diana.

Kitty went away, and an intermission ensued. When she returned things were worse.

"What are we going to do?" Sky kept asking. They were currying Kitty's horses.

Kitty was miserable. "I don't know. But I can't move in with you." Kitty lived far out in the valley, where she could keep her two horses and a shifting collection of stray dogs and cats. Behind her house, where they were now, a ramshackle stable sheltered her horses. Shooting on "Paradise" had been delayed; Sonny had been in the hospital. But it was resuming in a few days on the studio's sound stage. Soon Diana would be back from San Francisco.

"But it would be natural for you to live there," Sky insisted.

"Let it go for a while," Kitty counseled, sharply.

"Oh, why is this so hard?! We haven't done anything wrong."

"Most people will think we had," Kitty said. "Sometimes I think so myself."

Sky looked at her angrily. "I have those thoughts, too," she said, "but I am not going to give in to them!"

When Sky got home that afternoon, Lindy was waiting for her. "Mom," she cried, "where have you been? You forgot!"

"Oh, honey, I'm sorry!" She and Lindy were supposed to make cookies for the school bake sale. "We'll buy some!"

"No! I want cookies you and I made!"

Sky dreaded cooking because she knew nothing about it. "Okay, let's have at it!"

After false starts, bad guesses, and brave laughter, they turned out misshapen, flat, hard peanut-butter cookies that Lindy nevertheless pronounced good. "Thanks, Mom," Lindy said. "I know this was hard on you."

Sky called an architect. She asked him to design a separate house at the bottom of the garden between the fishpond and the edge of her property near the "lake." Sky was in a meeting with the architect for the "shack," as she referred to it, when Diana arrived.

"I need more space," Sky said. "It's an office for Kitty right now."

"You're building a house for Kitty?" Diana asked. "She's got her own house."

"It's an office, Mother."

"Well, how about Sammy or Ernie Ping? Why not build an apartment house, and then everyone could live here!" Diana looked at her daughter crossly. "You look nervous and distracted, dear."

"I've got a big scene tomorrow, Mother. That's all." Diana knew her daughter better, but she, too, had a lot

—308—

on her mind. It was late 1961, and the Freedom Riders were testing the segregation laws of the South by riding on buses in Alabama. Diana was helping to coordinate white California liberals, usually young college students or ministers, to take the places of riders who had been beaten too badly to continue. This work consumed her and, because of it, Diana saw nothing except that she had to compete with Kitty for Sky's attention.

"I came down here to get a little rest," Diana said. She was also helping coordinate the Southern Christian Leadership program at UCLA. "Is it too much to ask that I be made welcome?"

"Mother, you *are* welcome." Sky went back to her blueprints.

As the days went on, and Kitty was more often at Sky's little castle than she was at her own home, Diana saw that something between them had changed. Sky was enthralled with Kitty, laughing gaily at her anecdotes about the set or the cast or Beaudine. Diana felt excluded from Sky's life. When her attention wasn't on Birmingham, Alabama, she warned Sky that Kitty's influence over her wasn't healthy; it gave Kitty too much power. She complained to Sky how rude Kitty had been to her. But Sky just laughed: Kitty was the least rude person in the world!

"There you go," Diana said, "taking her part."

Diana watched the builders erect the "shack" at the bottom of the garden. It was all too fast. She shouted at Kitty, "Can't they be quiet? I'm on the phone here with Alabama!"

Kitty respected Diana but she dreaded Diana's certain discovery. Kitty didn't know if Sky was strong enough to defy her mother for such a socially unacceptable relationship. For her own part, Kitty wondered if she herself would have the face for the same battle with her father.

Diana embroidered all the exchanges she had with Kitty; Sky defended her. "You're against me now, aren't you, darling?" Diana said, her voice trembling. "You don't want me to be with you anymore. I can feel it. She's got you under her spell."

Sky ignited, lashing out at her mother. "Don't tell me what to do or who to like!" She pulled back. "I'm sorry,

Mother. But you have to face the fact that there are more people in my life than just you. It doesn't mean that I don't love you. It doesn't change my feelings for you."

Diana's bedroom faced the lake. She was drifting off to sleep one evening when a creak on the stairs awakened her. Someone was going downstairs.

Diana got out of bed and went to the window. She saw nothing except the shimmering still water of the pool and the garden beyond it. It was Diana's favorite time of day and her favorite view: the garden dressed in silver light from the moon.

From the back of the house, she saw them: Kitty and Sky in their white nightgowns, Sky carrying a bottle of some kind and two glasses. They darted around the end of the pool, past the gazebo, and down the path to the unfinished "shack." On a wave of soft laughter and shushes, they disappeared into the shadows. Diana looked after them for a long time.

"I am not living in this place," Kitty said softly. "It will make a very nice guest house."

"I am fully prepared to tell Mother all about us when it's finished," Sky said.

Sky and Kitty were sitting in the living room. The moonlight shone down through the unfinished roof; the air was humid, warm, and still. The dark doorway in the far wall led to a study-office where Kitty would keep track of most of Sky's personal and studio affairs. Off on the other side was the bedroom. They had uncorked the champagne and sat next to each other against the wall, their legs stretched out, Sky's arm around Kitty's shoulders.

"When I'm out here with you there isn't another person in the universe," Sky murmured, exquisitely happy. "This is the universe."

Kitty leaned her head against Sky's shoulder. "I've never been in love before," Kitty said. "I mean it. I love you. The real you—the here and here and here you." Solemnly, she put her hand on Sky's cheek, breast, and belly. Then she leaned in and gently kissed her. Sky responded passionately, her whole body tingling. She felt Kitty's tongue in her mouth and Kitty's hand on her breast. She lay back and gave herself to the floodgates that had been opened in the Bahamas, wrapping her arms around the woman who set her on fire.

Unseen, Diana stood in the doorway, silhouetted against the brilliant moonlight, witness to her daughter's embrace.

"Reed, dear," Diana said over the telephone the next day, "I wonder if you have time to have tea with me."

They met at his house in the hills above Sunset Boulevard. Mementos of his productions covered the pale walls of the living room—production pictures, one sheets, art directors' drawings, cartoons. Distant traffic from Sunset Boulevard rose like the hum of the sea on a far shore. Diana smoothed her gabardine suit and settled into a handsome Sheridan chair that faced the French doors.

"I heard that Sky was offered Teddy's play and refused," he said, serving her tea.

"Yes. Very loyal of her."

"And how's Sara?"

"She's in Rome doing an undistinguished movie." She took the cup he offered. "Reed, I came to talk about Sky. This is very difficult," she said, adjusting on her lapel a large gold pin in the shape of a stag. "I come to you out of my respect for you and your affection for Sky and, of course, my love for Sky." She shifted demurely. "To put it delicately . . . Sky is having an affair with Kitty."

Reed was astonished; it shivered across his face. "Sky told you this?"

"No. I saw them."

"Perhaps you mistook—"

"Reed, the only affair I ever had in my life was with Neddie, but I do know what I'm talking about." She adjusted her pin again. "I've never made judgments about what people should do. The director of our museum up north was, I'm sure, a homosexual, but that didn't impair his visual gifts or his ability to fund that museum. Of course, it's harder with your own child. One thinks of what one did wrong, about what terrible, superficial people say—"

"Who?" Reed asked, completely lost.

"The psychiatrists!" Diana said with venom. "Did she lack love, and all that!"

"Oh. Well, I can understand the—well—the surprise this must be to you—" He stopped and changed his mind. "What do you think of Kitty?"

"She's ordinary," Diana said promptly. "We don't agree on many things, except about the Freedom Riders, with whom she very properly has great sympathy."

Reed rose and began walking around the room, ending up at the glass doors to the terrace, his back to her.

"It's my feeling," Diana went on, "that Kitty should be dismissed in some fashion, perhaps by the studio, or sent on a production somewhere far away. Of course," she said, staring at the cushions in the couch, "this liaison is just a crush, but if it gets out—"

"It won't get out," Reed said to the window.

"Oh, how can you say that? Your own heart must be breaking and no one can guarantee that—"

"My heart is not breaking, Diana." He turned and walked back to her side of the room. He was quite tall, and his dark grace seemed to hold a quiet threat that put her off. "It would be most unwise for you to make an issue of this." He wondered how much he might tell her about her own need to control Sky, of Sky's need for a confidante, for a lover, for someone who did not threaten or detract from her work. Kitty was not the choice he would have made for her—a woman for a lover created more problems than it solved.

It was all very hard to take in, and he realized that Diana had said something he'd missed. He sat down beside her. "Do you have any idea how important you are to Sky?" he began.

Diana smiled tolerantly. "Sky doesn't listen to me."

"If you confront her with what you have seen, it will embarrass her. You'll force her to choose between you and Kitty. I think you know at this point who she'll choose."

Diana sat up very straight. She was angry because she'd hoped for a quick, hot reaction from Reed, one that would ally with her own sense of grief. "You are misreading the situation entirely," she said pointedly. "We have never had anything so disreputable in our family. It's unhealthy and scandalous. If you won't give her some guidance—"

"Sky's thirty-one, Diana!"

"Get the studio to send Kitty—"

"The studio won't send Kitty anywhere!" he said, rising and shoving his hands in his pockets. "That isn't how it works. Sky is far too valuable to make an issue out of it, and as long as they are discreet—"

"Discreet!" Diana snapped. "That's the last word I would have expected out of you. Don't you love her?"

He whirled on the infuriating woman who never raised her voice. "Of course I love her! But not in the way you want me to love her, and Sky doesn't love me in that way! I can't compete with Kitty. And she's not a cheap person. She's a woman of character and intelligence who probably has Sky's best interests at heart."

"Really, Reed! Kitty has seduced Sky for her own purposes, whatever they are. What kind of mother would I be if I just sat idly by? It's unthinkable!"

"I'm warning you, you will harm her if you do anything about this."

After she left he sat out on the terrace smoking a cigarette. He had weak lungs, and his doctor had told him to give them up, but Reed kept a pack around for "emergencies." This was an emergency. How he wished things were different, that he and Sky had married, perhaps had a child, worked together more often, fought the studios with greater courage. He wished a lot of things. He was glad he was starting a new picture, a musical that held new challenges. He crushed out the cigarette and shivered in the hot sun. Things really hadn't been good for Sky since Lila killed herself. He and Sky had talked about it. She couldn't forget Lila; she kept wondering if people blamed her for Lila's suicide. Its tentacles reached out of the past into the present. Even that unhappy picture Sky had been shooting then—*The Ginkgo Tree*—had bombed at the box office; the relentless press had pursued her until her good relations with them had soured and broken. The role Lila had lost to Sky, the one that had triggered her death, had done Sky's career no good. *Once in Nashville* had suffered from a dozen rewrites and a maniacal producer who had had the taste of a jackal. That film, too, had bombed.

He rose, went back into the living room, and stared at the tea tray. He felt that Sky's life was taking a bad turn—

—313—

not because of Kitty but because other forces were coming up from the shadows to demand payment. All he could do was stand by and help Sky as a friend if she needed him.

"We're back in the bungalow, Sky, and Rachel knows her life is falling apart." They were on the set and Beaudine was describing the scene. "Her husband's just left, drunk, for the boat. She knows now that he was the cause of her little boy's death. You're alone. Your life's in a shambles, and I want you to come apart. I want you to weep from your belly."

"I can only do it once," Sky finally said.

"I know." Beaudine put a hand on Sky's shoulder. "You tell me when you're ready."

Sky glanced at Kitty, then walked out on the set and sat on the edge of the bed.

After several minutes Sky lowered her head and nodded at Beaudine that she was ready. The camera rolled. She built the scene from a murmur and escalated to wrenching sobs that riveted even the hardened grips. Beaudine finally whispered "Cut." The crew burst into applause. Wiping the tears from her face, Sky smiled bashfully. Ace arrived with a towel.

Diana was waiting in the bungalow when Sky, Kitty, and Ace came bursting in from the set. She could not have picked a worse moment to have it out with her daughter.

"Sky just did a scene that'll be a classic!" Ace said.

"Darling," Diana said to Sky, "I need to talk to you."

"Shoot," Sky replied, sitting down at the makeup table. She always felt newly made when the tough scenes were over. Kitty was pouring her a glass of champagne.

"You drink too much champagne, Sky," Diana said sharply, "and you, Kitty, shouldn't press it on her that way."

"Ooops," Ace said, taking a glass of it, "party's getting rough."

"I wonder if I could be alone with Sky for just one minute," Diana said.

"Guess I'll be going," Ace said.

"Thank you, Ace," Diana said. She looked pointedly at Kitty. Ace took Kitty's arm.

—314—

"Hey!" Sky said, coming down from the scene fast.

"That's okay," Kitty said. "I'll be right outside."

"What the hell do you think you're doing?" Sky asked, arching an eyebrow at her mother. Ace and Kitty left.

"What I have to say is just so very, very important, and there's no time at the house. Kitty's always with us these days," she added darkly.

"What is it, Mother? Is Sara okay? Vail?"

"Everyone's fine, Sky. But you're not." The beautiful daughter that she had so carefully raised felt remote to her. She would bring her back. "I know about you and Kitty, Sky, and I want you to think about what you are doing to your life."

Sky felt the blood drain from her face. She turned away from her mother and found both of them reflected in the mirror. She pressed her fingers into a jar of cold cream.

"Did you hear what I said?"

"I heard. I don't understand what you mean," Sky said softly. The moment she had dreaded and sought to avoid had pounced on her. She was astonished at its power.

"Do I have to tell you what I saw? You and Kitty in that wretched little guest house you're building. It was two nights ago, Sky. I just wouldn't be a very good mother if I didn't have the courage to confront you with this foolish thing. You don't know what kind of jeopardy you're putting yourself into, the kind of ghastly scandal that can overtake you, kill your career—"

"Just stop." Sky was shaking from head to foot. She had been putting the cold cream on her face. Now she took a fistful of tissues and roughly wiped the cream off in great swipes. "I won't talk about this! This is none of your business."

"What kind of a person would I be if I ignored you when you were in trouble?" Diana said, rising. She started to pace the room.

"I'm not in trouble. I'm happy for the first time in my life. If that's trouble to you—"

"Is that all you can say?" Diana pleaded, her voice wavering and tears springing into her eyes. "What would people think if I just abandoned you? I'm trying to help, dear. I've talked to Reed, and he agrees—"

"You've talked to Reed about Kitty?" Sky gasped.

"Of course, dear. He cares very deeply about you. So do I."

"I won't have this!" Sky shrieked. She couldn't believe that her mother had gone to Reed. "Doesn't what I want—isn't that important to anyone?"

"You're acting like a child, and you're making a fool of yourself. Kitty just leads you around by the nose. Pretty soon this will get out—these things always do—and then you'll be gossiped about all over town!"

Sky shot to her feet. "I won't listen! Kitty is everything to me!" Sky started to stutter. Everything Diana said shamed and insulted her. She couldn't find her way back into all the carefully arranged phrases she'd rehearsed to say to her mother.

"Don't be ridiculous, Sky. I'm worried about you. I think Kitty should take a trip so you can get your bearings again—"

"So you can take control of me again; that's what you mean! I'm not fifteen! I want a life of my own! Isn't it enough that you and Daddy are living on my money? Sometimes I feel like you're eating me alive!" Sky choked on the sobs she was trying to keep inside.

"What do I have to do to make you see some sense?" Diana said through her teeth. She took hold of Sky's shoulders and shook her roughly.

Sky seized the jar of cold cream and threw it at the mirror, shattering it. "Get out!"

Diana stepped back. "I certainly *won't* get out. What's come over you? I suppose that Kitty has set you against me—"

"*Get out!*" Sky screamed, picking up another jar and throwing it at her mother. It missed and hit a wall. "I have a right to my own life!" In her rage she grabbed a folding chair and started beating it against the table. The door burst open and Ace and Kitty rushed in.

"You did this, you terrible woman!" Diana shouted at Kitty. "You're ruining her!"

"I want her out of here!" Sky stared at Diana.

Kitty. "I want her out of here!" Sky was sobbing, her face streaked with cold cream and tears.

Diana stared at her daughter incredulously.

Kitty said, "Sky, sweetheart, put the chair down."

"C'mon, Mrs. Wyman," Ace said. "Just for the moment, till Sky calms down."

Diana shook Ace's arm off and strode from the room, head up. Ace followed her and closed the door after them. Inside, Kitty took Sky in her arms and rocked her.

Sky wept. "Call Reed. I've got to talk to him. I won't go around lying to everyone and leading two different lives. I won't do it, Kitty. I want him to hear it from me." Her sobs and screams, filling the room so totally, like the air, didn't seem to Kitty to be coming from any one body. She thought that if she went outside the mountains would be ringing with the sound.

"I didn't want you to find out that way," Sky said.

"I know," Reed replied, taking her hand. Sky was curled up on the sofa in her bungalow, Reed beside her. "Don't feel you have to explain to me." He really didn't want to hear.

"But I wanted you to be—" she searched for the right words and actually looked around the room. "I didn't know how separated from everyone I felt until I met Kitty—I mean, I didn't know how lonely I was. I can't have friends, like just ordinary acquaintances—oh, I'm getting all mixed up." Her eyes were red, and she was smoking furiously.

"Give me one of those," he said.

"You're not supposed to have one." She plucked a cigarette out of a box on the table for him. He lit it and inhaled.

"Kitty—it was like having a friend who understood just the way Sara and Vail always understood. There wasn't any barrier between Kitty and me. She wasn't intimidated, and when she didn't agree with me, she said so, but she always had another suggestion, it wasn't just arbitrary."

"I know."

"And she's had a whole life of her own, she's not just someone who's never done anything. She's good at what she does, and she respects herself. We'd laugh and kid each other—we went to a drive-in movie and sat there and howled, and, oh, Reed, when we were in the Bahamas, it wasn't just being on a tropical island or any of that stuff, it just—it was like a natural extension of the respect we have for each other. This sounds like an apology doesn't it? It sounds like I'm ashamed of myself, doesn't it?"

"No, but it—"

"Oh, I care about what you think! If I could just feel that people wouldn't look at me now as though I'm some kind of freak. I mean, I know it'll get out, and I'm not sure people like me or my work enough to look beyond. I mean, are they going to think—how about Lindy—oh, God, Lindy. And Daddy? And Vail and Sara? I've done nothing but think about what they'll think of me—and Kitty—since we got back. I mean, how do I explain this?"

"Some of them will surprise you," he said. "What do you care about people you don't even know? Some people in the business may whisper about you, but not to your face. So what?"

"But Sara and Vail and Lindy—that's where I really get the quivers. It frightens me, Reed."

"Oh, c'mon, you're seeing ghosts. Can you imagine Vail and Sara, er, well, cutting you off because of Kitty? I can't."

Sky lit another cigarette. "No, I guess not. But what would they say privately? And Lindy," she moaned.

"That's different. That's much more delicate. But you'll find a way. Kitty's very sensible, and she has integrity."

"Kitty and I can't go anywhere together, not the way you and I did. I've thought of that a lot. Who'd invite both of us to dinner?"

He laughed. "Lots of people!" She was like a violin whose strings had just popped, flying out in all directions.

"I'm thinking of the benefits and the premieres and all that," she said. "I can't escort Kitty to—"

"I guess you'd better get acquainted with a different way of living. I'll escort you when you want, where I can. I'm kinda involved with Patricia right now," he said, mentioning the comedy writer he'd been seeing for the last few months. "Jim Fry will escort you or Kitty, he's crazy about Kitty."

She leaned back. "I don't want to bring all this down to escorts or dinner dates. That's not important, it's just one of the things you think about." She sat up and leaned her elbows on her knees. "I'm so worn out. I'm so tired of the

—318—

photographs and the snively press and the productions and pleasing a horde of people out there—" She waved one hand and put the other to her forehead. "And the feeling that I never belong to myself—myself! When I'm with Kitty, I'm with my pal."

"You've always pleased everyone. Now you are going to have to live with not pleasing some people. That can be hard. It's new to you." He was seeing a side of Sky that he'd not seen before: Sky had no sense of the consequences of her actions.

"Help me, for God's sake," she said, pitching into his arms suddenly. "Help me. I can't lose her."

Reed held her close; it was all he could do.

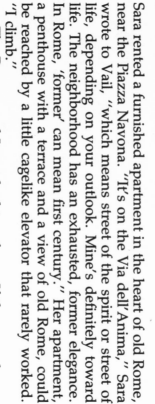

25

Sara rented a furnished apartment in the heart of old Rome, near the Piazza Navona. "It's on the Via dell'Anima," Sara wrote to Vail, "which means street of the spirit or street of life, depending on your outlook. Mine's definitely toward life. The neighborhood has an exhausted, former elegance. In Rome, 'former' can mean first century." Her apartment, a penthouse with a terrace and a view of old Rome, could be reached by a little cagelike elevator that rarely worked. "I climb."

The Roman god Janus had two faces. If the crazy buoyancy of Cinecittà was the sunny face of her days, the emotional baggage Sara dragged with her from New York cast on them a long nocturnal shadow. The passionate and debilitating years with Teddy had left her raw and grieving and hungry. She had been in a major Off-Broadway hit but had failed to translate it into a career. At night Sara thought about Sky refusing to do *Elephant House* and about Teddy rewriting for Anne Bancroft, for whom it was now being mounted.

It was in this conflicted mood that Sara took her first walk down the Via dell'Anima one Sunday. The thin midwinter sun felt tepid. Behind an iron gate, near a building that looked deserted, a mother cat kept a watchful eye on two thin kittens. Roman cats were numberless; many were wild, all were hungry. It was said that the ancestors of the cats in the Colosseum had arrived with the real Cleopatra. Sara reached into her pocket and pulled out a little sack of dry cat food. She shoved it through the gate at the mother cat, who nosed it suspiciously, then ate it hungrily with her kittens.

Around the corner the Piazza Navona bustled with tourists and residents. Two thousand years before, chariots had whipped around the track of Domitian's Stadium, cheered by the crowds from ringside seats. The huge piazza had been built over the oval. Later, in the sixteenth century, a powerful Umbrian family commissioned three fountains. The central one was Bernini's Fountain of the Four Rivers; it dominated the square. At the southern end of the piazza was the Fountain of the Moor; and at the north end, from the third fountain, Neptune rode on the back of an octopus surrounded by half-submerged horses galloping out of the water.

Compared to them, the rest of the piazza seemed tame. Three-story seventeenth-century buildings, ochre, yellow, ringed the square. The delicate dome and belfries of Saint Agnes's church rose opposite the Fountain of the Four Rivers. Sitting on its steps was a ragged child. Her face was smudged, her hands grimy, her arms like sticks. She was begging. On another day Salvatore had seen Sara give another child a thousand lire, a lot in Italy but less than two dollars. Salvatore was outraged: Give, yes, but not a thousand lire!

"Nobody begs if they have enough," Sara had replied.

"Ah, they are lazy gypsies," he had said.

Sara gave the girl on the church steps a thousand-lire bill, then she sat down at a restaurant on the square and ordered a coffee.

He was sauntering across the square, an impeccable dandy, his head tilted to one side, his gaze haughtily glancing at the women he passed. His eye stopped at Sara. He sat down at the next table and ordered coffee. His trousers were freshly pressed, his black hair and his cufflinks glistened in the sun. A handkerchief peeped from his breast pocket, a splash of red against his pale blue jacket. He looked beautiful and gloriously contemptuous. He smiled at her with disarming childishness. She smiled back. When his coffee arrived, he picked it up and glided to her table, standing beside it, holding the cup and saucer with a temporary air. He asked something in soft Italian.

"Americana," she responded, not knowing what he'd asked.

"Ah!" he exclaimed with liquid appreciation. He sat down. With almost no common language, they stumbled into a neutral territory of laughter and long looks and accommodating misunderstandings. He said his name was Giovanni; he was in business from Milano. "Voi—you, ah, you film star?" he asked.

"No," she said, "Cinecittà. Actress. Attrice. Sara Wyman."

He leaned back and lit a cigarette. "Sì. Signorina Wyman." He pretended not to care, then leaned in, his dark eyes gleaming. "Voi—you zee Queen White!" He reached out and touched her hair and laughed gently. "Negro—black? You change?"

It was an odd moment. Something snapped for Sara. Even years later, she couldn't decide if she'd simply stopped caring who compared her to Sky or whether she began to take on the role of being Sky to get something—or some-one—she wanted. She took him to her apartment. They arrived breathless from the climb, and an hour after that, they were in bed. He was overjoyed. He pleaded with her to come and meet all his friends. She refused. A week later she saw him waiting tables in a trattoria on the Via del Corso.

The Monday after the elegant waiter shared her bed, Sara saw her first rushes from the film. She thought she looked wooden on the screen. Pepper proclaimed himself very happy so far; Marco, the director, flattered her. So did Salvatore: Very photogenic; bella, he said, bella. But the rushes depressed Sara. As people filed out of the little screening room, she wondered if she'd deluded herself that things would be different in another country. She kept seeing the way Sky would have done the stupid role.

Marco saw her distress. "We go to Colle Oppia," he said. "Ristorante grande. You will like."

"I don't know what I'm doing here," she said.

"You are meeting new people," he exclaimed. "Having new experiences! You are feeding every cat in Rome!"

"Aha! There is gossip about me already!"

The Colle Oppia was a huge outdoor restaurant and nightclub frequented by Roman movie folk, overlooking the Colosseum. "See?" he said, "Sorpresa! A surprise." He unfurled the film's one-sheet. A Technicolor picture of herself, in her faintly Turkish outfit, showed her struggling against the ardent embrace of John Barrymore, Jr. At the top of the sheet, "Barrymore," and under it, "Wyman."

"Where's my first name?" she asked.

"Here," he pointed at the bottom of the list, where the major players' names were spelled out in small print.

He pretended not to understand. Indeed, she was never sure how much English Marco understood. "Beautiful, si?" He rolled it up again and gave it to her.

"No. Terrible."

"Do not be sad, cara. You can make many films here," he said. Nothing had ever sounded so depressing. "It is today! Fun today—divertimento!" A rushing waiter pulled to a stop beside their table. "We begin," Marco said, "with vino bianco—Frascati." They gorged themselves on *prosciutto e fichi* and thin bread sticks called *grissini*. Next, *spaghetti alle vongole* and *scampi alla griglia*, finishing with a salad followed by a huge bowl of fruit, from which Marco carefully selected a pear, cut it up, and doled out slices to her.

They ended up at her apartment. Marco's tender, passionate body made Sara forget deepening discontent with herself. They lay on the bed, spent, the doors open to the terrace and the strangely warm evening. She stared up into a luminous midnight blue sky that reminded her of Christmas wrapping paper. "Marco, even if this movie were not a piece of shit, I am still not as good an actress as Sky," she said. "I want you to tell me why not."

He turned over and stroked her head. "Is not better, not worse. You are different," he said. "You are more robust. More sexy. Ecco tutto.". He rubbed his lips against hers. He wanted her to be frisky and vivacious again, the way she had been that first day on the set.

Sara felt that she was drowning.

The Mongol movie ended. Marco asked Sara to play the lead in his next film, a historical costume drama. It was called *Lady of the Wild Things*, and it took place in ancient

Greece. Sara was reluctant; Marco took her to dinner in a restaurant near the Piazza Venezia.

"So who's the producer on this one?" she asked, feeling the effects of the strong wine Marco had ordered.

"Bruno di Cecco. He has made many, many films like this, is wealthy from them. He is socialist and he loves birds, hates people who shoots them, won't eat them." He laughed melodiously and stroked her cheek with the back of his hand.

"And what are your politics, caro?" she asked.

"Ah, communista," he said proudly.

"There are many communisti here, si?" she asked.

"Yes, but many socialists, too, and others. We have all kinds in Italy, all factions—fazione. You learn that. I speak part Italiano, part Inglese. You learn. Si?"

"Marco!" A man rose from an adjacent table and came over to them enthusiastically.

"Bud! Come state?"

"Molto bene, grazie." The man was very tall and thin, an American with a jutting jaw, a kindly smile, and crisp blue eyes. "E—" he said, looking at Sara.

"Posso presentarvi la Signorina Wyman, Signore Bud Graven, Associated Press," Marco introduced him. "Bud has covered Roma since Quo Vadis in—"

"Since 1950. Piacere," Bud said, taking her hand.

"Likewise," she said.

"Wyman is a well-known name in the States," Bud said.

"Yes," Sara said. "My sister's name. Sky. You've heard of her, no doubt."

"Of course."

"Join us," Marco exclaimed, the expansive host. Bud sat down, another bottle of wine was ordered, and more food. "How about an interview while I'm sitting here?"

"Sara's consented to play the lead in my next film, The Lady of Wild Things," said Marco, who danced in and out of the conversation like an acrobat. Bud lifted his eyebrows.

"So, shoot me," Sara said.

"Marco's films are always well made," Bud said. "Someday he might even take cinema seriously. But tell me, weren't you in Teddy Monroe's Off-Broadway play last year? Kind of a big success?"

—324—

"I'm resting," Sara said.

Bud heard the cynicism in her voice. "I thought you did high-tone stuff. It's refreshing that you're not a snob."

"I guess you get right down to the bone, don't you?" she said, paying more attention to him.

"But it's funny you're here and not there. Don't you want to do other plays?"

Sara switched the subject to *Cleopatra*. No one could open a magazine without finding a Taylor-Burton story, usually accompanied by a page of pictures. *Cleopatra* and its cast were on Page One of the *Daily Mail* and the *Mirror* and *Der Tag* five days in a row.

"But the Fox executives are very unhappy," said Bud. "They think the publicity will hurt the picture. Can you beat that?"

"Politics!" Marco cried. "We talk politics!"

Sara's interview got lost during the course of the meal, in the flow of the wine, followed by much grappa with the fruit. But Bud picked it up again when he asked about her youth, about growing up with Sky, about being a triplet.

"When you're a triplet you have instant comrades who understand the same things you do at the same time," Sara said, momentarily sentimental, remembering the big ranch at the foot of the Sierras. "Sky was sickly but so sweet. Vail, our brother, always liked to get people in trouble." She laughed.

"Telling fibs, was he?"

"Yes, but he was caught in the middle between Sky and me." She felt tipsy.

"And you?" Bud asked. "What were you like?"

"I was the actress in the crowd. I always wanted to act."

"How do you like Rome?" he asked.

Marco poured more grappa. "I love Rome," she said. "Better than New York."

"Better than being in New York plays?" he asked, mildly astonished.

"Sure! Much friendlier!"

Bud thanked her effusively as the three of them staggered out of the restaurant and into the night.

To celebrate the flamboyant end to the Mongol movie, Marco threw a huge party for the cast and crew on the set.

People wandered in and out from other sets, nobody cared, all were welcome. At one point, quite high, Sara threw herself onto one of the lush sofas and someone tossed a newspaper over her face. She pulled it aside, struggled up, went in search of an espresso, and was sipping it at the edge of the set when she focused on the newspaper she'd dragged along with her. "Sisters Vie for Roles?" the headline said, above Bud's byline. As she read on she felt her fingers turning to ice. She was instantly sober. Bud's article stated that Sara Wyman was picking up a little money in Rome by "waltzing through" one of the "laughable and repetitive" costume movies, a "craze started by *Hercules*" that was now raiding other stories in history and mythology.

"In speaking with Sara Wyman, sister of the American star, Sky Wyman, she told us confidentially over dinner that Sky had been a reclusive child with no perceivable talents, and that their brother, Vail (they are a set of triplets), was a liar as a child, a troublemaking prankster who kept all of them in hot water. We asked Miss Wyman what her brother was doing now. 'He's an aging beatnik,' the actress responded over after-dinner drinks. And was it true that the role that Teddy Monroe wrote for her in his new drama, *Elephant House*, had been offered to her sister Sky instead? Miss Wyman stated that she preferred Hercules-style movies to the American stage."

Sara looked around the crowded and noisy sound stage. Marco was a few tables away; he made enthusiastic and suggestive gestures about going to bed with her.

"How could you let me do this!" she cried, waving the paper. "I'd had too much to drink, it wasn't fair!" Marco shrugged; he didn't understand her. She was in pain with jealousy, he thought, watching her tear up the newspaper. He hoped she would get well soon.

Sara meticulously researched her jewelry and costumes for *Lady of the Wild Things*. Since she was playing an ancient Greek priestess, her calls were for 5:00 A.M. so that her entire body could be covered in sepia makeup. Her hair was dyed stone black. It was a shock when she sat down before the mirror to see her stiffly permanented hair sticking out in damp black coils: She looked like Sky. Only her hazel eyes gave her away.

The assembled cast was a group of monumental, bristling egos who managed, at the same time, to be loving and courteous. It was a curious mixture. Marco developed hives when his other female lead, a French starlet, resisted his direction. She could not find her floor marks without looking for them and constantly called Marco's directions into question, embarrassing everyone. One actor, from Spain, was always drunk. Then there was the Austrian male lead, Wolf, who learned his lines after he came on the set each morning just before doing the scene. The resulting tension this created in him made him feel that he was truly acting.

There were jealous arguments between Marco and di Cecco, the producer, regarding credits and publicity and budgets. It was January, but the picture was shot in an unheated studio. Salvatore was the director of photography. It was rumored that his photography for a film he'd shot last year might be nominated for an Academy Award. He hadn't been the same since.

The rotund, exuberant di Cecco usually sat with the crew; Sara often joined them. She especially liked the electrician, the wise philosopher of the set, who often praised the Americans' creative professionalism. They were sitting on the altar set one day when di Cecco took a script out from under his capacious coat and shyly offered it to Sara. "Maybe you show it to your sister," he said, smiling deprecatingly. Sara didn't say no, but when she got back to her apartment, she threw it into a basket where it joined a dozen others.

Carmen, who was working on a mythological film about giants with Pepper, often joined her for lunch on the terrace of the restaurant.

"It's official," Carmen said one day. "Fisher's bounced. And Burton's wife, Sybil, is flying to London. Taylor-Burton are going out in public for first time." Burton was fed up with everyone telling them to be discreet.

The next day the papers were crammed with pictures of Burton-Taylor going on the town. The Fox executives huddled in their battle stations, furious and fearful.

Midway through "Lady," Salvatore made a mistake on a scene that involved Sara. She shrugged it off but Salvatore yelled, "Sono uno nobile direttore di fotografo farò anche meglio!"

"So you're one of the greatest cinematographers in the world," said Sara. "But I was on my mark. You made a mistake." Salvatore exploded and insulted her. "Don't you dare!" she shouted.

In the deep silence, Marco took Sara's arm and led her to one side. Across the set Salvatore was ranting and raving, "I'm Salvatore Manzini! My filming may be Academy Award!" Sara began laughing at his display. He was absurd.

"Idiota!" he screamed at her as his assistant and the sound man started pulling him toward the door. "The only reason you're in the production is because Marco wants to reach Sky!" He licked his thin lips, pleased at the shock on her face.

"Bugiardo!" she shouted. "Liar!"

In her dressing room, Marco said, "Salvatore didn't mean it."

"He did mean it," she said. Her skin was allergic to the body dye; it itched, and when she sweated under the heavy costume, the rash stung.

He drew her into his arms. "I am not using you to reach your sister."

"It doesn't matter. I'm used to it." She disengaged herself from his arms.

"It matters. To have such a sister is a curse and a gift." Sara shrugged. "Let's get on with the scene," she said.

The next day, Marco wanted to shoot the French version of a scene. Sara was wearing a long, stiffly ruffled dress; the bodice was open to her waist, covered by a gauzy material. "The French version will be without this," he said, fingering the gauze.

"Bare-breasted?" she said. "Are the other women doing that?" He nodded. She didn't feel comfortable about it, but she agreed. She pointed at Salvatore. "I won't do it if *he's* around."

It was night when she left the studio and walked down the main street, under the lamps. A bent woman, wearing a shawl, a long skirt, and boots was coming toward her from the opposite direction. Her boots dragged painfully on the pavement as though she were carrying a heavy, invisible burden on her back. Sara hesitated. As she came abreast of Sara, the woman turned her battered old face up. It was a woman Carmen had pointed out, a once-famous Italian actress.

The old woman stared into Sara's face. The youth of an actress is the short season, Sara thought. She saw herself as the old, crippled woman, and it sent a chill straight into her bones.

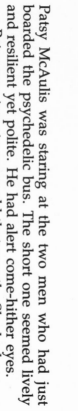

26

Patsy McAulis was staring at the two men who had just boarded the psychedelic bus. The short one seemed lively and resilient yet polite. He had alert come-hither eyes.

Patsy was twenty years old that month. She had grown up in Reno, Nevada, the daughter of a woman who dealt blackjack. Her father had jilted her mother when he'd learned she was pregnant. At seventeen, Patsy had joined the beat movement by running away to San Francisco with the idea of becoming a singer in one of the new jazz and poetry clubs. She had tied up with some of the beats, and now those connections had landed her on this bus, touring the West, living life as it came.

Patsy had a flat, heart-shaped face; round blue green eyes; and straight, stringy brown hair the color of bittersweet chocolate. She moved over to the empty seat next to the short man and asked him if he had any grass.

"No, sweetmeat, I don't do that shit anymore. Me and Bondy've been getting cooled out." He had a warm, soft voice.

"What's your name?" she asked.

"Vail. As in Vale of Tears."

"How romantic. Mine's Patsy." She curled up, put her head in his lap, and listened to Vail's conversation with Bondy. Vail was educated. His travels impressed her. The bus chugged through the wasteland of western Wyoming. Vail and Bondy had been hunting Buddha and the eight-fold path that relieved all suffering. Bondy was tired of suffering. Their efforts were sustained by checks from Diana. "Mom's way of keeping tabs on me," Vail had once sighed. Vail was still writing essays and reviews that he'd spin around the movies playing in Sweetwater, Wyoming, or in Fargo, North Dakota, sending them to the *Village Voice*.

When most of the latest check was gone, they had decided to find the eightfold path by surviving in the wilderness on wild lettuce, watercress, sunflower seeds, nuts, fasts, and meditation. "Find your soul, man," Bondy instructed him. Vail could only find memories of New York City with Sara and Teddy, of Sky and Teddy's new play, memories that made him cringe. What was happening to them all? Vail wondered. "Don't think of them," said Bondy. "Just get to your own bottom." They bumped into a movie company on location in the desert. The director looked a little nuts to Vail, and the company didn't seem to know what they were doing. High on something, he thought. Vail wrote some dialogue for them because their story had to do with beatniks. The director tossed his dialogue out: a written scene marred the movie's sharp improvised edge.

In the desert Vail had a vision of Sara surrounded by golden lights. He was sure it meant she was in trouble. "How can she be in trouble in Rome?" Bondy demanded. "It's the Eternal City, where one century flows effortlessly into another!" Even so Vail was moved to break camp. He and Bondy struck out for the highway, where they started to thumb rides. That's when the bus with the jagged streak of lightning painted on its side found them.

Bondy, who was one seat in front of Vail, said, "I'm going to Europe. Your sister has given me an idea. That's where the action is." Bondy's face looked like old leather, dried out and darkened. "I'm closing up my pad in Frisco and giving away my books and records and my hi-fi."

Vail sympathized. He felt done in, too. The bus meandered around the backsides of towns to avoid the fuzz, who liked to beat up beatniks or anyone with long hair. Patsy clung to Vail; she was soft and strong at the same time, but extremely young. It didn't seem to him that Patsy knew anything worth knowing. He made love to her in the back of the bus, which had been converted into a large couch divided from the rest of the bus by a curtain and some bead drapes. The windows back there were painted bright blue. Patsy nuzzled him like a kitten; she made him feel good.

Every day that they rode west on the multicolored bus, Bondy meditated about reconstructing his life, Patsy pan-handled for herself and for Vail each time the bus stopped, and Vail wrote an occasional article. Patsy combed Vail's hair in the morning and made him glasses of iced tea in the afternoon.

Vail felt disconnected from the others on the bus—they were ten years younger and had different dreams. Except for Patsy and the driver, Bo, Vail's fellow passengers seemed indistinguishable from each other. At moments on the long rides through high valleys, mountain passes, and pastures, he dreamed of Riva and of the early days. But now, beat was hip, jivey, even criminal. It had lost its purity. Beatniks on TV were lazy bums or hoodlums associated with drugs, even though the really big drug dealers lived in lavish Park Avenue apartments. America had packaged the beats.

Vail knew this was his last trip. "I'm heading back to California," he said one day. "I'm going to join the work force." The *Voice* printed his reviews; others would, too.

"Good man. Save yourself," Bondy replied. "Settle down and marry Patsy." Patsy was uneducated, healthy, honest, and sexy. Vail found these qualities in her attractive. But he was reluctant to do anything except sleep with her. Bondy had taken a real liking to her sweet, tough nature. "She can't express herself elegantly," Bondy said, "but she's sharp, man. And nonmanipulative." They were crossing the Truckee River in Nevada, headed for the home of a friend of Patsy's in Reno where they could park the bus without a lot of hassle from the cops. Patsy was pointing out all the places she'd known as a child, and whom the streets were named after.

Bondy and Vail walked downtown into a blaze of neon casinos. They ran into Jerry under Harrah's glittering mar-quee. "Jeez, man, what you doing here?" Jerry was stag-gering drunk. "You got a coupla bucks on you?" he asked, as though he'd just seen Bondy and Vail the day before yesterday instead of two years ago. Vail bought him a sand-wich with the last of his money.

"How're we going to make some bread?" Vail asked, looking around at an acre of jangling slot machines. Bondy had two quarters, which he stuck in one of the machines, without issue.

"Just go down to the wire services office," Jerry said. "Tell them you're Sky's brother. Or send Bondy, who'll say he can get an interview with you for a few bucks. I've done it," he added a little sheepishly.

"You've done what?" Vail asked.

"Well, I've told them—geez, I hope this was okay—that I had you sorta incommunicado, y'know, but that you'd talk to me, and I'd make up a little story and dictate it to one of the guys down there. Y'know, about being on the bum with you, your thoughts about Sky, like that."

Vail was astonished. No one had ever paid much attention to his being Sky's brother.

"It's all different now," Jerry said. "Sky won't give interviews anymore. They're wild to have any kind of information. I thought you knew."

"We been out in the goddamned desert, man," Bondy said.

"Sara's doing it, I guess," Jerry said. "At least there's a piece about her around. Came out of AP in Rome."

A kind of crazy enthusiasm for the plan took on its own life, and they ended up at UPI on Wells Street where Bondy informed a bored, bald man that Vail, brother to Sky Wyman, was announcing his marriage to a local girl, Patsy McAulis. They decorated the story a bit and made enough to buy a little grass and dinner at Harrah's. On the way out Vail remembered the story about Sara and asked if UPI had a copy. The man fished around and came up with a clip that Vail stuffed in his pocket, anxious to get out of there before they asked him more questions about his bondage to Patsy.

A couple of days later, Bondy, Bo, Patsy, and Vail were sitting on the grass next to the bus. Bo was reading a newspaper article aloud, all about how Vail Wyman, Sky Wyman's brother, was marrying one Patsy McAulis. "Man, you are a bourgeois betrayer," Bo said to Vail.

Patsy didn't see it that way at all. Her affair with him suddenly took on significance. Ecstatic, she threw her arms around Vail, kissing him. "I didn't know you were Sky's brother!" she squealed. "But even if you weren't, I'd love to marry you." She abandoned her role as beat chick. Bondy laughed and laughed.

"Don't take it seriously," Vail said to Patsy. "It's just a press thing. Happens all the time to us, because of Sky. Gotta roll with it."

Patsy's face fell, and she collapsed on the steps to the bus. "You were just using me," she said.

"No, no," Vail said, "but the press, they do funny things. You can't believe them." Bo stared at them. Not only had Vail betrayed the principles of the free life and free love, he was now compounding the error.

A moment of nutty hilarity was turning sour. Patsy began to cry. Vail put his arm around her. She threw it off and disappeared in the back of the bus where her sobs increased, audibly. Vail went back to try and comfort her, while Bo and Bondy went downtown.

The Reno police hated beatniks. Two of them arrested Bondy that night as he was coming out of a gas station men's room. Bo had fled. When Bondy hadn't appeared by morning, Vail went searching for him at the police station. They denied arresting him. Vail aggressively told them who he was and who his sister was and who his attorney was.

"Take him over to the morgue," the beefy desk sergeant said. "Maybe that's the guy."

Vail's heart stopped. He shoved his hands in his pockets and followed a slender, blond cop across a courtyard and into a building that smelled like formaldehyde. "It can't be Bondy," he kept saying like a mantra.

It was Bondy. His face was bruised, his eye blackened.

"What happened?" Vail demanded.

"He fell in the showers," said the blond cop. He had a nervous tic in one cheek.

Vail was about to make accusations, and threats of suit were bursting out of the grief that was enveloping him, but even the morgue attendant looked dangerous. The little blond cop was staring at him boldly. Vail didn't think either he or the people on the bus would get out of town if he said anything.

"I'm claiming the body," he said. Outside, he felt broken

—334—

and stunned, as though someone had hit him with a board. Patsy was waiting for him on the steps of the police building.

"They killed him," he said, tears rushing down his cheeks.

"If I never do anything else, I'll find out which one of those bastards did it and make him pay." Patsy put an arm around his waist and tried to hurry him away from the building where blue-suited officers with pistols were eyeing them.

"We gotta get out of Reno, Vail," she said.

"Not till I get Bondy away from them. I'm not leaving him on that slab down there."

Bondy had been a popular passenger on the bus, so most of them stayed for the little funeral Vail held for him at the first town over the state line in California. Sky had sent the money.

"I've known Bondy since Korea," Vail said, standing by the grave in the lush green cemetery. "I don't know how to live without him." He felt hollow. He felt as if life as he'd known it was over. He felt old.

Patsy looked up at Vail's slender, grieving face. She adored him. "May I be a substitute?" she said softly.

They said good-bye to the bus and got on a train for Los Angeles. Vail loved trains; they soothed him. He sat by the window, looking out, thinking about Bondy in Korea, Bondy in New York, and finally Bondy in Reno, talking about Patsy.

Patsy read Vail's moods. She didn't try to cheer him up, she just waited while he mourned.

The train was coming out of Santa Barbara when he asked her to marry him. It had really been Bondy's idea to begin with. Patsy made a high sound of showy delight. He knew Patsy cared for him, but he disliked seeing the new light of the supplicant in her eyes; she was too aware of his connection to the famous Sky. But that would pass.

"Do you love me?" she asked him shyly.

"Yes," he said truthfully. Not like Riva, he thought, not like Bondy, but different. "Won't Mother be surprised?"

To Patsy their affair had taken on a magical quality found only in books. When Vail made love to her in the roomette, she twisted with a pleasure larger than herself. Vail loved going down on her, and she went crazy, whimpering and moaning in ecstasy. Before Bondy had died, she and Vail had made love out in the woods, steaming together in the sleeping bag, but now they'd fallen off the edge of the world into a new life. She wanted to learn more about Sky and about Sara—her future sisters-in-law!—and about his childhood in San Francisco. Patsy laid siege to his memories.

"Here!" he said, feeling the unread clipping in his pocket that the UPI guy had given him. "Read about Sara, and quit bugging me."

She took it avidly. He got up and started pulling on his jacket. They were coming into Los Angeles.

"That's not very nice," Patsy said dully. She passed the clipping back. He read it. "But then," she said quietly, "you said these things in the papers aren't really true."

Vail was furious. "How could she *say* that?"

Coming on top of Bondy's death, Vail felt that Sara had betrayed him in a public and embarrassing way. "You don't know Sara," he mumbled. "I know her better than anyone alive." The weapon of the press was a lesson he would not soon forget.

The soft acreage of the carpet in Sheldon Winters's new office led the eye to a superb rosewood desk at one end, where two leather chairs and a leather love seat were grouped around it like suppliants. Sheldon and his wife collected art. A few of the precious objects—a de Kooning and an Isabel Bishop—were displayed at strategic points in the room. Mrs. Winters had recently discovered Pacific Northwest art and had purchased a George Johanson oil, which hung in a controlling corner, and a startling Ken Shores ceramic. It was the Shores that Sky noticed when she entered Sheldon's office on a bright February morning.

"New piece?" she said. "I hope he doesn't kill the birds to make it."

"No!" Sheldon exclaimed, horrified. He swung around to face the large silver-glazed clay disk mounted on the wall. Luminescent black feathers fanned across half its surface. "He collects the feathers," Sheldon said. Sheldon was aging well, and he still looked as sleek as a fine ship.

"Good," Sky said. She sat down. "You summoned me?"

He frowned. "Sky, I've asked Mel to join us—" A soft

polite buzz sounded on his desk. He flipped a switch. "Tell him to come in," he said.

The door opened, and Mel burst through it. While Mel rushed through life, Sheldon glided. They all went into Sheldon's private dining room for lunch. Sheldon examined his menu. "I'll have the London broil," he said to the waiter. Mel said he'd have that, too. Sky had the Caesar salad.

"Now, about *Easy Street*," Sheldon said, making a steeple out of his fingers. "I want us to come to an agreement on the script, Sky. I like it the way it is. It's a nice departure for you, a little comedy—"

"Sheldon, please can it," Sky interrupted with a smile. "We've been over this and over it. The script's funny at the expense of Mary's character. That doesn't make Mary funny. I'm not going to appear in this piece of shit unless there's another rewrite. Period." She smiled again, bewitchingly.

Sheldon sighed. Mel shifted in his chair. Sky had a habit of being infuriatingly right about the scripts, shots, location choices, dialogue changes, costumes, and direction. But her reputation was altering. Her last two pictures had not made big profits, and the advance word on "Paradise" was not great.

Over the years Mel had grown fond of Sky. He had tried to warn her that even a great actress could not survive a string of poor-box-office pictures. Her intractable attitude about the scripts was not paying off. Mel knew Sheldon. As long as she made money for the studio, she could continue to rewrite and make directorial demands. But if "Paradise" failed, too, her bargaining position would be precarious.

"I didn't like your writer's rewrite, Sky," Sheldon said. He untied his fingers, rewrapped them around his fork, and dug into the salad the waiter had just put in front of him. "If we shoot it your way, it'll fail. Period." His pale eyes scanned her.

"Don't threaten me, Shel," she said quietly.

Mel said, "Do you know how many scripts I have piled up for her, people who are dying to have her! I can go right over to Columbia or Paramount today and come out with a deal."

Sheldon sneered. "You'd have the same trouble there that you're having here, because the problem is Sky's."

"I don't have any damned problem, Sheldon, *you do*," she said.

"Name your price. My instincts are good, and I know you'll be great in this part. Just name your price." He looked over at Mel.

Sky said, "It's not the money, Shel! It's the role!"

"Are you turning down a million dollars?" he asked her coldly.

"If that's what you're offering, yes."

Sheldon stopped eating completely. "Well, I'll be goddamned."

"Sky!" Mel bellowed, outraged at her.

"I want a rewrite. Then," she said, meeting his gaze, "I'll do it for free."

"Sky!" Mel whispered, sinking back in his chair.

"I will not allow you to rewrite this script again," Sheldon said. He tapped his fork against the side of his plate. "You do it my way, or don't do it." He was very angry.

"Then I'm out!" she said, rising.

"Sky," Mel said hastily, also getting up.

"Call me at home," she said, striding out.

Sheldon eyed her. "Staying on top is a lot harder than getting there!" he yelled at her. She slammed the door behind her.

Mel sat down. "You know she's perfect for that part," he said.

"So is Elizabeth Taylor."

"Oh, for Chrissakes," Mel snapped. "She may never get out of Rome!" He calmed down and shifted his tactics. "Sky's comedic sense has never been tapped. She's one of the best professionals in the business, and she'd be even better if you'd only give her more range. She's one of a kind. The press will cream you and the studio if—"

"Mel. You know as well as I do that Sky's relationship with the press wouldn't get her a bus ticket to Santa Monica." The waiter brought in their entrées. When he left, Sheldon said, with respect, "That broad turned down a million bucks."

"You wouldn't have given her a mil, Shel," Mel said, looking at his London broil.

"No, but pretty near." He cut into his meat.

"The script *does* need work, Shel. She's right."

"I'm sick of her highfalutin notions about art and integrity that aren't worth warm piss at the box office."

"Her mind's on Vail's wedding!" Mel said, still eyeing his lunch. "Give it a couple of weeks, give her time to think it through—"

"Her mind's on Kitty Hightower and you know it!" Sheldon thrust some food in his mouth as though he needed the fuel but didn't like the taste.

"You shouldn't let her go, Shel."

"I'm not sinking any more preproduction money into that script. She said it, she's out, and frankly, buddy, I'm relieved." He reached for his water glass.

"She'll mount her own productions," Mel warned. "I haven't encouraged her, but she's—"

"An actress producing!" Sheldon sneered. "Actresses are the children and the idiots of the business! Their only use is to look pretty and take direction. And look at the trouble we get into for making them stars! Look at Monroe, for Chrissakes! Twelve years and what do we have to show for it? Wreckage."

"Sky's not Marilyn—"

"No!" Sheldon roared, angry. "She's worse. She's got pretensions about art, about scripts. Girls like that—they don't know a goddamned thing except what we print about them. If they'd just stick to their purpose in life—acting sweet, looking beautiful, fucking, and keeping their mouths shut." He let his arms drop and glared at his brother. "It's girls like Sky who are making an old man out of me."

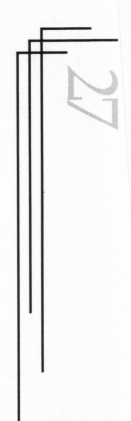

27

When Patsy walked into Sky's house, she knew she had entered a different world. She had seen pictures of houses like this. She had never thought she'd actually be inside one. She ran a finger over the edge of a velvet love seat. She carefully picked up a glass lion. Then Sky was upon them, and Vail was hugging the most famous woman in the world. Patsy felt like fainting.

Diana's preparations for the wedding had taken on the proportions of a state function. Putting her own work with Dr. King's group aside, Diana had invited the upper half of the Hollywood elite and many of her old friends from San Francisco. She had connected a new phone line to the upstairs study, her command post; she had lifted Lindy out of her more ordinary studies to learn the art of society weddings firsthand. Lindy entered into the enterprise gamely. She liked Patsy, and she'd always been fond of her uncle Vail.

Diana had taken Vail's selection of Patsy stoically. That he was getting married at all and was ready to settle down was gift enough. She dismissed Patsy as "a lovely child," malleable and willing, still enthralled with her sudden nearness to celebrities. Diana was sure that if the wedding were splashy enough, Patsy's common antecedents would go unnoticed.

Outside, Sara, Vail, and Sky were walking around the reservoir.

"But you called me a liar in print!" Vail said to Sara.

"Vail, I've told you—it wasn't quite like that, but I—it *was* my fault and I'm sorry," Sara said tensely. "Can we drop it?"

Sara, fresh off the plane from Italy, was wearing a wrinkled seersucker dress, a kerchief, and a lot of plastic bracelets. Her hair was dyed black—for the ancient Greek priestess role.

"You don't know what she called you," Sky said. "The press just makes it up."

"You were plenty upset when I showed you the clipping," Vail said to Sky.

"For a while," she answered, lighting a cigarette. "But Sara and I—" she took Sara's arm "—had a hard time in New York. But I didn't take the part, did I?" Sky's intelligence had told her the article was a silly tempest, but in her heart she had felt Sara's anger and envy. Sky had been more critical of Sara in front of Lindy during that time. The darts found their mark in the impressionable child.

Sky and Vail began swapping information about the pills Sky easily obtained from worshiping doctors. "Kitty's incensed about it," Sky said. "She thinks tranquilizers are 'dangerous.'" She didn't add that since Lila's suicide, a few little pills helped her cope with the pressure.

The water looked blue and fresh, and a soft March wind came over the top of the hill. Sky stopped walking. "I want to tell you something," she said. They stopped. Sky knit her hands together. She was most apprehensive about Sara's reaction. Would Sara fight to take Lindy back when she heard? "My arrangements at the house—" She hesitated. "Gee, this is tough."

Vail said, "Kitty."

"Why do you always know what people are thinking?" Sky asked, not sure if he'd taken her off the hook or put her on it. "Yes, Kitty. Kitty and I are, well, we're in love, and I hope—" her voice shot up shrilly "—it won't make any difference to all of us."

"I'm glad you mentioned it," Vail said. He had been wondering about Kitty and Sky, whether he should say anything or just stay out of it. But the triplets had always shared, and it was hard to make no comment on a major relationship. "Have you—how long has this been going on?" he asked, politely.

"Not long. Since the Bahamas. We've been friends for years, as you know." She looked at Sara who was clearly surprised. "Are you upset?"

"I don't know," Sara said.

"It takes some getting used to," Sky said.

"Yes, it does. I'm thinking about Lindy. She's ten now, and that's an impressionable age. Does she know?"

Sky shook her head. "She's very fond of Kitty."

"What are you going to tell her?" Sara asked.

"The truth. I don't want her to find out from anyone else." They started walking again. "Only Mother knows, and Reed."

"When did you tell Mother?" Vail asked.

"I didn't. She discovered us."

"In flagrante?" Vail whispered, shocked. Sky nodded solemnly. He threw back his head and let out a robust laugh. Sara was wrestling with it. She had seen Kitty with Lindy, had seen Lindy's delight in her. Sara herself liked Kitty.

"So what about Mother? What happened after she found out?" Vail asked.

"We had an excruciating battle. It's better now. We agreed to disagree. She behaves as though we didn't fight at all. You know."

"Well, Mom's another generation," Vail said.

"Mom's jealous," Sara said. "She doesn't want anyone to be really close to you."

"Trust Sky to come up with some dramatic twist on life," Vail said. He peered at her. "Do you ever do anything average?"

They all swerved away from the topic, temporarily. Sara was anxious about Lindy, but the flight had exhausted her, and her thoughts were jumbled. They all led such different lives. She remembered the three of them learning to ski in Switzerland. They'd glided down the mountain's cheek, three abreast, in unison. Would they ever do anything together like that again?

"Aren't we still close?" Sky said, picking up on Sara's

mood. But she had been thinking of Kitty. As Sky's life revolved more and more around Kitty, her rush for work had lessened. She'd relaxed into the wonder of love, the precious agony and the exuberant joy. "Thank you for being so great about Kitty," she said, taking Vail's arm so that the three of them were walking abreast.

"I think we're still close," Vail said. "Don't you, Sara?"

"Yes," she said, knowing they were not. She said, "I could take Lindy back to Rome with me. I've got plenty of room——"

"You want to take her out of school, away from all her friends?" Sky asked.

"No, I was thinking of the summer."

"Okay, if she wants to," Sky said. "Let's talk about Patsy! She strikes me as someone who looks soft but isn't."

"I think we can say that Patsy's sturdy," Vail said. Except in bed, communicating with Patsy was like communicating with an orange. She was sweet and juicy, but she didn't have any mystery to her.

"What kind of job are you going to get, Vail?" Sara asked.

"Same, writing essays, reviews—up in San Francisco. Patsy wants to work, too. I want her to go back to school."

"Reviewing doesn't pay much," Sara muttered. "Are you writing more plays?" They were approaching Sky's house, having made a circuit of the lake.

"Shit, no! That's over."

"The press. I'll be damned," Sky muttered, looking at the back of his head. "Who are you going to call on first?"

"To get a job? I've already done that. I've been thinking of stringing in San Francisco for UPI."

"San Francisco isn't exactly a hotbed of film interest," she said. "Except for Pauline Kael."

"Then what do you suggest?"

Sky thought about that. "There's Hugh Bliss, editor of one of the trade magazines down here."

"Shit, Sky, they don't pay anything either. You want me to work for the industry's mouth organ?" Vail demanded.

"I understand that you are too classy to work for them," she drawled, "but I thought you were just starting out. You're thirty-two and haven't ever worked! You got no track

—343—

"record, pal." She wondered if he'd expected her to come up with a fancy name out of *Time* or the *Los Angeles Times* to start him on his way. "My press contacts are extremely limited."

Vail stopped walking. They had reached the gate that led back through the trees and garden to Sky's house. "If you gave me an exclusive interview," he said, looking at Sky, "and I did a retrospective on all your films, I'd get a job."

When Sky had stopped giving interviews—even to her fan club magazines—the press had responded by making things up about her or getting secondhand copy. It was a war, and a dangerous one for her, as Kitty had warned her more than once.

Sara wanted to sleep. She pushed open the gate, and they all started up the path.

"Yoo-hoo! Sky? Vail? Sara?" Diana sounded excited. She emerged from the house as though blown out of it. "The most thrilling thing has happened!" she cried. She came to a stop in front of them. "Vail, dear, turn around so I can see you. Guess who just sent in their RSVP to the wedding?"

"We cannot imagine," Sky said laconically.

Nothing could dampen Diana's high spirits. "The Venners!"

Sara gazed at her mother, shading her eyes from the hot sun.

"Faith Venner? Your real mother?" Sara asked.

"The woman she thinks is her real mother," Sky said.

"Think? That was proved long ago!" Diana said. "Honestly, Sky."

"How many Venners are there?" Vail asked.

"Faith Venner and her son, Arch."

"Arch?"

"Yes, Vail," Sky laughed, punching him playfully, "Archie!"

"Isn't it exciting?" Diana exclaimed.

"Yes," Sara said, "but why are they suddenly coming to a wedding—"

"—of people they don't know," Sky finished.

"They are coming, actually, Arch is coming because,

well, I don't know! Do we have to analyze everything? People do change, you know." She whirled daintily. "*Oh!* I simply cannot describe to you how happy I am!" She clasped her hands together and knocked them against her breastbone. Her eyes were filling with tears. "I can't wait to tell Neddie."

"You know, under that patina she calls breeding, Mother's really very emotional," Vail said, watching Diana rush back into the house. Sara followed her.

Vail turned around to face Sky. "Please give me the interview, Sky."

"I'm worried about Sara," Sky said, looking after her.

"Because she's worried about Kitty and me and Lindy."

"Sara needs some time."

Sky thought Sara's dyed black hair was distressing. "She's emotional."

"So are we," Vail said.

Sky turned back to him. "I'll do the interview, but you have to give Kitty some publicity, too. A separate article, with pictures. She's done unusual work and she's a real pro."

Vail instantly agreed.

Arch Moberly was a large man—tall and broad and powerful. He had a noble quality about his brow and his nose, lively brown eyes, and thick blond hair. A bushy blond mustache handsomely completed the arrangement of his face. But his mouth, full and sensuous, said that he was one of those men who bolted into emotions and pleasures.

The distant, high screams of Sky's loyal fans could be heard in the street below the little castle. Hired help, under Mrs. Sho's and Kitty's able direction, were busily turning out pastries and canapés, arranging flowers, counting bottles of champagne, and generally scurrying from the house to the cypress grove, where the wedding was to be held. A hundred chairs had been set up in the back garden and long tables with flapping white linen lined the space between the chairs and the garden. Patsy was upstairs dressing, attended by Lindy, Ace, and Cage.

On the day of the wedding, Arch Moberly stood in Sky's

foyer, holding a dressy felt hat in his hand. Diana had choreographed her introduction to him. On his cue from Mrs. Sho, Vail moved in.

"Mister Moberly, I'm Vail Wyman, Diana's son," he said, shaking his stepuncle's soft, square hand. There was some current buried in the man, some instability held tightly in check. It intrigued Vail. All Diana's stories about the fabled Venners' wealth and power seemed even more exotic now: Arch Moberly was not superficial.

As Vail escorted him into the study, Diana froze. Her half-brother's attitude was one of intelligent courtesy—even humility—instead of the brazen pride of the rich. Sky was struck by a vague resemblance between Diana and Archie: the long eyes and nose, the same blond coloring.

Ned played his part in the little drama. He rose, shook Moberly by the hand, and introduced Diana, who rose, extending her long white hand. "Arch, so nice to make your acquaintance finally. And Faith?" she added.

"I am afraid mother's too ill. She couldn't make the journey. But the message I bear," he said with formality, "is that she extends to you her warm wishes and hopes you will be able to see her soon." He had a soft, gentle voice.

"Of course," Diana said, ushering him to a large chair, which he filled. "I've wanted to bring about, well, what should I call it, these things are so delicate . . . a reconciliation? I've wanted that for years."

Moberly nodded at Sky, who nodded back. "Oh, I am sorry, this is my daughter, Sky," Diana said.

"How do you do?" He smiled, showing his even white teeth. Sky shook his hand. Ned offered Arch a Bloody Mary. He didn't know where to put his hat. Vail took it and handed it out to Mrs. Sho, who was as curious about Arch as the rest of them.

"I hope Faith isn't ill," Diana said, fully in charge.

"Just frail." He looked around at the group and sipped his drink appreciatively.

"What line of work are you in?" Ned asked. He had wedged himself into a corner of the dark green love seat, holding his drink precariously.

"Medicine," Arch said. "More precisely, I'm a psychiatrist. In San Francisco." He smiled.

"It's really impossible to make light conversation, isn't

—346—

it?" Diana asked. "Perhaps you'd tell us about yourself. It's not every day that I meet my half-brother." She wanted to ask why it had taken them six years to do the right thing and come see her.

Arch smiled his gentle sneer again. He had been startled to see Diana but now he was getting used to her. She was the spitting image of his mother, and Faith was going to fall over or have a stroke when she met this woman, if that day ever came. "Why don't we just cut through?" he said. "I went to Stanford University, premed at UCLA."

Ned could be heard to sigh as he pried himself out of the corner of the love seat and went to the bar. "Drink, anyone?" he asked.

"I have a small practice," Arch went on. "I didn't want it to get so big that I lost touch with my patients as people." He glanced about the room. "This is a beautiful home," he said, gently running a hand along the carved arm of his chair.

Diana looked at her watch. "I suppose we'll have to postpone this until after the wedding. Vail, don't you think you should change?"

"If I must," he said. He rose and clapped Moberly on the back as he passed to the door. The man was solid as an ox. Sara came into the room.

"Sara, darling, come and meet Arch," Diana called out.

Sara looked at the large man who was rising out of a wing chair. "Arch?"

"Your uncle, sweetheart, Arch Moberly," Diana said, grabbing her wrist. "This is Sara, our third triplet."

Sara asked, "Uncle?" Much later she remembered thinking that he was handsome, but that his eyes looked as if his sensitivity had been stifled.

Diana was too thrilled to notice the edge in Sara's voice. Everything Diana had striven and hoped for was coming true.

On the lawn Reed was approaching Sara. She was laughing at everything and nothing, pretending to be silly and flip. She raved about the Italians, and spoke seriously about the necessity of having a sense of humor.

"Reed!" she said, kissing him on both cheeks, "how delightful!" He asked about her current film. "Minor amusement," she said. She didn't stop talking even to take a breath. "I'm doing a horror film next," she cried, "a lady vampire! Such fun!" He wanted to take her by the arms and shake her. "And have you met Patsy?" she asked, running on. "In some lights, she resembles Diana a little, don't you think? She's got a lot of character hidden in there somewhere." She laughed tightly. "Well, boys always marry their mothers. And when are you getting married, Reed?"

"Oh, I thought about it very seriously a couple of years ago," he answered easily. "We may still make it one of these days." Sky had called him about Vail's and Sara's reaction to Kitty, and he'd been glad for her. "How's Lindy?"

"Wonderful. So grown up in just two years. But these years make all the difference, don't they? I've invited her to spend the summer with me in Rome, but I don't think she's going to do it." She laughed nervously and took his arm. They started to walk around the garden. "It's a shame about the cheetah, though," she said, glancing at the jabbering guests.

"What about the cheetah?"

"Lindy. She left the gate open yesterday, down by the water. Nigeria ambled out—" she flung out an arm with too much gusto "—and raced all around the track, getting up a good head of steam, and knocked over a man who was taking his exercise. Frightened the fellow half to death. We couldn't find her until the pound called—Nigeria's been captured. She's in detention."

"Oh, Sky will be so upset," Reed said, sadly. "She loves Niger."

"It's worse. They won't let a full-grown cat like that within the city limits. She's just had her last run. Isn't that miserable? Sky has to give Niger to the zoo." Sara squinted up at him. "Of course, we're all in zoos, of one sort or another." She laughed again, another strangled sound.

Poor Sara, he thought. She seemed frantic and artificial. He felt she was on some long downslope, unfed and unloved. He wondered if she had the stamina and the guts to survive it.

That night, having seen Patsy and Vail off to the plane that would take them to Hawaii for the honeymoon, Diana lay awake on her bed in the upper front room, listening to Ned's breathy snores. Tears streamed down her face and sank into the pillow. They were tears of relief and joy. She had done it—she had brought the Venners back into her life, they who had begun her life. She was relieved that Arch seemed like an attractive man, even if he did have that slightly seductive air.

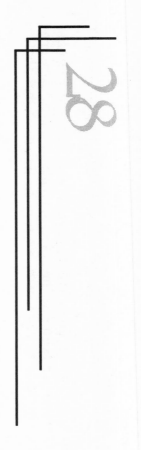

28

Arch Moberly had booked a suite at the Bel Air, a hotel he could not afford. But he had never been one to control his appetite for luxury. He was walking in the garden after a comforting supper, looking out over assertive gardenia shrubs and fat banana trees. He slipped a cigar out of his pocket, lit it, and puffed gently.

All his life he had lived with his own envy and with the slightly contemptuous tolerance of people who knew that he had no share in his family's former power. But a just God had brought Sky Wyman and her family to his door, and he was not about to let them slip away. His only problem was his mother—the legendary and now reclusive Faith Venner. Her snobbery and her shame stood in his way. But he would circumvent them.

He did not remember his grandfather, Harry Venner, the railroad king, for Archie had been born after Harry's death. He admired Harry from the distance of death and generation, and he hated him for what Harry had done to Archie's mother and, therefore, to Archie.

Yet he and his grandfather had common ground. Blond and fair like Harry, Archie also shared Harry's powerful build, aggressive jaw, and, though Archie took pains to hide it, a vindictive nature when crossed. To Harry money had been the fulcrum and the grease of life. But to his daughter, Archie's mother, he'd left practically nothing.

In the early 1900s, Harry had been a millionaire. He had two assertive, restless children, a son and a daughter. Faith

—350—

had maintained that her high spirits had been systematically smothered at finishing schools. Rebelling at eighteen in the only way open to her, she'd fallen in love with a railroad worker, a sort of roustabout in the San Francisco yard. It was from this uncommon union that Diana had been born.

Faith had been bundled off to a private hospital, where she was virtually imprisoned until she delivered a daughter, named Diana. The baby had been turned over to an adoption agency. Its unfortunate father disappeared without a trace. Arch suspected that he'd been killed.

Faith's indiscretion cost her a fortune. Her father cut her out of his will and left everything to his son. But Faith's brother died young within a year of their mother's death. When Harry died in 1920, he left millions to endow a university and a museum in memory of his son. To Faith, he left only a small stipend and the family mansion on Nob Hill.

Faith was in her thirties when Harry died. She married briefly and had a son, Arch. But her new husband abandoned her when he discovered she had no control of the fabled Venner railroad fortune.

The glow from Archie's cigar punctured the dark garden path. He wanted what remained of the Wyman money, and he wanted access to the rich, self-indulgent film industry folk in Los Angeles which Sky could give him. He was only forty-one—he and Diana were separated by fifteen years— there were good years ahead of him yet. He tapped the ash off his cigar and walked on through the shadowed, lush garden. Reconciliation between Diana and his mother, Faith, was the first and most difficult step. For years Faith had managed to hide from him all the overtures of Diana's lawyers. But no longer. He was in charge of the field now. Carefully, taking his time, he strategized.

"Actually, my first love was music," Arch was saying to Diana as they lunched at the Palace Hotel's Garden Court in San Francisco. He played the piano and was a big supporter of the symphony, he said. In the month since Vail's wedding, Diana had met him twice for lunch. She was trying to enjoy his studied courtesy.

Out of the corner of her eye, Diana saw Vail appear at

the etched glass double door. As he scanned the quiet diners under the vast, domed glass ceiling, he looked pinched and fretful.

"Oh, darling," said Diana, not pleased to see him. "Arch was just telling me about his music." Vail nodded at Arch brusquely. "Vail is working as a free-lance reviewer for a local film magazine," Diana said warmly. "He and Patsy have settled into an apartment on Russian Hill."

"The wrong side of Russian Hill," Vail put in gratuitously. Diana smiled tolerantly at Arch.

"Mother, could I see you a moment?" Vail requested.

"I've got to make a phone call," Archie said tactfully, rising.

When he'd left, Vail said, "Sara's in trouble." He had seen a wire release out of Paris describing Sara as "a short-lived theatrical actress" and as Sky Wyman's sister. The release noted that Sara was currently starring in *Lady of the Wild Things*, a racy film just this side of pornography. The French version of the film about the ancient and libidinous Greeks had been promptly released in France before the Italian-European version got out of the dubbing rooms. "It's getting a big press play because of Sky," he said.

"My God," breathed Diana. "What will Arch think?"

"What will Arch think?" Vail repeated, aghast. "What's wrong that Sara's showing her tits in public?!"

"Honestly, Vail, do watch your—"

"Can't you think of anyone except those goddamned Venners?" he demanded. "What will it do to *Sky*?"

"Vail, calm down," she ordered, sipping a glass of ice water. "I'm sure Sara hasn't done any of the things they're saying."

Vail looked around the table as if hoping to find assistance. "Mother, she plays some kind of Grecian wood nymph who presides over Dionysian orgies. Can I be more graphic?"

"Then why don't you go over there? Maybe you and Neddie. Maybe she doesn't have any money."

"Oh, Mother," he said, disgusted, "she's got money. She doesn't act for free over there, and the exchange rates are phenomenal! That's not it!" Sara was becoming an embarrassment again.

Diana groaned, considering all the ramifications of this

new problem. "Pornography? Oh, I think I'm going to have a heart attack." She was quite pale.

Archie returned. "Everything all right?" he asked.

"It's nothing," Diana said, smiling at him. "Just a little flap at the magazine Vail thought I would enjoy."

That afternoon Vail made his plans. He told his saturnine editor that he wanted to do a piece on the *Cleopatra* charade from the angle of "Can art be bought for twenty million dollars?" and that he would pay his own expenses. The editor was not about to look a gift horse in the mouth. Then Vail sent Sara a wire, telling her that his new assignment would take him to Rome. He wondered about taking Patsy with him.

A few of the paparazzi spun away from the Taylor-Burton orbit and took off after Sara when *Lady of the Wild Things* was rushed into release. It had never occurred to Sara that anyone would notice the film. But the celluloid image of Sara sprawled on the pagan altar, her breasts and thighs bared, sent the press into a fever: it was like seeing Sky's breasts. Sara was besieged by producers who wanted her to repeat her wood nymph role in various historical guises. But Sara wanted to work with Antonioni or Vittorio de Sica. She chased after them. They were polite, amiable but distant—someday they might work together, they said.

The ebullient Marco suggested she see the producer of *Sisters of the Night*. Sara found his office on the Via Minghetti near the Fontana di Trevi. A flight of rickety stairs led up to a dark and ancient hallway. The producer was a vibrant, plump man with a huge smile and bushy eyebrows. He was sitting in a large, airy room on the top floor, decorated with Italian Renaissance furniture. A telephone and an open script lay before him on a large carved table. Sara seduced him, showing her handsome legs, drawing her fingers languidly through her bronze hair.

"I like you," the producer said in heavily accented English. "How much do you want? Denaro?"

She told him, and he launched into the producer's eternal cry of pain: "*Yiiiiii!*" Instead of screaming back, she kissed him on the cheek and started to walk out, rolling her

—353—

hips. If she was going to take off her clothes, she was going to get paid a lot of denaro. The producer stopped her. She had the part. They shot it in a week and dubbed her.

When Vail's wire arrived, Sara had a momentary chill. "Lady" had been a lark; what was he so upset for? She tossed the wire away and sailed out to meet Carmen for dinner. Carmen had been posing for publicity stills: with an elephant, carrying a machine gun, dressed as a stick of gum or as a mushroom. Now she had a job as a production assistant on *Cleopatra* to make arrangements for the company's move over to Ischia, where they would shoot the exteriors of the Alexandria sequence. Carmen always cheered Sara up.

"They're millions of dollars over budget. Incredible pressures. Tempers very short," Carmen was saying as they settled into a little restaurant in the crowded Piazza di Trevi. From her position, Sara could see part of the fountain where gods, goddesses, Tritons, and horses rose out of the sculpted rocks in cascades of water. But she was thinking of Lindy at Vail's wedding, how pretty and somehow fragile she'd looked. Sara had wanted to scoop her up in her arms, tell Lindy the truth about her father, about herself. The fiction of Lindy being Sky's child was getting harder for Sara to maintain.

She glanced back at the fountain. Tourists sat on its lip, soaking their feet in the cool shallow water. Across the piazza a pharmacy dating from the fifteenth century was still open for business. The air was balmy. It was early spring.

Carmen skimmed over the gossip like a butterfly darting from one precious flower to another. "Everyone is working toward getting Liz up on the sphinx for the mighty processional scene. Six thousand extras for one scene!" Carmen looked down at her bright red nails. "Um, *Der Tag* quoted Taylor as saying she'd live in a cold-water flat to be near Burton. Oh! The big news is that Fox's New York offices have ordered their producer, Walter Wanger, to order Taylor and Burton to stop seeing each other! Bad for the box office!"

Sara exploded with laughter, rolling around in her chair, clutching at Carmen, tossing her head. "But hasn't it *made*

—354—

the box office?" Sara cried too loudly. "Everyone in the world will see the picture now." Still laughing, she poured them another glass of wine. That killed the bottle. She waved at the waiter for another.

Carmen put her feet up on the third chair and looked at Sara. "You have finished 'Sisters'?" Sara nodded, lighting a cigarette. "That film will do you no good," Carmen said. "Worse than Marco's Greek epic. You shouldn't do those films any more."

"Oh, what does it matter? It's all lunacy, it earns me money, and keeps me in Rome."

Carmen shook her head. "No, amica, they are bad for you. You are using them."

"You are a prude!" Sara barked, then laughed.

Carmen shrugged. Some essential innocence in Sara had vanished, and it saddened her. "You do not make them for good reasons. You make them for some other reason like you want—to—to discredit yourself."

Sara blew out a jet of smoke. "Well, don't you worry, amica, my family's arriving soon. They will do all the discrediting necessary. They've heard about ancient Greece, too!"

It was Palm Sunday. People thronged into Saint Peter's Square bearing palm leaves to be blessed. There were processions all over the city, special ceremonies in the Catacombs and in the Colosseum, and beautiful music floated out of the churches. Sara wandered aimlessly from piazza to church to trattoria, watching battalions of little girls dressed in white for their First Communion, their veils lifting in the breeze, their faces solemn and shining. She had awakened that morning thinking, or dreaming, of Teddy. His play, *Elephant House*, had opened on Broadway, and she imagined he was the toast of New York, since it was a raging hit. She was glad for him, but she felt completely disconnected from him. He was like a painfully bad dream whose interlocking parts did not make sense. She hadn't heard from him, and she hadn't called either, but she'd often caught herself feeling that he was standing beside her, his sardonic slightly disapproving face angled up at her, waiting.

—355—

Early in the evening, she walked down the Corso Vittorio Emmanuele, halting briefly in front of the pretentious monument consecrated to the unification of Italy. Begun in 1885 and not finished until 1911, it had been dubbed a "wedding cake" by World War II British troops. Its spanking white marble layers towered over the Piazza Venezia and the swirls of traffic. Each of the two topmost tiers bore a set of four horses drawing a carriage. A mighty woman of victory stood in each carriage, her bronze wings splayed out into the sky. The monument always had a mesmerizing effect on Sara: overpowering, ugly, grandiose, supreme.

She turned her back on victory and walked toward the Colosseum and the Colle Oppia to join her father, Patsy, and Vail for dinner. She found them in the restaurant garden staring up at the lighted ruins of the Colosseum. They gave her a glass of wine. Sara opened with the first sally.

"How much experience have you had doing reviews?" she asked Vail jauntily. "Isn't this a very important job, doing a series on *Cleopatra?*"

He affected an offhand, laconic air; inside, he was jumpy. He didn't know how to approach the matter at hand. "I did write for the *Voice*," he answered, "and I ran that poetry magazine."

"Into the ground," Sara said. They both laughed; one up for Sara. She sent another salvo across his bow. "And speaking of ruins, Vail," Sara went on, "how's Diana?"

"Spending a lot of time with her family, Archie," he said, displaying his thin smile.

"Patsy, try some wine," Ned put in. He poured her a glass and sipped his scotch. The waiter brought a sumptuous antipasto.

"This is thrilling," Patsy said. Sara focused on her. She was like a sweet pause between past and future. She watched everyone, picking up silverware and handling her glass just as they did it.

"What will you do tomorrow?" asked Sara, eager to keep the conversation rolling along.

"I don't know," Patsy said. "What will we do, Vail?"

"Museums." He didn't seem enthusiastic.

—356—

"Don't you like museums anymore? Whom do you cherish, or what, Vail?" Sara asked and immediately regretted it.

"I used to like you," he shot back, "but I think you've gone loco."

"I know what you're going to say. Just don't. It's not anyone's business what I do over here."

"It's everyone's business!" he snapped. Patsy looked distressed.

"Keep your voice down, Vail," Ned said. "Everyone's looking at us."

"They're not looking at us, Daddy, they're looking at me," Sara said. "I'm a kind of star over here."

"Because you," Vail said, "have made an utter fool of yourself, exposing yourself in that film! It's practically pornographic!"

"Wait till you see the next one!"

Their argument rose and fell, Ned playing the referee to whom neither paid much attention. Sara felt strangely disengaged from Vail's distress. She wanted to be close to him in the way they'd been as children, but the old bonds had been cut. Here he was essentially pleading Diana's case, Sara was sure, and Sky's, as though he hadn't spent all those years away from them trying to construct his own life. Well, she would show him how it was done.

"I don't think this is fair," Patsy said.

Vail ignored her. "You're making it extremely uncomfortable for Sky," he said to Sara. "Put yourself in her place!"

"I'd love to," she said. "Then I could be Lindy's mother."

"You don't have any consideration for any of us," he said.

"I have!"

The more he sought to bring her to the mark, the more she danced away from it. "You're very square, Vail, face it," she said. "And don't worry about Sky. I guess she'll just have to separate herself from me, won't she?"

"You're trying to drag Sky into the muck so you won't look as second-rate as you are!" he accused her.

Startled and wounded, Sara laughed. "Since when are you Sky's big champion? Believe me, she can take care of herself. She as much as told me at the wedding that nothing can touch her!"

"At least Sky doesn't have to be over here with the discards in the business!" Vail thrust forward his face, which, at that moment, resembled nothing so much as a weasel's.

"You bastard," Sara hissed, cut to the quick as she correctly sensed his enjoyment of the scene. "I'm not staying here and listening to this shit anymore." She shot up from the table and ran from the restaurant. Outside, she leaned against the wall, shaking. It was chilly, and she'd left her jacket inside.

A moment later Ned emerged. "Here," he said, holding out the jacket. They walked around the outside of the Colosseum, dodging traffic, then cut down a tree-shaded side street that eventually led to a tiny square. It had no way out except the way they had come in. Ned eased himself down on a stone bench.

"Chicken," he said. "You've done pretty much what you liked all your life."

"Dad, I haven't done anything wrong!"

"I'm not even debating that with you. I just want you to be content." He got up off the bench and looked around at the dark buildings. "The place smelled of endings. "This place gives me the creeps," he said.

They walked until they came to a strip of park near the Roman Forum. Ned gratefully fell into a rickety chair at an outdoor bar and ordered a double scotch. In the distance behind them, spotlights shown on three columns and the arches of the Forum.

"Dad, how are the horses?"

"Dandy. Good company, but I sure wish I could've won a few races. I sure wish that. But it's restful to go up there and work them out a little, take long rides."

"How many you got now?"

"Only six. You'd like the sorrel. She's a beauty." A silence fell, and Sara felt the bowl of the Forum behind her stretching into a corridor of long centuries.

Her father was looking at her. "I remember the day I married your mother," he said. "She was so beautiful, and her face, when we made love, was exquisite. She'd had such a hard time growing up, though she never talked about it much. But in those days, everything delighted her." He downed his drink. "I wish I could start all over. I didn't want you to grow up without me while I was traveling all those years."

"You weren't gone that long," Sara mumbled.

"For a child, a week is a long time. But I had the money then, too," he added, wistfully. Music from an outdoor concert drifted over the sound of the traffic. "You've got a lot to answer for, Sara. I suppose you feel bad about Lindy, but I never faulted you for leaving her with us. I've loved her just like I've loved you, and I've enjoyed her, too. But what you're doing now is perverse."

"Bullshit," she said crudely. "You're all a bunch of prudes! I'm a very sought-after actress over here!"

His dark hazel eyes nailed her. "I don't care that you're stark naked in a movie!" he said with sudden energy. "But I know it's your way of striking back—by degrading yourself."

"Oh, lay off, Dad. I'm not doing anything wrong!"

"No, you're not," he said, looking away. "Not really—but you *are* hurting yourself." He said it simply, as if she'd asked him for his opinion about the Kennedy administration.

His complacency was a kind of surrender, and she disliked him for it. She remembered all the long years that she'd desperately wanted to be first in his heart, wanted acceptance from him at any price. Now she saw the futility of those desires. "Have you ever done anything in your life that you're proud of?" she asked sharply.

"Not much, but I'm proud of you and Vail and Sky."

"Then leave me alone," she hissed, getting up. "I'm not explaining what I do to you or to Vail. How typical of Mother to send the two of you out here! I'm sure she's afraid I'm embarrassing her with the Venners or shaming Sky. The hell with them. The hell with all of you!"

She turned from the table, but he caught her wrist. "Sara! Listen to me. You are wasting yourself in envy. Let go of it before it's too late."

She wrenched her wrist away from him. "Let go! You're a weakling. You always have been!" She fled. But at the corner she looked back. He was still sitting at the table, the lighted Corinthian columns and the remains of the temple of Castor and Pollux behind him. Far beyond, above those remnants in the night, floating on white marble, a brace of four bronze horses pulled the winged women into space. Sara felt only defeat.

The city was jammed with Holy Week celebrants. But Twentieth Century-Fox and Cinecittà were hosting their own celebration: the long-waited processional scene of Cleopatra's entrance into Rome. The set looked as though all Rome had broken away from its devotions and turned time back. Wanger, the producer, had issued invitations to the cream of Roman society, who sat out in the hot sun under parasols on a platform behind the camera. The atmosphere on the mighty set was like the old days with the Christians and the lions. Reporters from the *New York Times*, the wire services, the *International Herald Tribune*, and every major newspaper in Europe thronged one whole section of spectators.

The vast set of Rome contained six thousand extras and scores of animals. The idea was that hundreds of slaves would haul the gargantuan sphinx bearing a brilliantly costumed Liz Taylor under the arch to Caesar's feet. Liz would then descend a golden staircase that led out of the sphinx. Mank, the director, was sweating and screaming from the crane as Roma, circa 1962, fanned itself in the grandstands.

Sara was late. She found Vail and Patsy by sheer chance in the crush.

"Where's Daddy?" asked Sara.

"Went home."

"Home? Back to the hotel?"

"Home. Back to the States," Vail said, coldly.

Sara was nonplussed. Patsy was reaching out to give her a kiss on the cheek. "I don't get it," she said to Vail.

"Came in late last night, said he was tired and wanted to get back to the ranch. He took a flight back this morning. That's all."

"Sit here, Sara," Patsy said, making room.

Distressed, Sara sat down. Ned had left because of what she'd said. She smiled gamely, feeling even more defeated. "That's a pretty dress," she said to Patsy.

"I'm glad you like it. I asked Sky to take me shopping so I could look better."

"Lindy would sure love this show," Sara said.

During the long, hot afternoon watching the giant sphinx bearing the minuscule Liz Taylor, Sara and Vail were struck by their uneasy truce. Since childhood they'd learned that no word or action of the three of them was sacred, safe from ridicule, or even lasting. But some invisible boundary had been breached last night. As the crowd shouted, the director screeched from the crane, and the gigantic sphinx rolled slowly forward, Vail knew that he and Sara might never get back to their former, safer, territory. He couldn't tell if Sara knew it, too, and if she did, if she even cared.

29

Carmen took Sara, Vail, and Patsy to the postprocessional party Fox hosted at the Villa d'Este in Tivoli. A holiday resort where the wealthy had owned country homes since ancient Roman times, Tivoli was about a half hour outside Rome, sitting on a hill overlooking the plain.

People were streaming into the estate when the four of them arrived. The villa had been a church until the son of Lucrezia Borgia, a cardinal, converted it into a magnificent palace in the sixteenth century. It was surrounded by gardens large enough to be called a park, arranged in a series of descending levels connected by tree-shaded staircases, walkways, and countless fountains.

Carmen had taken an instant liking to Vail and Patsy. She clung to their arms in her affectionate way and acted like their personal hostess. "My God," Patsy exclaimed as they entered the terrace that looked out from the central hall, a former throne room. Below them was a breathtaking view of the park, where lights played on brilliant blue fountains and the water dripped off the stone like liquid silver. Shrill laughter and the hum of hundreds of people partying filled the rooms and terraces. Waiters toured with glasses of *spumante*. On all sides, they could hear Italian, English, German, French, Spanish, Danish.

They ambled from one hall to another of the once-sumptuous palace still filled with frescoes, sculptures, and huge tapestries. Paintings by Raphael and of the Muziano and Zuccari schools stared down from the walls. They went on to the loggia, a roofed open gallery that formed the central part of the facade, and then down a stairway onto a terrace overlooking the park again, and found themselves in another hall. It had once been the library and still bore the cardinal's coat of arms in the center of the ceiling. From there the party flowed downward to a lower apartment and out into the vast, gemlike gardens.

"Carmen! Come state?" They were standing on the lower terrace. They turned to see a man who seemed effortlessly stylish. He had black hair and blue eyes. Carmen introduced Guido Arbitriano.

"Guido's an actor," she said. "So is Sara."

Guido kissed Sara's hand. He was extremely handsome, the kind of man who appeared in the pages of fashionable European magazines. "Carmen compliments me," he said. "I am *trying* to be an actor. I am just beginning."

"Let's eat something," Vail said. Sara was about ready to follow him back upstairs, but Patsy wanted to go into the garden, as did Carmen; they all disappeared.

Sara turned away from Guido, leaned her arms on the balustrade, and stared into the thick park, as he made easy conversation about American films. Cary Grant was his hero. He'd seen all his films. Sara wanted more wine. He found it for her. He wanted to know all about her; she felt uncommunicative. They started walking into the park below the villa along a narrow avenue called the Cento Fontane. On their right was an imposing triple tier of fountains rising from hundreds of spouts for the entire length of the path.

The garden was full of guests, laughing and joking and drinking. Because the garden was so vast Sara had no sense of being in a crowd. They ambled along, talking about his enthusiasm for acting. Guido struck her as being a sort of playboy, shallow and pretty. She kept looking for Vail and Patsy and Carmen.

"You have a husband, children, here too?" he asked as the corridor ended at the Fontana dell'Ovato. A sparkling waterfall fell from a top basin in a wide green pool below.

"No. Just me." They were back in the light now. He had a mobile face, and expressive eyes.

They started talking about families. "Triplets?" he exclaimed. "Ah, your poor parents!" A novel reaction, she thought, probably for her benefit. She asked him about his family. "They think I am crazy! They are horrified that I want to act. My grandmother said, 'What are you doing with all those strange people?'" He was a good mimic and made her laugh.

She finished her wine and drank the rest of his. They walked on, past the fountain of the four dragons, spewing out water in the center, and the fountain of birds decorated with niches, spouts, and arches. He took her arm. "In old times," he said, pointing, "the niche up there was full of bronze birds. By means of a water-activated mechanism, the birds sang very sweetly. Then an owl came out over there, and the birds would stop singing."

"All this to entertain the cardinal's guests?" she asked as they went down a wide marble staircase to another level.

"Sì! Big parties here in the sixteenth century!" He laughed, a sort of rolling sound that made her want to laugh too, but she resisted. Unaccountably, she wanted to get away from him.

The fountain of Neptune spilled out of an upper basin into three levels below it. An ornate facade jutted out above a terrace. From a central spot, a sheet of water fell to another level near where they stood, crashing into yet another pond.

"And now, turn," he instructed softly. Extending from the fountain was a line of shallow square ponds along a central corridor, an esplanade lined by ancient cypresses, some dating back to the sixteenth century. She looked up at the villa towering over them.

"You know this park very well," she said.

"Sure! We used to play here as children. There are hundreds of fountains here—a child's magic land—unique in the world." He took her arm again, but after a moment she moved away. "We have a family house not far away. Nothing like this, of course!" He started walking. "Food!" he said with energy. "We need food!"

They retraced their steps to the villa above. One of the halls had been turned into a dance floor. They found Vail, a wide-eyed Patsy, and a more neutral Carmen helping themselves to the food Fox had supplied. "No wonder they're over budget!" Sara cried, eyeing the feast. Guido excused himself and wandered away.

"You like him?" Carmen asked slyly.

"Not much, though he's pleasant. Who is he?"

"A prince," Carmen said.

"He's nice, Carmen, but I don't know that I'd describe him as a prince of a guy." She put a bunch of grapes on her little plate.

Patsy said, "Have you ever seen anything like this?"

"But he *is* a prince!" Carmen protested, pushing something rolled and gooey into her mouth. "The Arbitriano families can be traced back to the days of the Roman Empire. They have given the world popes, dukes, and patrons of artists like Bernini. His family owns castles but he's a black sheep because he wants to act. The family's furious."

"Well, I'm still lukewarm," Sara said. "He's probably a bad actor, just playing at it?"

"I've heard he's pretty good."

Sara took Patsy's arm and they strolled off. "How do you like marriage?"

"Oh, it's wonderful," Patsy replied. "And so many new things! Kitty wants to redo some of the furniture—new covers or something—and she's going to let me help." She smiled wistfully. "Vail—he's got a hard edge but you know how soft he is underneath. I'm going to go to night school!" she exclaimed. "Vail says it's okay."

"What are you going to take?"

"I don't know yet. I thought maybe I could help out as a secretary in a law firm or something like that. And I want to take some history and some art, so I can talk to Vail better." She put her arm through Sara's as she had seen Carmen do. "I want to make Vail happier," she confided. "He's so sad inside."

They squeezed through a crowded room where paintings from past masters glared down on them.

"It's hard for Vail to be as direct as he's been with you. He goes about things—circuitously. I don't mean dishonestly."

"He just wants me to do things his way," Sara said, amazed at little Patsy and, at the same time, pleased that she had judged Patsy to be deeper than her naive surface at first indicated.

—365—

"You gotta do what you gotta do!" Patsy laughed. "But Vail's really concerned about you."

"Vail's concerned about how things look."

"Yes, that, too. He's mysterious," she giggled. "I don't understand him sometimes. Other times, I can see right through him. For instance, I know when he's thinking about Korea and what happened there, because his face changes."

Sara drew back. "Korea? That was ten years ago."

"For Vail it was yesterday."

"What part of Korea are you talking about?"

"The beating," Patsy said as they passed a Bernini sculpture of the cardinal.

"What beating?" Sara stopped walking.

"I hope I'm not doing something wrong." She looked up at Sara. "I mean well," she said disingenuously. "He was almost killed but not the way he said. He was with a prostitute, and some men beat him up in an alley. He wasn't wounded in action." She bit her nail, then quickly removed her finger from her mouth, embarrassed. "Don't tell him I told you."

"Poor Vail," Sara said. "He never told us. He must love you very much to be so vulnerable."

"Well, he does, really, but he doesn't know it yet," she said with her disarming honesty. "He's probably being hard on you because he's so hard on himself."

"Patsy," Sara said, taking her by the shoulders, "you don't have to go to school."

"You're teasing me," Patsy giggled. "There's so much I have to learn. Your mother is a very fine lady, and a little critical."

"That's a nice way of putting it."

Guido called Sara every day, and asked her out every day. She refused. Finally she agreed to have a coffee with him.

"You do not like me?" he asked as they sat in a little outdoor restaurant.

"I just don't want to be involved with anyone."

"No involvement! That is good, too!" He clapped. "We will go to a movie!"

They went to the movie. Another week they went to a

play, and then another time to a minstrel show, and slowly Sara began to miss him when they weren't together. "You aren't just playing at acting, are you?" she asked him one evening.

"No," he said, serious. "It is my work and my joy."

They were walking to his car after seeing a play and having dinner in a little restaurant that smelled of fragrant white truffles. He opened the door to the car; she paused. She curled a hand around his neck and kissed him. It was only then that she knew she was really healing from Teddy. He drove out the Appia Antica to his house, fleeing from the city, his arm around her, a cigarette cocked in the corner of his mouth.

A fountain played in the moonlight in front of the large house. Still without talking, clinging to each other as if someone had threatened to part them, they entered through the front door. Inside it was still. Sara's heels clicked on the marble floor. Guido shut the door and put his arms around her tenderly. She could see the corner of his eye, the shape of his nose. "From the first moment I met you, dear Sara, I cared about you. But you didn't like me!" Very gently, his hands circled her face. His lips touched hers. This was no playboy actor; this was a mature and feeling man. She sighed against him, leaning hungrily into his kiss.

He put an arm about her and guided her into a soft sitting room off the hallway. The furniture was old and comfortable, the lamps shaded and ornate. She sat on the sofa, grinning, while he got them a glass of wine. She could not drink hers. She wrapped herself around him. He smelled her bright hair, kissed her neck. "I am too young for you," he said softly, teasing her.

"How young?" she asked, kissing his ear.

"I am twenty-five," he said, pulling away slightly to look at her.

"You're right. You are much too young for me." She reached out for him. Soon they were stretched on the couch, the wine forgotten, sailing into their own seas, her body arching against his. She felt alive again.

They saw each other every day and the pace, the temperature, of Sara's life in Rome changed. It would never be the same again. She loved his gentleness, his courage, and his compassion, his ability to cry and to laugh. Her Guido was tolerant and just.

One day he held out a kitten, a fluffy black-and-white ball with a pink nose and huge blue eyes. He said, "Cats are said to be the connections between lovers." She took the kitten from him and started to cry. "Oh, Guido," she sobbed.

"You feed so many anyway," he said. "You ought to have one of your own. We say here that cats are older than Rome." He embraced her. "I would also like to give you a child, since you take care of so many of them on the streets. You are a fine woman, Sara."

They went everywhere together—to the Cafe de Paris on the Via Veneto, where Sara, looking lovely and soft, got notes from admirers at other tables and Guido delighted in their senders' good taste. It seemed to her that the street was full of love and ease, that every human being there was connected. They ate truffle shavings and Parmesan cheese on ovoli mushrooms, which he said were gathered at the foot of the Alps, and drank frosty white wine. Sara told Guido about Lindy, about her guilt and her sense of self-betrayal, about her fear of the inevitable time when Lindy would discover the truth—that Sara had left her in sweet abandonment.

"You did what you had to do," he said. "We all carry regrets but they must not carry us."

She met his friends, a whole new group: fiery revolutionaries, former resistance fighters, novelists and poets, painters and filmmakers. One was shooting a film that attacked Italian family law, especially its prohibitions against divorce. Liliana Cavani, the director Carmen so admired, was a part of this group. She was making documentaries. An anarchist, she talked movingly about her plans to make a film on Francesco d'Assisi.

Pier Pasolini, a novelist, poet, and film director—an exuberant and erratic man—held regular discussion meetings at his duplex in Via Eufrate for "his group," which included novelists, painters, and filmmakers. Rifts in the group opened and closed, sometimes over politics, sometimes over love.

It was there, too, that Sara met Palmiro Togliatti, the long-time leader of the Italian Communist Party, who spoke about the loss of people's pure ideals. "Italian Communists," he said, "are living quietly like the middle class—comfortably compromising." Many mourned the loss of those days of struggle right after the war, when sharp ideals had shaped the vision of the "new realism" in films and books.

Sara had a hard time keeping the political parties straight. Sergio Segni had just been elected president of Italy. "Now who are the left wing?" she would say. "The Social Democrats?" "No!" Guido would reply. "They are the right wing! The Socialists are the left wing."

"Oh, that's right. All these democrats. The Social Democrats and the Christian Democrats band together."

But Fanfani, the new premier, had managed to form a left-center coalition. Many people had high hopes for his success.

It was June. Guido and Sara were soon going to Ischia, an island off the coast, where *Cleopatra* was shooting its last scenes. "I am now going to see Carmen," Sara said to him, "to give her her birthday gift, then I'll meet you later on the Veneto—si?" She kissed him and dashed off.

Carmen had been a prisoner on *Cleopatra* while Sara was being reborn in love. "Oh, Carmen!" Sara cried joyfully when they met later that afternoon. "I am so in love!" She danced. "I want to marry him."

Carmen was shocked. "But, cara, you can't marry Guido!" She looked at her friend. "He's already married, a dynastic marriage. She lives somewhere in Umbria, I think. It is one of the reasons his family is so angry with him." Sara's animated face turned to stone. "I am sorry," Carmen said. "Everyone knows he is married. I thought you were just having a good time."

Sara and Guido drove the three hours to Naples that night and took the hydrofoil across the bay of Ischia. "You are very quiet," he said softly on the ride across the bay.

"I don't want to talk about it now. We'll talk in Ischia." He took her hand and squeezed it gently.

They stayed in the Regina Isabella, an elegant hotel on

the water. The island had been invaded by the paparazzi who disguised themselves as waiters or guests.

Sara lay on their bed, facing the blue water. Guido sat down beside her. "See what a beautiful day we have, and you are sad. I have never seen you so sad!"

"I did not know you were married."

"Bah! What is that? It is nothing! A marriage made for reasons other than love." He took her hand and caressed her fingers. "I accepted it." He kissed her hand. "I love you, cara Sara," he said tenderly. "I would like to divorce, but Italy doesn't recognize divorce. You and I must take what we can get."

From their balcony, they could see the sets bobbing in the water—his and hers barges—Cleo's and Antony's. They were shooting only barge-top scenes and other exterior stuff since all the interiors had already been shot at Cinecittà. The open sea around the barges was filled with little boats of all kinds, manned by the press and sightseers. They drifted into camera range when a shot was being made, driving everybody crazy.

The port at sunset was a color-and-light show, streaks of beautiful magenta and dark crisp blues. Sara and Guido ate dinner on their own terrace or at little restaurants, staring into the glorious dusk. As the sun went down, at the old castle on the Ponte, the whole island turned out to watch the night shooting among the barges.

On their third day, the camera was shooting from Liz's yacht which was tied up next to her barge set. Guido and Sara could see Taylor throwing her costume over her bikini. Sara laughed and thumped Guido on his back. Each day La Taylor's sunburn got deeper. Sara said: "It isn't going to match the interior stuff they shot earlier—the footage that's supposed to go with these barge-top scenes." They were sitting on their balcony, eating a fish salad. "Ah, yes," said Guido. "I would not have thought of that. You have a director's mind."

The next day, Sara and Guido hired a yacht that slept six. The hotel packed up a lunch and a dinner, and off they sailed to anchor near the barges, eat cheese, drink wine, and make love. At night, they lay on deck and watched the stars and listened to the lap-lap of the water on their boat.

—370—

"I love you very much, my Sara," he said in his silky voice. "I shall try to divorce my wife. I do not think it will be possible, but I shall try."

When they returned to Rome, Guido applied for an annulment on the grounds that when he married his wife he hadn't believed in the sacrament of marriage.

30

"It's all arranged," Archie said to Diana over the telephone. "Mother will see you."

Diana was so overwhelmed by her final triumph that she had to excuse herself from the telephone. She was in the morning room of the Clay Street house. She sat very still, looking out the window into the branches of a hawthorn tree in bloom. She pressed a hand to her breast as tears came into her eyes.

Diana started to collect the triplets, bringing Sara back from Rome and Sky from Los Angeles. Vail was in town. They were to accompany her to Faith Venner's home when Diana, fifty-six, was to see her mother for the first time.

Lindy was visiting her grandparents when Diana breathlessly commanded her to come with them and meet her great-grandmother. But Lindy, as usual, had her own agenda; it did not include seeing her great-grandmother. She dared Diana to force her. Recently Lindy had become difficult. Her mischievous, deep eyes dominated her small face, narrow mouth, and turned-up nose. She led with her chin physically, too, for it finished off her delicate face with a determined tilt.

Ned was an even greater surprise. He was pleased for Diana but wanted no part of the audience himself. He did not like Archie, did not trust his motives, and had no case to press with Faith Venner. He went back to the ranch with Lindy.

Diana wore very little makeup, but as she and her children stood in front of the Venner mansion, looking up at the pile of Victorian masonry at the top of Nob Hill, two pink spots stained her cheeks. For an instant Sky thought her mother had used rouge. But when she heard her mother's breathless admonition to "join her at the door," she realized that Diana was in a state of high excitement. Diana was, in fact, afraid. Would her mother approve of her? Would she ask her about her childhood, and what would Diana say? Would she hug Diana?

To Vail the old family manse, compared to the imposing buildings around it, looked like a hanger-on from a desperately different era. It was three stories high with a square top and gabled windows. He counted five chimneys. He shuddered slightly. The cold, gray mansion had a forbidding air. Sara, who had just stepped off the plane from Rome that morning, sighed and straightened the straw hat Diana had clapped on her head. The frantic preparations of that morning had left her feeling like a child again.

A butler ushered them into the white-and-coral foyer. He took their coats and disappeared. A circular stairway of cherry wood and a curving beechwood railing wound down from the second floor. Ornamental plasterwork decorated the ceiling. The butler returned and showed them into the sitting room.

Miss Venner, as she preferred to be called, sat in an old-fashioned wheelchair near a cavernous fireplace at one end of the well-furnished room. Arch Moberly stood stiffly at her side.

"I am glad you could come," he said, giving Diana a kiss on the cheek and nodding subserviently at the triplets. "Let me introduce you to Mother."

Perched in her chair, Faith Venner was a small birdlike woman. Her peaches-and-cream complexion was scored with deep wrinkles. Age had arched her nose proudly and hooded her deep-set eyes. Her snowy white hair was piled loosely on her head. She was dressed in an ankle-length green velvet gown with a lace collar. Her long fingers were curled under from arthritis, yet she displayed them as though they were not afflicted. As the Wymans drew close to her, the old lady looked up boldly. Diana sucked in her breath; Faith Venner's eyes were pale gray blue with dark blue rings around the iris—the eyes Sky had made famous around the world.

"So you finally got into the house." Faith greeted her daughter with barely concealed contempt.

Diana's heart almost stopped, but she managed to say, "I am so glad to be here." The words sounded hollow. They were the ones she had finally chosen over "remeeting you," "seeing you again," or other phrases that carried too much freight. She introduced her children, pushing Sky forward especially. Faith nodded at each of them coldly. A door opened, and the butler came in with a large silver tray, glistening with the tea service.

"Please sit down," Moberly said to them.

"Serve the tea, Archie," Faith said, "and stop making a fool of yourself." Vail smothered a broad smile.

Her mother's ghastly greeting had almost unhinged Diana; she could feel the old, lonely hopelessness take hold of her again, but she fought it off and tried to keep her tears out of her voice. "I hope you've been well," Diana said.

"You never feel well past sixty," the old lady snapped, fixing her steely eyes on Diana. Each of the triplets took a cup of tea, a cookie, and a tiny, richly embroidered napkin.

There ensued a series of polite questions posed by Archie, followed by polite answers by Diana or the triplets. Diana worked hard to bring out the fact that the children had been tutored in Europe and had graduated from college. Faith Venner seemed uninterested; her eyes wandered to the fire, to her needlepoint, to a chair Moberly said Harry Venner had often occupied. But Faith warmed up when her two tiny white poodles bounded into the room. One of them leaped into her lap; the other set up as a sentinel below the cookie dish on the coffee table. Moberly kept everything going, but he was not adept at such maneuvers. Occasionally, when Faith thought no one was looking, Sara saw her fix her sharp eyes on Diana with an unnatural ferocity. Archie fawned, some of his handsome charm gone, his expression full of worry and service.

While Diana hunted for winning, convivial conversation,

the triplets took a good look around. The old manse was falling apart. There had been attempts to spruce it up, but the gorgeous old Aubusson carpet was threadbare, and high up in the corners of the room, ghostly cobwebs had gathered. The glazed chintz chairs and love seat in blue and biscuit stripes needed a good cleaning. The decorative tile facings for the fireplace were blackened.

"I think Archie needs a connection to us somehow," Sara said as she and Sky moved around the faded room. She thought the old lady hadn't caught on, or she had refused to dignify his ambitions.

Vail leaped into the silently contested battlefield, turning on his considerable male charm for the old lady. He sat on a footstool near her, his head on a level with hers, and chatted about the movies and plays of the twenties, a subject on which he had recently completed research for an article. He spoke about the Geary Theatre, the Jenny Lind, the Metropolitan, and the Music Hall. He chatted about tea at the Saint Francis and supper at the Fairmont. In the midst of his accelerating recital, he tossed in the term, "Frisco," whereupon Faith Venner put a rugged old hand on his arm. "No, no," she said in a surprisingly strong voice. "Only people who wear paper collars call this city Frisco." Diana struggled to impress on Faith that her children never called San Francisco "Frisco." Glancing with malicious pleasure at Sky and Sara, Vail took Faith's cup and poured her more tea with an extra helping of sugar, just as Archie had done.

Faith paid little attention to Diana, which stirred her to greater narrative feats about her children. At her first mention of Sky's fame, Miss Venner laughed. It sounded like a distant echo of what had been a rich, rolling, mocking laugh. Abruptly, the game was over.

"You cannot buy your way into my family on the back of your daughter, Mrs. Wyman," Faith said with remarkable hostility.

"Mother," Arch pleaded, but she silenced him with a look.

"I certainly have no intention of doing so," Diana said with just the right mixture of hauteur and courtesy.

"You want me to say that you are my daughter," Faith

went on, putting her cup aside with Vail's tender help. "If I had had such a daughter, do you really believe I would have left her to strangers?"

"They were kind strangers," Diana lied.

"Then keep them as your own!" Miss Venner said harshly, drawing a shawl around her lap and waving at the dying fire. Vail instantly sprang up to tend it in its blackened, ornate grate.

Diana was in agony and felt the tears darting into her eyes. She turned her head away and found Archie looking at her narrowly.

"You are all pretenders!" Faith hissed at the room. "I don't know what the crowd of you are doing here if not for some evil, deceitful purpose! I have no daughter!" she finished triumphantly. Her rage was magnetic and held them in its field. Sara, Sky, and Vail broke from it first and, as one, turned to look at Diana, who was slowly rising. The old lady cried out again, "I have no daughter!" Then a waterfall of cackles overcame her, and her frail body shook like an envelope of tendons and bones.

"Mother, she *is!*" Archie whispered urgently. "Look at Diana and see yourself!" He raced across the room and snatched a silver-framed photograph off the great grand piano. "Look at this! It's true!" He thrust the photo in front of her; Faith pushed it away. Archie handed it to Sky and Sara. It was a photo of, they presumed, Faith in her thirties. It looked remarkably like Diana at that age.

They handed it across the antique table to Diana who simply put it down on a nearby table without looking at it. "I am not interested in such things," she said in a low voice. "I know who my mother is." Diana could feel herself rising. "Come, children, we mustn't tire Miss Venner." Her voice was dreamlike. She seemed transfixed. Mechanically, she took up her elegant handbag, bought especially for this visit; then she faced Miss Venner. "I shall hope to have the pleasure of visiting you again, Miss Venner," she said, approaching the old lady and extending her hand.

Faith stared up at her, silent and alert. Diana was on the verge of turning when Miss Venner said, "I am sure that Archie will let you in." She started her derisive cackle again. The little poodle in her lap began yapping.

Diana turned. "Don't make fun of me." Diana felt outside herself. She watched her arm rise to point at Miss Venner. Her voice sounded high. "You left me! You left me with people who made me a servant, who beat me every day of my childhood, who never gave me a toy of my own, or a kiss, or a warm word." Sky, Sara, and Vail rose in astonishment, quickly setting aside teacups and plates, their eyes darting from their mother to Miss Venner, whose hands were drawn up in front of her like a begging dog.

"Get out!" Faith Venner hissed. "Archie!"

Archie was stunned, his eyes wide, his sensual mouth open. Diana couldn't stop. "Did you never think of me? Did you never wonder what had become of me? I thought of you, often, when I learned that you existed but didn't know your name. I imagined—" Diana's voice broke and she screamed: "I thought you would come for me! Oh, the foolish dreams of children!"

Sara broke first, taking her mother's arm. The dog on the floor was barking shrilly.

Diana shook Sara off. "Don't patronize me!" She glared at Miss Venner. "What did you do?" Diana yelled, a tower of rage and loneliness. "Sit in this house, not caring and not loving? I suffered! And when I learned as a child—by accident—that you existed, I bent every effort to become a person you would admire. So that you would love me. And you don't even have the courtesy to be kind. I won't have it!" Diana covered her face with her hands and began sobbing.

Miss Venner was waving a hand in front of her face as though she were ridding the area of smoke. "Archie," she kept saying, querulous and annoyed.

Sky took Diana's other elbow and with Sara they led their weeping mother out of the room. Vail hovered at the doorway, exchanging a last bewildered look with the old lady.

Archie stared after them. "Are you pleased, Mother?" he said with a sneer when they were gone.

"Oh, go away, for heaven's sake. Leave me alone!"

Furious, he slammed out of the room. Faith sighed and stroked the fuzzy head of her dog. "It's my life, isn't it, Peachy?" she said to the dog. "What right's he got butting into it?" The little dog stared at her with beady eyes. Faith leaned her head back against the chair. That woman personified the bloodstained spring of 1906 to her, and she wanted no reminders. "You wouldn't remember that, Peachy, but it was such a lovely spring. All the dogwoods were in bloom, and those big pink roses we had in the bottom garden." She could still hear the clop-clop of the horses on the pavement in front of the house. Faith used to meet Bill in the bottom garden by that big tree, sometimes at night, sometimes in the late afternoon before her father got home. She'd rush to him, her head whirling, her arms aching. And he'd grab her and lift her with a deep, satisfied laugh way down in his chest and swing her up, then bring her down into his embrace. It was wild and jubilant; it was everything her life had never been. "You would have liked Bill, Peachy. My Billy. We were going away to Alaska where Billy would make his fortune. . . . But they killed him," she said, sighing. The dreams of spring always ended in murder for Miss Venner. She knew Harry had had it done. She had run to meet her lover that spring night and had found Billy hanging from the dogwood tree, the rope cinched tight around his neck, his handsome face contorted. "Oh, what a storm of tears I sent up. Father was there, waiting, watching. Oh, it was a terrible time. It just broke my heart, Peachy."

In the car, as Vail drove down California Street, no one said anything. Diana was dabbing at her eyes with her dressy hankie.

"Mother," Vail said softly, "there's nothing to be gained there. It's very sad, but you've got us."

"That's all very well for you to say," Diana responded, blowing her nose delicately, "but you have a mother."

"Maybe the lawyers made a deal with Archie," Sara said, feeling deflated and wretched.

"Oh, don't be silly, Sara," Diana whispered.

Uncharacteristically, Sky flew into a rage. "That Archie is a bloodsucker! Can't you see that?"

"I don't know how you can say that!" Diana exclaimed, shocked. "Look at that house, those fine old antiques! The Venners made millions!"

"I don't think they have millions," Vail said, turning down Hyde Street.

—378—

Everyone started talking at once. Diana turned away from their recapitulations of the visit. Meeting her mother had brought back all the lonely, disappointed, abandoned feelings she'd had as a child. She began weeping again. "Oh, this is disgraceful," she said, hunting up her handkerchief again. "It's so humiliating."

Vail stopped the car. The triplets looked at their mother helplessly. "Maybe we should go somewhere for a drink," he said.

"I don't want to go anywhere but home," Diana moaned. She blew her nose and looked up. Vail put the car in gear. They drove on. Diana broke the silence as they neared the house. "If you think I'm going to give up, you are very much mistaken." She turned away from them, mumbling. "I'll bet she didn't lift a finger for women's right to vote, either."

The sorrel horse was screaming. Lindy turned over, in her sleep, shivering at the dream. She came awake when the other horses began screaming. She rushed to the window and looked out. High under the eaves, a tongue of fire vaulted from the side of the stables. "Granddad! Maggie!" she shrieked. "Granddad! Maggie!"

She tore out of her bedroom and down the stairs. By the time she got to the stables, the double doors were open. Ned came running out from inside the building, chasing two horses in front of him. His pajamas were smoking and singed. "Stay back!" he ordered her, then rushed back inside. But Lindy followed him without thinking.

The entire upper portion of the stable was on fire, the flames spurting up at the roof like jets. The noise of the fire and the screaming horses, combined with the smoke, made her fall back. Ned disappeared down the central walkway, unlatching stable doors as he went. Suddenly the new colt bolted out of his stable and came barreling toward her. She flung herself out of the way as he rushed past. Then she ran down to check the stalls. The sorrel was trying to get out through the wall. She slapped her rump, and grabbed her mane, then leaped on her back and rode her out of the stable, slid off, and tore back inside.

"Granddad!" she yelled. Another horse came out of the

smoky interior, wild-eyed, ashes and hot coals sizzling in its hide. She slapped it toward the front. "Granddad!" A coal fell on her arm. She shrieked from the pain. The stable was a caldron of flame and hot coals. The smoke was now so thick she couldn't see or breathe. Above her a timber cracked. Suddenly, she heard a horse pounding toward her. Her grandfather was on its back, clinging to it, his head bobbing against its neck. As it shot past her, Ned's arm reached down and swept her up, pressing her against the thudding shoulder of the horse. As they reached the door of the stable and she began to slip, Ned gripped her tight, his hand digging into her back hard.

Maggie saw Ned's grip on Lindy loosen as the wild-eyed horse emerged from the stable. Lindy fell to the ground; but the terrified chestnut kept running, Ned slipping from it until he fell against the paddock fence. Maggie tore off her bathrobe and flung it over Lindy. Her nightgown and hair were afire. Behind her, with a great crack, the roof of the stable gave in and came crashing down in a burst of fiery timbers.

Vail was asleep when the phone rang about midnight. Sky was at a dinner party at Reed's new home in Bel Air.

Sara had gone back to Rome. She lay curled in Guido's arms in his house on the Appian Way. Bright summer sun streamed in through the tall windows at the far end of the room. She had been awakened suddenly, unaccountably, and had lain for some time, listening to the sound of a lawn mower moving steadily forward and back at the bottom of the garden. Guido's petition for an annulment had been promptly denied. His family was up in arms about it. When the doorbell sounded, she rose reluctantly.

"Guido," she said, shaking him. "There's someone downstairs." The bell tinkled again insistently. An hour later, Guido was driving her to the airport. Lindy was badly burned. Ned had suffered a heart attack.

All the way back across the Atlantic, and then across the face of her country, Sara replayed her last look at her father as he sat hunched over at the little outdoor table near the Colosseum. She remembered too clearly her last sharp words and prayed that she would have the time to call them back, to make amends.

It was one in the morning when she arrived in San Francisco. Sky, in dark glasses, sat with Vail in the lounge, waiting for her. It had been Sky who'd sent the telegram. As they drove, Sara learned that the fire had been three days ago.

"But why didn't someone call me?" Sara kept saying, smoking one cigarette after another.

"Mother wouldn't let me!" Vail explained. "She kept saying that Dad would get better, and why upset you?"

"And Lindy? Didn't anyone think I'd want to be with my own daughter?"

"You know Mother," Sky said. "She didn't want to upset you."

"That's a lie!" Sara cried, furiously upset now. "She's punishing me—"

Sky said, "Dad did seem to be rallying!"

They were driving the long miles to the hospital in the town near the ranch. Sara felt bitterly excluded as the familiar road, the shapes of the trees on either side, spooled out before them.

"It's strange to make this drive again tonight," Sky said, voicing all their thoughts. "Who would ever have known that we'd be chasing out here at two in the morning after all the years we—"

"And Daddy being so—injured," Vail said.

"Don't they give him any chance?" Sara demanded.

"Yes, a little. Slim, they said," Sky whispered.

"He saved Lindy," Vail said.

They rode the curves in the road in silence.

"I always felt the ranch was an oasis," Sky said. "A safe place, didn't you?"

"No," Vail said, "I didn't."

"But we didn't have tutors or school or anything at the ranch. We could just be ourselves there," Sky said.

"I had to be Dad's pal there," Vail murmured. "Mother's little gentleman, Dad's little pal." Vail had not wanted to be like Ned, who wouldn't stick up for his children against his wife, yet whom else was he to be like but his father? Often he had hated Ned, and often he had loved Ned—his soft voice, his kindness to animals and to children.

Sara said, "Remember the day he gave us Peg?"

Sky grimaced. "Oh, yes." She remembered Ned holding the bridle proudly, hopefully, offering the beautiful horse. That image of him was so fresh. It encapsulated, for Sky, his entire relationship to the family: He was present, waiting just outside the front door. "Oh, God," she groaned as she began to cry softly.

"We can't go on like this," Vail said briskly, "crying in cars. So unseemly." He mimicked Diana perfectly.

"Darling," Diana crooned to Sara as they came through the hospital doors at three in the morning. "I'm so glad you could break away. Such a long, terrible trip to make alone."

"Why didn't you call me as soon as it happened?" she demanded. "How's Lindy?"

"She'll be fine. She has some burns on her arms, but otherwise she's fine. Well, her hair was burned."

"And Daddy?" Sky asked.

Diana's face sobered. "Daddy passed on about an hour ago."

"How could you?" Sara screamed. "You did this deliberately!" A nurse materialized to shush her. "I will not be quiet! I needed to talk to him! I'll never forgive you for this!"

Sara went first to her daughter's room. Lindy looked so fragile, lying on her back in the white, smooth bed, her arms and head bandaged. Sara sat beside her bed realizing how keenly she felt the bond between them.

"Lindy, sweetheart, I'm here, too," Sara murmured. "You were very brave."

She stirred and groaned. "Mommy?" she said weakly.

She opened her eyes. "Oh, Aunt Sara."

Sara started weeping. "Yes, it's me."

"My arms hurt, and my back."

"Don't move, Lindy, you've been burned, but you're going to be all right."

"Where's Mommy?"

Sara sighed. "She's here, too. I know you want to see her."

—382—

It was dawn when Sara walked to the end of a long, dark corridor on a lower level of the hospital. She opened a door. The room was small and cool. Her father lay on a table, covered by a sheet from the neck down. A single candle burned at the head of the table. The bed next to the table was rumpled, the pillow indented, as though he had just gotten up. The light flickered. Outside, very distantly but distinctly, a nightingale sang its repetitive song. It was such a lonely place to be, this small neat room, this terminus. She thought of her father's life. Not only was it over, but the living of it seemed so completely without meaning. He had died trying to save the horses he loved but that had never brought him any success, like so many things in his life. He was so alone in this room, it broke her heart. She reached out and stroked his head, combing back the hair. She felt the loss of him sweep over her in great waves, one after the other, each painful and engulfing. Now she would never know him. She ached for herself and for him. "Dad, I'm so sorry," she whispered. "I'm sorry for what I said in Rome. I wish it were different. I wish you could be here to forgive me. I need it. I didn't realize," she sobbed, "that we didn't have time for forgiveness."

It was Lindy who bore the living horror of the fire. For the next week Sara rarely left Lindy's room. She fed her, read to her, talked to her about Rome, and entertained her with stories from her childhood as a triplet, stories that, Sky said, had always been Lindy's favorites. Sky and Diana withdrew in an unspoken accord that Sara have her time with Lindy. But when Lindy wanted Mommy, Sky was there.

It was during this recuperative period that Lindy asked Sara again about her father. "Granny won't tell me anything," she complained. "Didn't Granny like my father?"

"No, she didn't. But Granny doesn't like a lot of people," Sara said. "That's just Granny's way."

"What happened?"

"He——" Sara stopped. What if she told Lindy the truth? No, not now when she was still so injured. Sara forged ahead. "He ran away to South America. He wanted to come back but he just never made it. I—We don't have the slight-

"est idea where your father is today. We hope he's all right, because he would be proud of you."

"Everyone has a father except me," Lindy pouted. She was improving, Sara saw, since she could pout now and insist upon having her own way. "I want him to come back."

The funeral was jammed with photographers and spectators hoping to catch a glimpse of Sky.

"Jesus Christ," Vail muttered as he took Sara and Sky by the arm. "It's a sideshow!" In every direction fans or reporters perched on the cemetery's tombstones, craning their necks, eating hotdogs, drinking coffee out of paper cups. When the triplets entered the cemetery behind Diana, the fans surged forward, shouting, groaning for Sky's autograph. Police backed them off. The graveside service was punctuated by flashbulbs going off, sprinkling the sullen overcast day with brief diadems of light. When Sky's head, sheathed in a dark veil, bent over her hands, a flurry of flashbulbs popped as photographers hoped to catch Sky weeping for her poor father.

"When I die," Sara hissed to Vail as soon as the minister had finished, "my obituary will read, 'Sara Bay Wyman, sister of Sky Wyman, died today after a short illness.'"

Vail looked up into the clouds as they waited for the police to help them out of the cemetery. "Only if you want it that way," he whispered. He was thinking of his father, of the teary woman named Willa who'd come out to the ranch, begging for her clothes and other belongings. Vail had helped her pack. Willa had practically lived at the ranch with Ned in the last years. He had checked Ned's will first, and since it had carried a bequest to Willa, he'd had the lawyer omit her name for Vail's when he read it. Vail had given the blowsy but kindly woman the money Ned had promised her. He had cleaned out his father's desk, had carried off and burned all the girlie magazines he'd found and the vodka bottles stashed long ago in closets and behind cupboards. He had made the place respectable for Diana.

"I know I wasn't much of a son," he thought, talking to Ned as the police formed a circle around the triplets and Diana. "But I promise to be a better one, Dad."

Sky was crying softly. "I can't stand it," she said. Sara didn't know if she meant Ned's death or the circus funeral. She took Lindy's hand.

Many things were over. Back in Rome, Sara took a cab out to Guido's house on the Appian Way.

"I'm so sorry," he said, enfolding her tenderly in his arms. They sat in the garden, drinking spumante, listening to the delicate birds singing, and to the bubbling fountain, and smelling the sweet grass. "We'll go to dinner," he said, taking her hand. "Somewhere quiet and happy. Do not think about grief. Just let it hold you right now." Guido was always dignified and compassionate.

"It is so beautiful here," she said wistfully. "But I came out to say goodbye, Guido."

Her words rocked him. "No!" he said. "You need me. And I need you. Don't leave!"

"Yes," she said, "that's all true, but I don't belong here." She caressed his face with her open palm. "I love you, Guido, always. But I can't stay anymore. I can't be a mistress. Isn't that amusing after all the outlandish movies I've—" She checked herself. "I can't watch another woman have your children. I can't stay with you. I'm so sorry, darling."

"Don't do this!" he cried, gripping her arms and shaking her. But her mind was made up. He clasped her head to his chest, holding her tight. Gently, she pulled away. "Are you going to stay in Italy?" he asked quietly, steeling himself in advance for the years ahead when he would see her and have to pretend she meant nothing to him.

"I think so. I don't really know."

"Why are you doing this?"

"I can't explain it. Everything's changed. Don't ask me how—it's just changed. All this time we've been together—it's as if I was dreaming with you. Living in a mutual dream."

He reached out and drew her back into his arms. "Respect yourself, cara mia. I have such boundless admiration for you."

As she stared out the window of the cab taking her away from Guido, she thought of the first time she'd seen the Appia Antica on her first day in Rome. The sun was setting now. A shepherd walked on a hillside behind a placid flock of sheep, near the skeleton of a ruined temple. She thought of the army of Spartacus that had been crucified all along the Appia Antica—thousands of men, dead and dying, hanging from bloodied crosses as the Romans passed beneath them on their way to the ancient Roman equivalent of a business meeting in town or to lunch at home. She swept by conical cypress trees, quiet meadows with their buzzing insects, hidden mansions behind walls gated by poplars. Goats grazed among rusting automobiles, and broken marble blocks from ancient buildings lay in pieces on the grass. She rushed along the road built twenty-four centuries before, back to the arms of Rome.

31

Sky had hired a writer to script a sequel to her celebrated Western, *Ride On*. The new version was called *Rider Blue*. It was a Western set in the 1930s in a small town suffering in the teeth of the Depression. Sky asked Reed to direct and was thinking about Jim Fry to produce it.

"Jim's never produced anything," Reed said. "Produce it yourself!"

"In effect, I will be. But producing seems so tiresome. I'd rather do the acting."

"You're afraid," he said.

"Maybe," she replied. But she knew he was right. "If this one's successful, I'll produce the next one." She looked at him over her shoulder.

She met Jim for lunch. They hadn't worked together since *Paradise Key*. His weight had shot up but not his temper; he was the same easygoing, sweet man. But he didn't want the job. "I don't know anything about producing," he said.

"I've already used that excuse," Sky told him. "Find another." When Sky made up her mind, she usually got what she wanted. He capitulated after dessert.

For the location work, the company chose the little mountain town of Truckee in Northern Nevada, a few miles northwest of Lake Tahoe, where Sky rented a luxurious house.

Sky was pacing the floor, gesticulating. "I don't care about the cost," she was saying. "It looks shitty—we've got to do it again!" They'd just seen the first rushes of one of the stunts. They'd been shooting for two weeks.

Reed was sitting on a couch, his elbows on his knees, his head in his hands. Kitty, who was coordinating the stunts, was standing by the great fireplace, keeping an eye on the level of whiskey Sky had in her glass. Ernie was lying on a hooked rug, one arm over his eyes.

Jim was eating a carton of ice cream. He'd spent a great deal of time staring at numbers for this production, and he did not agree with Sky. "We're already behind schedule—"

"The rider's style's no good!" Sky insisted. "I know riding, I grew up with riding! It's a crucial scene."

"Sky," Kitty said, "I let the stuntwoman go, and even if the weather holds—"

"I'll do it!" Sky shouted, pacing back and forth like a cat. "I want to do it!" Everybody sighed, thinking of the insurance rates.

Kitty watched Sky cutting from one end of the room to the other. She had had the feeling for some time that Sky didn't feel connected to life unless she was playing a role. Moreover, she was isolated—sometimes even good friends couldn't break through the barrier of bodyguards, lawyers, secretaries, servants, chauffeurs, and press agents who protected her. Her drinking had increased with her isolation.

"I don't like it, Sky," she said. "Let me get Marge back."

"Reed," Sky said, kneeling beside him, "you know I can do better than Marge. You know the scene isn't right yet."

Reluctantly, Reed agreed to reshoot. Everyone straggled away.

When they were alone, Kitty put her arms around Sky. "I'm against you doing the stunt. It's too dangerous."

"Nonsense! It'll be the best scene in the whole picture!"

Sky downed her drink and started putting on a thick jacket. "C'mon, let's take a walk!"

The lake was a few feet from the house. Huge fir trees towered from the shore and reached into the night. Winding in and out of the fir trees, they walked along the edge of the water, breathing in the crisp, autumn air.

"You know," Sky said, "when you're young and struggling, you don't know how precious anonymity is. Because a beginner can take risks, make mistakes—she hasn't any image or reputation to protect. She's got nothing to lose." They stopped and looked out across the lake. A full moon was rising. "Success doesn't tolerate mistakes. That's why I've got to do that scene over."

"You don't have to prove anything anymore, Sky."

"Who says I'm proving anything?" Sky cast an arm around Kitty and steered her along the edge of the lake. "I used to think that acting would bring me contentment," Sky sighed. "*You* have, my dear, but almost nothing else has." She kissed Kitty's cheek. Kitty smiled and put an arm around Sky's waist. "I was so naïve!" Sky mumbled.

Kitty was only half-listening. She was trying to figure out how to prevent Sky from doing the stunt. Unfortunately, the small train involved in the stunt was still in place. She wondered if she should talk with Reed again but decided against it.

"The first thing Reed ever said to me was about naïveté," Sky said as they walked. "It was the chief cause of every artist's sufferings, but it was the source of the creative spirit, too. He said, 'Study as hard as you want but guard your naïveté. It will be all you've got someday.'" She turned and slipped both her arms around Kitty's waist under her jacket. "Where would I be without you? Don't ever leave me!"

"Let's get some dinner into you, and then it's off to bed. It's late."

But Sky wanted to go to the lodge and eat in a real dining room, and nothing would dissuade her. "I'll put my hair under my cap, and I'll wear your glasses!" She clapped her hands. "Presto!"

The lodge had been built in the twenties out of stone and timbers. The rustic dining room was circular, its paned windows overlooking the lake. Sky ordered a bottle of wine and a huge dinner. Kitty became uneasy. The meal and the alcohol would keep Sky awake, which meant she'd be tired tomorrow. Kitty checked the cloudless night from the little windows beside their table. She was hoping for rain to delay Sky's stunt work, but the brilliant stars promised a glorious autumn day.

"Why, darling, I never dreamed I'd see you down here!"

It was Diana, who had taken rooms at the lodge for the shoot. "May I sit down?" she asked, sitting down. "You look cute with your hair up in that cap, honey." Sky ordered another drink.

Ever since the Venners had appeared on the family stage, Diana had rarely joined Sky on a location shoot. But when she did, the three of them declared an unspoken truce. There had been no scenes or recriminations since Diana's battle with Sky about Kitty. Mother and daughter treated each other courteously but coolly. After Ned's death, Diana had withdrawn into her civil rights work and into her efforts with Miss Venner.

"Are you selling the ranch?" Sky asked.

"I'm thinking about it, dear. Of course, Vail still objects."

"Maggie can come with us," Sky said.

"No, dear, Maggie wants to work with me—if I sell it, that is."

"If you do, give Lindy a last month up there. She loves it so," Sky said.

"Darling," Diana began, "I wonder if you would consider doing me a very big favor?"

"Sure, Mother."

"I want you to rethink that role."

"Which role?"

"That one about the little orphan." Kitty shut her eyes. Diana never knew when to give up. She had pressed her case relentlessly.

"I have no intention of taking that part, Mother," Sky said, loftily. "It's stupid, and the picture will be drivel."

Diana straightened her silverware daintily. "Well, if you can't find it in your heart to do it, why not make it possible for Sara? She could do it nicely, and wouldn't we love to get her out of Rome?"

Sky felt cornered. She compressed her lips. Kitty looked around for the waiter to get their food as fast as possible. "We don't even know if Sara wants that crummy role. I certainly don't want to see her in it."

"Why don't you help your sister? You've got your own success; you don't need to succeed at her expense anymore."

Sky stared at her mother. "Is that what you think? That my success was bought at her expense? My God, I can't

—390—

believe you said that." The elderly couple at the next table stopped eating and looked at them.

"What did I say?" Diana asked. Baffled and hurt, she looked at Kitty.

"Whatever I've got, I *earned*. I didn't take it away from Sara or Vail!" Sky was leaning toward her mother. "Furthermore, you don't want that role because it would be good for either Sara or me—you want it for some other reason!" Had it always been like this? Sky wondered. Had her mother always been emotionally caught up in Sky's ambitions, shaping them for what they could produce for Diana herself? No, she couldn't believe it.

"Don't get excited, dear," Diana cooed, taking a sip of ice water. "I just felt you owed me a little something, too. But never mind. I know when I'm licked." She smiled distantly at Kitty.

"Maybe I'm just a convenience you also like," Sky suggested sarcastically. Kitty touched Sky's arm but Sky made no attempt to lower her voice. "Is that it?"

"What a dreadful thing for a mother to hear from her daughter," Diana whispered, conscious now that people in the dining room were listening.

"Don't I give you enough money? Do you want me to start sending checks directly to Vail now instead of through you?"

"Why, I never—"

"I know you practically support them! With my money! Isn't it enough that you're selling the ranch?" She touched one hand to her head. "Have I been blind all these years?" Her voice dropped as if she'd just run out of energy. "But I did feel you loved me. I felt you respected my work."

"I do!" Diana cried, confused and frightened.

"I'm just an extension of you, aren't I?" Sky said, chillingly.

"Sky," her mother wailed, "you're making a scene!"

Sky rose from the table. "Fine! For once it's for free!" Sky turned to the room. "You will forgive my mother and me—this is the way we discuss things in our family—dramatically." She bent down and put her sleek face close to Diana's. "If I'm just an extension of you, who am I?" She jerked up again. Her cap fell off her head, and her hair

—391—

tumbled out. Who am I? she said to herself. She turned back to her mother and stared at her as she might stare at a stranger. Then she walked out of the old dining room.

Sky woke up in the middle of the night as she always did when she'd had too much to drink. The bedroom was rustic, too, with a fireplace and nubby curtains and knotty pine paneling. How much did she owe her mother? she wondered. How much did she not owe her? She felt used; she was shamed that she'd never seen it before. Had everyone seen it? Had Kitty? Had Sara? Or was she wrong now about being used? Was that too harsh? She turned her face to the wall. Had she really wanted to be an actress? She tried to think back to the early days, to her first role, to her screen test. They were cloudy and far away. Was she, Sky, living her own life or a life her mother wanted her to live?

She woke up at dawn thinking about Pegasus. After all these years, she could still see that bewitching horse: her white stockings on her narrow legs, the white blaze down her slender nose, and the clear intelligence in her eyes. She was such a sweet horse, even though their acquaintance had been so brief. She'd often wondered about where her mother had sold her. Why hadn't she asked? she thought, as she got ready for the day's work.

"Kitty," Sky said at breakfast, "why didn't I ask Mother where she sold Peg? Huh?"

Kitty was biting into a piece of toast. She put it down.

"Do you feel all right?"

"Sure. But why didn't I?"

"Maybe you didn't want to know."

The company had appropriated two streets and an old railroad siding, on which a locomotive suitable to the period of the thirties was hissing steam into the early morning. Crowds of locals were forming; the crew stood around the equipment trucks, sipping hot coffee from Styrofoam cups, reading newspapers or paperback books. Near the locomotive the script clerk, Paula, a young woman from Wardrobe, and two female bit players sat in canvas chairs playing a lively game of "desert pick."

"Who do you want with you on a desert island?" Paula asked, initiating one of the actresses who'd never played before. The game allowed players to express confidences normally hidden. It was also a great way to establish intimacies.

"Oh, Reed," the actress said. Paula sighed; that was boring. Everyone wanted Reed, but that gave the other players no insight into the men on the set the little actress was really attracted to. If she'd said Ping, that would have been fine grist for their rumor mill.

Sonny Somaine was Sky's costar again and had received second billing again, too. Reed was trying to convince Sonny to wear the boots chosen for him. Out of the corner of his eye, Reed saw Mrs. Wyman standing in the drugstore doorway, a beret on her head, a cup of coffee in her hand.

"They look dopey!" Sonny was yowling about the boots.

Kitty saw Sky coming out of her trailer. She was costumed and made up. Kitty braced herself.

"What are you doing in the duplicate costume?" Sky demanded of her.

"I'm riding in your place, Sky," Kitty said, pulling on her gloves.

"You are not! Christ, why is everyone telling me what to do?"

Reed came over to them. "Kitty's right, Sky, it's just too dangerous. Tricky timing. You haven't done your stunts for years. C'mon, be sensible."

Sky smiled and said sweetly, "Let's do it my way or I'll walk. I'll shut it all down." She took the reins of the gelding called Bob, which a wrangler was patiently holding.

Reed sighed. "All right, everybody, let's have a rehearsal," he called out to the crew leaning against the equipment trucks or sitting on canvas chairs on the sidewalk. They got up groaning. The locomotive engineer waved cheerfully from the cab and let out a jet of steam. The crowd was held behind ropes out of camera range. They waited for the action to begin, ogling Sky and Sonny.

"Sky, please get into position," Reed said. Sky walked the horse down the street, which was perpendicular to the path of the train's siding, toward a group of mounted riders.

The stunt called for Sky to gallop down the street, pursued by the other riders. When she drew alongside the moving train, Sky was to look back at her pursuers, then catch hold of the grab iron of the car and swing herself

—393—

aboard. They had already taken the scene directly following this one, of Sky standing on the steps of the little passenger car, waving her hat and jeering at her pursuers.

Sky entered into the rehearsal with gusto. Her first gallop toward the train was beautifully timed, but she had trouble getting hold of the grab iron. The gelding seemed a little train-shy. "I thought you said this horse was trained," Sky said to the wrangler.

"He is! I swear it!"

"Manny!" Reed called out to his assistant director. "Get that car moved out of there." He pointed to a Chevrolet parked at the side of the street near the tracks.

"I would have, but it's locked, and no one's owning up to it. It isn't in the shot, is it?"

"No, I just want it out."

"Well, I dunno what to do. Leave it, I guess."

The second rehearsal was perfect. Sky swung smoothly from the saddle onto the moving train as if she'd done it every day. The crowd applauded. Sky waved her hat triumphantly. The train started backing up to get into place again.

"Shit, why didn't I shoot that?" Reed muttered. "Okay, this is a take," he shouted. "She looks terrific, doesn't she?" he said to Kitty. "I guess we're out of the woods. It's not that hard a stunt anyway."

Down at the end of the street, Sky patted the glossy neck of her mount. The extras, her pursuers, congratulated her. "How can we make it more interesting?" she asked them. She rubbed her shoulder. She wasn't used to pulling herself up on trains and knew she'd be sore tomorrow.

"It can't be more interesting," one of the men said, "unless you make it a lot more difficult. It looks good as it is."

Sky looked down the street to where it bisected the tracks, to where one of the cameras was mounted surrounded by reflectors, lights, and a knot of production people. She felt good. Her hangover was gone; the wrenching and disturbing scene with Diana was fading. She kept her eye on Manny, who would give her the signal to start. She thought of Pegasus nostalgically, and of the ranch, and of Ned. She wondered what Sara was doing this morning. Manny's arm went down. Sky let out a whoop, and her horse plunged forward. She galloped toward the train feeling the wind in her hair. Timing, timing, she said, seeing the train coming into view and knowing she was a beat or two behind. She dug her heels into her mount and leaned forward. She was right next to the train reaching for the grab iron when she heard a shrill, screaming whistle. Her horse bucked, and she went flying. The train disappeared from view. She was sailing into the air.

Diana dropped her coffee cup. Reed screamed: *"Sky!"* Kitty started to run toward her as Sky collided face first with the windshield of the parked car.

Kitty reached her first. Sky was crumpled against the windshield like a doll. Someone's arms were reaching out for her. *"Keep away!"* Kitty screamed. It was Diana.

"My child!" Diana wailed. She hit out at Kitty with all her strength, then grabbed a handful of Kitty's hair. Reed jerked Diana away and bodily turned her over to Manny. Diana never stopped screaming—long, thin, trailing sounds shooting up from her like a fountain. Kitty, weeping, was feeling for Sky's pulse. Then she heard Sky groan. "Don't move, sweetheart," Kitty said, her voice shaking.

"Oh, my God," Reed was mumbling over and over. He was staring at Sky's blood leaking across the caved-in glass. The right side of her face and her shoulder seemed embedded in the concave windshield. Her legs were stretched out akimbo on the hood. Manny was yelling for an ambulance. Diana was still screaming.

TRIPLETS

PART THREE

32

In 1965 Robbie Beaudine, the elegant director of *Paradise Key*, found a script called *Foxglove*, which made him think of Sky. But she hadn't made a picture since her accident three years ago. Beaudine went to Sheldon Winters. They sparred, and Beaudine began to understand why Sky hadn't worked. He finally wrung a concession out of Sheldon, but it was an unbelievable insult to Sky.

"So Sheldon wants me to test," Sky said to Beaudine, who was handsomely draped on a small sofa in her study.

"It's appalling of him," Beaudine said.

Sky, at thirty-five, looked thin and rather remote. "He doesn't think I'll do it. But I'm going to surprise him. Let's get Ernie."

"I can't. He's on location in Africa."

"Damn!" She thought of all the hours she, Ace, and Ernie had spent lighting various makeup techniques to cover the scars that plastic surgery couldn't completely repair.

The young cameraman the studio had hired for her test was named Harold Pizer. He couldn't believe his eyes when Sky strolled into the old sound stage for he'd expected a fully made-up and costumed star with an entourage. But Sky was carrying a floppy hat and dressed in slacks and a silk shirt. The only people with her were Ace and Cage.

"I'm sorry," Harold said, flustered. "The dressing room's not very clean. I didn't know—"

The dressing room was filthy. The dusty counter before the long mirror was covered with makeup stains. A heap of discarded tissues lay on the floor in a corner. Sky sat down as though she were back in her old bungalow. She leaned forward and gently pressed the bridge of her remade nose. One side of her face was frozen, slightly out of alignment with the other side. The light in the dressing room was abysmal; she looked haggard. Sky called her accident "a mighty expensive face-lift."

One of the first people she'd seen after the accident had been Arch Moberly. He had had a look of solicitous concern on his ruddy face. She had shut her eyes. She didn't want to see anyone who looked so robustly healthy.

In the autumn of 1962, Arch had been vacationing at Tahoe when he heard about her accident. He'd immediately driven to the Reno hospital where the ambulance had delivered Sky. He was her uncle, a psychiatrist, he'd told them.

One side of her face was thick with bandages, her jaw was wired, her shoulder dislocated, and her back—broken—was braced in traction and a body cast. Moberly saw his chance clearly. "I will handle everything," he said contentedly. "You have nothing to worry about." She could barely hear him. Kitty was glad to have the help. She hadn't slept in thirty-six hours. Diana was under sedation.

People started to arrive. Vail was one of the first. He bent over her bed. "You are more myself than I am," he said. Sky dreamed that the three of them were together at the ranch. She moaned constantly for Daddy. She refused to see Diana until she believed she was dying.

Archie came every day, sat with her for an hour or two, let her talk, offered indulgent advice. Archie had a calming and protective manner that surprised Sky. When whole factories sent their prayers for her recovery and newspapers started carrying front-page boxes detailing progress reports on her condition, Arch read the telegrams and the papers to her. Slowly he became indispensable. Sky told him about her childhood, about her argument before the accident with Diana, about Reed, and the whole story about Belinda being Sara's child. Archie listened—his soothing talent—and he translated the "medical lingo," as Sky called it. She was transferred to Los Angeles, and when she was well enough he took her to elegant restaurants, sharing with her his love of comfort, gourmet food, and fine wines. Reluctantly Kitty made room for him; Sky seemed better after he'd been with her.

But privately Kitty didn't like Arch. Grace and crudity were the contesting plates of his nature. He was dishonest in a way she couldn't describe; he wanted something. She didn't know what.

Sky had had thirteen operations on her face and nine on her shoulder and back. In excruciating pain, she had complained that the doctors never gave her enough medication. Archie did. Slowly Sky recovered. But with recovery came another kind of shock. When Sky realized that many people had admired her more for her beauty than for her talent as an actress, the revelation had a more profound effect on her than the trauma of the freak accident or the agony of recuperation.

Two years after the accident, Sky made her first public appearance—at a party given by Sheldon Winters and his wife. As Reed escorted her into the huge, softly lit Bel Air home, the living room full of people from the industry fell silent. Sheldon welcomed her boisterously and kissed her cheek. The party began again. Everyone pretended nothing had changed; but when Sky wasn't looking at them, their eyes minutely searched her face for damage and alteration. Her face was public property and had improved the economic advantage of many there. The room buzzed. Some said she seemed more human, less flawlessly beautiful; others despaired: Her exotic good looks were frozen. Certainly Sky Wyman was changed.

"It's the effect of her face," Jim Fry murmured to Ernie Ping in the commissary the next day. "It's a mask. It doesn't move." Jim towered over Ping, even though he was hunching his wide shoulders and slouched down in his chair. He looked worried and unhappy.

"Enigmatic," Ping said. "But I think it's going to work in her favor."

"Let me check your pulse," Fry said. "You're a sick man."

"Beauty can work against a woman," Ernie replied. "They might begin to accept her as the fine actress she's always been instead of a sex symbol. It's not too late."

Archie visited Sky in Los Angeles once a week. He supplied "boosters"—vitamin B shots laced with uppers or tranquilizers; he listened, he pacified. He never lost his temper, he never wanted to talk about himself. Archie encouraged her to free-associate. Sky talked incessantly. She worried about the effect of her accident on Lindy, about her inability to be the mother Lindy needed and had come to expect; she wondered if she was acting because *she* wanted to or because, long ago, she'd wanted her mother's approval.

"I really want your opinion," Sky said to him.

"I don't think Diana's approval is important anymore."

Sky recommended him to a friend; Archie's practice in the Hollywood film community increased. From a man who felt he'd been deprived of his place in life, he declared (to his mirror while shaving) that he'd now come into his own by helping Sky and the celebrities she knew.

Kitty called him "Doctor Feelgood." She watched helplessly as Sky's addiction to the pain pills Archie supplied grew. Sky was not present in her life as she had once been. When Kitty argued and pleaded with her, Sky escaped into the roles she'd played, reenacting them in real life: the reclusive, introverted Rosa Morris in *The Ginkgo Tree* or the immature but stimulating Estelle in *The White Queen*. Sky didn't know how she herself felt anymore. Kitty wanted her to get out more, meet new people, wean herself from the drugs the doctors had started her on. Sky wouldn't do it. "Life is short—socializing steals time," she snapped at Kitty. Mrs. Sho shook her head: If Kitty couldn't get her to stop living in a private haze, no one could. And Kitty was almost burned out from the strain.

Ray Sordo had cut his producer's teeth on *The White Queen*, and had built a low-key but steady career. He was known as an "understanding" producer. His ingratiating grin was still stamped on his face, and he still kept his hands in his pockets. Ray was always looking around for flunkies to take the burden of the work off him. His eyes settled on Jim Fry, who had served as Sky's producer on her aborted Western.

Sordo had a script about a one-time Miss America who, in her thirties, decides to swim the English Channel. It was based on real life, and Sordo wanted Sky in the part. Ray wanted to be the producer who put Sky back on top. He was amazed to find that Sheldon's studio didn't want to back Sky in the part. Not only had Sky's last two pictures

—402—

before the accident failed at the box office but the costs of her aborted Western hung over Sky's ledger in chains of red ink. But it was Sky's rashness—the needlessness of the accident—that most enraged Sheldon Winters.

"Sky?" he said incredulously when Fry and Sordo were sitting in his office, pitching the project. "I wouldn't touch it if she paid *me!*"

"But the plastic surgery's good—" Sordo began, completely misreading Sheldon.

"I saw her last month!" Sheldon bellowed. "I know what she looks like! She's not beautiful anymore."

Fry was aghast. "Sheldon, she's just as beautiful as—"

"As a marble fixture!" Sheldon roared.

"But the part doesn't need a beauty—" Sordo said, grasping at anything so he could make the picture. "It needs an actress!"

"You want to make it with Sky," Sheldon said, "you take it to another studio."

"Aw, Shel," Sordo moaned. Sheldon was punishing Sky, and he knew that for a while no other studio would go against him.

Other producers came to Sky and to other studios with scripts for her. The studios appeared interested, but nothing happened.

Then Robbie Beaudine found the script called *Foxglove.* He wanted Sky to play the beautiful blind woman who was raped, knifed, and survived to testify in the final court scene. But it was the second lead—not the starring role. Before the accident, no one would have suggested Sky for it; Sky herself would have dismissed such a part. But Beaudine knew it was the role that would bring her back.

Sheldon was having his hair cut in his office dressing room when Beaudine outlined the picture, for which he already had the financing.

"Sky can't play that part," Sheldon said, gravely. "The audience won't accept a big star, even though she's a former star, in a small part. You know better than that, Robbie." But Robbie had wrung the test out of him anyway.

Now Sky sat in the dingy dressing room off the unused sound stage watching Cage gently put on her makeup.

"I'll show that Sheldon," she murmured. "No, Cage,

—403—

don't cover that," she said to him about a crescent-shaped scar on her cheek. "It'll be good for the part."

Foxglove went on to win five Academy Awards in 1967, and one of them went to Sky for best supporting actress. It was her first Oscar. "Sky's natural acting has set a tone and style for her time," her presenter said, "and for the actors who come after her. She is that rarity—an actress who makes history."

But even this success carried defeat: She was no longer perceived by the industry as a star. Sky never looked back. She would make a different kind of career—as a serious actress.

The month after the Awards, Kitty was coming in from the garden with an armful of daffodils and tulips. Sky was standing at the top of the stairs, one hand on the railing. She had an open book in the other.

"I didn't know you were up," Kitty said. "Aren't these lovely?" She held out the flowers.

"Where's Lindy?" Sky asked dreamily. Then she raised the book and started reading. "Incongruent hour of sweet loss. . . ' " Her voice trailed off, the book fell from her hand, and she swayed. Kitty watched the woman she loved tumble in a terrible slow motion down the stairs.

Kitty dropped the flowers and ran to Sky as her head cracked against the bottom step. "Sky!" she sobbed.

Later, at the hospital, Kitty learned Sky was loaded with Librium and alcohol. "She could have broken her neck," the doctor said. "She only broke her wrist—this time." Appalled and shaken, Kitty knew she had to find a way to separate Sky from Archie's medicine chest.

"My back is killing me," Sky complained. They were sitting on the terrace in the late afternoon sun.

"That's not all that's killing you," Kitty said, taking her hand. "Sky, if you don't get off those pain pills and the liquor, we won't be together next year. Remember where I come from. I've been up close to addicts and drunks—"

"I'm not one of those!" Sky shrieked.

"Not yet," Kitty said. "But you're losing control of your life, and I can't get it back for you. Archie is not helping. Please," she wept, "please stop. Think of Lindy. Please let me help."

Sky clutched her head dramatically and wailed, "Don't leave me, Kitty!" Slowly she pulled herself together. "I'll do anything for you and Lindy."

When Kitty told Archie that Sky was going to Europe with Reed for a few months, he looked at her with a tolerant air of condescension. "Her back is a mess, and she'll need medication for the rest of her life," he said.

Archie wore beautifully tailored clothes, Kitty saw. Sky's misfortune had put them on his back. The realization brought out all her anger. "You're killing her! Doctor Peterson doesn't think she needs a lot of medication. He thinks she needs work and physiotherapy. I'm going to see that she gets the best—in Switzerland. She almost died on those stairs, and if she dies, where will you be?"

Archie only stroked his silk Dior tie. "You don't know what you're talking about." He went into the study where Sky was pouring herself a glass of wine. "Are you both crazy?" he demanded. "You are under *my* care, Sky."

She looked at him a little sheepishly. "Yes, but Kitty's right, Arch. I've got to get straight. I hate to leave Lindy, but maybe this little trip will be good for me."

He wanted to shake her but wisely restrained the impulse. "You call me, day or night," he said softly. "I'll send you what you need."

In Italy, Sara had one arm around a marble column. She held a glass of red wine in her other hand and surveyed the party on the terrace. She was wondering which man she'd take home with her for the night. A group of young French and English actresses and actors surrounded her. It was a costume party. Sara wore a harlequin mask, a black wig, and a copy of a dress Sky had made famous in *Paradise Key*. She was laughing steadily.

"Let's get her home," Carmen said to Marco. They were furious at her, and saddened. But Sara wouldn't leave. She'd done this before at loud, big parties, but she'd never made quite as much of a fool of herself. Now she was standing between a French actor's legs: he was drunk as she, and they were clumsily embracing while spouting Racine in French.

Carmen couldn't bring herself to judge Sara harshly.

She'd been there when Sara received phone calls from complete strangers who "just wanted to hear the sound of Sky's voice," and Carmen had heard Sara make her voice sound even more like Sky's than it naturally was when she spoke to her mother in the States. Carmen had watched Sara resort to love by transference, by substitution, and by fantasy, and she firmly believed that Sara was unaware of what she was doing. But Carmen was wrong: Sara *was* aware of it. And though she seemed to be dedicating her life to love, Sara had, in fact, lost her belief in love. She was at rock bottom, and Carmen grieved for her.

The next day Sky and Reed arrived in Rome. Applause for *Foxglove*, capped by the Academy Award, was rolling over the world. Sara had just completed a multinational horror movie that reviewers had found laughable—when they bothered to review it at all. Sky was the last person Sara wanted to entertain.

Sara had moved into a large penthouse apartment near the Borghese Gardens in Rome. She'd decorated with modern Italian furniture—sleek and colorful. A wide terrace overlooked the city. The party at Marco's seemed like years ago.

Reed kissed Sara's cheek and said, "You've lost your naïveté."

Sara, surprised, said, "I thought you said that to Sky." She could still see Reed standing on the threshold of the theater dressing room the night Sara and Sky had first met him. Now he had deep lines scored in his cheeks, but his dimples remained, and Sara thought that he was better looking at forty-seven than he had been at thirty.

"Oh, so you remember that, do you? So long ago," he said. "I said it to both of you." Sara's once luscious mouth was thinner, but her bright, bold eyes held a shrewd, self-mocking, provocative glint.

In the last five years, Reed had married and amicably divorced; he had directed two films and produced a third. An uncle many times over, he kept a separate calendar on his desk to remember all his family's birthdays. He was at the top of his profession but privately he sensed his life was adrift; the close, intimate joy of realizing a script on film had left him. Almost no one he met revived his former delight in convivial companionship. He wondered about the meaning of life, and though he was not unhappy, and did not feel sorry for himself, he felt blunted.

Sara settled Reed and Sky on her terrace. Utterly Romanized, Sara had quantities of sweet cheese, hard slabs of Parmesan, pungent Gorgonzola, cool white Roman wine, and fruits. Sara had been devastated by Sky's accident. She had flown into Reno, had sat with her in the hospital, but had finally realized that Sky couldn't stand anyone seeing her vulnerability—her casts and her bandages, her helplessness and her injury. Sara had understood. She had comforted Lindy as best she could and had then gone back to Rome.

On the terrace Sara started singing Sky's praises. Everything in her rollicking conversation revolved around Sky—her roles, her hopes, her problems getting scripts. She had compassion for this and advice for that. Reed saw that Sky gave Sara little in return. But then Sara didn't ask very much from Sky. Observing them, Reed wondered at the depth of Sara's love and envy of Sky. The twin opposing strands in her were ingrained like strata in a rock fossil.

Sky didn't want to be in Rome. She missed Lindy badly; she felt like a patient with a caretaker—Reed. But Kitty had put their relationship on the line. Sky was torn between Kitty and Arch. She knew Kitty was right, but the pain in her back rippled over her in waves, her face itched, and the wine tasted like water. Sometimes just a tiny movement the wrong way could make her back or shoulder feel like someone had stabbed her. She needed Arch.

"How many bedrooms do you have?" she asked Sara abruptly.

"Three."

"Good. Ace and Cage are arriving soon. Maybe they can stay one night until they decide where they're going. I think they'll be heading to Portofino."

The next day, all three of them drove north to Siena. It was a brick red, medieval walled town where the streets, inside the walls, were as narrow as sidewalks. It was like a pretty and ancient maze.

The room clerk at the hotel was a film buff, and his mouth opened in joyous surprise when Sara and Sky, accompanied by the American director, came in out of the autumn rain that evening.

"You are traveling incognito," he whispered. "I shall not tell." Sky didn't care whom he told; she was in pain, and she retired to her room without ceremony. The adoring room clerk personally escorted her upstairs, then recommended a little restaurant to Sara and Reed. It was on the Campo, a huge, fan-shaped piazza at the center of town.

Reed was glum. Sara was thinking about how sad Sky looked. "What are we going to do? What the hell is the matter with her?" Sara asked.

"Some of it," he said and looked away. "Is it all pain?"

"It's a lot more than that, Reed."

"Of course it is. She's been used to a steady diet of codeine and God knows what else. One of her doctors said she'd be going through a moderate withdrawal. The other one disagreed. No one seems to know very much. She's taking a lot of aspirin."

Sara said, "We've got to get her acting again."

"First some physiotherapy," said Reed, "then another good role."

Sara stopped picking at the antipasto. "Acting's really a neurotic expression, isn't it? I suppose after you've developed the faculty, you go on being an actor because you're just too neurotic to do anything else."

"I don't think it's quite that bad." He served himself some sweet red pepper soaked in herbs and oil. "But actors don't seem to enjoy much else besides acting, and they're fairly inarticulate about acting itself!" He didn't want to talk at all. The trip was a disaster. He kept on talking and pushed the plate of antipasto toward her.

"It's narcissistic and self-indulgent," she said. "It's false love, too. I know Sky feels released by acting. She gets out of herself. I used to feel that way, too, but I don't anymore. I just feel bored. I wish I could do something else."

She didn't want to be talking to him. He bored her, too.

"You can change your life," he said. "Look at all the changes in cinema that are taking place in Europe! In America we try to make everything perfect, but it just comes out looking like a factory dress or a magazine ad—'the Hollywood Look.' But there's a European look, the new-wave look. It's exciting.''

Sara thought about the people she knew: Marco was a television director now, and a good one; Carmen was an assistant director on a first-rate motion picture; and Guido had become a superstar, a man whom the press and the public followed everywhere. Guido wasn't famous because he was handsome and decent; he was an actor of sensitivity and boldness. He had told her that his family had come around.

''Why don't you stop trying to compete with Sky, stop envying her? You're never going to be her—and you're very lucky. You don't really want to be inside her skin.''

''You're always so full of advice, Reed,'' she said. She finished off her wine. ''Why don't you and Sky just get married, and be done with it? Quit hanging around each other like brother and sister.''

''That's pretty silly,'' he said, smiling. ''Sky's in love with Kitty. She probably won't marry anyone.''

Sara poured herself a glass of mineral water from the bottle on the table. ''Why is that, Reed? I was so surprised when she told me about Kitty, and so moved, too. It also made me feel endangered. Isn't that crazy?'' She laughed falsely. ''I'll never know why I felt that way.''

Reed broke up some bread to mop up the olive oil on his plate. ''Oh, maybe you just didn't want to know—the way you don't want to know anything. It's more comfortable for you if she's famous and you're not. You're used to that. Then you can finish the rest of your life feeling sorry for yourself.''

''You're way out of line,'' she said, rising.

''Of course. Too truthful.'' Angrily, he threw some lire on the table and walked out behind her.

When they got back to the hotel, Sky had checked out.

''My God!'' Sara cried, her imagination leaping. ''Poor Sky. Where could she have gone?''

''Back to Arch,'' Reed said. He had put everything aside to accompany her on the trip, and he was profoundly distressed about her. The substitute room clerk shrugged miserably.

''That creep,'' Sara said bitterly. ''Mother sure brought

all the ravens down on us with him." She sat down in a lobby chair. "Of course, maybe she went back to Lindy and Kitty."

"Not Kitty," he replied. "They're having real troubles. Maybe Lindy." He glanced at the cheery, overstuffed lobby without seeing it. "I'm not leaving," Reed said to a flowered sofa. "Damn her."

When the film buff clerk returned from his dinner, he told them that Signorina Wyman had hired a car to drive her back to Rome, where she was joining up with "two people," he said, "Ace and Cage." They were going to Portofino.

The next day, Sara called her apartment and Sky answered briskly.

"Sky, for God's sake, you scared us!"

"I'm sorry. I just had to get out. Reed was like a nurse. I'll be better with some sun."

Sara, feeling deflated and disturbed, joined Reed for breakfast at the restaurant on the Campo. It was a beautiful crisp day with high white clouds.

"What are your plans?" Reed asked, sipping his caffe latte.

"I never make plans," Sara responded. "Are you still going to Florence today?"

"Yes, I want to know about the location site. I do have a little work to do, y'know," he said, smiling. "Have you thought much about bringing Lindy over here?"

"What are you, my conscience?" she said, irritated. The waiter brought a basket of hard rolls. "Oh, I've tried," Sara said, more sweetly. "She prefers her glamorous life with Mommy Sky and Granny Diana. She's a teenager now—fourteen. Glamour is important to teenagers."

"You of all people ought to know it's anything but glamorous!" He broke open a roll. "For Sky, the sun rises and sets on Lindy. Don't have any worries on that score. Sky's been a good mother."

"Oh, I know. I just wish—oh, I don't know what I wish." She eyed Reed as if she was trying to decide whether she liked him or not. His brow was crinkled, his hair mussed. For all his quiet strength, there was something boyish and imprecise about him, almost forlorn.

—410—

"How long are you going to keep up the deception?" he asked.

"Reed, I don't really want to talk about this. The deception, as you say, is firmly in place, and Lindy is Sky's daughter." He started to say something but she went on. "Yes, I feel wretched about it sometimes. No, I probably wouldn't do it again, knowing what I know now, but at the time, it really seemed best for Lindy. Best for me, too. But I am concerned about Lindy now. Sky isn't on deck for her the way she once was."

"I'm sorry about what I said last night," he said. "I was out of line."

"Forget it. How's your family?" Sometimes she imagined Reed's family as the only normal people left on earth. "Still living up there around Mount Shasta?"

"Yes, Dad's still pumping gas at the station, Mom's still handling the store and the bar. They won't let me help much, except I put a roof on the place last year. And I help with my youngest brother's college."

"And all the others, too, if I remember right." She grinned at him. She was relieved the conversation had shifted from herself to neutral territory.

"They've turned out great: two teachers, one carpenter—makes cabinets, Jed's great—one pediatrician, and one stewardess."

He saw that Sara had gone back inside herself. Reed sighed. He couldn't seem to reach her. She was sunk in a morass of self-pity and bitterness. Yet, in spite of that, she was still wildly generous with friends, family, and even with complete strangers, and she was bewitching. Her cool, piercing eyes didn't seem to miss much—except about herself; her high cheekbones, lightly rouged, narrowed to her little chin; her brassy hair, roguish and aberrant, flew out from her head and caught the light in a golden nest. He realized that his compassion was mixed with attraction. As they talked on, he found himself flirting with her, holding her gaze until she dropped her eyes, leaning forward into her space at the table. Surprised at himself, he began to imagine touching her narrow waist as thin as a whippet's and her round, full mouth. He would look away across the gently sloping Campo, brilliantly sunlit like a huge roller rink; then he'd look back at her, half-hoping that the crazy attraction had been cut. But it grew. She had a habit of rolling her eyes to one side and glancing out at a person, wistful and shrewd at once.

"I think I'll drive back to Rome with you," he said.

"Fine. You run off to Florence, I'll sit here a while, then we'll meet for dinner tonight and pack off to Rome tomorrow. How's that?"

After Reed had left, Sara turned her face up to the sun and had another cup of coffee.

The Campo was filling up with tourists. Local women carried string bags with the day's groceries, and local men lounged against the balustrade of the fountain, their hands arcing in the air descriptively. Her eye settled on a man across the clutter of outdoor tables who was gorging himself on cappuccino and rolls. For a thin man he had a big appetite. The way he moved his head and shoulders seemed vaguely familiar to her. But he was sitting with his back to her; she couldn't be sure. Maybe someone from school.

The man looked up at the waiter, and Sara saw his profile. "Jesus," she whispered. "I don't believe it." It was Vic.

For years, when Vic Oumansky caught sight of the color of bronze, he would glance furtively at the woman's face. But it was never Sara. Today the woman was smiling at him, a look of astonished recognition on her face. She was the one woman who belonged to the hair.

"I don't know whether to kiss you or sock you," Sara said.

"God, you look terrific," Vic said, sitting down.

She couldn't take her eyes off him. His nut brown hair was graying attractively; he had the same clear blue eyes. His forehead was tracked with horizontal lines, but he didn't look careworn at all; he looked polished. He still had most of his hair, swept straight back from his high forehead. His clothes were expensive. There was a happy, self-satisfied air about him.

"My former husband. I divorced you when you abandoned me, you cad. Where did you go? Make it good." No matter how good it was, it couldn't compare to the card she had up her sleeve: Lindy.

"I hope we can be friends," Vic said amiably. "And the name's Oliver now, Vic Oliver."

Sara frowned. "That sounds familiar."

"I hope so. I've been on the best-seller list." He smiled broadly. "I'm in Italy researching my next book."

She found herself feeling pleased about his success. "What kind of books do you write?"

"Adventure thrillers, action and suspense, with believable heroes," he said. "The Ringyard Trio, Season of Darkness."

"I remember seeing The Ringyard Trio on the racks in bookstores. Big gold and black cover?"

He nodded. "And where have you been all these years?"

"I'm not exactly invisible." She was hurt. "You haven't seen any of my movies?"

"No. But I spend most of my time in Ireland. I own some property there. We don't get a lot of movies out in the country. I'm sorry. I have heard," he quickly added, "about Sky. I even saw a couple of her movies. It was a very strange sensation."

"Well, I haven't made the kind of movies Sky has," she said. "How'd you get into writing thrillers?"

"I bummed around for a while, and then I was almost killed in a boating accident that turned out not to be an accident. I wrote a book about it, a thriller, and it sold well enough so that I could write another one." Vic flagged the waiter for another coffee. "And then, I was, well, on my way."

Vic was pliant and spoiled. Nothing disturbed him very much; he had no political opinions and no causes. He played around the world, smiling nicely, never staying in one place very long, except for Ireland, where he wrote his books.

Long-sealed memories of the time she had spent with him returned to Sara; she could see in his eyes that he, too, was remembering. He seemed curiously and aggravatingly free of regret. The two of them circled over the terrain of the past, but did not land on it.

They walked around Siena, looking into shops, sitting

on the edges of fountains, talking about everything except the unfinished business that hovered between them like a third person. Sara had never understood what happened, why Vic left without a word, why she had never even been able to find him. Vic had carried the guilt of leaving her, had deliberately never contacted her for fear that the reason he left would be forced out of him. He had been bought, and though it did not haunt him, it was not an act he was proud of. At last they settled into a restaurant for a late lunch.

Sara kept her voice light, and a smile on her face, but she couldn't wait any longer. "I don't care if you've sold more copies than Harold Robbins. How come you left me?"

"I see your sense of drama hasn't changed," Vic said, trying to stave off the inevitable. He knew he didn't have the courage to tell her the whole truth. "I'm not going to lie to you. I was a coward." He looked down at his manicured hands, delaying the impulse to tell her what had transpired with Diana. "I didn't know how to handle the situation."

"You didn't know how to handle *love*?" she said in a voice full of saccharine disbelief.

He shook his head. "No, I didn't. But I do now." He chuckled softly. "Older and better, I hope." He reached out for her hand and raised it to his lips, glancing at her over her fingertips. "I've thought about you a lot, Sara."

She felt herself surrounded by the artificial luncheon hothouse atmosphere that encouraged affairs, deceptions, license. She broke out of it and pulled her hand away from him. "Don't. That was a long time ago."

They were sitting on a banquette. He moved nearer to her, full of seductive glances and sighs. "We could bring it into the present, we could——"

"Vic, I think not," she said gently. It was tempting but unappetizing at the same time.

Vic, however, had a real need to make her into a lover again. It might wash away the memory of his bargain with Diana. He pressed her. "Sara, you are the most beautiful of women. We don't have to remain enemies."

"We're not enemies."

He put his arm around her and kissed her on the neck.

—414—

"Come back to my hotel with me. We could have such a lovely afternoon."

"Vic! I don't want this." She slid away from him and his playboy moves. "You always took everything so lightly. I'll bet your books are just packed with fantasy and heroes who are never cowards! This is real life, damn you." She saw herself back in the ratty little apartment they'd shared in Berkeley, where she'd come home to that huge empty moment on the day he'd disappeared.

"That day you left I was just bursting with news for you. But you'd gone."

Vic misjudged the depth of her feeling. He moved closer. "News? So tell me now. It's never too late." He took her hand again.

She took her hand back. "I was pregnant."

"Pregnant?" he gasped. It had never occurred to him. Sara smiled with satisfaction. That had reached him.

"Yes. I have a daughter. Her name is Belinda Wyman. You'll understand why I didn't let her have your name." Vic was staring at her, his composure gone. "And now," Sara said, "if you'll excuse me——"

"You can't leave! You can't just drop that and leave!" A waiter's eyes rolled; heads turned.

"Watch me," Sara said, rising.

"Please don't leave, Sara."

She relented and sat down. "You could have called or written any time, Vic. Whatever reason you left, it didn't prevent you from getting in touch years later. Frankly, I dislike you for *that* more than for leaving."

"Are you going to deny her her father?"

"Am *I* going to deny her a father?!" She turned to stare at one of the waiters with an expression of mock astonishment. "I didn't leave her—you did! You don't need her. You've probably got your own family. Don't horn into mine."

"But I don't have a family. Oh, sure, I was married a couple of times, nice women, but—I don't have any children!" It was hard for him to take it all in. He was a father! "Please tell me about her. I want to see her, get to know her."

His eagerness struck her as vulgar. "Really, Vic, it's too late." She wanted to add that it was a great deal more complicated than he could imagine, since Lindy was now—to everyone except the family—Sky's child.

"It's never too late!" he exclaimed. "I'll do anything—at least let me write to her."

All through the meal she talked about Lindy—about how she was high-spirited, a little stubborn, and had strong feelings. She described Lindy as if they'd spent every day together. Lindy had his hair, she said, and Sky's eyes, and, she added, stretching the truth, Sara's face. Lindy was smart—a real student, maybe a scholar. Vic drank it in, forming a picture of the daughter he hadn't known he had.

"But what did you tell her about me?" he asked.

"That you'd left. I told her the truth."

"You didn't tell her that I was dead or anything like that?"

"No."

"Oh, good. I'm relieved."

Sara laughed. Vic was kind of silly.

As they reached her hotel, Vic said, "I don't want to seem crass. But knowing about Lindy has really given me a new lease on life, Sara. I'll write you. I hope you'll let me write Lindy." He kissed her hand again.

"Please don't kiss my hand anymore, Vic. I'm Sara, remember? I knew you in the Sunset District of San Francisco when the only horse you'd ever been on was rented."

"Miss Wyman!" The hotel desk clerk came pumping out, waving a sheet of paper. "A call from Rome!"

"What's wrong?" Sara asked.

"Nothing! I make a special effort to find you." He was wheezing with exertion. "It is Stefano Chiaro!" He named the most acclaimed film director in Italy.

33

It was noon in San Francisco, and Patsy McAulis Wyman was leaving a class on criminal law. It was her second year of law school. She shifted the weight of the books in her arm, and hefted her briefcase.

Patsy had graduated from college in 1966, a year and a half ago. She could still remember that day as she looked out over the sea of graduation gowns and caps and clutched her college diploma. She had felt electric. She had done it! She had waved the rolled-up diploma at Vail, who'd been standing among a flock of coeds under a eucalyptus tree. He was well known in San Francisco as Sky's brother and as a critic. When she reached him, he had introduced her, but the coeds had not been interested.

"Patsy's going on to law school," he had said to one very pretty girl. Patsy had smiled at him. Vail was still trying to make his peace with her law school ambitions. In public he succeeded brilliantly. In private, life with Vail had been an uphill climb.

It had all begun when Patsy had first seen Sky's house and met the celebrated at the wedding. She had embarked on a self-improvement program. Looking back, Sky and Kitty had been very decent about it. They had become her teachers—clothes, furniture, books, plays, movies, food. Diana had not helped until she saw that Patsy was seriously remaking herself. Then Diana had taught her about jewelry.

During those early months as Vail's wife, Patsy had been aware that the other side of her adoration for Sky was dissatisfaction with Vail: Why wasn't he famous, too? They had quarreled; Vail always kept her off balance. She'd never known what set him off—the way she brushed her hair or painted her toenails, the release of a new movie, or the release of Albert Speer, former Nazi, from prison. She lived in fear of rupture or discovery. Patsy had wanted a child; Vail rejected it. Children were forlorn and a nuisance—a bad combination. She had wanted to take a night class in filmmaking so she would know more about his world and Sky's. He hadn't wanted her to know anything about it. She had watched television but was careful to have the set turned off when he got home.

She'd thought, at first, that Vail wanted her to be like his sisters because he needed a woman who, like them, knew what he was thinking and feeling before he even expressed it.

"I'm tired of this," she'd said. "We either live differently, or let's not live with each other at all. I'll never be able to be like your sisters. I don't know what you're thinking half the time, and I didn't share a womb with you." She had told him everything she had tried to do to be like them in the touchingly direct way that was natural to her. "I want to get a college degree," she'd said. "I want to be more like your sisters in *that* way." At last, he'd agreed.

Patsy had enrolled as a freshman at Berkeley. She found that she had a good mind. Her teachers had encouraged her. She had been only twenty-one in 1963; the other students had accepted her as one of them. She'd taken a heavy schedule and had graduated in three years.

But she had been so eager to prove herself to Vail, to reach his high standards, to be sophisticated, that she'd never thought about what it might do to their relationship. She had believed he would be proud of her. It was not to be.

Vail had mourned the passing of the minxlike girl he'd met in the bus with the jagged stripe of lightning. What had happened to *that* Patsy McAulis? That Patsy had been terrific in bed. That Patsy had respected him, had hung on his arm. This woman opened her own car door. This woman graduated cum laude and was going to be a lawyer. He hadn't wanted to marry a lawyer. As Patsy became more sophisticated, soaking up books and subjects like a drunkard, Vail became more self-conscious. She had opinions about him and his work, and she expressed them.

Beginning with his retrospective of Sky's pictures—a long interview with the star who wouldn't give interviews—he'd advanced from the obscure San Francisco film magazine to a sleazy entertainment sheet and then to a major newspaper. He had been good at picking up gossip and turning it into titillating or surgical prose pieces. He was now the newspaper's film critic. He was known for his barbed, almost indecent candor in his reviews and essays. He cared naught for the huge amounts the studios spent in his newspaper to advertise their movies. He positively enjoyed flaying pretentious films under his banner of honesty. It had been Patsy who'd pointed out—infuriatingly—that when he loved a film, he presented a reasoned and decorous review of conservative, joyless praise.

"Why don't you make your good reviews as passionate as your bad reviews?" she'd asked.

By the middle sixties, he had built a cult following of readers who protected him from the dislike of his coworkers and his city editor, who variously referred to him as "that wolf," "that weasel," or "that butcher." In some ways these were apt descriptions, because Vail's most celebrated (or reviled) reviews compared actors to animals. "Miss McCarthy has all the range of expression of a snail." Or, "Thirty frames of Mr. Benson's sick seal look is a moving experience, but ninety minutes is to enter a sea of nausea."

Patsy had known that Vail's stiletto reviews in those early years stemmed from the feeling that he had sold out. He was no longer the pure artist—the playwright, the poet—bumming around America and cataloging his observations and his emotions about life. He reported on other people's creative endeavors.

Her briefcase was heavy. She transferred the books to her other arm as she made it up the walk to their little house. When Vail got home that afternoon, Patsy was gaily unwrapping her purchase: a set of glassware identical to the kind Sky owned, thick Waterford highball glasses. Vail picked up one of the glasses.

"Who sent you these?" he asked, frowning.

"No one. I bought them."

"I didn't like these glasses at Sky's, and I hate them here," Vail said, examining the glass in his hand. He could feel his anger rising. "Why are you always buying this stuff that Sky or Mother has? If I'd wanted you to be like them, I would have married someone really like them, not an imitation!" He flung one of the glasses against the kitchen wall.

"You're just doing that because you don't want someone educated!" she fired back.

"Educated," he sneered. "You are stupid!" He threw a second glass. "You're envious and shallow!" Smash!

Patsy started to cry, squeezing the tears out between little gasps. Sometimes Vail could be so sweet and solemn, but at other times, he was a terror. As he continued to hurl the glasses against the wall, she wailed and sobbed, crumpling on the kitchen table, burying her head in her plump arms.

He stopped breaking the glasses and listened to her rich sobs as he might to a distantly familiar piece of music that had once moved him. Over all these years her crying had given him a feeling of physical pleasure. Vail dropped into a kitchen chair, remembering his mother sitting by his bed when he was six. She had been weeping because—why? Had he broken something that time, too? And then he'd gotten sick.

Now, hearing Patsy, the law student, sob, he could not bring back the reason his mother had been crying, but the sounds then had been as musical as Patsy's now. He realized he picked fights with her to inspire her crying, which was deeply but not lastingly satisfying to him.

He felt ashamed. He put an arm around her shoulders.

"I'm sorry, honey."

"You only married me because of Bondy," she moaned.

Vail had to admit she was right. But it was a lot more complicated than that. He had been attracted to her healthiness, to her ignorance and sweetness. She wasn't manipulative, like some people he could mention; she wasn't like his mother or his sisters. She had not known a Waterford glass from a jam jar, and he had liked that.

—420—

Patsy slowly stopped crying and swallowed noisily. He gave her a tissue.

"Vail, if you can't love me the way I am now—the way I really am, and the way I want to be, then we should separate." She got up from the table and left the room. He heard the front door open, and he leaped up.

She'd left! "Patsy!" He ran outside. "Patsy!" She was wearing her coat, and she had her briefcase, and she was on the front walk. "Where are you going?"

Her eyes and nose were red. "Out. Away. You take me as I am, or don't take me at all."

He knew she meant it. It was a crisis. Suddenly he didn't care. "Then go, damn you!" he said.

He spent the next week worrying about her until he found out she'd taken refuge in the Metropolitan Club in downtown San Francisco. Stubbornly he refused to call her. But he thought about her constantly, about all the nights she'd stayed up, studying, coming from far back in the field. His minx on the bus was gone. The new Patsy had discipline and staying power.

"Oh, Christ," he mumbled. He went down to his mother's club, praying he wouldn't run into Diana. The front desk called upstairs for Patsy, and a few minutes later she walked out of the elevator.

He took her arm. "I'm an ass," he said, brushing a damp lock of hair away from her eye. "I don't want you any way but what you are or will be."

She looked at him hard, her little mouth set. "Are you sure?"

"Yes." He clasped her hand. A touch of the younger Patsy lit in her face as she embraced him. They had crossed a fragile, breaking bridge safely. They were, he felt, on the other side, at least for now.

Vail embraced her again.

In the car, as he drove her home, Patsy said, "Your mother doesn't give you enough credit for the career you've made. She almost never mentions Sara." Diana was a trial. "I wish she could talk about something other than President Johnson's 'war machine' and Sky."

"I'm thinking of a new piece for the paper," he said. "I want to do something nice for Sky and Sara." Patsy perked

—421—

up. This was the side of Vail that few people ever saw. "I thought I'd write something about how hard it is for women to get really decent roles."

"There's *Bonnie and Clyde* and *Valley of the Dolls*," she said.

"Yeah, you're very alert. Are those the only kind of women we make movies about?"

The image of the snow leopard leaped in his imagination. He hadn't thought of it for years. It was a good sign.

Diana stared at Maxine, the owner of the Sutton Street beauty shop Diana had patronized for years. "You don't know who Shirley Chisholm is?" Diana asked. "She's declared for Congress—election is next year. If she wins, she'll be the first black woman ever to be in Congress."

Maxine pretended to care. "Civil rights is one of the most important issues in the country," Diana went on. Maxine *was* mildly curious about the connection between Dr. King's campaign for civil rights and his outspoken stand on the Vietnam War. She didn't understand how those two combined, but she didn't want to get Diana started.

"You mark my words," Diana told her, shaking a finger, "Johnson won't run again. This war is killing him as surely as it's killing those poor boys over there." She had forgotten that Maxine's grandson was in the Marines in Vietnam.

Diana had a facial, had her eyebrows plucked and arched, had her hair styled, and had her nails manicured. She was putting on her gloves when Maxine called her to the telephone.

"Mother died this morning," Archie said without preamble. Diana sat down. She felt as if she'd turned to stone. Over the years since her first explosive meeting with Faith Venner, she'd regularly visited every few weeks, bringing little amusing anecdotes about the triplets, often coercing Vail, whom Miss Venner seemed to tolerate well, into accompanying her. But Diana had never received a single response from her mother except a cold or eccentric dismissal. "I have no daughter" remained her declaration until she died.

When Diana arrived at the old house, Archie let her in.

He glanced at her shrewdly. She looked like a woman whose last disappointment had just locked into place.

"How did the end come?" she asked.

"Quietly. She died in her sleep." Archie led the way upstairs.

Faith's bedroom was a large front room that looked over the tree-lined street. The bed had been made, but the spread, an antique crocheted piece, was rumpled. Little tables were cluttered with medicines and magazines; a once-glorious Chinese carpet was gray with wear. The tall windows were sheathed in heavy drapes and fringed shades. The room was more lived in than any other Diana had seen in the old house.

She walked around hesitantly, almost shyly, lifting a music box or a figurine gingerly, then replacing it as if she were in a shop whose articles were too expensive for her. She stopped at a half-finished crocheted doily stretched on the needle, the other embedded in the yarn. "She loved her needlework, didn't she?" Archie nodded abstractly. He was thinking of the plane he had to catch to Los Angeles. Diana glided on to a small bookcase containing leather-bound volumes of Balzac and Poe.

"Don't think she didn't like you, Diana," Archie said briskly. "She just couldn't face her own past."

"Don't analyze us," Diana said evenly. "Save it for Sky."

Before Sky's accident, it had been Diana who had brought Sky and Archie together at a dinner when Archie had come to Los Angeles. After the accident, their relationship had mushroomed into something private and secret; it excluded Diana. Neither Archie nor Sky talked about each other. She wondered what had happened to his practice in San Francisco, and she supposed that he was replacing it with bejeweled and needy women in Los Angeles.

"She was very fond of her books," Archie said.

"Fonder of them than she was of me." Diana picked one of them up and opened it. "I guess you've gotten everything you wanted," she said, putting the book down. She felt drained by the long pursuit and its fruitless, meaningless end. One of her greatest gifts, denying reality in order to surmount difficulties and obstacles, came to an end in Faith

Venner's bedroom. She glanced over at Archie; he was certainly better dressed than he had been when she'd first met him. His blond hair had been styled, and his fair skin looked slightly tanned. He glowed with good health and success, but his expression of sad concern for her was patently false. She tightened her jaw and turned away from him. It was unconscionable that he should look so well while she had nothing but an empty room.

34

Stefano Chiaro began making films after the war when the Italian neorealism movement was in full swing. But Chiaro had soon branched away from it, exploring a universality of life, particularly the "little betrayals in relationships between people," as the *New York Times* had quoted him in an interview in 1965. "We all wonder what our purpose is in life—yes? We wonder what our lives are all about," he had said. His producers and his financiers, the backers of his films, varied as the market widened to the international, but his loyalty to his own poetic vision never changed or diminished. His first international feature, *Diabolo,* won the Palm at Cannes and had been distributed in the States. Lines formed around the Murray Hill Theater when the film opened in New York City. Chiaro was one of the few directors in the world who was as famous as his actors.

When Sara met him in his office at Cinecittà, she saw a casually dressed, unpretentious man in baggy clothes. He had thinning black hair, a high forehead, and dark, lively, and penetrating eyes. He was casting a new film titled *Sollazzo.* It meant "amusement."

"Thank you for coming," he said with an enchanting smile. "Ah," he sighed, staring into her face, "ah. I have seen you before, but I didn't see you, si? And now, the new movie—" He pronounced the word "moooo-vie." "Please, sit here in the light." She did so. He asked her to turn this way and that. "Oh, I love your face," he cried happily. "Face is the big clue to a human being. Lines of joy, lines of disappointment, all there. In a movie, everything is said "through the face," he went on. "Faces express feelings, and there is so much feeling in your face. I choose all my actors by face, even the bit players. Very important. Yes! I saw your face in a movie last week, movie terrible, movie about bats, you remember?"

"How could I forget?" She grinned.

"But you are a trained actress, you are very good actress."

"Thank you, maestro," she said, referring to him by the name that everyone used.

"You are not making movies that challenge you," he stated.

"No, maestro."

"I like to disturb my audiences!" he shouted, dancing back to his desk on nimble feet. He had started life as a dancer and always wore highly polished, soft shoes. "That is sometimes not so very popular. You have a face that is full of contradictions—warm, open, closed, cold. Tough and gentle. Brava, ragazzina!" He clapped his hands together joyfully. "You want to be in my film?"

"Of course!"

"You want to know about the part?"

"Whatever it is, it will be the right one."

He clapped his hands and smiled at her.

Sollazzo was to be shot in Venice, and her part was one of two leads. "The part of Gucciano will be played by Guido Arbitriano. You know him?" Chiaro asked shyly. Sara smiled. She'd seen a lot of Guido at Cinecittà, and occasionally at parties. But since that afternoon in his garden they had not been together. It had been agony for her at first, and she knew it had been for him, too. Now the father of two, he was a big family man in the press. She didn't regret her decision, though she'd often missed him brutally.

"I think he is a glorious actor," she said. "He has worked hard."

"The film is about a woman and a man who are trying to come to terms with life, to reach an agreement with life, with love, you understand. Trying, as we do, to make friends with themselves and each other. They have no fear, but no hope either. It is an inside story, interior, but it has joy, too."

Sara came out of his office spinning. Looking back in later years, trying to pinpoint what had turned her from her downhill path, she would cite Chiaro and his confidence in her during the making of *Sollazzo*. But it had been more than that and, as happens when life takes a diverging route, the change comes from a culmination of sources and impulses.

One of them was Reed.

"Life is so capricious, isn't it?" she said to Reed that evening with a kind of wonder.

He had driven down from Siena with her, listening to her ranting about Vic. Now they were driving out of Rome to dine with Chiaro at his home near Tivoli. "You can meet someone around the next corner in the next minute, tiny distances from you that reverse everything. What made us breakfast yesterday out on the Campo and meet Vic, instead of eating at the hotel?" Sara rattled on and on. Reed was silent, feeling her presence next to him in the car. He watched his headlights penetrating the darkness ahead on the old road and the hulking shadows of trees coming on, then swishing past them.

"But you'd met Chiaro before, hadn't you?" he asked her. Chiaro was a man for whom Reed had enormous respect.

"Yes, but I guess we weren't fated to really communicate then. Oh, he was very polite and amiable. I came close to working with de Sica once, too."

How fragile, thought Reed, are our chances in life, made of nothing more than tissue paper, an accidental meeting, a word not spoken, a glance not taken. Sara was like a woman roused out of a long sleep—and all because Chiaro had been casting about for a particular part and had seen her in that wretched bat film.

"If Sky hadn't been famous," he asked, thinking about the vagaries of fate, "what would have changed for you?"

"I wouldn't have married Vic, probably, although I was very taken with him then. I certainly wouldn't have had affairs with some of the men I had affairs with," Sara said. "Except one, that is." She looked out the dark window, thinking of Guido. "The others didn't want me for myself."

Suddenly, up ahead, a huge dog rushed out and stood in the middle of the road, mouth open, daring them to hit him. Reed swerved the car, hit a stone mileage marker, and came to rest in a ditch.

"You okay?" he asked her. Sara nodded, shook herself, then climbed out of the car, looking back.

"I guess you missed it," she said to him. She couldn't see the dog anywhere. Reed got back in the car and tried to start it up, but the front end was badly damaged from the stone marker.

They were far out in the country. They started to walk. "We'll phone him as soon as we find a house," he said. "There must be houses out here." They walked along the edge of the road for a while, trying to flag the few cars that passed them to stop, without success. "Let's make for that hill over there," he said. "Maybe we can see lights from it."

"We must be crazy," Sara grumbled half way up the hill. She'd taken off her high-heeled shoes, which she held in one hand, and hung onto Reed's arm with the other. "Most people would simply stay at their wrecked car, you know . . ."

"Praying. C'mon, Sar', that's not our way," he laughed, struggling up the hill. "We're probably walking over some old second-century mansion right now."

"So what?" she wheezed.

"So, it's just an odd sensation, walking on top of the past."

"We do that every day," she said.

When they got to the top of the hill, gasping, they could see a clutch of lights about a mile away. "Is that where we want to go?" he asked.

"I haven't the faintest idea," she said. A drop of water fell on her face. "If we are really lucky, it'll begin to rain."

The downpour began immediately. They ducked under the one tree on the hill. Reed took off his jacket and threw it over her shoulders. "Put your shoes in the pockets," he said. The rain pelted down in thick, corpulent drops, smacking the leaves above them like lead pellets. "Oh, God," Reed groaned, "why are things always like this in Europe—disorganized and impromptu?"

"This is vital! Besides, who suggested we leave the car?" she chuckled. She looked out at the pouring rain. "Chiaro will understand."

—428—

"We were caught in a rainstorm after our car refused to run over a huge Baskerville dog," Reed said, putting an arm around her shoulders.

"He'll congratulate us for our quick reflexes. Not everyone can hit a mileage marker at a moment's notice." She started to laugh and couldn't stop. She laughed and clung to him, and hit her side, and grabbed at a wet branch that promptly deluged them with fresh rain. And she laughed at that. He caught her by the waist in her paroxysm, pulled the funny, wet hat off her head, and kissed her fully on the mouth. He could feel her laughter bubbling inside her lips, then slowly subsiding as she began to kiss him back. He ran a hand through her sopping hair. His breath rushed past her cheek, warming it. There was no light, but even so Sara could see Reed's eyes and the bridge of his nose. Something happens in the eyes when you connect completely with another person. She felt bound to him in the cool autumn night; she pressed her face against his, licking at the rain, and felt the joyful freedom of not caring about getting wet. She clasped this tall, gentle man to her and felt a surge of desire toward him.

Sara gently disengaged herself from his arms. She tilted her head up with a tight half-smile. "Want a little taste of Sky?" she murmured, her eyes slipping toward him slyly.

"No!" he said, drawing back, shocked.

"Oh, it's okay. Though I did think that you'd know the genuine article from the fake." She laughed, a hollow mockery of the merry sound that had come from her before.

He clutched her shoulders with both hands. The rain was dripping off his face. "Shut up," he said clearly. "Just once, you're going to have to be brave enough to trust another human being." He loosened his grip on her and then pulled her to him. "I know it's hard," he said gently, hugging her, "but you're too good to play these silly games anymore." He had his lips pressed against the top of her ear, and she could feel his warm breath again. "Something very powerful was happening to me yesterday in Siena. It was like you'd—like someone had opened a door and there you were, standing on the other side! I was so drawn to you. I still am. Let's be friends. Maybe lovers later, but really close friends now." She shivered against him. "C'mon, Sara,

"I'm worth loving, and I never saw anyone more in need of loving than you. Be bold."

He held her a moment longer, then hooked his arm through hers. "Shall we strike out for those lights?" he asked, pointing to the house lights about a mile away from them.

"Yes, sure." She felt breathless and giddy. She fell into step beside him.

All through the zany and intense filming of *Sollazzo*, Sara remembered Reed's words and the feeling of his embrace.

Chiaro's good humor never waned. Was Venice rainy for a week. "Buono! Perfetto!" he declared. Was it cold? "Meraviglioso!" They shot in narrow cluttered streets, in majestic piazzas like San Marco, from gondolas, on bridges, and in musty, towering, damp stone palaces. Chiaro's crew was a well-oiled machine, having made five films together. When Chiaro said, "Not deep enough," or, "More shadow, like a graveyard," they knew exactly the tone or texture he wanted.

Working with Guido allowed Sara to relive the love they had shared, to air it out, face it, cherish it, and, finally, to let it go. He was a tremendously giving actor, lively, responsive, and funny. She met his children when their tutor brought them to the set one afternoon and found that she could enjoy them fully.

Sollazzo became more than the entertainment its title suggested; it was a rejuvenation for Sara, a joyful housecleaning of herself, dusting out the crowded, lonely attic and throwing its trash onto the bonfire of the film. *Sollazzo* was memory and death and laughter all at once.

"If you two would stop giving each other the scene, I could get the shot," Chiaro would say playfully. "This is your scene, Sara. Don't give it to Guido."

"Oh, he deserves it," she said, laughing.

"No, no, it's yours," Guido cried, leaping out of a chair.

"But you give me all the scenes, Guido."

"Very tender, very special," Chiaro said after they'd completed the scene on the Rialto Bridge over the Grand Canal. He wiped tears from the corners of his eyes. "Much better than bats."

— 430 —

35

The summer of 1969 was unseasonably warm for San Francisco. In a brightly lit, downtown bookstore, Vic Oliver was autographing copies of his new book, *Blackfriars Bridge*. Flying over the table where he sat, a colorful banner depicted the book's heroic team, Marge and Matt Pouls. They were in midstride, holding hands, looking back, their coats flying out behind them. The store throbbed with shoppers, secretaries, businessmen.

Vic had signed at least a hundred books; his hand was tired, his smile automatic. He was thinking about Belinda and Sara. He had called Sara again in Rome, but she had refused to discuss his sudden reappearance with Lindy over the telephone. It would have to wait until she was back in the States. He had agreed that was best. Sara had gone off to make her movie with Chiaro, and he'd gone back to Ireland.

Then, in March, he had telephoned Sara to say he was planning a national book promotion tour that would take him to San Francisco and Los Angeles. He wanted to see Lindy. Sara had reluctantly agreed. Lindy was celebrating her sixteenth birthday this summer, Sara had told him, but the party wouldn't be held until August, the month the whole family could get together. Diana could not break away from her mobilization of senior citizens against the war, so they were all meeting in San Francisco. "Great," Vic had said. "See you in August!"

Vic handed the freshly autographed book to a woman

in a dark suit. "Next," he said, smiling woodenly. The line for books didn't seem to have any end. Vic was not going to be put off any longer. He had decided to appear at the old Clay Street house and deliver Lindy's gift personally. He was quite excited about it.

In another part of the city, Sara was being interviewed about her role in *Sollazzo*. The picture was opening in a week. From her seat next to the interviewer under the lights, she glanced at Reed at the back of the studio. He wore a jacket over his shoulders and carried a hat and valise; he'd just flown in from London. His face looked creased and handsome. She hadn't seen him since the dinner with Chiaro, on the night they'd shared a kiss under the dripping tree. But they'd talked on the telephone. Slowly. Though they'd known each other for years, they were just getting acquainted.

For his part, Reed was surprised how much he'd anticipated seeing Sara again. She was becoming dear to him. From the back of the studio, he watched her head tilting, the light bouncing off her brassy hair, and fantasized making love to her.

"Okay, I'm finished!" she cried. He came forward, put an arm around her shoulders, and kissed her politely. "Dinner at the Clay Street house," she said, "with the whole family! But first—"

"First, I get to have a drink with you alone." He lightly brushed a hand over her hair. "Gosh, it's good to see you," he said.

Belinda's slender, oval face bent over the large pad of paper in her lap. Her long, straight brown hair fell against her cheeks. Fierce concentration lit her face as she drew the pen across the paper in a broad stroke, lifting it slightly at the end of the line: Archie's nose and forehead. She laughed. The sketch had just the right mixture of sarcasm and compassion—that personal style that was all Archie.

Archie filled a large wing chair in the cream-colored living room of the Clay Street house. "Smile," Lindy ordered. Archie complied. Then he examined his nails closely. The high buff he liked was dimming.

The Queen-Anne-style Wyman house had not changed much since 1925, when Diana had first seen it. Its large downstairs rooms smelled of old woods, wax, and roses.

Lindy's caricatures were sly, knowing, and deft. She sketched in Archie's wide sensual mouth, turning it up at the corners in a charming sneer. She looked at the caricature through narrowed eyes, then exaggerated the mouth. She liked Archie; he was part of the family now. Lindy looked up and caught Arch staring at her. He winked.

"When do I get to open presents?" Lindy asked.

"I don't know what's planned," Archie replied. "All I know is that everyone's coming together today and leaving tomorrow." He moved his bulk around inside the chair and gazed at Lindy. It was a distinct pleasure. She had a little lift to her head, brave and irreverent at the same time. He hadn't seen her in a year. A year made a great difference in a young girl's manner.

"I hear you're graduating high school a year early. How's that feel?" he asked.

"Great. Everyone thinks I'm a brain."

"Aren't you?"

"Yup. Straight A's."

Diana had urged Lindy to apply to Mills College, where she could study art, but Lindy thought the school stuffy. She wanted to go to Cal at Berkeley, where, as she said, the students and faculty had joined the twentieth century: They protested the Vietnam War and didn't dress in fifties cardigans.

Lindy was spoiled, brash, moody, and very bright; she had no difficulty maintaining an A average; she could discuss art or history with equal interest; she was intensely involved in school programs on the Vietnam War and on counterculture debates. She was thinking of changing her name to Rainbow.

Upstairs, Sky's head felt big and heavy, and her mouth fuzzy. She gulped a glass of water. It was hard to button her blouse so she took it off and put on a bright red turtle-neck T-shirt instead.

When she'd left Reed and Sara in Siena, she'd spent a long month with Ace and Cage in Portofino, had gone on to Switzerland, and then home. By that time, she had needed

Kitty—and she needed Archie's pills. Kitty had been over-joyed to see her, but they had had rocky times for a while. Kitty had lined up appointments with other doctors who recommended more surgery to relieve the pain. Sky refused. A picture called *Foreign Service* had been offered her—a thriller about a love affair between a defecting Russian scientist and the wife of an ambassador. Kitty had admitted that Sky had been right to take it: The picture was good therapy.

Sky looked at herself in the mirror of her teenage bed-room, the bedroom that had been hers for every year of her life until she left for Hollywood. Diana had framed some of the posters from her major films and hung them on the wall. Sky turned and straightened her shoulders. *Foxglove* had restored her career; *Foreign Service* had restored her confi-dence. Scripts flowed in to her now—even Pitcher Steinmetz was chasing her for his new picture. But she didn't want to work with Pitcher again. Their last picture, *The Ginkgo Tree,* always reminded her of Lila's suicide.

But Sky's work didn't satisfy her. In her worst moods, she told both Kitty and Archie that her work did nothing to influence life, improve the goodness in people, or lessen the larceny in the human heart. She had lost her belief in the audience as intelligent and discerning. She played her roles by depending on her technique. And her technique was so good that no one demanded more of her.

She swiped a brush through her dark hair and started to cry. This was awful, she moaned. It always came on so suddenly. A whoop went up from the kitchen where Vail and Patsy, Maggie and Kitty were somehow collaborating on dinner. Sky pulled herself together.

In the kitchen, Vail was making a tray of smoked salmon and oysters, cheese and crackers. Patsy, standing next to him, was buttering a cut loaf of French bread.

"Let's do 'Hey Jude!'" cried Kitty, who flung herself into festivities and carried everyone else with her.

Vail immediately started singing in his high, sweet tenor. Kitty and Maggie, who stood at the sink peeling potatoes, joined him a couple of notes lower in harmony. Patsy, hav-ing finished law school, had the air of someone who'd been reprieved.

"Kitty!" Lindy called out from the living room. "Your turn! I'm doing the whole family."

Kitty went into the dining room and poked her head around the double door. "You have a mean streak in you," she said to Lindy, shaking her finger. "I'm not sure I should risk being drawn!" Lindy smiled up at her. She liked Kitty.

"Then Vail! C'mon Vail!" Lindy called. He joined Kitty at the dining room doors.

"I'm not through with the platter—oh, hi, Arch. I didn't know you were here." Vail tolerated Arch benevolently, even though in some circles it was said that his practice was constructed on the backs of celebrity patients. But Sky called him a miracle, and if he brought Sky a little comfort, well, fine. Arch was winding a pen knife around his nails. Vail glanced at Kitty; she always looked grim when Archie was around. "Forget him," Vail mumbled and went back into the kitchen to finish his cheese platter.

The doorbell rang. "I'll get it," Kitty shouted. A moment later she appeared in the kitchen. "Vail," she said in an urgent voice. "It's a man called Vic who says he's Lindy's father."

"Vic?" Vail said, incredulously.

"Where is he?" Maggie asked, afraid Kitty had taken him straight on into the living room.

"I told him to wait in the hall. Is this really the notorious Vic?"

Vail went out into the foyer and saw the man who, with Sara, had changed his life so greatly. If Sara hadn't eloped, he would never have joined up for Korea so impetuously. They shook hands. "What the hell are you doing here?" Vail asked.

"I'd like to meet my daughter." Vic told him about meeting Sara in Italy.

Vail now noticed that Vic was carrying a small, beautifully wrapped box. "You can't just walk in there," Vail said. Agitated, he led Vic to the study and shut the door. The room was mahogany and oak with walls of built-in bookcases. Vail turned on an antique lamp and raised a shade. The room was a mess from Diana's anti-war work. Flyers were stacked on the table and on the floor; a half-finished press release was sticking out of the typewriter. "Sit down," he said to Vic. "Did Sara tell you—"

"Sara suggested I call here first," Vic said, "and I tried, but the line was always busy, and I figure I have a right to see my daughter."

As Vic rattled on, Vail cataloged him. He had the air of a playboy, slightly corrupted but not overly concerned or soured by it. He was elegantly dressed—sleek jacket, designer tie, ruby pinky ring.

"You can't see her unless you agree to some ground rules," Vail said.

"Sure, sure."

"Not 'sure, sure,' " Vail replied, "this is serious."

At that moment, Sky walked into the room. "This *is* a surprise," she said with no delight in her voice. Vic had improved since his days as stage manager when he carried a pack of cigarettes rolled up in his T-shirt sleeve. He rose and shook Sky's hand.

"I was just explaining the new ground rules to Vic," Vail said, then turned to him. "You left Sara, and now Lindy is Sky's child."

"*What?*" Vic muttered, confused.

"Sara couldn't care for Lindy. But Sky could. She's cared for her like a mother all these years. Lindy believes Sky is her mother. Now, you either play along, or out you go."

Astonished, Vic looked at Sky.

"That's it, Vic," Sky said distastefully. He was the last person she wanted to see; the echo of Sara's early warnings about his reappearing came rolling home to her.

"I don't believe it!" Vic said. "Sara didn't mention anything like this!"

"It's true," Vail said.

"But—why? I don't—"

"Why, why," Sky snapped. "The why is not important. Don't you think I gave Lindy a good home?"

Vic stared at them. "Yes," he said, "of course. It's just a lot to get used to."

"Do you agree to honor it?" Sky demanded.

"Were *we* married?" he asked her.

She turned uncomfortably. "I suppose that has been the understanding. Of course you weren't supposed to come

—436—

back! No one ever heard from you. And frankly, I resent it deeply that you think you can just waltz in here and be a father!"

"Well, I admit it's late—"

"*Late?*" Vail yelled at him. "You bet it's late! You don't have any rights here at all! You left Sara—"

"But I didn't know she was pregnant!"

"That doesn't matter!" Vail pressed him. "You left her, so you just play along or get out. What's it to be?"

Vic agreed.

Vail went into the living room and sat down beside Lindy, who was finishing Arch's caricature. "Belinda," Vail said, "there's someone here who wants to see you." Lindy looked up from her drawing.

"Mike?" Lindy asked, naming a current beau.

"No. You don't have to see him unless you really want to. Or you can see him some other time after you've had a chance to think—"

"Jeez, Vail, who is it?" She arched her eyebrow at him and gave the drawing to Archie.

"Oh, great," Arch said, looking at it.

"It's your father," Vail said. Archie's blond head snapped up.

"Here?" she asked, astonished. "Jeez, does Mom know?"

"Yes."

Lindy glanced at Arch, who always had advice for Sky. "It's your choice, Lindy," Archie said. "You can see him or not, or see him later. It's not really fair for him to—"

"I want to see him." She had become quite pale. She put her pens and pad aside and rearranged herself in the chair. "Show him in," she said in a voice strikingly similar to Sky's.

Vail brought Vic in. Lindy looked at him fully, up and down, completely self-possessed. She put out her hand. "How do you do," she said.

Vic was dismayed by her grown-up manner. He shook her hand. It was soft and cool. Then he offered her the gift. "Oh, thank you," she said, taking the gift. "Is this supposed to make up for all the time you've been away?"

"No, of course not," Vic said hoarsely, realizing with a shock that she resembled him, except for her eyes, which looked like Sky's. "It's just something I picked up in Paris that I thought you might like. I saw your—ah, Sara in Italy." "Do you travel a lot, too?" she asked, liking the fact that he might.

"A little."

"What do you do?" Lindy asked him, admiring his fine coat.

"I write books."

"Oh. Where you do live?"

"In Ireland." He sat down. He was bombarded.

"So what are you doing here?"

"I came to see you." His heart was pounding.

"Well, where have you been all this time?" she asked brashly, in her manner.

"That's a very long story, but I'll be glad to tell you later."

Patsy, who had come into the room with everyone else to watch the momentous scene, felt a natural break had occurred, so she introduced herself and said, "Drinks?" She went to a cart that bristled with liquor bottles and glassware. Vail's eyes followed her.

Archie was looking at Lindy. Her cheeks were flushed, and she was caught between anger and need. She was turning the wrapped gift over in her hands. She wanted to open it, to have something from the father she'd dreamed about for hundreds of hours. He had a nice smile and a graceful bearing. He fit the romantic picture she'd constructed of him all these years. But faced with the moment, she found herself unwilling to do what he wanted.

Lindy thrust the gift back at Vic. "You haven't earned the right to give me things," she said.

Vic didn't know what to do. To take it back was to admit a defeat that was painful and hard. Not to take it would create a scene. He looked at his child, who was a woman, and saw she was close to tears. "I'm sorry," he said. "I've done a lot wrong, I guess, by coming here so suddenly. I don't have much sense about such things. But I meant well. You're my only child."

It sounded kind of wishy-washy to Lindy, who lived on a sharper edge. But Vail was moved. Archie rose. "Perhaps we could all have a drink, and

Lindy can put Vic's gift away until she feels the time is right to open it. How's that?"

"Fine," Vic said. Patsy gave him a drink.

Lindy still held the gift. "Okay," she said, handing it to Patsy who put it in her apron pocket.

The moment was breached. Sky sat down on the arm of Lindy's chair protectively. "Did Auntie Sara know you, too?" Lindy asked Vic.

"Oh, yes," Vic replied. "Sara and Sky were at the summer stock theater."

"You again," Sara said, coming into the room with Reed and seeing Vic. She was stunned but carried it off well. "Lindy, dear," she said, kissing her cheek. "What a big surprise." She turned to everyone in the room. "Will you excuse Sky and me for a moment?"

In the study Sara faced Sky. "It's time the charade ended," Sara declared.

"No! We can't! It's never to come out," Sky said. She was desperate. If it came out, she feared she would lose Lindy's love. "I didn't ask him here, you did! I didn't tell him about Lindy, you did! You *have* to go through with it!"

"Don't you see how impossible this is? It's one thing for you to have raised Lindy, but it's quite another to maintain this fiction forever."

"We have to! I can't tell her on her sixteenth birthday that I'm not her mother—can *you?*" Sky said. "You had plans; you didn't want to be a waitress or stay home and marry someone and be a mother—you wanted to be an actress! Well, there are payments due—"

"You don't have to tell *me* about payments, Sky!"

The door opened. It was Lindy. Sky and Sara stared at her.

"Why are you arguing?" Lindy asked. "Is it about Vic? Don't you like him?"

"We don't like what he's done, Lindy," said Sky. "Just bursting in here—"

"It's my fault," Sara interjected. "I met him by accident in Italy, and I told him about you."

"You never should have done that!" Sky yelled. "He never would have known—"

Lindy shut the door. "Everyone will hear you," she said.

—439—

"Oh, let them," Sara said. "I'm disgusted with it all."

"I'm glad you told him, Sara," Lindy said. "I'm glad to meet him. I've heard about him for years, and everyone had a different opinion about him. So I wanted to see for myself." She kissed Sara's cheek. "Thank you for telling him."

Tears sprang into Sara's eyes. She turned away. "He's not a bad man, Sky," Sara said. "He's a little shallow."

"He really wants to get to know me," Lindy said, brightly. He was romantic, an author of best-sellers, handsome, mysterious. He intrigued her.

"We can get him to leave," Sky said.

"No, I don't want him to leave," Lindy said. "But I wish I could be invisible and just watch him without him watching me."

Sara looked at her smart, pretty child. "I'm sorry he did it this way. He was supposed to have called me. And then I would have called Sky and—"

"He's put everyone in an awkward position, Lindy," Sky snapped.

"When he said he might come this summer, I couldn't tell you, Lindy, that your long-lost father was arriving and then not have him show up!"

"Okay, I get the picture! You're right! Let's just have a good time—okay?" Lindy yelled, flustered. Everyone was upset.

"Calm down," Sky said. She mimicked Diana. "You always get so emotional." Sara laughed.

They were coming out of the study when the front door flew open. "Mother!" Sara cried. Diana stumbled into the hall. "Vail!" Sara called out. Everyone came running.

Diana's hat was tilted precariously on her head, her hair was all messed up, her stockings torn, her skirt twisted, and the sleeve of her coat was ripped.

"Jesus, Mother," Vail whispered, "what happened?"

"Just let me sit down," she said. "I'm all right." Vail and Sky helped Diana into the living room.

Diana was in her early sixties, a stylish dowager queen in her smart conservative suits, heavy jewelry, and fine Hattie Carnegie hats. She fell into the chair, one hand aimlessly feeling her pearl necklace. She sat bolt upright. "Well, I never!" she said. "I'm missing an earring." She was wearing her usual full complement of bracelets, rings, and neck-laces. She checked them all.

"Everything else there?" Patsy asked.

Diana nodded. "Perhaps a glass of sherry," she said to Vail. But Archie got to the bar first.

"What happened?" Sara demanded.

Diana turned to Patsy. "Oh, Patsy, how lucky you de-cided to stay here. But you missed a lot of excitement."

"It's exciting here, too," Patsy said.

It was at that moment that Diana noticed the surprising and unwelcome addition to Lindy's birthday party.

"Why, Vic," Diana said. "How astonishing to see you." Her voice was very cool. Vic went over to Diana and shook her hand. "You've met Belinda, I presume," she said.

"I have," he replied guardedly. "Sky has done a lovely job," he added, cuing her that he knew.

"Mother! What happened to you?" Vail demanded.

Diana was getting her bearings back. Archie brought her the sherry. "It was a little spontaneous protest demonstra-tion. I had nothing to do with it! I was shopping. Anyway, a nice-looking young man in Union Square was speaking out against the war, and a crowd gathered. He was saying that one hundred Americans are killed each week now in Vietnam. Well, some other man, he looked like a banker, so well dressed, he started arguing about how Nixon's bring-ing home seventy-five thousand soldiers—" She broke off and clasped her hand to her forehead. "Oh, God, I can hardly believe that man is president." She stopped mourn-ing suddenly and looked up. "Out of nowhere, the police arrived, and they tried to disperse the crowd, and, well, it was a melee." She looked around at them brightly. "I man-aged to get out on Post Street but I fell down—I didn't see the curb, can you imagine? Finally, I got a cab, and here I am." She showed them her torn sleeve. "A policeman did that."

"They're pigs!" Lindy said. She had strong feelings on the subject.

Diana smiled at her. "Yes, well, if I'd called them that—I'd be in jail! I did feel like it because everyone was very peaceful until they came along. They would have clubbed me the way they did that nice young man!" She held up her glass. "I'll have another one of these," she said, giving her glass to Vail. "Oh, look, my stockings!" she wailed. Her legs were scratched. "But never mind. It was thrilling!"

There was an uncomfortable pause as if someone had made an embarrassing sound. Then everyone erupted, debating police tactics, combat deaths in Vietnam, and the war that couldn't be won. "We're killing them because they're Orientals," Sara said at one point. She had backed up next to Reed; his presence gave her strength. "We don't care about human life at all!" As arguments whirled around him, Vic felt he'd been caught in an electric fan. He'd forgotten how keyed up life was with the Wymans.

Sky was trying to remember the old, old days in San Francisco, and she wondered what had attracted Sara to Vic. She let herself float. She liked to feel disconnected, traveling slightly above ground, out of pain's reach, beyond gravity. She opened her eyes and found Kitty looking at her. Everyone was still arguing now about the war. Sky squeezed out a smile for Kitty and thought about their days in the Bahamas.

"Have you seen it, Sky?" Reed was asking.

"Seen what?"

"Sara's film!"

"Oh, yes! I saw it at a screening last week. Very good. What are you doing for an encore?"

"An encore?" Sara asked. "This film hasn't even opened yet! God, I don't know how you stand it over here. The pressure's so intense. An actor's only as good as his last picture, not the body of work he might produce over twenty years. Frantic." She watched Lindy sneaking looks at Vic.

"We get used to it," Sky muttered, floating.

Archie and his little pills, Kitty thought. That's how we get used to the pressure.

Reed gamely described the differences between working in America and working in the more relaxed European studios. But his eyes said to Sara, Tell them, tell them.

She knew what he meant. She had told him about watching Carmen directing a short in Naples. Sara hadn't been able to forget the image of Carmen waving her arms and peering through the lens. Watching Carmen in Naples and acting in Chiaro's movie had changed Sara's life. He wanted her to tell them.

"I'm going to do something different," Sara said. "I am going to direct a film."

"What?" Sky exclaimed, opening her eyes.

"Brava!" Vail cried, uncharacteristically. "I hope it's not a horror film."

"Hardly," Sara said.

"Tell them what Chiaro said," Reed murmured.

"Well, he's going to help me. I've found a script that has to do with bigamy. It's called *Winter Wheat*. It sort of explores the outrageous expectations we all have of marriage," Sara said. She didn't yet know how she was going to pull it off; she was scared and excited at the same time. She was hoping to convince Guido to play one of the leads, and possibly Marco to produce. She knew it would be a year or more before she could actually start shooting. But she was jubilant about her new prospects, and she couldn't keep the triumph out of her voice.

"You mean," Diana said, as though she'd just come into the conversation, "that you are going to direct a film, like Reed directs a film?"

"No, Mother. Reed would do it differently. But I am going to direct a film."

Reed kept his face impassive as he watched Diana and Sara duel. Sara needed to resolve a great deal of unfinished business with her mother: she needed to forgive her. Sara couldn't grow or love until she did.

"Times are changing, Diana," Reed said. "And so are films. Women directed many films in the States before the twenties. They ought to do it now. Even actresses are different now. No one wants a pinup woman anymore."

"Nobody but the Americans," Sky put in.

"But do you think you're up to it, dear?" Diana asked Sara. It all seemed so unlikely to her. Sara had been a mediocre actress. Sara was the one who always needed help, the one who was out of step.

"I'm up to it. I'm looking forward to it," Sara said.

"Gee, I think that's great," Lindy said.

Diana shifted her attention to Vic, who was sitting slightly outside the circle of sofas and chairs, looking in. At least he'd made something of himself, she thought. He had obviously not told Sara the real reasons for his abrupt departure from their marriage. Diana sniffed and fingered her necklace. She had done what she considered to be in the best interests of her daughter, and she'd do it again. Belinda, however, was at that excitable age when she might do something rash—as her mother had. Diana was afraid Lindy might join some hippie group in Oregon, or end up on the Santa Monica pier, where those strange Krishna devotees begged and chanted.

Diana was even more concerned about Sky's big mood swings. She didn't understand them. The change she'd seen in Sky since her accident prompted her next ill-advised remark.

"Sky, darling, now that Sara's changing her goals so courageously, why don't you get back into the theater?" She plucked at one of her bracelets. "You could do something with depth again." Kitty stiffened.

"Haven't I done enough for you?" Sky asked in a dangerously soft voice.

"Of course, darling. I didn't mean it that way. I meant you could branch out, do something different. I expect you're bored."

"Sky isn't bored," Archie drawled. "She's fatigued."

"I'll talk to my own mother, if you please," Sky snapped. She hated being interpreted.

"Calm down," Vail said.

"I am perfectly calm!"

"Sky, please," Kitty said, reaching over and stroking her arm.

"Stop that!" Sky felt at once goaded and overprotected. "As a matter of fact, I might take the lead in Pitcher's new film."

Reed groaned. "You never liked him, Sky. He's hard to work with." Pitcher had turned into a gifted but irascible producer-director.

Vail said to Vic, who hadn't spoken for an hour and looked uneasy, "The picture is about a famous film star making a comeback."

"Do you really want your public to see you as a has-been?" Archie asked.

"It's only a *role!*" Sky shouted. "It's not my life!"

"Roles are your life," Vail interjected.

"He just asked you yesterday," Kitty said delicately. "You should think about it more."

"Oh, Sky," Sara said. "Don't do anything hasty or ill-advised. Whatever we do now is more important and lasting than what we did when we were twenty."

"You're just saying that because *you'd* like to do a picture with a great American director," Sky said, regretting the words as they came out of her mouth.

"Mommy," Lindy said. "Aunt Sara—" She glanced at Vic who looked distinctly ill at ease.

"I'm sorry," Sky apologized.

Vail said, "Vic, let's you and I get the barbeque going." After they left, Archie said to Sky: "Sara's right. It's hasty. Think it through."

Kitty turned to them all. "It's a very hard shoot, all over the West, even in Death Valley, and Pitch has got a lot of stunts that stars did routinely in the twenties, like floating down real rivers on ice floes—"

"*I'm* not going to do the stunts!" Sky bawled.

"I certainly didn't mean—" Diana began hesitantly.

"I don't care a rat's ass what you meant, Mother!" Sky said, exasperated. "You're always doing this—pitting us against each other!"

"Why, Sky," Diana whispered, shocked and hurt. "I don't do anything of the kind! I only asked what—"

"You didn't only ask' what I was doing next! You had a little plan because you didn't feel I was out front enough! I'm so damned sick of it—" Embarrassingly, Sky began weeping. She was infuriated at her tears and at her mother. "Why don't you just stay out!"

Archie put his arm around Sky, then moved her toward the stairs.

"Stop right there!" Kitty commanded. She wanted to throw a decanter at Archie. "We never finish anything around here because you're always hauling Sky away. She's plenty strong enough to stand up for herself."

—445—

Sky turned. "Oh, please, Kitty, I just want to lie down for a little while. Then we can all have a nice dinner—"

Kitty spun away and marched into the kitchen.

Angry and bewildered, Diana watched Archie helping her daughter upstairs. "Very well," she whispered. "I know when I'm not wanted anymore."

"Oh, Mother, Sky's letting off steam," Sara said, suddenly very tired.

A while later, Vic came back into the house. "I guess I should be going," he said to Lindy. "I hope you'll have dinner with me some night. I'll be in and out of town for a while."

"Maybe," Lindy said, looking at him bashfully. She knew she would. She liked the drama of getting to know this handsome stranger, her father.

Upstairs Archie gave Sky a pill and a glass of water. "You're overexerting yourself, Sky. I don't want to have to tell you again." He drew the shades.

Lindy was coming up the stairs as he left Sky's room.

"Is Mommy all right?" she asked.

"She'll be fine."

"I hate it when we have scenes."

"She's high-strung, like you in a way." He smiled at her. He knew she liked to be compared to Sky. "What did you think of Vic?"

"He's okay. At least he's good-looking. He's going to send me copies of his thrillers."

"Do you like thrillers?" Arch asked, looking at the way her straight silky hair fell all the way down to touch the points of her breasts.

"Sure!" Lindy said, feeling his eyes sweep over her.

Diana was alone in her house again. Everyone had scattered.

"You look all in," Maggie said. Diana was standing in the living room, holding the only thing she'd taken from Faith's bedroom: her crocheting. The day Faith had died, Maggie had heard Diana crying like a child in her bedroom.

Diana put the crocheting down, and started picking up all the framed pictures of Sky in the room—one of her as a child, one of her as a teenager in the school play, two taken of her on two different sets in Hollywood. She left the pictures of Sara and Vail in place.

"Help me," Diana said in a hollow voice.

Maggie took some of the pictures from her.

"Children can be so cruel," Diana said from the landing. "First I lost the mother I never had, and now I'm losing Sky. She doesn't pay any attention to me anymore, and she doesn't need me. I just cannot bear to look at her many faces."

Diana stripped her bedroom, the upstairs hall, the library, and the guest rooms of Sky's pictures. She came upon a picture of Sky at eighteen. "I'll keep this," she said faintly, as if the stuffing were leaking out of her.

36

After *Sollazzo* opened to fine reviews, Sara returned to Rome. She plunged gamely into work on *Winter Wheat*. Guido agreed to play the lead. But Marco could not produce it, though he would advise her if she needed it. She called Ernie Ping and asked him to be the director of photography, and he agreed. Finally, she called Reed: Would he produce "Wheat"? If she could hold everyone together until late 1970, when he was free, he would. Sara put down the telephone; she felt a sudden rush of terror: What was she getting herself into?

Meanwhile, spurred by her own rash announcement in front of the family and by Sara's fresh start, Sky began negotiations to play the lead in Pitcher's movie, *Lady Blue*. As usual they were lengthy and tangled. Sky didn't care; secretly she hoped they would founder. But as they ground on, she was able to spend Lindy's last year at home with her. Sky was proud of her academic success, proud of her lively mind, and even proud of her stubborn passions. Lindy would brook no interference in her choice of school, either: In the fall of 1970, she went to Berkeley.

"No reason," Arch said, as he seated Lindy in a small San Francisco restaurant choked with greenery so thick they couldn't see the people at the next table. Huge Boston ferns in giant baskets hung from the ceiling. It was like eating in an enormous greenhouse. "I just thought you'd like to get

—448—

away for lunch." A solicitous waiter was bending over them. "We'll have two martinis, please, with olives."

"The young lady?" the waiter asked uncomfortably.

"Yes, she's eighteen," Archie lied, waving him away.

"Certainly, Doctor Moberly," the waiter said.

"Well," Archie said to Lindy, "you're almost eighteen." Belinda looked younger than her years. Archie liked that about her. Lindy hated it. "They always ask," Lindy sighed. She groaned and made a face. "I've had martinis before," she fibbed. She was wearing tie-dyed bell-bottom jeans, a turtleneck sweater, and a long, fringed leather vest. A beaded headband held her long hair in check. Etched on the back of her vest was Make Love Not War.

"Martinis—at school?" Archie asked.

"Sure. On dates."

"Are you still dating Mike?" He flashed a warm smile.

"Sometimes," she hedged. Mike was a real radical rabble-rouser. She'd known him since high school. He was older than she was, now a junior at Berkeley. He'd spoken at the Berkeley march last spring, mobilized after the Kent State killings. She had gone up to Berkeley for the demonstration and had been chased across campus by the Alameda storm troopers who were gassing and clubbing protester and bystander alike. "How do you feel about the war?" she asked him.

"It's evil," he said easily, knowing her opinion of it.

"Jeez, you're the only person from your generation—no, that's not so. Granny's against the war." She put her hand against her cheek. "And Mom."

"And Reed. And millions of others who don't march. Vail's dead set against it. We talked about it." Lindy nodded. Their martinis arrived. Arch raised his glass. "Here's to you!" When he smiled, his whole face lifted. When he frowned or looked thoughtful, Lindy felt he looked disillusioned.

She sipped her martini. She liked the look of the glass in her hand, but she didn't like the taste. She managed to look smoothly across at Archie, who was relishing his drink.

"How do you like my beard?" he asked her. His pale face was now wreathed top and bottom with blond hair.

"I can dig it." She felt good about being out with a mature man.

Lindy, seventeen, chatted on about university life, about her essay on Proust, about a new Poli Sci teacher, about the Pentagon bombing Cambodia. Archie had arranged his face in an attitude of complete interest, but he wasn't listening. He was peripherally focused on her rounded breasts going up and down with her gestures. She flicked her hair back with one hand, a gesture at once natural and self-conscious. In his listening attitude, he examined her gray blue eyes, so deeply set and rather close together, and watched her pink mouth. He fantasized those delicate lips kissing him and had to rearrange the napkin in his lap to cover his erection. He desired her intensely.

"Jeez, no, I wasn't lonely," Lindy was saying. "I mean, Kitty was around when Sky was on location, and Maggie, and Mrs. Sho, and Grandma and Grandpa. I miss Grandpa a lot."

The waiter put their salads in front of them.

"How do you feel about all those dreadful movies Sara made?" he asked.

"Kinky, huh?" She grinned at him. "I liked a couple of the horror films. I like to be scared." She wasn't being completely candid, and Archie knew it.

"Now, I can't believe you wouldn't have liked to grow up like every other girl in America with a mother and father—"

"Well, it would have been great to have a father," she admitted. "What gripes me is that Sky and Kitty still treat me like a child. Granny too. It's a lousy rap."

"Well, of course," he said, "they all think of you that way, but in fact you are a grown woman. You have a woman's body—I'm speaking now as a doctor, you understand—and a very fine adult mind. It's hard for them to see that."

Lindy was flattered. Even though Mike, her boyfriend, was fiery and committed, it was delicious to sit with a real professional like Archie and know that he thought well of her. Archie was so unruffled, so soothing. Mike was always excited or mad about something, and he never listened to anything she said. She'd been right about the distribution plan for the posters for the Moratorium march, but did Mike listen? No. She told Archie about Mike and the other guys in the antiwar group at Cal.

He ordered another martini for them. "Is Sky going to do Pitcher's film?"

"Oh, yes. It's taken a while to get things going," she said with a cavalier air. "You know, contracts, availabilities. They're starting in the spring."

"Is it true," he asked, paraphrasing a popular antiwar advertisement, "that girls say yes to boys who say no to the war? Have you gone to bed with Mike?" he asked in his soothing doctor's voice.

"Well, Archie!" she said, pretending to be shocked.

He ignored that. "I would expect that you have, because you are a delightful young woman, and he'd be a fool not to have asked you."

"Well, yes, he did, and we did!" She laughed.

"I hope he was loving and skillful." He sipped his martini. "Here's to love. Make love not war and amen." She drank, wondering if Mike had perhaps not been skillful. There was no way to know; Mike was the only boy she'd ever had. "Do Patsy and Vail expect you to be with them tonight?" Arch asked.

She shook her head. "Vail's giving a speech about endangered mountain lions—his new bag. And Patsy's studying like crazy for the bar. Would you ever have thought Patsy would be a lawyer?" She leaped back to Vail and remarked that there was a campus campaign against fur coats.

"I'm glad you care about such things," Archie said. "That's what's special about young people today—caring. And knowing that today is really all we have." He smiled at her. "Anyway, I was asking because Sara's movie, the Chiaro film, is back in town. I thought it might be fun to go together."

"Oh, sure," she said. When it had opened, she'd seen it with Mike, hoping to impress him. *Sollazzo* was still a big foreign hit. "Didn't you ever see it?"

"No, just too busy with patients." He was consumed with passion for her. It had started that summer Vic had suddenly appeared. He knew it was wrong, but when it came to pleasure, Arch rarely denied himself. The danger of his desire made it even more compelling. He had taken her to lunch a few times during her last year of high school.

Today was the first time he felt some interest from her— nothing definite, but it was there. She was drawn to older men, as some girls always are, especially those who had had no fathers or whose fathers had been emotionally unavailable.

"What's happening with Sara?"

"She's starting to shoot soon. Imagine, a director! That's so cool."

"Do you think of having a movie career?"

"No. I think ambition sucks."

"I've got an idea," he said, his blond eyebrows lifting as if he'd just thought of it. "We'll go to the movie this afternoon and then have cocktails at the Top of the Mark and dinner out. How's that sound?"

They ate dinner at Ondine's, a restaurant in Sausalito that perched out over the water. Archie ordered white wine and clams and Caesar salads. Lindy discovered that Archie had a sad side to him. He told her about his childhood alone in the "mausoleum" on Nob Hill, about his favorite playmate who had been killed by a cable car on Hyde Street, about his dog that died of leukemia, about his failed marriage and the fact that his wife could never have children, about his stifled hopes until he'd met his real family, the Wymans. "I was blond," he said, "like every California boy ought to be, but I was big and clumsy as a teenager."

"You're handsome now," she said.

"Thanks. But underneath, I'm just a lonely guy who knows that half his life is over."

They were driving back across the Golden Gate Bridge. "Talking with you," Arch said after a silence, "is wonderful, Lindy. You have such a rich understanding of life. I hope I'm not taking advantage of your generous spirit."

"You're not!" she replied with energy. Tonight she'd been allowed to see a distant, respected adult as a lonely human being. His attention, his grave confidences, his flattery attracted her. She knew, too, that he was sexually attracted to her. The knowledge of such forbidden emotions made her feel excited, sinful, powerful, guilty. "You're a very interesting man."

"Interesting." He laughed. "I wonder what that word

really means?" He drove off the bridge exit and plunged into the San Francisco streets.

"I don't know," she said, nervously. The air between them in the privacy of the car felt loaded, tense.

"It's only eight o'clock," he said. "Come over to the house for a minute. Okay?"

Lindy was surprised. His nearness charged her. She pushed her misgivings aside and waited.

The mansion on Nob Hill, sandwiched between the apartment buildings, had had a new coat of paint. "Are you keeping it, then?" she asked as he ushered her inside. The foyer echoed. It was chilly and dark.

"For a while. Let's go in here." He indicated a small room off the foyer. "Mother used to call it the family room. She and I were the family."

The room was soft and comfortable. A handsome Victorian sofa in dark blue striped material sat against a wall, with two pale blue chairs beside it. A small tiled fireplace rested between two built-in bookcases. Lindy sat in one of the chairs. She looked at him pertly. "I was up here a couple of times," she said. She was ambivalent about being with him, alone, willing and unwilling, tempted and afraid.

Archie was moving about the room. "But you weren't in this room. This is a private room," he was mumbling, opening a cabinet. "I used to keep sherry in here." He was thinking: I must stop. This is wrong, this is mad. But Archie had never been able to delay any sensual satisfaction—slippery oysters, fragrant wines whose spicy perfume melted into his tongue, pearly grains of caviar, satin coverlets, a woman's soft yielding body in his arms. Archie's list of delicious sensations in life was long and heady, but paramount was his desire to woo the unlikely, the unsuitable, the unwinnable, and then, winning, to mount, to command, and to explode inside those women. Women had snared and seduced his senses more than any other pleasure.

He turned, faced her, crossed the room, sat down on the sofa next to her chair. "I have a very special feeling for you, Belinda. I've had it for a long time." His heart was beating like a sledgehammer. He reached out and touched her hair, letting his hand trail down its length to her breast.

He dropped his hand. "I'm going to say something to you, and I don't want you to be scared." His eyes looked at her with soft longing, an appeal. "I'll be so gentle with you, if you'll have me."

He couldn't stand it any longer. He rose from the sofa, pulled her out of the chair, and pressed her slender body to his. Her head only came up to his chest. "I know how to make you feel so good." He kept his voice low and comforting and needy. He kissed her cheek and neck. Lindy stood on her tip-toes to put her arms around his neck. He smelled of shaving cologne, and his beard was softer than she'd imagined. This was definitely illicit and intemperate, but she felt tingly all over. Her body thrummed with desire for the forbidden man.

He lifted her up off the floor and buried his lips in hers, thrusting his tongue inside. She leaned back in his arms and let him kiss her throat. "Take this off," he said, fondling her breasts through her clothes. His passion for her was rampant. When she emerged from her jeans and vest, standing on the rug nude, sylphlike, raising her hands above her head and turning, he grabbed her. "I knew you would like this," he said, kissing her with his thick, wide mouth, running his hands possessively up and down her body.

Later, she thought, lying on the rug of the family room, Mike wasn't very skillful. She nuzzled against him. One of his hands was cupped over her breast. He took her chin in his other hand and turned her face to him. "This is our secret," he said. "No one must know."

37

"It's good to be working together again, Sky," Pitcher Steinmetz said when he arrived at her house in the early spring of 1971. She gave him a kiss and a drink.

Pitcher made fast-paced, occasionally profound action pictures. He personified the rugged American auteur-director of the early seventies. Despite his success he had not outgrown his insecurities; he covered them with the image of a big-drinking, he-man's he-man who played the ponies—an avocation for many Hollywood directors. Actually, Pitcher didn't care much about horse racing. He *did* care about his films.

"Jesus, you look great!" he declared. She hadn't gained a pound, and her black hair set off her ivory face in the same soft curls. He would never have known her face had been through a glass meat mincer.

Conversation roamed over the picture, *Lady Blue;* the Santa Anita racetrack; over *Ginkgo Tree,* the only picture they had made together; and ended on poker. Sky thought he seemed calmer and more flexible, but then Pitch had always had two faces, aloof and aggressive at once. He dyed his hair now, except for the gray at his temples, and he'd gained some weight that hadn't helped his blood pressure problem.

"Have you cast the aunt yet?" Sky asked him.

Pitcher's bushy eyebrows peaked over his eyes playfully; he could animate them separately. "I know what you're going to say," he said. "She called me, too."

Anne Abbott, sixty, hadn't worked in five years except for a few undignified small parts in films about grisly murders or the occult in urban settings. She'd sold her house and was living in an apartment on Western Avenue not far from Paramount.

Sky went to bat for her. "Just give her the role. It's five pages; she'll do it well."

"She's difficult."

"Aw, she's old. We all get old."

"I've only got enough for scale," Pitcher said.

"Give her double, and take the extra out of mine," Sky said. "But don't tell her."

Sky was as generous as people said. He wondered if the other things he'd heard about her were true, but just looking at her he couldn't believe she was on drugs or drinking too much. He'd never given any credence to the rumor that Kitty was anything more to her than a glorified friend-secretary. He figured people were jealous of her. He had a blasé confidence in his own opinions and judgments.

"Here's the way it breaks out," he said, hunching forward on her sofa and knotting his hands in front of him. "We'll shoot on Stage 9 for twelve days—all the penthouse stuff. Then off to the desert for the flashbacks, the silent movie stuff—about two weeks. Then up to the river location, and then back here for the other interiors. It's not an easy picture. Get your track shoes on." His beady eyes narrowed.

"Don't worry, Pitch. I'm hale and hearty." Sky smiled at him warmly. "But why can't we shoot the river stuff in the tank?"

"Oh, you know me, I hate that process stuff. We gotta get right out there in nature, the way they used to do it! We're making a picture about a great silent movie star on the rerise, a star coming back whose first movies were all shot out in nature!"

The night before Sara was to start shooting *Winter Wheat*, she had thrown up twice. She imagined the worst. Most of the actors were experienced, older and wiser than she, she thought. Would they make trouble for her? Would they approve of what she asked them to do? Would they laugh behind their hands at her? She kept imagining the crew, asking her about the first setup. Would she remember where she wanted the camera?

Sara had felt strangely isolated when she told the crew where she wanted the first setup. When she first called "Action!" and "Cut!" she felt lonely and silly. But she had gained confidence by the second day out, and by the third, she was fully in charge.

They were shooting on the Via Sistina in front of the Grand Hotel. The scene was between Guido and two other actors. Ernie, always calm, had framed up in a medium shot, and she was peering through the lens. Guido made a face at her, knowing she was looking at them.

"Buono," she said, then stepped back. She went over to the actor standing next to Guido and ruffled his hair a bit with her hand. An assistant came up to her, wondering if the mirrored glass in the background of the shot needed to be resprayed. An actress who was going to walk into the scene was worried about her shoes. "They won't be seen," Sara said. She glanced around. The end of the street had been roped off, and a crowd of spectators stood against the rope, sighing for Guido.

"Let's do it!" she exclaimed. I sound as if I know what I'm talking about, she thought. She'd told Ernie that she didn't want Hollywood-like magazine pictures in bright colors; she wanted muted colors, lots of north light. She wanted economy. "I want every light or shadow to contribute," she'd said when Ernie had come over to Rome and they'd met for the first time in years.

"I'll throw away my gelatins," he'd said, smiling.

"The street stuff should look cold, real," she'd said, flipping through pages of the script. Ernie saw how nervous she was, afraid of making mistakes. "But inside I want to leave things to people's imagination. Does that make any sense?" She'd stared at him quizzically.

"Yup."

On the Via Sistina, Sara watched the actors doing the take. She was thinking about the next take and the one after that. She felt as if her eyes never shut, her mind never stopped.

The take went well, but she made another with slightly different business from Guido just to give herself options.

There was a turnaround at the end of the street a few steps away. "Avanti!" she cried, then whispered to Ernie, "Just as we discussed, at the entrance to the turnaround. And then after that, we do the dolly shot. I want the audience to ride down this street—Jesus, the tracks!"

"They're okay, Sara, believe me." He chuckled. She bounded ahead, concentrating on where she wanted the camera set up. Guido caught up with her and threw an arm over her shoulders.

"I have not seen you as happy as these last weeks," he said into her ear. "Such a busy woman!" Sara had never felt as good about herself or her work. She smiled up at him, thinking about the business with his ring in the next scene.

The crew applauded when Sky arrived on Pitcher's set. That first morning was like the old days. Guests milled about behind the cameras, superstar politicians escorted this time by the governor of California, Ronald Reagan, who knew his way around a set. Anne Abbott was walking two yapping Yorkies on silver leashes, but she had no adoring young man in tow this time. Sonny Somaine was playing Sky's on-screen lover-husband-manager. He'd aged well, still a trim hunk, still a happy-go-lucky, rather vacuous man who often said he didn't have an enemy in the world. Jack Nicholson, who had a wicked smile, was playing a twenties movie director. Gig Young had a good supporting role, as did Dyan Cannon.

A new young actress called Lorna Portland was playing Sky's daughter. She had lots of curly dark hair and a cute little face.

They started to shoot. Lorna stumbled over her lines and was shaking visibly. She reminded Sky of herself twenty years ago.

In the afternoon, Anne Abbott had her only scene with Sky. Abbott was playing the aunt as an old dowager. She wore a high-necked blouse and many strands of beads. She had not cleared her bracelets with anyone.

The scene began with Abbott entering the penthouse set and greeting her niece effusively. The aunt's hidden agenda was her need for a check, an objective with which Abbott could identify.

"Just come in this way," Pitcher instructed Abbott, "move to here, and embrace your niece. That's for the long shot. Then we'll go to the close-up. Got it?"

Abbott swept in in full regalia—hat, gloves, purse, fox furs—playing the part to the hilt. Sky began her first line, but it was drowned out in a jangle of silver bracelets. Shit, Sky thought, waiting for Pitcher to cut the scene. But he did not. Abbott was standing in front of her, raising her mighty arms for the embrace.

"Oh, darling," Abbott boomed over the noisy percussion of bracelets.

Sky started to say her next line, but by that time Abbott was lowering her arms. The jangling jewelry drowned her out. Sky started laughing.

"Cut!" bellowed Pitcher. "Strike the bracelets!"

Abbott drew herself up. "My character wouldn't be caught dead without jewelry," she said. The bracelets pealed again as she spoke.

"Your character will die on the cutting-room floor if you don't get rid of those goddamned bangles now!"

Sky was trying not to laugh. Her eye caught Kitty's, who was standing on the sidelines, also trying to smother her laughter. But Abbott was pathetic, too, and that silenced Sky's giggles. Anne, trying simply to be noticed, had succeeded.

They did the scene, sans bracelets, five times. Abbott was letter perfect. Sky had an unusually hard time with her lines. Sky was also overstepping her marks. She'd always landed right on them before. Pitcher attributed it to the first day's jitters. He knew he could count on the famous current between Sky and the camera when they were really rolling.

Sky had, as usual, developed all her character's eccentricities: the egoism, the indulgence, and the passionate warmth. As the days progressed, Sky began to play her character off the set, too. She had done this before, but now she merged her persona completely into the personality of the role of Mary Leland. Mary was desperate to remain young and in the public eye; Mary was a hard woman to live with.

"Can't we just turn it off for dinner?" Kitty snapped one evening about ten days into the shoot.

"It's the only way I can get the performance," Sky stated, smiling loftily like Mary Leland.

"It just seems that the line between fantasy and reality has blurred," Kitty said, thinking of the night Sky screamed like a stuck pig "in character" when a fly fell into her wine glass.

The last day on the set before going off for location was a nightmare. Sky couldn't believe it was happening to her.

Pitcher was directing her with barely controlled fury. The crew, on overtime, stood around in silent knots. The script supervisor, Wanda, had read Sky the line a dozen times in a muted, sad voice, and Sky still couldn't remember it. It was the twenty-ninth take. The line was, "Mark, aren't you more than a little infatuated with her?" Easy. But Sky kept saying "infatuated," and when she got the word right, her intonation on the line was wrong. Sonny, playing Mark, was demoralized, out of embarrassment for her.

"Blackboard it," Pitcher snapped.

"I know the line, Pitch!" Sky groaned.

The assistant to the assistant director quickly chalked the line on a board and held it up in Sky's sight line.

"Action," Pitcher said, spitting the word out.

Sonny made his turn, and Sky said, "Mark, aren't you infatuated with her?"

"Cut! Cut!" Pitcher screamed. "What the hell's wrong? The line is 'more than a little infatuated'! The line is not a demand, it's a question!"

Kitty writhed and prayed.

"Take Thirty-one!" the clapper snapped.

"Action," Pitcher drawled. He settled for take Thirty-one and left the set.

Vic was back in San Francisco. Archie hadn't wanted him to join them for dinner, but Lindy had insisted. She had seen Vic twice since he'd entered her life. She enjoyed him.

Archie was afraid that Vic would pick up on his affair with Lindy and make a big scene about it—belated parental responsibility. Actually, Archie didn't want to share any of his precious "Lindy time" with anyone. He was intensely curious about what she did when she was away from him at Berkeley, and he interrogated her about Mike as well as anyone else in her classes or in the radical antiwar group she hung out with.

Lindy was nervous about the dinner, too, but she wanted to be seen with Archie; she'd grown impatient with their pattern of eating a hamburger and then hitting the sack at the old mausoleum.

They were dining at John's, an old restaurant off Market Street. She watched Archie's courtliness with Vic, his amazing fund of information—he could talk about practically any city in the world with Vic, discussing anything from the Pentagon Papers to Northern Ireland. She gazed first at one man, then at the other, warmly, and was moved to steal her hand under the white tablecloth. She placed it on Archie's muscular thigh. He soon put his hand under the cloth and played with her fingers.

"Isn't she something?" Vic said, waving his hand languidly at Lindy. "I just can't believe it."

"Why not?" she said with an insolent charm. She flicked her hair back over her shoulder.

"So tell me about all the men you have on the string over there at Cal," Vic said to Lindy, pretending to concentrate on the job of cutting up his steak.

"Oh, only a dozen or so," she said, dangerously, feeling Archie stiffen beside her. She'd stopped sleeping with Mike, which had outraged him, so he'd cut her off from the inner circles of the campus demonstrations. "But they're not important. I want to be an artist."

"I've got it!" Vic said, proudly. "You could design the cover for my new book."

"Could I?" she asked excitedly.

Archie was impatient for the dinner to be over. He wanted to get her into bed, to feel the curves of her body, to feel her bones and skin moving under his hands. His passion for her had not subsided—it had grown in direct proportion to his desire for secrecy. He cautioned her each time they were together—so much so that she'd started to deride his "obsession," as she called it.

"Maybe I could come to Ireland," she declared, "and do the sketches there."

"You ought to stay in school," Archie counseled. "Every-one has a degree these days. Even in art."

Vic was surprised at how quickly Archie had moved in on her remark. Archie had done it with an attentive charm, but Vic began to look at them with new eyes. He didn't know how he felt about his daughter being ploughed by a man twice her age. *Were* they sleeping together? Did the boys her own age bore her? But wasn't Archie Sky's ther-apist? Wasn't he a relation of sorts through Diana? There was power underneath his smooth facade—power and hun-ger. He could see why a young woman might be attracted to his knowledge, though Vic thought him a trifle boring. He watched them shrewdly and soon saw that when Lindy's hand was in her lap, one of Archie's hands was under the table, too.

"I think it would be a great idea for you to come to Ireland," Vic said. "Stay a couple of weeks—maybe a month." When Vic saw Archie's mouth set and his huge shoulders square, he knew he was right: They were lovers.

Archie moved them off the subject of Ireland. They talked about the conviction of William Calley for the Mylai mas-sacre in Vietnam for a while; then Vic said to Lindy, "I'm going to have a little cocktail party the night before I leave. Some old friends from when I was growing up here. You could come and bring whatever current boy friend you have. And you come, too, Arch," he finished.

Lindy said promptly, "I'll bring Arch. He's my boy-friend." She looked at him mischievously.

"Oh?" Vic glanced at Archie for confirmation.

"Well, well," Archie said, having been tossed into a very cold creek, "I'm very flattered." He forced out a laugh and glanced at Vic to see what his reaction was.

Lindy felt denied. Deceitful relationships were against everything she and all her friends believed. They were old-fashioned and damaging. She pushed her plate away and faced Arch. Her little mouth thinned. "Don't do that," she said in a voice at once pained and sharp.

"Do what?" Archie asked, floundering.

"Don't lie about me."

"Why, I'm not lying. I'm very flattered that you'd want to take me to Vic's party."

"That is not what I mean."

Vic was sorry he'd started it. It was plain that Archie felt strongly about Lindy but was embarrassed about it. "Look," Vic said equitably, "I'm sorry. Bring whoever you want. It's none of my business."

"How can we get to know each other if you don't know about the most important person in my life?" Lindy asked Vic.

"Lindy!" Archie groaned; he shot an abashed half-smile at her father.

Lindy was angry now. "I'm in love with Archie, and he's in love with me," she declared. "But Archie wants to keep it a secret."

"There is a rather large difference in your ages," Vic said, called upon to say something, "but that's not an insurmountable—" Archie's face had gone beet red. The man was actually sweating. "I think it's a fine idea! Congratulations!" Vic said, raising his glass, making the best of it. He wondered if he was supposed to give her advice. "If you're happy, Lindy, I'm happy for you."

Vic thought about their dinner long after it had ended. He wasn't sure he'd done the right thing. He hadn't known what the right thing was. Should he have counseled her to stick to boys her own age? Should he have been displeased? He wondered if he should get in touch with Sara. Finally, he dismissed the whole business. He didn't know what to do.

Pitcher was addicted to realism at any price. Since shooting on location was his drug, he'd brought them to the Mojave desert in late June without worrying about the climate. Discomfort would be good for the picture.

It was a furnace—always hot except at night, when it was cold. In every direction, the desert is surrounded by low, barren mountains where only twisted juniper and Joshua trees grow. But on the valley floor, there is nothing except cactus and dry, wiry brown bush.

"It was an ancient interior sea!" Pitcher told his people jovially. He was always full of geographical information. Ace growled as he helped Valerie out of the car. Cage bounded out after them.

"I knew you shouldn't have come, Valerie," Sky said.

"It's going to be—"

"Just like the old days," Valerie said, looking around. "You know Von Stroheim, that crazy old coot, shot *Greed* out here? It was a hundred thirty-two in the shade."

"What shade?" Ace griped, who loved his comforts.

"Under an umbrella," Valerie said. Her peaches-and-cream complexion was like crinkled satin paper, and her soft blue eyes danced. "I think they could only get water from Furnace Creek!"

The company "made camp" just outside Baker, a little town in the middle of the desert. All the trailers for cast and crew were parked there; buses took them out to the desert for the day's shoot. It was torture. The normally silent brotherhood of the grips groaned and sweated; by noon the gear was too hot to touch; the film had to be rushed back to Hollywood by car each day to preserve it. The cameraman, Barney—a stranger to Sky, since Ernie was shooting with Sara in Rome—refused to wear a hat for some reason and collapsed on the second day. After that he wore a hat. Water was trucked out to them. They couldn't shoot much in the afternoon because a strong, dry wind blew across the valley floor, sweeping up dust and sand.

Sky and Pitcher were sitting in canvas chairs under huge umbrellas next to the camera and reflectors. Everyone moved in slow motion except Pitcher, who wore a wool vest under his shirt. "That's what the Bedouins do," he said, proud of his triumph over the heat. He never seemed to sweat.

"You're just remarkable, Pitch," Sky said during a time out. It had never taken Sky thirty-one takes to do anything before, and the feeling on the set just before they'd left for location haunted her. She was making an intense effort to put her shame behind her and to win Pitcher's confidence back. "I suppose all your leading ladies have been in love with you."

"Why?" he asked, tipping a bottle of water and drinking.

"Oh, I don't know, but it could happen." She took a swig from the bottle and patted her face with a wet handkerchief. "You're a handsome, energetic man, Pitcher."

"The heat's getting to you," he said, tilting back in his chair. Sky had always been unapproachable or had seemed that way to him. But that didn't mean that he hadn't entertained fantasies about her.

"No, really," she said, turning the proven force of her smile upon him like another sun. "I can see it on the screen."

"You can?" My God, she's flirting with me, he thought.

Pitcher had often romanced his actresses. His attentions had been one way to control them, even when the flirtation went unconsummated. It was certainly one way to counteract the intense boredom.

In the incandescent Mojave, Sky was an angel. She spent many hours with Pitcher after the end of a day's shooting, sitting outside her trailer, drinking Canadian Club, listening to old war stories from former shoots. Kitty had gone back to Los Angeles and wouldn't be joining them until they were up on the Russian River, the next challenging location Pitcher and his production manager had selected. So Kitty wasn't there to see what a fool Sky feared she was making of herself with Pitcher.

By the time they pulled up stakes in the desert, Pitcher was directing Sky with his arm around her waist and entertaining serious visions of sleeping with her. The picture was ten days behind schedule.

It was now July. They should have been back in Los Angeles on the day they arrived at the cold, fast-running river in Northern California. Everyone was so happy to leave the desert that no one complained when the weather shut down: it was wet and bleak. The wind snapped the summer trees around, and when it stormed, sheets of rain billowed into their faces. Their feet were numb, and it took energy just to keep warm. The sites for the scenes were at different places on the river; they motored around by car and bus from one spot to another. Most of the roads were dirt roads.

Pitcher, like all directors, established the atmosphere on his shoots, but since he felt that all actors were cattle—excepting only his leading ladies—his shoots were often laden with boisterous insults and demands. Messages from Hollywood, clocking off how far behind schedule he was, did not improve his temper.

"They sit in Hollywood with a slide rule making out the fucking schedule and send wires up here that we're behind schedule," Pitcher sneered, waving the latest telegram. "They have no idea of the location complications because they've never been on location."

He was particularly hard on Wanda, the script coordinator, whom he abused mercilessly as the rain made them even further behind schedule than had the desert heat. Sky could usually joke him out of it and often took Wanda's part, but day by day, the normally crazy interpersonal relationships, the practical jokes, and the levity of the shoot vanished. Sky began keeping vodka in her thermos to ward off the unseasonable damp cold and seal herself off from the tension around her.

Days passed without a single foot of film being shot. Wanda was sleeping with the cameraman, and Lorna and Sonny were having a rather argumentative affair until his wife arrived. Pitcher often came to Sky's trailer out by the river during the day when they had hoped to shoot and could not. He also spent time with her in the evenings at the rustic hotel where they were "encamped" for the nights. He thought she seemed receptive to him, and sweet.

Sky telephoned Arch and asked him to come up with some "supplies." He arrived with friends of his Sky had never met. She had them into her trailer to please him but his presumption irritated her.

"Where's Kitty?" she said as he was leaving. "I miss her a lot."

"She's coming up tonight, Sky. But I can't stay. I gotta get back." He glanced at her. "What's wrong?"

"Nothing," she said. "Everything. Bad shoot. You don't have time to listen."

They were now a month behind schedule. They'd shot one scene that morning during a break in the rain and then

—466—

they had all headed back to the "Hilton-on-River," as Sky called the hotel.

Kitty was waiting for her in her room. "Oh, I'm *so* glad to see you!" Sky yelped, drawing her friend into a huge hug. "God, I thought you'd never get here. Pitch is about to bore me to *death*." She drew back and looked at Kitty. "But I am being very nice and patient, even though he only talks about horses and baseball."

"Are you teasing him?" Kitty asked playfully.

"Oh, no, not really. Just a simple location flirtation. It's all harmless." She kissed her and hugged her tight.

"I should stay away more often," Kitty said. It was like having her Sky back. "Location shooting is good for you. How's it going?"

"Great! And awful! Which room are you in?"

"Just down the hall."

"Don't be a stranger."

Sky, elated to see Kitty, lifted everyone's spirits at dinner, mimicking Sheldon during the old days. She and Lorna did a takeoff on Pitcher that amused everyone, and she finished with a rendition of "Buttons and Bows." As Pitcher watched her, he wondered how, years ago, he could have been so in awe of her. She was behaving like a girl, a delicious girl.

The weather was promising to clear up the next day. After everyone had turned in, Pitcher sat in the lobby's knotty-pine and fir-stump bar, drinking. Being behind schedule didn't really worry him that much; it happened to productions. He was far more concerned with the quality of what they were shooting, and he knew from long experience that if he had it on the screen, no one would care about *Lady Blue* being over budget. He knew he was creating a film that was the perfect merger of art and commerce; it would be a big hit, it would have power and depth. It would say something about picture making.

He chugged his drink down and headed for the stone stairs that led to the second floor, where most of their rooms were. As he passed Sky's, he stopped and knocked. There was no answer, and he was about to go on when he tried the knob. If he hadn't had that last couple of drinks, he probably wouldn't have entered her suite. It was dark, but he could hear what sounded like Sky turning or talking in her sleep in the bedroom. He nervously adjusted his baseball cap and opened the adjoining door.

The ambient light from the front of the old hotel shone on Sky's face. She was lying, nude, on a pillow, her dark hair disappearing into shadow behind her. The covers had fallen off the end of the bed. Kitty's head lay on Sky's breast, and both her arms were passionately wrapped around the woman Pitcher desired. They were entwined.

Pitcher could feel his heart pumping. He knew his blood pressure was shooting up as he stood there. "I'll be a son-ofabitch," he said. He whirled and slammed the door behind him.

"I ought to go after him," Sky said to Kitty.

"Pitcher's a big boy, Sky. He'll be shocked for a couple of days, maybe, but he'll be all right," Kitty said, gathering up the covers at the foot of the bed. Outside, it started to rain gently.

38

Pitcher was ice cold to Sky the following day. The weather cleared by midmorning, and they shot on the river as long as their light lasted. When the grips were hauling away the reflectors and winding up the cables, Sky jumped into Pitcher's jeep. "Am I still welcome for the ride back?" she asked. He mumbled something and put the car in gear.

The trees bent over the dirt road that wound away from the river up to the old two-lane highway. The air was cool and the sun slanted through the boughs of the fir trees far above them.

"You made a fool of me," he said.

"I didn't mean to, Pitch, and if you feel that way, I'm really sorry."

"Carrying on with your pretty eyes, and shaking your breasts——"

"I never shook my breasts at you! Don't make things up!"

"You're a goddamned phony, that's what you are!"

"I am not a phony!" she cried. His accusation struck at her most vulnerable point.

He swung the jeep roughly around a bend. The setting sun hit the windshield. "You've always struck me as kinda naive, and now I can see why." He reached out and stroked her thigh.

She pulled away from him. "Pitch, please!" Sky said. "This is your fault, too! You just barged into my room——"

"I knocked——"

"I never invited you in! I'm sorry you saw us, but, well, it hasn't exactly been a secret about Kitty and me—"

"I don't want to hear. It's childish. Your problem, Sky, is that you've never had a real man." He was sounding like a gruff, insulted father. He stopped the jeep suddenly at the side of the road, reached across for her, and tried to pull her to him.

"Pitch!" she cried. "Stop this!" He was terribly strong. She clung to the edge of the door, twisting away from him. This was awful—he was like some wounded, angry old bull. "Pitcher!" He released his grip on her. Behind them the truck with the gear had caught up. It honked lightly.

"Hey, Pitch!" the top grip yelled, leaning out of the window, "you got engine trouble?"

Pitcher waved out the window, ground the gears angrily into first, and took off down the road.

"If you'll just relax, Sky, we can have a great relationship. You need a real man. You just don't know it." He didn't sound half as concerned about her as he sounded eager for the challenge. He accelerated the jeep.

Sky put one hand over her eyes and stared under it at the tree boughs brushing past the car. They were nearing the highway. "Pitch, please understand that I don't need rescuing."

He reached out again for her knee. She lifted his hand away. "It's going to be okay, Sky. Trust me." His hand moved to the back of her neck.

"Don't reform me!" she said with more energy and heat than she'd intended. "I care about you," she said more calmly, if not completely truthfully. "You're a great guy, and I'm not repulsed by men. But I don't desire you—",

"You will," he said, stroking the back of her neck.

"Dammit," she snapped, moving to the far side of the jeep. "Quit massaging me!"

He pulled the jeep to the side of the road and waved the truck past them. Sky watched it trundle on, wondering if she should get out and run after it. Pitcher turned the engine off, leaned against his door, and faced her. Then, without warning, he sprang at her, trying clumsily to hug and kiss her. He smelled of bourbon and cheroots. She protested, wrestling with him, which inflamed his desire even more. "Don't fight me," he kept saying, "just relax. It's going to be all right."

"Get away from me!" she yelled, then slapped him hard.

He jerked back, shocked. Very quietly, he said, "What was it then, all an act?"

Sky, panting, felt near tears. "No, Pitch, it was friendship, it was interest, respect, good conversation—didn't you ever have any of those things with a woman?" I'll never flirt with anyone again, she thought. I swear it, please God spare me, I'll never do it again. "It all started with that horrible day, thirty-one takes. I felt so low. I wanted you to like me again—you were really hard on me. I'm sorry, Pitch. I'm human. I made a mistake." She knew she was babbling, but she couldn't stop. "Lots of people flirt on location, for God's sake, it's no big deal. And I care about you. I just don't want to sleep with you. I've been with Kitty for years, Pitcher, and you've been married for years—"

"You're a fucking tease, and you used me," he said softly, dangerously. He started the jeep again and jerked it out onto the road. Its rear wheels spat up mud and gravel.

The next day at the same location, Pitcher drove the cast and crew like a man possessed. He looked at Kitty as if he wanted to kill her; he insulted and bullied Lorna until she was in tears, and he screamed at the cameraman. For Sky he reserved the most abuse, throwing up his arms after her scene as if pleading with an indifferent God in heaven. "When, oh, when are you going to do this scene as we rehearsed it? It's such a simple scene!" His voice dripped with exasperation and sarcasm. By the end of the day he was shrieking at her, "A has-been playing a has-been!" They were on the twelfth take of the scene, and the light was going. Even Pitcher's assistant director, a man who was known for his pandering to directors, tentatively stated that he thought the take was good.

"I don't care how big she is," Pitcher muttered, "or how big she's been. I'll break her."

Ace, Cage, Valerie, and Kitty sat in Sky's hotel room that night. "I've never seen anything like it," Ace said, shaking his head. "He's mad." Sky was crying, and Kitty stood by her chair, a hand on her shoulder.

"No, he's not," Valerie said. "He's rejected in love. It's a very dangerous state to be in."

The next day the weather still held, but Pitcher's mood was even worse. People fled from him or leaped to perform what he demanded like slaves afraid for their lives. When Pitcher wasn't yelling insults at Sky, he was pointedly ignoring her or whispering about her. The production had turned into a raw, debasing contest of wills.

The major scene on the river was one in which Sky, held by wires around her waist to prevent her from falling, stood in the shallows of the river, about knee deep, not far from the bank. The mountain water was cold, but the shot was a short, simple one. It was all part of the flashback sequence as the star recalls the rigors of being a silent movie actress.

The cameraman signaled that he was ready, and the fake ice floes were released into the river by the prop man. Sky waded into the water, feeling the wires attached to the hidden belt around her waist tighten. When she was in position, Pitcher called for action. Sky looked out at the ice floes floating past, then back to the shore. That was the entire take, since the actual swim by her character was to be done by a stuntman in a wig.

"Cut!" Pitcher yelled. He approached the bank. "Can't I have just a little energy, a little fear on your face, Miss Wyman?" She raised a hand up for a lift out of the water. "Stay where you are! We're doing it again!"

"I'm freezing my fucking ass off!" she yelled back.

"Good! Maybe I can get something printable outta this day. Places! Camera!"

They did six takes; she was in the water for two hours. That night at the hotel, Pitcher sat in his room, drinking; knots of cast and crew hovered around the bar, murmuring, and Sky was bundled up in her bed.

"I'm not going to be beaten," Sky said to Kitty and Valerie. "He won't do it to me."

Out in the sitting room, the house phone rang. "I'll get it," Kitty said. "You sleep."

She shut the door behind her and lifted the receiver.

—472—

"Kitty?" It was Lindy. "I'm downstairs. Can I come up?"

"No, not right now," Kitty said, astonished. "I'll come down. Have you had dinner?"

Lindy was chewing on a cocktail straw when Kitty joined her in the almost deserted dining room. "Well!" Kitty said, sitting down. "What brings you up here?"

Lindy looked tired and nervous. "The trip up to this godforsaken place was harder than I thought," she said. "All twists and turns." Lindy hated driving, but there'd been no bus or anything into the woods, so she'd hitched a ride. "How's it going? Can I watch tomorrow?"

"It's not going well," Kitty said. "Did you order some food?"

Lindy nodded. "What's wrong?"

Kitty was distracted. "It'll be all right. It's a tough shoot, that's all."

Lindy's food arrived, steamy and hot from the kitchen. She stuck her fork in the mashed potatoes. "I'm glad I got you on the phone instead of Sky," she said. She wanted help, but she didn't know how to approach it. "Something's happened. . . ."

Kitty was thinking about the war between Sky and Pitcher.

"Did you hear me?" Lindy asked, her voice rising.

"I'm sorry," Kitty said. "What?"

"I'm pregnant."

"Oh, Jesus," Kitty moaned. "How do you feel? Who's the father?"

"That's the problem." She stopped, biting her lip and sticking her chin out. "Do you promise not to tell anyone?"

Kitty's dark eyes surveyed her. "I'll promise for a while," she said carefully. "And if I think it must be told, then I'll talk to you first."

Lindy switched her long, straight hair back over her shoulder. "I guess that's okay. It's Archie."

"Archie?!" My God, she thought, incredible! She rubbed one hand against her forehead. "How long have you, were you, er, lovers?"

Lindy told her. "We're in love, Kitty. And I want to have the baby, but I don't know what to do because I don't think Archie will want it."

"Why?"

"Because he's been very secretive about the whole thing."

"As well he might," Kitty said heavily. "So you haven't told him yet." Lindy shook her head. "Your food's getting cold. You'll need nourishment."

Lindy sighed. "It's hard to eat. I get sick." She looked up. "Were you ever pregnant?"

"Once. I miscarried."

"Should I talk to Sky?" Lindy asked.

"Look, Sky's having a very hard time up here for a lot of reasons. Telling Sky now about Archie and you just wouldn't be a good idea. Believe me, it wouldn't."

"But I don't know what to do! I'm about six weeks gone."

"There's time. Can you just do nothing for ten days? We ought to be out of here and back home. Can it wait ten days?"

"No! I've got to do something."

"I can't leave here now, Lindy. When I get back, we can get the abortion—"

"I don't want an abortion," Lindy said, disgusted.

"What do you want?"

"I guess if I told Sky how Archie and I feel about each other, that if he doesn't agree about having the baby, Mom could convince him that—"

"Sky's too upset to hear that her shrink has been sleeping with her daughter!"

"You don't have to get angry," Lindy said, her face collapsing as great, round tears started running down her cheeks.

"I'm not angry," Kitty said, putting her arm around her. Kitty felt helpless and exasperated. She loved Lindy, but Lindy could be headstrong in ways that were inspired and destructive. "You don't think Archie loves you enough to want the baby?"

"I don't know."

"No matter what Archie says, it's ultimately your decision. You understand that?" Lindy snuffled loudly. "So a few days won't make any difference at all. But they would mean a lot to Sky. Won't you do this for her?" she pleaded.

—474—

Lindy roughly brushed her tears away. Her face looked closed and set. She didn't want to wait; she wanted people to rally to her. She wanted everything out in the open. She could already see herself diapering a child in the mansion off California Street. "I want some help so Archie won't—"

Kitty peered at her, bewildered. "Won't what?"

Lindy shrugged. "See, if Mom came around to my way of thinking and told Archie he'd better do what's right, then he'd probably want the baby."

"But you wouldn't want Archie under those circumstances, would you?"

"No, I guess not. I don't know what to do."

First of all, Kitty just couldn't conceive of Archie and Lindy being truly in love, and second, she couldn't see Archie dancing with joy over Lindy's pregnancy under any circumstances. She could see an Archie paralyzed with anxiety over it and demanding that it be hushed up. Oh, Jesus, whatever had possessed this stubborn, passionate child to involve herself with him? She knew only too well what had inspired his involvement with Lindy, but his rashness truly amazed her. "Many men aren't too keen about having a child," she said, trying to be patient. "Your mother had to have you all alone—"

"I don't want to repeat that!" Lindy said with fury. "I want to have a home for it with Archie."

After an hour Kitty finally wrung a promise from Lindy to wait until they all got home. "We'll have a powwow and do what's right," Kitty said.

In a small, dark room at Cinecittà, Sara was looking at the final cut of her film, *Winter Wheat*. She groaned. "Oh, it's not what I had in mind. It's not good enough."

Guido, sitting next to her, said, "But, cara, be happy. It is quite nice."

"Nice, what's *nice*?" She laughed. The rough cut rolled on. "Oh, wait, here's that—" She watched a scene of Guido's on the screen intently. When it was over, she murmured, "Good."

"It's all good," he hissed. "It has charm and magic and disappointment and hope."

When the lights came up, Sara put her head in her hands. Guido bent over her and kissed her hair. "I go now to see you later."

"Why did I use that angle in the bridge scene?" she muttered into her hand. She sat up slowly, then rose. "Reed!" She had noticed him suddenly out of the corner of her eye. He was sitting behind her with his feet up on the row in front of him, a cowboy hat perched on the back of his head. He was smiling. "You just fly all over the world these days!"

He nodded. "I was on my way to England and got sidetracked." He grinned. "Good show."

"Oh, don't mock me. It's terrible!"

"Okay, it's terrible."

"Didn't you find anything to like in it?" she asked.

"A lot. You can improve. No one's a director overnight. You ready to listen?"

When Lindy refused to stay, Kitty arranged for her to get back to San Francisco. "Call me every night," Kitty said, kissing her cheek. "Everything will be just fine. We'll all help. Just sit tight."

It was hot in San Francisco when Lindy got in. She took a cab to the campus and thought about canceling her standing Tuesday night date with Archie. But at the same time she was eager for the confrontation, eager to have it out.

"Oh, honey," he said when she entered his house early that evening. "I missed you." He swept her up in his arms and kissed her. Lindy felt her pulse hopping as she antici- pated the importance of the scene about to be enacted. "Let's get you out of those nasty old jeans and into something—" he smiled sideways "—more comfortable."

"Archie, I've got something very important to say," Lindy whispered as they went arm and arm up the curling stair- case.

"Let's not talk. Let's—"

"It can't wait." They approached his bedroom. He opened the door.

"Yes, it can," he said, ushering her into the large, dark room with its mighty mahogany four-poster bed.

"No, it can't." She walked to the bed, turned, and leaned

against one of the posts. He was pulling at his tie. "I'm pregnant." His hand stopped in midtug.

"But I got you the pills!"

"Well, sometimes I forgot." She went up to him and pressed her hands against his deep chest. "Aren't you glad?"

"Glad?" He took her hands away. It would mean that everything would come out; he'd lose Sky and his practice. "No, I'm not glad. Having a child will ruin your life, you're too young."

"I'm eighteen!"

"That's too young for a talented girl like you," he said, slipping into his soothing doctor's voice. "Now here's what we'll do. I'll arrange everything. We'll go to a friend of mine, a doctor, and he'll do the abortion. It won't—"

"I don't want an abortion!"

"It won't hurt! It's just like bad cramps."

"How do *you* know?" she asked. "You never had cramps. And besides, I don't want an abortion! I want to live with you, right here, and have the child. Oh, Archie, it'll be great!"

Archie stepped back, appalled and afraid. "That's out of the question. Who have you told about this?"

"Only Kitty," she said, realizing his worst fears.

"Jesus! You can't do this to me! Don't tell anyone, do you hear? No one!"

"I'll tell whoever I like! It's our child—yours and mine!" She was over at one of the tall windows. She reached out and grabbed the shade and let it go. It shot up to the top of the window and snapped into a tight roll.

"Lindy, listen to me," he begged.

"No! You don't love me."

"I do! But a baby—that wasn't our bargain. Now be sensible!" She seized another shade and jerked it. It shot up and snapped. "Stop that!" He grabbed her by the wrist. "Listen to me. Don't ruin everything."

"I'm not ruining everything," she said angrily. "*You* are."

"Now just calm down," he said, desperate, "and listen." He held her tightly against him. But she struggled and tried to get away. "We'll do it your way, if that's what you want."

She looked up at him. "Do you mean it?"

"Just look at it with me, honey. It will mean you'll have to quit school—"

"Archie, I want this baby. Please don't try to talk me out of it—"

"But I'm looking out for your welfare. I'm thinking of you!"

"No you're not! You're thinking of yourself!" She flung herself on the bed and broke into long, high sobs. He stood in the middle of the room, willing himself to stay calm. No matter what he did he was entirely at her mercy. What would Sky say when she learned? Oh, God, he groaned, how could he have endangered everything for this rash child? Why hadn't he delayed the impulse to have her? As he faced Lindy, he wanted to cry at the ruin she threatened to make of his life. But Archie didn't know how to cry anymore.

39

Vic proudly put an arm around Lindy and sauntered through the chattering guests in his hotel suite. He was proud for many reasons: his new novel, which was Number Nine on the best-seller list and climbing; Lindy's acceptance of him; and being able to invite the people who represented his youth to a suite at San Francisco's majestic Fairmount Hotel—an impossible dream for a poor boy from the Sunset district. The looks of admiration he received warmed him physically.

"And this is my daughter, Belinda Wyman. You all know her mother, Sky Wyman," he was saying. A stack of his latest novel, each one signed, sat on a table in the foyer.

"Where's Archie?" Vic whispered to Lindy as he moved her away from the crowd.

"I couldn't get him on the telephone," she said.

"Maybe he's out of town," Vic said, glancing around at his guests appreciatively.

"No, he's not." Archie had been avoiding her. His excuse was the beginning of group sessions, but she knew better. She'd waited outside his house last night and had seen him enter it at midnight with a young girl she knew was a patient of his. Since that moment she hadn't slept or eaten but had revolved in an inner cyclone of fury and grief and fear.

To Vic, impervious in the golden glow of the self-made author, Lindy seemed sad and lonely. He put an arm around her shoulders. "Romances sometimes come to abrupt endings, but at your age you'll get over it. There's lots more fish in the sea!"

Lindy looked up at her father. He had clear blue eyes. "I wish I knew what to do now," she said, miserably.

"We'll have dinner later," he said, squeezing her shoulder, "and you can tell me all about it." His high school math teacher who'd nearly flunked him had just come into the suite. Vic wanted to make every sweet moment count.

But when the guests had gone, and Lindy had told him everything, Vic had got up from the table abruptly, a sharp flash of panic in his eyes.

"I'll give you the money for an abortion," he said.

"So you think that's best, too," she said.

"Of course it is! He's a cad! Don't ruin your life over him." Vic returned to the table and chugged some red wine into his glass. "I'm sure your mother would agree with me. Or, listen, how about this? You could go to Europe, see Sara. It's much easier and safer to have an abortion in Europe. I'll give you the money."

"I don't want an abortion."

"Come come, now, be sensible. Have you talked to Sky yet?"

"She's getting in from location tonight. I'm going down there tomorrow."

"That's good. You talk to Sky." He smiled and glanced at the clock. "I'm off to Deauville early tomorrow," he said regretfully. "But I know you'll do the right thing."

Sky leaned her head back against the chair and let out a long sigh. "Jesus, it's good to be back home."

The "Descent of Pitcher Steinmetz," as Sky called the experience now that it was over, had been extraordinary. Demanding, tyrannical, petty, cutting at the actors and screaming at the crew, he had managed to alienate everyone while making them feel sorry for and respectful of Sky at the same time. Insisting on take after take of the same shot, he'd tried to wear her down; when she would not break, he had increased the pressure. Rumors of what was going on had reached Hollywood; wires arrived on location every day, demands that he complete the location work and get his ass back. Pitcher had replied that he was creating a great film and that no one but he could possibly understand the difficulties. Finally Sheldon Winters had flown in. "Wrap it up in three days," he had said. And Pitcher did.

Kitty saw the lines of exhaustion on Sky's face. Her scars showed more when she was tired.

"When's Archie coming in?" Sky asked.

The moment Kitty had been dreading was upon her.

"Sky, we've got a serious problem." And she told her.

Sky physically recoiled. She felt she'd been punched. "Oh, no, it must be that Mike, that antiwar guy," Sky said at first. Gently, persuasively, Kitty told her everything Lindy had said. *"That bastard!"* Sky yelled, rising out of her chair. "I'll kill him!"

Jubilant guests—Marco, Chiaro, Carmen, Guido, Reed, and many others—filled the rooms of Sara's apartment in Rome to celebrate the final cut of her film, which was going to be released in both Europe and the United States. Reed sat cross-legged on a soft couch watching Marco playing a harmonica while Chiaro did a two-step with a beautiful Roman actress who'd played a small part in Sara's film.

Chiaro had described *Winter Wheat* to the press as an intimate film of "humor and cutting insight." Reed thought that Sara was finding her way at last, but success was a new feeling for her; she was used to envy and failure. When she started second-guessing her feelings of elation, trying to find problems that weren't there, Reed had warned her, "Don't do that! Just ride the wave—you've earned it."

Sara danced over to him. She was wearing a sleek gold dress that matched the color of her hair. "I am proud of you," he said. Reed had just arrived from Pinewood Studios in England and was due for a two-week stay in Rome on his latest picture.

"Sara—telephone!" Carmen yelled happily. "It's Los Angeles."

"The news is everywhere," Reed murmured.
Sara went into her bedroom and picked up the extension.
"Yes? Sky! Oh, how wonderful of you to call!"
"Sara, I'm sorry—" Sky began.
Reed was standing in the doorway, gazing at her happily. Someone had put a paper hat on his head. He looked

ridiculous. He saw Sara sit down on the edge of the bed, the bed Reed was dreaming of sharing with her when the time was right. He saw the color drain from her face and the lines around her mouth deepen.

"My God, no!" Sara said. "How could he? How could she?" Sara put a hand on her forehead and tipped her head back. Reed took off the paper hat and sat down beside her.

"Send her over here. I'll take care of everything. Where is she? I must call her."

When she hung up, she lay back on the bed. Reed closed the door. When Sara had explained the situation to him, she said, "They don't know where Lindy is. They think she's going to Los Angeles tomorrow, but they couldn't reach her tonight in her dorm."

"She's a strong and determined girl," Reed said. "If she doesn't want an abortion, no one will make her have one."

He stroked her forehead.

"I'm going to leave for the States tomorrow," she said. "She needs me. I'll bring her back here." He knew it was no good advising her to stay. Sara let out a long sigh. "Poor Lindy. What is it with young girls and older men?"

"Fantasy, remembrance," he whispered.

Lindy was with Vail at his office. He sat behind his desk. He was facing a deadline. Groveling assistants rushed in and out with snippets of research for him. One delivered a huge basket of fruit from a gratefully ecstatic actor to whom he'd given a warm review. "Here, Lindy, take it back to the counterculture." He pushed the basket toward her. "I've got five minutes." He checked his watch. Then I've got to finish this review, and Patsy's due here any second. She's got a job, did you know? She's a real attorney with some great firm, I forget the name, it's as long as your arm. What's up?" When he heard, he laughed. "Archie?" he squealed, holding his sides. "Old Archie?"

"He's not old," was all Lindy could think to say.

"Well," he spluttered, "he's a good sight older than you." He checked himself. "Look, I'm sorry you feel rotten, of course you do, but it's not the end of the world." Vail knew what the end of the world felt like. It was the sense that half his life was over, that he wasn't handsome any more, that people fawned around him but didn't respect him, that one of his sisters was in some kind of gruesome contest with her director and that his other sister had taken leave of her senses and had decided to be a director. It was moments like these that made him feel old and impotent, that threw all the intimate, youthful hopes up against a screen and exposed them for the unattainable charades they really were.

Vail had had lunch with Schurl that day, a long overdue meeting that had made him feel even more corrupt than he normally did. Schurl had left his comfortable life in Marin and was now a leading antiwar mobilizer. He'd been wired with energy and commitment, chopping at the air over their lunch vigorously, describing the duplicity of Kissinger and the Department of Defense. Even old Schurl had kept his compact with his principles. As Bondy had. The lunch had left Vail angry and grieving.

Vail physically shook himself. "I'm just an old sellout," he said to Lindy, who had begun to cry. "The damage has already been done, Lindy. Just what do you want me to do?"

"I want him back. I want revenge. Oh," she wailed, "I don't know *what* I want anymore."

"Nonsense," Vail said, irritated. "Charge a ticket to my account and go see Sara and get an abortion in Europe."

"She's ten thousand miles away!" She had no habit of consulting Sara, though she trusted her, and she would have said, if pressed, that she loved her.

"Just don't elope with Arch!"

"Don't worry," she wept. "He won't even answer my phone calls."

"The son of a bitch. Well, I never liked him." He tented his fingers. "What did you see in him?" He peered at her, interested.

She snuffled and dragged out a torn tissue. "I felt protected and—" She started crying again.

Flattered, Vail said to himself, she was flattered by the old goat's attentions. He leaned across his desk and gave her a fresh tissue from his pocket. "Look, sweetie, you want to have the child, great. Everyone will help. You don't want to, fine. Everyone will help. It's your choice——"

Patsy opened the door. She was beautifully dressed in a pale gray business suit. She carried a briefcase.

"You look lovely, dear. Help Lindy," Vail said. "I'll be back." He grabbed some papers and flew out of the room.

"What's the matter, Lindy?" Patsy asked, sitting down beside her like a bird landing on a twig.

Lindy glanced up at Patsy's sweet, confident face. She didn't think she had the energy to describe everything all over again. She was sick of talking about her problem; she wanted action.

"Why do you stay with Uncle Vail?" Lindy asked Patsy abruptly.

"Because he needs me and I love him," she said quietly. "I know he seems excitable and not very nice sometimes—," she laughed lightly "—but he's got a very soft and vulnerable nature. A lot of the noise is just an act." Patsy brushed a hand over her perfect hair. "Are you in trouble?"

Lindy launched into her story, but as she was telling it she wondered if she'd toured the family not only to get help but also to get some attention. That was not very attractive of her, she thought. She realized that since she'd seen Archie with his young patient, she'd avoided the one person she should have faced.

Patsy heard her out. "Do you want to have the child?"

"I don't know anymore."

"Then you shouldn't do anything until you know that. What's Archie think? What's he say?"

"I guess I better try and see him again."

"After you've seen him, call me," Patsy said, handing Lindy her new business card. "It's got both my phone numbers on it."

Pitcher and Sheldon were sitting in Sheldon's private screening room. They'd just looked at the rough assembly of *Lady Blue*.

"You know it and I know it," Sheldon was saying. "It's not great, Pitch. Sky's stiff, Lorna looks like she just came outta the woodwork and is trying to figure out where she is. Nicholson looks good, and so does Gig Young—the cameos." He turned around in his chair and fixed Pitcher with a cold stare. "But you're way over budget. What the hell—"

"It was Sky's fault, Shel, I'm telling you. She caused constant delays. She was uncooperative, spoiled. She argued about everything—ask anyone. She's just a broken-down old actress."

"You're an outrageous son of a bitch, Pitcher. Two months ago you were dying to have her." Sheldon could smell fear in seconds, and he knew that Pitcher was afraid. "You can't lay all of this at Sky's door."

But Pitcher was agile when his back was to the wall. He could see his livelihood slipping away from him if *Lady Blue* wasn't released. Then he'd be just another director who hadn't made it as a producer; he'd be living off his last picture, which had been released three years ago. He had to get another picture out there, and he had to duck the reputation of being a director who couldn't control his productions.

He locked eyes with Sheldon. "I'm going to sue her for ruining the artistic integrity of my picture," he said, grinding his jaw. "She's not going to get away with it, and you're going to back me up."

Late that night, Archie decided to go for a walk after his cab dropped him off in front of his home. He strode purposefully down California Street, swinging his arms, inhaling the sea air, trying to feel in control of his life.

Sky was back from location, he knew. He was debating whether he should call her or just go down there tomorrow as if nothing had happened. He was almost certain that Kitty had told Sky about Lindy. That meant that his relationship with Sky was over unless he could figure out a way to make her see it as an unfortunate human accident, one he regretted. He turned various scenarios over in his head as he made a left and walked down Stockton to Sutter Street. Sky would need her medication soon, but she could talk another doctor into prescribing.

He passed art galleries and glittering antique shops, winding his way through the downtown streets. He missed Lindy, her lithe and imaginative little body and her sharp mind had filled a real vacancy for him. He was fond of her, and even at this terrible moment in their lives, he longed to be making love to her. He'd miscalculated Lindy's at-

—485—

tachment to him. He regretted that. He'd hoped that the couple of weeks of silence had begun to break her dependence on him. She had good family, people who would help her.

Perhaps he was going at this all wrong, he thought, turning onto Mason and heading downhill again. Maybe he should play the indulgent elder suitor, a little ashamed but still adoring, eager to marry Lindy and raise the child. He doubted even that script would keep his Los Angeles practice for him. He returned to the more convenient script for him—that in a few months it would all blow over, Lindy would have come to her senses and had a quiet abortion in Denmark, and his practice would be moderately undisturbed.

But no matter which course of action he played out, he knew that Sky was lost to him. He ground his teeth and scowled, heaping abuse on himself. How could he have sacrificed Sky for Lindy!

Lindy was sitting in the garden of Archie's home, huddled against the granite wall that partially sheltered her from the cool, damp breeze. The moon was cut in half, but it was bright, and a nightingale sang from somewhere near the dogwood tree. Lindy had decided to give Archie another chance to do the right thing, to be the person she'd believed he was. If he didn't, then she'd go to Los Angeles and talk to Sky, and maybe she'd fly to Rome. It all sounded good in her head, but she was keyed up, conscious of making final decisions. Her heart banged against her ribs.

She got up and shook out her cramped legs. An upstairs light had just gone on. Archie was home. She went around to the front of the house, climbed the stairs, and rang the bell.

"Lindy," Archie said, opening the door. "It's best if we don't—"

"Is she with you?" Lindy demanded, amazed at herself. She hadn't intended to mention that patient of his.

"Is who with me?"

"Your new girlfriend!" Just looking at him made her feel furious and used.

Archie was alone. He let her in. "You're upset. Maybe we can talk when you're less—"

"The least you can do," she said, her voice rising, "is to talk to me!"

"All right," he said, soothingly. "We'll go in the study. It's warm."

The house was always cold, and it always echoed, as now, when people moved from one vast section to smaller, warmer terminals.

The study was a small room toward the back of the house. It had dark, narrow-striped wallpaper, Tiffany lamps, a couple of oil landscapes in heavy gilt frames, and leather furniture. Its heavy opulence was decidedly masculine. Archie sat on the sofa and patted the space next to him. But Lindy spun away and landed in a playful sulk behind his desk.

Very gently, he said, "Well, Doctor Wyman, what words have you to say to me?" He smiled warmly.

She tilted her head, and her large round eyes glinted in the light from the glass lamp. "I wanted to give you a chance to come to your senses," she said, mimicking his words of two weeks ago to her.

"I am in full possession of my senses," he said. He watched her little hands creep across his desk. She was desirable and delicious. He forgave himself his passion for her. He selected an avuncular tone. "You will see that these little agonies pass quickly. I know it's painful now, and I do feel for you, but we don't belong together as man and wife. What we had was very special, and in a way we should congratulate ourselves for our courage—the courage to fly in the face of social customs, to please each other, and to know each other." She had picked up his letter opener and was smiling faintly. "But we're not parents—"

"I'm a parent already!" she said, putting the letter opener down and sliding open the top drawer of the desk. She made a show of being interested in the paper clips and envelopes.

"You don't have to be a parent either! This is nineteen seventy-one—not the nineteenth century. Quit playing the martyr! You can go on with your life. I want you to. I want you to be happy."

She looked at him sharply as she closed the top drawer and opened another. She could feel her pulse racing as she stared at his blond hair and his round face, gently lit by the lamp beside the sofa. She looked down and saw the revolver nesting in a cloth-lined box.

"I'm not going to let you make me the fall guy," he said, angry at her. "I've spent a lot of years getting where I am. You've got a problem—",

"We've got a problem!"

"We can still go to Sara."

"Sara? She doesn't have anything to do with this! Don't keep pushing me off on other people," she said shakily.

"Why did you mention Sara?"

He laughed. "Slip of the tongue. Oh, Lindy, quit making this into a dramaturgy. You're such a smart girl! Grow up!"

"I want you to marry me and be a proper father, or I'll tell Sky everything. She won't want you as her therapist, and the others down in L.A. won't either!"

"Don't threaten me!" he bellowed, goaded by her increasingly shrill demands.

"I will! I can! You deserve it! You're just throwing me away!"

"Don't be stupid! When something's over—"

"It's not over! Wait till Mother and her friends—your patients, Archie—hear about everything we've done together!"

"You idiot!" he yelled. "Sky isn't going to fire her therapist!"

"She will!" Lindy shouted. "She'll be on my side when I tell her how you seduced me, how jealous you were of me, how you like making love on the floor, and what we did on the floor." Her narrowed eyes carried the bolt of a hundred dark and thrilling intimacies.

"She won't believe you!"

"Yes, she will! She's my mother!"

"She's not your mother!" Archie roared.

He couldn't believe he'd said it. Lindy was staring at him.

"What do you mean she's not my mother?" she gasped.

"She's not. She's just—"

"She is!"

"No, she isn't! Sara is your mother!" Once it was out

the momentum of it shot him forward recklessly. He sprang off the couch. "You think your mother's a movie star, the famous Sky Wyman? The woman the world worships? You've enjoyed that, haven't you? It's brought you friends and parties and money and respect you wouldn't have had without Sky, hasn't it?" The glazed shock on her face satisfied him deeply. "She's not your mother! Your mother's an Italian porno queen who spread her legs for all the pizza boys—"

"You're a liar!" she shrieked. He was robbing her. He was setting her on fire. She seized the gun from the drawer. He lunged for her. Lindy pulled the trigger. The gun went off, flying up out of her hand.

Archie staggered back, clutching his throat, wheezing horribly. She could see the blood seeping between his fingers. She watched him as if she were floating above the scene. He tumbled to the floor, his eyes staring up, wide open, astonished. He blinked. He coughed and gasped. Lindy went around the desk and picked up the gun. She aimed it at him again. He was waving his arms.

She fired.

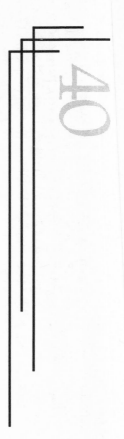

40

When Sara saw her daughter, Lindy was in jail. In her jeans and jacket, she looked like a sad little street urchin—dark circles under her eyes, her long straight hair hanging down stringy and uncombed. This is it, Sara thought. This is where my life ends.

Lindy had made no effort to escape. She had been sitting on the study floor when the police arrived, called by a neighbor who'd heard the shots. That had been two days ago. Now, Sara stood outside the visitors' room, looking through a one-way mirror in the door. She had flown into town, expecting to give Archie a piece of her mind and to take Lindy back to Europe.

A slender and rather young matron stood a few feet away.

"I can't go in," Sara whispered.

The matron looked interested but remote. "Why? She's expecting you."

The moment Sara realized she'd once longed for—in a romantic, youthful way years ago—and had dreaded as Belinda grew older—had arrived. It was time to be honest. She pushed open the door.

Lindy looked up coldly. "Well, well, Mom's here."

Sara sat down at the bare table. She reached out to stroke Lindy's hand, but Lindy pulled it away.

"Haven't we been friends all these years?" Sara asked.

"At least friends?" Lindy made no answer. "I'll do whatever needs doing," Sara said.

—490—

"Don't bother," Lindy replied in a flat voice. "It doesn't matter."

"You matter to me, Lindy. Always. No reservations." There were so many things Sara wanted to say, but Lindy was sealed off in a private world where no one—particularly Sara—could reach her. "I know what a terrible shock it was for you to learn you weren't biologically Sky's child—"

"A *shock?!*" Lindy said. "Shock doesn't begin to describe it."

"I wanted to tell you a long time ago."

"Don't bother giving me all the reasons why you didn't," Lindy said, twisting away from the table and going over to the grimy window. "I *would* like to know when the handoff occurred between you and Sky."

"I was about your age. You were a few months old," Sara said.

Lindy turned. "I don't want to talk to you. I don't want to be your daughter. I'm Sky's daughter."

Sara rose. "No reason, no matter how good it seemed at the time, looks good now. I never dreamed we'd be talking about it in this place," she murmured. "I'm going to keep trying to see you," she went on, trembling, "because I have loved you since the day you were born. I hope you will understand someday why I did what I did. I am as responsible for your being here as you are."

Lindy had turned her back to stare out the window at the brick wall a few feet away. She heard Sara knock on the door for release, but she didn't turn around.

Sara went back to the Clay Street house, avoiding the press who were clustered noisily outside by going through their neighbor's backyard. From there, she crossed into Diana's yard and let herself in the back door.

In the kitchen, Maggie was just pouring herself a cup of coffee. She gripped a stack of papers under her arm. They exchanged a look.

"She'll come around," Maggie said. "Lindy's stubborn, but she's generous. You'll see."

Sara just shook her head sadly. Out in the hall, Sara heard the low murmur of voices coming from the living room. One belonged to Roger Banning, the attorney she,

Sky, and Vail had hired. Diana's voice was sharp and querulous.

"I don't understand that at all!" Diana was saying as Sara came into the living room. "She was not in her full mind! Who would be? He drove her to it!"

"Mrs. Wyman, I'm not saying," Banning replied coolly, "that we cannot plead not guilty for reasons of insanity. I'm saying that the fact that she shot him twice, once while he was lying on the floor, mitigates against an insanity plea."

Sara nodded at Sky, who looked wan, thin, drawn out. They were all distressed, but Sky was getting up and tinkering with objects in the room, chewing on her nails, nervously aware of every tiny sound. Vail was hunched over in his chair, his hands knotted in front of him, elbows on his knees.

Sara sat down and smiled at Patsy. It had been Sara who had insisted that Patsy be part of all their meetings. Banning, from the distinguished firm of Banning, Bode, Carter, and Nye, had been hired on his own merits, a top criminal defense lawyer. But Sara had felt that Patsy, even as the newest member of Banning's firm, would give Lindy a sense of security, a familiar face among strangers. Vail had been the first to agree, Sky and Diana somewhat more reluctantly. They had little confidence in Patsy's abilities.

They were discussing "avenues"—Banning's word—approaches to strategy for Lindy's defense.

"Why can't we just get her out on bail?" Sky asked.

"It's possible," Banning said. He was a thin, tall man with curly gray hair and sharp dark eyes. "But she has been arraigned on first-degree murder."

"She's just a little girl," Sara whispered.

"In the eyes of the law, she's an adult. She's eighteen," Banning replied. "I'm working on bail."

The family began marshaling its considerable resources. Carefully picking his way, shoring up his arguments with cautions that nothing could be guaranteed, Banning began to point the way. Lindy could get a conviction of first- or second-degree murder or of manslaughter. He thought the chances that a jury would acquit her for reasons of self-defense or insanity minuscule.

—492—

"Now what does all this mean?" Diana asked. She was seated in a large wing chair, her white hair swept up on her head, her fingers glistening with her two favorite rings. She looked more alert and ready for battle than anyone else in the room.

"It means that we have some important choices. We can plead insanity, but the result, if we could win on it, may be to no one's liking: lifetime imprisonment in a state mental institution."

Sara started to cry silently, the tears falling down her cheeks steadily. She wiped them away but they kept coming. Sky went over and stood behind her like a sentinel, one hand to Sara's shoulder. But a few moments later, she drifted away and sat down next to Vail.

"Pleading *not* guilty immediately takes us into a jury trial," Banning said briskly. "On the other hand, we might consider pleading guilty to manslaughter right now, instead of not guilty." His slender white hands pushed at some papers spread out on an ottoman in front of him.

"Why?" Sky asked angrily. "Why would we plead guilty?"

"Because," Patsy said softly and clearly, "manslaughter is a much lesser charge. A judge might look favorably on such a plea given Lindy's youth and her completely crimeless—"

"Yes, yes," Diana said impatiently, "but what kind of penalty?" She was looking at Banning.

"If the district attorney allowed us to plead guilty to manslaughter, the lesser charge, remember," Banning replied, "it could mean imprisonment for a period of years or a fine and a shorter imprisonment."

Patsy sat up. "Roger, could we plead Lindy guilty of manslaughter and tell the court Lindy would voluntarily commit herself to a mental hospital to show that she wants to get well?"

"That's exactly what I wish to propose here." He glanced at Patsy and then at Diana.

"I don't understand," Sky said.

"If she pleads guilty, she avoids a trial," Patsy said.

"Then it's up to a judge to determine the sentence for the crime to which she pleaded guilty," Banning explained.

"What I'm trying to construct here is a plea and a sentence that don't confine her to a mental hospital or to a prison for the rest of her life." Sky and Sara gasped. "I am hiring three psychiatrists to testify about Lindy's mental state. Fortunately, the deceased isn't someone the community loved. His career as a therapist here in San Francisco is checkered, to say the least."

"Oh, God," Sky moaned, "I feel so responsible." Vail saw his mother look at Sky with contempt.

Later that afternoon, after Banning and Patsy had left, Sara asked Sky to take a walk with her. "I want to talk, Sky." They started down Clay Street, the first street they had ever seen or known. It was unchanged.

"I know you feel responsible, and I do, too," Sara said. "I was worried about Lindy, after your accident, about the—well—the atmosphere in your house—"

Sky stopped walking. "Do you mean Kitty?" she demanded.

"I do not. Of course not." Sara said. "I'm talking about Archie's influence over you, all the pills you took—"

"For pain! Have you ever been in constant pain, Sara?"

"I understand! But you were drinking, too. Maybe you still are! I didn't think that kind of atmosphere was a great influence on a young girl!"

"My house was good enough when you were traipsing around going to drama school and living in New York."

"That was years ago, Sky! We've both made mistakes!"

"I'm devastated by this, Sara. Don't you think I've asked myself—"

"I know you have, Sky." Her sister's eyes glittered like snow under sunshine.

"I love Lindy like my own daughter!" Sky said. A man passed them on the quiet, tree-lined street and stared.

"My mistake was letting Mother talk me into your raising her as your daughter, and Lindy never knowing that she was mine!" Sara said. "We both gave Archie ammunition—"

"I thought you wanted her raised as my daughter!" Sky said.

"I never did! I wanted to take her to New York with me when I—before things got rough—"

—494—

"You see? Things weren't any better for you with Teddy than they were for me later," Sky said.

Sara stopped talking and looked at Sky sadly. "Lindy used an expression this morning that cut me right to the bone. She asked when the 'handoff' happened. She feels like an object passed between us."

"You can't have her! You can't take her back!" Sky started to walk furiously.

"Sky!"

"I can't stand this. It's killing me," Sky called back.

Sara raced after her. "Sky, stop." She reached out and grabbed her shoulder. It was like a collection of bones under her hand. "I can't get her back! She told me today that you're her mother. She doesn't want me."

They stared at each other. Sky fell into Sara's arms, moaning. "I'm so sorry," she said. "I'm selfish. I know it's agony for you, too."

"It's been like that for me for a long time—hearing Lindy call you mama, being with her but never being able to approach her honestly. Now, for the first time in her life, I can be myself. It's just so—if I can't do that now, a very big part of me will just dry up and die. Please understand. Please help me. Help Lindy. The charade's over, Sky. We have to let Lindy decide now."

"Yes, I see," Sky said softly. She put an arm around Sara's waist. "I guess it all had to end sometime."

"It's not ending!" Sara cried. "She needs us both! She needs to hear from you why you adopted her, why you raised me as your child. Why you insisted on that."

"It was because—that, well—" Sky stammered, "because she needed me! Because you didn't want her! You couldn't take care of her!"

"Why did you insist on that?" Sara repeated.

Sky countered. "If Lindy needs to know anything, it's why you gave in to it."

"Answer me!" Sara demanded.

Sky buried her face in her hands and moaned. "I don't know why I insisted. Mother thought—I just had to have her."

Sara backed away. "Because she was *mine*," she insisted.

—495—

"No! That wasn't the reason!" Sky's voice echoed on the street.

"Yes!" Sara said, chilled. "It *was* the reason."

The woman's movement was just barely getting its footing in the early seventies. In San Francisco the first wave of women lawyers was being graduated from law schools in the Bay Area—women with long straight hair, shining faces, and demanding principles. Women who already used words like "chairperson" before they were common currency elsewhere in the country. "Oppression" was a state that these women had perceived and faced; they were translating for other women who hadn't yet caught on that being a house-wife was unpaid labor. It was a vigorous time.

The Wyman case got a lot of publicity, yet Lindy had refused to give any interviews. As speculation wore thin, interest in Lindy's crime dwindled. Emma Rosenthal worked for a small San Francisco newspaper and went to law school at night. She was looking for an angle on the Wyman story to write a long, in-depth article on Lindy. She wrote Lindy a note and was granted, exclusively, Lindy's first interview.

Lindy refused to see Sara until Sky and Vail insisted.

"Gee, practically the whole family," Lindy said when Sara, Sky, and Vail entered the reception room in the jail. "Everyone's caught up in the Wymans' horrifying drama?"

"We brought you some goodies," Vail said. "They're out at the desk being searched. You know, the file and the pistol buried in the cake." He grinned and kissed her forehead.

"Patsy came this morning," Lindy said. "It's really great to see her instead of the shrinks, all those strange old men."

Sky hugged Lindy and Lindy returned it warmly. "Sit down, sweetie," Sky said.

"Is this a family confab?" Lindy asked guardedly.

"In a way." Sky looked anxiously at Sara and Vail.

"I wanted to tell you why I let Sky raise you as her daughter," Sara said, slicing right into it.

"I don't want to go into that!" Lindy bolted from the table.

"Sit down and listen," Vail said. Even if you don't want to know, he thought.

Lindy retreated to the window as Sara spoke about Vic

—496—

and his disappearance, about her own desires, about the heady, happy, nutty days of Sky's first picture, about the money Sky was making and how tempted Sara had been by Diana's proposition.

"I didn't hand you off," she stated, wanting to punch through to her daughter. "I did what I thought was best—no, that isn't true. I did the easiest thing that I thought would also work out for you. Deep down I knew it was wrong, Lindy, I knew the day when you found out was coming. I think we all did."

Lindy remained impassive, her back turned. Vail walked over to her and physically turned her around. "You listen to your mother!"

"She's not my mother!"

"She is! You've got to admit it! I've spent a lot of my life not admitting things to myself, and I can tell you, that way lies disaster. You ask Patsy about that."

"Sky!" Lindy shrieked, holding out her arms.

Sky rushed to her. "Nothing's changed, darling."

"Dammit, Sky, things have changed!" Vail snapped.

"I mean, I'm still here," Sky said to Lindy. "We all love you. That's what we came to say." The look on Sara's face stopped Sky cold. It was a look of intense misery and fury and surrender all mixed up. "Lindy, that's just one of the things we wanted to make sure you knew. I want you to know that Sara didn't give you up easily. There was a lot of pressure." Lindy straightened up and moved out of Sky's arms. "I was so desperate to have you."

"If you'd really wanted me you would never have given me up," she said to Sara.

"I was young and selfish and I didn't know any better," Sara said. "I didn't know what it would mean. Believe me, I've paid a million dues for it and I'll pay a million more. I can't change it! I wish it were different!"

"You never said anything either, Vail," Lindy accused him.

"No, it was their decision." He sat down next to Sara. "But in some ways, it was a good decision. I mean, it had its up side," he stated. "Nothing's ever all bad." He saw Lindy tip her face up to Sky, frantic, adoring. Archie had taken more away from Lindy in that second's revelation than anyone had imagined. She had had a famous and gifted mother all these years whom in one instant he had snatched from her. "You haven't lost Sky," Vail said to Lindy. "You've gained Sara. Sara's got a lot to offer."

Seeing all three of them that day, and Vail's timely and sensitive perceptions, made a dent in Lindy's adamantine sense of betrayal. Shortly after, Banning got her out on bail; she returned to Diana's house. Sara visited day after day, sometimes with Sky, sometimes with Vail. By October, when Sky was forced to return to Los Angeles, Lindy was talking to Sara.

"Don't guilt-trip yourself, Sara. At least I didn't know I was abandoned," Lindy said. She smiled at Sara. They were sitting in the living room. "What I really missed was a father. Have you heard from Vic?"

"Oh, yes," Sara replied. "He's shocked, of course. He babbled about how he probably should have called me himself."

"When he and I talked that night at the hotel?"

"I guess so. He wasn't making much sense. But he cares about you in his own way. He's a single man, Lindy. Raising children is completely outside his universe."

"Outside yours, too," Lindy snapped. Underneath, her bitterness and doubt remained.

"Yes, that's true," Sara said.

"I didn't go there to kill Archie," Lindy said suddenly. "That just happened when he said Sky wasn't my mother. I don't really remember it very well. I remember wanting to get *through* to him, when we started talking, and then he said something, and I realized that he hadn't really cared about me, that the baby was my problem, and that we were an inconvenience. He thought he could just use me and throw me away. I told Emma that, and it's true. Well, they can't do it anymore."

Sara stared at her daughter and realized that she didn't know her at all. For centuries, women had put up with the results of lovemaking, had been stranded or abused, ignored or indifferently tolerated. Whatever the treatment, it gave no woman the right to kill a man, but Sara had to admit that when Vic had abandoned her, an essential piece of her intrinsic dignity, and her trust in the power of love, had been destroyed. No one and nothing had ever fully taken its place again.

"Being rejected didn't give you the right to kill him," Sara said, softly. "Hearing a terrible truth, no matter how viciously or mistakenly meant, didn't give you that right."

"I don't remember killing him! And I know I'll be punished. But the way he talked to me made me feel dirty, stupid, like I'd been a good time and wasn't any fun any more. He gave himself the right to tell me about you and Sky! He wasn't dumb! He knew that would hurt me the most." Her chin trembled as tears formed in her eyes.

"It's so sad," Sara murmured. "I would do anything to change it for you."

"If that old gun hadn't been there it never would have happened," Lindy sighed.

Pitcher was suing Sky.

"That I," Sky was yelling at Mel Winters on the telephone, "I ruined the artistic integrity of Pitcher's film? I caused it to go over budget?" Sky and Kitty were on the patio of their house in Hollywood. They'd only been back a few hours. "You must be joking! Pitcher damn near killed me in that fucking Russian River! Ask anyone!"

"It's serious, Sky," Mel said. "You have to get over here this afternoon." Pitcher was also busily campaigning by rumor about her all over town. "It's very damaging. I want you to give a few select interviews, and we have to decide what kind of response we're—"

"That film had no artistic integrity to begin with until I got into the act!" She reached out for a bottle of aspirin and shook several into her palm. She hadn't had any Librium in days, and she felt like she was going to come apart like a puppet. "He wants to make me the scapegoat for his mistakes." Mel started to interject but Sky went on, "I'll sue him right back."

"Please, Sky. Come into my office today. He's making you look very bad. It's just possible Sheldon will back him up. This is serious business!"

"Do you believe that?" Sky demanded, hanging up the

telephone. "Pitcher is suing me for causing *Lady Blue* to go over budget?" She gulped down three aspirins. "I'm going to sue his ass off."

Kitty said, "Countersuits are expensive and usually ill-advised."

"Well, what would you have me do? Just keep silent? I can't do that."

Mrs. Sho came out of the house. "There's a Patrick somebody to see you, Sky. Quit taking that aspirin. I told you they're bad for you." She glanced around the terrace, taking in the scattered towels, books, trade papers, cigarettes, coke bottles, and scripts. "Look at this place!"

"Hey, Sky," Patrick said, appearing in the doorway behind Mrs. Sho.

"How're you doing?" Sky asked. He looked thinner. His blond hair was grayer, and his blue eyes looked wary and desperate. "It's been a while, hasn't it?" she asked, trying to calculate how many years it actually had been since she'd seen him.

"You sure do have a great place here," he said, glancing around him. "That front room—wow! Beautiful decoration."

"You want a drink?" she asked. "You remember Kitty, don't you?"

"Oh, sure." He stuck out his hand. "How're you?" Patrick asked, with a trace of his old charm. "Yeah, I'll have a drink."

Sky went inside to make it. Kitty said to him, "You were in a lot of Sky's early films with her, weren't you?" She was trying to bring the two images—the young and the old Patrick—together. "Oh, you were here the night Lila—"

"Yeah, yeah. Bad night." He looked down at the tiled terrace.

Sky returned with a tray of drinks and they all sat down. Patrick's hand shook when he took his glass. "How are your folks?" Sky asked.

"They're fine, I guess. I never hear," he said with a hatred that resonated in the calm afternoon. "Dad cut me off without a cent."

"I'm real sorry to hear that, Pat," Sky sighed.

"Mom sends money now and again—Mom was always kind." He drained his drink. "The town's gettin' so tough these days. Got to give everyone blow jobs before they'll even let you read."

Sky stared at him coldly.

Patrick's fury, just below the surface, was a raging river. He jerked his eyes away from Sky and looked out over the pool toward the trees, fantasizing about living with Sky in this beautiful, remote place. Everyone would admire him. If he lived with Sky, they wouldn't turn away from him.

Behind Patrick, Sky and Kitty exchanged a look.

"Sky," Patrick began uncomfortably, "I've hit a run of bad luck. I really need some work."

Sky had figured as much, and indeed, over the years, she had gotten him work. As a cloud moved in front of the sun, she saw that his face hadn't merely aged, it was bleached in a strange way. "Sure, Pat, I'll see what I can do," she said, knowing that no one in town would hire him.

"Even extra stuff," he mumbled.

Sky thought about stringing him along and then decided not to insult what was left of him. "Pat, let's be honest. I can't get you work."

"Sure you can! You got all the studios on the string!" he yelled. "Why won't you help me?"

"I'd like to, but you've just dug your own grave all over town. Look what you did to Ray over at Universal. Ray would laugh in my face if I asked him to give you some work." Ray was head of casting and had, a few years back, given Patrick a job for old time's sake. Patrick had repaid the favor not only by getting drunk on the job, but by pushing the director into the tank where he nearly drowned. Sky could recite a list of such incidents, including the one where he punched out his agent and demolished his office into the bargain. "You've got to get into some kind of treatment center."

Patrick lurched out of the deck chair. "Jesus, I come here with my hat in my hand and whaddaya give me? Nothing! I've just been through a really tough, shitty time, Sky. You've been there, from what I hear; you know what it's like. Can't you help me out?"

"You get into a program and I'll pay for it."

Patrick stared at her, hating her; he could feel his memories crowding at his back, of being with her, of kissing her.

Had he really kissed her or had that been a fantasy? "You're all alike," he sneered, throwing his glass into the pool. "You get so high and mighty, you don't have time for old friends who didn't have it so easy. You're all scum!" Kitty was on her feet. "Don't worry, tiger," Patrick slurred. "I'm going. The sooner I'm away from here, the better. I can't stand the stench."

Thick clouds bumped off the horizon and rolled into town. In San Francisco, Patsy collected depositions and helped deal with the postponements. She and Banning huddled with the district attorney, confirmed the agreement for Lindy to plead guilty to a reduced charge—a triumph—but failed to get a sentencing agreement. The probation report—a full investigation of Lindy—was begun; Banning prepared for the sentencing hearing before the judge. But in all the preparations, one thing kept needling Patsy and she couldn't shake it. On the surface it didn't look important, but her instinct kept telling her it was. Finally, she decided to go with her instinct. She called Vic.

Reed came in and out of town, offering Sara what support he could. Then he went down to Los Angeles, where he found Sky suing Pitcher and beginning her own round of depositions, charges, and countercharges.

The week before Lindy's hearing, Emma's first article appeared in the newspaper. "Archie Used to Pay the Price," screamed the headline.

"Jesus Christ," Emma's astonished editor and publisher said. "We've sold out and are going for a second edition!" The paper's small circulation rocketed. The other papers in the Bay Area picked up her story. Soon it was news again. In no time Emma had turned Lindy's case into a feminist cause célèbre: "Lindy Was Used and Discarded," blared another headline. Underneath that, in smaller type, "Women Take Stand with Lindy." "Archie Used Secret Against Lindy." "Cheap journalism," Emma said to Lindy. "Sorry." Lindy agreed but pointed out that Emma was establishing a climate of sympathy.

Lindy was the Number One topic of conversation all over the city. People argued in coffee houses and bars. "But she killed him!" both men and women exclaimed. "Women aren't going to put up with abuse any longer!" came the reply. Sky and Kitty had flown up for the hearing. They were sitting in the Sir Francis Drake Hotel when they overheard a matronly woman driven to distraction by her son and daughter, students at Berkeley, who were enthusiastically outlining the debate that had so fired the town.

"I don't know how you can defend a murderess," the matron said, her words formed by her lips since her beautiful jaw didn't move much.

"That's not the point, Mom!" her daughter protested. "There's got to be a change. That old stuff about suffering and about it's always being the woman's job to make sure there's no kids—that's over!" The matron from Connecticut looked shocked.

In the chilly house on Clay Street, big with child, Lindy began looking forward to the hearing.

41

Patsy had told Sara privately that Banning's questioning of her at Lindy's hearing could be hard on her. Patsy had been right.

"And what happened in nineteen fifty-three?" Roger Banning asked Sara, who sat in the witness chair in one of the sleek, modern courtrooms in the Federal Building in San Francisco. The defense had challenged the probation report on Lindy as being incomplete ("fucked," Banning had called it privately). He and his team, which included Patsy, were bringing forward witnesses to try to show the matrix in which Lindy's crime had occurred. Even though it was a sentencing hearing instead of a trial, it was just as demanding. The judge, about fifty-five, a black woman named Fern Lanier, had been making copious notes, but now her pen stopped moving. She looked up expectantly.

"In nineteen fifty-three I left my child and went to New York—back to school," Sara said, looking at Lindy, who, very pregnant now, sat at one of the gleaming oak tables in front of the judge and the court recorder. Behind her, the small, wood-paneled court room was crowded with press and spectators. Patsy sat at the defense table with Banning's assistants.

"You separated yourself from your child."

"I did. I was very young, but that was no excuse." Sara looked at the judge, then at Diana, who wore a smart blue suit and hat. She sat next to Vail in the row directly behind

Lindy. Diana's back was straight and she looked at the proceedings unflinchingly.

"And then what occurred?" Banning asked.

"My sister, Sky, was having a tremendous success at the time. My mother convinced me it would be best for Belinda if Sky raised her."

"And you agreed to this arrangement?"

"I did. I didn't—well, I felt uneasy about it."

"Why?" Banning asked.

"I was told the only way my sister would agree was to raise Lindy as her own child."

"But you did agree."

"Yes."

"And did you make attempts to take care of your child?"

"Objection," Samuels muttered, the prosecuting attorney, a young, aggressive man with wavy hair. His short, square fingers were wrapped around a ballpoint pen.

"Your Honor," Banning said, "I am drawing the picture here of a young woman, the defendant, whose mother— for whatever reasons—abandoned her as a baby. The defendant did not learn of her true parentage until the deceased told her in a moment of fury. In that moment the defendant, Belinda Wyman, was herself pregnant. I am submitting that her concern for her child's welfare would be overwhelming given the circumstances of her own upbringing—"

"Yes, I can see the path, Counselor. Overruled," Judge Lanier said to the prosecutor.

"Did you attempt to take care of your child in *any* way?" Banning repeated.

"Yes," Sara said, "I saw her whenever I was here, but I couldn't afford to have her with me in school, nor would it have been allowed."

"But she has never lived with you, isn't that right?" he pressed.

"That is right," Sara said softly.

"She was, in effect, and as far as she knew, Sky Wyman's child."

"That's right." Sara looked down at her hands. "Your Honor, could I just say something here?"

"Objection!" the prosecutor shouted, rising. "This is not a forum for soap opera confessions—"

"Oh, Mister Samuels, I think in this hearing we can afford a little latitude," Judge Lanier said. "Don't you? Continue, Miss Wyman."

"I just wanted to say, Your Honor, that I didn't love my daughter any the less by at first leaving her with her grandmother and grandfather, and later with Sky. Sky adored Lindy and gave her a good home and a fine education. Had that *not* been the case, I would have kept her." Sara stopped and collected herself. It was so hard to put all the decisions made almost twenty years ago into a few sentences. She continued hesitantly. "Her father abandoned both of us. He simply vanished." Sara felt her throat constrict. "I've always regretted not having taken care of Lindy myself as a proper mother would have done. In a way Lindy paid a steep price for my life and my work. And if Lindy is to be judged here, I, too, should be judged. She should have been told whose child she was long before Archie hit her with it."

"Oh, Your Honor, really. It recalls the weepies in the movies. The defendant shot and killed—" the prosecutor objected.

Banning snapped, "No further questions, Your Honor."

Reporters were scribbling rapidly, the spectators buzzing, Samuels snapping his pen. On that wave, they rode into cross-examination.

"Miss Wyman, isn't it a fact that your daughter had an excellent education surrounded by loving relatives, one of whom she believed to be her mother, a woman who gave her practically anything she wanted?" Samuels demanded.

"Yes, but she—"

"Just answer my questions, please." He glanced down at his notes. "And isn't it a fact that she was known as a willful, stubborn, and often recalcitrant child?"

"Objection!" Banning roared. "Leading!"

"I'll rephrase, Your Honor," Samuels said. But for the next hour, he failed to shake Sara's calm demeanor or her iron grip on her own contribution to the present unhappy circumstances.

During lunch Patsy again drew Sara aside. "Hang onto

your hat. It's going to be a bumpy afternoon," she said, paraphrasing a line from one of Vail's favorite movies.

In the afternoon, Banning called Vic Oliver to the stand. Urged by Patsy and Banning, he had flown in from Ireland the day before and had met privately with both of them.

Banning moved around the defendant's table to the far side of the room so that his body did not block any spectator's view of Vic Oliver.

"Mister Oliver," he began coldly, "would you please tell this court why you left your wife?"

Victor was nervous. He could feel the sweat popping out on his palms. He looked at the triplets sitting together and at Diana. Then he gazed at Lindy, who seemed so young and tiny compared to her powerful relatives.

"I didn't know Sara was pregnant," he said, clearing his throat. "I left because Sara's mother paid me to leave."

The court room exploded. Samuels fell back in his chair; Sara, sitting next to Vail, gripped his arm; Diana's gloved hand flew to her mouth, and Judge Lanier banged her gavel.

"Would you explain that, Mister Oliver?" Banning demanded loudly.

"Sara and I had been married about six months. I was in school at Berkeley. Sara was working in an office on campus to help put me through. Mrs. Wyman came to me privately one morning and offered me five thousand dollars if I would leave—just vanish. I was appalled, naturally, and very angry. But she kept talking about how talented Sara was, about how marriage at her age was a mistake, how Sara needed to have an education herself, that I and my plans were thwarting Sara, that Sara had been blinded by her sister's sudden success—" Vic glanced at Diana, who was leaning back in her seat, her eyes never leaving his face, her lips pressed together tight. "She said that I and I alone could save Sara's life—by leaving."

"So you took the money and left," Banning murmured.

"Finally, yes, I did," Vic said. "It wasn't very admirable, but five thousand dollars was a lot of money in those days. I knew that Sara didn't belong with me. I was the kid from the wrong side of the tracks. I knew she loved me but that she'd married me for a lot of reasons, primarily to escape her family. I also knew that she and I probably wouldn't stay together." Sara had put a hand over her face and her shoulders were shaking.

"Why was that?"

"Because I didn't love her. I admired her, and I liked her. She knew I didn't love her, too." He looked at Lindy. "I had no idea she was pregnant. I'd like to think I would have acted differently if I'd known that."

"And now that you've met and become acquainted with your daughter, what is your opinion of her?"

"She's an intelligent, decent young woman."

Banning seemed pleased with himself. "No further questions."

Samuels muttered, "No questions, Your Honor." He was slouched sullenly in his chair at the prosecution table. His assistant was combing through a large file.

"Defense calls Mrs. Diana Wyman," Banning said, not looking at her.

Sara, hunched over, watched her mother rise, tuck her crocodile purse under her arm, and move smoothly to the witness stand as if she were going to a slightly boring luncheon. She removed one of her gloves to take the oath and then settled into the chair.

"Mrs. Wyman," Banning began, "I wonder if you could tell us about the events of your daughter's elopement."

"Irrelevant and immaterial, Your Honor," Samuels interjected.

"Your Honor," Banning said crisply, "we're here today because Lindy Wyman has pled guilty to manslaughter. It is now up to the wisdom of this court to determine what punishment is to be meted out to her. I am trying to show that the events leading up to that dreadful moment in Doctor Moberly's home began before the defendant was born. I think it's important that you have all the information in order to make your judgment."

"Overruled," Judge Lanier declared. Samuels sighed and sat down. The reporters scrawled furiously on their note pads.

Diana said, "She eloped with Vic Oumansky, as his name was then. What more do you want to know about it?

Did I expect it? Of course not. Did I like it? What mother would?"

"Did you, as Mister Oliver has said, pay him money to leave your daughter?"

"I did what I thought best," Diana said, head up, lips pursed, hands folded in her lap. Sara stared at her mother.

"Perhaps you could expand on that statement," Banning suggested.

"My daughter eloped with a man not one of us knew, someone who seemed unsuitable. She was impressionable and headstrong, not unlike Lindy, and she had, in my judgment, made the worst mistake of her life. I didn't think that a mother who really cared would just stand around and watch her daughter's life be ruined. If Victor had refused to take the money and leave, I wouldn't have pressed it any further. But he took the money." She looked at Lindy. "I had no idea Sara was pregnant."

"And if you had known?"

Diana took a hankie from her purse and pressed a point of it against her eye. "I don't believe the outcome of the marriage would have been much different."

"Mrs. Wyman, was that your decision to make?"

"Oh, of course not, Mister Banning. What do you take me for?" she snapped. "But it's agony for a mother to see her child just throwing away her life and not to try to do something about it!" She pressed the point of her handkerchief to her other eye. "I may not have done the right thing but I don't regret doing something!"

"Your Honor," Samuels said in a fatigued voice, "how long are we going to follow this maudlin road of the past, which has so little bearing on the case at hand? We are now two generations removed from the murder of Arch Moberly."

"Yes," Judge Lanier said, "I do think we are fairly far afield, Mister Banning. Make the connections."

"Your Honor, indifference and interference brought Lindy into the study that evening with Doctor Moberly! They are important and relevant. We contend that psychiatric help is now needed for the defendant, which the defendant herself has agreed to."

Banning, Samuels, and Judge Lanier droned on. Sara rose from her seat and walked out of the courtroom. She leaned against the wall in the corridor and lit a cigarette. A reporter came by. Sara said, "No comment on anything," then walked away and shut herself in the rest room down the hall.

Inside the court Diana watched her daughter leave. Shortly after that, the judge took everything under advisement and adjourned until further notice. Diana left the stand, walked past Vic, Sky, and Vail without a nod, and went into the hall. Sara wasn't there. Reporters began jumping around her. She was distantly aware that Vail was putting his arm through hers and guiding her through the excited and energized press. She saw the rest room sign. "Wait here," she said, and went in.

Sara was vomiting into one of the basins. Diana went up to her and put a hand on her daughter's forehead. Sara pulled away.

"I really felt it was for the best," Diana said, a note of panic in her voice. "I hope you believe that."

Sara was pressing a damp paper towel to her face. "You just never stop, do you?" she said softly. "How did you know if Vic and I would separate? We might have stayed together. None of this would have happened!"

"Oh, Sara, that's a very comforting thought for you—"

"Of course it's comforting!" she shot back. "But Lindy would not have grown up believing herself to be Sky's daughter, she might never have met Archie, and he certainly wouldn't have had any such appalling, shocking 'truth' to throw at her! We don't really know what would have happened if you had just stayed out of it, do we?"

Diana turned on the cold water and put her wrist under the tap.

"Do we?" Sara demanded.

"I guess not. But don't you stand there and revile me! You don't have the right—"

"I don't have the right? Are you crazy? I have *every* right! You've interfered with my life and with Sky's and with Vail's and none of us are the better for it! God knows what Lindy thinks of you today. She missed having a father and she can really lay that one at your door. Don't you think we're able to run our lives?" She searched her mother's long, still-beautiful face. "I guess you don't. Do you even like us?"

"I won't listen to any more of this. I only came in to tell you that I didn't mean you any harm." She patted her wrist dry. "I know that sounds weak and silly now, but it's true."

"Just get away from me. I don't want to see you for a while. Maybe not ever."

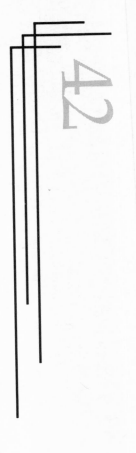

42

As Banning had predicted, Judge Lanier sentenced Lindy to an indefinite period in a local mental health institution for psychiatric evaluation and care. Vail attributed the leniency of the judge's decision to Vic's revelations, which Patsy had made possible.

Vail put his arm around his wife. "Lindy has a lot to thank you for," he said to Patsy. "So do I."

Shortly after the judge's decision, *Winter Wheat's* distributor held a press and industry screening of the film just before it was to open in New York and Los Angeles.

"I'm not in the mood," Sara told Vail and Sky. "Besides, I've seen it," she said. The court hearing for Lindy's sentencing, and all that had come in its wake, had left her numb. Reed was back in Europe; she wanted to be on the next plane.

"You're the director! You've got to be at the screening and be interviewed," Vail said. "There's nothing you can do here for Lindy."

Sara went down to Los Angeles with Vail and Patsy. The screening was being held at the Directors Guild Theater on Sunset Boulevard. When they arrived, the lobby outside the auditorium was full of guests—industry executives, press, and "opinion makers" whose word of mouth would boost the film.

"Sara!" It was Ray Sordo, the producer who'd taken the triplets to dinner at the Brown Derby a lifetime ago, the man who'd produced *The White Queen.* "If I could just speak with you a moment?" He made motions to draw her aside from Vail and Patsy, who were about to go into the auditorium. "Congratulations!" he said enthusiastically. "I hear you have a great little picture with lots of depth."

Sara correctly assumed that the only depth Sordo was acquainted with was the deep end of his pool. "What is it, Mister Sordo?" she asked.

"It's about Sky's problem with the studio."

"Sky doesn't have a problem—Pitcher has a problem," Sara said.

"She's got to save her career!" Sordo cried. "All this suing back and forth, and the damaging reports about her in the trades. Very bad for her." He looked at Sara brightly. "I've been instructed to make a proposition to you—" If he disliked his role in this matter, it didn't show.

"Mister Sordo, my own picture is about to begin. Can't we discuss this later?"

"It'll only take a minute." He glanced furtively around. "I've been instructed to tell you that a word from you about Sky's, er, difficulties since her accident would give you great access to distribution for your next picture. Maybe even financing."

Sara, in the middle of turning away from him, stopped. "I don't believe it."

"Yes, yes!" he said, completely mistaking her. "A great connection to a major U.S. studio!"

"If I just what? Sign something that says my sister couldn't find her marks and that's why the picture went over budget?"

Sordo got her drift. "Well," he said haplessly, sticking his hands in his pockets, "it's a great offer."

"You know, Ray, there was a time when I might have signed your thieving paper. But not now."

"Really, it's good for Sky because she's got to put this thing behind her."

The last of the crowd was filing into the theater. "You miserable crumb-bum," she said, pushing at him. "You're a despicable shit." He backed into a wall, his eyes sad and panicky.

"It was only an offer!" he shouted after her as she swept into the theater.

Sky's battle with the studio had seesawed back and forth. Aside from the tension of overseeing the charges and countercharges, giving depositions, watching the studio flacks drop damaging "revelations" about her in the press, and constantly huddling with her attorneys, Sky felt that her life had become a winding cloth that she could not escape. Offers for her work had dwindled. Her career halted. Mel kept saying it would all be forgotten after a few months, but Sky knew better. Producers didn't know what had happened on the Russian River or who was at fault, and they didn't particularly care. It came down to how few enemies they could all keep from making, and none of them wanted Sheldon or his studio brass angry at them. That meant avoiding Sky. Sky was "a problem." No producer could afford to take the chance of hiring "a problem."

The press treated Sara's film with respect. In print Vail pronounced it "a carefully observed delineation of contemporary relationships." *Winter Wheat* was much more successful in Europe. But by the time Reed and Chiaro had each sent her clippings from Europe, Sara was back in San Francisco: Lindy was in labor.

Edward Andrew Wyman was born in a mental health institution just before midnight in February of 1972. He was named for his grandfather and for Lindy's doctor, of whom she had become fond. Eddie had curly blond hair and slate blue eyes. And he had no fingers on his left hand.

"Why?" Sky gasped when she heard. They were sitting in the hospital's visiting room.

"There isn't any reason except birth defect," Vail said.

"Cool it."

"I love him even more because of it," Lindy said. "He's never going to feel that he's not whole. I don't want any of you pampering him because of his hand." Patsy was holding Eddie in her arms as Vail, Sara, and Sky looked on.

"Right," Vail said, staunchly. "What else is new?"

"Not much in this joint," Lindy replied. "Go to therapy. Go to class—they have art classes here. Do my work—I'm assigned to the office, where I type things. And I nurse Eddie." She looked at him lovingly.

Sara was thinking how quickly people adapt to circumstances. Here they all were, visiting her daughter—confined to a mental hospital for shooting her lover—and cooing over her baby, the product of that ill-starred affair. Here was Sky, watching her career being swallowed up in a welter of attorneys, briefs, and expert witnesses, behaving like a proud grandmother to little one-handed Edward. And here was she, mother of the daughter who killed, pouring out the coffee, joking with Patsy, and looking forward to the trip back to Europe as if the time spent over here had been a vacation instead of the emotional vise it was.

"Has Diana been here?" Sky asked.

"Oh, yes, she comes about once a week." Lindy looked at Sara. Sara had not seen Diana since the day of Vic's testimony.

Vail was playing his old role as mediator and interpreter between his sisters and his mother.

"You really must not leave without coming to some kind of terms with Mother," he said to Sara.

"You mean, forgive Mother for bribing my husband to leave me?"

"Ooooh," he said, "so bald."

"It's true."

"Let's not go into this now," Sky suggested nervously.

"She's old," Vail pressed on. "She could have a heart attack and die. And then what?"

"Trust me. She won't die while Nixon's in office," Sara said.

Lindy did not want to ignore Sara. Her doctor had told her that one of the ways she would get well would be to accept Sara as a person. "When are you going back to Europe?" Lindy asked her.

"Soon. I'm not sure when, exactly," Sara said. Throughout the horror of the last months, Sara and Lindy had begun to shape a relationship with each other.

"You should get on with your work," Lindy said. "I want to see more of your movies. But I can't if you don't make them."

Sara had decided to go back to Italy. She'd done everything she could here for Lindy. And there was another reason to return.

Reed was in Europe. Carmen had sent Sara a note from a British gossip column which noted that the "well-known American director was last seen kissing Julie Christie in the

Connaught bar." On another occasion they were seen stroll-ing hand-in-hand in St. James's Park and lunching at Simp-son's-in-the-Strand for lunch. Reed's telephone calls to Sara had dropped off sharply. Sara was surprised at how un-happy the silly column made her feel.

"How's the suit coming, Sky?" Lindy asked.

"It's not. sometimes I think I'll never work again."

Everyone was worried about Sky. Her visits to Lindy had become less frequent, and she looked haggard. She had stopped trying to cover up the deep scar on her cheekbone.

"Any word yet on Lindy's next hearing?" Sky asked Patsy.

"Not yet," she replied. "Sometime next year." The hear-ing before the judge was to evaluate Lindy's progress and the length of her sentence, but there were no guarantees.

"Look how sweet-tempered Eddie is," Patsy said. She rose and pushed the gurgling baby into Vail's arms.

"I don't know how to do this!" he protested, balancing the baby like a sack of eggs in his hands.

"Hold his head!" Sara said. "Put your palm under his head."

"Somebody take this," he said, holding the baby out. No one moved.

"Let's have a cup of coffee, Patsy," Sky said with a trace of her old spirit. She looked at Lindy mischievously. "You want to come, Sara, Lindy?"

"Hey, wait! You can't leave!" Vail shouted. "What am I supposed to do with this?"

"This' has a name. It's Edward, just like yours. Deal with it," Patsy said, taking Lindy's arm. "I wish someone had a camera. We could get front-page space," she said to Lindy as they left the room. "Don't worry. He'll be real careful with Eddie."

—516—

43

"But there are lots of things you can do!" Kitty implored, exasperated and frightened. Two years had passed; it was the spring of 1974. "You can offer yourself for roles in Europe. You can start looking for plays. You can write a book—you write well. You can teach!"

Sky lay on the hammock strung between two trees in the side yard. Beside her, under a pillow, she had a bottle of brandy and a collapsible silver cup. It was a brutally hot day in Los Angeles. The smog sat on the city like a lid, pressing down indifferently.

Sky didn't have any idea where Mel was in her suit against Pitcher or where Pitcher and the studio were in their suit against her. She had no work, so wherever they were, the result for her was the same. Unable to sustain the taxing battle, and unable to rise above it to rebuild her career, she was suspended in a private purgatory.

Another link in the rancid and unhappy chain of events occurred when Valerie died in her sleep that spring. From the moment Sky had met her in wardrobe on her first day at the studio, Valerie had supplied Sky with the uncritical support of a mother—the kind of loving advice and admiration Sky had always wanted and never received from Diana.

Valerie's funeral marked the first time Sky had appeared in public in months. Her friends and longtime associates had been shocked to see her—pale as paper, her hand trembling slightly, too thin. Some friends thought the look in her eyes was one of tremendous surrender. Ace had been especially furious. He'd spent the last year on location, and had come in from Hawaii for Valerie's funeral.

"How could you let her go out like that?" he demanded of Kitty after the funeral. Sky had looked like an ethereal caricature of herself.

"Easily. She refused to call someone to do her hair, and she refused to do it herself."

Ace was a lean and good-looking man in his late forties.

"Shit. I'm sorry, Kitty. I know she's in a bad way. What can I do?"

"Talk her into working."

"But if no one out here will—"

"She can work on the stage. It might get her out of her self-pity. Or you can take her with you to Maui. Me, I'm going up to the reservation, where the action is." Kitty's elderly father was building a house on the Fort Belknap Reservation, where the Assiniboins and some of the Sioux shared a slice of government-administered parsimony.

"How long are you going for?" he had asked, upset.

"Oh, not long, relax. I can't be away from Sky, no matter what kinda shit she's pulling, you know that."

"Why don't you take her with you?"

"Up there among all those drinkers?" Kitty had replied.

"Up there with all that fresh air and all those good people."

Now the events of the last year were racing through Kitty's head as she stared at her best friend lying in the hammock, slightly drunk. She knelt down beside her. "Sky, honey, don't do this to yourself."

"Leave me alone," Sky groaned, distinctly. "I just want to be left alone and watch the fleecy white clouds in the sky." The meaninglessness of her life as a commercial actress in the movies had caught up with her.

Kitty wanted to slap her. She hadn't done anything except mope around and drink.

"There are no clouds in the sky," Kitty said.

"There are over this Sky," she said, giggling.

Kitty started to cry. She put her head down on the edge

of the hammock and wept. Sky's hand fell heavily on Kitty's head. "Don't waste your tears, babe. I got nowhere to go but down."

"You're already down as far as you can go."

"Then you don't know the Wymans," Sky said. "Watch me."

Kitty got up and stumbled back into the house. The doorbell rang. She wiped her tears away. When she opened the door, there stood Patrick.

"I'm real sorry to disturb you," he said softly. He had an infected scratch on his cheek. "Can I see Sky?"

"She's not here, Patrick." What a pair, Kitty thought.

"I gotta see her! I know she's here!"

"Damn you, she's not! Leave her alone!" Kitty stabbed her fist into her jeans pocket and brought out twenty dollars. "Here. Now get lost. Sky's got problems, too."

He took the money. "Sky," he mumbled. "She doesn't know what problems are, the selfish bitch." He was halfway down the stairs when he turned. "You know Sky and I were going to get married," he said plaintively. "If things had worked out, I'd be living in this house instead of you." His lips curled up in something resembling a smile. Kitty shut the door and went back into the house to find Mrs. Sho.

"Mrs. Sho!" Kitty called, standing in the doorway to the study where the air conditioner was going full blast. Mrs. Sho was lying on the sofa reading Kurt Vonnegut's new novel. "I'm going to take Sky up to my pop's."

"Good idea," Mrs. Sho said, barely looking up from her book. "Think she'll go?"

"Can you think of anything else?"

Mrs. Sho put her book down. "Call Vail and Sara. Enlist them. Then go up to Montana."

Montana means mountain country—high granite peaks, lakes like sapphires, green forests. Massive beauty. Once the grass had been high and had fed the buffalo; now it was short and fed the cattle.

The reservation was in the high plains where the regal Blackfoot, Sioux, and Crow used to fight over adjoining territory, and where a million beavers used to be trapped each year by the Astor Company franchisers. Pop High-tower, Kitty's father, was tall, lean, gnarled, and taciturn. He wore faded jeans, water-stained cowboy hats, and checked shirts. The foundation of his house had been laid in the lee of a small rise. Kitty and Sky stayed at Mrs. Wells' place, a shingle-and-stone house. It had running water and a new washer-dryer set, but no electricity.

At first Sky just sat at the kitchen table drinking coffee with Mrs. Wells. Then she started to take walks, on which she looked around at the ragged homes dropped by national disinterest and guilt into the gemlike mountain land. Poverty and beauty were cellmates here. No one cared who Sky was or what she'd done before: What could she do *now*? Could she cook? Could she sew? Could she cut wood or refill the kerosene lamps? Could she lay a floor or drive a pickup?

"I'm not going to make it here," Sky said to Kitty one night. But for Kitty's sake, she tried. She hauled water and chopped wood and hefted sacks of cement. She worked every day, but she knew that only another picture would save her.

Sky and Kitty returned from Montana, stopping off first in San Francisco to see Lindy. A revived Sara, just back from Italy, was there. She told them that Marco, her old friend who had been her first director in Rome, was producing a new picture, and he wanted Sara to direct it.

They had all spent the day with Lindy and with two-year-old Eddie. Later, in Sky's hotel suite, Kitty asked, "What's the picture about?"

"Two women working in the Italian underground who escape the Nazis in 1944," Sara replied. "Based on a true story. It's called *Torino Express*."

"That doesn't sound very commercial," Sky commented.

"People don't think that two women can carry an adventure film."

"Oh, Sky, those old attitudes are changing," Sara said.

"Those old attitudes never change," Sky said.

"Where's the money coming from?" Kitty asked.

"France, mainly. Italy, too. I'm over here to ask Ernie if he'd do the photography." Carmen had agreed to be her assistant director. Sara felt high with the possibilities. "Marco's talking about getting Alida Valli."

"Oh, she's wonderful," Kitty said. "You got a copy of the script? I could use some reading that would improve me."

"Isn't Alida Valli a little old?" Sky asked. "She must be fifty."

"But that's fine," Sara said.

When Sky excused herself and left the room, Sara said, "I take it Montana didn't agree with her."

"It wasn't that," Kitty said. "She worked like a Trojan, and I think that was good for her. But only a picture will cure her. Everything left her life at once—Lindy, her career, Valerie."

"But I thought that thing with Pitcher was over. Isn't the suit settled?"

"Sure, but people don't know what to believe about Sky. Did she wreck Pitcher's movie? Didn't she? They'd rather play it safe and get someone else."

"I'm sorry. I didn't realize."

"Her career's stalemated. I'm afraid for her."

That night, after both Kitty and Sky had read the script, Sky said, "It's a minefield of a picture. It would explode in my face if I did it." The lead had no glamour. It was totally unlike anything she'd ever done.

But Kitty said, "You're crazy if you don't ask her for it."

"I don't want Sara to direct me," Sky said. "I don't trust her as a director."

"Don't you remember Winter Wheat? It was a beautiful little film. If you don't go after this one, you might not make another picture."

The next afternoon Sky met Sara outside the mental hospital. "Can we go somewhere?"

"I only have a couple of hours before my flight," Sara said.

"So what? Can't we go somewhere?" Sky demanded. They ended up in a coffee shop. "I read your script last night."

Sara was sorting through her bag for her passport. "Did you like it?"

"Yes. I want to—well, would you consider me for Salvina's role?" she asked, referring to the Italian American part.

"Marco's already asking Valli! Why would you—"

"I need a role desperately," Sky said. "You know that. I have to prove that I can work again—to myself as well as to the industry."

"But Sky—"

"I don't take pills anymore, and I can stay off brandy. I'm still a good actress—"

"Oh, you don't have to—"

"I'll do anything if you'll give me this part!"

"It's not mine to give, Sky," Sara said, lowering her voice. The steamy little coffee shop was very small, but Sky seemed unaware that she could be heard, that heads were turning.

"C'mon, Marco wanted you to direct this, right? He'll listen to you about casting."

"Sky, I just can't—" She was embarrassed. Not only was her gifted sister begging her for a part, but people were staring, and she knew that some of them recognized Sky.

"Sara, I'm pleading with you."

"Oh, please, don't—" Sara whispered.

"Help me. I only need one chance. Please give it to me." Sara looked at Sky. "Why should I?"

"Because I never meant to hurt you. Be honest; you didn't really want to be a mother. I did. I loved Lindy from that first moment I saw her." Sky glanced around the hermetic coffee shop. "Whether you approve of the way it was done or not, I was there and willing when you needed a place for Lindy. I loved her and fed her and educated her, and I would do the same for Eddie if it came to that."

Sara looked at her sister, at the thready wrinkles on her brow and around her eyes. She felt resigned, almost peaceful. Between them, it was more than Lindy. "It's you and "me," she whispered, knowing with an iron certainty that she could never refuse to help Sky, just as Sky could never ignore Sara's pleas for help. "You're more important to me than anyone, except Vail." It was the three of them; it always came down to that.

In Rome the weather was hot and humid. Marco and Sara were walking down a tree-lined street next to the Tiber. An imperfectly played Chopin polonaise drifted out of a high window.

"But Marco, since Alida Valli isn't free to do the role, why can't we think of Sky?" Sara was saying.

Marco's hair was thinning, but his expressive eyes and his dynamic energy were unchanged. "I have loved you like a good friend," Marco said. "We discuss this a lot since your return. But this I cannot do."

"Don't just say that! Sky would be riveting in this part."

"That is not the issue," he said. He knew Sara to be brave; she had weathered many battles. If she said she wanted Sky in the part, then he trusted her ability to make it work. But this was different. "Listen to me. We are still looking for the rest of the backing. Putting Sky in the picture will make it much harder to raise what we need."

"Sure, in the States, but here she—"

"No, not even here. I have checked—"

"Oh, Christ!"

"I am sorry."

"But there must be a way around that, Marco."

He laughed. "Sara, be sensible. We need a million dollars." Sara stopped walking. "If you have it in your pocket, we will go ahead." He threw back his head and laughed again. "Do not worry. There are other fine actresses—"

"Marco. Sky will waive her fee. So will I. Let me try to get the rest."

"You are pazzo."

Sara caught up with Vail in the lobby of the Algonquin Hotel in New York City. It was an old shrine where the sharp cadences of crackling wit from writers and critics echoed around the dusty Georgian chairs and over the threadbare rugs. Staying at the Algonquin made Vail feel he was part of something larger than the present.

At forty-four, he looked at the peak of his form. He hadn't gained a pound or lost any hair, and his hazel eyes still twinkled and snapped to show that he was two steps ahead of everyone. He was wearing a smart suit that said "successful bicoastal critic" all over it. They settled into a Victorian love seat. Vail pressed the bell on the spindly table in front of them.

"The idea's ludicrous," he said, happily, grinning at her, his arms folded against his chest. "Sara Wyman directing Sky Wyman—it sounds like a stunt. I'm not saying it's not a generous idea—it is! But two women fighting off all the Nazis in Naples—please!"

"Spare me your cutting review," Sara said. She was irritated with him, but over the years, especially since Lindy's hearing, Vail and Sara had found a lasting friendship. "Help me raise a few hundred thousand." She disliked sitting out in the open like this with Vail; people were always coming up to him and talking about his reviews, his insight, his spleen, his enjoyment (and theirs) of his cut-and-slash techniques, which he had honed to a fine art.

An elderly waitress took their order for two sherries. When she'd left, Vail said: "Why did you agree? It's such a risk."

"Because of Lindy," Sara said. "She needs Sky back on her feet. Because of Sky—she's our sister. She's done a lot wrong, but never cruelly. Would you let *me* sink without a trace? If pressed, would Sky let either of us go? No, she wouldn't." A man passed them carrying a transistor radio from which Senator Ervin drawled a question to Bob Haldeman. The Watergate Hearings were in progress.

"But you directing Sky," he said, puzzled. "Can you get her to do what you want?"

"We'll see. It's a fine part for her."

"If you can't, your career goes down the tubes! You can't stand a failure either. Remember? What you follow the first success with is even more important. It proves you can do it! But you're risking your second picture on Sky, and she hasn't worked in years."

Sara nodded. "Vail, she begged me."

Vail stared at a flower arrangement. "Then I suggest you see Teddy."

"Teddy?" she repeated, startled.

"He's on his way to Hollywood to adapt one of his plays—he did five Broadway plays, you know." She knew. "His royalties alone must be astronomical. Someone out at Columbia has hired him to adapt *Sudden* for the screen."

"My play?"

"Of course, if Sky wasn't in limbo, Columbia would have asked her to play it. In fact," he said, taking his sherry from the waitress's little pewter tray, "I know they would have."

"Oh, poor Sky. She knew, didn't she?" Vail nodded and sipped his sherry.

"She doesn't have such a bad life, Sara. She's well off, and she's got Kitty. She sees Lindy every month, and she loves Eddie. Mother wrote me that Sky offered to take Eddie if the judge doesn't let Lindy out this time."

"You and Patsy should take him."

"Don't get started! That's all I get from Patsy." Vail polished off his sherry and lit a small cigar.

"At least he doesn't look like Arch," Sara said. "I think he looks like Dad's family," thank God."

"Reed will help on the money thing," Vail said.

"Yes. He was happy to do it. As were Kitty, Ace, Cage, and Ernie. But I haven't got enough."

"How about Mother?" he asked, slanting his long eyes toward her.

"I won't ask her."

Vail smoothed his tie. A tall, thin man who spoke very fast in abbreviated sentences came over to their table and said how much he enjoyed Vail's reviews. "Literature," he called them. After he left, Vail said, "Stage director." He started rooting around in his jacket, which was flung across the love seat. "Here," he said, with a trace of embarrassment, "I thought you'd like this."

She unwrapped the gift. It was a review copy of his first book: the collected wisdom—in print—of Edward Vail Wyman.

"That's wonderful!" she exclaimed. "Aren't you proud?"

He peered at her quizzically. "I'm not sure how I feel. It was Patsy's idea to make a book out of them," he added, pleased.

Sara put off meeting with Teddy. The prospect unnerved her yet tantalized her, too. She hadn't seen him for more than ten years. Teddy had once occupied 150 percent of her thoughts; now she thought of him only when she heard some sixties music, like "Moon River," or when she read press reports on him.

But as her stay in New York lengthened, as she found herself walking on the blocks she and Teddy had known so well, as she passed the Circle in The Square Theater, she knew she had to face him—for herself much more than for Sky.

Teddy was still living in the Village. She found him at the White Horse, propping up the bar. He looked older and had a slight paunch, but seemed essentially unchanged until she got close: There was fear in his eyes.

"I was surprised to hear from you," he said, leading the way across the room to a table and chairs. "Have you had a nice life?" He giggled, which didn't sound quite as charming as it had when he'd been twenty.

"Varied and interesting" would summarize it." They sat down.

"Where did we leave off?" he asked, waving toward the bar. A waiter came over. "Paul, this is one of my wives. I think she drinks wine."

"One of your wives?" Sara asked when Paul had left.

"We weren't married, as I remember."

"Oh! That's right!" he said, happily. "I always *felt* we were married."

"How about your other wives?"

"Marissa was a brief marriage, I am proud to say. Then there was Sally, and finally Ann. Thank God one doesn't have to marry now to have a relationship."

"One didn't have to then," she said. There was gray in his hair. He was wearing a well-clipped beard and mustache that gave him a precise look. "Do you have children?"

"Yes. Several." He changed the subject quickly. "I suppose you heard that *Elephant House* was a big hit with Bancroft," he said. "She was good, too, though not quite what I had in mind." *Elephant House* had been followed by four other plays, not such big hits. "I'm one of the oldest angry playwrights still living in America," he said.

"You are certainly one of the most successful."

"Sara!"

She looked up. A man about fifty pounds overweight, sporting a wild blond beard and wired with nervous energy, was making his way toward them.

"You remember Bertie," Teddy said, saving her. "Bertie's a character actor in television."

Bertie kissed her cheek but didn't sit down. "I'm off for a casting call. I closed up a sitcom just last week, and I'm back on the streets again."

"What ever happened to Annie Mehan?" Sara asked, seeking conversation.

"Annie Mehan! Don't you know?" Bertie yelped with exaggerated surprise. "She's one of the biggest comedy actresses in television. Plays an amateur detective. She's very funny." Sara tried to picture Annie being funny. "I saw the film you directed—*Winter Wheat?* Mighty impressive!" His pale blue eyes glowed. A moment later, he was gone.

"Yes, that movie of yours was good, m'dear," Teddy said. "I couldn't have done it."

"What ever happened to everyone else we went to school with?" she asked.

"Well, Dirk died of leukemia. John's a speech teacher and very hostile about it. GW's retired and spending his money on Off-Off-Broadway flops. Georgie, I'll bet you want to know about Georgie. He married one of his students and moved to the Midwest and was never heard from again."

"And Irene?" she asked.

"Poor old Irene. She got arthritis bad. She's living in some home for old actresses on Long Island. Can you imagine what they all talk about out there?"

Sara could still see Irene serving her giant martinis. She felt sad. "That's how it's going to be, I guess, for all of us."

"I'm on my way to Hollywood, I expect you've heard. Screenwriting." He nattered on, leaving the painful memory of Irene behind. "Maybe I'll write an original screenplay after I do *Sudden*." He glanced quickly up at her. *"Sudden* was always my favorite." Sitting with him, she had the nutty feeling that if she walked outside, she'd see a brand new set of 1960 cars honking along Seventh to Eddie Cochran songs, and that *Bye Bye Birdie* and *The Best Man* would be playing up on Broadway. She was glad to see that he wasn't living on the pavements somewhere, or inside a straitjacket at Bellevue.

Teddy was looking at her.

"I'm sorry," he said. "About all the pain I gave you. I suppose it was pain. Maybe it wasn't."

"It was hell, Teddy," she said, suddenly drenched in emotional memories.

He screwed his face up. "I didn't think it was that bad."

She looked away. She still cared about him in a small space deep inside. "Yes, it was. I loved you desperately." She began to think about what might have been and veered away from that dangerous and threatening bog. "Teddy, I'm trying to put a film together with Sky."

"Yup, Vail told me when I ran into him yesterday. Now *there's* someone who's cleaned up his act. He's a good reviewer, now that he isn't such a cad. Jesus, he would crucify people when he started out."

"That's how he got popular."

Teddy was reaching into his pocket. "I had this crook who does my taxes and things make out a check for you. If you run out, let me know. There's more." He handed her the folded check.

It was for a hundred thousand dollars. She looked up at him and caught him staring at her with that half-smile cocked on his face. "Thank you, Teddy." For a moment, she could see a trace of the sweet youth she'd fallen in love with so many years ago.

—528—

44

In 1975 *Torino Express* chugged into production.

Sara's art director was a middle-aged man with wispy hair and a soft voice. He had designed sets all over European sound stages for twenty years. His name was Pierre Morielle, and his hobby was breeding rare tropical fish. She asked him to design a miniature of each set, which she took back to her apartment to study. Little balls of paper represented the actors, and she moved them around to prepare for the next day's shooting.

"Here's the plan," Sara said nervously when she had her cast and crew assembled. Sky sat on a couch in Sara's apartment, her chin in her hands; Ernie was on one side of her, Ace on another. Marco, the producer, sat in a commanding ladder chair in a corner; Guido, who was playing Sky's occasional lover in the film, lounged on a rug, smoking cigarettes. Maria Cortelli, a friend of Carmen's from Naples, was playing the role of the younger woman; she was buxom, cheerful, and vibrant. Sara hoped Maria would make a good contrast to Sky's cooler, more interior acting style.

"We'll start on Stage 9 at Cinecittà for the apartment sequences," Sara said. "The winter sequences in the graveyard are going to be shot in an ice plant downtown."

"What fun," Guido remarked lazily.

"This is where I came in," Sky said. "I've already shot in one of those. It was sheer hell." Everyone looked at her. Sky had brought a grumpy, show-me attitude to the meeting.

"I remember," Sara said, lightly. "That's what gave me the idea. You'll have fur-lined clothing. Pierre's designed a set that will fit right into it."

"Into the icehouse?" Guido asked.

"It's a big place," Sara said, already completely visualizing the graveyard set—sinister and offbeat with Ernie's early-morning light effects. "Then we go up to Torino for the train sequences. We've got a train set out on a spare branch line beside an abandoned prewar railroad station. It's perfect." No train would ever be "perfect" for Sky again, since her accident. Her gloom deepened.

Everything went wrong their first week on the apartment set on Stage 9. Sara wanted soft, low-key lighting in the apartment where so much action between the women took place. But the lighting had to vary according to the time of day and the mood of the scene and according to the increased danger of the characters' situation.

But Pierre had unaccountably built an apartment set so solid and realistic that they couldn't take the walls out.

"So what are you telling me?" Sara asked him on the first run-through. "That I have to shoot into some rooms through the windows? I don't want to shoot through windows! I might as well have used a real house!" Unlike her first production, this one seemed completely out of control. "If we're using a studio set of an apartment, Pierre," she said, "why can't it be pliable enough to take walls out so I can get around in it?"

But she was stuck with it and she knew it. Ernie solved part of the problem by putting the camera on a small dolly and making it a mobile unit inside the set. "I want the light to come from the correct source," Sara told him. "Let's not cheat unless we have to. I want this to look truthful, lifelike, and scary at all times."

Something was off from the very beginning, but Sara couldn't put her finger on it. She tried telling as many bad jokes as she could remember to put everyone at ease, but unrest—discord yet to happen—hung in the air.

As an actor Sky knew all the tricks of the trade—the perfect fabrication of emotion through technique. But when Ernie's camera came in for a close-up, she knew if the real emotion wasn't there, the close-up would reveal her deception. But Sara hadn't begged her to play this role; Sky had talked her way into it. For this reason Sky demanded more of herself and became more self-critical. She wanted deeper, more penetrating emotions, but she couldn't let them control her or her performance would be phony, even ludicrous. She had always relied on her instinct to get the balance between these two extremes. But her instincts were rusty. She was frightened.

Sara watched Sky battling self-doubt but Sara was a captive of her own fears. If the picture didn't work Sky would be criticized, yes, but it would be said that Sara had not been able to handle her, that Sara had lost control of her own picture.

"Cage, less makeup!" Sara called out on the set. "Ace, let her hair fall naturally. It's the Allied invasion of Italy. The beauty salons are not making appointments!" Sky fought her. Sara prevailed.

Word got around the other stages at Cinecittà that Sky was acting in Sara's picture. Soon American, British, French, and Italian actors and crews were stopping by the "Torino" set. They had a great residue of feeling for Sky, a mixture of respect, affection, awe, and sorrow.

At first Sara was tempted to close the set, but then she realized that the constantly shifting audience was having an effect on Sky. When they applauded a scene spontaneously or stopped to chat with her between takes, Sky came alive. When no one was there, Sky's work was mechanical.

"I want another take," Sky announced after a scene that involved a lot of tricky camera movement.

"Sky, it was fine," Sara said.

"No, it didn't feel right."

"It will take hours to do it again—"

"I don't care! I want another take," Sky yelled. Suddenly Sara realized that Sky was afraid her public wouldn't accept her in a dark, naturalistic picture so antithetical to the Hollywood star vehicles she'd acted in for so long. She was afraid she would look silly or misused or ugly.

"Lunch," Sara called out. She whispered something to Ernie, then said to Sky, "Let's walk."

"Let's not," Sky said. She strode off to her dressing room. Sara followed her.

"You're trying to second-guess every shot, and I won't have it. Either you trust me or you don't."

"I'm trying to, but directing isn't something you just pick up like a hand of cards and play. You don't have a lot of experience."

"You're just scared that this movie won't bring back your career. You're scared because your instincts are off, and you think I can't rescue you. Sky, I'm telling you, no director can rescue you. All you're doing now is demoralizing everyone. You either do the work here and agree to my concept of the picture or you walk."

"Then I walk."

"You can't do this!" Sara screamed.

"I don't want to, but I'm not going to be made a fool! You're lighting me so bad, I look like a witch! You don't let Ace do what he knows best, and how about Cage?"

"How about giving me some real emotion out there? Then no one would care what you look like!"

Angry and frustrated, Sara canceled the shoot for the rest of the day. She found Ernie in the studio restaurant behind the bar. "Ernie, I need your help," Sara said as she sat down at his table. After she'd told him the news, she said, "It's a matter of trust in me and trust in her own instincts."

Ernie sighed. He was a shy man, not given to demonstrative feelings or declarations. "I don't know what I can do."

"Tell her what you think of her in this picture, and I don't want to be there. It's the last stand."

"Don't you want to know what I think now?"

"No. I think I already know."

They went back to the sound stage. Sky was taking off her makeup.

"Sky, Sara's asked me to tell you what I think of your performance, and I offered to tell her before we came here, but she wouldn't let me." He sat down on a folding chair and touched her shoulder. She stopped snatching at tissues and looked at him in the mirror. "We've done about—what?— ten pictures together? Twelve?" Sky nodded, wary. "All I can tell you," he said, "is that you never looked better through the lens. You *have* looked more beautiful."

—532—

"I'm a wreck. I shouldn't have even tried this."

"But never *better*."

"Don't horseshit me, Ernie."

"I'm not. This picture may open up a whole new career for you."

"No one in Hollywood believes I can hack it anymore, and they're right," she said, pressing a tissue to her eyes.

"That's because they don't have a tough no-nonsense script like this for you." Ernie smiled at her.

"I've lost it, Ernie," Sky said. "I can't feel the part."

"You're not concentrating, Sky," he said.

"You're crazy, Ernie. I'm concentrating my brains out."

"Do you think I'm lying?" he asked, laying it out.

"No."

"Okay then."

"Okay," Sky said softly.

The next day on the set, Sky dove into her part as though the previous week had been a rehearsal. When Sky made up her mind, she gave her all. She became fiercely committed to the picture and never looked back.

Maria, much younger, was in awe of Sky. She watched her work carefully. During one scene, Sky dramatically paused before saying the last line. It was a pause which went on a beat longer than anyone expected, yet when the line came, the pause felt just right. "We will have to meet in other lives," Sky's line went. She put a sob like a faint exclamation point at the end of the sentence.

Maria cataloged these techniques diligently. In a later scene, she managed to incorporate an overly long pause between two of her lines and ended her last line with a short sob.

"Cut," Sara said. She and Sky exchanged a look.

"Won't you come to my dressing room and have a drink, Maria?" Sky said to her.

Maria was thrilled. Sky must have noticed her additions to the scene and liked them! She entered Sky's dressing room, her heart pounding.

"You know that line where you paused?" Sky asked her. She was seated at her dressing table, running an emery board around her nails.

"Yes, yes," Maria said, tingling.

"I think only one of us should pause," Sky said dolorously.

Maria's heart stopped. She had offended Sky Wyman. She didn't know what to say. Sky poured her a glass of wine, took a fresh white linen napkin from a drawer, and brushed an invisible grain of dust from her costume. "And about that sob you put at the end of the line," Sky said, handing Maria her glass.

"Yes, I thought the character—" Maria said, breathlessly. Sky shook her head mournfully. "I think not."

They were five days behind schedule when Sara moved the production to the icehouse. Sara got her white clouds of breath on film, just the way she wanted, but at a price. Cast and crew were freezing even in the fur-lined, leather-covered suits they wore under their costumes. The brandy Carmen freely doled out made everyone slightly looped for the duration. The real problem, however, was the lights: They shattered in the cold.

Next, the production moved up to Torino in northern Italy, where they shot at first on the streets and then on a bridge with shimmering lights and fog. By the time they started shooting on the little spare branch line for the all-important train sequences, they were nine days behind schedule. But Sara and Sky were working as if this were their tenth, not their first, picture together.

The little station had been built around the turn of the century. Pierre had had it repainted and repaired.

"I think I want to get rid of the clouds," Sara said, looking up at the sky. Ernie was busy inside the railroad compartment, balancing the light from interior to exterior for the window shot.

"Sky," Sara said, "this is the scene—it's the last time you see Maria alive. And in a way you know it . . ." Sky nodded dreamily.

The atmosphere on the shoot had taken a jovial turn, with much lighthearted joking around—a contrast to the scene Sky had to play now. As the gaffers and grips crawled around the train, as the extras played cards and drank coffee, as Ernie shouted for his lights, and as Sara ran this way and that, Sky sat inside the carriage facing Maria, burrowing into herself. She shut out everything around her, isolating herself for the tears she needed to summon. Sky rummaged inside herself, seeking a well of emotions she hadn't tapped for years. Distantly, she heard Sara call "Action!" Sky swung out, sailing into that uncharted, horizonless landscape of the heart.

"Cut!" Sara called. The small cluster of people around the train applauded. Sara bounded over to Sky and kissed her tear-stained cheek.

"Come along," Reed said, putting a coat around Sara's shoulders. She had struck the "Torino" shoot; cast and crew were heading back to Rome by train or by car for the final scenes on the Cinecittà sound stage.

"Where are we going?" Sara was annoyed. "I've got a million things to do!" She was frazzled, exhausted, and insecure about what she had on film.

"I am taking you to the train south," he said calmly. "Aren't you glad to see me?" He bundled her into a cab.

"Of course," she said, smiling. "I'm just harried. I don't know what's wrong with this shoot. It goes from the extraordinary—mainly because of Sky and Ernie and Marco—he's just wonderful—to the absurd, mainly because of Sky and Pierre. I don't seem to have a grip on it. They're going to murder me in the press." She was sitting bolt upright. "I'm dreading the rushes. It has got to look like we're really back in the forties in the German occupation and there's menace around every ordinary corner." She leaned back a little. "And Sky in that train, saying goodbye to Maria, not knowing if she'll ever see her again, fearing she won't, and finally admitting how dear the woman is to her—God!" She squirmed around. "Have you seen Lindy?"

"Oh, yes. She's fine—considering. You'll have to be patient." Reed had been back in America for the last six months. "Her doctors have good reports, and she may very well get another hearing before the judge—but not for a few months."

Sara's face fell. She bit her lips and looked out the window of the moving taxi. The arcaded sidewalks of Torino slipped past. "I just want her to be well, to get another chance at bat."

"What you need is a fine dinner in a dining car, and a long rest in a private first-class compartment."

She glanced at him suspiciously. "Is Julie Christie on this train?"

"No," he said, smiling.

"Are there going to be people from my movie on this train?"

"Nope!" he replied airily.

"Thank God." She closed her eyes.

When Sara had started preproduction on *Torino Express*, she had met Reed in Rome as he was on his way back to America. "Just pretend I don't exist," Sara had said to him. He knew what she meant. Directing or producing a film was like being on a long, mad boat ride far out to sea, trapped with people who showed themselves to be better—or far worse—than first meetings could predict.

In the last year, the pace of Reed's life had become frenetic. Quite abruptly, he had stopped working; he refused every offer and retired to his house in Los Angeles. He had been in the trenches too long.

He decided to do the garden over and plunged into the task with a Japanese gardener. The planting of the plum and almond trees and crape maple, and the landscaping of the rock garden, gave him time to contemplate his mood but did not provide him with the solutions he sought. To a man half his age, Reed's options would have seemed unlimited; but to an insider in his early fifties, his options seemed few. He wanted to change his life but knew he couldn't change it too much: He could continue to produce and direct; he could start his own independent production company, an option that fatigued him just thinking about it; or he could become a studio executive and join the ranks of the enemy—no option at all. Or he could quit the business entirely.

He thought a lot about Sara, about their mutual reluctance to surrender to intimacy despite their growing bond of friendship and camaraderie. He thought about working with her again. He saw all the cities he'd worked in—London, Rome, Paris, Trieste, Hollywood and a dozen other American sites—roll past the inner screen of his memory. He remembered shooting at Pinewood, the studio just outside London where acting was an honored profession. He thought about Pinewood's beautiful old dining room for the

—536—

casts and crews, with a bar, no less, an appendage unheard of in Hollywood. Pinewood was a much saner atmosphere in which to work. He cataloged the four films he was proud of out of the twenty-six forgettable ones he'd directed.

As the trucks dragged away an old sycamore tree or rolled into the garden with more ground cover, he realized he wasn't tired or bored or disillusioned. He wanted something different. He couldn't shake his vague discontentment. Sometimes it is the most simple, obvious aspect of a life that is off balance or out of focus. Slowly, Reed recognized what he wanted. He brought the re-creation of the garden to a halt and booked a flight to Europe. He ended up in Positano in southern Italy, where blankets of bougainvillea tumbled from the balconies of homes that clung to the jagged cliffs above the sea. When his sabbatical in Positano ended, he just had time to fly to Torino.

45

The train nuzzled into the station like a silky, sleepy snake and hissed to a stop. Railway workers shouted back and forth in Italian as Sara and Reed boarded the daily luxury express that would carry them straight to Rome.

"This is great, Reed." She was delighted as the porter showed them into the first-class double compartment.

Later, as the train pulled out of Genoa, starting the coast route south to Rome, Sara and Reed were sitting at a table looking out over the high cliffs that shot down to the sea. It was sunset, and the water glowed with a burnished blue. Nervously touching the real rose that peeped out of a vase fastened to the table, Sara talked about her production—about how she wanted Maria's hair to flow out from her head underwater in a certain way, about how she wanted the scene to play when Sky learns the name of their betrayer, about how she wanted a dolly shot to look in the scene where Sky escapes Gestapo headquarters.

Reed listened with half an ear, the glow of the sunset on one side of them, the soft interior light of the dining car on the other; the tinkle of glassware and silver blended with the metallic click-clack of the train on its tracks. What if he'd done everything only to hear her say no? She had, after all, never expressed any need for any of it. He watched passengers regarding her as they entered the car. She'd done her hair up on the crown of her head, which accentuated her long sultry eyes under her bronze brows. When she talked, her whole face lit up.

"Sara," he said gently, interrupting. "Shut up. Your movie's fine."

"I'm not so sure," she said, misinterpreting his comment as an introduction to a new turn in the conversation. "Sky's uneven and I can't tell—"

"Intermission!" He hunched toward her, commanding her attention. "Do you recognize me?"

"How silly of you."

"Who am I?"

"Reed Corbett, director-producer. You're riding on a—"

"Look into my eyes," he said.

Reed's eyes always looked as if he knew the secret of life but wasn't sure anyone would believe him if he told them.

The waiter arrived and Reed cursed his wretched timing. They ordered, Sara taking an interminable amount of time to decide between fish and beef. Hastily, he ordered a bottle of white wine. The waiter left.

"If I ask Ernie to move the camera to Sky's point of view in that—"

"Hush," he commanded. "You were looking into my eyes."

"Right," she drawled, adjusting her napkin while reaching for a roll.

"Sara, marry me."

She stopped moving. "M-marry you?" she stuttered. "Oh, no." She put her elbow on the table and her chin in her hand. "Marry you?" she asked again, frowning. "Why on earth should we do that?"

"Because I love you and you love me. Admit it."

"I don't love you," she said. She took her chin out of her hand. "We like each other. You've been gardening too long."

"Yes, we do like each other," he agreed, his mobile mouth moving upward, the lines around his eyes crinkling. "That's the beauty of it. We also love each other. Admit it."

"Well, as a favor to you I might marry you, I mean,' if you feel strongly about it—" She glanced at him, smiling slyly. "But Reed, I think this is very hasty of you. No, I'm not going to marry you."

The waiter returned. "Oh, would you just leave us alone for a moment?" Reed asked him.

The waiter, baffled, backed off. "Leave the wine," said Sara. He did so and then went off again.

"First of all," Sara said, "thank you very much for—"

"Please don't organize this," he said. "Just marry me."

Sara felt little prickles inside her nose and throat. "My God," she said, as her eyes filled with tears. She floundered around in her pockets and purse, hunting for a hankie. He pulled one out of his pocket and handed it to her. She blew her nose, but her eyes were overflowing. A clutch of waiters at the end of the section stared at them.

"Will you?" he asked again.

"I've got to get out of here," she said, rising and lurching into a waiter as the train went around a bend. She was making for the door.

Reed jumped up. "We'll be back," he said to the waiter. "Keep the wine chilled."

She was one car ahead of him on her way back to their compartment. "Wait up!" he yelled. She paid no attention. She flung doors open and fairly raced through cars. Heads swiveled as she dashed past. Reed followed grimly.

At last she pulled open the door of their adjoining compartments and flung herself inside. Reed dashed into the room and slammed the door behind him.

She was facing the window that looked out on the reddened, glowing sea. She whirled around. "I couldn't stay there another minute," she said, weeping, her voice shaking and heaving. "I've never been so happy in my life. I had to hold you!" She threw herself into his arms.

They locked the door, made love, lay in each other's arms a long time without speaking. At one point, Reed stirred. "I know you," he whispered softly, looking at her in the dim light. "I know you as I know myself. You are my other me. I know what you are feeling, and I know we belong together."

"Well, it's on a cliff—" Reed was saying.

"Isn't everything in Positano?" she laughed, pressing her cheek against his hand. They were sitting in the club car later that evening. Reed had just retrieved their bottle of wine from the steward.

"Almost. The beach is below it, down a long, long flight of steps. There are flowering vines climbing its walls. Oh, I love you, Sara," he whispered. "And almost every room overlooks the sea. The terrace is ideal for sunbathing."

"And when did you buy this madly beautiful house?" she asked, watching the way his mouth moved. The steward couldn't keep his eyes off them.

"About a week ago." He kissed her fingers. They couldn't stop touching each other. "My idea is—"

"Oh, I know. You want a bicontinental existence." She smiled broadly. "I've got to stop being so happy and start thinking of my movie!"

"Don't stop being happy," he said. "See, it came to me while I was doing the garden in L.A. that I wasn't doing it just for myself. It was for you. And once I recognized that—the rest followed."

"But why Positano?"

"You mentioned it once, and you had a special sound in your voice. Like it was unreachable, too perfect," he said. "Too good for you."

"I'm telling you, Sky," Sara yelled, "the advance press in Europe is amazingly good."

Sky was afraid to believe it. "The American press will murder us," she said. "Or they'll ignore us. I don't know which is worse."

"They're not going to ignore any film you make. You are beating the system." The telephone line crackled, and for a moment she thought their connection had been broken.

"We've got to get Vail cranked up," Sky said.

"I'll be over there in a week or so. There's quite a lot of babble about it here—I think it's awfully good," Sara said, trying to put Sky at ease.

"Do they like me?"

"Yes! Relax!"

Sky had returned from Europe to find a small cluster of fans in the street around the entrance to her "castle," just like the old days, she had quipped to Kitty.

—541—

"That bus that takes the tourists around has put us on their Home of the Stars map," Kitty said.

"I want to go riding!" Sky exclaimed. "First thing tomorrow morning, let's ride!" She squeezed Kitty around the waist with one arm.

But the next morning, she and Kitty were in a San Francisco hospital. Diana had had a heart attack. She lay in the bed like a pale figurine, her hands resting outside the white blanket, her face turned upward. "Put those pillows behind me, Vail, or crank up this platform," she said.

"The bed?"

"Yes. It feels like a platform."

Her voice was weaker, but it still had reserves of power embedded in it. Vail cranked up the bed. "Now over there on that table—hand me my mirror. And the powder."

"Mother, it's Sky outside, not your maker," Vail said.

"I'll just do this my way, if you don't mind, Vail." She extended a limp arm toward the table. He got her powder and mirror. After she had slowly and weakly adjusted her face, she asked for her bed jacket. He helped her put it on.

"Now," she said.

He opened the door. Sky entered. "Sky, dear," Diana Wyman said softly.

Sky took her mother's offered hand. "You gave us a big scare," she said.

"Then you scare easily. It's just a little nudge," Diana said.

Vail backed away and sat on the radiator cover. "Vail, turn that television set off," Diana commanded. "I don't know why they have those things in a sick person's room. Television is bad enough when you're well; it's repugnant when you're sick."

"You control the set, Mother, by that thing on your bed."

"Well, it gets buried; I can't find it," she said, her voice shaking impatiently. She was older now. Vail found the remote control and shut off the television.

"I want to see Sara," she said to Sky. "You can make her see me. I won't leave the hospital without seeing her."

"You're not leaving anyway, for a while," Vail said from his perch on the radiator. He fingered the light scar on his temple, the one Korea had given him.

—542—

"She's on her way," Sky replied. "I called her. She was dreadfully upset."

"Sara's always emotional. I guess she'll never get over it," Diana said.

The hospital reminded Sara of the night Ned had died. She rode up in the elevator thinking of her flight that night, also from Italy, and of her mother standing like a duchess in the waiting room, announcing his death. Too late. Now here she was again, riding these cold metal elevators, walking down frigid halls where metal wagons delivered dinners while people with mops roamed about swishing and cleaning. And yet, boiling emotions of birth and death shook the hospital's cold frames. People died here, people suffered, babies were born here. Why weren't hospitals, such crucial depots, more resonant of those major junctures in life—birth and death? She was wondering about this when she arrived at her mother's room.

Diana was sleeping. Sky and Vail had gone off to the cafeteria. "Mother," she said. Diana opened her eyes.

"I've been hoping you'd come," she said faintly. Her wrinkled, handsome face looked up at her daughter. "I had to tell you about Vic, just in case."

"You don't have—" Sara stopped. Of course she had to. "What, Mother?"

"I interfered in your life, and I'm sorry you are so upset about it—"

"I'm getting used to it." Sara sat down on the edge of the bed.

"But I'd do it again," Diana said. "You would have stayed years with him because you're stubborn, and your only hope was to get out. And look what you did when I got you out."

"I went to New York," Sara stated, not following.

"Yes! See? It wasn't until you eloped with that silly man that I realized how jealous you were of Sky." Sara said nothing. She had not seen her mother, or talked to her, since that day of Lindy's hearing.

Diana groaned. "Oh, I would have given anything if my mother had talked to me like I'm talking to you. To have had from her just a fraction of the concern I have for you." She looked up at Sara sharply. "You think I interfered too

—543—

much with my triplets, don't you?" Sara nodded. "You wouldn't if you'd grown up without a mother." She closed her eyes, then opened them. "That's all I have to say."

"That isn't enough! Don't you see? What you've done to Lindy is to repeat what your mother did to you!"

"You are a hard child, Sara Bay."

"And you are a hard mother."

Silence came into the room between them like a cold wind.

Three weeks later, Sky, Vail, and Sara were in Sky's screening room off her study. It was a comfortable room with leather furniture, pale blue walls, thick rugs. Sky had asked a few trusted friends: Ernie Ping, Ace, Cage, Mrs. Sho, Reed, and Mel.

The screen rolled out of the ceiling, and people settled into the big chairs or onto the couch, their faces lit by the screen's flickering lights and shadows.

Torito Express was a fast-paced film about courage, survival, and the payments betrayal exacts—in war, in death, and in peace, another kind of death. The film followed the two women—one a teacher, the other her student—from their initial distrust of each other, into their first frightening ordeal, which forces them to work together in the Underground, and on into their growing affection and trust for each other as their exploits become more dangerous. Then Guido's weak betrayal causes Maria's death, which she chooses in order to protect Sky. And then on into Sky's ultimate, though bitter, triumph.

A huge closeup of Sky came up on the screen; she was pressed against a stone wall, her head tilted up. The scar on her forehead and her cheek showed, and her eyes glittered as one of her hands came up into the frame to push back a lock of hair. She pushed herself off the wall and started walking down a deserted street. She shook her hair out as the camera panned with her. A car appeared and followed her slowly, the driver calling out to her. She shook her head, her back still toward the camera.

The angle changed as she reached the end of the street where a cadre of German soldiers waited. Behind them were the Germans' captors. They were not waiting for Sky but being marched toward her. She passed them in the middle of the street, without looking in their direction. The camera followed her, getting gradually higher as she walked determinedly forward, swinging her arms.

Sky turned the lights up in the screening room as the music came up and the last credits rolled. Everyone applauded, immediately rose, and, talking excitedly, started drifting out of the room toward the buffet and the bar.

"I've never seen anything like it!" Ace exclaimed. Sky repressed a smile. Ace always said that. When he didn't like a film, he said nothing.

There had been a lot of intra-industry gossip about *Torino Express*. Some of it had praised Sky and Sara; some of it had debunked the movie as a gesture on Sky's part to help Sara or on Sara's part to rescue Sky. In Europe, "Torino" was an artistic and controversial success. But there was still no American distribution.

Sky was wearing a silver lamé jumpsuit and a pair of large diamond earrings that flashed whenever she turned her head. She was afraid of the film: It might put the last nails in her career's coffin or it might make her a star again. As she listened to the warm congratulations of her friends, she pretended that the outcome wasn't important. She couldn't tell from their reactions what they thought. They all said they loved it.

Vail was stunned by the film. Sky had revealed herself so much that it made him feel he was a fake. Moreover, Sara was a fine director. Compared to their work, he thought his was a hopeless joke.

When the guests had left and only the family and Reed remained, Sky said: "This was a lousy idea. What did I *think* they would say about the film? Did I think they'd say what they really thought if they didn't like it?"

"You thought they'd tell you how good it was. Which they did," said Mrs. Sho. "And it is. It's got a good feeling at the end, too. Satisfying."

"Thank you, Mrs. Sho," Sara said. "Think you'd pay a couple of dollars to see it? How about Sky? You like her?"

"I sure do. Sky, I've seen every one of your movies, and

you've never seemed so real up there. Like a person, not a goddess." She took a cracker from the table and scraped some cheese across it. "You people can stay up if you want to, but this person's going to bed."

"Night, Mrs. Sho," they chorused as she left.

"Do you think I'd tell you it was good if I thought it was bad?" Reed asked.

"No," Sky admitted. "What *did* you think?"

"It's a raw, cold war that has trapped human beings," he said. "It's one of the best jobs you've ever done. You'll get some work from it."

Patsy had seen Vail warring with his emotions, and she knew the nature of the battle. She took his arm. "Let's go," she murmured.

"Don't you want to know what I think?" he asked his sisters.

"Vail," Patsy said. "Later."

"It's a copy of the Italian neorealism style of movies with none of their warmth," he said. Sara and Sky stared at him.

Patsy tugged on him. "No, Vail, let's go home."

"Sara's direction is pathetic and stiff. This whole room knew that you were trying to capitalize on a great star in her sunset years."

"Vail!" Sara whispered, stricken.

"No one would hire Sky," Reed said, "until Sara put this together. You even helped her do it. What the hell are you saying now?"

"Just because I helped doesn't mean I have to like the result," Vail said.

"You're being disgraceful, Vail," Patsy said.

Sky moved toward Kitty. "Would I have made this picture twenty years ago?" she asked her. "Am I lost or am I honest now?"

"This is the best thing you've ever done," Kitty said, glaring at Vail.

"C'mon, Vail," Sara said, "you don't think it's that bad, do you?"

"What do either of you really care?" He sat down heavily. "I'm sorry." His face was collapsing. Patsy rushed over to him. "It's good, it's very good. I hope you win awards and get work out of it, as Reed says. I wish I could have made it." His hands flew to his face, and he started to sob. "All my life I wanted to create, not sit on the sidelines and criticize or review."

It was an excruciating moment. Reed excused himself, knowing that Vail's embarrassment would be even more acute if he remained. Kitty left with him. Sara and Sky stared at each other.

"Oh, Vail," Sara said, sitting down on the floor beside him. "How selfish we've been all these years. We value your opinion. You've always been there for us—"

"Oh, I have not. Don't get maudlin." He wept.

"A lot of the time you've been there," Sky said. She stood nearby, gazing at him.

Vail's tears slowly subsided. Sara put her hand on his knee. "I never thought how hard it might have been for you sometimes," she said. "I was an insensitive pig."

Patsy, sitting on the arm of the chair, her arm around Vail's shoulders, took a handkerchief out of her pocket and gave it to him. "Here, honey."

Vail never did the expected, Sara was thinking. How lonely he must have been in the beginning when she and Sky were all wrapped up in their work, gaining applause, striving and battling. And, more recently, there'd been Vail's constant reminders to both of them about settling things with Diana. Had he left things unsaid and undone with Ned that made him so acutely aware now?

"Vail," Sara said, "it's not that I depend on your opinion of my work or need you to tell me if I've done something good or bad. It isn't that I want to rub your nose in it, either. But you—of everyone I know—always have the unusual comment—"

"Please," he said, looking at her and blowing his nose. "Just drop it. I'm sorry."

Strangely, Sky hovered near them and yet was distant from them. I do need people's opinions, she thought, before I know whether I'm good or not. That's the big difference between Sara and me now. In the instant that Vail said the film was bad, she had thought it was bad, too. Now she thought it was better.

"Vail," Sara said, "do you remember when we were small and traveling around Europe?" He nodded. He looked terribly sad. "And Mother found a drawing of a naked woman, I think it was. We had made a pact. If she or anyone accused one of us, we'd all take the blame. Remember?"

"Yes," he said.

"Shouldn't that also be true of the good things in life?"

Out in the kitchen, Kitty and Reed were leaning against the drainboard, drinking orange juice. "Tough," Reed was saying. "Tough on him. Never thought of it."

"It's Ned and Diana," Kitty said. "That man never once stuck up for his kids against her. And she kept up the pressure, the incessant goading. I understand why she does it, she really can't help it, but they have to forgive her or they won't be able to live with themselves."

"On the brighter side," Reed said, "Sky's going to have a good year, don't you think?"

"After Torino?" She pushed herself off the drainboard. "You bet!"

Reed and Sara stood in the front doorway. Vail and Patsy had left. "Lunch tomorrow," Sara said. "The six of us. We'll celebrate!"

Sky nodded. "I don't care what people say. If the critics kill me or if they praise me—and I don't mean Vail—I'm grateful to you, Sara."

Sara moved out to the porch, and Reed took her arm. She was anxious to leave, but Sky stopped her. "Why do you have to go? There are so many things to talk about."

"Oh, I can't talk about the picture anymore tonight," Sara said. "And I don't want to talk about Vail."

"No, I mean, about us," Sky said, "about you and me." She'd been thinking about the ways in which her fame had damaged Sara's life, and Lindy's. "Sara, please stay and talk, like we used to do."

"Tomorrow," Sara said. She kissed Sky's cheek and danced down the steps with Reed.

Sky watched their descent into the street.

46

Sara paused to look up at her sister, backlit against the hallway, her hand raised. Then the door closed. Reed tightened his grip on Sara's arm.

"I feel so sad about Vail," Sara said.

"Vail's got a big burden, honey."

"I never saw it before in quite the same light as tonight."

"Your movie's not perfect, you know that, but it's honest, and Vail's hue and cry all these years has been 'Honesty! Truth!'" Reed opened the car door. "I was a reference point for him with you and Sky." They got inside the car.

"Yeah," Sara said, leaning her head back against the seat. "He and I had a big fight about that once. It was always easy for him to trash what Sky was doing because 'Hollywood's never honest,' and what I was doing because—well, I certainly failed the 'honest' test for years."

"But I like Vail," Reed said as he started the car and drove off. Sara watched Beechwood Canyon fly by as they descended the hill to Franklin. She felt that she had a grip on her life. She looked forward to a long talk with Sky tomorrow. She had a lot to say about Lindy, and she thought Sky was ready to hear it.

"Success is all interior, isn't it?" she murmured to Reed.

"It doesn't have much to do with the outside trappings." She thought about the quiet joy of living from the inside out.

Sky was all keyed up. "I think I'll go for a walk," she said.

"It's after midnight," Kitty muttered, picking up some of the glasses and putting them on a tray.

"Yeah, I know, but I want to walk and think." Sky grabbed another tray and started picking up. "I want to think about the movie."

"I love that movie," Kitty said. "You looked like a woman of standards and strength up there." Sky smiled and kissed Kitty's hair. "You want company on your walk?"

Sky shook her head. They carried their trays out to the kitchen. "I won't be long," Sky said, "but don't wait up."

"You going to walk in your silver lamé jumpsuit?" Kitty asked, pointing to her.

"Sure. Why not?"

"Take a coat or something."

Sky went out the back way, crossed the garden to the edge of the reservoir, then walked east until she hit the path that circled it. There was a nearly full moon and blissful silence except for the sound of her shoes on the path.

Maybe Vail had been telling the truth about the picture the first time he spoke, she thought, and then sought to hide his feelings for fear of hurting Sara. She doubted that the film would restore her career but at least she looked like herself. Maybe it was a good picture; she wished she knew.

The old guilt about Lindy returned. She blamed herself for Archie's influence in the family with her, Archie's deadly proximity. Suddenly, she was thinking of Nigeria, the cheetah. She saw again her small head, the long, dark lines running from the corners of her eyes to her mouth, her powerful shoulders. She had had a sweet, playful nature. When Lindy had let her out Sky had forgiven her but had wept in her bedroom—for her own selfishness for loving and keeping the animal, for the crushing fate that awaited her at the zoo where she could not run and could not push her head against a loving hand. She had gone up to see her once; she had not been able to do it again. Niger in that cage reminded her too much of herself.

She heard running footsteps behind her and turned.

"Sky! Sky!"

It was Patrick. "Where did you spring from?" she asked, irritated.

"Oh, I often walk around the reservoir," he said, pulling up to her. They fell into step together. "It's nice up here. I think about all the things I didn't do, or what didn't work out, and other things. . . ."

His sharp, handsome profile was melting into middle age. They walked in silence until they were about halfway around the reservoir. "See?" he said. "It's like we're together, like we mean something to each other, walking along like this."

"Well, we're friends, aren't we?"

"I mean—being—well, close," he said, his face alight with an intense adoration. She picked up her pace; he matched it. "I don't know how to explain it. Like I'm you and you're me. I've just come out of the house and met you and we're going to walk all the way around 'Lake Hollywood,' and then I'll go back into the house." He giggled. "Or, maybe you really *are* Sky, and I'm Patrick, and you will go back inside the house."

A chill swept through her. She glanced at his profile and walked faster.

Patrick's heart was beating thunderously. Which one of them was Sky? Was the woman walking beside him an impostor? Was he Sky, and had this woman stolen his life and his fame? It had all seemed so clear a while ago as he listened to the laughter and chatter coming from the house. Sound carried so beautifully onto the reservoir. Maybe the woman was Sky and he was Patrick. But that didn't sound right to him. She was walking awfully fast; had she read his thoughts and did she know that she had been discovered?

"You can't get away," he heard someone saying as his hand reached out and grabbed her arm.

Sky, terrified, broke into a run. She could see the lights of the house where Kitty waited, but it seemed very far away.

"Don't run!" he called out, seizing her arm and jerking her around to him. "I want my life back!" He was breathing heavily. She beat at him with her fists, kicked him. She started to scream. His hands closed around her throat like a vise.

From across the lake, they appeared to be struggling passionately in silhouette, soon to surrender to the embrace overtaking them.

Kitty awoke with a start. Her neck and shoulder ached; she'd fallen asleep on the living room sofa. She glanced up at the window; it was dawn. Slowly she rose and went upstairs. But Sky's bedroom was empty. Puzzled, she checked all the rooms on the second floor, then went back downstairs. "Sky?" she called. She surveyed the study. Sky was not there. Nor was she in the kitchen or in the screening room. Now Kitty was afraid.

She stood in the garden, scanning the edge of the lake. She started walking, her heart pounding, trying to think of all the ordinary reasons Sky would not have come home. Maybe she had come home, sat in the living room, and read until dawn. Then she had gone out to—where? Another walk? Breakfast? Sky disliked breakfast and avoided it. Where would she go at dawn? Kitty broke into a run, a feeling of dread surrounding her. She looked at the thick shrubs as she passed, and down into the water, knowing this was no way to hunt for someone. Could she, dear God, could she have had a heart attack? Panting, Kitty drove herself on, past the halfway mark. And then she stopped.

Sky was lying face down across the path, her black hair in the dirt, one arm under her, the other flung out toward the lake, one leg bent at the knee, one shoe gone.

The howl that soared over the lake tore into the morning. The husband-and-wife writing team who had just rented Lila Lewis's old house woke with a start.

—552—

EPILOGUE

Sara was staring at Detective Rollins, who still stood just outside the front door.

"May I come in?" he asked.

The murmuring sound of Sky's fans clustered below the house floated up to them. "Yes, of course," Sara said, vaguely. She heard Diana come out of Sky's bedroom and halt at the top of the stairs.

She followed Detective Rollins into the living room. He stopped in the center of it, his feet slightly apart, a notepad in his hand.

"There has been a development," he said in his clipped but oddly lonely voice. "Is your brother here?" He looked around for a chair in a room full of chairs.

"Not yet. Soon." Sara was watching Diana coming into the room. Her mother's face was pale and lined. "Mother, just remember you haven't been out of the hospital that long—"

Diana shrugged with irritation.

The front door opened and banged shut. Vail came into the room. It was instantly apparent to Rollins that Vail was in charge, and that he was not used to being in charge. Sky had made him the executor of her estate. He stopped when he saw Rollins. "Someone has confessed, hasn't he?" he said.

"Yes," Rollins replied, "how did you know?"

"Just a guess."

For Vail, Sky's death was like an ax separating his arm

from his body. With the rush of agony came the pain of remembrance: the circular window over her staircase landing, the succulent palm fronds behind it, his vision of a woman struggling against an unseen assailant on the other side of the water. He had seen it and not seen it. He had forgotten it for years. His waking dreams, which had been so frequent in childhood, came to him rarely as an adult, and had not come at all for years.

"Who's that behind you, Vail?" Diana asked.

A rather chilly, effeminate man smiled distantly.

"This is Alden Butterfield, Mother, Sara," Vail said. "I've asked him to write Sky's story."

"Well, honestly, Vail," Diana snapped. "Isn't this a little early?"

"Mother, I'll handle this." Butterfield stirred uncomfortably. "I'll join you in the study," Vail said to him. "It's right through there." He pointed at the foyer.

"Now that everyone's here," Rollins said, "I think you ought to know that Patrick O'Mara has confessed."

"What? Patrick!" Sara cried. "No, not Patrick!" She reached out for a chair. Vail grabbed her. "Oh, God, no," she moaned.

"You all knew him, I gather," Rollins intoned in his wintry voice.

"Patrick was a *friend*," Sara gasped. She saw his cold Long Island home and his brutal father as they had been on that ill-starred weekend so long ago. Vail was holding out a jigger of scotch.

"Drink this." His face was ashen.

"It's one of those celebrity—" Rollins glanced sharply at Diana, who was standing by the window. "One of those acts of killing a fantasy of glamour in order to—"

Diana turned. "In order to what?"

"To have it himself, the doctors think, to sort of absorb personality by killing it." He looked at them miserably. It was a vulnerable and explosive theory. Rollins did not mention how satisfied Patrick had seemed with himself.

"Are you sure?" Vail asked. "Maybe he's just pretending. He'd been pretty off his beam for the last few years."

"We're sure he did it," Rollins replied. "There will be an announcement this afternoon to the press."

"Will that stop them from speculating that Sara will take her sister's place on the screen?" Diana asked. "It will not."

The mother's a powerhouse, Rollins thought. Miss Wyman was anyone's accomplice, Mrs. Wyman," Rollins said.

"Well, I should think not!" Diana snapped.

"I can assure you—" he began, then dropped it.

"Patrick," Vail murmured. "Jesus Christ." He looked at Sara.

"I'm all right," she muttered. But she knew this final blow would be a long time leaving.

People began coming and going. Condolence notes and cards began filling the silver tray beside the door. Suddenly Ace was standing in front of Sara. He wondered shyly if there was some small object of Sky's that he could have. "Of course," she said.

"Wait," Vail said. "I want to try to keep some order in here."

"Ace and Cage were with Sky for twenty years."

Vail relented. Drinks were poured, food offered. Knots of people stood around in the living room, their voices soft. Ernie Ping arrived, shook hands, embraced Sara, began weeping, and left with Ace.

Diana suddenly looked old, frail, and vulnerable to Sara. As she accepted condolences, Sara kept thinking of her mother, who had never really been a mother just as she had always been too much a mother. Even with Diana's controlling spirit, her fantasies, her deceptions, it was disheartening to see her as a deposed monarch. Vail reveled in his ascendancy. How did Diana feel about Vail, Sara wondered, as she heard him making plans to execute the will immediately, to close the chapter. The shift in family power was unmistakable and uncomfortable.

Reed slipped through the front door. He put his arms around Sara. "Don't go out on the streets," he said quietly. "The news about Patrick has been leaked to the press." Rollins hovered. Sara watched him. Why was he still here?

Mrs. Sho, her eyes red from weeping, came into the room. "Sara?" she said and beckoned. They went into the kitchen.

"Kitty!" cried Sara. "And Patsy!" She hugged them both. Kitty's hands were shaking. She looked drained.

Patsy said, "I thought Kitty might have missed this." She held out the newspaper. "I just gave it to Mrs. Sho."

It was Vail's review of *Torino Express*. Sara sat down. When she had finished, she said, "Sky would have liked that." Kitty nodded, her eyes filled with tears. "He's in there right now, throwing his weight around."

"Oh, that's just his way of grieving," Patsy said. "It's much harder for him than you think. Because of his premonition, or whatever you want to call it. He blames himself for not—"

"I don't want to talk about that." Vail was standing in the doorway.

"Oh, Vail," Sara moaned and went to him. "Such good things you said about Sky and me in the review, and so hard for you. . . ." He endured her embrace, glad of it, while psychologically refusing it.

"Kitty," he said, "where are you staying?"

"With friends."

"She left you the house. You should be staying here." Kitty shook her head. "Maybe later."

"Well, Mother and I are going back to San Francisco tonight. Now come into the living room. People are wondering where you are."

"I—well—your mother—"

"Don't worry about her. She's well in hand," he stated. "What about the potential biographer?" Sara asked.

"When did you do that?"

"The day after she died. I've given him access to her papers, that's all."

"But Vail, it's so sudden—" Sara began.

"We've got to do it our way before someone else does it their way. The subject is closed."

"But Kitty's got to live here—"

"Kitty can put up with it, can't you?" he said. "It's got to be done."

"I think it's nonsense," Sara said.

Reed poked his head in. "Your mother wants you," he said to Sara. "She's in the study."

"I thought the biographer was in the study."

"I sent him upstairs."

"Into her bedroom?" Sara asked, appalled.

"No, Sara," Vail said, patiently, "into the sitting room where the photographs are."

"It's creepy having him here," Sara said, then left.

The study had always reminded Sara of a forest glade. The sun slanted through the far window, brightening the dark green wallpaper. Diana was pouring herself a glass of sherry. Sara shut the door behind her.

"You think I've done a lot wrong," Diana said abruptly. She turned. "Well, I have. Sky was not my favorite child, as you and Vail believe, but fate favored her and I helped it along where I could."

Sara was about to hear from her mother what she had been demanding just an hour ago when they had been alone. But now she wasn't sure she wanted to know. "Don't you think Vail should be here?"

"This is just between you and me. He's out there running the show and Sky gave him that right. She knew it was the most she could give him, and I understand it. My life is over."

Is it? Sara wondered. Much of her mother's power had been given her by Sky's unique stature, yet she didn't look submissive or flattened by grief. There was something else eating at her.

"You feel wronged," Diana said to Sara. "So you were. I had none then, but I have doubts now about what I did. I had a lot of time to think in the hospital. Hospitals do that to you—encourage summations."

"Are you talking about Vic? Or about Lindy? Or about both?" Sara asked.

"Especially Lindy." She sat down on the love seat and crossed her legs primly. "I can't change any of it. Anyway, it all seems so meaningless what we do—useless, now that Sky's dead."

"I'm alive," Sara said.

"You don't understand! I was trying to tell you that upstairs. We strive to do what's right, to make use of what comes to us, and then something like this happens and makes a mockery of striving, of struggle, of ambitions. It could have been you, you know. You could have been in Sky's place."

"I don't want to talk about that, Mother, really I don't."

Diana took a little box out of her pocket. "Sky didn't know herself very well. She acted every day of her life. That's just the way she was. You didn't think I'd admit that about her, did you?" She smiled sourly. "Mothers know everything." She extended the box to Sara. "I had this made up for you, Sara Bay."

Sara didn't want to take the box. Diana held it out shyly.

Sara took it.

The diamond and pearl pin nesting inside was shaped like a winged horse.

"I thought of having a pin made in the shape of a flute, but I knew you loved the horse more. Also, I wanted to return what I had taken from you."

Sara slid into a chair, remembering that fateful summer day when she and Sky and Vail had flown on the forbidden horse. She looked up to see her mother's dark eyes under her pencil-thin brows staring at her hard.

"I lost a lot more than my two front teeth and the ability to play that flute," Sara said. "I felt I lost my place in your affections that day because I couldn't play anymore."

"I know it seemed like that," Diana responded dreamily.

"Maybe it was, for a while."

"You pressed me and pressed me to play the flute, Mother, until I hated it."

"I wanted you to use your gifts, to do well. That's all I ever wanted for any of you. It's a sin to waste your gifts," Diana looked away. "I may have asked too much."

Sara's eyes filled with tears. "No, it was that you gave so little." Her mother's deeply lined face looked shocked. "But it means a lot to me that you have doubts—about what you did—Vic, Lindy. About what you did to my family. It makes me feel less lonely."

Diana waved her hand. "I can't imagine why you are lonely. Look at the boost Vail's given you in that wonderful review, and look at Reed. You have a very full life, and I hope someday you are magnanimous enough to thank me for it." Sara smiled and cried some more.

Diana finished her sherry. "I want to talk about Vail. We have to decide what to do."

"What do you mean?" Sara asked.

"About Lindy's little boy!"

"I still don't see——"

"The boy," Diana said softly. "Your grandson. He cannot stay with your daughter any longer in that wretched institution. I think Vail and Patsy should take care of him until that judge comes to her senses and lets poor Lindy out. Don't you?"

"Mother, stop running things. Just stop it."

When Sara and Diana left the study, the biographer was standing in the foyer. "Oh, Mrs. Wyman," Butterfield said, "am I being too disrespectful to ask you about this?"

He thrust a photo of Sky, Sara, and Vail at her. "Oh, yes," Diana said. "That was taken up at the ranch we used to own in Northern California. They're about fourteen there, I think."

"What are they doing in the picture?" he asked.

"Dressing up!" Diana said. "They were always actors—especially Sky. She wanted to be in the movies in the worst way. She was a natural actor."